R.D. Wingfield, who is married with one son and lives in Basildon, Essex, is a prolific writer of radio crime plays and comedy scripts, some for the late Kenneth Williams, star of the 'Carry On' films. He is the author of five books featuring DI Jack Frost. The series has been successfully adapted for television as *A Touch of Frost* starring David Jason.

www.booksattransworld.co.uk

Also by R.D. Wingfield

- FROST AT CHRISTMAS
- A TOUCH OF FROST
- NIGHT FROST
- HARD FROST
- WINTER FROST

and published by Corgi Books

HARD FROST
and
NIGHT FROST

R.D. Wingfield

HARD FROST and NIGHT FROST
A CORGI BOOK : 0 552 14918 7

This W H Smith edition first published 2001

1 3 5 7 9 10 8 6 4 2

including
HARD FROST
Originally published in Great Britain by Constable & Co Ltd

Corgi edition published 1996
Set in 10pt Linotype Plantin by
County Typesetters, Margate, Kent.

HARD FROST
Originally published in Great Britain by Constable & Co Ltd

Corgi edition published 1992
Set in 10pt Monotype Plantin by
Phoenix Typesetting, Ilkley, West Yorkshire.

Corgi Books are published by Transworld Publishers, 61–63 Uxbridge Road, London W5 5SA, a division of The Random House Group Ltd, in Australia by Random House Australia (Pty) Ltd, 20 Alfred Street, Milsons Point, Sydney, NSW 2061, Australia, in New Zealand by Random House New Zealand Ltd, 18 Poland Road, Glenfield, Auckland 10, New Zealand and in South Africa by Random House (Pty) Ltd, Endulini, 5a Jubilee Road, Parktown 2193, South Africa.

Printed and bound in Great Britain by Cox & Wyman Ltd, Reading, Berkshire.

HARD FROST

The man crouching by the window at the back of the house gritted his teeth as he forced the blade of the screwdriver between the wooden frames. Through the glass he could just make out the cot on the far side of the darkened bedroom. He couldn't see the kiddy, but knew he was in there. He had watched in the dark from the end of the garden, hands sweating with excitement, as the mother put the boy to bed.

The blade was in far enough. He took a deep breath and levered. Wood splintered and he felt the screws tear free. A sudden swish of noise from behind him almost made him drop the screwdriver. He turned in fright, ready to duck low and run zigzagging across the garden. But it was a firework, a rocket soaring up to the night sky where it burst in a cluster of bright green puff-balls.

His heart hammered and cold sweat trickled. A long, deep breath to calm himself, then, very carefully and very quietly, he eased open the window, heaved himself up on the sill and swung inside. Three careful steps across the room and he was able to reach the blue-painted chair next to the cot and wedge it under the door handle to stop anyone from coming in. At the door he listened. The late night film on television. Just the woman on her own – he'd checked.

The cot creaked as the child snuffled and wriggled. He froze and held his breath. A tiny yawn, then shallow breathing. He relaxed. The child had settled into a deep sleep . . .

He took the knife from his pocket. Quietly he tiptoed over to the cot.

1

Hallowe'en, 31 October

A lone sky rocket clawed its way up to the night sky, scrabbled feebly as it started to lose height, then burst into a cluster of green puff-balls.

PC Mike Packer, twenty years old, barely gave it a glance as he turned the corner into Markham Street. This was his first night out on the beat on his own and he had other things on his mind. He patted the radio in his top pocket, reassured he could call for help if he needed it.

A clatter of footsteps. Two teenage girls, heavily made up and dressed as witches, tottered past on high heels trailing a cloud of musky perfume. They whistled and called to him, blowing wet-lipped kisses. On their way to some Hallowe'en party and already drunk. Someone was going to score tonight. Grinning ruefully, Packer wished it was him! But no such luck. He was on duty on this cold and windy night, pounding his lousy beat until six in the morning. He drew his head tighter into the snug warmth of his greatcoat and watched until the girls turned the corner. The wind snatched away the last whisper of their perfume and he was on his own again.

He cut through the narrow alley which brought him into Patriot Street, a backwater of small lock-up shops and an empty space that was once a second-hand car site.

The street was dark, its single street lamp vandalized long ago.

The hollow echo of his footsteps pattered behind him

giving him the uneasy feeling he was being followed. Once he even stopped suddenly and swung round, but there was no-one there. Outside the shops, piled up on the pavement, were plastic bags of rubbish, ready for collection the following morning. Packer weaved his way around them and flashed the rock hard beam of his brand-new torch into shop doorways, rattling the odd handle to make sure all was secure.

The end shop, long empty and boarded up, was once a butcher's. A faded sign, swaying gently in the wind, said 'This Valuable Property To Let'. The doorway was piled high with rubbish sacks which had obviously been dragged there from outside adjacent shops. Why, wondered Packer, had someone taken the trouble to do that? Again he clicked on his torch, watching the beam crawl slowly over the pile. He half expected to disturb a dosser or perhaps even the boy they had been told to look out for, the seven-year-old who had gone out with his guy and still wasn't home at eleven o'clock at night.

Packer stiffened. There was someone crouching behind the bags in the corner. Someone keeping very still. 'All right – I can see you! Come on out.' No movement. Keeping the torch handy for use as a weapon if necessary, he started pulling bags out of the way. Then suddenly the figure lunged at him and the face . . . God . . . it wasn't human . . . it was green and malevolent. Dropping the torch he fumbled for his radio. The radio . . . he couldn't find the bloody radio . . .

'Denton police.' Police Sergeant Bill Wells stifled a yawn as he lifted the phone to his ear and muttered into the mouthpiece. He wasn't really concentrating on what the caller was saying as he was still simmering with rage. He had been going through the new duty rosters to the end of the year and was livid to see that Mullett had yet again put him down for duty on Christmas day. Well, Superintendent flaming Mullett had another think coming. Let some of his blue eyed boys do their share of holiday nights for a change because the worm was about to turn. He frowned at the agitated voice buzzing away in his ear. 'Try and take it easy, madam . . . just tell me what happened . . . What? . . . Where? How bad is he?' His pen scribbled furiously. 'Don't worry. I'll get someone over there right away.'

He snatched up the internal phone and jabbed the button for Wonder Woman's office . . . Detective Sergeant Liz Maud. Let that flaming tart do some work for a change instead of painting her lousy fingernails. He'd noticed from the roster that she had all of the Christmas period off and she'd only been here two bloody weeks.

'Yes?'

The impatient edge to her voice always put his back up, so his tone was curt. '17 Crown Street . . . break-in and stabbing – little boy, one year old.'

'I'll need back-up,' she said.

'We haven't got any,' said Wells, happy at last.

Packer was sweating with relief, thankful he hadn't been able to get to his radio. They would never have let him live it down. It was a guy, a child's guy, and the green face was Guy Fawkes. He pulled some of the sacks away to get a better look. Behind the guy a rubbish sack, propped up against the shop door, looked wrong. He touched it and his hand jerked back as if he had received an electric shock. He had never seen a dead body. Part of his training would involve a visit to the mortuary to view a post-mortem, but this had not happened yet. Burton had said that the pathologist always cut a long slit under the corpse's chin so he could peel the face off like a rubber mask. Packer hoped he would be able to see it through without fainting when the time came. But now, before he was ready, he knew he had a dead body. Too small for an adult. A child.

As he reached out, it toppled over and he thought he heard a grunt. Still alive? Was it still alive?

He tore off his gloves with his teeth and fumbled at the cord tying the neck of the sack. Then he was staring at a face. A young boy. Brown masking tape bound round the eyes as a blindfold. More masking tape, pulled tightly into the mouth forcing the lips back into a mockery of a grin. Vomit dribbled from the mouth and nose. Packer dropped to his knees and gingerly touched the flesh. Ice cold and no sign of a pulse. The brown dribble of vomit had a naggingly familiar hospital smell which he couldn't quite place. He opened the plastic sack wider, holding it by its extreme edge, and shone his torch inside. The boy, knees bent, was naked.

He straightened up and pulled his radio from his pocket, then took a few deep breaths and called the station. To his surprise he managed to keep his voice steady. He sounded as if he met death in the street every day. 'Packer here, Patriot Street. I think I've found the missing kid . . . and he's dead. Looks like murder.'

'Stay there,' ordered Wells. 'Whatever happens – stay there!'

Packer moved out to the street and waited. An eerie silence seemed to hang over the area, and the tiniest sounds were magnified. The rustling of the wind on the exposed plastic sacks. The creaking of the 'For Sale' sign over the butcher's. The hammering of his heart.

Then, just audible but getting louder, the wailing siren of an area car. Wells wasn't going to send out the murder team until he had checked. Not on Packer's first night out on his own.

At the station it was chaos with Bill Wells in near despair. Everything was going wrong. A murder investigation and no senior CID officers available. Detective Inspector Allen, who should have been on call at home, had left a contact number which rang and rang but no-one answered. Jack Frost was on holiday and that supid cow Liz Maud must have switched her radio off as he had gone near hoarse calling for her. He was now ringing the Divisional Commander's home number, but knew he would get short shrift there. He could hear Mullett's sarcasm now. *Surely you are competent enough to sort this out for yourself, sergeant?* The phone was hot against his ear and the ringing tone went on and on. Then he was aware of a tapping on the desk in front of him. A little tubby man in a camel-hair coat trying to attract his attention. 'Be with you in a minute, sir.'

'You'll deal with me now, sergeant. I'm in a hurry.'

Wells groaned. One of those pompous little bastards. Just what he needed tonight . . .

His attention was snatched back to the phone. Someone had answered. Not Mullett, but his half-asleep, disgruntled, toffee-nosed cow of a wife peevishly demanding to know who it was. 'Sorry to disturb you at this time of night, Mrs Mullett, but is the superintendent there? . . . No? Do you have a number where I could contact him? Yes, it is urgent.' *Of course it's urgent, you stupid cow. Would I be phoning if it wasn't?* 'Thank you.' He scribbled on his pad and hung up.

The man was glaring at him. 'I am still waiting, sergeant.'

'Please take a seat, sir. I'll deal with you as quickly as I can.' He looked up hopefully as PC Lambert came in from Control.

'Still no answer from that Inspector Allen number, sarge.'

'Keep trying. Any luck with Wonder Woman?'

'Not a dicky bird!'

'Bloody cow's useless.' Wells ripped the sheet from his pad. 'See if you can get Mr Mullett on this number.'

Lambert frowned. 'This is the same number I'm trying for Mr Allen, sarge.'

Wells looked at it again. Lambert was right. 'Mullett

and Allen, both out together at eleven o'clock at night. I wonder where?'

'A cut-price knocking shop?' suggested a familiar voice, helpfully.

Frost! Jack Frost in his crumpled mac and maroon scarf beaming at them.

'Jack!' cried a delighted Wells. 'I thought you were on holiday.'

'I am. I've just nipped in for some fags. Did you get my comic postcard?' He struck a pose and declaimed:

> 'I cannot get my winkle out
> Now there's a funny thing.
> The more I try to pull it out
> The more I push it in!'

Wells grinned. 'I stuck it on the notice-board, but Mullett made me take it down. He said it was near pornographic.'

'There's nothing pornographic about a man eating winkles,' said Frost. 'So what's all the panic?'

'Patriot Street. Body in a dustbin sack.'

Frost grimaced. 'Where did people hide bodies before dustbin sacks were invented? We find more bloody bodies than rubbish in them these days.'

'This one's a kid,' said Wells, 'a boy, seven years old. We've got a murder investigation, a detective constable in sole charge, the pathologist on his way and Mullett and Allen conveniently unobtainable. A proper sod-up!'

'Not as good as some of my sod-ups,' said Frost, 'but I'm glad I'm on holiday. I'll just nick some of Mullett's fags and go.' He disappeared up the corridor.

Seeing Wells with nothing to do, the man in the camel-hair coat sprang across to the desk.

'Perhaps you can now spare me some time. I've lost my car – a metallic grey Rover, registration number—'

'Stolen car, right,' said Wells, pulling the forms

towards him. The quickest way to get shot of him was to take the details.

'I didn't say it was stolen. I just don't know where it is. I drove down from Bristol for the firm's function. I parked it down a side street somewhere. I must have got confused – I can't find it. My wallet, credit cards, everything, are inside it.'

'It's probably been pinched by now,' said Wells cheerfully.

'I'm sure it hasn't, sergeant. It's fitted with anti-thief devices.'

'And you've no idea where you left it?'

'If I did, I wouldn't be here, would I?'

Wells put his pen down. 'So what do you want us to do about it?'

The man sighed as if explaining to an idiot. 'I would have thought that was obvious, sergeant. If one of your men could drive me around the side streets, we could look for it.'

'I've got a better idea.' Frost had returned with one of Mullett's best cigarettes dangling from his lips. 'Why don't you piss off and go and look for it yourself? We've got more important things to do.'

The man spun round angrily, jabbing a finger at Frost. 'I'll have you,' he spluttered. 'I've got friends in high places. I want your name.'

'Mullett,' said Frost. 'Superintendent Mullett.'

'Right,' said the man, scribbling this down. 'You haven't heard the last of this.' He stamped out of the station.

'You bloody fool, Jack,' said Wells.

'He won't take it any further,' said Frost, but now beginning to have doubts himself. 'Anyway,' he brightened up, 'I'm on holiday so Mullett won't suspect me.'

'If you were dead he'd still suspect you,' said Wells grimly.

Lambert slid up the dividing hatch to the Control

Room. 'Still nothing from that number, sarge. I got the exchange to trace it for us. It's the Clarendon Arms, that big pub and restaurant over at Felstead.'

Wells's eyes narrowed. 'What the hell are they doing there? Those two are up to something, you mark my words. Why isn't anyone answering the phone?'

Lambert shrugged. 'There could be a fault on the line. We'll have to send someone over there to pick Allen up.'

'We can't spare a bleeding car,' said Wells. He groaned. There was no other option. 'All right – send Charlie Baker. We want Allen back here. Tell him it's a murder enquiry.'

The hatch slammed shut. Wells spun round quickly, just in time to catch Frost before he sidled out. 'Hold it, Jack.'

'I'm on holiday until the end of the week,' said Frost.

'We've got to have a senior officer over there . . . Please, Jack. I only want you to hold the fort until Allen arrives – fifteen minutes, half an hour at the most . . .'

'All right,' sighed Frost reluctantly. 'But if he's not there in half an hour, I'm off.'

'You're a diamond,' said Wells.

'I'm a prat,' said Frost.

The door was closing behind him when Lambert slid up the hatch. 'I've got hold of Liz Maud, sarge.'

Detective Sergeant Maud was late arriving at the house. She still didn't know her way around Denton and the ancient, well-thumbed street map Sergeant Wells had given her was falling to pieces with lots of the street names unreadable. After twice retracing her route, she pulled up outside the front door just as the doctor was leaving. 'Kiddy's not too badly hurt,' he told her. 'Couple of superficial wounds to the upper arm, which only required a dressing.' He glanced back and winced at the hysterical shrieking and sobbing from inside. 'That's the mother. She's in a worse state than the kid. I offered her a sedative, but she chucked it at me.' He edged past her. 'I wish I could stay, but I've got other calls.' He plunged out into the street, relieved to get away from the noise.

Liz switched off her radio. She didn't want her interview with an overwrought mother interrupted by trivial messages. She homed in on the crying which was now accompanied by a banging noise. It led her to the child's bedroom, a small room with a single cot, its walls decorated with nursery wallpaper.

The banging was caused by a middle-aged man who was hammering nails into the window frame which had been forced open by the intruder. A young woman, the mother, jet black hair, slightly olive skin, was sitting in a blue-painted chair, rocking from side to side, moaning and sobbing continuously. Liz sighed. She obviously wouldn't be much help.

A plumpish woman in her fifties was standing next to the mother, holding the child, wrapped in a blanket. The child, a boy, barely a year old, his face flushed and tear-stained, had cried himself to an exhausted sleep.

'Detective Sergeant Maud,' announced Liz, holding out her warrant card.

'Took your time getting here,' said the man, knocking in one last nail and putting down the hammer. He gave the window frame a testing shake. 'That should keep the bugger out.'

'If you could try to avoid touching things,' said Liz. 'There could be fingerprints.'

'You wouldn't need fingerprints if you got here earlier and caught him,' said the man.

Liz ignored this. 'Are you the husband?'

'I'm her next-door neighbour – George Armitage.' He nodded at the woman with the baby. 'And that's my wife.'

Liz addressed the mother. 'What's your name, love?'

It was Mrs Armitage who answered her. 'Lily – Lily Turner. She's in a bit of a state, I'm afraid.'

'Is there a husband?'

'Well – there's a father. Not sure if he's actually her husband, if you follow my meaning.' She lowered her voice. 'He's inside . . . doing eighteen months – stealing radios from cars.'

Liz gently touched the mother's arm. 'Lily, I'm from the police. Can you tell me what happened?'

The mother's only response was to moan louder.

Liz turned to the other woman. 'Perhaps you can tell me what happened, Mrs Armitage.'

'Half a mo.' She gently laid the boy down in the cot and pulled the bedclothes over him, careful to avoid touching the injured arm with its strip of pink plaster. There were tiny flecks of blood on the sheet. 'Lily was in the other room watching telly when she heard little Tommy crying. When she tried to get to him, she couldn't get the door open.'

'The bastard had jammed that chair under the door handle,' said the man, pointing to the chair the mother was sitting on. Liz made a mental note to ensure it was fingerprinted, and nodded for the woman to continue.

'The kiddy was screaming and she could hear someone moving about. She thought it was burglars. Anyway, she came running in to us and George went straight back with her and managed to kick the door open.'

'Let me tell it now,' said the man. 'I kicked the door open. That window was wide open with the wind roaring in. I nipped across and looked out, but there was no sign of him. The kid was crying fit to bust, so she picked him up and then she spotted the blood and next she was yelling and screaming louder than the bleeding kid. I got my wife to phone the police and the doctor. The rest you know.'

Liz walked over to the window and looked out on to a small back garden. There was a gate in the rear fence leading to a lane. Easy to get in and out without being spotted. The window had been crudely levered open, exactly the same as the other three stabbings. 'Do you know if she's noticed anyone watching the house, or following her?'

'We're not on speaking terms,' said Armitage. 'We wouldn't be in here tonight if it wasn't an emergency. I was one of the people her old man nicked a car radio from, so we're not coming in for tea and biscuits and a chat, are we?'

Liz snapped her notebook shut. She would have to come back again tomorrow when the mother had calmed down. 'Well, thank you very much. Try not to touch anything. There'll be a fingerprint man here in the morning.'

Mrs Armitage walked with her to the front door. 'Do you think you'll catch him?'

'We'll get him,' said Liz. She wished she shared her spoken optimism. A maniac who had a thing about seeing blood on children. They had no description, no fingerprints – they didn't even know if it was a man or a woman, and all of the known sex offenders she had painstakingly questioned had cast-iron alibis. 'We'll get him all right.' The front door slammed shut behind her, but she could still hear the mother wailing.

In the car she switched her radio back on and they told her about the dead boy. She fished out the map and tried to find how to get to Patriot Street.

'She had her damn radio off!' said Wells incredulously. 'What does the silly cow think we give her a radio for – just to keep in her bloody handbag?' The phone rang. 'Yes?' he snapped.

It was Mullett and he sounded just the tiniest bit drunk. 'My wife tells me you've been trying to reach me, sergeant.'

Wells clapped his hand over the mouthpiece and yelled for Lambert to call back the area car. Then he told Mullett about the murdered boy.

* * *

Mike Packer stamped his feet and flapped his arms. It was damn cold. He wished he could go back on his beat and walk around to keep warm, but he had been delegated to stand with a clipboard and record details of everyone who approached the body. So far he had recorded himself, PCs Simms and Jordan, DC Burton and the two Scene of Crime officers in their white overalls who had screened off the area, plus, of course, the police surgeon who was in and out in a flash, simply confirming the boy was dead and the circumstances were bloody suspicious. Across the road Jordan and Simms, in the warmth of the area car, were waiting to be told what to do. No sign yet of the pathologist, nor Detective Inspector Allen who should be in charge.

An old Ford Escort wheezed round the corner and shuddered to a halt. Simms nudged Jordan who climbed out of the area car, ready to send the newcomer away. But the man getting out of the car, maroon scarf streaming in the wind, was Detective Inspector Jack Frost. What was he doing here? He should be on holiday.

Burton, kneeling by the body, heard the car draw up and swore softly. Control had told him that Detective Sergeant Liz Maud was on her way over, so this must be her. The pompous little cow would soon start taking charge, lording it over everyone and barking out her orders. But that raucous laugh that came slicing across the gloom had him hurrying out. There was only one person with a laugh like that.

Frost took a quick look round the scene. Everything seemed to be in order. The street was cordoned off and a tent-like structure erected around the shop doorway. A small generator installed by the SOC men chugged away, providing the emergency lighting, and everyone seemed to be doing what they ought to. He nodded happily to himself. DC Burton was competent enough to handle all the fiddling details.

'Right,' he said, after lighting up one of Mullett's cigarettes for Burton, 'I'd better know what we've got, just in case some nosy bastard asks.'

'Dead boy, aged about seven,' said Burton, leading him to the body. 'Believed to be Bobby Kirby, reported missing from home. Mother separated from husband. She and her boyfriend nipped out to the pub for a couple of hours leaving Bobby watching telly. When they got back around ten o'clock, Bobby wasn't there.'

The body was still in the plastic sack and wouldn't be removed until the pathologist, a stickler for insisting on things being left exactly as found, had examined it. Frost knelt down and looked at the white face, the brown plastic masking tape round the eyes and mouth still in place. He shook his head sadly. 'Poor little sod. Have the parents been told?'

'Not yet,' Burton told him. 'We're waiting for Mr Allen.'

'Rather him than me,' said Frost. He peered more closely, his face tight with compassion. 'What dirty bastard did this to you, sonny?' He examined the tape binding the mouth, and the dribble of vomit. He sniffed. That smell. What the hell was it? He knew it from somewhere . . . Of course, the hospital. It was always lingering around the ward when he went to visit his wife, when he sat by the bed for hours on end to watch her slowly dying. He worried away, trying to identify it, but gave up. It wasn't his case, so it wasn't his problem. 'Cause of death?'

'The police doctor thinks he might have choked to death on his own vomit.'

'How long dead?'

'Wouldn't commit himself. He said ask the pathologist.'

'Helpful bloody bastard.' Frost straightened up and squinted at his watch. 'Where the hell is Allen?'

'He and Mr Mullett are on their way over now, sir,' Burton told him.

'Mullett? Don't let him see your fag, son . . . he might recognize it as a long-lost friend.' Frost took one last look at the body. 'I'm only the token inspector, so just carry on until Smart-arse gets here.' He found a dustbin to sit on while he waited.

Detective Sergeant Liz Maud skidded round the corner. She knew she was driving too fast, but she was in a state of high excitement. A murder case! Her first. And Inspector Allen unavailable. Now was the time to make her mark.

As she parked tight into the kerb behind a police car, she glanced across the road and frowned. The area was supposed to be cordoned off, but there, sitting on a dustbin, hunched up against the wind, was an old tramp dragging on a cigarette. How had the fools let him get so close? Heads would roll for this. She flung open the door of her car and sprang out. 'Hey – you!' The man, who was in the process of flinging his cigarette end into the gutter, looked up briefly, then, ignoring her, rose to walk towards the canvas enclosure where the body was. She frowned in disbelief as the two fools in the police car in front of her just sat and watched.

Liz raced across the road, fumbling in her shoulder bag for her warrant card. 'You in the mac – hold it!' She shoved her warrant card in his face.

Frost barely gave it a glance. 'No thanks, love – I've already got one.' Then he was yelling at two uniformed men who were starting to shift the sacks of rubbish out of the way. 'Leave them be! I want them checked for prints and examined.' He turned to Liz and introduced himself. 'Detective Inspector Frost. You must be new?'

She managed to keep her voice calm, but inwardly she was boiling. Her one big chance and this idiot had to come back from holiday early. 'Detective Sergeant Liz Maud. I was transferred from Fenley Division last week.'

Frost eyed her. In her late twenties, a bit on the thin side, her dark hair scragged back emphasizing her sharp features. But she wouldn't be a bad looker if she took a bit of trouble and wore something different from that drab grey and black striped skirt and jacket.

'All right if I have a look at the body, inspector?'

Frost spread his hands. 'Be my guest, love. I'm only keeping it warm until Allen turns up.'

She winced at the 'love' but tried not to show her annoyance. Before she could move, a sleek black car slithered round the corner. A Rolls-Royce. The pathologist had arrived.

'Shit!' muttered Frost. 'It's Dr bleeding Death. I'd better take over. He's insulted if he has to deal with sergeants.' He looked longingly up the road, hoping to see the headlights of Allen's car roaring to the rescue, but no such luck. Lighting another of Mullett's specials, he mooched across to the tented area, Liz following hard on his heels.

A man in white overalls stopped them. This was PC Reg Evans, a Scene of Crime officer. 'There's about twenty rubbish sacks there, Mr Frost. Do you want us to fingerprint them all?'

'Better than that, Reg. I want you to take them all back to the station and open them up as well. The killer might have dumped the kid's clothes in one of them.'

Dr Samuel Drysdale, Pathologist for the Home Office, had wasted no time. He was out of the car and kneeling by the body before Frost returned. He studied the face very closely, watched by his female secretary who was directing a torch to augment the spluttering emergency lighting. 'Steady,' he snapped as the beam wavered. Above him, the canvas flapped angrily in the wind, almost drowning the constant radio chatter from the police car in the street.

The dribble of vomit from the nostrils and the corner of the mouth held his attention. He lowered his face until his nostrils were almost scraping the boy's cold flesh, then sniffed carefully. He nodded. He was able to place the smell which had baffled Frost. Next, he transferred his attention to the taped mouth. Behind it, the skin round the lips was an inflamed red and there were tiny filaments of white fibre.

'How's it going, doc?'

Drysdale stiffened. He didn't have to raise his head to identify the speaker and the shower of cigarette ash which floated down confirmed it. He flapped the ash away angrily and slowly looked up. There he was. Detective Inspector Jack Frost in the same battered mac, a button hanging loose, a maroon scarf trailing from his neck. Drysdale glowered. 'I thought this was Mr Allen's case . . . and kindly put that cigarette out!'

'We're trying to find Allen,' said Frost, pinching out the cigarette and crouching down beside the pathologist. 'He's attending a piss-up somewhere.' He jabbed a finger at the boy's face. 'What are those bits of white?'

'Cotton wool,' said Drysdale. Before he could elaborate there was a scurry of activity outside with car doors slamming and the buzz of voices. Detective Inspector Allen, in evening dress, a white scarf round his neck, made a slightly unsteady entrance into the tent, bringing with him the strong reek of cigar smoke and whisky. He nodded curtly to Frost as he made his apologies to Drysdale. 'Sorry for the delay, sir. I was off duty.' He stared down at the body, shaking his head sadly. 'What can you tell us?'

The pathologist straightened up. 'The child was anaesthetised.' He pointed to the lips. 'Those white fibres are from the pad of cotton wool which was used to apply the anaesthetic. It was clamped over his mouth and nose. When he was unconscious, a gag of cloth was inserted into the mouth, then the plastic tape was applied to keep it in place. Unfortunately, this meant that when the boy was sick the stomach contents couldn't escape and he choked to death on his own vomit.'

He moved to one side so Allen could examine the

mouth, which he did with difficulty, his eyes trying hard to focus. He nodded. 'I see.'

Must have been a bloody good booze-up, thought Frost.

'Any sign of sexual assault?' asked Allen.

'I haven't been able to examine him in detail. This isn't the place. Get him to the mortuary. Don't remove him from the sack and leave the plastic tape in place.'

'We'll need the sack for fingerprints,' said Frost.

'After I've removed it from the body.'

'Time of death?' asked Allen.

'It's a cold night, which tends to slow rigor down. I would suggest he has been dead somewhere between seven and eight hours. I can be more precise once I get him to the mortuary.'

Allen studied his wrist-watch very carefully, holding it much closer to his eyes than he usually did. 'Which makes the time of death . . .' Brow furrowed in concentration, lips moving, he did mental sums.

'About five or six o'clock this evening,' offered Liz Maud.

'I can do my own sums, thank you,' snapped Allen, who was a long way from calculating the answer. 'Did he die here, Mr Drysdale?'

'No,' said Frost, buttoning his mac, ready to leave them to it. 'He wasn't dumped here until six at the earliest.'

Drysdale scowled. The question had been addressed to him. 'Share your medical expertise with us, inspector.'

'You don't need medical bleeding expertise,' said Frost. 'The shops don't shut until six and that's when they put their rubbish sacks out.'

A grudging nod from Drysdale. 'Yes. He died elsewhere and was dumped here probably four hours ago.'

A burst of wind rattled the canvas and creaked the metal stays. Frost wound his scarf round his neck and lifted the canvas flap. 'I'll leave you to get on with it. I'm off home.'

'Hold it, Jack.' Allen followed him to the street where the wind was like ice on his flushed, sweating face. 'You couldn't do me a favour, I suppose?'

No way, thought Frost. When have you ever done anything for me? 'A favour?' he asked warily.

'Flaming hell, Jack – I've been drinking. Look at me. I'm in no state to take over tonight.'

Hard bloody luck, thought Frost. You knew you were on call. You sweat it out, mate, I'm on holiday and I'm off home.

'Just for tonight, Jack. I'll take over again first thing in the morning.'

No way, decided Frost. You wouldn't lift a finger if it was me asking you. But he said nothing. He stared at Allen, his face impassive.

'And look at me, Jack. Evening bloody dress . . . half cut . . . How can I break the news to the kid's parents looking like this?'

Frost dropped his gaze. Allen had him there. A man stinking of whisky and cigars, in evening dress, swaying, speech slurred, telling you that your seven-year-old son was dead . . . murdered and probably sexually assaulted. Bloody hell. The bastard had got him. 'All right,' he grunted.

Allen squeezed his arm. 'You're a good 'un, Jack. I owe you one.' He walked unsteadily towards the police car that had brought him from Felstead.

There was another passenger in the car, a man also in evening dress sitting bolt upright in the back seat. Frost managed to get there before Allen opened the driver's door. He sniffed and wrinkled his nose, winking at the driver. 'What a stink of cheap booze in here, driver. Get your prisoner to the drunk cell and then come straight back.' He paused and reacted as if he suddenly realized who the 'prisoner' was. 'Mr Mullett! Sorry, super – didn't recognize you in the monkey suit.'

Mullett kept his face expressionless, not giving Frost

the satisfaction of showing his annoyance. He stared straight ahead at the back of the neck of the police driver who was almost choking as he tried to suppress a snigger. A curt nod to Frost as Allen clambered in and dropped heavily on the seat beside him. A few muttered words to the driver and the car sped away.

Liz Maud, seeing Allen make his exit, had renewed hopes that this would mean she would be in charge, but was disappointed to see Frost, grinning all over his face, return to the tented area where Drysdale was pulling on his leather gloves. 'There's something you should see.' He took the torch from his secretary, crouched by the body and shone it inside the bag. 'Take a look.'

Frost squatted down beside him. There was something white, covering the boy's right hand, fastened around the wrist with yet more masking tape.

'What is it?' asked Frost.

'It looks like a small plastic bag,' replied Drysdale. 'I can't make anything of it at the moment, but once we get him on the table, I can take a better look.' He straightened up and clicked off the torch. 'You can remove the body now, inspector. I'll do a brief examination at the mortuary tonight, then a full post-mortem at ten tomorrow.'

'I'll let Mr Allen know,' said Frost. This was getting too complicated for him and he would be glad to dump it back in Allen's lap. He beckoned to Burton. 'Whistle up the meat wagon.'

As the Rolls-Royce slid away, its place was taken by the undertaker's plain, unmarked van. Frost checked that the undertaker and his assistant were wearing gloves before they touched the plastic sack and watched as it was lifted and zipped in a black body bag.

PC Evans, the SOC officer, squeezed past to take photographs, and to examine the area on which the body had been lying.

Frost drew Liz to one side. 'Get back to the station and

open up the murder incident room. Then ask Bill Wells for our list of known child molesters.'

'I've already got it,' replied Liz. 'Some pervert has been breaking into houses and stabbing toddlers in their cots.'

'Right,' said Frost. 'Round them all up . . . any with their dicks out still warm and throbbing, treat with suspicion. Burton, you come with me.'

Liz hesitated. 'Wouldn't it be better if I came with you and Burton opened up the incident room?' If Frost was leading the enquiry, she wanted to stay with him.

'You're not missing any fun,' said Frost. 'We're going to break the news to the parents – a job that Mr Allen wriggled out of. You're welcome to come if you like.'

She shook her head. She couldn't face any more hysterical mothers tonight. 'I'll get back to the station.'

It was easy to spot the boy's house in Lacey Street. It was the only one with its lights still on. Even before Frost's Ford had scraped its tyres to a stop along the kerb, the front door was flung open and a woman came rushing out.

Wendy Kirby, the boy's mother, aged around twenty-five, eyes swollen from crying, had wrenched open the door. 'Have you found him yet?'

'Let's go inside, love,' said Frost, lighting up the cigarette he needed to bolster up his courage.

'We only went out for a quick drink. We hardly ever go out.'

Frost nodded sympathetically. A man in his mid-twenties was at the door. He wore a black, imitation leather zip-up jacket. 'Have you found the little sod? I'll wring his bleeding neck . . .'

'Are you Mr Kirby? asked Frost.

'No, I'm damn well not. I'm her boyfriend. That kid's ruined our bloody evening.'

The boyfriend! Shit, thought Frost. He was hoping it

was the father so he would only have to break the bad news once. 'Let's go inside.'

They were taken into the lounge where the mother dropped into an armchair and grabbed at a table lighter. She had difficulty lighting her cigarette. Frost leant over and lit it for her. Burton stood by the door, watching, feeling superfluous.

'It's bad news, isn't it?' said the mother. 'I know it's bad news.'

'You're always bloody negative,' said the boyfriend. 'Always looking on the black side. Be bloody positive for a change.'

That's right, thought Frost. Raise the poor cow's hopes so I can smash them down again. He took a deep drag, then slowly exhaled. He couldn't put it off any longer. 'Mrs Kirby . . .' he began.

The woman had taken a framed picture from the side table and was holding it to her chest, rocking slowly from side to side. Frost paused. 'Is that Bobby?'

She nodded.

He held out his hand. 'Could I see it?'

She handed it to him. A school photograph. A freckle-faced boy with light brown hair grinning shyly at the camera. 'Taken last week,' she said.

Frost studied it, then handed it to Burton.

Burton raised his eyebrows in surprise.

It wasn't the dead boy.

2

'We haven't found your son yet, Mrs Kirby,' said Frost, 'but we might have found his guy.'

'Oh – bloody marvellous,' said the boyfriend. 'Bring the guy home, put it to bed and that's the end of it.'

'Why don't you shut your mouth?' said Mrs Kirby. 'It was your bloody idea we should go to the pub.'

'You didn't try to talk me out of it, did you? I hadn't finished suggesting it before you had your hat and your bloody coat on and were half-way up the street.'

Frost stretched out his arms like a referee parting two boxers. 'Can you save the squabbling till later? We're very concerned about your son, Mrs Kirby, and we want to find him as quickly as possible. Now, his guy – white and green plastic zip-up jacket?'

She nodded. 'Bobby's old one – he'd grown out of it.'

'And the mask – Guy Fawkes with a green face?'

'Yes.'

'We found it in a shop doorway in Patriot Street. Would Bobby have gone there with his guy?'

'I wouldn't have thought so. No-one goes through there at night. He was after money. He usually hangs about around pubs and bus stops.'

'Tell me exactly what happened tonight.'

'We've already told it once,' said the boyfriend.

'And now you are going to tell it again,' snapped Frost, 'and if I want you to tell it twenty bloody times, you'll tell it twenty bloody times. What's your name, by the way?'

'Green – Terry Green.'

Frost waited while Burton noted this down, then turned to the mother. 'What happened tonight, Mrs Kirby?'

'Bobby had his tea at five and then he wanted to go out with his guy. I said no. It was too dark and there's been this weirdo out at night stabbing kids.'

Frost nodded vaguely. This must be the case Liz Maud was rabbiting on about. 'And how did Bobby take it?'

'He swore at me.'

'Don't know where the little bastard gets it from,' said the man. 'Anyway, I gave him a clout, so he swears at me – said I wasn't his bloody father and I said I was bloody glad I wasn't otherwise I'd have strangled him at birth—'

'OK,' said Frost, cutting him short, 'spare us the happy families stuff.' Back to the woman. 'What happened then?'

'Bobby sat and sulked in front of the telly. Just after seven, Terry suggested we went out for a quick drink. I told Bobby that as soon as his programme finished he was to go straight to bed. Me and Terry went out and were back just after ten. I went upstairs to check Bobby was all right – and he wasn't there.'

'Little sod – just did it to spite us,' said Green.

'Did the officers who came earlier do a search of the house? Sometimes kids hide, just for the fun of it.'

'They turned the place upside down. He isn't here. We've been out pounding the streets, looking for him. We've been round to all his friends' houses and they haven't seen him!'

His friends. Could one of them be the dead boy? 'None of his friends were missing, I suppose?'

She looked puzzled. 'No – we spoke to them all.'

'I see. And you've absolutely no idea where Bobby might be?'

'I know where he is,' said Green. 'He's round his bloody father's moaning about us.'

'If he was there, Harry would have phoned,' said the woman.

'Hold on,' said Frost. 'The father – he lives locally?'

'He lives in Dane Street with his slag Chinese girl.'

'Suzie bloody Wong,' added Green.

'Are you telling me the father lives in Denton and you haven't checked to see if your son is with him?'

'If Bobby was with him, he'd phone me.'

'And you haven't told him Bobby's missing?'

'If he knew we'd left Bobby in the house on his own while we went to the pub, he'd come round and cause trouble. He's already threatened to smash Terry's face in.'

What better reason to go round and see him, thought Frost.

Outside, in the car, he radioed through to Liz Maud to tell her that the dead boy wasn't Bobby Kirby and that the search for him should continue. 'If we don't find him tonight, get Bill Wells to organize a search team for the morning. We'll have to pull men in off their rest days – tell him to clear it with Mullett.'

'Right,' she said.

'Circulate all forces with a description of the dead kid. Ask if anyone has reported him missing.'

'Right.'

'Anything you can't manage, let me know.'

'There's nothing I can't manage,' she snapped. 'Over and out.'

'What do you reckon to Ms Maud?' asked Burton, as he tried to get the engine of Frost's car to cough into life.

'Maud can come into my garden any time she likes,' said Frost. 'Hooray!' This because the engine suddenly belched and fired and they were away. 'Put your foot down, son. I can't wait to see what this Chinese slag girlfriend looks like. Oriental nookie turns me on.'

'Oriental women are old and wizened at thirteen,' said Burton.

'Then let's hope she's only eleven,' said Frost.

The house looked promising. Gone midnight, but lights were on downstairs. Burton thumbed the door bell and after a short while a woman's voice called, 'Yes?'

'Police,' said Burton. The door opened on a chain and he pushed his warrant card through the gap. 'I wonder if we can have a word?'

The door opened. She was a stunner. A Chinese girl in her late teens, a doll's face and shiny black hair flowing loosely down her back. She had just showered and she glowed, squeaky clean and wholesome, in a white towelling bathrobe. She smelled of Johnson's baby powder. Her name was Koo Chen, a nurse at Denton Hospital, and she was getting ready for night duty. 'How can I help you?'

Bloody easily, thought Frost, but he let Burton do the talking. 'Is Bobby here?' Burton asked as she led them through to a tiny kitchen, everything spotless and gleaming.

'Bobby?' A flicker of concern darkened her face. 'Bobby is with his mother.'

'Could we speak to his father – Mr Harry Kirby?'

'He asleep. But I fetch.'

Harry Kirby was thickset with tight fair curly hair. Some six feet tall, he towered over the tiny nurse who looked up to him with obvious pride. Straight from bed, he had pulled on a pair of jeans and a grey sweater. 'What's this about Bobby?'

'Is he here, Mr Kirby?' said Burton.

'Here? Why should he be here?' He glared at Frost. 'What's happened?'

'He's gone missing, Mr Kirby,' said Frost.

Kirby listened, mouth agape with incredulity, anger reddening his face as Frost told him what had happened.

'That cow left my seven-year-old son alone in the house while she and that dickhead went to the pub?' He looked down at the nurse. 'Shoes!' he commanded.

Her eyes widened in alarm. 'Where you go?'

'Round to see that cow and her ponce of a boyfriend and smash their faces in.'

She thrust out her chin. 'No – you stay here.'

'He's not your son – he's mine. Get those shoes!'

'Hold it,' said Frost wearily, his head aching from all the squabbling. 'No-one's going anywhere. We're going to search the house.'

Kirby stared open-mouthed at Frost. 'You think he's here? You think I'm hiding my own son in my girlfriend's house? Where is he – behind the attic wall like Anne flaming Frank?'

'He's missing,' explained Frost patiently. 'We don't know where he is. He might have sneaked in without you knowing. So, for everyone's peace of mind, we're going to do a search.' The father went to follow them, but Frost jabbed a finger directing him back to the kitchen. 'Stay here, please.'

Burton checked the ground floor while Frost went up the stairs. First he checked the bathroom. Nowhere a child could hide, or be hidden. Just a wash-basin and a shower. A tin of Johnson's baby powder stood on the window ledge and the nurse's tiny damp footprints showed on the carpet tiles. Next to it was the spare bedroom, not much more than a boxroom, with a single bed and a small, white-painted chest of drawers. Opposite this was the nurse's bedroom, clean, neat and small like the nurse herself. It was just big enough to hold a double bed, jammed tight against the wall to save space, and a dressing-table. In the corner a built-in cupboard. Frost pulled the door open. Men's and women's clothes swinging hangers, a stack of ironing on the shelf and two empty suitcases. He knelt and looked under the bed. Something yellow and wispy was on the floor. A very short, skimpy nightdress with a heady perfume that was not Johnson's baby powder. The thought of slipping into that double bed with the soft, compliant little nurse made Frost almost forget what he was there for and he jerked round guiltily as Burton came into the room.

'Nothing downstairs,' reported Burton.

'Nor up here,' said Frost, 'apart from this!' He held up the nightdress. 'The naughty nurse's nightie . . . Cor, I bet her little bottom pokes out from under that like a couple of honeydew melons.'

Burton grinned. The joy of working with Frost was that he never let the circumstances of the case he was working on get him down.

Downstairs in the kitchen, Kirby was pulling on a thick duffle coat, anxiously watched by the nurse.

'I come with you,' she announced. She had a slight lisp which Frost was finding disconcertingly stimulating.

'No,' snapped Kirby. 'You get on to the hospital. You could well have two more patients in Emergency, by the time I've finished with them.'

'Go to bed and save your bloody energy,' said Frost. 'If we don't find Bobby tonight, we'll be organizing a search party first thing in the morning and we're going to need all the help we can get, which means you and Dickhead.'

As they stepped out into the street they could hear the car radio pleading for them to answer. 'Can you get over to the mortuary, inspector. The pathologist wants to see you urgently.'

The mortuary, a sombre-looking Victorian single-storey building, was situated in the grounds of Denton Hospital. Burton parked alongside the Rolls-Royce, which gleamed and sneered at Frost's mud-stained Ford. 'Looks like a bloody hearse,' sniffed Frost. There were other cars, a dark blue Audi which Frost recognized as belonging to Evans, the Scene of Crime officer, and the Vauxhall belonging to Harding from Forensic.

Most of the autopsy room was in darkness, but strong lights glared down at one of the tables where a gowned Drysdale, a green waterproof apron round his waist, beckoned the inspector over. Behind Drysdale, notebook in hand, was his ever faithful secretary. Drysdale preferred to dictate his notes rather than use cassette recorders which had let him down on more than one occasion. Evans, also wearing a green mortuary overall, hovered in the background with his camera. Alongside Evans, similarly gowned, was Harding from Forensic.

The tiny corpse of the boy seemed lost on the large autopsy table.

'I want you to see this,' said Drysdale. He bent over and carefully lifted the boy's right hand, the hand that had been covered by the white plastic bag.

Frost stared and his mouth sagged open. Behind him, Burton gasped. Where the boy's little finger should have been was now a bloodied stump. The finger had been hacked off just above the knuckle. Very gently, he took the cold, waxen hand from Drysdale to study it closer.

'A clean cut,' said Drysdale, almost with a note of admiration at the craftsmanship. 'I imagine a sharp blade was rested on the finger, then hit with something heavy. A single blow was sufficient. The wound was then doused with disinfectant, wrapped in cotton wool and strapped with sticking plaster. The bag was put on, I imagine, in case any blood leaked out.'

'Was it done before, or after, death?'

'Definitely before.'

'Poor little bastard!' said Frost.

'I doubt if he knew anything about it. I imagine that was why he was chloroformed.'

'Would it have required some degree of surgical skill to sever the finger?' said Burton, peering over Frost's shoulder.

'No,' said Drysdale. 'Just a high degree of callousness.'

'So a nurse could have done it?' suggested Frost.

Drysdale frowned. 'Anyone could have done it . . . a nurse, a plumber, a television repair man.'

'Would there have been much blood, doc?'

Drysdale pursed his lips and shook his head. 'Very little. You would get more blood cutting yourself shaving.' He nodded to his secretary who flipped over her notebook. 'Let's get on.' He glanced up at the clock. 'Examination of the body of Robert Kirby commenced at 1.57,' he dictated.

'Oh!' interrupted Frost. 'Sorry, doc – should have told you. This isn't Bobby. We don't know who he is.'

Drysdale glowered, his lips tight. 'Thank you for sharing that information, inspector. I find these little details rather important.' As he turned back to the table, Frost thumbed his nose at him.

Very slowly, Drysdale inspected the body, lifting the hands to examine the fingernails, searching for cuts, abrasions, any marks of injury. He raised the head and his fingers explored the scalp.

'If you could hurry it up, doc,' urged Frost. 'We don't know who the poor little sod is yet, and we want to get photographs off to the media.'

Ignoring him, Drysdale dictated his findings to his secretary. 'Little finger of right hand severed, but no other signs of external injuries.' He bent over the face. 'Vomit exuding from nose.' He took samples and passed them over to Harding. 'Mouth and eyes covered with brown plastic masking tape approximately 50mm wide.' He moved to one side. 'You may remove the tape now.'

Harding carefully eased it off with tweezers, first from the eyes, then the mouth. A sour smell of vomit and chloroform. The boy's mouth, distorted by the tape, had been frozen into a grotesque teeth-baring grin. The flash gun crackled and the film-winding motor whirred as Evans took pictures.

Drysdale studied the area around the lips and nostrils, pointing out where small fibres of cotton wool still adhered. He tweezered them off and passed them over to Harding. 'The anaesthetic was poured on a pad of cotton wool and clamped over the mouth, causing a slight burning of the flesh . . . here . . . and here.' He forced open the mouth and shone a small pen torch inside. 'Particles of undigested food and vomit . . . looks like ground meat, onion . . .' Then he tweezered out a piece of sodden cloth and held it aloft before dropping it into the large glass container Harding was holding out for him. 'The gag,' he announced. Then, with agonizing slowness, he extracted more samples from the mouth and nose.

'Any sign of sexual interference, doc?' asked Frost impatiently.

'I'll tell you when I'm ready,' murmured Drysdale, 'and not before.' He then proceeded to work even more slowly.

Frost sighed. The man was a bastard. He wandered off to a side room and helped himself to a mug of coffee from a thermos he found on the table. He had no wish to see the body opened and the organs removed and weighed. All he wanted was the findings . . . He sipped the coffee and smoked and tried to think of anything he should have done, but hadn't. He poured another mug of coffee, then wandered back to the autopsy room. The pathologist had finished and was washing his hands at the sink, while the mortuary attendant was busily suturing the gaping wounds. 'Brief findings, doc?' He stressed the 'brief'. Drysdale was inclined to be long-winded.

Drysdale tugged at the automatic towel dispenser. 'No sign of sexual assault. If that was the intention, then it wasn't carried out.'

'Good,' nodded Frost, although this meant there was

no way of knowing if they were looking for a sex attacker or not.

'His last meal was a proprietary hamburger – sesame seed bread roll, ground beef, onion rings, eaten very shortly before death.'

'How shortly?' Frost asked.

'Half an hour at the most.'

Frost thought this over as he tried to rub some life into his cheek. It was freezing cold in the autopsy room and his scar was starting to ache. The kid had a hamburger half an hour before he died. They'd have to check all the likely places – McDonald's, Burger King – in the hope someone might remember serving him amongst their hundreds of other customers . . . You're bound to remember him, he bought a hamburger! A forlorn, bloody hope, he knew.

'There's a very faint mark around the hair-line,' said Drysdale, leading him back to the body. 'You can hardly see it.' He slipped a finger under the hair to lift it and showed Frost what he meant . . . a barely perceptible white mark, just under an eighth of an inch wide, running across the forehead.

'What do you make of it, doc?'

'Something elasticated pulled over the hair. My secretary suggested a shower cap.' He nodded to the woman, who blushed and went back to writing out labels for the specimen jars.

'A shower cap?'

'Doesn't make much sense, but something like that. You'll get my fuller report in the morning.'

'Send it to Mr Allen,' said Frost. 'Not me – it's not my case, thank God!' Then he remembered what he meant to ask. 'Chloroform. Do they still use it in hospitals?'

Drysdale shook his head. 'Not for many years. It's been superseded.'

'So where would you get it – a chemist?'

Another shake of the head. 'Only if they've got some

very old stock they haven't got around to throwing away yet. Years ago it was used in certain prescribed medicines, but not any more. Anything else?'

Frost scratched his head. 'That's all I can think of, doc.'

'I'll bid you good night then.' He jerked his head to his secretary, who followed him out.

Evans began to bag up the materials removed from the body . . . the masking tape, the cotton wool and sticking plaster . . . The mortuary attendant came out to take the body back to the storage area, but Frost held up a hand to delay him. 'Take a couple of Polaroid shots of the face,' he instructed Evans. 'I want them faxed out to all forces in the hope someone can identify the poor little git.' He moved out of the way as the flash gun fired. One last look at the body. He lifted the hand with the severed finger. 'Why the hell would anyone want to do this?'

'Liz Maud has got a weirdo breaking into houses and stabbing kids,' said Burton. 'Could be him.'

'Could be,' said Frost, not sounding very convinced. 'I'll have a word with her.'

On the way out they passed Drysdale and his secretary in the midst of an angry exchange with the mortuary attendant who was hotly denying helping himself to coffee from their thermos flask.

In the car Frost settled back into the passenger seat and offered his cigarettes to Burton. 'I want you to check up on that little Chinese nurse. Find out where she was from four o'clock onwards, today.'

Burton frowned. 'You surely don't suspect her?'

'Sticking plaster, cotton wool, chloroform, things you'd find in a hospital. And she'd certainly know how to lop off a finger.'

'But what on earth would her motive be?'

'I don't know, son.' The cigarette waggled in his mouth as he spoke and sent a shower of ash down the front of his mac. 'Perhaps she was jealous of Kirby's son – perhaps he was spoiling their relationship.'

'But this is a different boy.'

'They all look the same to us – maybe our kids all look the same to them. Perhaps she got the wrong kid.' Even as he said it, it sounded weak. 'Just check her out, son. It'll give us something to do. We've got no other leads at the moment.'

A disgruntled Bill Wells grabbed Frost as soon as he entered the station. 'If you want me to do anything for you, Jack, like organize a search party, do me the courtesy of talking to me direct. I'm not having that stuck-up tart telling me what to do.'

'Sorry,' said Frost, knowing how prickly Wells could be. 'Have one of Mullett's fags and we'll say no more about it.' Wells took one and let the inspector light it for him. He was still not mollified.

'And where is the good lady in question?' asked Frost.

'Lording it up in the murder incident room.'

Frost nodded and breezed off down the corridor. 'I'll give her your love,' he called.

He sailed into the incident room. Liz had done a good job getting it organized, and under way. The fax machine in the corner was chirping away, spewing out yards of messages; two uniformed men were taking calls and another phone was ringing on an unoccupied desk. As Burton followed Frost in, she yelled, 'Answer that phone.'

Sullenly, Burton snatched it up. Like Wells, he wasn't happy taking orders from a woman.

'Be with you in a minute,' she called to Frost, putting down her phone and galloping over to the fax machine. She skimmed through the messages, shook her head in disappointment and dumped them in an already full wire basket. She was annoyed. 'We fax all forces asking if they've had a boy answering our description reported missing and they send us details of every missing boy they've got on their books whether he fits our description or not. Some have even sent details of missing girls!'

'Anything remotely like our boy?'

She pulled a fax from the pile. 'Just this seven-year-old, Duncan Ford, reported missing this afternoon from Scotland.'

Frost took the fax. 'Last seen in Montrose just after four thirty,' he read. 'Well, unless Concorde has changed its route, we can rule him out.' He gave her the Polaroid shots taken at the mortuary. 'Fax these around.' Then he remembered the photograph of Bobby the mother had given him. 'You'd better send this out as well.'

As she busied herself at the fax machine, he riffled through the heap of faxes received, then pushed the tray away. His gut feeling told him that the murdered child came from Denton and they were wasting their time enquiring elsewhere. When Liz came back he asked her about her child stabber.

'We've had four cases over the past week,' she told him. 'He breaks into the house, usually through a window, and stabs the kids while they sleep . . . just cuts their flesh. I think he gets a sexual kick out of seeing blood.'

'Do you think he'd get a bigger sexual kick cutting off a finger?' She shuddered as he told her about the dead boy and of Drysdale's findings. 'Let Mr Allen know tomorrow – and tell him his company is requested at the post-mortem, 10 a.m., top hat, white tie and tails.' He yawned. It was nearly three o'clock in the morning. 'I'm off home.' A wave to everyone. 'See you next week.'

As he left, she was yelling for one of the PCs to start checking through the rubbish bags stacked in the car-park to see if the dead boy's clothes had been dumped inside.

'Bossy little cow, isn't she?' whispered Frost to Burton.

'Too bleeding bossy,' muttered the DC.

'Still,' added Frost, 'I wouldn't kick her out of bed on a frosty night.'

Burton sniffed derisively. 'I wouldn't have her in my bed in the first place.'

It wasn't until he got home and the front door slammed behind him that he suddenly remembered Shirley. Shirley, who had been on holiday with him and who was going away again with him in the morning. He had left her in the house while he went off to the station to nick some fags from Mullett's goody box. Bloody hell! He had told her he would only be a couple of minutes and that was nearly five hours ago.

She wasn't in the living-room. He looked hopefully in the bedroom. The unmade bed was empty. Sod it! He snatched up the phone and dialled her number. The engaged tone. She had left the phone off the hook. Sod, sod and double sod. He considered driving round to her place, but was too damn tired. What a bloody fine holiday this was turning out to be. Piddling with rain all the time he was away, a murder case, a post-mortem and a solitary bed. He undressed, letting his clothes fall on the floor by the bed, then flopped down on the mattress.

He slept soundly until seven thirty when the insistent ringing of the phone brought him reluctantly to the surface. It could only be Shirley. But at this time? He lifted the phone.

'Frost,' he mumbled, sounding very contrite.

It wasn't Shirley. It was the station. Mullett wanted him to report there right away.

'Tell the silly sod I'm on holiday,' said Frost.

'The silly sod knows that,' answered Bill Wells. 'But he still wants to see you and he's in a real right mood.'

Frost's heart nose-dived. 'He's not been counting his bloody fags, has he?'

It was ten past eight and still dark as he turned the Ford into the car-park at the rear of the station. Usually half empty at this time of the morning, it was now jam-packed with alien vehicles of all kinds. Bobby Kirby was obviously still missing and the search party was assembling. Every available officer had been called in to help, including off-duty personnel and officers who could be spared from neighbouring divisions. All very efficiently organized. Frost was glad it wasn't his case. Organization and efficiency weren't his strong point. He'd have made a complete sod-up of it all.

As he bumped along, looking for somewhere to leave the Ford, a stray dog in the kennels started to bark and was answered by suppressed whining from the dog-handler's van over in the far corner. Space was at a premium, but he managed a clumsy double-park which effectively boxed in Mullett's blue Jaguar.

In the lobby, a weary-looking Sergeant Bill Wells, who should have gone off duty at six, was directing a group of constables from Thorrington Division up to the canteen where the main briefing was to take place. 'Follow the smell of stewed tea and burnt bacon – you can't miss it,' called Frost.

Wells beckoned Frost over, his eyes glinting as they always did when he had an item of tasty gossip to impart. 'Did you hear what happened last night?'

'You got your leg over with Liz Maud?' suggested Frost.

'She should be so lucky!' snorted Wells. He leant across the desk. 'That booze-up that Mullett and Allen attended. It was some sort of senior police do – top brass from all divisions were there.'

'My invite must have been lost in the post,' said Frost.

'Anyway,' continued Wells, getting to the meaty bit, 'my information is, they sunk a lot more booze than was good for them and they were all well over the limit. Chief Inspector Formby from Greenford Division was giving four of them a lift back. He was in no fit state to drive, but that didn't stop him. Just outside the hotel car-park there's a lamp post. Formby wraps the car round it and turns it over.'

Frost beamed. 'I like happy endings.'

'It's even happier,' continued Wells. 'They're all in Felstead Hospital with broken arms and ribs – Formby's leg is broken as well.'

'Serves the bastard right,' said Frost. 'If he had an inch of common decency he'd have given Allen and Mullett a lift as well and broken both their bloody legs.'

Two more uniformed men swept in. Wells steered them up the stairs to the canteen, then leant over to Frost, lowering his voice. 'Here's the best bit, Jack. The ambulance was called and the Traffic boys turn up anxious to breathalyse the driver – the car just stunk of malt whisky.'

'Bloody hell,' said Frost. 'I'd give up my pension for the chance to breathalyse a sod like Formby.'

'He wasn't breathalysed, Jack. Someone pulled rank.'

'There's no justice,' said Frost.

'Anyway, five senior officers in hospital is going to make them a bit thin on the ground for a few weeks.' The internal phone rang. Mullett. 'He wants you,' said Wells.

'He can't have everything he wants,' said Frost.

Mullett dropped the Alka Seltzers in the glass of water and winced at the headsplitting fizzing noise. He shouldn't have drunk so much last night, but the other officers were so insistent and he didn't want to appear the odd man out. A perfunctory tap at the door and before he could say 'Enter' Frost had shuffled in. Mullett groaned. Was that the only suit the man had? He squeezed out a thin smile and waved Frost to a chair, then swilled down the Alka Seltzer.

'Have a good holiday?' he asked.

'Peed with rain all week,' grunted Frost.

'Good,' said Mullett, who wasn't listening.

'Did you get my comic postcard?' asked Frost.

Mullett frowned. Yes, he had got the card. And torn it up immediately. 'It was extremely rude,' he muttered.

Frost looked puzzled. 'Rude? You must have spotted some double meaning I missed.'

Mullett flapped a hand. 'Be that as it may. Sorry to drag you in, Frost, but things happened last night. Five of our top men involved in a car accident.'

'So I heard,' said Frost. 'The car had a fight with a lamp post.'

'Yes – a patch of oil on the road. They skidded.' Mullett, not a good liar, didn't sound very convincing.

'Was Formby breathalysed?' asked Frost. 'I understand he'd had a few.'

'Oh – Chief Inspector Formby wasn't driving,' said Mullett, carefully avoiding Frost's eye. 'His daughter was driving and she hadn't been drinking.'

Frost smiled and gave a conspiratorial wink. 'Bloody clever! You're a lot of crafty sods, sir, that's all I can say.'

'What do you mean?'

'It's obvious. Formby was driving. He didn't dare be breathalysed, so you brought his daughter in from home to pretend she was the driver.'

Mullett tried to sound suitably shocked. 'That's a libellous thing to say, Frost. His daughter was driving. We all gave statements to that effect.'

'Then the witness who claims to have seen it all differently is telling lies?' said Frost. He put on his innocent expression. 'What did you want to see me about?'

But Mullett was now in a high state of agitation. 'What witness? What does he claim to have seen? You must tell me.'

'If what you say is true, then he couldn't have seen anything, could he, sir?' said Frost blandly. 'It would be your word against his anyway, even if he is a vicar.'

Mullett stared hard and jotted a note on his pad. He would have to talk to Frost about this later – man to man on a friendly basis. He hadn't wanted to get involved in this wretched deception anyway, but they had pulled rank and twisted his arm. He cleared his throat. 'The result of this unfortunate accident is that five senior officers are nursing broken bones in hospital.'

'Then it wasn't all bad,' said Frost.

Mullett ignored this. 'Obviously, this has meant some temporary relocation of personnel. In our case it means that Inspector Allen has been seconded to Greenford Division as acting chief inspector until such time as Mr Formby is fit enough to return.'

'When is he going?' asked Frost.

'He's already gone. It was arranged last night.'

'Do you mean to tell me,' said Frost, 'that Allen knew he wouldn't be here when he conned me into taking over his cases on a temporary basis last night?'

'I don't know anything about that,' said Mullett, again not meeting Frost's eye.

'The bastard,' said Frost, banging his fist on Mullett's desk which jolted the headache into overdrive.

'Please!' Mullett held his head. 'You will take over all his cases.'

'That still leaves us a man short.'

'There will be a temporary replacement for Mr Allen . . . a detective sergeant as acting inspector. We haven't finalized the details yet.'

'The sooner the better – we're pushed enough as it is.'

Mullett waved a hand of dismissal. 'I'll leave you to it then. Sorry to have to cut your holiday short, but it couldn't be avoided.'

'A few less drinks last night and it would have been,' said Frost, pushing himself out of the chair.

As the door closed, Mullett heard a startled cry from his secretary and a raucous laugh from Frost. 'Caught you bending there, Ida!'

The Divisional Commander shook his head sadly. What could you do with a man like that?

Frost took a quick look in Allen's office on his way up to the briefing. He shuddered. The room was so neat and tidy it almost hurt. Desk tops clear, wall charts meticulously entered, and the prissy smell of lavender wax polish. A cold, heartless room, which matched its former occupant, and which made Frost itch to get back to the warm, untidy fug of his own office. He delved into Allen's in-tray, and pulled out a neat stack of forms and returns which had to be completed and sent off to County by the third of the month. Trust the sod to leave them behind. He put them back and went across the corridor to the incident room where Liz Maud, still in her drab grey outfit, was surprised to see him.

'I thought you were on holiday, inspector?'

He explained about Allen. Her eyes narrowed. If a detective sergeant was to be made up to acting inspector, then who better than her!

'There's a few returns and things in his office,' said Frost vaguely. 'Perhaps you could see if you could handle them.'

'No problem,' she said. 'I'll move in there.'

'I take it we didn't find Bobby Kirby?'

'No. The briefing for the search party is in five minutes.'

'Right – I suppose I'd better do it.'

She concealed her disappointment. In the absence of Allen, she was hoping she could take this over.

'Have we identified the dead kid?'

'No.'

'Damn.' He lit up a cigarette and stared out of the window on to the car-park. 'A young kid, eight years old at the most and dead for nearly fifteen hours. Why haven't his parents reported him missing?' He sucked hard at the cigarette as he had a thought. 'It could be because it's his parents who killed him.' He spun round to Liz. 'As soon as the schools open, get on the phone to the head teachers. I want to know if there's any seven- or eight-year-old boys who haven't turned up for school today.'

'Right.'

'But don't tell them he's dead – not until we've traced and informed the parents.'

'Of course not.' Give her credit for some common sense.

'Any joy with the rubbish sacks?'

'Plenty of prints, but we're checking with the shop people today to eliminate them. And no sign of the clothing.'

'Has everyone in the briefing got copies of both photographs – the dead kid and Bobby?'

'Yes.'

'And the guy? People might not have noticed the kid, but they could remember the guy.'

'Yes. And I've sent copies of the photograph of Bobby to the press and TV and we're having a pile of "Have you seen this boy" posters run off. Also some extra large ones to stick on a loudspeaker van to tour the neighbourhood.'

'Good,' nodded Frost. He had forgotten about that. 'Right, let's get the search party briefed.'

The canteen was packed. He snatched himself a mug of tea and a bacon sandwich and elbowed his way through to the front. 'Your attention, please!'

There were murmurs of surprise. Everyone had been expecting Inspector Allen.

'First the good news – and I must ask you to promise not to laugh. Chief Inspector Formby was injured in a car crash last night and is in hospital with two broken arms and a broken leg.' He paused as delighted laughter roared out. 'And this will really make you laugh – he's in quite a bit of pain.'

There were one or two cheers at this. Formby with his sneering manner and sarcastic tongue was not a popular officer.

'The bad news is that Inspector Allen has been seconded to Greenford as acting chief inspector and I'm in charge of this missing boy enquiry. You are looking for Bobby Kirby, aged seven. You all have a photograph and a description. His parents have split up and he lives with his mother and her boyfriend. Last night the mother and the boyfriend nipped out to the pub for a quick one, leaving the kid alone in the house. When they returned just after ten, the kid wasn't there. Apparently he sneaked out with his guy to collect money. About eleven o'clock last night we found the guy behind a pile or rubbish bags stacked in a shop doorway in Patriot Street. Next to the guy was a boy's body in a rubbish sack. The boy, aged around seven or eight, had been chloroformed and gagged with plastic masking tape and had choked on his own vomit. He was naked, but there was no sign of sexual assault. The boy was not Bobby Kirby and up to now he has not been reported as missing so we don't know who he is. We'll be checking with schools as soon as they open. So our task is twofold. To find Bobby and to find out all we can about the dead boy.'

He deliberately didn't say anything about the severed finger. There'd be floods of hoax calls and fake confessions and he wanted there to be something that only the real murderer would know.

'About half an hour before he died, the boy ate a hamburger. It's going to be a bloody waste of time, but we've got to check all the fast food joints in Denton and ask if they remember serving something as unusual as a hamburger to the boy in the photograph around, say, four to five o'clock. I'm sure this will give us about three hundred useless leads, but it's got to be done. Any questions?'

A duffle-coated PC from Lexton Division put up his hand. 'You think there's a connection between the dead boy and Bobby?'

'The dead kid was found next to Bobby's guy. That's the only connection we've got at the moment. It could be a coincidence, but it's good enough for me. I say there's a connection.' He looked around. No-one else had any questions. 'Right. You've been allocated your search areas, so the very best of luck.'

He watched them file out clutching the copies of the photographs. He was hoping for the best, but he had a nasty feeling at the pit of his stomach that they were not going to find anything.

3

Phones in the incident room were ringing non-stop. The TV appeal for Bobby's return made by his distraught parents, the tear-stained mother with her husband's arm firmly around her, Terry Green and the Chinese nurse tactfully absent, had provoked a terrific response from people convinced they had seen Bobby. None of the leads seemed very hopeful, but all would have to be followed up.

In the same TV bulletin, a photograph of the dead boy was shown with a statement that the police were anxious to identify him. No mention was made of the fact that he was dead, nor that there might be a connection with Bobby.

DC Burton, his ear sore from being constantly pressed against the phone, scribbled some details and thanked the caller. He tossed the form into the main collection basket.

'Any news from Forensic?' asked Frost, dropping in the chair next to him.

'Nothing worth having. The masking tape on the boy's face is run of the mill stuff and there were no prints on it. The cotton wool is a standard type. The plastic bag round his hand came from Bi-Wize supermarket and there were no prints on the rubbish sack the body was in.'

'If we didn't have a Forensic Department,' said Frost, 'how would we know we had sod all to go on? What about the prints on the other rubbish sacks?'

'The only prints found so far came from the shop staff.'

'This bloke is too bloody clever to leave prints,' said Frost gloomily. He glanced up at the clock. Nine twenty-five. The kid had been dead for some sixteen hours and no-one had yet reported him missing. 'Who's in charge of checking the schools?'

'Wonder Woman. She's in Mr Allen's office.'

'Right, son.' Frost pushed himself up from the chair. 'Let's go and see what she's got – if you'll pardon the expression.'

Bill Wells was distributing the internal mail. From force of habit he knocked on the door of Inspector Allen's office and a red light signalling 'Wait' flashed. Dutifully, he waited. Then a green light bade him 'Enter'. He went in and stared goggle-eyed. Sitting at Inspector Allen's desk as if she owned the bloody place was Liz bloody Maud. The cow! Flicking the switch to make him wait. Who the hell did she think she was?

She didn't look up, just waggled her finger at the in-tray. 'In there, please.' Fuming, Wells flung the mail in. As he reached the door, she called him. 'Sergeant!'

He turned. She was holding up a red folder and beckoning for him to come over. 'Do you mind taking this to Mr Mullett?'

'Yes, I bloody well do mind,' he snapped, and his slamming of the door echoed around the building.

Liz shrugged. She knew Wells resented her. Well, he would just have to learn to start taking orders from a woman, because her immediate aim was to be made up to acting detective inspector during Allen's absence. She had seen Superintendent Mullett and explained why she was the most suitable person for the temporary promotion. He had nodded vigorously and agreed wholeheartedly with everything she had said. 'The decision is not up to me,' he had told her, 'but it will receive my strongest personal recommendation.' As she didn't yet know Mullett very well, she believed him.

Spluttering with indignation, Wells buttonholed Frost as he came out of the murder incident room and poured out his moans about Liz Maud. 'In Allen's office – and with the red light on.'

'Perhaps she's turning it into a knocking shop,' suggested Frost.

But Wells was too angry for jokes. 'Who the hell does she think she is? She's only a flaming sergeant and she's acting like a . . .' He stopped open-mouthed as the almost unthinkable thought struck him. 'Flaming hell, Jack. You don't think she's going to be made up to acting DI, do you?'

'Could be,' said Frost. 'I saw her coming out of Mullett's office with her knickers in her hand.'

'I wonder she wears any,' snarled Wells, stamping off. 'I bet that's how she was made up to sergeant.'

Frost went into Allen's office without knocking although the red light was on. 'What news from the schools?' he asked.

'Five boys in the right age group didn't attend for lessons today,' she told him. 'Three they know about – one to the dentist, one in hospital and one the mother phoned through this morning to say he had a cold . . .'

'Check that one,' said Frost. 'The mother could be lying. What about the other two?'

'I've sent Collier round to the houses. I'll let you know as soon as he reports in.'

Ten o'clock. A lull in the incident room. The phones had stopped ringing and Frost was sitting on the corner of a desk, watching Liz who was stretching across to stick coloured pins into the wall maps, to mark the progress of the various search parties, and was showing lots of leg into the bargain. 'I wouldn't mind sticking something in her,' he murmured to Burton.

Progress was slow. Everything up to now was negative. The five boys who were away from school had all been accounted for. The fingerprints on the rubbish bags all came from the shop staff, except for two which were too blurred to provide any positive identification but like the others probably came from a shop assistant. The little Chinese nurse was reported to be very fond of Bobby and wouldn't lift a finger to harm him. A missing boy and a dead boy and no leads to follow on either.

The phone rang. He looked up hopefully, but it was Mullett asking for a progress report.

'Tell him it consists of two words,' grunted Frost, 'and the second is "all"!'

'Still following up leads, sir,' translated Liz. 'We'll let you know as soon as we have something positive.' She went back to her wall map.

Bill Wells came in, grinning all over his face. 'Control have just had a phone call from a motorist. Said a naked girl tried to flag him down in Hanger Lane.'

Frost brightened up. Naked girls interested him very much. 'Did he pick her up?'

'No. He couldn't stop. Said he was in a hurry to keep an appointment. He phoned us on his mobile.'

Frost frowned and shook his head in disbelief. 'A naked girl and he didn't stop? I'd have stopped if she was only half naked . . . Bloody hell, I'd have stopped if she was fully dressed with one titty hanging out.'

'You're all heart, Jack,' said Wells.

'Some people say I'm all dick,' said Frost, 'but I try not to brag.' A snort of disgust from Liz Maud made him pull a face at Wells.

'I've sent Jordan and Simms to pick her up,' said Wells.

'Some people have all the luck,' said Frost.

Another phone rang. Liz answered it. She listened and her expression changed.

'What's up?' asked Frost.

'That naked girl. It's not as funny as you thought it was. She's only fifteen. She was abducted last night by a gang of men. Her parents had to pay a £25,000 ransom to get her back.'

'Shit!' swore Frost. 'We've got enough on our flaming plates without this . . .' He stared at her thoughtfully before reaching a decision. 'You can handle this one, love,' he said, 'if you don't mind me coming with you.'

They went in Liz's car, Frost sitting next to her and Evans, the Scene of Crime officer, in the back seat. It was a white-knuckle drive as she slammed the car in and out of the tight country lanes, trusting to luck there was nothing coming in the opposite direction. Frost sank down low in his seat and tried not to look at the blur of greenery flashing from side to side across the windscreen as she spun the wheel, slammed on the brakes and skidded, narrowly avoiding catastrophe after catastrophe.

'Left here,' he murmured.

'No – right,' said Evans from the back seat.

She turned right. Up to now, Frost had been wrong with his directions every time and she'd had to slam on the brakes and do a reverse.

'There it is,' said Evans.

Liz turned the car into a long drive leading to a large, ivy-clad Edwardian house standing alone and surrounded by fields. Frost stared at the house. He'd been here before, but couldn't remember when, or why. A police car was parked just outside the front door. She slowed and parked behind it. Frost and Evans staggered out. PC Jordan came from the house to brief them.

'Family of three – husband, wife and fifteen-year-old daughter. Husband and wife travelled up to London last night to see a show. They got back home around three in the morning. The house had been ransacked, jewellery and furs valued at £50,000 missing. They found this on the kitchen table.' He gave Frost a sheet of A4 white paper which had been slipped inside a transparent folder to preserve any prints. The message had been printed on a bubble jet printer, and read:

> TO MR & MRS STANFIELD
> WE HAVE YOUR DAUGHTER. IF YOU GO TO THE POLICE WE WILL GANG RAPE HER. ONE OF US IS HIV POSITIVE.
>
> IF YOU WANT HER RETURNED UNHARMED YOU WILL GO TO YOUR BANK AS SOON AS IT OPENS AT 9.30 AND WITHDRAW £25,000 IN USED NOTES. YOU WILL PUT THE MONEY IN A SMALL SUITCASE. AS YOU PASS THE WHITE GATE IN CLAY LANE YOU WILL THROW THE CASE OUT OF THE CAR INTO THE DITCH. YOU WILL DRIVE STRAIGHT HOME. YOU WILL NOT LOOK BACK.
>
> IF YOU DO ALL THIS AND THERE ARE NO TRICKS WE WILL RELEASE YOUR DAUGHTER UNHARMED. IF YOU TRY TO TRICK US SHE WON'T BE WORTH HAVING WHEN WE RETURN HER. THE ENCLOSED IS TO SHOW WE MEAN BUSINESS!

'This was with it,' said Jordan, handing Frost a Polaroid photograph, also in a transparent cover. It showed the girl, kneeling on the floor. A hand of someone out of sight had grabbed her hair and pulled her head back. The other hand held a knife which was pressed against the girl's throat. Her eyes were closed and her mouth sagged open. She was naked.

'They ripped her nightdress off with a knife,' said Jordan.

'I usually use my teeth,' grunted Frost, passing the photo and the message to Liz.

'The family are in the lounge with Simms,' Jordan told him. 'Do you want to see them?'

'Show me round the house first,' said Frost, hoping it might jog his memory as to when he was here before. 'How did the gang get in?'

'Through the back door – I'll show you.'

Jordan walked them down a side path to the rear of the property where a small patio with tubbed plants backed on to the lawn. The back door had one of its glass panels smashed. The gang had punched a hole in the glass, reached in and turned the key which had been conveniently left in the lock.

Frost squinted through the smashed pane. 'Stupid bastards! They install an expensive, six lever mortice lock, then they leave the flaming key in it.' He waited as Evans, his hand gloved, opened the door for them. They stepped over broken glass on the mat, into the kitchen, Evans staying behind to dust the door for prints. A pine wood table had been laid the night before with cups and cereal bowls for a breakfast that had not been eaten. Frost picked up the cereal packet. 'All Bran – nature's laxative. I bet no-one needed that this morning.' Jordan laughed, but Liz didn't find it funny. 'How many of them were there?'

'Four, we think,' said Jordan, taking them through a door leading to the hall. 'The first thing they did was to turn the electricty off at the mains.' He opened a small cupboard door under the stairs and revealed electricity and gas meters, side by side, with the central heating control box just below.

Frost frowned. 'Why did they do that?'

'So the girl couldn't call the police. She had a phone in her bedroom – it was one of those cordless models. If the electricity is off, they don't function.'

'I thought they were battery powered,' said Liz.

'The handsets are, but most base units are mains powered – without electricity they just don't work,' Jordan told her.

'I thought they only didn't work when I dropped the bleeding things on the floor,' said Frost, checking the clock on the central heating timer with his watch. It was only a couple of minutes slow. 'It wasn't switched off for long, then?'

'Once they got the girl, they switched the power back on. They needed the electric light so they could ransack the rooms.'

Evans rejoined them, shaking his head sadly. 'No-one leaves fingerprints any more.'

'Crooks today have no consideration for the police,' said Frost. He still couldn't remember why he had been in the house. 'Let's see the girl's bedroom.'

A typical teenager's room. Posters on the wall advertising past pop concerts and a large one saying 'Save The Whale'. A black ash wall unit held a hi-fi system with two tiny Wharfdale speakers and a 10-inch colour TV set. The room had been turned over. Drawers gaped, their contents strewn all over the floor. Frost's nose twitched. The girl's perfume lingered. A bit sexy for a fifteen-year-old, and so were the pair of scanty briefs he bent and picked up. He showed them to Liz. 'You'd have a job stuffing your hankie up the leg of these.'

Jordan grinned, but Liz stared stonily. The man was an ignorant pig.

Frost flicked the briefs across the room and they butterflyed delicately down to the carpet. 'What was taken from here, Jordan?'

'The girl's too upset to check, but her mother doesn't think anything is missing.' He pointed to a heap of chunky beads, bangles and necklaces tipped out on the floor. 'It's all junk, not worth pinching.'

'I'm surprised they didn't take that little telly,' said Frost. 'I wouldn't mind having that myself.'

'They were after bigger fish,' said Jordan. 'Jewels and furs from the parents' room. I'll show you.'

The main bedroom was a bigger shambles than the girl's, with drawers dragged open and clothes strewn about apparently just for the hell of making a mess. On the big double bed the contents of a drawer had been tipped out – underwear, perfume bottles, cosmetics, in an untidy heap. 'The jewel box was in that drawer,' said

Jordan. 'They took the lot, box as well . . . fifty thousand quid's worth, they claim – including the fur coats from the wardrobe.' He nodded towards the far wall where the sliding door of the woman's wardrobe was open, showing a jumble of coats and dresses on the floor and empty hangers swinging above.

Frost picked his way through the mess on the floor to take a closer look. 'Why did they drag all these dresses off?' he asked. 'They could have got to the furs without doing that.'

'Some people get a kick out of leaving things in a mess,' said Liz.

Frost grunted. It could be the answer. He peered through the large picture window which overlooked the garden and the fields and the winding lane which was the only access to the house. Some more houses in the far distance, but not a soul to be seen. He was fumbling for his cigarettes when a man's voice bellowed from downstairs.

'When you've finished sodding about up there, what about talking to us – or aren't the victims important any more?'

He went to the landing and looked down. An angry-looking man was glaring up at them. Robert Stanfield, early fifties, sallow complexion and a tight, thin little mouth.

Frost frowned. He'd seen Stanfield before . . . in this house, but still couldn't recall the circumstances. He clattered down the stairs, followed by Liz and Jordan, Evans staying behind to photograph and check for prints. Then it all came back to him. He smiled broadly. 'We meet again, Mr Stanfield.'

The man's eyes crawled over Frost's face. A brief flicker of apprehension, then a thin, scornful smile. 'Ah yes – the arson attack. Let's hope you are more successful this time, inspector. In here . . .' He jerked his head to direct them into the lounge.

PC Dave Simms, sitting by the door, jumped up as Frost entered. It was a large and comfortable room with a recently lit log fire crackling in the grate. Wide casement windows gave a view across the garden. In the corner stood a large screen television set on a stand, beneath it a video recorder, its clock, not yet reset, flickering on and off showing there had been a break in the current.

Stanfield hurled himself into an armchair by the fire and swilled down a glass of whisky which had been perched on the arm. Opposite him, in a settee drawn close to the fire, sat his wife and his daughter. His wife, Margie Stanfield, dark-haired, in her early forties, wearing a red and black satin housecoat, was flashily attractive. Frost couldn't remember seeing her before. But it was the girl, Carol, PC Simms's greatcoat draped around her, who held Frost's attention. She looked much older than her fifteen years. Her dark brown hair was long and flowing and uncombed, giving her a wild, untamed appearance. She kept her head down, but her eyes, narrow like her father's, were watching Frost suspiciously and reminded him of a cornered animal with nothing to lose and ready to fight back.

Somehow I don't trust you, my love, thought Frost as he gave her his warm and friendly smile.

'I want you to get these bastards,' said Stanfield. 'They've stolen my wife's jewellery and fur coats, they've subjected my daughter to hours of terror and they've blackmailed me into giving them £25,000.'

'Not your day, sir, was it?' said Frost.

Stanfield opened his mouth to reply when he noticed Liz Maud who had followed Frost in. 'Who the hell is she?'

Liz took the warrant card from her handbag and handed it to him. He looked at it and gave a contemptuous sneer as he handed it back. 'A bloody woman sergeant! I'm not being fobbed off with second best, am I?'

'No,' said Frost. 'I'm second best – she's class. And it's her case.' Stanfield's snort showed what he thought of this. He hadn't invited them to sit down, so Frost dragged the other armchair over to the fire and offered it to Liz while he sat on the arm. 'Ask the gentleman your questions, sergeant.'

She opened her notebook. 'Tell me everything that happened.'

'I've already told that police officer.' Stanfield nodded at Simms. 'He wrote it all down.'

'We can't read his writing,' said Frost. 'So tell it again.'

'My wife and I went up to London to see a show – *The Phantom of the Opera*.'

'Just you and your wife?' interrupted Liz. 'Not your daughter?'

'As she was bloody abducted while we were away, it's obvious we didn't take her.'

'I know you didn't take her,' said Liz through clenched teeth. 'I'm wondering why.'

'If I'd booked the tickets myself, I obviously would have included Carol. Friends of ours had two tickets but found they couldn't go, so they passed them on to us. Satisfied, darling?'

She gritted her teeth at the 'darling' and nodded.

'We left just after four yesterday afternoon, drove up to London, saw the show, had a meal, and came home.'

'What time did you arrive back?'

'A little after three in the morning. I parked the car, Margie went upstairs to switch on the electric blanket and found the bedroom had been ransacked.'

'Perfume, make-up, dresses, just thrown anywhere,' said his wife. 'I screamed for Robert. He charged up and made for Carol's room to see if she was all right.'

'The bastards had got her,' said Stanfield. 'My first thought was to phone the police, but I couldn't find the cordless phone – it should have been by Carol's bed.'

'They threw it out of the window,' said the girl. She spoke almost mechanically, staring straight ahead. Her mother put an arm round to comfort her.

'Anyway,' continued Stanfield, 'I couldn't find it so I went to use the phone in here.' He pointed to a phone next to the TV set. 'A note and a photograph were propped up against it.'

'We've seen them,' said Liz.

'Then you know what the bastards threatened to do if I called the police. I had no choice. I did exactly what they wanted. We sat in here, staring at each other until the bank opened. It was the longest bloody night of my life. I drew out the money, chucked the case out in Clay Lane, then roared back here to wait. We were going mad with worry – and then your two officers brought her back.'

'£25,000? You had that sort of money in the bank?'

'Yes – I run a used car business. Most of my suppliers insist on hard cash.'

Liz then turned to the girl, who had been staring down at the floor all the time her father was talking. 'Right, Carol. Can you tell me what happened to you?'

Carol drew Simms's greatcoat tighter around her and Frost realized she was naked underneath. Her voice was not much more than a whisper and they had to strain to hear what she was saying. She had gone to bed just after midnight and was just dropping off when she heard the sound of breaking glass from downstairs. She thought it might be her parents back early, so she clicked on the bedside lamp. Almost immediately the lamp went out. Then she heard men's voices from inside the house. She fumbled in the dark for the cordless phone and dialled 999, but nothing happened. The phone was dead. Heavy footsteps pounded up the stairs . . .

'I jumped out of bed and tried to wedge a chair under the door handle, but he burst in on me and there was this light in my eyes and the knife . . .' She started to shake. Her mother held her tighter.

'Take your time, love,' said Frost.

'I opened my mouth to scream, but he jabbed the knife at my throat and said if I made a sound he'd slice through my vocal cords. I must have passed out.' The recollection made her shrink back inside the greatcoat. 'The next thing I remember was being bumped about. I realized I was in the back of a van, being driven at speed. I was blindfolded and I was cold. They'd thrown a sack over me, but I was freezing. I tried to get up, but a hand pushed me down and a man's voice said, "I think she's with us again." They pulled the sacking back.'

'*They*?' queried Liz.

'There were two of them in the back with me. They pulled the sacking back and they . . . they did things . . .'

'The bastards,' exploded her father.

'What things?' asked Liz.

The girl shook her head. 'I'm not going to talk about it.'

'Did they rape you?' asked Liz.

'No.'

'How many of them were there?' said Frost.

She switched her gaze to him. 'Four. Two in the back with me, the other two in the front.'

'And all men?'

'I only heard men's voices.'

'How old would you say they were?'

She shrugged. 'I don't know – late twenties, early thirties.'

'And you didn't recognize any of the voices?'

'No.'

Liz waited patiently for Frost to finish. 'I'd like a doctor to examine you, Carol.'

'No.'

'If they raped you, there are DNA tests that would help us identify them.'

'They didn't rape me, I told you . . . I'm not going to talk about it any more.'

'All right,' soothed Liz. 'What happened then?'

'The van stopped and they changed places . . . the other two men came in. I pretended I'd passed out, so they didn't do anything much, just sat and smoked. After what seemed such a long time, someone banged on the side of the van and called, "We've got the money." The van drove off, then it stopped and I was pushed out. By the time I'd got the blindfold off, it was out of sight. A car came . . . but it wouldn't stop . . . and then the police car picked me up.' She wrapped the greatcoat around her like a cocoon.

'I really would like a doctor to take a look at you,' urged Liz.

'No!' She screamed the word out. 'I'm all right. Just leave me alone.' With an abrupt shrug she shook off her mother's arm. 'Just leave me alone.'

'She's upset,' said her mother.

'That's right,' exploded Stanfield sarcastically, 'explain it to them. They wouldn't bloody know otherwise.' To Frost he said, 'Right inspector, you've had a nice sit-down – now go and catch the bastards.'

'Just a few more questions,' said Frost. He smiled at the girl. 'You heard breaking glass. You switched on the bedside lamp and tried to dial 999. The lamp went out and the phone was dead—'

'Because they'd switched off the current,' said Stanfield, as if explaining to an idiot.

'Exactly. Between the time you heard the sound of glass breaking, which was them getting into the house, and the phone going dead, how much time elapsed?'

'I don't know . . . seconds . . .'

Frost nodded. 'They were bloody quick, weren't they? They knew exactly where the meter was.'

'It wouldn't take a bloody mastermind to work that out,' exclaimed Stanfield. 'Most people have their meter cupboard under the stairs.'

'Yes,' agreed Frost, 'but these people had to be sure.

They had to do it bloody quickly otherwise Carol would have made her phone call. There's only one way out of here – along that four mile lane. The police would have been waiting for them. How did the gang know that the phone in Carol's bedroom was cordless?'

'I've had this house up for sale for the past four months,' said Stanfield. 'We've had estate agents in and out measuring up, we've had prospective buyers and every nosy sod imaginable poking and touching everything with their grubby fingers . . . any of them could have been casing the place.'

'We'll need names,' said Liz.

'Then get them from the estate agents, darling. They didn't leave flaming visiting cards, just sticky bloody finger marks on the wallpaper.'

'When did your friends offer you the tickets for the show?' asked Frost.

'The day before yesterday. He had to go to Paris on business. Why?'

'I'm wondering how the crooks knew Carol would have been alone in the house last night.'

'They could have been watching the place and picked their moment. We do go out at night from time to time.'

Frost pulled a face. He didn't think much of this explanation. Before he could ask another question, Jordan was beckoning from the doorway. 'Sorry to disturb you, inspector, but it is urgent.'

Frost stood up. 'What was the value of the jewellery they nicked?'

'I haven't added it up – around £50,000,' said the woman.

'But you are insured?'

'It's not the money, is it – it's the sentimental value.'

'Of course,' said Frost.

Stanfield sprang to his feet. 'And just what are you insinuating?'

Frost switched on his look of injured innocence.

'Nothing, Mr Stanfield. Nothing at all. Now, if you'll excuse me . . .'

He followed Jordan into the hall, closing the door behind him. 'What is it, son?'

It was a radio message from Control. A woman had just phoned in reporting her eight-year-old son had been missing since the previous afternoon. Her description matched the dead boy.

Frost swore softly. 'I suppose no-one's given the poor cow any hint that he's dead?'

'No, sir,' said Jordan.

'We'll go in your car,' said Frost. 'Sergeant Maud can stay and finish up here.' He went back into the lounge and quietly explained the position to Liz. 'Got to go,' he told Stanfield. 'Something important has come up.'

Stanfield stared incredulously. 'Something more important than this?'

'Yes,' sighed Frost. 'Something more important than this.'

Jordan negotiated the car round the twists and turns of the narrow lane with much more care and skill than Liz had done. Frost was sitting alongside him, smoking, lost in his thoughts. If the dead boy was her son, how was he going to break it to her? Eight years old . . . God . . . He had radioed for Burton to meet him outside the house. He would have preferred to have a woman police officer with him, but they were all out helping with the search for Bobby Kirby. Still, breaking news like this was a job he had done many times before. Too many bloody times.

Jordan dragged him back from his brooding thoughts. 'What do you reckon is behind this abduction, inspector?'

Frost took the cigarette from his mouth and dribbled smoke down his nose. 'I'm not even sure there was an abduction, son.'

Jordan frowned. 'What do you mean?'

'I've come across Stanfield before. He runs this second-hand car business. About four years ago the Customs and Excise were suspicious that he was working some VAT fiddle. The day before they were due to examine his books there was a mysterious and very convenient arson attack on his office. All his receipts and records were destroyed.'

'And you believe he started the fire himself?'

'I bloody know he did, son, but I couldn't prove it.' He wound down the window and chucked the cigarette end out. 'If you want my utterly biased opinion, last night's escapade was an insurance fiddle . . . hide the furs and jewels and claim the insurance.'

'But if it was an insurance fiddle,' protested Jordan, 'the girl would have to be in on it as well.'

'Ten out of ten,' said Frost.

Jordan spun the wheel and the track wriggled before turning into Hanger Lane. 'This is where we found the girl . . . standing in the middle of the road, starkers.'

'You're only saying that to make me jealous,' said Frost. A thought hit him. 'Stop the car!'

The car coasted to a halt and Jordan watched as Frost poked and prodded amongst the undergrowth of the grass verge, then disappeared from view as he squeezed through a gap in a hedge. Rustling sounds, then a whoop of delight and Frost emerged carrying something grey. He climbed back into the car. 'What do you reckon to this, son?'

'A blanket,' said Jordan. 'From a single bed.'

'Exactly.'

Jordan stared at it blankly. He hadn't the faintest idea what the inspector was on about.

'Listen,' explained Frost. 'You're a fifteen-year-old girl, all throbbing thighs and tits. You've been dumped in the road by your father to flag down a car. You're starkers and it's freezing and Dawn's icy fingers are toying with your privates. So what do you do? You take a blanket with you to keep yourself warm. When you hear a car, you chuck the blanket behind a hedge, step in the middle of the road and waggle your dugs. If the car doesn't stop, you retrieve the blanket and wait for the next one.'

'It's possible,' said Jordan, begrudgingly.

'Sniff it,' said Frost.

Jordan lifted the blanket delicately to his nose. 'Perfume?'

'And what's the betting that if you sniffed Simms's greatcoat where it was wrapped round her naked, hot, rampant little body, you'd smell the same perfume?'

'But the gang could have taken the blanket from her bed and wrapped it round her.'

'So why wasn't it still wrapped round her naked little figure when she was flagging cars down?' He sighed. 'But that little mystery must wait, son. We're putting off the pleasure of telling a mother her son has been murdered.' He tossed the blanket on to the back seat and smoked silently until they reached the address given to them by Control.

Kenton Street consisted of large, three-storeyed houses, converted into flats. Burton was waiting outside number 3a. Frost steeled himself and reached for another cigarette. A few quick delaying drags before he would have to confront the mother. But like Bobby's mother the night before, the woman had seen the police car draw up and was already on the doorstep. Frost gave a deep groan and poked the cigarette back in the packet. 'They can't wait for bloody bad news, can they?' He nodded at Burton. 'Come on, son. Let me do the talking.'

Joy Anderson, a plump, bouncy little brunette in her twenties, anxiously watched them approach, trying to read some sign of hope from their expressions. 'Have you found him?'

'Give us a chance love,' said Frost. 'We've only just got your message.'

They followed her up the stairs to a largish room which overlooked the street. It was basically furnished like a hotel room, with few signs of personal belongings. Two large suitcases stood beside the two-seater beige moquette settee.

Frost parked himself in a chair by the window. 'How long has Dean been missing?'

She sat opposite him, staring out of the window as she answered, leaning forward hopefully every time someone turned the corner, slumping back when it wasn't her son. 'About half-past two yesterday afternoon.'

'But you didn't report him missing until this morning,' said Burton.

She took one of Frost's cigarettes. He lit up for both of them. 'It's all my bloody fault. I thought he was in bed.' She held the cigarette up vertically and watched the smoke wind up to the ceiling.

Frost didn't prompt her. He let her take her time.

'I've got this job at the Coconut Grove. It's a casino near Denton Woods.'

'Yes,' nodded Frost. 'We know it.'

'I'm one of the dealers on the blackjack tables – eight in the evening until four in the morning. Not much of a job, but you've got to grab what you can get.' A cylinder of ash fell from her cigarette. She blew it off the polished table top. 'Dean gets himself to bed. I usually look in on him when I get back, but I didn't this morning. I . . .' She hesitated, then lowered her eyes. 'I brought a bloke back here.' She glared at Frost defiantly. 'I'm not a prostitute – just now and then. I need the money.'

'Sure,' said Frost. Baskin at the Coconut Grove employed plenty of girls like her. Punters went to the casino for a gamble, then some sex, and Baskin provided both. He probably owned this flat. Frost nodded for her to go on.

'I didn't let him know I had a kid . . . it puts some people off. They don't even know at the Coconut Grove that I've got Dean. Me and the bloke went to bed. He left just after six this morning and I was so bloody tired, I went straight off to sleep. I didn't wake up until half an hour ago, I staggered into Dean's room to see if he wanted any breakfast. His bed hadn't been slept in.' She smashed the cigarette out in a heavy glass ashtray. 'He's got himself lost, that's what's happened. We've only been in Denton for two days. He doesn't know his way around yet.'

'When did you last see him?'

'Yesterday afternoon. He was fed up being stuck in here on his own, so I gave him the money for the pictures. He went off about half-past two.'

The cinema! Of course, thought Frost. That would be where he bought the hamburger. Probably ate it as he watched the film. 'Weren't you worried he hadn't returned home before you left for work?'

'I had to have my hair done and be fitted for my uniform. I left here just after five. He knows how to work the microwave if he wants anything to eat.'

'How was Dean dressed when he left here?'

'Black trousers, Jurassic Park T-shirt and a red and white zip-up shell jacket – and blue trainers.'

Burton noted the details. Frost showed her a photograph of Bobby Kirby. 'Would your son know this boy?'

She dragged her gaze from the window to look at it. 'I don't think he knows anyone yet. He hasn't even started school here. Why do you ask?'

'It's not important,' lied Frost, crushing out his cigarette alongside hers in the glass ashtray. He took a deep breath. Now for the moment of truth. 'Do you have a recent photograph of Dean, Mrs Anderson?'

'Miss,' she corrected, 'not Mrs.' She reached for her handbag which hung from the back of her chair. 'Taken about three months ago. He's filled out a bit since then.'

Frost looked at it, then passed it to Burton. Burton's eyes flickered, but his expression didn't change as he handed it back. Not the slightest doubt about it. It was the dead boy.

'How old are you, love?' asked Frost.

'Twenty-four.'

Twenty-four. She would have had the boy when she was sixteen. 'Where's Dean's father?'

'With his wife back in Birmingham.'

'Does he support the boy?'

'No. He claims Dean isn't his. I can't even be sure myself.'

'Any friends, or family, who can help you?'

'No!' She stood up and glared down at him. 'Look – I don't want any help. I just want you to find my son.'

Frost stood up and took her hand. 'I've got some bad news for you, love,' he said.

She looked at him. 'How bad?'

'Bloody bad,' said Frost. 'As bad as it bloody well could be.'

She shook her head. 'No!'

'He's dead, love,' said Frost. 'We found him last night, but we didn't know who he was.'

'No,' she whispered. And then she shuddered and tears streamed down her face. 'No . . .'

Frost took her and held her close to him. 'You poor cow,' he said. 'You poor, poor cow . . .'

4

A blown-up photograph of eight-year-old Dean Anderson, wearing the red and white zip-up shell jacket and bright yellow Jurassic Park T-shirt he was last seen alive in, grinned down at them from the wall of the murder incident room. It was a skilful combination of two photographs using another eight-year-old boy. Next to it was the enlarged school photograph of the missing Bobby Kirby.

As Frost breezed in, people swarmed around him with messages. He warded them off with a fried egg sandwich. 'I'm having my dinner.' He found an empty desk. 'Right. What have we got?'

'No luck with the missing boy, yet,' said Burton.

'I guessed that,' said Frost, digging in his pockets for a cigarette for his dessert, 'otherwise someone would have told me. What else?'

'Stacks of phone calls,' said PC Lambert, offering him a heap of scribbled messages.

Frost eyed them with distaste. 'You don't expect me to read them, do you? Anything positive?'

'All of them, if you want to believe the twenty-three people who claim to have seen him. Trouble is, there were a lot of kids just like Bobby out with guys last night. We've had so-called positive identifications all over Denton. We're following them all through.'

Frost took another bite at his sandwich. 'Right. Until something definite breaks, we've just got to pin our hopes on one of the search parties finding him. So let's concentrate on the dead kid.' He stood up and waved his sandwich at the blow-up. 'As most of you know, we've had a positive identification. Dean Anderson. His mother, Joy Anderson, is a single parent, a blackjack dealer and, for the want of a better word, a "hostess" at the Coconut Grove. They've only been in Denton two days. The kid knew no-one here and barely knew his way around the town, although apparently he knew how to get to the cinema.' He gave them the details, pausing as the phone rang and Liz answered it.

'Search party three covering sector two. Nothing found. Now moving to sector three. Denton Woods.' She shifted a coloured pin to a new position on the wall map.

Frost went cold, remembering an earlier occasion when they were combing the woods, then in deep snow, for a missing girl, eight years old, who was dead when they found her. He uttered a silent prayer that the pattern wouldn't repeat itself with Bobby . . . surely one dead kid was enough? But his prayers were seldom answered these days. He turned back to the photograph. 'The first thing to do is see if the mother's story checks out. In the absence of anyone else, she's our sole suspect.'

'What possible motive would she have for killing her own son?' queried Liz.

'He could have been getting in the way when she brought men home,' said Frost. 'It puts a man off when he's half-way up a woman's leg and the kid comes in for an ice lolly.'

You callous bastard, thought Liz.

'It may not be very probable,' continued Frost, 'but let's check her out. Did anyone see the boy leave the house at the time she said? Did anyone see her leave for the Coconut Grove? What time did she get there . . . what time did she leave? And we'll need to question her client.'

'They don't usually leave their name and address,' Liz pointed out.

'The Coconut Grove is a gambling club – you've got to be a member. And knowing the way they work, the punter probably paid for her services by credit card so he could clock up some air miles. There'll be no difficulty getting his name and address.' He shuffled through his notes. 'Someone was going to check with the cinema.'

Jordan elbowed his way through. 'I did it. They think they remember seeing Dean yesterday afternoon. They often get kids in the afternoon who have sneaked off from school. The ticket seller thinks she sold him a ticket about three-ish. The tart in the hamburger kiosk says Dean could have been one of the kids who bought food . . . but all kids look alike to her.'

'Right.' Frost took a last bite at his sandwich before hurling the crust in the bin. He wiped his fingers on his jacket and lit up the cigarette before sitting down again. 'Let's assume he went to the cinema around three and saw the film through. What time would he leave?'

'Between half-past five and six.'

'By which time it was dark, most of the shops shut and the town looking like a morgue. I reckon he would want to go straight home.' He swung his chair round so he was facing the large street map of Denton on the wall. 'He doesn't know the area too well, so he takes the main road, not the back doubles.'

'But that wouldn't take him anywhere near Patriot Street where we found the body,' said Burton.

Frost nodded. 'You're right, son. So let's try this for a working hypothesis. He's walking home. Some bastard in a car toots his horn and says, "Do you want a lift, sonny?" He gets him in the car, gives him chloroform, kills him, panics and dumps the body. So . . .' He jabbed the wall map. 'Let's set up a road block here tonight. Stop all cars. "Were you here this time last night, sir? Did you see anyone give a lift to a kid?" You know the form.'

'I'll lay it on,' said Burton, scribbling on a pad.

'Hold it!' said Frost, spotting a snag. 'It's not as simple as that, is it? The kid has only just moved into Denton. He could have been going the wrong bloody way. He stops a bloke. "Excuse me, kind sir, can you tell me how to get to Kenton Street?" "You're miles out of your way, sonny. Hop in, I'll give you a lift – mind that bottle of chloroform and the knife."'

'I'll get Traffic to cover all roads in all directions,' said Burton. 'It'll mean more overtime. Mr Mullett won't like that.'

Frost flapped a dismissive hand. 'Don't worry. I'll sort old Roughchops out. Next, we'll put out an appeal over the media. Anyone who was in the Curzon Cinema between, say, two and seven, we want to hear from you . . . All calls treated in the utmost secrecy just in case kids playing truant might not want to come forward . . . and say we'll accept reverse charge calls if they don't want to phone from their parents' home.' He rubbed some life into his scar. 'Anything I haven't thought of, do it anyway.'

'Do we still need to check out all the hamburger outlets?'

'I think so, son. Forensic are comparing the stomach contents with a sample from the cinema, but until they confirm it's the same we'd still better check them out.' He stifled a yawn. He hadn't got to bed until the early hours and had then been dragged in at the crack of dawn by flaming Mullett. He realized quite a few of the team looked as if an early night wouldn't go amiss and they were only into the first few hours of the murder investigation. 'Split up into two groups – half of you snatch a few hours' sleep, then relieve the others. I don't want you stumbling around like bloody zombies – there's enough useless people in this station as it is.' He looked up as Mullett entered and, without changing his expression, said, 'Hello, sir, we were just talking about you.'

Mullett smiled and nodded to the team, wondering why some of them seemed to have difficulty in keeping their faces straight. A surreptitious peek to check that his zip wasn't open. 'A quick word, inspector.'

'Be with you in a tick, sir.' Back to the team. 'One last thing. On no account must we let anyone know that the poor little sod had his finger hacked off. We'll soon be swamped out with phone calls from weirdos and cranks confessing they killed him. Most of them will be time-wasters, but if anyone mentions a missing finger we jump on the bastard.'

They clattered out. Liz answered another phone call from a search party reporting negative results. She resited a yellow pin on the wall map. Mullett took Frost's arm and moved away from her. This was to be confidential. 'Any progress?'

'Everyone's sweating their guts out, but nothing definite achieved so far,' grunted Frost.

'It would be helpful if we could get this tied up very quickly, Frost. With all the overtime involved, the cost of these searches is astronomical. I take it we do need all these men from other divisions? The cost goes on our account, you know, not theirs.'

'Tough!' said Frost. 'And yes, we do need them all. If we want to find him alive, we need to find him quickly. It's bleeding cold out there . . . you probably noticed it as you staggered out of the boozer last night.'

Mullett's face reddened. That was something he didn't want to be reminded about. 'Do you think you will find him today?'

'I'm not a bleeding fortune teller.'

'I can cover the overtime from our budget for another eight hours. After that, I'll have to go to County, cap in hand.'

You can go with your dick in your hand for all I care, thought Frost, but aloud he said, 'It'll take as long as it takes. I can't hurry it.' He felt this was not a good moment to tell the superintendent about the extra overtime needed for Traffic tonight. He yawned again as another wave of tiredness washed over him. 'And when are we going to get a replacement for Inspector Allen?'

Liz Maud, hovering in the background, pricked up her ears. This was what she was anxious to know. As Mullett turned his head in her direction, she pretended to be engrossed in the contents of a folder.

Mullett lowered his voice. 'I'll have news on a replacement for Mr Allen very shortly. I'm only waiting for confirmation from County.' He gave Liz a thin smile as he went out. She beamed back, reading the secret message in his smile. She knew that the temporary promotion was hers. Frost had come over to her. She closed the folder. 'Yes, inspector?'

'Your abduction case. It might be a good idea to chat up the girl again.' He told her about finding the blanket.

'And you're suggesting it was all a fake? She wasn't abducted? There was no robbery?'

He nodded. 'The titty-grabbing bad guys knew too much . . . where the meter cupboard was, that there was only a cordless phone upstairs. They knew the parents would be away and they knew they wouldn't be back until well after midnight.'

Liz shrugged. 'There are ways they could have found that out.'

'The ransom was £25,000. Do you know how much Stanfield had in his current account? I phoned the bank and they told me – £25,000, give or take a few quid. If the gang had asked for more, he couldn't have paid it.'

'It still doesn't prove anything,' she said stubbornly. 'What father would put his daughter through all that for an insurance fiddle?'

'A father called Robert Stanfield,' said Frost. 'Get tidied up here and we'll go and pay them another visit.'

* * *

He was on his way to his office to see what junk Mullett had dumped in his in-tray when Bill Wells called him. 'Lady to see you, inspector.' He nodded in the direction of a small woman in her mid-seventies in a faded brown coat, who rose wearily from the hard bench in the waiting area and shuffled over. 'It's me again, Mr Frost,' she said apologetically.

'Who the hell is she?' whispered Frost, always worried when people asked for him by name. He rarely forgot a criminal face, but members of the public were just not recorded in his mental filing system. But before Wells could reply, she had shuffled across to him. 'Have you managed to get them back yet?'

Then he remembered. The robberies – the con man who wangled his way into people's houses by pretending to work for the Water Board. This old dear had had her jewellery stolen, plus her late husband's war medals. Her husband had been an RAF pilot during the Battle of Britain and had been awarded the Distinguished Flying Medal amongst other decorations. Frost tried not to meet her eye as he shook his head. 'No luck yet, love – but we're still trying.' Why was he lying to the poor old girl? He'd dropped that case months ago.

She looked as if all hope had been drained out of her. 'I don't care too much about the jewellery. It's the medals. He was so proud of them.'

'I know,' said Frost. The last decoration had been awarded posthumously. A tracer bullet had penetrated the fuel tank and the heat-warped canopy had jammed. He screamed to his death in the blast furnace of a burning Spitfire, crashing to merciful oblivion in a field in Kent on a blazing hot summer's day in August 1940.

'How long before you catch the man who stole them?'

'Can't really say, love. We're following several leads.' More lies. He didn't have a bleeding clue! 'I'll be in touch as soon as we have anything.' Which would probably be bloody never! 'Sorry I haven't better news.'

'I'm sure you're doing your best,' she said.

He walked her to the door and watched her hobble across the road, fumbling for her bus pass. She realized she was being watched and turned to give him a wave.

He slouched back to his office and screwed up the two niggling memos from Mullett he found lurking in his in-tray. Staring through the dirty grime of his window he wished it would hail or snow or pee with rain, anything to match his mood. But the sun glinted off the grime. He couldn't even get that right.

Liz poked her head around the door. 'Ready, inspector?'

'Yes,' he nodded. 'I'm ready.'

They took Frost's car and he cowered down in the passenger seat as Liz did her Monaco Grand Prix stuff. The thin sun zipped backwards and forwards across the windscreen like a typewriter carriage as she hurled the car down the zigzagging lanes. Away to the left, flying past, he could see the distant figures of one of the search parties spread out across a field. Liz screamed the car round a tight corner, shooting him forward as she suddenly slammed on the brakes. 'Stupid, stupid, stupid!' she snarled. She had almost run into a cluster of cars parked in the lane. Over on the right another search party was clambering up a steep hill.

'Half a mo!' Frost fumbled to get his seat belt off and slipped out of the car. Just ahead, on the grass verge, Detective Sergeant Arthur Hanlon, in charge of the search team, was bending to tie up his shoelace. His back was to Frost, his tight trousers providing a target the inspector was never able to resist. Frost's stubby finger shot forward, hitting its target with unerring accuracy. 'How's that for centre, Arthur?' he cried, triumphantly.

With a yelp of outrage, Hanlon sprang up abruptly, indignation evaporating as he recognized Frost. 'You sod, Jack. No matter where I am, I've only got to bend over and you appear!'

'Fatal attraction, Arthur. The moving finger pokes, and when it pokes, moves on.' He squinted up at the men now disappearing over the top of the hill. 'Where are you going to search now?'

'Those old bungalows behind the hill.' This was a site long abandoned and the huddle of decaying, pre-war jerry-built shacks were now mainly roofless and little more than shells. The area should have been cleared and flattened years ago when the last residents were re-housed, but the Council had better ways to spend its money. 'What's your gut feeling about our chances of finding him alive?' asked Hanlon.

'Don't ask, Arthur. It would only depress you.' He took one last look at the straggle of men disappearing over the top of the hill. 'If we don't find him by tonight we'll start dragging the river and the canal tomorrow.' A brief nod to Hanlon and he returned to the car.

Carol Stanfield was now dressed in tight jeans and an even tighter grey woollen sweater. Her hair had been brushed back over her shoulders and as she passed close to Frost she smelled just like the blanket. Her mother and father were still sitting on opposite sides of the fire. Stanfield looked up with irritation. 'More questions? We've told you everything. Now go out and catch the bastards.'

Frost plonked himself down on the settee and loosened his scarf. The heat in the room was oppressive. 'We've found something.' He pulled the blanket from the plastic carrier bag he was holding and offered it to the mother. 'Did it come from here?'

She examined it with a frown. 'It could be ours.'

'It *is* ours,' said the girl from the far side of the room. She was staring out of the window, her back to them. 'They took it from the bed.'

'You never mentioned it,' said Frost.

She shrugged. 'They wrapped it round me in the van.'

'Bloody nice of them,' said Frost.

'It was freezing in there. I was naked.'

'It was a darn sight colder outside the van, but they took it off when they booted you out.'

'I expect it fell off.'

'Then it would have been in the road. We found it on the grass verge.'

'Then they probably chucked it out as they were driving off.'

'You must have seen it,' said Frost.

Her father's head snapped up. 'If she had seen it, she would have wrapped it around her, instead of standing there starkers, freezing to death.'

'But how could you miss it?' insisted Frost. 'It was lying there in the open.' He was hoping to catch her out. Hoping she would say, 'It wasn't in the open, I hid it behind the hedge,' but before the girl could answer her mother had chimed in. 'It couldn't have been all that obvious. Your policemen didn't see it this morning.'

'Silly me!' said Frost, forcing a smile as he pushed himself up out of the settee. He stuffed the blanket back into the carrier bag. 'We'll hang on to this for a while – let our Forensic people give it a going over.'

He held his feelings in check until they were back in the car. 'The scheming bastards. They went back to recover the blanket and realized we had found it.'

'There's always the possibility they're telling the truth,' said Liz, spinning the car into a reverse turn.

'No way,' said Frost, wincing at the thought of the rubber they were leaving in the road. 'There was no robbery and no abduction. I want it tied up quickly. We've got more important things to do than sod about with this.'

They were passing a small isolated house when, suddenly, she slammed on the brakes. His head hit the windscreen. He had forgotten to put the seat belt on. 'What the hell . . . ?'

'Sorry,' she said, getting out of the car. 'That house. There was no reply this morning when I knocked to ask about the van. Someone's in now.'

'Oh – the non-existent bleeding van loaded up with naked tart,' said Frost, rubbing the bump on his forehead. 'Well, make it quick.'

He watched her walk up the path and knock on the door. An elderly man answered.

'Control to Mr Frost.'

He picked up the handset. 'Frost . . .' He listened. It wasn't good news.

Liz was scribbling down the details the old man was giving her when the car horn blasted out repeatedly. She tried to ignore it, but it went on and on. Frost was waving frantically and yelling for her to return. Muttering apologies to the old boy, she raced back to the car. What was up now?

Frost, now in the driving seat, had the passenger door open for her. 'Get in,' he yelled, and the car was away even before she had the door shut.

'Why did you drag me away?' she protested. 'I was getting details. The old boy saw the non-existent van going towards the Stanfield house late last night. Even gave me the colour – light brown.'

Frost skidded the car round a tight bend and removed several inches of hedge in the process. 'I've had Control on the radio. Arthur Hanlon's search party – those old bungalows. They've found a body.'

Liz went cold. 'The boy?'

'Life's not that bleeding simple,' snorted Frost. 'It's not a boy – it's a man, probably a dosser. It never rains flaming bodies, it pours!'

The car wheezed its way up the steep gradient of Denton Hills, its engine making unhappy noises and giving off the smell of burning oil. They were behind the woods in a barren section of the district. Years ago a sprawl of pre-war bungalows and weekend shanties had occupied the area, their dwellers living in primitive conditions without mains drainage or electricity. These substandard dwellings were deemed unfit for human occupation and some twenty years earlier the Council had rehoused the occupants and compulsorily acquired the land for a building project for which it had long since given up trying to raise the money. The empty properties were quickly vandalized and opened up to the weather and were now of no interest, even to the local tearaways. Roofless, windows smashed, doors torn off their hinges, the flimsy buildings cowered under the wind and weather. The whole area was overgrown with vegetation and stunk of damp, rot and decay.

Arthur Hanlon and a uniformed man were waiting for them, hands in pockets, stamping their feet for warmth. The sun was a watery yellow in a clear sky. It was going to be a freezing cold night.

Hanlon led them across what was once a front garden, overgrown grass slapping at their legs. It fronted the shell of an asbestos-walled bungalow, painted in now-faded pink. Frost peeked in through the glassless windows on to strewn rubbish and charred floorboards where someone, years ago, had tried to start a fire, but the wood was too damp to burn. 'I wish my place was as tidy as this,' he muttered.

They trudged round the side to the rear. Other overgrown gardens could be seen, many of them with ramshackle wooden structures like sentry boxes. 'Outdoor privies,' said Hanlon. 'The old bucket and wooden seat – there was no mains sewerage.'

'The body's not in one of them?' asked Frost apprehensively.

Hanlon shook his head.

A sigh of relief from Frost. 'If he'd known I was going to be on the case he'd have died head first down an unemptied privy bucket.'

Hanlon grinned. Frost had an affinity for mucky cases.

'He's in a bunker, Jack.'

'A bunker? It's not bloody Hitler, is it?'

'A coal bunker. Over there.' He pointed to where a uniformed officer stood guarding a taped-off section. The undergrowth was almost waist-high, but had been trampled down to form a path leading to an almost concealed brick-built coal bunker, four feet long, three feet high. A rusted sheet of corrugated iron that had once covered the open top was propped to one side. A strong smell of putrefaction drifted out to greet them.

Frost wrinkled his nose. 'Bloody hell, Arthur, what have I told you about changing your socks?'

Hanlon giggled. 'We reckon it's probably a dosser – crept in there to sleep and got hypothermia.'

Frost took a deep breath and looked inside. 'Bloody hell!' He moved back and sucked in great gulps of clean, cold air. He passed his cigarettes around and moved a few steps back, but the smell seemed to be following him. Liz pushed forward to take a look, but Frost held out a restraining hand. 'Best if you don't, love.'

Angrily she shook his hand off. 'I've seen bodies before.' She took a breath and looked down. Huddled at the bottom of the bunker, in some inches of soupy rain water, were the remains of a man. The body was in an advanced state of decomposition and the face, covered with black mould, was unrecognizable. She moved back, exhaled slowly, then took some deep breaths. She fought back the urge to be sick.

'Are you all right?' asked Frost.

'Yes,' she snapped. 'Perfectly all right.'

'Remind me to tell you of that dead tramp I found in a heat-wave,' he said. 'You could have poured him away. It made this one smell like Chanel Number 5 in comparison . . .'

'Don't let him tell you that story, Liz,' said Arthur Hanlon. 'Not on a full stomach – I was sick for three days after I heard it.'

'You're thinking of the other one,' said Frost. 'The bloke who drunk the contents of the spittoon for a bet.'

Hanlon went white. 'I'd forgotten all about that one.' He pulled a face. 'If you value your stomach, Liz, don't let him tell you that story either.'

A short tubby figure carrying a medical bag came puffing towards them. Frost waved. 'Over here, doctor.'

Dr Maltby beamed when he saw the inspector. 'I thought you were on holiday?'

'They couldn't do without me, doc.' He jerked a thumb at the bunker. 'There's your patient.'

Maltby took a quick look. 'I confirm life is extinct.'

'Is that all we get for our bloody money? How long has he been dead?'

The doctor shrugged. 'No idea, Jack. Weeks – probably months. Was that corrugated iron sheeting on the top when you found him?'

'Yes,' confirmed Hanlon.

'Sun beating down on that would make it like an oven – and there's a good two inches of water down there to speed things up. Decomposition could start in hours.'

'Cause of death?'

'No idea. If you drag him out I'll take a further look, but if you think I'm going to climb down inside . . .'

'Sod it!' sighed Frost. He pulled Hanlon to one side. 'Pathologist, Forensic, SOCs, the works, Arthur. You know the drill.'

'You think it might be murder?'

'There's water and broken bricks at the bottom of that bunker, Arthur. A dosser would have to be pretty hard up for a bed to sleep on that.'

'I'm off then,' said Maltby, backing away.

'Thanks, doc,' said Frost. 'If you hadn't told us he was dead we'd still be pushing aspirins down the poor sod's throat.' He waved him off, then returned to Hanlon. 'You'd better handle this one, Arthur. It was your team who found him, you can suffer the consequences.' He took one last look at the bunker and shuddered. 'I'd hate to be one of the blokes who have to lift him out. Don't pull him up by his arms, they might come off in your hand . . . and for the same reason, don't lift him by his dick.'

Liz screwed up her face in distaste. She didn't find death the least bit funny.

'We're going to need some more help, Jack,' Hanlon called after them.

'Our beloved Divisional Commander has it all in hand,' said Frost. 'We're getting another detective inspector.'

As they climbed back into the car, Liz had an awful thought and consulted Frost for reassurance. 'You don't think Mr Mullett is going to upgrade Sergeant Hanlon to acting DI?'

'No,' said Frost, wriggling down into the passenger seat. 'Arthur's a lovely bloke, but, like me, he hasn't got the making of an inspector and Mullett knows it.'

'Oh,' said Liz. She smiled to herself. Then it would definitely be her.

Bill Wells sipped his mug of tea and took a sly drag at his cigarette. His first chance to relax all afternoon. Mullett had been flapping in and out, wanting to know if anyone had been asking for him, but not explaining who he was expecting. A blast of wind as the main doors opened. With practised skill, he pinched out the cigarette and slid his mug of tea under the counter top. 'Can I help you, sir?'

The man, carrying a suitcase, walked across to the desk. Fair-haired, thickset and in his early forties, he gave a curt nod.

A cry of recognition from Wells. 'Jim Cassidy! What are you doing back in Denton?'

Cassidy put down the suitcase and twitched a wan smile. His manner was far less enthusiastic than the sergeant's. 'Hello, Bill.'

'I've heard you've been in the wars – some bastard stabbed you?'

Cassidy nodded, his expression making it clear this was something he didn't want to talk about. 'I'm here to see Mr Mullett.'

So this was why Mullett had been flapping. And not a word to a flaming soul! 'May I ask what about?' said Wells, picking up the internal phone and dialling Mullett's number.

Cassidy frowned. Surely the news should have been out by now? 'I'm back in the division for a while. I'm going to be your acting detective inspector.'

Well's jaw dropped. Cassidy! Acting detective inspector? Cassidy who was a trainee constable while Wells was already a sergeant. Some people, if their faces fitted, would always rise in the ranks. While others who flogged their guts out, worked all the hours God sent, were bunged on the rota every bloody Christmas . . . He realized Mullett had answered and was barking angrily in his ear. 'Detective Sergeant Cassidy to see you, sir . . . Yes, sir.' He put the phone down. 'Go straight through, Jim. You know the way.'

Cassidy nodded and slid his suitcase across the counter top for safekeeping. At the swing doors he paused. 'Important point, sergeant. While I'm acting inspector, I want to be treated as such. Call me inspector, or sir – not Jim.'

Forcing a smile, Wells seethed inwardly. You bastard! Pulling rank on me! 'Very good . . . sir,' he said, through clenched teeth. 'By the way . . . sir. I saw your wife – sorry – your ex-wife in town the other day.'

Cassidy stiffened. He wouldn't turn round. He had no intention of letting the sod know how deeply that shaft had hit home. 'Did you, sergeant? How was she?'

'She looked great. Her new husband was with her. They both looked very happy.'

The swing doors closed shut behind him and Wells

chortled with wicked delight. 'Game, set and match,' he beamed, retrieving his mug of tea.

'What was that all about, sarge?'

Wells turned his head. PC Collier on his way up to his meal break had seen the little drama enacted.

Normally Wells would have told him to mind his own business, but basking in the warm glow of his little victory he was only too pleased to explain. 'That big-headed git you just saw go through is Jim Cassidy. He was a detective constable here some four years ago – before your time. Career mad . . . nothing was going to stop him getting on – and he didn't give a toss who he stepped on to get there. Grabbed all the credit, even when it wasn't his, and worked all the hours going without claiming overtime, which made him Mullett's blue-eyed boy. Anyway, one night he'd promised to take his teenage daughter out to see a film she'd been dying to see, but a job came up so he cried off. She went out on her own and got knocked down and killed by a hit and run driver. He went to pieces and his marriage broke up. He started criticizing everyone here because we couldn't trace the hit and run driver and became impossible to work with. So he was transferred to Lexford, at which point we stopped hating him and they started.'

'And now we've got him back as acting detective inspector?'

Wells nodded grimly. 'And that will put the cat amongst the pigeons, I promise you.' There was a bit more to the story, but Wells was keeping it to himself. He couldn't wait to see Jack Frost's face when he told him Cassidy was back. The internal phone rang. Mullett. Demanding two coffees.

Wells looked round, but Collier had gone. 'Sorry, sir, I've got no one to send.'

'And some biscuits,' said Mullett, putting down the phone.

* * *

'Come in, Jim, come in,' said Mullett warmly, hand outstretched. 'Good to have you back in the division.'

Cassidy shook the offered hand and noted with relief that there was a hard-seated chair in front of the polished mahogany desk. But to his dismay, Mullett waved him towards one of the two deep-cushioned armchairs reserved for important visitors. Damn! He could lower himself in it all right, but the effort of hauling himself from its depths would trigger off the pain again. He gritted his teeth and sat down. No-one must know he was still suffering from the after effects of the stabbing, not if his promotion to Inspector was to go through this time. He turned a grimace into a smile of thanks as a ripple of pain sizzled across his stomach. The seat was lower than he thought and there was no support and it was pulling on his wound.

Mullett took the other armchair, concerned to see Cassidy looking so drawn. 'Sorry to hear about the stabbing. Are you all right now?'

'I'm fine,' lied Cassidy. He was learning to mask the pain. He had fooled the police doctor and should have little difficulty in fooling Mullett and his pack of dummies. 'I'm anxious to get started, sir. I understand Inspector Allen was handling a murdered boy enquiry. When can I take over?'

'One dead boy, one missing boy,' corrected Mullett. He paused as a sullen-looking Sergeant Wells came in with the coffees and banged them down on the desk, spilling some into the saucers. He waited until Wells had left before continuing. 'You'll be working with Mr Frost on this one.'

Cassidy's head snapped up. 'Frost! Jack Frost?'

Mullett saw something very interesting to look at through the window – the blank wall on the other side of the road. 'Er – quite so.'

'My understanding was—'

'Circumstances have changed,' interrupted Mullett. 'I

had intended you would be taking complete charge of Mr Allen's cases and working on your own—'

'That was the only reason I agreed to come back here,' cut in Cassidy. 'You will appreciate that Denton has many unhappy memories for me.'

'I understand that, but nevertheless you will be working under Mr Frost.'

'Under? I'm an acting detective inspector. I didn't come all the way back here just to stay a sergeant.'

'The Chief Constable is a little concerned as to your fitness . . .'

'I'm perfectly fit.'

'. . . and he has a much higher opinion of Frost than, perhaps, those who have to work with him have. He wants you to work under Frost's authority as he considers this is a case requiring the leadership of an experienced officer.'

With difficulty Cassidy pushed himself out of the chair, his anger overcoming the pain. 'I am sorry, sir. I would find it impossible to work with Frost. The way he mismanaged the investigation into the death of my daughter . . .'

Mullett gave a deep sigh. 'I know you weren't happy at the way he handled the case. I agree he's unorthodox.'

'Unorthodox,' exploded Cassidy. 'He's more than unorthodox. He's sloppy, lazy, inefficient, devious—'

'That will do!' An angry Mullett pounded his fist on the desk. It was not that he disagreed with the views expressed – he, himself, might have gone further – but he wasn't having this sort of talk from a sergeant, especially one from another division who could well carry a report of the conversation back. He was concerned that Frost's deficiencies should not be too widely known, otherwise his chances of dumping the man on another, unsuspecting division would be minimal. 'Whatever your feelings, Cassidy, you will put them to one side. The Chief

Constable has decreed that you will work with Mr Frost and that he will be the senior officer.'

'I am not happy with this, sir.'

'I take note of your unhappiness,' said Mullett, 'but would advise you to take full advantage of this opportunity.' He gave his crocodile smile. 'Any successes that you achieve will be duly noted and, should the time come for Inspector Frost to be replaced . . .' He spread his palms significantly and let the option hang. 'However, if you decide you cannot work with him, I am sure County can find some other sergeant who would be only too pleased to improve his promotional chances by acting as inspector.'

Cassidy grunted. 'I'll work with him.'

'Good man,' beamed Mullett. 'Well, I expect you will want to get started. You'll be in Mr Allen's office. You know where it is.' He stood up to indicate the interview was over. 'I'm glad we've had this little chat.'

A stab of pain caught Cassidy by surprise as he pushed himself up. He winced and gritted his teeth.

'You all right?' Mullett asked.

'Leg a bit stiff after the journey,' explained Cassidy, forcing himself not to limp as he crossed to the door.

'Oh – one other thing,' said Mullett, making his carefully rehearsed speech sound like an afterthought. 'That business with your daughter . . .'

Cassidy turned slowly to face the Divisional Commander. 'Yes?'

'Over and done with – all in the past.' Mullett gave Cassidy's arm a 'man to man' squeeze.

'Yes,' said Cassidy, tersely. 'All in the past.' There was no one in the passage outside so he was able to allow himself the luxury of a limp back to Allen's office.

Thomas Arnold, assistant branch manager at Bennington's Bank, blinked nervously at Frost through thick-lensed glasses. By his side stood the cashier who had attended to Stanfield when he withdrew the £25,000 that morning. He waited for his secretary to give Frost and Liz a cup of lukewarm instant coffee, then nodded for the cashier to proceed.

'Mr Stanfield was waiting outside the bank when we opened at nine-thirty,' the cashier told them. 'He handed me his withdrawal request. I raised my eyebrows and said, "Rather a large sum!" And he said, "Just get it!" I obviously didn't have that amount of money in my till and it was more than I like to count out over the counter, so I took him round to Mr Arnold's office to wait while we fetched the money from the vault.'

'That's correct,' said Arnold. 'I offered him coffee, but he refused.'

Frost pushed his half-empty cup away from him. 'I'm not surprised.'

'How did he seem?' asked Liz.

'In what way?'

'She means,' said Frost, 'did he look as if his daughter was going to be raped if he didn't cough up the cash, or did he behave normally?'

'He seemed very impatient – but then he usually is,' replied the assistant manager. 'It only took eight minutes to provide the cash.'

'I brought it in, but before I could hand it over he snatched it from me,' said the cashier. 'He didn't bother to count it, just stuffed it in his suitcase and left.'

'You didn't think it strange he should withdraw such a large sum in cash?'

'To be quite honest,' said Arnold, 'I thought he was going to do a runner . . . leave the country. I believe Customs and Excise and the Inland Revenue are breathing very hard down his neck . . . but that is strictly off the record, of course.'

They nodded their thanks and left.

'Well,' smirked Liz when they got back in the car. 'He was agitated, and impatient – it's starting to sound genuine.'

'Of course he looked agitated. You'd hardly expect him to be whistling "Happy Days are Here Again". He knew we'd check.'

'Then what about my witness who saw the van?'

'I don't care if he saw a hundred bloody vans. I still reckon this is a tax and insurance fiddle.'

'We'll see,' she smiled, determined to prove him wrong.

He dropped her off at her digs. 'Get a few hours' kip. I'll see you back at the station later.'

He drove to his house for a quick cup of tea and flopped wearily in an armchair to drink it. He was dead tired. He leant his head back on the cushion and closed his eyes for a second. He woke with a start. His untouched tea was stone cold. Outside it was already dark. The phone was ringing.

'Frost,' he said, shaking the sleep from his eyes.

It was Johnnie Johnson, who had taken over from Bill Wells as Station Sergeant. 'You'd better get over here, Jack. Another child's gone missing.'

'On my way,' said Frost.

5

He slouched into the incident room rubbing sleep from his eyes. 'What's all this about another missing kid?' he yawned.

'Judy Gleeson, fourteen years old,' said Burton.

Frost collapsed into a chair, relieved that it wasn't another eight-year-old boy. 'Tell me about it.'

'Mother goes to work. She came home at five. No sign of her daughter and no table laid, which the daughter usually did. She assumed the kid was with her mate. Half-past six, still no Judy, so the mother gets worried, phones around and learns that Judy hadn't been at school all day.'

Frost chewed this over. 'I can't see it tying in with our missing boy. Sounds like your average girl doing a runner to me.'

'Probably, but we can't take chances. Detective Sergeant Maud has gone round to the house to get details. Should be back soon.'

'Right,' said Frost. 'And how are things going with the search for Bobby Kirby?'

Burton told him the position. The search parties had plodded on until it was too dark to see properly. All the more likely areas had been covered and they were now moving on to the less likely ones.

'I've laid on the frogmen team for tomorrow morning.'

Frost nodded his approval. 'What about our appeals to the Great British Public?'

Lambert came forward. 'Thirty-five more positive

sightings. Eight of them were kids with men.'

'Probably fathers taking their sons home. What about the dead kid? Did anyone see him?'

'There's a snag,' Burton told him. 'Both kids left home wearing similar clothes. People are reporting seeing kids in zip-up jackets and it could be either of them.'

'Or neither,' said Frost. 'The cinema?'

'Three kids playing truant from school are pretty certain they saw Dean in the Curzon yesterday afternoon. He was sitting on his own. They didn't pay much attention to him and didn't see him leave.'

Liz stuck her head round the door. 'That missing girl. I've circulated details, but it looks as if she's just run away from home. I spoke to one of her friends who reckoned there had been some friction between Judy and her parents, but the mother denies it.'

Frost waved a hand in acknowledgement. Kids running away from home were all too common these days.

Liz went back to Allen's office to check the in-tray and was irritated to find someone had been in and removed all her stuff from Allen's desk and dumped it back on the small desk in the corner. Probably whingeing Bill Wells up to his bloody tricks again. Seething with annoyance she moved it all back and was just reaching for the phone to ask Wells what the hell he was playing at when the door crashed open and a thickset sandy-haired man in his early forties barged in.

'Do you mind knocking before coming into my office,' snapped Liz.

The man glowered at her. 'And do you mind getting out of my bloody desk,' he roared.

Cassidy had dumped his suitcase at his digs and had then taken a drive round Denton to see how much the place had changed since he was here last. He drove past his old house, the house he had had to make over to his wife as part of the divorce settlement. The downstairs blazed with light and the front lawn looked immaculate. Very different from when he lived there and there was never any time for gardening. He stopped the car and stared up at the small bedroom window, his daughter's room. Today would have been Becky's eighteenth birthday, not that anyone else would have remembered.

He passed a florist's that was just closing and, on impulse, stopped and bought a small bunch of flowers. She loved flowers.

It was getting dark, but he managed to find the grave without much difficulty. A small white headstone. 'Rebecca Cassidy – aged 14 years.' To his annoyance there was already a large, ostentatious bouquet of pink carnations lying by the headstone. The attached card read: 'On your birthday, darling, from Mummy and Geoff.' Geoff! The new bloody husband! He was shaking with rage. How dare that swine give my daughter flowers. He never even bloody knew her! Cassidy snatched up the bouquet and tore the card to shreds, then gently laid his own small offering in its place. Fourteen! Fourteen years old, all her life in front of her, and some bastard, probably drunk, had mowed her down and didn't bother to stop to see if she was alive or dead. And then Frost had sodded up the investigation.

He walked away, clutching the carnations, looking for a bin where he could dump them. He passed another grave, overgrown and neglected. He stopped. Talk of the devil! It was the grave of Frost's wife, the grass overgrown, long-dead stalks of flowers in a vase. The callous bastard hadn't been back to tend it since the day she was buried. As he tore up some of the long grass to make room for the carnations, he winced. The cold night air was getting to his wound, triggering off the hurt. He hurried back to the warmth of the car.

Mullett marched into the incident room and headed straight for Frost. 'Another missing child?' he barked, making it sound as if it was all Frost's fault.

'Yes, sorry about that, super. I'll try and see it doesn't happen again.' He scooped up some papers and headed for the door, but was called back.

'Traffic are talking about extra overtime. I haven't authorized it. Do you know anything about it?'

'Ah yes,' said Frost, who had forgotten all about it. 'I was going to come in and see you about that.' But he was saved by the bell. Liz Maud came in, not looking at all happy, and behind was – Flaming hell! Jim bloody Cassidy. Where did he spring from?

'Ah,' said Mullett. 'In case you don't know, our old colleague Mr Cassidy is taking over as acting detective inspector – only until Mr Allen gets back. I'm sure we're all delighted to have such a worthy addition to our team.'

The news was greeted with stunned silence, broken by Liz. 'If I could have a word, sir,' she said, her eyes smouldering with resentment. Mullett had as good as offered the promotion to her and she wanted to know why he had gone back on his word.

'Later, later,' said Mullett, backing hurriedly to the door. 'Make an appointment with my secretary. I'm a bit tied up just now.' He scuttled back to his office and switched on the red 'Engaged – Do Not Enter' light. Cassidy might be trouble, but there was no way he was having a woman detective inspector in his division, even if the promotion was only temporary.

'Good to see you, Jim,' said Frost. He didn't hold out his hand as he knew Cassidy wouldn't take it. He introduced him around. One or two people knew Cassidy from his previous time in Denton, but did their best to hide their dismay. 'And, of course, you've met Detective Sergeant Maud?'

Cassidy flicked her a brisk nod. 'I'd like an office on my own. Perhaps she could move in with you.'

'Of course,' agreed Frost. This wasn't the time or place to start a row.

'And I'd like someone assigned to me to do my filing and odd jobs and things.' He pointed to Burton. 'He looks a likely chap.'

'We all do our own filing and odd jobs and things,' said Frost. 'I can't spare anyone – we've got too much on.'

Cassidy's expression did not change. 'I see. Well, perhaps you had better brief me on just what you do have on.'

He sat at a desk and listened, without comment, making neat, copious notes, as Frost gave him the details of the two boys, the dubious abduction, the weirdo who was stabbing sleeping kids and the body in the bunker. When Frost had finished, Cassidy capped his fountain pen and gave a sour smile. 'You don't seem to have made much progress with any of them.'

Before Frost could answer, the phone rang. Arthur Hanlon calling from the mortuary where the post-mortem on the body in the bunker was taking place. 'You'd better get down here right away, Jack. There's something odd about the body.'

'Two dicks?' asked Frost. 'I'll send Liz.'

'The tops of three of his fingers have been chopped off. After death, the pathologist says.'

Frost backed into the parking space outside the mortuary, squeezing in between Drysdale's Rolls-Royce and a hearse. The mortuary attendant, busy writing up records in his cubby-hole, waved him through. Frost was a frequent visitor.

At the far end of the darkened autopsy room, under the splash of overhead lights, a cluster of men stood at a discreet distance from the post-mortem table where a green-gowned Drysdale was bent over, cutting carefully with a scalpel. The atmosphere was oppressive and worsened rapidly when the pathologist opened up the stomach. Overhead the extractor fans whirred, but were fighting a losing battle. Drysdale's gloved hands removed something from the corpse.

'Got any pieces for the cat, doc?'

Drysdale stiffened. That damn Frost again, making his tasteless jokes. He affected not to hear and carried on with his task.

Frost's scruffy figure emerged from the gloom. 'Bloody hell. He doesn't improve with keeping, does he?' The rasp of a match as he lit a cigarette.

'Please don't smoke,' snapped Drysdale. 'There are things I need to smell.'

'Whatever turns you on, doc,' said Frost, shaking out the match, but keeping the cigarette in his mouth. 'So what's the verdict?'

'I have already given my preliminary findings to the sergeant,' said Drysdale. 'I am not in the habit of repeating myself.'

A white-faced Arthur Hanlon came round the table to Frost. The post-mortem was making him decidedly queasy. 'Dead for some time, Jack, two, even three months. Died as the result of a heavy blow to the back of the head which fractured the skull. Killed elsewhere and the body dumped in the bunker shortly after death.'

'He died about an hour after consuming his last meal,' added Drysdale, transferring something horrible to a jar and handing it to his secretary for labelling. 'A substantial meal – dinner or lunch.' He stepped back and peeled off his rubber gloves. 'I've finished with him. Sew him up, please.'

Frost waved the mortuary technician back with a hand holding a match, ready to light his cigarette. 'Give us a minute, please.' He turned to Hanlon. 'What's this about fingers cut off, Arthur?'

Hanlon indicated. He wasn't going to touch the puffed, squashy flesh. 'His right hand, Jack.'

Frost stared, then bent over to study the hand closer.

The thumb and little finger were intact, but the tops of the three middle fingers had been hacked off at the upper joint. 'This couldn't have been an accident, doc – shut his hand in a door, or something?'

'No,' said Drysdale, bridling as always at being called doc. 'No. This occurred after death and was deliberate. A knife, or something sharp, laid across the joints, then struck with a hammer or something heavy. Whoever did it had to have a couple of tries – just below the joint there's the marks of an attempt that failed.' He pointed to a bloodied indentation running parallel to the severed ends.

Frost straightened up. 'I suppose the missing bits of finger weren't dumped in the coal bunker? You have looked, Arthur?'

Hanlon hadn't, but he fished out his radio and gave instructions for this to be done.

The body was of a man in his mid-forties, a little over six feet tall, overweight, with long, lank, water-blackened hair. 'Biggish bastard, isn't he?' mused Frost aloud as he studied the bloated face with its purple lips, the eyes little more than wet swimming slits in the puffed and mould-stained flesh. A buzzer sounded at the back of his brain and tried to stir his memory. He stared at the face, trying to imagine how it might have looked in life. 'I know this sod from somewhere. Any identification on him?'

'Nothing, Jack. He was wearing a jacket over a boiler suit, but the pockets were empty. I'll get Forensic to give it the once-over.'

Frost signalled to Evans who was keeping as far from the body as possible and answered Frost's summons reluctantly. 'I'm afraid you're going to have to touch it. Fingerprint the fingers that are left and check with records to see if we've got him on our books.' He stubbed out his cigarette. The smoke was tasting of the body. 'Let's get out of here, Arthur.'

As they moved away, the mortuary technician, whistling tunelessly to himself, began sewing up the incisions made during the post-mortem, leaning to one side in mid-stitch so Evans could gingerly take fingerprints.

Outside the night air had a clean, fresh smell. But it was cold. Bitterly cold. And they still hadn't found the boy. 'We're not going to break our necks on this one, Arthur,' said Frost, pausing as Drysdale, followed by his secretary lugging a metal specimens case that seemed far too heavy for her, strode past to the Rolls with only a curt nod to the two detectives. 'He's been dead for weeks,' continued Frost, 'so another couple of days won't make any difference. We'll keep it ticking over and look busy if ever Mullett comes sniffing around, but we'll concentrate our efforts on trying to find Bobby Kirby and the bastard who killed the other boy.' He shivered. The cold was beginning to get to him. 'Let's hope that poor little sod isn't out in this.'

All they had for him in the incident room were more negative reports. The few sightings they had been able to check had all turned out to be false leads.

'What about the dead kid's mother, the blackjack dealer? Have we checked her out?'

'I saw Harry Baskin, this afternoon—' began Burton.

'Harry Baskin?' said Cassidy, who had been sitting at a corner desk, listening and scribbling notes. 'Is he still running the Coconut Grove?'

Burton nodded. 'Baskin says she started work at the club at eight, worked through her meal break and finished around three in the morning. She left with one of their clients.'

'By eight o'clock her son was dead,' said Frost. 'She could have killed him before she went to work. I want to interview her client to see if he noticed anything in the flat when he went back with her, like the smell of chloroform or a severed finger on the bread board.'

'Baskin refuses to give the bloke's name. Says he respects people's rights to privacy.'

Frost stood up and grabbed his scarf. 'This is a murder case. He'll give me the punter's name or I'll run him in for living on immoral earnings.'

'Hold it!' called Cassidy, rising to join him. 'I'm coming with you.'

'Sure,' nodded Frost. 'Glad to have your help.' But he wasn't happy. This could open old wounds. It was just outside the Coconut Grove where Cassidy's daughter had been run down and killed.

They travelled in Cassidy's car and it was a silent, uncomfortable ride with Cassidy making it tacitly clear he was only tolerating Frost's company. The Coconut Grove was busy, with the car-park three-quarters full. They brushed past the bouncer who wanted to know if they were members and ignored the leggy blonde who tried to take their hats and coats, making straight for Baskin's office. A sign on the door said 'Private – Do Not Enter'. They went straight in without knocking.

Harry Baskin, dark and swarthy and in his late thirties, looked up from his desk with a frown. 'Can't you bloody well read?' Then he saw who it was and he gave a deep sigh. 'What the hell do you want?'

Frost dragged out a chair and sat down. He pointed a thumb to his companion. 'You remember Mr Cassidy?'

For a moment Baskin looked startled, but quickly composed himself. 'Mr Cassidy! I heard you were back in Denton.' He waved a hand. 'Sit down.'

But Cassidy had moved to the window behind Baskin, a window that overlooked the road running past the club. He stared out at the cars that sped past, on to the straight section of the road before it curved towards Denton. He spoke, almost to himself. 'That's where it happened.'

Baskin shot a glance across to Frost, whose face remained impassive. 'It was a long time ago, Mr Cassidy.'

'Was it one of the drunken bastards from your club who was at the wheel, Harry?'

'We've had all this out before, Mr Cassidy. The driver didn't stop. We don't know who he was.' He swivelled his chair to face Frost. 'Is this what you've come to talk to me about – ancient bloody history?'

'We're here to talk about Joy Anderson,' said Frost.

'The new girl! If I had known she had a bloody son, I never would have employed her.'

'She hasn't got a son any more, Harry,' said Frost. 'He's dead.'

Baskin spread his palms, the chunky gold cuff-links on his wrists clanking as he did so. 'Tell me about it!' he moaned. 'Bloody fine advert for the club, isn't it . . . have your blackjack cards dealt by a girl whose son was murdered. It puts a damper on the bloody place. I'm not a hard man, Mr Frost, but I'm getting shot of her.'

'No, you're not, Harry,' snapped Frost. 'The poor cow has suffered enough without losing her job as well.'

'All right.' He tried to sound reasonable. 'She can stay away for a few days – I might even pay her – but when she comes back she'd better not go around with a long bloody face. We need to keep the punters happy.'

'Of course you do, Harry – so we want to know the name of the punter she kept happy last night.'

'As I told the other copper, people who come to this club have a right to privacy. Whatever arrangement the gentleman made with Joy Anderson after she left the club is a matter entirely for him.'

Frost gave a sweet smile. 'Let me put it plainly, Harry. People come to your club for a gamble and a bit of the other and you are happy to provide both so long as they pay. Most of the girls who work for you are known prostitutes. You take at least half of what they earn on the side, probably more if the client pays by credit card. You also provide the girls' flats at exorbitant rents. So what say I nominate you as Pimp Of The Year and charge you with living off immoral earnings?'

Baskin's face flushed a dark red. 'This is a respectable club. I could have you up for defamation of character . . . but if it will help you catch the boy's killer . . .' He scribbled something on a pad and tore off the sheet. 'There's his name and address – now piss off!'

Frost glanced at the note, then stuffed it into his mac pocket. 'Thanks, Harry. I knew I could appeal to your better nature.' He stood up and looked over to Cassidy. 'Ready?'

Cassidy was still staring out of the window and seemed to have taken no interest in Frost's conversation with Baskin. He frowned as if dragged out of a reverie. 'What?'

'Let's go.'

'Sure.' One last look out of the window. 'Sure.'

Joy Anderson's client lived in Lexington. Frost radioed through to Lexington Division to send someone round to question him. They had barely got inside the station when Arthur Hanlon came running up to them, beaming all over his face and falsely raising Frost's hopes that the boy had been found. 'You were right about the body in the bunker, Jack. We've matched his prints – we know who he is.'

'Are you going to tell me his name, Arthur, or do I get three guesses?'

'He's Lemmy Hoxton.'

Hanlon offered the form sheet to Frost. Frost didn't take it. He stared at Hanlon open-mouthed. Lemmy! The bloated balloon of the putrefying face swirled in front of him as he tried to compare it with the living Lemmy Hoxton, a vicious and habitual petty criminal he had arrested many times. 'We won't try too hard on this one,' said Frost. 'Whoever killed him deserves a medal.' He fumbled for a cigarette.

'He's been dead over two months and his wife hasn't reported him missing?' observed Cassidy.

'Probably couldn't believe her bloody luck,' said Frost. He sighed. 'But you're right. She's got a hell of a lot of explaining to do. Let's pay her a visit.'

The house was a semi-detached, two-storeyed dwelling, its front garden asphalted over to provide parking space for Lemmy's metallic bronze Toyota which was still parked there. The place was in darkness and all the curtains were drawn. It looked empty, but Frost thumbed the door bell anyway and waited. Nothing. He tried again, egged on by Cassidy's impatient shuffling of his feet, implying that if he rang it, the door would open. Still no reply. Frost lifted the letter-box flap and squinted through. All dark inside. Then he stiffened. He could have sworn he heard a door at the back of the house quietly click shut.

'Let's take a look round the back.'

They went down the side of the house to the rear garden. Frost stopped abruptly and flapped his hand at Cassidy for silence. He pointed. Cassidy peered into the darkness. Movement. There was someone clambering over the rear wall into the garden, someone who didn't want to be seen. They watched as the figure darted across the lawn, then darkness swallowed him. The sound of a sash window being cautiously raised and closed.

'A flaming burglar!' moaned Frost. 'Just what we bloody need!' He sent Cassidy round to the front door to guard that escape route while he tiptoed across the straggling grass of the lawn, probably last cut by Lemmy some three months ago. A small patio of chequer-board paving stones led to the back door, which he tried; it was locked. Further along was a small window. The curtains were only partially drawn and he was able to flash his torch beam through to show a small utility room with a washing machine and a dish washer.

To his relief, the window slid up easily. He squeezed through, closing it carefully behind him and turning the catch to stop the intruder from getting out again that way. A door to the right took him into the darkened hall. A rustling sound. He froze. The sound was coming from a door to his left. He tiptoed over and pressed his ear tight against it. More rustling. Someone moving stealthily. He padded across to the front door to let Cassidy in, his finger to his lips as he pointed to the room. Cassidy nodded, eyes aglow, all eager for action. Frost reached for the handle, turned it silently, and gingerly inched the door open. The room was in pitch darkness but the radiator had been going full blast and it was hot and stuffy and . . . his nose twitched. Sweat. The strong smell of male sweat.

His hand slid down the wall trying to locate the light switch. Got it. He shifted his grip on the torch to use it as a club, if necessary. A sudden cry. A woman in pain. He pressed the switch.

A large, candy-striped settee was in the middle of the room and on it, two naked figures, blinking at the light, were frantically trying to disentangle themselves. The woman, reddish hair, freckle-flecked body, all buttocks and floppy breasts, was in her early fifties. The man . . . no, not a man . . . a youth, fifteen, sixteen at the most, probably younger, had pushed himself free of the woman and charged at Frost with a knife.

All confusion. The woman screaming, 'No, Wayne!', and Cassidy yelling 'Police!' while seeming to be rooted to the spot, and Frost belting the knife arm with his heavy torch, and the youth shouting obscenities.

Cassidy froze. He couldn't move. He could just watch . . . It was the knife. The cold steel of the knife that jabbed and jabbed . . . He suddenly realized he was terrified of being stabbed again . . . or was it that he wanted to see Frost get hurt? Frost, the bastard who had fouled up the investigation into his daughter's death. He gritted his teeth and forced himself to move, but before he could do anything Frost's knee came up sharply and the youth dropped the knife with a scream of pain and fell to the ground, hugging his groin.

Quickly, Frost pocketed the knife, then turned to the woman who was struggling to cover her nakedness with a dressing-gown. She scowled at him. 'Don't look, you dirty bastard!'

'Dirty bastard!' echoed Cassidy. 'That's rich, coming from you, Maggie. We've just caught you having sex with an under-age kid.'

'He's not under age. He's sixteen.'

'Inches, perhaps, but not years,' said Frost, looking down at the speechless youth who was still rocking in agony. 'Cover yourself up, son, you're making me feel inadequate.'

The boy crawled over to the settee and began to pull on a pair of faded jeans, wincing as he did so.

'You've no right to come barging in here,' said Maggie Hoxton.

'We rang your bell, but got no reply,' explained Frost. 'We saw super-dick climbing through your back window and thought you had burglars.'

'We've got nosy flaming neighbours. Tongues would start wagging if he came in the front door.'

'And his dick started wagging when he came in through the back.' Frost turned to the youth, who was dragging a red T-shirt over his head. 'So what was the idea of the knife, sonny boy – protecting your gran?'

'She's not me gran,' mumbled the boy.

'She's bloody old enough to be.'

'I thought you were her husband. He's supposed to be a mad sod.'

Frost nodded. 'He'd have broken you in two, sonny. You wouldn't have left here with all the bits you came in with.' He told Cassidy to take the boy into the other room and question him so he could talk to the woman on her own.

'Well, Maggie?'

She looked worried. 'I've done nothing wrong. He's my toy boy.'

'I know,' said Frost. 'I saw you toying with his dick.' He parked himself in the armchair and loosened his scarf. 'I didn't come about him. It's about Lemmy.'

'Oh?' She tried to sound unconcerned, but her nervousness showed. She wouldn't look at Frost as she dug down in the dressing-gown pocket and found a cigarette then crossed to the mantelpiece for her lighter, keeping her back to him.

Frost was watching her every movement. He wished he could see her face. 'Lemmy's dead, Maggie.'

Her back stiffened. For a brief second the lighter paused an inch from her cigarette then, hand shaking, she lit up and turned slowly to face him. 'Dead?'

He nodded. 'He's been dead for three months.'

She sat in the other chair, facing him, and inhaled deeply on her cigarette. 'How did it happen?'

'Someone smashed his skull in.'

She gave the tiniest twitch of a shrug. 'Oh dear.'

'I must say, you're bearing up bravely to your sad loss, Maggie.'

She snorted a sarcastic laugh. 'If you're waiting for me to break down and cry, don't hold your bloody breath. Lemmy was a bastard, a vicious, sadistic bastard and if he's dead, I'm glad . . . I'm over the moon.'

'When did you see him last?'

Her brow furrowed in thought. 'Beginning of August. We had a row and he walked out.' She flicked cigarette ash towards the fireplace and seemed unconcerned when it fell short on to the carpet. A woman after my own heart, thought Frost.

'Lemmy walked out . . . just like that? Leaving his house . . . his car?'

'Yes.'

'I find that very hard to believe, Maggie. What was this row about – theological matters?'

'He'd been seeing another woman.'

'What's her name?'

'I don't know her name – Lily, I think.'

Behind Frost the door opened and closed as Cassidy came back in.

'Where does Lily live?'

'I don't know her address. Someone said he'd been knocking about with another woman. I questioned him about it, we had a row and he walked out.'

'I've got a better suggestion,' said Cassidy, walking across the room and standing over her. 'Lemmy couldn't satisfy you so you started paying young kids to have it away. Lemmy came home early one day and caught you at it. There was a fight and you killed him.'

Maggie was up on her feet, shouting at him. 'That's a bloody lie!'

'Is it?' smirked Cassidy. 'I've been talking to your toy boy in the other room. All the kids round here know about you and your depraved habits. You pay them ten quid a time, don't you? It's been going on for months – even when Lemmy was still alive.'

She glared at him. 'If – and I'm not admitting anything – if I had it off with kids, they were all over age.'

'Did they come with their dick in one hand and their birth certificate in the other?' asked Frost.

Cassidy scowled. This was a serious murder enquiry and he could do without Frost's infantile jokes. 'He caught you at it once, didn't he, Maggie? The kid only just got out of the house in time. Lemmy beat the living daylights out of you.'

'All right – so he caught me at it. So bloody what?'

'He finds you with a kid and he beats you up, but when you tell Lemmy you've heard he's having it off with another woman, he meekly legs it away, not even bothering to take his motor.'

'Yes.' She thrust her chin out defiantly at Cassidy. 'That's exactly what happened.'

'Get some drawers on, Maggie,' said Frost. 'We'll continue this down at the nick.' When she went upstairs to dress, he asked Cassidy about the boy. 'Is he under age?'

'He says he's sixteen.'

'We'll check him out when we get to the station.'

'I'll do the questioning,' said Cassidy. It was a statement, not a request.

'This is Arthur Hanlon's case,' said Frost.

'Hanlon is only a sergeant.'

Frost shrugged. What the hell . . . Arthur would be only too pleased to get shot of it. 'Sure . . . take the case over.'

Cassidy smiled his satisfaction. Maggie's story was so weak, he was sure he could get a confession out of her without any trouble. Nice to be able to go in to Mullett and say, with the right touch of diffidence, 'I've cleared this one up, sir.'

'We'd better get a team over to search the house,' said Frost. 'If she killed Lemmy there might be the odd drop of blood or bits of finger knocking about she forgot to wipe up.'

He had just finished radioing instructions through to Control when Bill Wells took over the microphone. 'Jack – you're just round the corner from the old Rook Street housing estate?'

'Is that so?' grunted Frost. 'I was wondering where I was.'

'That missing girl – Judy Gleeson. Just had a phone call. Bloke wouldn't give his name, but reckons he saw a man dragging a young girl into one of those derelict houses in Rock Street.'

'Which house? The street's full of them.'

'That's all he told us, then he hung up.'

'Bless his bleeding heart,' said Frost. 'It won't take us more than four or five hours to search through the lot. I'll need help.'

'Wonder Woman and Burton are on the way.'

'I'll meet them on the corner,' said Frost.

The Rook Street estate had been built in the early fifties using a new French method of construction which involved preformed concrete slabs and metal binding rods. It was cheap and quick. The finished estate looked like a prison block, but people desperate for housing were pleased to have anything. Over the years serious faults began to develop.

It transpired that the wrong mix of cement had been used in the construction. The concrete slabs started disintegrating and the metal binding rods corroded and crumbled, making the structures highly dangerous. Experts said there was no economical cure, so the properties were condemned and the tenants rehoused.

The street was now a double row of decaying properties with damp-blackened concrete and the doors and windows boarded up with 18mm blockboard held in place by six-inch nails. An empty, miserable street, exuding the damp musty aroma of desolation.

Slowly, Burton drove down the road with Frost and Liz flashing torches on the houses as they passed them, looking for signs of forced entry. Nothing. All doors and windows appeared firmly sealed. 'I suppose we checked this place when we were looking for the boy?' Frost asked.

'One of the first places we looked,' said Burton. 'But I think they only checked that the doors and windows were still boarded up.'

'Better do it thoroughly tomorrow,' said Frost. 'Let's take a look round the back – that's where I'd break in.'

As they climbed out of the car, the wind kicked ancient sheets of newspapers across the road in front of them and dribbled an empty tin can along the kerb.

A high wooden fence protected the rear area. Frost clambered over it, hissing with annoyance as his mac caught on a nail and tore. He leant over to help Liz, but she ignored him, insisting on climbing over on her own and then offering her hand to Burton who was making heavy weather of it. They thudded down into a junk-littered jungle that once was a garden. The harsh moonlight shone on a row of boarded up windows and doors, all looking secure and untouched. Scrambling over dividing fences, they checked each house carefully.

They found the point of entry in the third house they examined, where the boarding had been newly wrenched away from a downstairs window. Frost signalled for Burton to go round to the front in case anyone attempted to get out that way, then swung over the sill and dropped inside. Liz followed. The intense darkness of the boarded-up house seemed to swallow up the light from Liz's torch as they padded across bare floorboards. A door swung ajar. Frost pushed it gently, then flapped his hand for the torch to be extinguished. Floorboards creaking above. Someone was moving about upstairs.

A muffled voice. Then a scream. A long, chilling, almost animal-like scream of pain.

'Come on!' yelled Frost.

They rushed up the stairs, taking them two at a time. A crack of orange seeped out weakly from under a door on the landing. They charged through it, into a room, its windows boarded, the darkness eased only by a candle stuck on the mantelpiece. In the flickering light they could just make out the back of a man bending over someone on the floor. A girl. A young girl. The room still echoed from her screaming.

At their entry, the man swung round, candlelight glinting off the knife in his hand.

Shit! thought Frost. Not another bloody knife!

He advanced gingerly, jerking back as the knife blade slashed the air, just missing him. The man's eyes were wild. He didn't seem to be in control of himself. 'Keep back or I'll rip you open . . .'

'Drop it.' Liz had managed to work her way behind him and had grabbed the knife arm. Furiously, he tried to shake her off, but she hung on with bulldog tenacity and forced the arm back. 'Drop the knife or I'll break your arm.' With a howl of rage he again tried to shake her off. A sickening cracking sound and a shriek of pain, then a clatter as the knife dropped to the ground. Frost, for the second time that day, scooped it up.

'Leave him alone, you bitch,' screamed the girl from the floor.

'Police,' announced Frost, flashing his warrant card. 'Are you all right, love?'

The girl was lying on the floor covered with a couple of coats. Her face was glistening with sweat and her lip was bleeding where she had bitten it.

A yelp of pain from the man as Liz snapped handcuffs on his wrists. 'You've broken my bloody arm.'

Frost ignored him. He was more concerned with the girl. 'What did he do to you, love?'

Her lips moved as if she was going to answer, then her eyes widened and she opened her mouth and shrieked, arching her back, almost shaking off the coats that covered her.

Frost yelled to Liz, 'Get an ambulance.' As she radioed through, he bent over and pulled the coats from the girl, then his jaw sagged. 'Shit! . . . She's having a bloody baby!'

Liz stood frozen to the spot, still gripping her handcuffed prisoner. The girl was now in convulsions, sweating and shaking from the pain and the terror at what was happening to her fourteen-year-old body. Her head thrashed from side to side as convulsion after convulsion racked her.

Frost moved back. He felt helpless. He didn't know what to do. He didn't even want to stay in the same room. He beckoned to Liz. 'Help her!'

Liz's face drained of colour. She went as white as

Frost. 'I don't know anything about having babies.'

Frost buzzed Burton on the radio. 'She's having a baby. Can you help?'

'Yes,' said Burton.

'Then bloody get up here – and quick.' The airless room was becoming hot and suffocating, smelling of blood and sweat and burning candle. Liz looked ready to pass out.

'Take him to the car,' yelled Frost. He didn't want another patient on his hands. He turned back to the girl, who was gripping his wrist, her nails digging into his flesh, hurting as the pain forced another scream out of her. 'Come on, Burton,' pleaded Frost aloud. 'Come on . . .!' The sound of the baby crying coincided with the approaching siren of the ambulance as it turned into the street.

6

'Any joy?' Wells asked as Frost mooched in.

'They had the bleeding joy nine months ago,' said Frost. He filled Wells in on what had happened. 'Fourteen years old. Too young to buy a packet of fags, but not too young to have a baby.' He shook his head sadly and dug in his pockets for his own cigarettes. Only three left. Another forage into the superintendent's office was called for. 'Is Hornrim Harry in?'

His question was answered by the booming voice of Mullett who came striding through the swing doors, beaming all over his face. 'I understand Cassidy has cracked the Lemmy Hoxton killing. That's what I like to see, Frost, quick results – something that is sadly lacking in other officers.' He gave the inspector his meaningful stare which Frost pretended not to understand.

'Are you telling me Maggie Hoxton has confessed to killing her old man?' asked Frost.

'Not confessed as such, but it's just a matter of time. Mr Cassidy tells me it's an open and shut case. She never reported him missing, she's been forging his name on cheques and if that wasn't bad enough, she's been buying young boys for immoral purposes. Even without a confession we've got the strongest possible case.'

'I never knew she'd been forging his cheques,' said Frost.

Mullett gave his thin sour smile. 'Sergeant Hanlon found evidence of it in the house. You really should keep yourself up to date, inspector. You are supposed to be in overall charge.' He spun on his heel to return to the old log cabin, tightening his lips and pretending not to hear what sounded suspiciously like a moist raspberry.

Frost hurtled down the other corridor to the incident room to find Arthur Hanlon sitting at one of the desks making a list of the contents of a large cardboard box which contained items found during the search of Lemmy's house. 'Who's been crawling round Mullett telling him things I don't know, Arthur?'

'The forged cheques, you mean? I've only just found them, Jack. I haven't even had a chance to let Acting Inspector Cassidy know yet.' He stressed the word 'acting'. 'Look at this first.'

He showed Frost a sheet of lined notepaper on which someone had been writing the signature 'Lemmy Hoxton' over and over again, getting more like the real thing each time. Then he produced a white envelope and tipped out the contents – a wad of cancelled cheques returned by the bank. Frost riffled through them. They were all dated later than the date of Lemmy's death. 'Here's an old cheque,' said Hanlon, pushing it across. 'That is a genuine Lemmy. These later ones are forgeries.'

Frost studied them and nodded. 'Maggie must have been bloody sure Lemmy wasn't coming back to have tried this lark. What else have you got in the box? If it's worth having, we share it fifty-fifty.'

Hanlon grinned and hauled out a carrier bag which he tipped on the desk. 'This was poked behind Lemmy's cold water tank. A few old friends there from the stolen property list.'

Frost poked through the pile of assorted bric-à-brac; necklaces, compact cases, dubious-looking strings of pearls, wads of family photographs, letters tied with ribbon. There was a rolled gold cigarette lighter which Frost flicked a couple of times, dropping it back when it refused to work. 'Nothing worth pinching here. Hello –

what's this?' A small, black rexine-covered case, the letters DFM in gold on the lid. He opened it. On a bed of blue plush was a medallion. He took it from the case and examined it. The Distinguished Flying Medal, awarded to Flight Sergeant J.V. Miller. Miller was the name of the old lady conned by the fake Water Board man. So Lemmy must have been involved in that scam, but he didn't match up to the description she had given. The man she described was small and thin with a moustache. He replaced the medal and pushed the case across to Hanlon. 'Let her know we've got it back. It'll cheer the poor old cow up no end.' He stood up. 'Where's Hopalong Cassidy?'

'Still questioning Maggie in No. 2 interview room.'

'I think I'll stick my nose in – if only to irritate him.'

But he was too late. Cassidy had just left the interview room and PC Collier was about to escort Maggie Hoxton back to her cell. Frost beckoned him outside. 'How's it going?'

'She hasn't cracked yet, but Mr Cassidy is sure she will.'

'Let's see if I have any luck,' said Frost. He went back into the interview room with Collier. Maggie, seated at the table, arms folded, looked up at him defiantly as he flopped into the chair opposite her and treated her to his disarming smile which immediately put her on her guard. He pushed across a cigarette and lit up for them both. 'Things don't look too good for you, Mag.'

She smirked. 'If they look so bloody bad, why haven't I been charged? You've nothing on me, not a damn thing. Like I told that other git, we had a row, Lemmy walked out and I haven't seen him since.'

'When he walked out on you, Mag, did he say, "Maggie, dearest, I'm never coming back, not ever"?'

'No. He slammed the door and went.'

'He didn't even do a typical, lovable Lemmy thing,

like putting your hand in the door frame as he slammed it shut?'

'No.'

'Didn't it strike you as strange that he left his home, his clothes, his change of underpants and his bronze Toyota?'

Maggie shrugged. 'Perhaps he didn't need them. Perhaps his new lady friend has lots of money.'

Frost beamed. 'Funny thing that, Mag. I was going to ask you about money. Did he leave you anything for the housekeeping?'

'No.'

'Did he send you a cheque from time to time?'

'No. He didn't give a sod about me.'

'Oh come, Maggie. You do that noble man an injustice. Lemmy was so concerned about your welfare that even though he was dead, rotting away and stinking the place out, he still insisted on signing cheques so you could entertain your toy boys.' He produced the cancelled cheques from his pocket and dumped them on the table. 'He's been dead for three months, yet there's one here dated last week.'

She stared at the cheques, her mind whirring, trying to find an explanation that just wouldn't come. 'All right. So I forged his name. How was I supposed to live? The sod had walked out on me.'

'If you believed Lemmy was still alive, you wouldn't have dared forge his name to his cheques. He'd have broken every bone in your body. You knew he was dead. You knew because you killed him, you and young Superdick.' He gave her a sweet smile. 'So I'm going to charge you both with murder.'

She snatched the cigarette from her mouth and leant across the table. 'You're not pinning this on me. I never killed him.'

'Then who did, Maggie?'

'I don't know.' She leant back and took a long drag at

her cigarette. 'All right, I'll tell you the truth. We didn't have a row. He went out one day and never came back. Well, you don't look a gift horse in the mouth. He'd been a bastard to me, knocked me about and kept me short of money. I didn't give a damn what had happened to him, I was just thankful he'd gone.'

'What did you think might have happened to him?'

'At first I thought he'd been arrested. I knew he'd gone out that day to do a job.'

'Nicking stuff from old age pensioners?' suggested Frost.

'Sounds his bleeding mark, but I don't know what it was. Anyway, he never came back – end of story.'

'So you started forging his cheques?'

'After a week. I had to live, didn't I?'

'Didn't it occur to you that Lemmy might be dead?'

'Occur to me? I was bloody banking on it.'

'So why didn't you tell the police? If you and young Rent-a-dick didn't kill him, you had nothing to lose.'

'If I told the police and they found his body, Lemmy's flaming wife would have copped the house and all his money.'

Frost gaped. 'His wife? I thought you were his wife?'

She shook her head. 'He walked out on his real wife over ten years ago. The greedy grasping cow – she'd have had me out of the house and on the street before the ropes came off the coffin handles.'

'So he went out, never came back and you did sod all about it?'

She glared at him defiantly. 'I don't think there's any law against that.'

'There's a law against forging cheques,' said Frost.

'I was his common-law wife. I had no money. I don't think any jury's going to convict me on that, do you?'

Frost tapped his empty cigarette packet on the table. 'You might be telling the truth, Mag. Trouble is, you still fit nicely into our frame. We reckon Lemmy came home unexpectedly, found you and little Wayne having it away. There was a fight, you killed him and disposed of the body. You then proceed to lead a life of unlimited dick and luxury.'

She snapped her fingers at PC Collier. 'Give me my handbag.' She opened it and took out a window envelope which she gave to Frost. 'Have a look at that!'

He unfolded the printed sheet inside. It was a Visa credit card statement made out to Lemmy Hoxton. The amount outstanding was £699.99 covering a purchase from Supertek Discount Warehouses, Denton. He looked at it, then back at her. 'So?'

'Lemmy never let his credit card out of his sight. It was in his wallet which he always kept on him. If he was dead in August, how come he spent nearly seven hundred quid in October?'

Frost looked again at the statement. The date against the purchase was 12th October. 'Are you saying you didn't buy this?'

'I didn't have his bloody credit card, so how could I? I reckon whoever killed him took his wallet. Check with the store – they ought to remember who they sold seven hundred quid's worth of stuff to.'

Frost refolded the statement and popped it back into the envelope. 'OK, Maggie. I'll check it out.'

He ambled back to the incident room where Arthur Hanlon was putting the finishing touches to a sheaf of schedules which he waved at Frost.

'Do you want to OK the arrangements for dragging the lakes and canals tomorrow, Jack?'

Frost shook his head. 'No thanks, Arthur. If you did it, I'm sure it's impeccable.' He yawned. 'I'm going to get my head down for a couple of hours. If any more bodies turn up with limbs or dicks cut off, let Mr Cassidy handle them.'

He drifted into his office on his way out. Liz Maud's things, following her expulsion from Allen's office, were neatly stacked on the spare desk. He took a cursory glance through his in-tray. More piddling little memos from Mullett and a wad of returns demanding to be filled in. In the middle of his desk Liz had left a list of the jewellery and furs allegedly stolen from Stanfield's house, together with a copy of their claim to the insurance company which suggested they had been robbed of the Crown Jewels. He skimmed through it and put it back on her desk. There were more important things to think about than that at the moment.

He almost made it to his car. As he was unlocking it Wells charged out, yelling his name and waving a message sheet. 'Another kiddy stabbed in his cot, Jack.'

'Give it to Liz Maud,' said Frost. 'It's her case.'

'She's off duty. Mr Mullett wants you to deal with it.'

'Me? Why?'

'You're an inspector. The kid's father is a friend of his.'

'Any friend of Mullett's is an enemy of mine. Tell him you just missed me.' But as he spoke he could see the Divisional Commander watching them both from his office window. He heaved a sigh of resignation, took the message sheet from Wells and climbed into his car.

The address was an expensive-looking bungalow with a large garden whose rear boundary backed on to Denton Golf Course. A police car was outside. As he slid in behind it another car skidded to a stop behind him and Liz Maud got out, her hair all over the place. She had heard the call over the radio and driven straight over.

PC Jordan let them in. They could hear angry voices. 'That's the father,' explained Jordan. 'He's throwing his weight about . . . a real right bastard.'

'Of course he is,' agreed Frost. 'He's a friend of Mr Mullett's.' Not feeling an immediate desire to go inside to be shouted at, he asked Jordan to tell him what had happened.

Jordan flipped open his notebook. 'Family name is Wilkes. Him and his wife were down the golf club – the annual dinner and dance or something – leaving the nanny to put their four-year-old daughter to bed. Around half-past eleven the nanny hears the kiddy screaming. She tried to get into the nursery, but the door was jammed. Anyway, she managed to give it a kick and burst in. The nursery window was wide open, the kiddy screaming with blood all over her pyjamas. Nanny looked out of the window and saw someone scrambling over the garden fence on to the golf course.'

'How's the little girl?' asked Liz.

'No real damage, thank God. She's gone back to sleep now, I think.' He frowned his disapproval at the angry shouting still coming from the other room. 'Assuming she can sleep through that damn row.'

'Show me where he got in,' said Frost. Jordan led them round the back of the bungalow, past the patio windows of the lounge where they could see the father striding up and down and yelling at PC Simms. He glared at them as they quickly scuttled past.

The end casement window was wide open and outside it the SOC man was closing up his case of equipment. He shook his head to Frost. 'No prints other than the mother's and the nanny's.'

'You're bloody useless,' said Frost, looking through to the nursery which was decorated in pink and white. A pink and white wooden chair lay on its side in front of the open door. The matching pink and white bed by the wall was empty. 'Where's the kiddy now?'

'In the nanny's room.'

Frost turned to look across the garden to the golf course. 'She saw him clambering over that rear fence?' It wasn't a very high fence.

He swung his leg over the sill and dropped into the nursery. Liz and Jordan followed. 'He wouldn't have to be much of an athlete to get in here, would he?' muttered

Frost as he padded over to the bed. He looked at the circus motif counterpane. One of the grinning, white faces of a clown was freckled with tiny drops of blood. Frost peered at it closely, then nodded. He had seen enough. 'I can't put it off any longer – let's go and talk to Mr Mullett's mate.'

The mother, an ash blonde in her mid-thirties, wearing a low-cut emerald green evening dress, was sitting hunched by the electric wall fire. Her husband, dark-haired, with a trim black moustache, wore a white dinner jacket and a black bow tie. His face was flushed and he spun round angrily as they entered. 'It's too damn late now. He's miles away. If you'd have got here sooner instead of sitting on your fat arses doing nothing, you might have stood a chance of catching him.'

Frost dropped uninvited into a vacant chair and beamed up at him. 'I would hardly describe my lady colleague as having a fat arse, sir – it's smaller than yours.'

The man's face darkened. 'Don't come that tone with me, inspector. Some perverted maniac has broken into my house and stabbed my four-year-old daughter. Instead of sending twenty men to surround and search the place, we get two men in a car. It's pathetic . . . bloody pathetic.'

'We couldn't send twenty men even if we wanted to, sir,' replied Frost. 'At the moment, all we have got is eight men covering the whole of Denton. The rest have been out all day from early this morning, searching for a missing boy. They only stopped when it was too dark to continue. They are now getting some sleep and will be out again early tomorrow morning.'

The man wasn't interested in facts and figures. 'Someone's going around stabbing babies,' he yelled. 'Get some more police in . . .'

Frost held up his hands in mock surrender. 'Let's calm it down, shall we, sir? You want him caught, we want to catch him. We won't achieve that by yelling at each other. You and your wife were out when it happened, so let's have a word with the nanny. She, at least, saw him.'

Frost had imagined the nanny to be a grey-haired little old lady in a nurse's uniform, reeking of wintergreen, and was pleasantly surprised when a strapping Swedish blonde in her late teens came in carrying the sleeping child wrapped in a blanket.

'Flaming hell,' he whispered to Liz. 'She can breast feed me any time she likes!'

Liz pretended not to hear and hoped the family hadn't heard either. Frost had a genius for tasteless jokes at the wrong time.

'Helga's English is not too good,' said the man.

I bet she knows how to say, 'Yes please,' thought Frost. He smiled encouragingly. 'So you heard a noise, Helga, and you ran to the nursery?'

She nodded, eyes glowing at the chance to recount her adventure. 'I hear Zoë cry. I run to nursery, but door is jammed. I kick and it opens. There is blood on Zoë. I look out of window and there is man climbing fence into golf field.'

'Can you describe him?' asked Liz, pen poised.

'No. Too dark. Too far. I phone Mr Wilkes at golf place.'

'That's right,' nodded Wilkes. 'I called the police from there and we came straight over.'

'If it was too dark and too far, could it have been a woman?' asked Frost.

Her eyes widened in astonishment at such a question 'Would a woman do such a thing to a little child?'

'They want equality with men,' said Frost. 'How bad was Zoë hurt? Did you call a doctor?'

'Three little stab marks on her bottom,' said Helga. 'I put on sticking plaster.' She pulled down the child's pyjama trousers to show them the plastered wound. It didn't look too serious and the sleeping child hardly stirred.

'I shudder to think what that pervert might have done if Helga hadn't disturbed him,' said Wilkes. He turned to his wife. 'First thing tomorrow – security bars on all these windows.'

'It will make it look like a prison,' she objected.

'I don't give a damn. Until these plods catch him I'm taking no chances.'

Frost ignored the 'plod' jibe. 'These aren't the pyjamas she was wearing in bed?'

'No. They had blood. I changed.'

'Perhaps you'd get them for me,' smiled Frost.

She returned in a few minutes after putting the child back to bed. She held a small bundle of Care Bear pyjamas. Her breasts bounced delightfully as she crossed the room and Frost wished he could think of more things for her to bring back. He took them and held them up. There were blobs of blood on the bottoms corresponding to the stab wounds. He examined them closer. The cloth was intact – no sign of tear marks made by the knife point. 'When you got into the bedroom, were these trousers pulled down?'

She shook her head and her blonde hair shimmered from side to side. 'No. Bedclothes pulled back. Zoë lying on her face, but pyjamas not pulled down.'

Frost smiled his thanks. 'I see.' He passed the pyjamas to Liz. 'We'll take these with us if you don't mind.' He stood up. 'We'll see ourselves out.'

'And that is it?' demanded Wilkes. 'You're not going to search the area?'

'For what?' asked Frost. 'For a man whose description we haven't got?'

'So what are you going to do?'

'We've got a few promising leads, sir. We'll follow them up and let you know.'

'I'd like to remind you that I'm a personal friend of

Police Superintendent Mullett,' said Wilkes.

'Don't worry, sir,' said Frost. 'We won't hold that against you.'

Outside the house he said to Liz, 'Those other kids that were stabbed . . . were their wounds the same as this one – little jab marks?'

'Yes,' replied Liz.

'I thought they were stabbed – slashed?'

'No,' said Liz. 'It's all in my report – on your desk.'

'You know I don't read bloody reports,' said Frost. 'Were any of the others stabbed in the buttocks?'

'Two in the buttocks, one on the upper leg and three on the upper arm.'

Frost opened his car door and slid into the driver's seat. 'And did he ever stab them through their clothes?'

She thought for a while. 'No. He pulled the nightdress or the pyjamas away and jabbed their bare flesh.'

'This little girl tonight . . .' He was rifling through the dashboard compartments hoping to find the treasure trove of a cigarette end. 'The bloke must have pulled down the elasticated bottom of those pyjamas while he stabbed her, then let it zip back.' To his delight he found a sizeable butt which he poked into his mouth, frowning at the heavy nicotine staining of his fingers.

'Is all this significant?' asked Liz, straightening up, her back aching from bending to talk to him in the car.

'It could be,' said Frost. 'Follow me back to the station as quick as you can.'

A fuming Acting Detective Inspector Cassidy was hovering in the corridor outside his office when they returned. 'A word, please, inspector,' he snapped, marching into Allen's office and waiting for Frost to follow.

'Sure,' called Frost, going into his own office and waiting for Cassidy to join him there. After a couple of minutes of waiting, Cassidy twigged what had happened and barged in. 'You will excuse us, please, sergeant,' he barked at Liz.

'Chase Bill Wells up on those files, would you, love,' smiled Frost. When she had gone he spun his chair round. 'What's up now?'

'I was in the middle of questioning Maggie Hoxton about the death of her husband. I take a break and when I come back, what do I find? I find that you have had the nerve to carry on questioning her on evidence that was not made available to me.'

'You weren't there,' replied Frost.

'But that doesn't give you the right to take over my case, to question my suspect, to use my evidence.'

'Sorry, son,' said Frost. 'I never seem to have time for the niceties. You're right. It is your case and I won't interfere again.'

Cassidy sank down into the spare chair. He had expected Frost to bluster and had intended hauling him before Mullett, but the man's contrite apology had thrown him completely off balance. 'It's not good enough,' he said weakly.

'Quite right, son – in fact it's bloody diabolical,' said Frost, warming to his theme.

Cassidy's mouth opened and closed. He couldn't think of anything else to say and was glad of the distraction when Liz Maud returned, followed by Bill Wells, each bearing a stack of dusty folders which they dumped on Frost's desk.

'They should be in alphabetical order,' explained Wells, 'but they got mixed up when we had the burst tank and the flooding in the old records room.'

'You've always got a bloody excuse,' said Frost. 'If you had any respect for the job, you'd come in on Christmas Day and sort them out.'

'I'm already due to come in on Christmas Day,' said Wells, taking the bait. 'Every bleeding Christmas I'm on that rota.'

'So you are,' said Frost. 'I forgot . . . you should have mentioned it.' He split the files into four piles and handed them around. 'We're looking for Sidney Snell's file.'

Cassidy's head came up. 'Who?' The name had rung a bell.

'Sidney Snell – Slimy Sid – child molester. Used to pretend he was a doctor.'

Cassidy snapped his fingers. Now he placed him. 'He called at the house and told the mother he was from the Health Department. Said the kids had to be vaccinated.'

'Vaccinated?' asked Liz.

'Yes, sergeant. He was a pervert. Liked sticking needles in little bottoms or little plump arms. It gave him a kick to see them bleed, to hear them cry.'

'He injected the arms and buttocks?' said Liz, still not taking it in.

'He only had water in the syringe,' said Frost. 'The object was to make them bleed. He did it to about six or seven kids before we caught him. Prior to that he used to expose himself to mothers with kids in pushchairs.'

'We had a couple of complaints this morning,' said Wells, 'about a bloke exposing himself to women in the park.'

Liz leant back and snatched up a sheet of typescript from her desk. She waved it angrily at Wells. 'I asked you for a list of all known sex offenders against children. This is what you gave me. Why isn't Snell's name on it?'

'Because he's ancient history,' retorted Wells. 'This all happened some ten . . . eleven years ago—'

'Even so—' Liz cut in.

'If you would kindly let me finish,' sniffed Wells. 'Snell doesn't live in Denton any more. When he came out of prison about five years ago, he moved up north. Too many parents in Denton had threatened to do him over if they ever saw him back here.'

'Oh!' said Liz, crestfallen. She had really thought

Frost was on to something. She transferred her annoyance to him. 'Then why are we wasting our time looking for his file?'

'I've an idea the sod might have sneaked back to Denton,' Frost told her. 'I think I saw him yesterday.'

'And you didn't think it worth mentioning to anyone?' asked Cassidy sarcastically.

'I wasn't sure,' said Frost, shuffling through his stack of files. 'It's been ten years since I last saw him.' He looked up as Wells cried, 'Bingo!' He held aloft a file and flipped it over to Frost. Frost blew off the dust, then turned the cover so he could see the photograph affixed to the inside. The photograph showed a podgy-faced man in his early thirties scowling at the camera. Frost jabbed it with a nicotine-stained finger. 'I was right. It was Snell I saw.'

'Are you sure?' asked Liz, getting excited at the thought of an arrest.

'I'm positive,' said Frost. 'It's been ten years, but he's still got the same little piggy eyes.'

'He used to live with his mother,' said Wells. 'Proper little mummy's boy.' He leant over Frost's shoulder and pointed to the address on the file. 'Ten years ago it was 39 Parnell Terrace. I don't know if she's still there.'

Liz picked up her handbag and checked that the street map was inside. 'I'll go and find out.'

'Hold it!' Now Cassidy sounded excited. He was staring at a typed sheet in the folder. 'You've overlooked something, inspector.' He held out the arrest sheet.

'What's that?' asked Frost, quickly skimming through it.

'Snell used to carry a genuine medical bag around with him when he posed as a doctor.'

'I know,' said Frost.

'Do you remember what was in it?'

Frost shrugged. 'Syringes, bandages, iodine . . .'

'And a bottle of chloroform,' said Cassidy with a smug

smirk. He pointed out the entry on the arrest sheet.

Frost whistled softly. 'Bloody hell! You're right. I'd forgotten about that.'

'Chloroform?' asked Liz.

Frost nodded. 'No evidence that he used it at the time. Apparently he had an uncle who was a doctor. The uncle died and Slimy Sid pinched his bag.' He chewed at his thumb as he thought this over. 'Chloroform! I can't see our luck running that way, but it would be bloody handy if it was Sidney who stabbed the kids and killed Dean Anderson.' He stood up. 'I'll drive.'

'Hold on!' Cassidy was buttoning up his jacket. 'I'm coming with you.' There was no way he was going to miss out on this. 'Two more cases solved,' he would tell Mullett with studied modesty. 'I spotted the reference to chloroform and put two and two together . . .'

'It doesn't need three of us,' said Frost.

'Sergeant Maud can stay here and look after the administration,' said Cassidy.

Liz was indignant. 'This is my case!'

'The murder of the boy takes precedence,' said Cassidy. 'You'll be more useful here, helping Sergeant Wells put these files in alphabetical order.'

She looked in mute appeal to Frost who shrugged and went out followed by Cassidy. She picked up a file and hurled it with all her strength against the wall where it fluttered papers all over the place. She looked to Wells for support. Wells's delight at the smug cow's frustration fought with his hatred for Cassidy. His hatred won. 'The bastard!' he said.

Cassidy swung the car into Parnell Terrace, pointedly fanning his hand to drive away the smoke from the stale cigarette Frost had found in the torn lining of his jacket. The car crept between a double row of identical and ugly terraced buildings made of preformed concrete. Not a light showed anywhere. The houses stood sullenly silent and an unnatural stillness hovered over the street. Cassidy's heart sank. The street was derelict. Every house was empty and boarded up with contractors' chalked notices saying 'Gas Off . . . Electricity Off . . . Water Off . . .'

'All that's missing is "Piss Off",' said Frost gloomily.

'What the hell—' began Cassidy.

'Concrete cancer,' explained Frost. 'The same as the houses in Rook Street where the fourteen-year-old had her baby.' He now remembered the article about it in the local paper. 'They've rehoused everybody.'

Muttering audibly about the complete and utter waste of time, Cassidy drove to the end of the road where he could reverse and head back to the station.

If Frost hadn't been looking up at that precise moment, he would have missed it. A flicker of light from one of the houses as a curtain was twitched back and quickly closed. A brief glimpse of a white face looking down at them.

'What light from yonder window breaks,' whooped Frost, nudging Cassidy and pointing. 'There's someone in that house.'

It was the only house in the street where the doors and windows were not boarded up. It was number 39.

Four empty milk bottles stood in a line on the doorstep, waiting vainly for a milkman who no longer called. Frost jammed his thumb in the bell push and leant his weight on it. A bell inside shrilled edgily. He gave the door a couple of kicks and yelled, 'Open up – police!'

A light clicked on inside and showed dimly through the grimed fanlight over the front door. The sound of someone stumbling down the stairs.

'Who is it?'

'The Avon Lady,' said Frost. 'Come on, Sidney, open up . . . you know damn well who it is.'

A chain clinked and the door opened a fraction so a bleary eye could study the warrant card held out by

Cassidy. The chain was unhitched and the door opened wide. A meek-looking man in his early forties, wearing a dressing-gown over red-striped pyjamas, thinning brown hair falling over his eyes, blinked at them. 'What is this all about?'

'Hello, Sidney,' beamed Frost. 'Long time, no see.'

Snell peered at the inspector. 'Sergeant Frost!' He shivered and drew his dressing-gown more tightly around him. 'I'd hoped I'd never meet up with you again.'

Frost pulled a face. 'I don't seem to endear myself to people, do I?' He stepped into the hall and kicked the door shut behind them. 'Can we come in?'

There was a musty smell to the house. Snell led them to the lounge, a cold room with old, worn furniture. Two battered suitcases and a pile of bulging carrier bags stood on the floor. A picture of Snell as a young boy, in the garden with his mother, stood in the centre of the sideboard. He switched on a two-bar electric fire and motioned them to chairs. 'I'm sure, if I wait long enough, you'll tell me what this is all about.'

'We were passing, we saw your light and we knew we'd get a friendly welcome and a fairy cake,' said Frost. 'But I'm forgetting my manners. How's your mother?'

Snell's lower lip quivered. 'My mother is dead.'

'My sincere condolences,' said Frost, remembering that this was the old cow who used to provide Sidney with watertight alibis all those years ago.

Snell knuckled his eyes. 'On the generous assumption that you are being sincere, I thank you.' He sighed. 'It's hard coming to terms with it.'

'Sudden, was it?' asked Frost.

Snell shook his head. 'She'd been in hospital for nearly two months. Three weeks ago they phoned me to say she was dying. I came straight away. She died half an hour before I got there.' He covered his face with his hands. 'We never said goodbye.'

'Three weeks ago? And you've been in Denton ever since?'

He nodded. 'Don't worry. I'm not staying. I couldn't, even if I wanted to. The Council are tearing this entire street down.'

'That's a bit drastic, just to make you move on,' said Frost.

Snell ignored him. 'Mother was the stumbling block. She wouldn't leave. As soon as they heard she was dead – she wasn't even buried – the Council slapped a demolition order on the place. I'm disposing of her effects, not that she had much, and I go back to Newcastle tomorrow.' He nodded towards the suitcases and carrier bags. 'So you needn't concern yourself with what I might do.'

'It's not a question of what you *might* do,' said Cassidy, deciding it was about time to make his presence felt. 'It's a question of what you've already done.'

Snell stared at Cassidy, his eyes blinking in puzzlement. 'Perhaps you'd kindly explain yourself.'

'The day after you returned to Denton, we had complaints of a man exposing himself to mothers and children. Isn't that what you used to do?'

'Coincidence.'

'Coincidence has a long arm, but a very short dick,' chipped in Frost. 'Two of the mothers said it was the smallest they had ever seen, which immediately made us think of you.'

Snell flushed brick red. 'Now you are being insulting.'

'And then,' continued Cassidy, raising his voice to let Frost know he was doing the questioning, 'we had instances of children being stabbed in the arms and buttocks, just as you did when you pretended to be a doctor.'

Snell slowly stood up, trembling with outrage. 'I committed my crime ten years ago. I was caught and I was punished. I've learnt my lesson.' He turned to

Frost. 'They don't like child molesters in prison.'

'Not too keen on them myself,' said Frost.

'I got beaten up – buckets of filth thrown over me. I'm not going to risk that again.'

'Where were you this morning around half-past eight?' asked Cassidy.

'In here, sorting out mother's things.'

'And where were you earlier tonight – from about ten o'clock onwards?'

'In here. I never went out.'

'Got a girlfriend, have you?' asked Frost.

'No.'

'Boyfriend?'

'No.'

'So if you're not sticking pins in little kids, hearing them cry, watching the blood spurt out of chubby little arms and bottoms, what do you do for kicks?'

With a disdainful smile, Snell opened the sideboard drawer and took out a bible which he waved in the inspector's face. 'Nothing you would understand, Mr Frost, but I get my kicks, as you call them, from the Good Book. I'm a born again Christian.'

'It wasn't your bible you were waggling at those women this morning,' said Frost. 'It was your little winkle.'

'How many times do I have to tell you – I never went out this morning . . . I'll swear to it on the bible if you like.'

'I bet you would, you bastard!' snarled Cassidy.

Snell glowered. 'I don't have to put up with this harassment. You haven't got anyone for these crimes, so you're trying to fit me up, even though I've gone straight for the past ten years.'

Cassidy pulled two photographs from his inside pocket. The first was of the missing boy. He handed it to Snell. 'Where did you pick him up?'

As Snell studied it, Frost watched him closely, noting

an expression of puzzlement followed by relief. If you're acting, you're bloody good, he thought.

'I've never seen him before.'

'Then what about him?' Snell took the photograph of the dead boy, but his eyes were on Frost who had got up from the chair and was now mooching about the room, pulling open drawers, rummaging inside. 'Do you have a search warrant?' he called.

Frost flashed a beaming smile. 'Of course not, Sidney. This is just a courtesy call.'

'The photograph,' snapped Cassidy, tapping it with his finger.

Snell gave it hardly a glance before returning it. 'Never seen him before.'

'He was chloroformed,' said Cassidy.

'So?'

'There was chloroform in the medical bag you used to carry around with you.'

'Was there? If there was, I never used it and that was ten years ago. I've taken my punishment and I've turned to the Lord. If he can forgive me, why can't you?'

'Perhaps the Lord didn't know you had these,' called Frost from the sideboard. He was holding up a coloured photograph he had found in the drawer. Two young children, aged about five, hand in hand and crying. They were both naked. He thrust it at Snell's face. 'Given it up, have you, Sidney?'

Looking disgusted at the suggestion, Snell snatched the photograph from Frost. 'A perfectly innocent snapshot of two sweet young children. What sort of mind have you got to see something dirty in that?'

'The sort of mind,' replied Frost, 'that looks at a born again Christian and sees a dirty lying bastard!'

Snell moved forward indignantly. 'I don't have to put up with this.' He spat out the words. 'This is sheer harassment.'

'Shut up!' barked Frost, poking Snell in the chest.

'And sit down!' Snell flopped in the chair. 'Now listen and listen carefully. You are a hypocritical bastard, trying to hide behind the bible. But you've been up to your old tricks again, haven't you, Sidney?'

'No, I—'

'Yes, you bloody have! Exposing yourself, stabbing little kiddies. Sadly for us, Sidney, this is your lucky day. At the moment we are so flaming busy we haven't got time to put trash like you away. When are you going back to Newcastle?'

'Tomorrow.'

'Then make it first bloody thing in the morning, because if one more kid is molested, one more mother sees a man with a microscopic dick exposing himself, I am going to throw the bloody book at you, whether you did it or not. Do I make myself clear?'

'Now hold on a minute!' said Cassidy, rising angrily from his chair.

'Shut up!' Frost waved him to silence. 'Well, Sidney?'

'I swear on the bible that I have committed no crimes since I've been in Denton, but as you wrongly and unjustly suspect me, I shall return to Newcastle first thing tomorrow. I hope that satisfies you.'

A curt nod from Frost. 'OK. We'll show ourselves out.'

Cassidy hurled himself into the driving seat and punched the dashboard in rage and frustration. Why did Frost always interfere at the critical time? 'I was questioning him—'

'He had nothing to do with the boys,' said Frost. 'They were far too old for him. Anyone over six is old and wrinkly to Sidney.'

'How can you be so damn sure?'

'I was watching his face when you showed him the photographs. He looked so relieved that you were veering away from the stabbings. He did the stabbings all right, but he knows nothing about the two boys.'

'So why don't we arrest him?'

'We've got no proof.'

'We can find proof.'

'We haven't got the time, son. We're struggling with a missing boy, two murders and an alleged robbery with violence.'

'We can get him for exposing himself,' insisted Cassidy. 'The woman should identify him.'

'It's too bloody petty to worry about.'

'Was the hit and run killing of my daughter too bloody petty to worry about?'

Frost ignored this. 'Tomorrow morning he'll be gone and he won't be our problem any more.'

'And the minute he gets back he'll be up to his filthy larks again.'

'Don't worry. I'll tip Newcastle CID the wink. They can do all the work and when they nab him, he'll confess to our crimes as well.'

'And they'll get the credit.'

Frost shrugged. Credit didn't interest him.

'I'd like to put on record that I disagree utterly with what you have done.'

Frost shrugged. 'If you like, son. It's a free country.' He yawned. 'Take me home, would you.'

Cassidy drove in frigid silence to Frost's house.

Frost yawned again. 'I shall go off to sleep the minute my head hits the pillow. You're in charge. Don't wake me unless it's bloody urgent.'

He was woken at three o'clock in the morning by the insistent ringing of his phone and someone banging at his front door.

It was bloody urgent.

7

Two o'clock in the morning and cold. Bitterly cold. The moon glared down from a cloudless sky on to a frost-rimmed landscape where a raw, cutting wind moaned and punched the side of the dark green Ford transit van as it turned the corner into Cresswell Street and drew up outside a small bungalow. The man sitting next to the driver climbed out and went to the back of the van. This was Mark Grover, twenty-six years old, married with three children, a fourth on the way. He opened the rear doors and took out his metal tool box. Closing the doors, he banged on the side of the van. Without looking back the driver acknowledged with a grunt and a curt wave as he drove off. Grover watched its rear lights disappear as it rounded the corner, then, humping the heavy tool box, he turned towards the house.

He shivered. It wasn't just the cold. He had the uneasy feeling that someone was watching him. He stared up and down the street. Moon shadows rippled across the pavement as the wind shook the trees, but no sign of anyone.

The front gate was swinging back and forth, creaking in the wind. He frowned, trying to remember. He was sure he had closed it when he had left earlier that night to go to work. He hurried up the path, tugging the front door key from his trouser pocket. But he didn't have to use it. The front door also was swinging ajar. Something was wrong. Something was very wrong.

He stepped into the dark of the hall, and was fumbling

for the light switch when a loud crash made him drop the tool case and spin round. The front door had slammed shut behind him. A strong blast of wind hit him in the face. A door or a window at the back of the house must be open somewhere. He hurried along the passage to the kitchen. There it was. The back door to the rear garden was wide open. He looked outside. Crystals of frost on bushes glinted in the moonlight. The gate in the wall leading to the path running along the rear of the properties seemed to be firmly closed. He closed the back door and turned the key in the lock. Then he saw that the piece of plywood he had nailed over the broken door pane was loose. The nails had been wrenched out of the woodwork. Someone had broken into the house.

He ran into the passage and called his wife's name. He flung open their bedroom door. She wasn't there. Across the passage to the children's room. He opened the door. He listened . . . Silence. An awful silence. Steeling himself, he clicked on the light.

The woman in the house opposite couldn't sleep. Another one of her blinding migraine headaches. She lay in bed, biting her lip against the pain, then flung back the bedclothes and went to the window where she stared out into the empty street which was almost as bright as day under the moon. Headlights. Then the transit van pulled up. She watched Mark Grover get out and walk to his front door while her mind debated whether to take a second sleeping tablet. Lights came on in the bungalow. She had often watched the children playing on the front lawn. Beautiful children, but noisy. Their mother didn't seem able to control them.

She checked the time. Five past two. Another six hours of tossing and turning. She went to the bedside cabinet and shook out two more sleeping tablets, swilling them down with a glass of water.

A piercing, animal-like wail of agony drew her back to

the window. The man came stumbling from the bungalow. He was carrying something in his arms. Good God! It was a child, its arms flopping limply. He must have taken leave of his senses to bring it out in the bitter cold.

Grover was yelling and shouting. She couldn't make out what he was saying, it was incoherent and he seemed to be crying. Lights came on in other houses and windows were raised. The woman in number 25 shouted angrily for Grover to stop that bloody row before he woke up her kids.

Someone phoned the police and complained about the noise. A yawning Bill Wells sent a car across to investigate.

Frost staggered down to the phone and yelled to the police motor cyclist who was banging at the front door that he would be there in a minute.

Bill Wells on the phone. He sounded grim. 'Nasty one for you, Jack. Three kids killed in their cots and the mother's gone missing.'

Frost slumped down in the chair by the phone. 'How old were the kids?'

'The eldest was three, the youngest a few months.'

'Bloody hell,' said Frost. 'Bloody, bloody hell.'

Most of the houses now had lights showing and curtains were twitching back as curious neighbours watched the comings and goings. A few, wearing dressing-gowns, were clustered at front gates, talking in hushed, disbelieving voices and shaking their heads sadly. One neighbour who ventured across the road was abruptly turned back by the police. 'Please keep to the other side, madam. Nothing to see here.'

The line of vehicles parked opposite the bungalow were filled with duffle-coated reporters and photographers with flashy Japanese cameras fitted with enormous telescopic lenses. Standing apart from the representatives of the big London dailies was Sandy Lane, Chief Reporter of the *Denton Echo*, his ears tuned to what the big boys were saying, but hoping to use his local knowledge to talk to the people who mattered. This was a big story which he could sell to London with a by-line, although it would be too late for the morning editions.

The man in the BBC Television van, an early arrival on the scene and able to park almost directly opposite the murder house, drained his cup of thermos coffee and mounted his video camera on his shoulder to film the arrival of Detective Inspector Frost. He panned the approach of the Ford as it coughed exhaust and jerked to a halt behind the police cars. He focused sharply on the figure at the wheel wearing a none too clean mac with a maroon scarf, then zoomed in to show him climbing wearily out and surveying the murder house which had lights blazing from every room.

Outside the front door Mike Packer, the young PC who had found the body of eight-year-old Dean Anderson, moved to one side to let the inspector pass. 'Sergeant Hanlon is inside, sir.'

Frost looked back at the knots of people outside the other houses. 'Don't waste time here, son. Go and knock on doors . . . talk to people . . . Most of the street are up anyway. It'll save time in the morning.' Relieved to be doing something useful, Packer hurried off.

The duty police doctor, anxious to get away, was waiting for him in the hall which had its grey carpeting covered with plastic sheeting. From a far door came the heart-rending moan of a man in the depths of despair. 'The father,' explained the doctor. 'He's in shock. I've given him a mild sedative but he needs to go to hospital. The ambulance should be here shortly.'

'Can I talk to him?'

'I don't advise it. He'll be out cold soon, anyway.'

Frost nodded as if he accepted this, but he intended to

question the father as soon as the doctor had departed. 'The children?'

'Asphyxiated, probably by a pillow being held over their faces. They've been dead two to three hours. You'll need a pathologist.'

'Drysdale's on his way,' said Frost.

The doctor snatched his bag and made for the door. 'Then you can manage without me.' Like Frost, he was not over-fond of the Home Office Pathologist.

Detective Sergeant Arthur Hanlon emerged from the door where all the wailing was coming from. Usually perky whatever the circumstances, he looked shattered. 'It's a mess, Jack. Three little kids dead and the mother's gone missing.'

Frost rested against the wall and fished out his cigarettes. He hated this type of case. 'She killed the kids and did a runner? I wonder what drove the poor bitch to do that. We're looking for her, I hope?'

'Yes,' said Hanlon. 'I've circulated her description.'

Frost rubbed his hands together to restore the circulation. The pervasive breath of death made the house seem very cold. Outside with that saw-edged wind it was colder. 'How was she dressed? Was she wearing a coat?'

'No idea, Jack. Haven't been able to find anyone who saw her leave yet.'

A row of clothes were hanging neatly from hooks in the hall: a man's raincoat and anorak, lots of brightly coloured children's coats and hats and, at the far end, a woman's thick red woollen coat with chunky black buttons. Frost patted the pockets and took out a suede leather purse which contained about £19. 'I reckon this is the coat she would have worn, Arthur. So it looks like no coat and no money – probably just wearing a dress. If we don't find her soon, the poor cow will freeze to death. Has she got any friends, or relatives living nearby, she might have gone to?'

Hanlon shrugged helplessly. 'We can't get any sense

from the husband and none of the neighbours have come up with anything yet, except to say she kept herself to herself and she loved the kids.'

'Never mind,' said Frost. 'I doubt if she's gone to anyone. I can't see her saying, "Can you put me up for a few days, I've done in the kids."'

'I'll show you the bodies,' said Hanlon

Frost took another deep drag at his cigarette. 'There's no hurry – they're not going anywhere.' He coughed as the smoke irritated his lungs. 'Fill me in on the facts, first.'

'Married couple. Mark Grover, aged twenty-six—'

'He's the one making that bleeding row?'

Hanlon nodded. 'The father – he found them. The missing wife is Nancy Grover, aged twenty-one. They had three kids, two boys and a girl, the eldest is three, the youngest – that's the girl – eleven months. Difficult to get details, but from what I can piece together, the husband is a self-employed carpet fitter. He had to go out at eight last night on a rush job.'

'Funny bleeding time to lay carpets?'

'That's what I thought. Anyway, he came home just after two this morning and found the front door wide open. The back door was open as well. He dashed to the kids' room . . .' Hanlon straightened up. 'I'll show you what he found.'

Frost took one last, long drag at his cigarette and pitched it out into the street. 'Let's go.'

Hanlon opened the nearest door, which was painted a nursery blue. Frost followed him into the small children's bedroom with its nursery wallpaper and heavy duty orange and brown carpeting, also covered with plastic sheeting. It held two single beds and a cot. Frost found himself tiptoeing across and holding his breath as if afraid to wake the tiny children lying in them. At the nearest bed he touched the cold, slightly swollen, face of a boy who could not have been more than three. He was lying on top of the bedclothes and wore white, knitted cotton pyjamas with Dennis the Menace figures printed on them.

'His name was Dennis,' said Hanlon in a soft voice, 'aged three.'

'Was he found like this – on top of the bedclothes?'

'No, Jack. When we arrived the father was cradling the dead kid in his arms. We had a job getting the boy away from him. We put him back here.'

Frost nodded. The room had a lingering smell of Johnson's baby powder which reminded him of the little Chinese nurse. God, was that only last night?

They moved across to the other bed, by the window. Another boy, fair-haired and slightly chubbier than his brother. His eyes were wide open and there were small dots of blood in his ears and nose. The bedclothes were drawn up to his chin.

'Jimmy, aged two,' murmured Hanlon.

Frost shuddered and shook his head. 'Poor little bleeder!'

A crumpled pillow lay on top of the bedclothes at the foot of the bed. There was a slight discoloration in the centre. It had been used to smother the three children.

The sound of a car pulling up outside. Frost looked through the window to see if it was the pathologist, but it was a black Vauxhall which he didn't instantly recognize. He turned back and went over to the cot.

Sandy Lane, stamping his frozen feet on the pavement, looked up as a black Vauxhall pulled in behind Frost's car. The man who got out and scowled at the press looked familiar. Cassidy! Detective Sergeant Cassidy who had been transferred from Denton some four years back after his young daughter was killed in a hit and run accident. So what was he doing back here? Sandy made a mental note to ask around.

* * *

The baby in the cot, so still and small, looked like a child's doll. Her arms, covered by the sleeves of a pink nightdress, lay on top of the bedclothes.

'Linda, aged eleven months,' said Hanlon.

Very gently, Frost touched the pale cheeks. They were ice cold. He felt he couldn't take much more and found something interesting to study out in the street, his eyes misting. Why the hell did he become a copper? 'Poor little bastards!' he muttered. It was all he could think of to say.

Angry voices from the hall. He frowned and went to look. Cassidy was snarling away at young PC Packer.

'He was supposed to be guarding the front door,' called Cassidy. 'Any Tom, Dick or Harry could have walked in.'

'Then we'd tell the bastards to walk out again,' replied Frost. 'I asked him to get statements from the neighbours.'

'Well, I've told him to come back on the door.'

Frost exchanged a sympathetic glance with Packer, but said nothing. He wasn't going to row over trivialities with three dead children in the house. He could have done without flaming laughing boy tonight. If he had known Cassidy would want to come he would cheerfully have let him handle the case.

Cassidy was out of sorts, annoyed that Frost had managed to get here before him. He went with Hanlon into the children's room, then emerged, tight-lipped, and they all went into the parents' bedroom with its large double bed and scarlet duvet. The bed, neatly made, its matching scarlet pillows plumped with nightdress and pyjamas folded on top, hadn't been slept in.

Frost wandered across to the window and parted the velour curtains to look out on to the rear garden which was lit up from the lights streaming from the bungalow. Beyond it there seemed to be fields and woodlands stretching to the horizon. At first he couldn't orientate himself as to where they were, then he realized he was looking at the golf course and on the far side was the bungalow of Mullett's golfing friend where the little girl was stabbed. 'Get someone to search the golf course. The mother might have wandered out there.'

'Doing it now,' said Hanlon, pointing to little pinpricks of bobbing lights from distant torches.

They went back through the hall to the dining-room where the father was sitting by the table, staring straight ahead. He was quieter now that the sedative had started to work, but from time to time he shook convulsively and seemed to have no control over his hand which was drumming a tattoo on the table top. His zip-up suede jacket was grease marked and scruffy. There was the tiniest smear of blood across the front.

'From when he carried the body of his son out to the street,' whispered Hanlon.

'Someone make some tea,' said Frost, drawing up a chair to sit opposite the man. 'Mr Grover. My name is Frost. I'm a police officer.'

Grover stared straight through him, his lips moving, but saying nothing.

'Mr Grover . . .'

Grover's head came up slowly, his face wet with tears. 'My kids. She killed them.'

Someone must have given him whisky. Frost could smell it on his breath. 'Who killed them, Mr Grover?'

'That bitch . . . that lousy bitch . . .' His fingers flexed and clawed as if squeezing someone's throat.

'Do you mean your wife?'

Grover suddenly stared at Frost as if seeing him for the first time. 'Who are you?' He slumped forward, buried his head in his hands and started to sob.

Frost wriggled uncomfortably and fished out a cigarette stub. Grover wasn't going to be of any use to anyone. Where was that flaming ambulance?

More commotion from outside then a tap at the door. PC Packer looked in and said, 'Ambulance is here, inspector. And there's a bloke outside who says he's able to help us. His name is Phil Collard. He was working with Mr Grover tonight. He drove him back here this morning.'

Frost took an instant dislike to Collard the minute the man waddled in. Balding and in his late thirties, Collard was running to fat, had a beer gut and an air of oily concern. 'Mark! It's not bloody true, is it? God – tell me it's not true!'

Grover looked up at him and gave a chilling, mirthless smile. 'They're dead,' he said simply. 'They're all dead.' Then he saw the ambulance man and stood up. 'I've got to go to the hospital.' Without another glance at any of them, he walked out of the room with the ambulance man. The passage crackled with blue flashes as the waiting pressmen took their photographs of the bereaved.

Frost waved Collard into the chair vacated by Grover. 'How do you fit into this, Mr Collard?'

'Mark's my best mate. We went to school together and now we work together.'

'Carpet fitting?'

'Yes.'

'So what can you tell us about tonight?'

'Not much. We usually go to the pub, but just after seven we had this phone call from Denton Shopfitters asking if we could help out with a rush job.'

'What rush job?'

'Fitting a new carpet in the restaurant at Bonley's department store. It's been completely refurbished. Tomorrow is the grand opening – David Jason cutting the ribbon – but the special carpeting got held up by Customs at the docks. It wouldn't reach the store until well after ten. They wanted us to work all night and lay it. Two hundred quid each, no tax – so we jumped at it.'

A tap at the door and a rattle of cups. Packer with

the tea. He handed it out in the mugs he had found in the kitchen and put a bag of sugar on the table. 'Thanks,' grunted Frost, nodding for Collard to continue.

'I called round with the van just after eight to pick him up. Nancy had the hump. Sat there sulking, not saying a word . . . the kids screaming and shouting.'

'Why did she have the hump?'

'She said she was frightened – she didn't like being left on her own all night. She was always moaning about being left on her own, even if we only went to the pub for a couple of hours. Anyway, we got to Bonley's about a quarter past eight and fitted all the grippers and underlay. At five past ten the delivery van turns up with the special new carpeting. We worked like the clappers to get the job done and finished about ten to two. I drove Mark back, dropped him off outside here, then went off home. Later I hear all the police sirens so I goes out to take a look and someone tells me Nancy's done the kids in. I couldn't believe it.'

'Did she ever threaten anything like this?'

'She threatened to do herself in – we had all the bleeding dramatics – but never the kids.'

Frost showed him the red coat from the hall. 'Is this the coat she usually wore?'

Collard nodded. 'Mark bought it for her last Christmas.'

'Any idea where we might find her?'

He pursed his lips and shook his head. 'I heard she'd legged it, but she's got nowhere to go.'

'Friends . . . relatives . . .?'

'She didn't make friends. She was a funny cow, very moody. Relatives?' He shrugged. 'Not as far as I know. When she was fourteen her mother's boyfriend started getting fruity so she ran away from home and never went back.'

Frost took a sip at his tea. 'Just for the record, Mr Collard, is there anyone at Bonley's who can confirm you were there all night?'

'The night security guard – he's on duty until six.' Then he realized the implication. 'You're not suggesting . . . ?'

'Just for the record, Mr Collard,' smiled Frost. 'We have to check everything and everybody, innocent or guilty.' He thanked him and let him go, then lit another cigarette. 'I'm beginning to feel a lot of sympathy for the poor cow,' he told Hanlon. 'Three kids, no friends, a husband who's either round the pub or out all night.'

'I can't feel sorry for her,' said Hanlon. 'They had all their lives in front of them, and she killed them.'

'Something must have snapped, Arthur.' He lifted the mug of tea to his lips when he saw it was a child's mug. It bore the name Dennis. He put it down and pushed it away. He didn't feel like tea any more.

Frost got PC Collier to phone Bonley's and listened to PC Jordan who had been knocking on doors and talking to the neighbours. 'The mother didn't mix with anyone, inspector. She and her husband were always rowing – someone heard them quarrelling tonight just after seven. Another witness thought she heard raised voices just before midnight this morning, but couldn't be sure if it was coming from this bungalow or not. Oh – the woman at number 22 said she was getting undressed a couple of nights ago when she saw a man staring in at her through the window.'

'Did she report it to the police?' asked Cassidy.

'No – she didn't think we'd do anything about it.'

'How well she knows us,' grunted Frost. 'Any description?'

'No. She screamed and he legged it.'

Frost nodded. 'Thank you, constable. You've been sod all help.' He looked up as Collier returned to report he had tried to phone Bonley's but could only get the answerphone.

'Send a car round,' ordered Frost. 'I want to know what time Collard and the husband arrived and what time they left – and check that they were there all the time.'

'You're surely not suggesting they've got anything to do with this?' asked Hanlon.

'Just being thorough,' replied Frost. 'Mr Mullett suggested I gave it a try in case the novelty appealed to me.'

Cassidy finished his tea in silence, staying aloof from the others, then went back into the children's bedroom. He wanted to take a thorough look around. He was bending over the body of the three-year-old Dennis when he spotted something that Frost, in his usual slapdash manner, had missed. On the upper arm of the pyjama jacket, a small stain. A bloodstain. His eyes glinted. Very gently, he lifted the arm and tugged back the sleeve until he could see a small blob of blood from a recent wound on the upper arm. It looked as if Dennis Grover had been jabbed with something sharp, exactly the same as the little girl in the other bungalow.

He pulled the pyjama sleeve down and lowered the tiny arm. What to do about it? He smiled grimly and decided he would keep this titbit to himself for the time being. He began feeling happy for the first time since he arrived in Denton.

Cassidy walked back to the dining-room where Frost was staring moodily up at the ceiling. 'I'll take over now,' he said.

'Thanks,' said Frost, trying not to sound too grateful. This was the sort of case he was only too happy to give up. Not much satisfaction in arresting a poor bitch of a mother who just couldn't take any more and getting her locked away in a mental institution.

He bumped into Liz Maud in the hall. 'Sorry I'm late getting here,' she told him. 'I lost my way. I couldn't find Cresswell Street on my map.'

'Apologize to the bloke who kicked you out of your office,' said Frost. 'He's in charge now.'

He walked back to his car, deaf to the questions of the waiting reporters. Then everyone's attention was diverted by the arrival of a gleaming black Rolls-Royce. Flash guns fired as Drysdale and his secretary walked into the bungalow. They flashed again when the bodies were brought out, bodies so tiny the undertaker was able to accommodate all three in a single coffin shell.

Frost drove back past the golf course, all silver and black in the moonlight. The flag on the club house was whipped out stiff and straight by the wind. No longer any sign of police with torches looking for the mother. The search had proved fruitless.

He detoured to skirt Denton Woods, a place where the mother might make for. His headlights picked out the odd small animal furtively crossing the road, but no sign of the woman. He shivered and turned up the heater. Something white caught his eye, something moving behind one of the bushes. He braked sharply, but it was only a plastic carrier bag blown by the wind.

As he turned into Bath Street he caught sight of the blue lamp outside the police station. He reversed and drove into the car-park. It would be warmer there than in his cold, empty house. He found the station a relaxing place to be in the wee, small hours when the phones were quiet, the office empty, and he could prowl around and read the contents of other people's in-trays to see what was going on. And best of all there was no Mullett to keep finding fault with everything he did.

'Nasty business with those kids,' said Wells, taking the offered cigarette.

'Yes,' grunted Frost. 'Any tea on the go?' He was munching away at the tuna fish sandwich Wells had brought in for his own consumption. The canteen wouldn't open until five so the night shift had to fend for themselves.

Wells clicked on the wall switch with his foot. The

kettle was already plugged in. 'Did I tell you that Mullett's got me working here on Christmas Day again?'

'Yes, I believe you did mention it,' said Frost. It was Wells's sole flaming topic of conversation these days. Frost was not really sympathetic. He always got the Christmas Day shift, but didn't mind. It was just like any other day to him with the added bonus of the absence of the Divisional Commander.

'I'm going to have it out with him,' continued Wells. 'I can be driven just so far.' He picked up a written message. 'We've had two more sightings of the missing boy – one in Manchester and one in Sunderland.'

'Thanks,' grunted Frost gloomily, stuffing the message in his pocket. 'In a couple of hours we start dragging the canals and the lakes. God knows how many dead dogs and horses we're going to turn up.' He watched Wells drop a tea-bag in each of two mugs and fill them with hot water and his mind drifted back to the bungalow. 'That place was spotless. The nippers were well nourished . . . clean . . . bags of toys.' He sighed. 'Poor cow. Better if we do find her dead. How can you carry on living knowing you've killed your own kids?'

Wells nodded sympathetically as he brought out the carton of milk. Then he stiffened. He had heard something. A car door slamming in the car-park. 'That sounds like Mullett's car.'

'You're just trying to frighten me,' said Frost.

But it was Mullett, shiny and polished in his uniform, chin pink and smooth and freshly shaved. 'I've just come from Cresswell Street.'

'Ah!' Frost gave a knowing nod. Cassidy must have told the publicity-hungry Mullett that the press and TV boys were there in force with half a million quid's worth of Japanese cameras. 'Get your photograph taken, did you, super?'

Mullett smoothed his moustache. 'I thought it advisable to take advantage of the TV cameras to appeal for help in tracing the mother.' He flashed a smug smile. 'I think it went very well. It'll be shown on breakfast television.'

That should put people off their cornflakes, thought Frost.

'Ah, tea!' beamed Mullett. 'You must have known I was coming, sergeant.' He picked up the mug Wells had poured for himself. 'I'll take it with me.' His smile clicked off abruptly. 'And I'd like a word in my office, Frost . . . now!' He spun on his heels and marched up the corridor.

'He's found out about the fags,' said Frost, horrified.

'Don't implicate me,' called Wells. 'I had nothing to do with it.' He looked at the cigarette smoking in his hand and quickly stubbed it out.

But it wasn't about the cigarettes. 'Sit down,' began Mullett, but he was too late, as usual. Frost had already slumped into one of the visitor's chairs, putting his mug of hot tea on the polished top of Mullett's desk. Mullett hastily put a sheet of blotting paper under it.

'Cassidy seems to think these unfortunate children might not have been killed by their mother.'

'Oh?' said Frost. 'First I've heard about it.'

'He detects strong similarities between these killings and the spate of child stabbings we've had over the past weeks.'

'Stabbings?' said Frost. 'The kids were asphyxiated.'

'There was a stab wound on the eldest boy's upper arm.'

Frost frowned. 'I never spotted it.'

'But Cassidy did. We're fortunate in having him, Frost, otherwise goodness knows what vital clues might be missed.'

'Kids always get knocks and scratches,' said Frost.

'This was definitely a stabbing wound . . . and the Home Office Pathologist says it was inflicted after death.'

That bastard Cassidy, thought Frost. He's deliberately

kept this from me. 'No doubt when we find the mother she'll tell us what happened.'

'*If* the mother was responsible. Cassidy is beginning to suspect Sidney Snell.'

'Snell? Rubbish!'

'Consider the coincidences, Frost. Snell likes jabbing very young children on the arms or buttocks. This boy was jabbed in the arm. Snell likes staring in windows, watching women undress. There was a report of a man doing just that in the same street. The previous stabbing was in a bungalow by the golf course . . . This also was a bungalow by the golf course. Too many coincidences to be ignored.'

'Snell gets his kicks from seeing little drops of blood on chubby arms and legs. He doesn't kill with pillows.'

'There's always a first time for everything,' retorted Mullett. 'Something could have gone wrong tonight. The children all woke up and started crying. He panicked and tried to silence them with a pillow.'

'And the mother?'

'Mr Cassidy thinks she could have heard the commotion and come running in, so he had to kill her as well.'

'And then he took her body away in case someone tripped over it?'

Mullett flapped away the awkward question. 'We don't know the exact details.'

'The mother killed her kids and did a runner,' said Frost firmly. 'Snell had nothing to do with it.'

'I hope, for your sake, you are right,' said Mullett. 'I understand Cassidy wanted you to arrest Snell, but you were content to warn him off. Might I ask why?'

'We've got too much on at the moment to sod about with Snell. Let Newcastle handle him.'

Mullett took a sip of his tea. 'If we find that the man you couldn't be bothered to arrest then goes out and murders three innocent children, I will personally throw the book at you, Frost.'

Frost gave him a sweet smile and stood up, ready to go. 'I wouldn't expect anything else of you, sir.'

Bill Wells could hear raised voices rolling down the corridor and was deciding whether to take a stroll past Mullett's office in the hope he could overhear what was going on. But a sudden blast of cold air that ruffled the papers on his desk made him look up. A little old woman had toddled in from the street. Frail-looking, in her eighties, she clutched a large empty shopping bag. Her feet flip-flopped across the lobby. She was wearing pink bedroom slippers with large red pom-poms.

'What's happening with the buses?' she demanded in a shrill voice. 'I've been waiting ages at that bus stop for a number 6 and nothing has turned up – nothing. I've got to get to the shops before they close.'

Wells sighed and shook his head sadly. 'It's four o'clock in the morning, Ada. The buses stopped running long ago and the shops are all shut. Everyone's in bed – and that's where you should be.'

The old woman blinked at him in confusion. 'But I've got to get dinner ready for my husband. He . . .' Her voice tailed off. Her husband had been dead for more than sixteen years.

The phone rang. 'Yes,' said Wells, 'she's just walked in here. I'll get someone to drive her back.' He put down the phone and went over to the woman. 'That was your daughter. She's worried about you.'

'Did you tell her I'd gone shopping?'

'I think she knows,' said Wells, taking her arm and sitting her down on the bench.

Frost came charging through, still seething after his bout with Mullett, but he brightened up when he saw the woman. 'Hello, Ada. What are you doing here?' He gave her his mug of tea.

'I'm doing my shopping.'

'Shopping? Not the sex aids shop again – you cleaned them out of mechanical dicks last time.'

She giggled and slurped her tea. She liked Frost. He made her laugh.

'Any chance of giving her a lift home?' whispered Wells.

'I've still got things to do here,' replied Frost.

A brisk clatter of feet as Mullett bustled through. Frost called him over and spoke quietly. Mullett frowned and looked across to the old woman sipping noisily from Frost's mug of tea. 'It's on your way, sir,' wheedled Frost.

'Very well.' Mullett wasn't too happy about it. It would take him well out of his way, but one had to do one's duty to the public. He walked over to her and shouted in her ear. 'If you'll come with me, madam, I'll drive you home.'

'I'm not deaf,' she snapped, gathering up her shopping bag. 'Can we stop at the shops on the way?'

'They're closed, madam,' said Mullett, ushering her out.

As the swing doors closed behind them, Wells turned in agitation to Frost. 'Did you warn him, Jack?'

Frost frowned. 'About what?'

'About Ada – she's incontinent.'

Frost sounded surprised. 'Is she?'

'You know damn well she is. The last time you took her home she piddled all over your front seat.'

'I thought that was Mrs Mullett,' said Frost innocently. Then he snapped his fingers as if he had just remembered. 'No, you're right . . . it was Ada.' He smiled. 'I suppose I shouldn't have let her drink my mug of tea.'

Wells's jaw sagged. 'You gave her tea? Bloody hell, it'll go straight through her.'

'Let's hope he drives fast,' said Frost. 'Them blue velvet seats don't half stain, and Ada's output always seems to exceed her input.'

Feeling considerably bucked, he wandered into the

incident room where Burton, the only occupant, was sitting by the phone, reading a paperback as he munched on a sandwich. He looked up guiltily as Frost entered. 'It's all right, son.' Frost dropped into the seat beside him. 'Anything happened? Has the kid been found, but it slipped your mind to tell me?'

Burton grinned and pointed to a filing basket brimming over with the night's phone messages. 'Sightings galore, most of them worthless, but we're following them up. No joy from the road blocks. Too many kids out with guys for anyone to recall one specific boy.' He tugged out a message from under the stapler. 'This bloke phoned a couple of hours ago. Wouldn't give his name, but was most insistent we should follow it up. He said he and his girlfriend were having it away under the canal bridge off Union Street when they heard a car draw up overhead. He heard some grunting and groaning as if something heavy was being lifted from the car, then something was chucked into the canal. It sunk right away. He reckons it could have been a body.'

'Grunting and groaning?' said Frost. 'I reckon him and his girlfriend were doing all the grunting and groaning.' He took the message and skimmed through it. 'We've got the frogmen arriving tomorrow, they can start off looking by the bridge.'

He poked a cigarette in his mouth. 'Having it away under the canal bridge? Some people pick the most romantic spots – it's cold, it's damp and it stinks. I'm not fussy, but even I would think twice.' He stood up and stretched. 'Let's go home, son. Early start tomorrow. The briefing is at eight.' He consulted his wristwatch. 'Just under four hours time.'

8

The early morning TV news showed pictures of the 'sad bungalow of death' and of the undertakers carrying out the bodies in a single coffin. Interviewed neighbours said how shocked and saddened they were and what a loving family it was and how everyone was shattered. A photograph of the mother filled the screen and a grim-faced Superintendent Mullett explained that the police were concerned for her safety and appealed to members of the public to look out for her.

Mullett clicked off the set with a nod of approval. An impressive performance, he thought. He picked up his gloves and patted his pocket to make sure he had his car keys. A final check in the hall mirror, a slight repositioning of the knot of his tie to dead centre and he was out to the car. As he opened the driver's door, he frowned and turned his head away, his nose wrinkling. The blue velvet seat cover on the passenger's side had been removed and was in soak with lots of disinfectant, but the smell still lingered. He vigorously squirted the interior with air freshener and drove to the station with the window open in spite of the cold. That damn woman! And Frost! Frost would have known all about her. He had set this up deliberately. He smiled grimly. Well, Detective Inspector Jack Frost was due for the biggest dressing down he had ever received.

His car purred down Bath Hill and glided into Cork Street. A young, uniformed officer spotted his car and gave a smart salute which Mullett acknowledged with a smile and a wave, delighted to see that the officer was in uniform. He had noticed two officers entering the station in their street clothes and would have a few sharp words with Sergeant Wells about that.

The car-park was crowded with vehicles of all types, most of which belonged to members of the search party. It was still dark and they would be having breakfast in the canteen before the main briefing. In the far corner two men were offloading aqualung cylinders from a van. The frogmen had arrived. Mullett had difficulty manoeuvring into his own parking space. As he locked the doors and tested the handle he was almost run down by a dirt-streaked Ford which squealed to a halt within inches of his heels. His face darkened when he saw Frost, a cigarette dangling insolently from his mouth, climb out.

'Frost!'

Frost looked up, startled. He hadn't expected to see Mullett in so early. A quick check confirmed that Hornrim Harry's seat cover was missing. A warm glow started up inside him. God bless incontinent old ladies. 'Good morning, super!' he called cheerily.

'That woman you induced me to take home—' spluttered Mullett.

'Yes, very kind of you, sir,' interrupted Frost. He smacked a palm to his forehead as if the thought had just struck him. 'Meant to warn you about Ada, although I'm sure it isn't necessary in your case. I was going to say don't get sexy with her. If you rub your knee against hers, tickle her groin, or anything like that, she'll pee all over your front seat.'

Mullett's mouth opened and closed. He never quite knew how to take Frost.

'What was it you wanted to say to me, sir?' asked Frost innocently.

'Nothing,' snapped Mullett. 'Nothing.' He spun on his heel and stamped off into the building.

In the incident room, PC Jordan was waiting to report

to Frost. He had got the information from the Discount Warehouse on the posthumous purchase made with Lemmy Hoxton's credit card. 'That was flaming quick,' said Frost, 'I thought they didn't open until nine.'

'Mr Cassidy said I should drag the manager and his staff out from their homes,' said Jordan. 'He reckoned a murder enquiry shouldn't have to wait for the store to open up.'

'Quite right,' said Frost, wishing Cassidy wouldn't poke his nose in. Lemmy had been dead for months, so what was the point of dragging people out of bed to save a few minutes? 'So what have you found out?'

'The item purchased was a 28-inch Nicam Stereo Panasonic TV set. But after two weeks no-one at the Discount Warehouse had any recollection of the purchaser or what he looked like.'

'They wouldn't have known what he looked like after two flaming minutes,' said Frost. 'All they look at is your credit card. You could walk in those places with your dick hanging out and they wouldn't spot it.'

Jordan had asked the credit card company to fax a copy of the actual Visa docket and this was clipped to his report. Frost compared it with a genuine Lemmy signature. It was an all too obvious forgery. 'You'd think the store would have queried the different signatures,' he muttered. 'I suppose there's no chance the set was delivered and we've got an address?'

'No, it was collected.'

Frost swung from side to side in his chair, sucking at his fourth cigarette of the day. Someone had used Lemmy's credit card to buy an expensive large screen TV. So was Lemmy killed for his credit card? Hardly likely. The card was only used once and that was months after his death. More likely that someone with a reason had done Lemmy in and the credit card was a bonus. Or perhaps the killer had thrown the card away and someone else had used it? He flapped the Visa docket to shake off cigarette ash. He couldn't work up much enthusiasm in finding Lemmy's killer. The sod deserved to die. A thought struck him. 'Check with Panasonic. See if the guarantee's been registered.'

'He'd be a bloody fool to do that,' said Jordan.

'It's the sort of stupid thing I'd do,' said Frost. 'Check it.'

Burton stuck his head round the door. 'Time for the briefing, inspector.'

A fair-sized crowd waited for him in the canteen, not quite so many as the day before when hopes were high that the boy would be found alive. Frost noticed that Liz Maud was there, alone at a corner table, snatching a hurried breakfast, even though she must have been up until the small hours with the tragedy in Cresswell Street. He bought himself a hot sausage sandwich, its melted butter making the bread soggy, and took it, with a mug of tea, to the raised section at the end. He yelled for silence. As the burble of conversation died down he let his eyes drift around the room, checking who was present. He couldn't see Detective Sergeant Hanlon.

'He's in the toilet,' someone told him. Almost on cue there was the rumble off of a cistern emptying and Arthur Hanlon, looking a mite bedraggled, stumbled into the canteen, doing a mock bow to the applause that greeted his entrance. 'Sorry I'm late, inspector,' he apologized.

'Flaming hell, Arthur,' said Frost. 'You always come out of the toilet looking as if you've just gone twelve rounds with Mike Tyson. Which reminds me . . . did you hear about the constipated mathematician? He had to work everything out with a pencil and a piece of paper.' A roar of laughter, the loudest coming from Frost himself who then almost choked on a lump of sausage sandwich. Mullett, who had just come in and was standing at the back, frowned. This was not the time nor place for poor taste jokes.

'OK,' said Frost as the laughter subsided. 'That's probably the last laugh any of us will have today.' He jabbed his sandwich at the enlarged photograph of Bobby Kirby on the wall. 'We didn't find the poor little sod yesterday. My gut feeling is that he is either dead, or he's being held captive somewhere. As you all know, another boy, Dean Anderson, was found dead near where Bobby went missing. Dean's naked body was stuffed into a black plastic dustbin sack and we've got to consider that the same fate might have overtaken Bobby. This means that some of you are going to have to go down to the Council refuse depot and start examining the hundreds of filled rubbish sacks collected by the Council yesterday.' He gave a nod to Burton. 'DC Burton will tell you which of you lucky lads and lassies have drawn the short straw.' He took another sip at his tea. 'But let's hope Bobby is still alive . . . in which case we've got to find him bloody quickly, so the sooner you get started the better.'

Mullett moved forward and indicated to Frost that he would like to say a few words.

'Bit of hush for Mr Mullett,' called Frost. 'You've seen him on the telly, now hear him in the flesh.'

The thinnest of smiles from Mullett. 'Inspector Frost forgot to mention that we are also looking for this woman.' He waited as Liz Maud rose from her table and pinned up a large photograph on the wall by the side of the boy. 'A tragic case. Her three children dead and she has gone missing. You have other priorities, I know, but please keep an eye out for her.' A brisk nod to Frost and he strode back to his office.

Frost sat on the corner of a table, legs swinging, watching the main group file out. He wiped the front of his jacket where the melted butter from the sandwich had dripped, then wandered over to the table where Liz was doing her crossword puzzle. He leant over her and pretended to read a clue. 'Four down – "Little Richard that ladies love big?" That must be Dick!' She found herself looking at four down before she realized it was another of his childish jokes. Too tired even to fake a laugh, she knuckled her eyes and took another sip from her mug of black coffee.

'Did you get any sleep last night?' Frost asked.

She shook her head. 'I was questioning neighbours until six and the post-mortems are at eight thirty.' She took the offered cigarette. 'Mr Cassidy suggested I attended.'

Frost clicked his lighter. 'The kids? I'll get someone else to go if you like.'

Her eyes blazed. 'Do you think I'll faint? I've been to post-mortems before.'

'I've been to the dentist before,' said Frost, 'but that don't make me anxious to go again. It's worse when it's children, love. Wild horses wouldn't drag me if I didn't have to.'

'Very kind of you to be so concerned for me, but I'm going,' she said, firmly.

He drained his tea then dumped the crust from his sandwich in the mug. 'Any developments after I left last night?'

'Nothing particularly helpful. The father is still in hospital, heavily sedated, so we haven't been able to question him. I've found two more neighbours who say they heard raised voices from the bungalow just before midnight. They thought it was the husband and wife having one of their frequent rows.'

Frost frowned. 'The husband? Could it have been him?'

She shook her head. 'Mark Grover never left the department store until just before two.'

'Are we sure about that?'

'I've spoken to the night security guard. He confirms that the two men were there until a little before two o'clock in the morning.'

'Could they have got out without his knowledge?'

'No. All the main doors are security locked and he would have to operate the release switch.'

'Damn,' said Frost. The wife rowing with another man around midnight was a complication he would have preferred to be without.

'And I've spoken to the owner of Denton Shopfitters,' continued Liz. 'He phoned the store just before midnight to check on their progress and spoke to the husband.'

'You're very thorough,' said Frost ruefully.

'Mr Cassidy is suggesting that the man the neighbours heard could have been Sidney Snell.'

Frost treated this with scorn. 'You don't have a row with a man who breaks into your house . . . you scream and shout at the bastard. Did the neighbours think she sounded frightened?'

'No. They said it was a heated row.'

'Well then . . .' He stood up. 'Sidney Snell is not a killer. Don't waste your time going down that road.' He glanced up at the clock, then flicked his scarf over his shoulder and stood up. 'Frogman time . . . if anyone wants me I'll be paddling in the canal.' At the door he paused, trying to remember what it was he intended asking Liz to do. Oh yes. He wanted her to check with the Council to find out who used to live in the derelict houses where Lemmy's body was found. But the poor cow looked ready to drop and she had a three-body post-mortem to attend. He'd get someone else to do it.

PC John Collier pulled at the oars and winced as his blistered hands throbbed. He wished he hadn't volunteered for this. He'd thought it would be pleasant, scudding the boat across the water, watching the frogmen plunge in with a kick of their flippers. But it was hard, back-breaking work. There was a strong wind blowing the boat in the opposite direction to which he wanted it to go.

'Steady as she goes, Number One.' PC Ken Ridley,

systematically prodding the murky bottom of the canal with a long pole, was doing his captain of the battleship act which got progressively less funny with constant repetition. Ahead of them a line of bubbles marked the progress of one of the police frogmen.

Frost sat on the bank, moodily surveying the proceedings and sucking at a cigarette while tossing small stones into the water. It was cold and windy and he had the strong feeling this would be a waste of time. The canal at this point was crossed by the road bridge which made it the ideal point from which to hump junk out of a car boot and chuck it into the black soup of the stagnant water. Much of this had been retrieved by the frogmen and the towpath was cluttered with foul-smelling heaps. There were sodden mattresses, a couple of bundles of carpeting that looked almost new, but which would never lose the ripe canal smell, a black plastic bag which turned out to be full of offal from a butcher's shop and the bloated carcass of a long-dead goat. Particularly revolting was a soggy cardboard box crammed full with maggoty chickens' heads and feet. 'All we want now is a few spuds and we've got ourselves our dinner,' he commented bitterly, pulling a face as the wind changed and drove the smell of putrefaction straight at him. Many years ago, when he was a small child, he had sat on this same towpath, probably not far from this same spot, and had fished for tiddlers. But there was nothing living in the water now. Denton Union Canal, long since abandoned by the once thriving barge trade, was now a choked, evil-smelling backwater.

A frogman's head broke the surface. He had been tying a rope to something enveloped in mud at the bottom and was signalling for Collier and Ridley to haul it up. A bulging, black plastic dustbin sack was dragged into the boat. Frost's heart sank. It was the right size and shape for a young boy's body.

The boat bumped against the side of the towpath and

the two policemen lifted out the sack which streamed water from holes, apparently punched in it to make it sink. They laid the sodden mass alongside Frost who regarded it gloomily, dreading to think what was inside. He stood up, chucked his cigarette into the canal, then gave the sack a tentative prod with his foot. Something soft and yielding, like flesh . . . He crouched down and sliced through the string tying the neck of the sack with his penknife. He peered inside. A sodden mass of water-blackened human hair. He looked up at Ridley and nodded grimly. 'It's the boy.' He pulled the neck of the sack open wider, then the cold sweat of relief flooded through him. He looked up again at Ridley. 'I'm a prize twat!' he said. It wasn't human hair. He reached inside the sack and pulled out a heavy sodden fur coat. He had no idea what a mink coat looked like, but this, even dripping with filthy canal water, looked expensive. As did the silver fox cape which was under it. At the bottom of the sack was a grey plastic bag which was tied tightly with clumsily knotted string and held something heavy. His penknife sawed through the string, leaving the knot intact so Forensic could submit it to their scrupulous examination and come up with sod all. Inside was a brick, put there to ensure the sack sunk, and also a jumble of jewellery. The haul from Robert Stanfield's house.

Frost stared at it. Why had it been stolen, then dumped? It suggested an insurance fiddle, although the furs and jewellery looked genuine enough. He put everything back inside the plastic sack. 'Trot it down to the station. We'll get Old Mother Stanfield in to identify it.'

Ridley's pole had prodded something that belched up large, rancid-looking bubbles which burst to exude a stomach-churning smell. He signalled to the frogmen, but before they could respond, Frost's radio squawked. Control calling him urgently. 'Can you get back here at once, inspector. We've received a ransom demand for the missing boy.'

'What's the betting it's a bleeding hoax?' muttered Frost, clicking the radio off.

He took one last look at Collier and Ridley, who were hauling up something slimy and phosphorescent that broke in half as they tried to get it into the boat, then made for his car.

There was quite a crowd waiting for him in the incident room including Cassidy, Hanlon, Burton and Harding from Forensic, all looking grim. 'So where's this ransom demand?' asked Frost.

Cassidy pointed to a padded envelope lying on the desk. 'It came in this morning's post.' The typed label was addressed to The Missing Boy Officer, Denton Police Station.' The postmark, date-stamped the previous evening, was that of the main Denton post office. 'This was inside.' He handed Frost a sheet of white A4 paper which had been slipped inside a transparent cover for protection.

The message was printed out on a dot matrix printer in draft mode. Frost read it aloud.

> 'To the officer in charge:
>
> 'I have the missing boy – the enclosed should enable you to convince Sir Richard Cordwell, Managing Director of the Savalot supermarket chain, that this is genuine.'

Frost paused. 'What was enclosed?'

Cassidy shook out a matchbox from the padded envelope and, holding it carefully by the corners, passed it to Frost without a word. Frost pushed open the tray, and stared in horrified disbelief. 'No!' On a bed of blood-flecked cotton wool lay a severed human finger. He looked away, then back again in the hope it wouldn't still be there. A tiny finger, the flesh waxen, grime under the nail, dried blood caking the severed end. It almost looked too small to be real, but Forensic confirmed it was from a child of seven or eight years old.

Frost stared at nothing, lost for words. Then, very carefully, he closed the tray and handed the matchbox back to Cassidy.

He poked a cigarette in his mouth to compose himself before he resumed reading the letter.

'I am sorry about the first boy. That was an accident, but if Bobby Kirby is to die, that will not be an accident. It will be because you have failed to carry out my instructions.

'1. For the safe return of the boy, I require to be paid the sum of £250,000. This money is to be paid to me by Sir Richard Cordwell, Managing Director of the Savalot supermarket chain. This money will be a flea-bite to him.

'2. I have also written to Sir Richard Cordwell explaining how the money is to be paid. If he refuses to pay, the boy will die and his company's name will be mud.

'3. Your job is to convince Sir Richard he must pay and then to stay out of it. You will take no further part in the proceedings if the boy is not to be harmed further. Any sign of the police when the money is handed over to me – even if a police car should accidentally pass by – then the boy will die. I will be monitoring all police radio calls to ensure you keep out of it.

'4. Any attempt at stalling for time and the boy will lose another finger.

'5. The boy is well, but in some pain. He is hidden where you will never find him. Do what I request and I will tell you where he is. Ignore my requests and you will never see him again.

'6. I am sending a copy of this letter and a cassette tape to the *Denton Echo* so the public are aware that it is up to Savalot whether the boy lives or dies.'

'Give credit where credit's due,' muttered Frost, 'but he's a cold, calculating, business-like bastard.' He read it through again, silently this time, then tossed it on the desk. 'He forgot to sign it.'

'There were no prints on it,' said Harding from Forensic.

'Never mind,' said Frost. 'It's not entirely your fault.' He pinched the scar on his face as he thought things over. 'Someone get on the phone to Sandy Lane at the *Denton Echo*. I want that letter. He's not to open it or play the cassette – he's to bring it straight over here.'

'Already done,' said Cassidy. 'He should be on his way over now.'

Frost tapped the matchbox. 'Have we confirmed that this is Bobby Kirby's finger and not the dead boy's . . . or even some other boy we don't know about yet?'

'I've sent someone over to the mother's house to get prints from Bobby's room,' said Harding. 'We're also checking with the prints of the dead boy in the morgue.'

'For Pete's sake don't tell the mother about the ransom demand,' said Frost.

'Of course not,' said Harding.

Frost spun his chair round and looked at the wall map which charted the progress of the search parties. 'Call off the search.'

'We haven't checked this is the boy's finger yet,' protested Cassidy. 'It could be some medical student's hoax.'

'A hoax? We should be so bloody lucky,' said Frost. 'It's genuine, I promise you.' He waved a finger at Arthur Hanlon. 'Call it off, Arthur.' Back to Cassidy. 'What about the letter he's sent to Sir Richard Cordwell?'

'I've been on to Savalot's main office. They're going

through all their post now. I've also spoken to his private secretary. She's going through the personal mail.'

The internal phone buzzed. Sandy Lane from the *Denton Echo* was here.

Bill Wells ushered him in. Lane was carrying a padded envelope, identical to the one in front of Frost. He handed it over. It had been opened.

'We asked you not to open it,' said Cassidy.

'I didn't get the message until I'd just slit the flap,' lied Sandy.

'Did it photostat all right?' Frost asked.

'Perfectly,' grinned the reporter. The postmark was the same. The envelope was addressed to 'The Chief Crime Reporter, *Denton Echo*'.

'Chief Crime Reporter?' queried Frost.

'That's me, Jack – Chief Crime Reporter, Chief Sports Reporter, Jumble Sales and Church Fêtes.'

'I expect your bleeding fingerprints are all over it,' said Frost, letting Harding extract the contents and slip them into transparent folders. There were two letters and a cassette tape. The first letter read:

> To The Chief Crime Reporter.
>
> I have the boy Bobby Kirby. The police will confirm this. I require £250,000 from Sir Richard Cordwell, Managing Director of Savalot supermarkets. His company can well afford this sum. If he refuses to pay, the boy will die and I am sure it will make an interesting story for your newspaper.
>
> Let the police have the tape after you have listened to it. Copy of my letter to the police enclosed.

'I suppose you've played the tape as well?' said Frost.

'I might have accidentally listened to it,' affirmed Sandy.

Burton took the tape and poked it into a cassette player. Everyone quietened down.

For a second or so, nothing, just the hiss of raw tape and the rumble of the recorder motor, then a boy's voice. There were lots of pauses and clicks. The recorder had been switched on and off a few times while the man obviously told the boy what to say. Bobby was clearly distressed and it made harrowing listening.

'My name is Bobby Kirby. I'm tied up and blindfolded. The man says if you do what he tells you, he will let me go home. He says you know what will happen if you don't do what he says. I want to go home. Please . . . I want to go home . . .' A click and the sound of raw tape without the recorder motor noise. Burton switched the machine off.

Harding leant across and fast-forwarded the rest of the tape on cue and review. There was nothing else on it. He removed the cassette and carefully examined it. 'I think that was the first recording on a brand-new tape, but I'll get it checked in case we can pick anything else up.'

'Any idea what sort of machine it was recorded on?' asked Cassidy.

'Judging by the sound quality certainly not a state of the art hi-fi. I'd guess at a cheap portable model with a built-in microphone – that's why it's picking up the sound of the motor.'

'Are they rare?' asked Frost.

'There's millions of them,' said Harding.

'What about the cassette? Could we trace the shop where he bought it?'

Again Harding shook his head. 'One of the commonest types . . . sold in their thousands. I'll replay it back at the lab and boost up the background. It might give us a clue as to where it was recorded.'

'Get a copy made,' said Cassidy, 'and take it to the mother – see if she can identify the voice.'

'No!' said Frost. 'Why upset the poor cow? If the fingerprint matches, we'll know it's genuine.'

Cassidy scowled. He resented being contradicted in

front of everyone. He resented even more the fact that Frost was right on this occasion.

'What's this about the boy losing another finger?' asked Sandy.

Frost filled him in. 'But I don't want it reported. We've got to keep that up our sleeve. In fact, I don't want any of this reported until we've got the boy back safe.'

'Bloody hell, Jack,' the reporter protested, 'it's the biggest scoop I've ever had. I could make a bomb selling it to the London papers.'

'It'll still be a scoop when we get the boy back. You can have it as an exclusive.'

Sandy sighed. 'All right. I'll make do with that.'

'How do you know you can trust him?' asked Cassidy when Lane had left.

'I can trust him,' said Frost firmly. He read through the letters again. 'The bastard's on to a winner here. Kidnap someone – anyone. It doesn't matter if the parents have got any money because you then blackmail some large corporation into coughing up the cash, knowing the public will think them shit if they refuse and let the kid die.' He groaned inwardly as Mullett came bustling in. He could do without another dose of Horn-rim Harry this morning.

'I've just come from your office, Frost,' said Mullett. 'There's a terrible smell in there.'

'You don't have to apologize, super,' said Frost, pretending to misunderstand. 'We all have the odd accident.' Mullett glared and Frost snapped his fingers. 'Oh – sorry. You mean the stuff we fished from the canal. It's the loot from the Stanfield robbery. I'm getting the insurance assessor over to have a look at it.'

'I understand there's been a ransom demand?' said Mullett, trying not to show his irritation at the suppressed giggles from some of the others in the room.

Frost pushed the letter across, then showed Mullett the contents of the matchbox. Mullett's face creased with concern which grew as he listened to the tape. He took his glasses off and pinched his nose. 'I do hope Savalot agree to co-operate.'

'They'll co-operate,' said Frost. 'They daren't risk the bad publicity.'

'Bad publicity?'

'When the papers print the story that they've refused to come up with money they can well afford and the kid dies.'

'It's blackmail,' said Mullett.

'All ransom demands are blackmail,' retorted Frost.

Burton, the phone pressed to his ear, called him over. 'Savalot. Sir Richard Cordwell's private secretary. She's been through all his private post – nothing. The main office has opened up all the general mail and there's nothing there either.'

'It's got to be!' frowned Frost. 'It's bloody well got to be.' He scrubbed his face with his hands, trying to think . . . 'Wait a minute. He must have sent it to Cordwell's house. Get the number.'

The number was ex-directory which the secretary refused to pass on, but she did condescend to phone the house herself and was back within two minutes. The letter, marked 'Strictly Personal and Confidential', was waiting for Cordwell who was still in bed.

'Tell him not to touch it – we're on our way over,' said Frost. She started to suggest he made an appointment, but Frost had slammed the phone down.

The internal phone rang. 'There's a Mr Hicks here to see you,' said Bill Wells.

'Send the sod away,' said Frost. 'We're too busy.'

'He says you asked him to come,' insisted Wells. 'He's the claims assessor from Cityrock Insurers.'

Frost snatched his mind away from the kidnapping and on to the furs and jewels dredged from the canal. 'Send him to my office. Tell him to follow his nose – he can't miss it.'

Hicks, a jolly little man wearing heavy horn-rimmed glasses, beamed as Frost tipped out the contents of the plastic bag. He held the furs at arm's length, his nose screwing up at the smell, nodded, then let them drop to the ground, more interested in the jewellery. His smile widened as he compared each item with his typewritten list. 'Looks as if it is all here, inspector.'

'Is it worth what they're claiming?'

A firm shake of the head. 'They're claiming £75,000. I'd put it at £35/40,000 top whack.'

'An insurance fiddle?'

Hicks pursed his lips. 'Not a very clever one if it was. We'd have knocked the claim down to something nearer £35,000 which is what the items are worth. They could have sold them for that and there'd have been no need to chuck them in a canal.' He zipped up his briefcase. 'As far as my company is concerned, the stolen items have been recovered and we don't have to pay out. Mr Stanfield can carry on paying the premiums for his own inflated valuation, but should they be "stolen" again, we'll settle on the basis of my own figure.'

'What about the money he claims he handed over to get his daughter returned?'

Hicks shrugged. 'If he was insured for such a loss then it wasn't with my company, but I don't think any insurers give cover for money held in a bank.'

Frost drummed the desk with his fingers. He still wasn't convinced this was a genuine robbery and abduction. If it was genuine, why steal stuff then dump it? He thanked Hicks, and steered him in the direction of the street.

Back in the incident room Burton was on the phone. He put his hand over the mouthpiece as Frost entered. 'Forensic were on. The prints check. The finger is from Bobby Kirby.'

Frost grunted his acknowledgement.

'And I've got PC Ridley on the phone. He wants to

know what we should do with all the stuff we pulled out of the canal.'

'He shouldn't have to ask,' replied Frost. 'There's a Keep Britain Tidy campaign in force this week. Tell him to chuck it back in the canal.'

Burton relayed the message and hung up. 'All search parties stood down,' he reported.

Frost nodded and walked over to study the photographs of the two boys. 'He intended Dean to be the kidnap victim. He chloroformed him, but the kid died. This didn't put the bastard off, he just looked for someone else – and he found Bobby.'

'What made him pick Dean Anderson in the first place?'

Frost took a deep drag at his cigarette then pushed out smoke. 'Any kid would have done – that's the clever part. The money is coming from a rich supermarket chain – pay up or your customers will know you let a kid die. This bloke is a clever bastard and he's on to a flaming winner.' He dropped his cigarette on the floor and crushed it with his foot. 'Come on, son, let's find out how the rich people live. We're off to see the Supermarket King.'

Mullett stopped them on their way out. He had been told the result of the fingerprinting, but not by Frost as he should have expected.

'Can't stop, super,' grunted Frost, edging past. 'We're on our way to see tricky Dicky.'

A concerned frown from Mullett. With someone as important as Sir Rirchard Cordwell involved, he was wondering if the uncouth Frost was the right person to handle the interview. 'He's a very influential man, Frost, and I understand he can be quite nasty when he likes, so handle him with kid gloves.'

'Don't worry, super,' said Frost, sidling past him towards the door to the car-park. 'I shall treat him with my usual tact.'

Mullett's smile tightened to vanishing point. This was exactly what he feared. 'I think I'd better come with you,' he said.

The Manor House was an imposing edifice, solidly Victorian, forests of chimney pots, standing in extensive grounds and enclosed by a high stone wall thickly coated with ivy. The black, cast-iron gates were firmly closed and a video security camera scrutinized them closely as Burton announced who they were into a microphone. Their credentials established, the gates swung back, closing again immediately they were inside. They coasted up to the main entrance behind a gleaming, pearl grey Rolls-Royce. Frost checked its tax disc and seemed disappointed to find it was current. Up stone steps to the front door where a female secretary hovered and led them directly to Cordwell's study, a large, high-ceilinged room with tall french windows opening out on to a billiard table lawn, a rose garden, and a large fish pool with a weathered stone fountain in the shape of a boy with a dolphin.

Cordwell, a thickset, coarse-featured man in his early fifties, was at an antique mahogany desk, its green leather top scarred with cigarette burns. As they entered he was bawling down a white and gold phone and didn't give them a second glance. 'If he's not measuring up, then chuck him out – you can find a reason. I'm not carrying bloody passengers.' He banged the phone down, grabbed an enormous cigar from a silver box and lit up with a lighter fashioned from a genuine flintlock pistol, then flapped a hand for Frost and Mullett to sit. Cordwell had started business selling broken biscuits from a barrow in street markets and, by cheating, scheming and doing down his associates, had worked his way up to owning one of the largest cut-price grocery chains in Britain. A grunt and a snap of his fingers signalled the hovering secretary to place a folder in front of him. He slid it across to the two policemen. 'The letter.'

Frost opened the folder. The envelope had been slit open and the letter was fastened to it with a paper clip.

'We asked you not to open it,' he said.

Cordwell gave him a sweet smile. 'Nobody tells me what to do.'

While Frost read the letter, Cordwell was back on the phone tearing some other poor devil off a strip. 'Cancel the bloody order!' he barked. 'I don't care if they have got a binding agreement – there's bound to be a bloody loophole somewhere, so cancel it.' As he slammed the phone down he shouted across to his secretary. 'What's that prat's name?' She told him. He scribbled the name on his pad. 'Next lot of redundancies, he's got pole position.'

Frost shut his ears to this as he and Mullett skimmed through the letter. Similar to the others, it read:

> Dear Sir Richard Cordwell:
>
> I have the boy Bobby Kirby. The police will confirm this is genuine. For his safe return I require from your company the sum of £250,000 in used notes . . . no marked money or the boy dies. Be near the public telephone kiosks in the shopping mall outside your Denton store at 8 o'clock tonight with the money and I will phone you with instructions for the handover. Just you – no police – I'll be checking to make sure. If you do not comply, the boy will die. The press have been informed and the public will know the consequences.

'We'll keep this,' said Frost, closing the folder and daring Cordwell to refuse, but this was agreed to with a wave of the hand.

'Is it genuine?'

'We believe so,' said Mullett.

'*Believe* so? I'm not sodding about with it if it's a try-on.'

'It's genuine,' said Frost. 'He sent us a tape of the boy.'

Cordwell flicked a long cylinder of ash from his cigar on to the carpet. 'And you reckon he'll carry out his threat to kill him?'

'Yes,' said Frost.

Cordwell beamed. 'Good. You got a photograph of the kid?' Frost slid one across the desk. Cordwell studied it through a fog of cigar smoke and nodded his approval. 'Nice-looking kid – I was afraid he'd be an ugly little bastard with a squint and bad teeth.' He flipped the switch on his intercom. 'Roberts – come in!'

A tap on the door and Roberts entered. A lean, mean-looking man in a sharp silver-grey suit. Cordwell showed him the photograph. 'The kidnapped kid,' he grunted.

Roberts looked at it and nodded. 'Nice-looking kid . . . and a good photograph. Should come up well in half-tone . . . I think we should go ahead.'

'So do I,' said Cordwell. 'This is what I want you to do.' He barked his orders. 'Check with the parents and see if there are any more photographs – the kid as a baby would be nice. Then a press release for tomorrow to all the London dailies – Supermarket Chief To The Rescue, you know the sort of thing. And get me some television interviews – me and the boy.' He dismissed Roberts then turned back to Frost. 'If you give a press conference you can quote me as saying that to save the boy I'm giving the police my unstinted, wholehearted co-operation.'

'You're too good for this world,' said Frost. 'Can you get the money together in time?'

'No problem.'

'How soon can you get it over to us?'

Cordwell frowned. 'Why should I let you have it?'

'We've got to mark the notes and record as many of the

numbers as we can. We also need to put a small radio transmitter inside the case.'

'No!' Mullett winced as Cordwell's fist thumped down on his desk top making the silver cigar case rattle. 'The object of the exercise is to save the kid, so no tricks, no marked notes and no transmitters.' He reached over and clicked on the intercom again. 'Roberts! You can add this to the press release. "The police wanted the notes to be marked, but supermarket chief, Sir Richard Cordwell, said no. Even though the ransom money is being paid by Sir Richard, his first and only consideration is for the safe return of the boy."' He clicked Roberts off in mid-acknowledgement.

'Now, listen to me—' began Frost.

'No!' snapped Cordwell. 'You listen to me. I'm not doing this for the love of humanity. This bastard has grabbed a kid and is on my back for the money. He thinks he's blackmailing me, but he's not – I'm doing this of my own volition, because it suits me to do so.'

'Hardly,' smirked Mullett. 'What would the public say if you refused?'

'Sod the public. They wouldn't desert Savalot. Knock tuppence off a tin of baked beans and they'd be fighting to come in whether the kid's dead or not. I don't usually give in to blackmail, but I can get some publicity out of this. For a lousy two hundred and fifty thousand quid I can get a million quid's worth of publicity and that's the sort of bargain I like. So you either do it my way, or I'm out!'

'All right,' said Frost reluctantly. 'We do it your way.'

'No police involvement in any shape or form until the kid is safely returned?'

'No police involvement,' agreed Frost.

'Do I have your word?'

'You have my word.'

Cordwell jabbed a stubby finger at Frost. 'Cross me and I'll crucify you – do you read me, buster?'

Frost put on his hurt look. 'I've given you my word,' he said.

They were curtly dismissed and ushered out to the car by the secretary. As Frost settled himself down in the seat, Mullett turned to him angrily. 'You had no business giving him your word, Frost.'

'Don't worry, super,' said Frost, 'I have no intention of keeping it.'

Mullett's eyebrows soared. 'What?'

Frost gave the same sort of sweet smile that Cordwell had given him. 'No-one tells me what to do,' he said. As the black gates closed behind them, he dug down in his pocket and produced three cigars. He stuck one in his mouth and offered the others to Mullett and Burton.

Mullett hesitated, but they were excellent cigars, probably costing something like £9 each. He accepted a light from Frost and inhaled with deep satisfaction. Soon the interior of the Ford was hazy blue and redolent with the rich Havana aroma. He thought wryly of the smell in his own car from that wretched woman last night. He took another drag and beamed with a glow of well-being. There was something about a good cigar . . . Maybe it wasn't Frost's fault. Perhaps, at times, he was too hard on the man. He took the cigar from his mouth and contemplated the glowing end. 'An excellent smoke, Frost. Where did you get them?'

'I pinched them from Cordwell's box when he wasn't looking,' said Frost.

9

When Frost got back to his office he nearly tripped over the fur coats the insurance assessor had dropped on the floor. Mullett was right, the office did stink. He opened the window a fraction to let in some fresh air, while he made a few phone calls. Liz was still attending the post-mortems where, no doubt, Drysdale was being his usual thorough self with all three tiny bodies. Bill Wells confirmed there was still no sign of the missing mother. Frost drummed the desk in thought – had he called off the dragging of the canal too soon?

The jewellery was still on his desk. He'd have to get Margie Stanfield down for a formal identification of her property and the sooner she took back her skunk-smelling furs, the better. Margie! She must be Stanfield's second wife. He seemed to remember an entirely different woman when he was at the house all those years ago for the arson case.

He stared at the jewellery. Damn. This phoney abduction case was irritating him. He wanted to get it out of the way, but he couldn't wait for Liz to come back from her autopsy treat so he collared Burton from the incident room.

'Where are we going?' asked the DC, sliding behind the steering wheel.

'Bennington's Bank,' Frost told him. 'I want to take a look at their security video for when Stanfield was drawing out all that cash.' The car slowed at traffic lights. 'How are you getting on with Sergeant Liz?'

'She tore me off a strip today,' said Burton, moving forward as the lights changed. 'I put the wrong date down on a report.' He grinned. 'I think I'm starting to fancy her.'

'She wouldn't be a bad looker if she tarted herself up,' mused Frost. 'Reminds me of those old Hollywood films where the heroine is a schoolmistress with no make-up, thick glasses, her hair in a bun and a flat chest. When she has her first kiss from the hero, she takes off her glasses, lets her hair down and her tits swell up to twice their previous size.' He started unbuckling his seat belt as the bank loomed into view. 'The same thing could happen to our Liz.'

Burton grinned again as he turned the car into the 'Staff Only' car-park behind the bank. 'I wouldn't mind being the bloke who makes it happen.'

The bank manager brought in the videotape and fed it into the player for them. 'I'm rather busy, so I'll leave you to it, inspector.'

'Yes, you go and foreclose on some poor sod,' answered Frost. 'We'll manage.' He pressed the play button.

On the monitor a black and white picture of the customer area of the bank. It was a minute to opening time so no customers. A running clock superimposed on the corner of the picture showed the seconds zipping on to 9.30 a.m. A cashier walked across the customer area, checked the time with the wall clock, then opened the doors. He was shoved to one side as an impatient Stanfield, barging his way through other customers, managed to reach the cashier's window before anyone else. He was carrying a large briefcase.

It was a wide angle shot taken from behind the counters. Other customers went to different cashiers, but the two detectives kept their eyes on Stanfield who pushed across a withdrawal slip, drumming his fingers impatiently on the counter as the cashier read it through. He snapped some angry remark and then moved to the end of the counter. The cashier came out and led Stanfield to the assistant manager's office and out of camera range. 'He's waiting in there while they're getting the money out of the vaults,' explained Frost.

More people came into the bank. Queues shuffled forward, cashing cheques or paying in money.

'What are we looking for?' asked Burton.

'I haven't the faintest bloody idea,' admitted Frost.

Ten more minutes of watching people come and go and Frost's attention was starting to wander. He began to read a confidential letter on the manager's desk. 'There he is!' said Burton. He was all attention again.

Stanfield moved back into the picture. The briefcase bulged and seemed heavier. He snarled at someone who dared to get in his path as he barged his way through the crowded customer area. The doors closed behind him and he was gone.

Frost let the tape run for a couple of minutes, then fished out his cigarette packet. 'There's something there, son, something screaming at me . . . but I don't know what it is.' He wound the tape back to the start and played it through again, only half watching as he dribbled smoke from his nose. Suddenly, he stiffened. 'Yes I do!' His finger jabbed the freeze frame button making the picture quiver and stop. 'In the corner, there – at the automatic cash machine.' The frozen picture was quite blurred and Burton couldn't make out who Frost meant. Then he saw a figure right in the corner of the screen drawing money from the service till. The person's back was to the camera. They could just make out light-coloured trousers and a dark duffel coat with the hood up.

'So?' asked Burton.

Frost pressed the play button again. The figure, not much more than an out-of-focus blur, seemed to be getting money from the machine, then a swirl of customers hid him from view. Frost forwarded the tape. The superimposed clock had moved on another six or seven minutes. The crowd suddenly thinned. 'Look!' said Frost. 'The bastard is still there . . . What's he doing now?'

The figure had now moved away from the service till and was by the automatic deposit machine where he seemed to be finding difficulty in filling in one of the bank's forms, screwing up the current effort and starting on a new one. He was still there as Stanfield emerged from the assistant manager's office carrying the briefcase. Stanfield left. The man screwed his form up, tossed it in a bin and sauntered out of the bank.

'He followed Stanfield in,' said Frost. 'He was here all the time Stanfield was in the bank. When Stanfield left, so did he.' He zipped back the tape, replaying some of it, freeze-framing from time to time.

'Assuming he was involved,' said Burton, 'the picture's nowhere near good enough to identify him.'

'There's more than one way of skinning a banana,' said Frost. He called the manager back into the office and pointed at the shape on the screen. 'I want to know who he is.'

The manager gave a shrug. 'I've no idea.'

'Yes you have,' said Frost. 'Look – he's using his cash card to draw money from your cash machine. You can see the clock – that gives the exact time he took out the money. You've got to have a timed record of all money withdrawn from that machine.'

The manager went to a computer terminal on a small table by his desk and rattled away at the keyboard. 'Yes. 9.34. £5 withdrawn.' He peered at the screen. 'That's strange. At 9.39 it was paid back in again.'

'He was stalling for time,' said Frost. 'I want his name, address and inside leg size.'

The manager twitched an apologetic smile. 'I can't

give you information about our customers. You will have to go through the proper channels.'

'Tell me that next time you come whining to me because you've got a parking ticket,' said Frost.

The manager clicked away at a few more keys and the screen display changed. He stood up. 'I have to go out for a few minutes. Please do not look at this screen. It contains classified customer information.'

Frost beamed his thanks and was at the computer even as the door was closing behind the manager. His eyebrows rose in surprise. The customer was a girl. Tracey Neal, 6 Dean Court, Denton. She had a balance of £25 in her account. Her date of birth was shown. She was fifteen, the same age as Carol Stanfield. Burton scribbled down the details.

'Mullett banks here,' said Frost, sitting down in the chair by the computer. 'I wonder how much he's got in his account. What's the betting he's in the red? Let's see if he's made any cheques out to ladies of ill repute.' He pulled the keyboard towards him.

Burton looked nervously towards the door, expecting the manager to return any minute. 'Do you really think you should . . .?'

Frost ignored Burton's concern. 'Do you reckon we just type in his name?' He pressed a key and the words ACCOUNT NAME? appeared on the screen. Frost started to peck out M . . . U . . . L . . . when the computer let out a high-pitched buzz, the screen display kept flashing on and off, and a Dalek-like, electronic voice bawled: 'Unauthorized input . . . unauthorized input . . .'

'Flaming hell!' Frost leapt from the keyboard to the vacant visitors' chair on the far side of the room. As the manager came running in, looking angry, Frost gave a puzzled frown towards the computer. 'What the hell is up with that?' he asked with all the innocence he could muster.

* * *

Liz was sitting at the spare desk when he got back. She looked shaken, but was busying herself with heaps of papers. She accepted the cigarette Frost tossed over to her.

'How did it go?'

Her hand was unsteady as she put the cigarette in her mouth, but she tried to sound calm. It had been a harrowing experience. Drysdale was always thorough, even when the cause of death was obvious, and to watch him being thorough three times, and on the bodies of tiny children, was almost too much. Even Cassidy had been affected and had mumbled some excuse about a phone call, leaving her to see it through, and she had managed a smug smile as she watched him leave, but now she felt shattered. 'Asphyxiated with a pillow, probably while they were sleeping. They wouldn't have cried out and they wouldn't have known anything about it.'

'Poor little sods.' He saw she was having trouble in striking a match, so leant across with his lighter. 'What about the stab marks on the boy's arm?'

'Not very serious and made after death. That's all he could say.'

'Time of death?'

'Between 11 p.m. and midnight, Drysdale will be able to pin it down closer when he knows the time they had their last meal. I'm seeing the father later on, he should be able to tell us when she usually fed them.' Liz shuddered as she thought of the mother preparing their food, cooking it ever so carefully, the last meal they would ever have . . . 'They all died within minutes of each other.'

'And still no sign of the mother?'

'No.'

'Let's hope she's killed herself. It'll save everyone a lot of sodding about.'

Liz winced at Frost's apparent callousness, but she knew what he meant.

'What about that row people heard? Has anyone owned up to it?'

She shook her head. 'I questioned our witnesses again and they still say they thought it was the wife and husband quarrelling, but as we know, the husband wasn't there.'

Frost scratched his chin. 'The man who never was. Ah well . . . one of life's little mysteries.' He switched to the Stanfield case. 'I've got a job for you.' He told her about the girl hovering about in the bank when Stanfield drew out the money. 'Check her out.'

Glad of anything that would take her mind off the memory of those three small bodies on Drysdale's autopsy table, she inserted her papers in a folder and grabbed her handbag. She had to squeeze past Burton who was coming in and who hadn't left her enough room to get through easily.

'You enjoyed that, didn't you, son?' grunted Frost.

'Never thought I'd fancy a sergeant,' replied Burton, pulling Liz's chair up to Frost's desk and sitting down.

'Is it still warm from her lovely bottom?'

'Red hot!' grinned Burton. 'Right. The phone booths at the supermarket. I've had them all bugged, as you asked, ready for when the kidnapper makes contact. Every phone call in and out is now being recorded.'

'What about bugging the money case so we can track it?'

Burton took a padded envelope from his pocket and carefully tipped out a small, grey plastic object, not much bigger than a fifty pence piece, and put it on Frost's desk. 'Self-powered . . . range up to two hundred yards.'

Frost prodded it with a nicotine-stained finger. 'Doen't look much. You sure it works?'

'Positive. I tested it on the way over. But how will we get it in the suitcase with the money if Cordwell refuses to co-operate?'

'Leave that to me, son. One of Savalot's security guards is going to slip it in for me.'

'Which one?' Burton asked.

'A bloke called Tommy Dunn. He used to be a copper – took early retirement under pressure from Mullett. He'd been taking back-handers.'

'Can you trust him?'

'No – but he'll do anything for a bottle of whisky. Tommy's done a bit of nosing around. The accounts manager is going to make the ransom money up from today's takings at the store. It will be put into an overnight case ready for Cordwell to collect. Tommy reckons he can slip the homing device under the lining so no-one will notice it.' He returned the tiny transmitter to its padded envelope and handed it back to Burton. 'Get over to Savalot, and ask for Tommy Dunn . . . Drop it in his pocket and leave.'

As Burton went out the internal phone rang. Bill Wells from the front desk. Mrs Stanfield was here to identify the furs and jewellery fished out of the canal. 'Right,' said Frost, but as he spoke, panic set in. His eyes began a swift search of the office. Liz had picked the sodden furs from the floor and had hooked them over the hat-stand, but where was the flaming jewellery? 'Hold on a tick, Bill.' He put the phone down and started to ransack the place, looking everywhere, even where he was sure he hadn't put it. £40,000 worth of jewellery and he'd left it lying on his desk in full view where anyone could see it and the door open . . . Don't say some bastard has nicked it, he silently pleaded. A sudden thought. The insurance assessor. He must have taken it. A quick phone call. 'No, inspector. It was still on your desk in a black plastic bag when I left.'

'Oh yes – of course,' said Frost, trying to sound as if he had just spotted it. He lit up a cigarette for inspiration then realized angry noises were coming from his internal phone. Bill Wells was still hanging on. 'Tell her to wait,

Bill. I'll call back.' He banged the phone down and again searched everywhere he had searched before, hoping that, in some magical way, the bag would suddenly appear.

His internal phone rang again. Mrs Stanfield was getting impatient. 'She'll have to come back later,' said Frost. 'Tell her the insurance assessor has got to check it first.'

'But I thought—' began Wells.

'Just tell her!' snapped Frost.

'OK,' said Wells, miffed by Frost's manner. 'By the way, Mr Mullett wants to see you.'

'He wasn't carrying a black plastic bag by any chance?' Frost asked.

'As a matter of fact, he was.'

Frost put the phone down, relief mingled with irritation. It was his own stupid fault, but if you couldn't leave stuff unattended in a police station, where the hell could you leave it? He was trying to work out his ploy with Mullett when Cassidy stormed in. Flaming heck, thought Frost dolefully. Not more bloody moans.

Cassidy jerked a thumb at the spare desk. 'Where's the girl?'

'Doing a job for me,' said Frost. 'Why?'

'Call from the track inspector at Denton railway station. There's a body on the track. It could be the missing mother.'

'Let's hope it is,' said Frost. 'We haven't got time to keep looking for her.' Cassidy could handle this on his own.

The phone rang. This time an angry Mullett demanding the inspector report immediately to his office. Frost put his hand over the mouthpiece. 'Hold on – I'm coming with you,' he called to Cassidy. Back to the phone. 'Sorry, super – urgent call.' He hung up quickly.

As they drove down the road running parallel with the railway track all signals were at red. There was a stationary passenger train, its windows studded with heads of angry passengers trying to make out what the hold-up was. Cassidy parked the car on the stone-walled bridge which continued the road over the tunnel and the two detectives slithered down the embankment to the mouth of the tunnel where two railway track inspectors in fluorescent yellow jackets were waiting for them. Cassidy looked nervously at the gleaming rails. 'Is the current off?'

The senior track inspector nodded. 'Yes – and it would help if you could be as quick as possible. This is playing havoc with our train schedules.'

Emergency lights were on in the tunnel, but did little to dispel the gloom. A strong wind roared noisily past their ears and they had to shout to be heard. Frost wrapped his scarf tighter around his neck and squinted his eyes against the dust and grit which the wind was hurling through the tunnel like bullets.

'There!' The railwayman stopped and pointed, turning his head away. He had seen it before and that was more than enough. He squeezed against the wall so they could get past him.

She was some thirty yards into the tunnel, a crumpled heap, one arm lying across the rail and partly severed. As Frost bent to examine her he realized that she had been decapitated and the head was a few feet forward in the middle of the track. So cleanly was it cut, it could almost have been done with a very sharp knife, but was the result of a high speed train going over her. The train would have barely quivered as it sliced its way through. Frost pulled his eyes away from the bloodied stump of the neck and gingerly touched the flesh of her arm. Hard and ice cold. She was lying lengthways along the rail and wore a black acrylic jumper and green slacks. He forced himself to look at the head. The eyes were open and staring, the face bruised and battered, light brown hair all over the place and matted with blood. He checked with the photograph in his pocket. No doubt about it. She was Nancy Grover.

'Could she have been hit by a train as she walked through the tunnel?' asked Cassidy.

'No way. If a train had hit her while she walked, she'd have been sent flying and would probably have been cut in half as it went over her,' replied one of the railwaymen. 'My guess is she jumped from the bridge. I can't tell you the number of suicides we've had to bag up from here. It's all flaming copy-cat. One does it, the others read about it in the paper, then they all do it.'

'They used to jump from the top floor of the multi-storey car-park,' said the other track inspector. 'Sod that for a way to die, strawberry jam all over the concrete.'

'This is worse,' put in the first railwayman. 'You could end up with your arms and legs cut off by the train and still be alive.'

'So if your bum itched you couldn't bloody scratch it,' added Frost. 'So come on . . . how would she have ended up half-way down the tunnel?'

'They go to the bridge, climb on to the wall and wait for a train, then jump down in front of it. Only I reckon this poor woman left her jump too late, fell on top of a carriage and as the train took the bend, she was thrown off and smashed against the tunnel wall. Then she slid down, her head fell over the rail and the wheels sliced it off.'

'Wouldn't the train driver or any of the passengers have heard her crash on the roof?'

'Not over the noise of the train.'

Frost shuffled forward to take another look at the head. The face looked strained and in torment. 'You silly bitch,' he whispered. 'You've properly sodded this up.'

The senior of the track inspectors was muttering into a mobile phone. He beckoned Frost over. 'There's a log jam of trains going right back to four stations. We'd like to get her shifted out of here so we can get things moving.'

'I bet you would,' said Frost. He scratched his chin, working out the distance from the tunnel to the woman's home. She couldn't have walked here in less than half an hour. The kids were killed around midnight, which meant she must have done her diving act at half-past midnight at the earliest. 'So what train did this to her?'

'There's one at five past midnight.'

'Too early,' said Frost.

'Then it would have to be the 00.35. That's the last through train until 5.22 this morning.'

A yell from the mouth of the tunnel where a disgruntled passenger, fed up with waiting in a stationary train, had walked along the line to complain. 'How much bloody longer? We've been here nearly an hour already.'

'Get back in the train,' shouted the track inspector.

'I'm going to report you,' called the passenger.

'And I'll bloody report you – it's an offence to walk on the track. Now get back!' He turned to Frost. 'Can't we move her?'

'Not until the police surgeon has certified she's dead.'

'Dead? Her bloody head is off!'

'If it was a man and all we had left was his dick, we'd still have to wait for the doctor to certify he was dead.' He shouted down to the mouth of the tunnel where Cassidy was in contact with Control on his radio. 'How long's the doctor going to be?'

'He's on his way,' called back Cassidy.

'Can't we cover her up and let the trains go through?' pleaded the senior track inspector. 'This is causing one hell of a disruption.'

'All right,' said Frost. 'But shift her head off the track first.'

The man shuddered. 'I'm not touching her head.'

'Then we wait,' said Frost.

They didn't have to wait long. Dr Slomon, the on-call

police surgeon, was scowling because this was miles out of his way and he had slipped on the mud coming down the embankment, smearing his light brown camel-hair overcoat. He looked anxiously at the rails. 'Is the current off?'

'Should be safe as long as you don't pee on the live rail,' said Frost, moving back so Slomon could see the body. Slomon shuddered as he eyed the trunk, then the head. Why did Frost always have to be involved with the messy ones? He remembered only too well the tramp in a toilet swimming with urine. He bent down and briefly touched the hardened flesh. 'Been dead some time – nine, ten hours.'

'Did the decapitation kill her?' asked Cassidy.

'Well, it certainly didn't help,' sniffed Slomon. 'You'll need a post-mortem to find the exact cause.' He scribbled on a pad and tore off a sheet. 'She's dead. You can move her.' He scrambled back up the embankment, glad to be away from the macabre scene. Cassidy was radioing to Control to get them to contact an undertaker to remove the body and to arrange an autopsy.

Frost wandered off, happy to let Cassidy attend to all the detail. The suicide tied up the case nicely. He clambered up the embankment, then realized he had travelled in Cassidy's car and would have to wait for him to get a lift back to the station. Damn. Down to his left he could see clusters of angry passengers arguing with the guard on the halted train. The sound of a car approaching. A bit too soon for the undertaker, surely? He hoped Control had warned them there was a severed head to collect as well. Some of them were a bit fussy about the state of the corpses they transported. But it wasn't the undertaker. It was Liz Maud. She braked to a sliding halt alongside him.

'We've found the mother?' she asked.

Frost opened the passenger door and slid in beside her. 'Yes, love. Parts one and two – she jumped in front of a train.' Liz made to get out, but he restrained her. 'You don't want to see her.'

She shook off his hand. 'Why not?'

'The poor cow is in two bloody halves.'

'But if Mr Cassidy is down there—'

'Sod Mr Cassidy. The case is all tied up. It's the fiddling, messy tying up the ends now and he's quite capable of doing that on his own.' He heard footsteps echoing from the tunnel below. 'Let's get out of here . . . I think he's coming.'

She drove off, swerving to avoid a battered black van that lumbered towards them. The undertakers didn't use their shiny black Rolls-Royces for messy jobs like this.

He lit up. 'Have you seen that girl – Tracey what's-her-name?'

'Not yet. I called at her house, but she's at school. Denton Grammar – the same school as Carol Stanfield.'

Frost pulled the cigarette from his mouth. 'Same school, same age – they must be in the same class. Very interesting.'

'It's probably a coincidence. Half the girls of her age in Denton go to the same school.'

Frost's eyes glistened. A school full of pubescent, busty teenage girls had the edge on following a maimed corpse to the mortuary. 'Let's visit the school and question her there. I want to get this lousy case tied up so we can concentrate on more important matters.'

The head teacher, Ms Quincey, was not too pleased. This scruffy man, who appeared to be a detective inspector, seemed more interested in watching the fifth-form girls playing handball in the gym through the glass partition of her office, than in listening to what she was saying. She cleared her throat noisily and snatched his attention away from the spectacle outside. 'It's just as a witness you wish to talk to her?'

Frost nodded. 'She might have seen something that would help us.'

Ms Quincey was still doubtful, but was relieved there was a woman police officer with him. She would have preferred to have sat in on the questioning, but had to take 4B for Social Studies while their normal teacher was away having an abortion. 'Ah – here comes Tracey now.'

Tracey pushed through the swing doors into the gym and hurried past the excited, squealing, flush-faced handball players. She was wearing her school uniform, a light brown jacket over a white blouse with a black skirt. She looked a lot younger than the figure on the bank security video.

'Come in, Tracey,' said the head teacher.

Frost flashed both his warrant card and his frank and innocent smile. 'Won't take more than a couple of minutes, Tracey. You might have seen something that could help us.' The girl sat down and crossed her legs, with an almost too studied expression of unconcern. Frost squinted up at the wall clock where the minute hand was quivering on the hour. He was itching for the bell to signal the start of the next period so Ms bloody Quincey would leave them alone. 'Better just take your name and address for our records.' He tried not to show his delight as the bell jangled.

'I'll have to leave you now,' said Ms Quincey, gathering up some books from her desk. 'Perhaps you could see yourselves out.'

'Of course,' nodded Frost, disappointed to note that the bell also signalled the end of the handball game and the girls had all disappeared into the dressing-rooms where . . . God! . . . they'd be having showers! All those sweaty little nubile fifteen-year-olds, stark naked . . . Then he realized the girl was talking to him and was snatched back from his fantasizing. 'Sorry – what was that?'

'You wanted my name – Tracey Neal, 6 Dean Court, Denton.'

He scribbled it down although it was unnecessary as they already had her details from the bank. 'You were in Bennington's Bank just after nine-thirty yesterday morning?'

'That's right.' She flicked away a strand of chestnut hair that had fallen over her face and tried to look bored.

'You know Carol Stanfield, don't you?'

'Yes.'

'And you heard about the robbery at her house?'

'It was on the radio. They kidnapped her and stripped her . . .' Her eyes widened as if she had just realized. 'Her father – when I saw him in the bank – was he picking up the ransom money?'

'So you saw him?'

'Only briefly. I don't know him that well. I sort of gave him a smile, but I don't think he noticed me.'

'You're being a great help,' said Frost. 'Did you notice anything suspicious – anyone hanging about – apart from yourself, of course?'

She screwed up her face to show she was trying hard to remember. 'There were lots of people there. I didn't notice anyone especially.'

'When you left the bank, did you spot anyone hanging about outside, or in a car . . .?'

She shook her head. 'Sorry.'

Frost beamed his deceptively reassuring smile. 'Not your fault, love. Oh – just for the record. What were you doing in the bank?'

She frowned. 'Why? What has that got to do with it?'

Frost spread his hands vaguely. 'Just routine. We have to check out everyone who was in the bank at that time, even if it is obvious they weren't involved. So what were you doing there – getting money out?'

'Yes.'

'You weren't at school yesterday?'

'No.'

Frost noticed she was starting to wriggle and look uneasy. He fished out his cigarettes and pretended to be preoccupied. Actually, he was looking through the glass to the doors of the dressing-room where the first of the damp-haired, squeaky clean girls were scampering out. 'Why didn't you go to school?'

She shrugged and looked up at the ceiling. 'Didn't feel like it.'

A sympathetic smile. 'As good a reason as any. So what did you do with yourself all day? Read the bible – take soup to the sick?'

'I went round a boy's house and we listened to some music.'

'That's terrific,' said Frost. 'Then he can vouch for you – save us doing a lot of checking. What's his name?'

'Ian Grafton.'

'Address.'

'23 Fairfield Road.'

'Right.' Frost scribbled this down on the back of a supermarket till receipt, then suddenly seemed to think of something else. 'This may sound silly. You took £5 out. What did you want the money for?'

'I was going to the disco at Goya's. It's a big night.'

'The disco was in the evening. Why did you draw the money out in the morning?'

'Why not?' she said defiantly. 'It was as good a time as any.'

'I suppose so,' said Frost, grudgingly. He worried away for a while at his scar. 'After you drew it out, you waited a few minutes, then paid it back. Why was that?'

'I suddenly realized I had a standing order coming up and if I withdrew the money it couldn't be met.'

'So you had to give the disco a miss?'

'No. Ian lent me the money.'

'Good old Ian. Did you go straight to the bank from your house?'

'Yes.'

'Your mother seemed surprised when we told her you were at the bank. She thought you would have been at school.'

'I don't tell her everything.'

An understanding smile. 'I bet you don't. Did you go straight from your house to the bank?'

'Yes.'

'Right.' He started to scribble this down, then paused. 'Wait a minute. Your mother said you left the house at your usual time for school and you were wearing your school uniform.'

'Yes – well, I wanted her to think I was going to school, didn't I?'

'And you went straight to the bank.'

'That's right.' She wasn't so quick with her answers now.

'We've got a witness . . .' He shuffled through some pieces of paper and pretended to read from one. 'Ah yes . . . an old dear. Not very reliable, I'm afraid . . . half blind and didn't have her glasses with her. She says she could have sworn you were wearing jeans and a dirty old duffel coat . . . not your nice smart uniform.'

'Then she was mistaken.'

'So you were in school uniform – the one you are wearing now?'

'Yes.'

Frost turned to Liz Maud as he scratched out what he had just written down. 'You see, sergeant – that silly old dear got it all wrong.' He patted the papers together and stuffed them in his pocket, then swung the chair round to face the girl and smiled with a nod as if that was all he wanted her for. As she got up to go he suddenly snapped his fingers. 'I'm a stupid git – I'm getting all confused. It wasn't the old lady who said you were in casual clothes, it was the bank security video . . . black duffel coat with the hood up and light trousers.' He beamed at her. 'So either you – or the bank video camera – are telling me porkies.'

She stared at him, her lips moving silently as she tried out alternative answers. At last she said, 'I took different clothes with me and changed in the public toilets.'

'So what did you do with your school clothes – flush them down the pan? They weren't with you while you were in the bank.'

'All right, all right!' She was almost shouting. 'Ian met me round the corner from my house in his van. My mother doesn't like me going out with him. I changed in the back of his van while he drove me to the bank. He waited for me, then took me to his place. Satisfied?'

'Perfectly,' said Frost, standing up. 'I just wanted to get the incongruities straightened out. Thanks for your time.' He gave the girl a brisk nod, then he and Liz left the school.

In the car, Liz said, 'She was lying.'

'Of course she was,' said Frost. 'So let's nip round and see Ian what's-his-name and find out what sort of lies he's going to tell us.'

There was a van parked outside the house, a battered, rust-riddled light brown Ford with the name of the previous trader crudely erased with black paint.

'Your witness said the van he saw was light brown,' said Frost.

'I thought you didn't believe him,' sniffed Liz.

'I can be flexible when it suits me,' smirked Frost. 'Sometimes I'm flexible when it doesn't suit me.' He pressed the door bell.

Ian Grafton was eighteen, tall and wiry, wearing his black greasy hair in a thick pigtail. He took them to his upstairs flat.

'I expect Tracey's phoned you about us, Ian,' said Frost, noting the pay-phone on the landing. 'Just wanted to confirm a couple of things.'

Grafton occupied a bed-sit. He was unemployed. Social Security paid the rent. His last job was doing deliveries for a local furniture shop, but the job collapsed when the firm went bust some twelve months ago. He hadn't worked since. They sat on the bed in his small room with its pop posters and the midi hi-fi unit and went through the motions of scribbling down his confirmation of Tracey's story. He agreed every word of it and Frost was sure he too was lying.

'You waited outside the bank for her?' asked Frost. 'Now, thinking back on it, did you notice anything suspicious . . . any weirdos hanging about?'

'The only weirdo was a fat tart of a traffic warden who gave me a flaming ticket for parking on a double yellow line.' He snatched it from a shelf and waved it at Frost who squinted at the date and time. It tallied.

'Thank you, Ian. We might want to speak to you again.'

He took another look at the van as they left. The same colour as the one the witness saw, but if it received a parking ticket at 9.35, then it couldn't have been the van the naked Carol Stanfield was held in. He worried away at this, but the pieces refused to fit.

He didn't have time to brood for long. As soon as Liz opened the car door, there was a radio message. Would Frost get over to the mortuary right away. The mother hadn't committed suicide. She had been murdered.

'Murdered?' said Frost.

The hospital pathologist, who had thought he was going to carry out a routine autopsy, nodded. 'Come and see.'

The body was on the autopsy table and much of the blood had now been washed off. Her clothes had been removed and the head had been put in place, ready to be sutured back on to the torso to make her presentable for relatives. The junior technician who had been summoned to perform this task was hovering in the background.

Frost and Liz looked down at the body. With the

clothes removed, the pathologist had no need to explain. There were stab marks all over the abdomen and the area of the heart. The lower incisions were encrusted with dried blood. Frost did a quick count. She had been stabbed eleven times.

'Shit!' This was a complication he could have done without.

'The incision through the heart would have been enough to kill her,' said the pathologist. 'She was dead before she went over that railway bridge.'

Frost gave a deep sigh. 'Any chance the wounds were self-inflicted, doc?' He knew it was a stupid question, but he wanted to cling to his suicide theory.

The pathologist shook his head. 'Look at her hands.'

Frost knew he should have checked before he asked. The backs of the hands showed slashes and stab wounds. They were inflicted as she tried to defend herself.

'This is right outside my league,' said the pathologist. 'You'll have to get Mr Drysdale to do the autopsy.'

'All right,' said Frost. 'Put her back in the fridge until he gets here.'

The junior technician helped the mortuary assistant to slide the torso on to a trolley then, with a look of distaste, carefully picked up the head and dropped it into a large polythene bag which he also placed on the trolley.

They met Cassidy as they were walking back to the car. 'Stabbed,' said Frost tersely. 'About eleven times. Dead before she was chucked in front of the train.'

Cassidy barely concealed a smirk. 'I knew this case wasn't as straightforward as you tried to make out.'

'Nothing I touch turns out to be bloody straightforward,' said Frost ruefully.

'Have they done the autopsy?'

'They've sent for Drysdale. If it's anything more complicated than an ingrowing toenail, this bloke doesn't want to know.'

'I'm going to pull Snell in,' announced Cassidy.

'Don't be a prat,' said Frost. 'You want to start putting pressure on the husband.'

'The husband couldn't have done it. Snell broke in, started to stab the kid when they all woke up and started screaming. He panics and silences them with the pillow. The mother runs in and he has to kill her as well.'

'Then why didn't he leg it and leave her? Why try to make out her death was suicide?'

'I don't know, but I'm going to find out.'

'I'll give you a better scenario. The husband comes back from work to find his wife smirking all over her face. She tells him she's killed his kids to pay him back for leaving her on her own, night after night. He takes it amiss and goes berserk, stabbing her again and again. He realizes suspicion must fall on him, so he carts the body away and tries to make her death look like suicide.'

'He couldn't have done it,' repeated Cassidy, stubbornly. 'He's got a watertight alibi. Three people can confirm he was in that store until nearly two o'clock in the morning.'

'Then recheck his alibi . . . see if we can break it.' He turned to Liz. 'Is he still in hospital?'

'Yes. They should be releasing him tomorrow.'

'Good. He was taken there straight from the house, so he was still wearing the clothes he had on that night. Get those clothes. I want Forensic to do a proper job for a change and go over every inch of them for bloodstains . . . there must have been one hell of a lot of blood.' Back to Cassidy. 'You'd better hang on for the autopsy. Drysdale should be here any minute. I'll make my way back to the house and wait for Forensic and the Scene of Crime boys.'

Cassidy wasn't happy at the way he was being ordered about. After all he was, if only temporarily, the same rank as Frost. But he decided to swallow it. It looked as if there could well be some embarrassing foul-ups with this case so it would be better if Frost was in charge. 'Right.'

He went back through the swing doors of the mortuary to wait for the Home Office Pathologist.

Liz dropped Frost off at the house in Cresswell Street and drove on to the hospital. The constable on duty, young PC Packer, handed over the front door key. 'Go and get yourself a cup of tea or something,' said Frost. 'I'll be here for at least an hour.' Packer nodded gratefully. It was boring standing on guard, nothing to do, no-one to talk to except when he was fending off questions from the inquisitive. There was a burger bar in the main road. He'd nip off there for a bite to eat in the warm.

Frost let himself in and closed the door behind him. In the oppressive background of silence small sounds seemed to be exaggerated. The lounge door creaked as he pushed it open. The curtains had been drawn to stop people peering in and the room was in darkness. He clicked on the light. Was the woman killed here and taken away? If so, there should be blood, but he couldn't see any.

He clicked off the light and went along the passage to the kitchen where there were still unwashed mugs on the small table. He should have got someone to tidy up after they left. Blue polythene sheeting had been laid over the floor to protect it from the feet of everyone tramping in and out. He hitched a section back and peered down on to blue and white vinyl. Blood would have screamed. There was none. The white surface of the tall fridge freezer gleamed coldly. He took a look inside. Near the top, an opened tin of Heinz baby food.

Over to the back door. At some stage one of its glass panes had been broken and a makeshift repair of a sheet of plywood nailed over the gap. The bottom of the ply was loose where the nails had been wrenched out, making it possible for anyone outside to squeeze a hand through and reach the key. This had been noted the night before, but not much attention was paid to it as the case then seemed uncomplicated.

He left the kitchen and went down the corridor, the soft padded creak of his footsteps following him. The children's bedroom still breathed Johnson's baby powder. The beds, stripped of their clothes, were icy to the touch. Across the room, on a shelf, a row of soft toys, animals, golliwogs, dolls, stared reproachfully at him. As he turned to leave, his heart froze. A child's voice cried, 'Mummy.'

It was a doll. A bloody doll on the floor and he had trodden on it. He picked it up and put it on the shelf with the others.

Shaken, he hurried off to the darkened lounge where he sat and smoked. The heavy curtains insulated the room from outside noises, but kept in the stifling silence of the house. It was chilly and he shivered. At one stage he was jolted from his thoughts by a sound like a child giggling, but when he listened hard there was nothing.

Footsteps up the path and someone knocking at the door. The Forensic team. 'Not today, thank you,' he said. 'I never buy at the door.'

He went back to the lounge and left them to it. Painstaking, methodical work was not his forte and he got impatient with people who had to work this way. Young Packer reported back and was sent to check with the neighbours about what they saw or heard last night. If the mother was killed in the house she would have had to be driven to the railway bridge, so did anyone see or hear a car?

A tap at the door. 'We'd like to do this room, inspector.' He was getting the distinct impression he was in the bloody way.

He moved on to the kitchen. Harding from Forensic was out in the garden examining the door in the wall that led to the outside lane. He saw Frost and hurried over to him. 'Something to show you.' It was the back door. With rubber-gloved hands Harding eased back the plywood panel and pointed to its jagged bottom edge.

Dots of red and flecks of skin. 'Someone forced back the wood to get a hand through so they could turn the key from the inside. The edge of the ply grazed the back of his wrist, drawing blood. Whoever did it would have a nasty scratch on the back of the hand.'

'It could have been the father . . . or even the mother,' said Frost. 'Forgot their front door key so came in through the back.'

'Possible,' said Harding. 'We should be able to do some DNA testing on the skin fragments. Find a suspect and we could match him to this. You wouldn't need a confession.'

'Science is wonderful,' grunted Frost. 'It's making the rubber truncheon obsolete.' Two men from the Forensic team in their gleaming white boiler suits came in. 'We'd like to do the kitchen now, inspector.'

Nowhere where he could sit and think and be undisturbed. He let them get on with it and caught a bus back to the station.

Cassidy was waiting for him in the murder incident room. He had the results of the post-mortem on the mother. 'Numerous stab wounds to the abdomen and heart. The wound to the heart killed her and she would have died almost instantly. Stab marks on her hands where she fought off her attacker.'

'What sort of knife?'

'Single edge, sharp-pointed. Could have been a kitchen knife.'

'Time of death?'

'Between eleven and one o'clock last night.'

Frost told Cassidy about the back door panel. Cassidy's eyes glinted with satisfaction. 'I want to bring Snell in . . . now.'

'He should be back at Newcastle,' said Frost. He hoped and prayed Snell would be there, sitting in his flat, reading his bible, the backs of his hands entirely without a scratch . . .

'He isn't,' said Cassidy. 'The Newcastle police have checked.'

Frost stared out of the window. With low-lying, heavy black rain clouds, it was already dark outside. 'All right. Let's try and find him.'

10

A few minutes past four o'clock in the afternoon and it was already dark with the ominous rumble of thunder in the distance as Cassidy pulled up outside Snell's house in Parnell Terrace. Only one of the street lights was on, the other had been vandalized, its metal cover forced off and the spaghetti of coloured wires wrenched out. No lights shone from the house and there was no reply to Cassidy's pounding at the door. Outside the front door five bulging dustbin sacks lolled against the wall.

Frost crouched to take a peek through the letter box into more darkness. 'We'd better take a look round inside.'

'Do you have a key?' sneered Cassidy.

'Don't need one, son. What's that?' He pointed into the darkened street. As Cassidy's head jerked to look there was the sound of breaking glass; when he turned back Frost seemed to be replacing an empty milk bottle on the step and the glass pane of the front door was shattered. 'Looks as if someone has tried to break in here,' said Frost. 'We'd better check.' He stuck his hand through the broken pane and unlocked the door from the inside.

Cassidy didn't want to get involved with any of Frost's corner cutting, but there seemed to be no chance of anyone finding out, so he followed him inside.

The hall light came on when Frost tried. There were two preprinted postcards on the door mat, one from the Electricity Board, the other from the Gas company. Both were dated that day and each said that their service engineer had called at 9 a.m., 'as requested by you for the purpose of taking the final meter reading and cutting off the supply. He could obtain no answer. Please contact our office to make a fresh appointment.'

They moved through to the living-room. On the table were six carrier bags packed with the mother's personal effects. There was food in the fridge in the kitchen, a Marks and Spencer chilled meal and an unopened carton of milk. The bed was made with folded pyjamas on the pillow.

Frost poked around a few drawers, but they had been cleared out. 'He hasn't been here since last night,' he decided. 'The bed hasn't been slept in.'

'He could have made it after he got up,' said Cassidy.

'No, son. He was going back to Newcastle today. He was all packed up, ready to go. He might make the bed after he got up, but he wouldn't fold his pyjamas and bung them on the pillow. And he'd have opened up the milk for a cup of tea.' He chewed his thumb knuckle thoughtfully. 'He went out last night, but didn't come back. Why?'

'I'd have thought that was obvious,' snapped Cassidy. 'He killed the kids, then the mother and he's now on the run.'

'I can't buy that, son. Why should he try to make the mother's death look like suicide? It doesn't make sense.'

'You're looking for a rational explanation. The man's a nut-case.'

'If he chucked her in front of the train to make it look like suicide, why then has he done a bunk?'

'Perhaps he saw the train hadn't gone over her. He wanted the body all mangled up so we wouldn't spot the knife marks. When that didn't happen, he ran.'

Frost chewed this over. It was as plausible as some of his own stupid theories, but it would mean that Snell, who up to now had been content with drawing pin pricks of blood, was suddenly a frantic mass murderer. He poked in one of the carrier bags on the kitchen table. On the top was a silver-framed photograph of the eight-year-old Sidney Snell in a sailor suit, hair combed, face washed for the camera, clutching the hand of his young mother. A sweet and innocent child . . . who grew up to be a pervert. 'OK,' he sighed. 'Get on to Newcastle. Ask them to keep an eye on his place and if he shows up, arrest him on suspicion of murder. Tell Control to radio all patrols – if they see him, arrest him on sight.' He took one last look round the room. 'And get someone to check this place from time to time in case he comes back for his milk.'

The front door slammed behind them, echoing in an empty street. As their car turned the corner, a furtive figure emerged from the shadows of a derelict house on the opposite side of the road. Sidney Snell, shaking with fear. He had come back to the house to retrieve his belongings when some sixth sense warned him to wait. Sweat had broken out from every pore of his body when he saw Frost and Cassidy forcing their way in. He couldn't hear their car any more, but he hesitated, racked with indecision . . . Should he risk it and dash over to the house, or were they lurking round the corner waiting for him to do something stupid like that? He was tired and he was hungry. He'd had no sleep at all last night. The back of his hand was bleeding again. He sucked it and wound the dirty handkerchief tighter. What to do? God, what to do . . . ?

The old woman was waiting for Frost as he pushed through the doors to the lobby. She hurried towards him, eyes glowing. 'You've got them back. The sergeant says you've got them back.'

He smiled, but she had wrong-footed him. Who the hell was she? Then he placed her. Of course . . . the old dear who'd had her husband's medals pinched. Bloody hell. He hadn't had time to sort out half the stuff they'd found stacked behind the cistern in Lemmy Hoxton's house. 'Your medal – yes, love . . . If you'd like to formally identify it . . .'

He took her into the main interview room and they waited for Burton to lug in the large cardboard box. The medal, in its black case, was near the top. It deserved more respect than being piled on top of the other junk. He gave it to her.

She beamed her delight. 'I never thought I'd see this again.' She took the DFM out and held it close to her cheek. 'He wanted our son to have it. There was going to be a baby, but I lost it when our house was bombed and I had a miscarriage. The doctor said it would have been a boy.'

Frost nodded in sympathy and explained they would have to hang on to the medal for a little while. 'Don't worry, love, it'll be safe here. I'll look after it.' Look after it! He grinned wryly to himself . . . as well as I looked after forty grand's worth of jewellery from the Stanfield robbery? Which reminded him of the treat to come. He was going to have to face Mullett about that.

'And you've found the photographs. That's such a relief!'

Photographs? What was she on about?

There was a wad of photograph wallets held together with a rubber band in the box. Frost had only skimmed through them briefly. Most of them looked like family snaps. It seemed Lemmy had scooped up everything he could lay his hands on, whether it was of value or not.

She had pulled out the top wallet and was shuffling through the photographs. 'I'd hate to think of these falling into the wrong hands.' She gave Frost a conspiratorial wink and nodded towards Burton. 'Do you think he's old enough to see these?' She handed them over.

Frost stifled a yawn as he took the photographs. More

black and white family snaps. Then he sat up straight. 'Bloody hell!'

Black and white postcard-sized prints, but not for family viewing. They showed a young, pert, dark-haired girl in a bedroom. Completely nude. 'Bloody hell!' he said again as the girl in the photograph cupped her breasts with widespread fingers to reveal rosebud-like nipples, or turned her back, peeping over her shoulder and showing a lovely tight bottom. Then his jaw dropped. He recognized her. He pointed to Mrs Miller. 'It's you!'

She nodded roguishly. 'My husband did his own developing. He used to get his chemicals and paper from the RAF photographic section. It was hard to come by during the war.'

'Bloody hell!' repeated Frost for the third time. 'You were a little cracker.' He showed them to Burton who grinned his approval. Reluctantly, he stuffed them into the wallet and handed them back to her. 'You'd better take these with you, love. They'll get us all too excited if you leave them here.'

She dropped them in her handbag and snapped it shut. 'I wasn't always old, you see,' she said wistfully.

'Good job I wasn't around then,' said Frost. 'Your husband wouldn't have got a look in.' He showed her out. When he returned to the interview room, Burton was packing the stuff back in the box.

'Hold on, son,' said Frost. 'Let's see what other goodies Lemmy had stacked away.'

In an old chocolate box they found lots of pornographic photographs, some involving children. There was a set of photographs of a man dressed in women's underwear. Frost showed them to Burton. 'I like his frilly knickers, but the beard puts me off.' There were letters. Frost read through one and whistled softly. 'This is a blow by blow description of what this couple got up to while her old man was away,' he told Burton. 'And I use the word "blow" advisedly.'

'This one's a bit naughty too,' said Burton, showing him a deckle-edge sheet of light green notepaper.

Frost found another letter, still in its envelope which gave the name of the recipient. An address Frost recognized. Inside was a letter and a Polaroid colour print of a woman bending over an armchair. A big, hefty woman. Her skirt was up and her knickers were round her ankles. A man in a mortar-board and gown was standing over her, wielding a long leather strap. Frost skimmed through the letter. The writer, a man, was arranging to call round the following evening and was detailing the punishment he meted out to naughty girls. His name and address were not included. Stapled to it was the carbon of a letter to him from the woman explaining how naughty she had been. 'Some old tom!' sniffed Burton.

'Not an old tom as it happens,' corrected Frost. 'She's a retired civil servant . . . lives in one of those posh houses in Charter Street.'

'You know her?'

'Not as a client. You know her too, son. She's a friend of Mullett's wife – they both serve on the same hospital committee or something. She reported some money stolen from her bedroom after a man from the Water Board called . . .'

'I remember now,' interrupted Burton. 'The very next day she claimed she was mistaken and nothing was pinched after all.'

'That's her,' nodded Frost. 'We never suspected it at the time, but I reckon she must have received a blackmail threat – pay up or we send the photos to the vicar, sort of thing.' He pulled the photograph towards him and studied it. Behind him the door creaked open.

'Inspector Frost!'

Frost groaned. Flaming Hornrim Harry, ready to give him a bollocking for leaving the loot unattended. He turned with a surprised smile. 'I was just on my way in to see you, super.' He held up the photograph. 'Just for the purposes of elimination, the man in the mortar-board isn't you by any chance?'

Mullett took one look at the photograph and flushed angrily. 'You know damn well it isn't. My office – now!'

Mullett's voice droned on and on as Frost sat in the chair, his face a look of rapt attention, his mind miles away, trying to filter out Mullett's drivel as he turned over the day's events in his mind. If Mullett's wife's mate was being blackmailed, it was a near certainty that Lemmy had been putting the squeeze on others for stuff pinched from bedrooms during his Water Board scam. Which meant Lemmy was a blackmailer as well as a thief and here was a strong motive for murder. Perhaps one of his victims had decided that enough was enough. He opened his ears, but Mullett still hadn't finished.

'. . . not the sort of behaviour I expect from an officer under my command . . .'

He clicked the sound off again. The first thing to do would be to call on this woman and see if she could throw any light on Lemmy's death. Come on, Mullett hurry up and finish . . . I've got work to do. He became aware of a welcome silence. Mullett had stopped at last and was looking at him questioningly.

'You've finished, sir? Good – sorry and all that. Won't happen again.' He snatched up the bag of jewellery and made for the door before the superintendent could think of any more of his shortcomings to moan about.

'Wait!'

It was a tone that could not be ignored, even by Frost. He turned slowly. 'Sir?'

'That photograph you showed me . . . there was something familiar about it.'

'Don't worry, super . . . I'll try and keep you out of it.'

Mullett tightened his lips and stretched out a hand for the Polaroid print. 'Let me see it again.' He studied it, then took off his glasses and polished them slowly. 'It's Mrs Roberts.'

'Top marks!' cried Frost. 'I would never have recognized her just from her bare behind . . . although, of course, I've never seen it before . . .'

Mullett reddened. 'I recognized the room,' he snapped.

'Of course, sir,' said Frost. 'Whatever you say.'

Mullett glowered. 'My wife and I have been there many times . . . those pictures . . . that bookcase . . .'

'Oh, I see, sir,' said Frost, leaving a lingering tinge of doubt in his voice to annoy Mullett further. 'You probably sat in that self-same chair she's bending over. I hope excitement doesn't make her dribble.'

Mullett wiped his eyes wearily and replaced his glasses. 'Look, Frost, this is all very embarrassing. She's a friend of mine and she's very big in the town.'

'She's even bigger round the buttocks,' said Frost.

Mullett ignored this. 'What do you intend doing with it?'

'I'm going round to her house to show it to her.'

Mullett stared hard at the surface of his desk and moved his fountain pen a fraction of an inch. 'I think it would be better if I handled that. She's a good friend, but she could also be a very bad enemy. If I could return the photograph and let her know we were keeping her name out of it, it would make things go a lot smoother in our later dealings.'

'Sorry, super,' said Frost. 'You're too late. I think she's been blackmailed already. In fact it could be the reason Lemmy Hoxton was killed.' As he filled Mullett in, the superintendent became more and more agitated.

'I'd prefer it if you would drop it, Frost. I'm sure she's not involved in murder. Dammit, she's a family friend.'

Frost adopted his air of puzzled incomprehension. 'Is this a bit of the Judges' Rules that I've missed, sir – that I shouldn't question any murder suspect who happens to be a friend of yours?'

Mullett leant forward, his face creased with anger. 'You know damn well that's not what I meant. Of course you must question her. If, by some remote chance, she is involved, then you have my full permission. But if this goes wrong, if it blows up in our faces, I'll come down on you like a ton of bricks.'

Frost retrieved the photograph and slipped it into his pocket. Mullett, as usual, had covered himself both ways and couldn't lose. 'I knew I could rely on your full support, super.'

He looked in the murder incident room and yelled for Burton to come with him. Mrs Roberts was a big woman and he didn't fancy tackling her on his own.

Mrs Emily Roberts lived in a small, semi-detached house at the end of the road. A neat front garden fronted by a trimmed hedge led to a porch and a front door with coloured leaded lights. The bell push surround was polished brass which Frost smeared by jamming his finger on it. After a pause, the door opened suspiciously on a length of chain and even his warrant card wasn't enough to gain admittance. She snatched it from him and went off to phone the station to make sure they were not imposters. She still remembered the fake Water Board official, but even he looked the part while this scruffy individual who thrust a dog-eared warrant card at her looked nothing like a policeman.

She had demanded to speak to her friend Stanley Mullett, the Divisional Commander. Mullett, who had sounded a trifle edgy on the phone, confirmed that Frost was one of his officers, although he wasn't exactly sure what case the inspector was on at the moment.

They were ordered to wipe their feet, which Frost did very perfunctorily, and were marched into the living-room where a cheery coal fire blazed. She meant for them to sit in the hard chairs, but the scruffy one made for one of her large, leather armchairs. 'Lovely chair,' remarked Frost, sinking down. 'Feels brand spanking new.'

Her heart skipped a beat. Was it her imagination, or

did he stress the word 'spanking'? She smiled bleakly. 'How can I help you?'

The room looked exactly as it did in the photograph, but the woman, large, almost mannish, in her tweed trouser suit, seemed light years away from the baby-talking writer of the letter imploring 'teacher' to correct her errors. 'You reported a robbery some months ago, Mrs Roberts,' said Frost. He wished she would sit down. She was standing, towering over him, making him crick his neck as he talked to her.

With an airy wave of the hand she dismissed the nonsense about the robbery. 'All a mistake, as I told your officer at the time.'

'We're wondering if it was a mistake.'

She frowned. 'What do you mean?'

'We think there was a robbery, which you reported, but you then realized he had taken certain items you didn't wish the police to know about.'

She drew herself up to her full height, towering over him even more. 'There was no robbery. Nothing was taken. I can't help you.'

'Why don't you sit down?' said Frost. 'Or is your little botsy-wotsy sore?'

She stared, mouth gaping. At first she thought she hadn't heard him correctly and then her eyes widened in stunned shock as he produced the envelope and the photograph.

'Not exactly full face,' said Frost, 'but we're pretty certain this is you.'

She tried to snatch it from him, but he drew his hand back. 'How dare you!' she hissed. 'How dare you.' Her mouth opened and closed, but that was all she could think of to say.

'Sorry about this,' said Frost, sounding as if he meant it, 'but when you lift stones, all sorts of nasty things come crawling out. I'd just like to get a couple of things sorted to help with our enquiries.'

'I'm not saying another word.' She dropped down in the armchair opposite him and folded her arms defiantly.

'Fair enough,' smiled Frost. 'Bank up the fire and get your hat and coat. We can continue this down at the station. It's not very private there, I'm afraid, but if you're not ashamed of what you've been up to, then what the hell . . .'

She said nothing, but the defiant look withered.

Frost took a folder from Burton and flipped it open. 'On 5th August you telephoned your personal friend, Mr Mullett, to report a burglary. A man posing as a Water Board engineer gained entrance to your house and after he had left you discovered valuables missing from your bedroom. Within twenty minutes of your phone call you received a visit from Detective Sergeant Hanlon. You gave him a list of stolen items – brooches, pearl necklace, gold powder compact, silver bangle . . . total value nearly £2000.'

He tugged out the list. 'This is what you said were stolen.' He held it in front of her. She stared straight ahead as if it wasn't there.

'Your very good friend, Mr Mullett, then called me in and ordered me to pull out all stops to apprehend the criminal. But the very next day you phoned, and subsequently signed a statement . . . this statement,' another sheet of paper was waved in front of her, 'which states that it was all a mistake and nothing was taken . . . you had misplaced the articles and had then found them in another drawer. Mr Mullett then instructed me to take no further action and I immediately complied.' He replaced the papers in the folder. 'My fault. I don't look for work, but I should have followed it up. I should have asked to see the items you now claim to have found.' He beamed at her. 'If I asked nicely, could you show them to me now?'

She stared at him, then lowered her gaze to the floor. 'No.'

'The stuff was stolen?'

'Yes.'

'So what happened to make you tell us it wasn't?'

She stood up and went over to a small coffee table where she took a cigarette from a black and gold lacquered box, lighting it with an onyx cigarette lighter. Before she turned round, Frost had lit up one of his own. 'That night I received a telephone call. A man. He read me a part of that letter and described the photograph. He said he was thinking of sending them to the press, but wondered if I would like to buy them back.' She dragged deeply at the cigarette. 'I asked how much. He wanted £500 in used notes. I said I would pay.' She crushed the barely smoked cigarette out.

'And . . .?' prompted Frost.

'He said there was a litter bin next to the bus stop in Stacey Street. I was to hide the envelope containing the money between the bin and the wall. If I returned there the next day, in its place would be the letter and photograph.'

'And?'

'I did what he said. I left the money. But when I returned the next day, the money was still there. It hadn't been picked up . . . The following day the same. So I retrieved the money and waited for him to phone again. I never heard another word from him.'

'And what did you do with the money?'

'I paid it back into my bank account.'

'Do you have copies of your bank statement?'

She glared and went over to an oak-veneered bureau where she took some papers from the top drawer. These she handed to Frost who passed them to Burton.

'Do you think I am a liar, inspector?' she asked, icily.

'People do lie to us,' said Frost. 'They tell us robberies haven't taken place when they have.' He looked across to Burton, who nodded. The payments in and out were recorded exactly as she said.

He showed her Lemmy's mug shot. 'Was this the man who robbed you?'

She studied it carefully. 'I think so . . . I can't be sure. I didn't pay a lot of attention to him at the time . . . one doesn't when it's workmen.'

'And the last time you saw him was when he left your house on . . .' He consulted the file. '5th August, the day you reported the robbery, and the day before you then reported it never took place?'

'Yes.'

'We think he might have come back here . . . the next day,' said Frost. 'We think he demanded money and threatened to send the photograph and the letter to the press if you didn't pay.'

'I've already told you what happened.'

'But are you telling me the truth?'

'I'm not used to having my word questioned and I'm not going to say another word unless you have the common courtesy to tell me what this is all about,' she snapped.

Frost smiled his reasonable smile. 'Of course. The man I asked you to identify is Lemmy Hoxton, a known criminal. We found your letter and the photo with other stolen goods, hidden in his house. We also found some jewellery that might be yours were it not for the fact that you had told us it hadn't been stolen.'

'My reason for silence no longer applies, inspector. Yes, I was robbed, as I have admitted.'

'What I didn't tell you,' said Frost, as if suddenly remembering something not too important, 'was the reason we went to Lemmy's house in the first place. Would you like to know why?'

'Not particularly, but I imagine you are going to tell me anyway.'

Frost took a long drag at his cigarette. 'It was because we had found his decomposing body feeding the maggots in someone's back yard. Someone – perhaps to avoid being blackmailed – had murdered him.'

She stared at him, open-mouthed, the colour seeping from her face. 'Murdered? You surely don't think that I . . . ?'

'Why not?' asked Frost. 'If I was in your position I would cheerfully have murdered the bastard, especially if I thought I could get away with it.'

She picked up the poker and began belabouring the coals on the fire as if it was Frost's skull she was smashing. 'I've told you what happened. I've nothing more to say. You have property of mine. I'd like it back.'

'All in good time, Mrs Roberts.' He studied her through narrowed eyes. A hefty woman, as strong as an ox. One blow from that poker would certainly make Lemmy's eyes water and she wouldn't have too much difficulty humping the body out to her car. But it might not have been so easy to carry Lemmy from her car to the coal bunker on her own. She might have needed help. Then what about her bottom-smacking chum in the mortar-board?

'I'd like you to give me the name and address of your gentleman friend in the photograph.'

'No!' She was firm on this. 'I'm not having him involved.'

Frost considered insisting, but decided against it. He thought about getting Forensic in to give the place a going over, but decided against that also. Too much time had gone by and, in any case, she wasn't denying that Lemmy had been here. Forensic had plenty of better things to do so he decided just to let her sweat for a while.

'What size television set have you got, Mrs Roberts?'

'Television set?' She stared at him as if he was mad. 'I haven't got a television set. I wouldn't have one in the house.'

'Then you won't mind if my colleague takes a look.' Frost nodded to Burton, who left the room. He stood up. 'I'll want you to go down to the station some time today and give us a full statement about the robbery and the blackmail attempt.'

She coloured a deep crimson and pulverized another piece of coal with the poker. 'A statement? Is that really necessary?'

'You needn't be specific – some of our young officers are easily shocked. You can just refer to a letter and certain activities it mentions you would prefer were not made public.'

Burton returned, shaking his head. No TV set of any size in the house. They showed themselves out, leaving her looking decidedly uneasy.

At the station Mullett was flapping about in a state of high agitation awaiting their return. He grabbed Frost and hustled him into his office. 'Well?'

'She could be involved,' said Frost. 'But I haven't got any hard evidence, yet.' He filled Mullett in on the details.

'There were other compromising letters and photographs – have you checked to see if those people were being blackmailed by Hoxton?'

'It's on my long list of things to do,' replied Frost, who hadn't got round to thinking of that aspect.

'The sooner we can clear Mrs Roberts . . .'

'As I am sure you would wish, sir, clearing Mrs Roberts is right at the bottom of my list of priorities,' said Frost.

'Of course, of course. The letter and the photograph – you didn't tell her I'd seen them?'

'She never asked.'

'Good.' Mullett dabbed at his brow with his handkerchief. 'It would be very embarrassing if she thought I knew.' He rearranged the blotter on his desk to show he was changing the subject. 'What's the procedure for the ransom handover tonight?'

'We've got all the public telephone kiosks in the

shopping mall bugged, so whichever one the kidnapper calls we'll be able to hear everything he says. I've also arranged for a homing device to be slipped inside the suitcase with the money.'

'How did you manage that?'

'Remember Tommy Dunn – used to be with us in CID?'

Mullett pulled a face. He did indeed remember Dunn, an inefficient officer with a drink problem and the strongest of hints that he took irregular payments. Dunn had been arrested on a charge of driving while well over the limit, but Mullett had managed to get the charge dropped in exchange for Dunn's resignation. A pity, he thought wistfully, he couldn't do something similar with Frost. He also recalled that Dunn was one of the investigating officers four years ago when Cassidy's daughter was killed and there were vague whispers he was bribed by the hit and run driver. 'I remember Dunn. What about him?'

'Tommy works for Savalot as a security guard. He's going to slip the homing device in the suitcase for us.'

'Why should he do that? He owes us no favours.'

'He's doing it for three bottles of Johnnie Walker and the cancellation of a couple of parking tickets.' It was six parking tickets actually, but he wasn't telling the superintendent this.

'I don't want to know,' said Mullett hurriedly.

'I'll bung the cost of the whisky on my petrol expenses,' said Frost blithely, 'so don't query it if it looks a bit high.' He was also going to sneak in the cost of petrol bought while he was on holiday which would make it higher still.

Mullett flapped a hand. 'Spare me the details. I'm not happy that Dunn is involved in this, Frost. You can't rely on him.'

'He's all we've got,' said Frost. But he shared Mullett's concern. Tommy had sounded half cut when he agreed to do it.

'So,' continued Mullett, 'if things go as you hope and Dunn runs contrary to past form, we will have a homing device hidden in the ransom money?'

'Yes. We'll be able to track Cordwell to the handover point and then keep tabs on the kidnapper after he's picked it up.'

'What about his claim he can monitor police radios?'

'I don't believe him, but just in case he does we'll be scrambling all our radio messages.'

'The safety of the boy is paramount,' insisted Mullett.

'We won't make a move until we know where he is and are assured he's safe.'

Mullett scratched his chin thoughtfully. It sounded foolproof, but when Frost organized things, nothing was foolproof. 'Well, I'll leave the details to you,' he said, so he could deny any knowledge of them should things blow up in their faces. 'The only stipulation I make is that things must not go wrong.'

'That's a bloody good stipulation!' said Frost in mock admiration as he walked to the door. 'I'll bear it in mind.'

While Mullett was trying to determine if there was a tinge of sarcasm in this, he heard an indignant squeal from Miss Smith, his secretary, then a cry of 'How's that for centre?' and a guffaw from Frost. He shook his head sadly. How could you work with a man like that? He looked up in sympathy at the scarlet face of Miss Smith as she burst in to complain.

Liz was waiting in his office and pushed a pile of reports over to him. Without looking at them, he pushed them back. 'Just tell me what they say, love. My lips get tired when I read.'

She took them and gave him a précis of each. 'I saw Mark Grover in hospital and broke the news of his wife's death.'

'Shit!' said Frost. 'I should have done that. Sorry to dump it on you, love – how did he take it?'

'He took it very well. He said it served the cow right.'

'You didn't tell him we suspect it was murder?'

'No. I just said it looked as if she had fallen in front of a train. He told me she had kept threatening to kill herself – the doctor had prescribed her pills for depression.'

'They don't seem to have worked all that bloody well,' sniffed Frost. 'I'll check it out with her doctor.' He scribbled a reminder on his pad. 'What else?'

'You told me to take his clothes to the lab. They're still doing tests, but if there's any blood, they haven't found it yet.'

'Did you ask him about the row the neighbours heard?'

'He says it wasn't him. He never left the store until nearly two o'clock. I've spoken to his workmate who again confirms this. Then I checked with the security man at the store. No-one can get in or out until he operates the electronic locking system and he's definite that he didn't operate it at all that night. And just in case you might still have doubts, I contacted their boss at the shopfitting firm. He phoned at twenty past midnight to find out how the job was going and Mark Grover answered the phone.'

Frost chewed this over. There was not a lot of support for his theory that Grover killed his wife. But he was only giving Liz half his attention. His mind was still on the ransom handover. He didn't want another of his usual cock-ups on this one.

'Which means,' Liz continued, 'that we can concentrate on our number one suspect Sidney Snell, who seems to have done a runner.'

'I just can't see Sidney killing anyone,' said Frost. 'The mother was killed in a frenzied attack. Sidney might stamp his foot and say "knickers" but he wouldn't get into a frenzy.'

'Three children, all in one room – that could have worked him up to a sexual state where he'd do anything.'

'A bit of bare thigh does the same for me,' sighed Frost. He saw there was more to come.

'We've got a key witness. An old boy walking his dog who swears he saw someone running from the house and driving off in a blue car.'

Frost's head jerked up. 'What time was this?'

'About ten minutes before two o'clock.'

'In the morning? What was the silly sod doing walking his dog at that time?'

'He used to be on shift work before he retired and old habits die hard.'

Frost tugged the man's statement towards him and read it. The old boy seemed pretty definite as to what he saw. 'He's sure the man he saw came out of the Grovers' house?'

'He's positive . . . And to back it up, Mark Grover says that when he came home last night the front door was wide open.'

Frost dug in his pocket and found a half-smoked cigarette hidden in the lining that had been there a long time. It was stale, but better than nothing. He lit up. 'And what colour is Snell's car?'

'Dark blue,' replied Liz.

He sucked in smoke and coughed, shaking ash all over a memo from Mullett complaining about the inadequacy of his daily call reports. 'Could be a clue there, somewhere.' He heaved himself up and snatched his scarf from the hat-stand. Something was nagging away at him, something just out of reach, something he knew he should have picked up, but the more he tried to remember, the more it crept back to cower in the dark, inaccessible recesses of his mind. He had to get out of the office and think. 'I'm off to see her doctor. Let's find out if he agrees with the husband about her suicidal tendencies.'

The waiting room was crowded, people hunched up coughing, snuffling and groaning in counterpoint to children running around, screaming unchecked. If you weren't ill when you went in, you certainly would be after a few minutes of this.

The receptionist was flustered. Patients were annoyed with her because the doctor was running late, the phone was ringing nonstop, and this scruffy man, claiming to be a detective, wanted to nip in in front of people who had been waiting for nearly an hour. 'I don't know when he will be able to see you. We're very, very busy,' she said.

'That makes two of us,' said Frost.

She looked up as a patient emerged from the surgery clutching a prescription form and was about to ask the next patient to go in when this scruffy man scooted in before the surgery door closed and before she could warn the doctor.

'I thought I was next,' said one of the women indignantly. 'I'm writing to the General Medical Council about this.'

The doctor, a plump young man in his early thirties, was at his desk, scribbling something in a register. He didn't look up as Frost entered. 'Please sit down, Mrs Jenkins. What's the trouble?'

'The sex change operation didn't work,' said Frost, sitting as requested.

The doctor looked up startled. 'I thought—'

'I'm not a patient,' said Frost, sliding a warrant card across. 'Police.'

The doctor stared at the warrant card as if Frost had just dumped a hand grenade with the pin removed on his desk. 'Look, officer. I think my solicitor had better be present. I never touched that girl. She stripped to the waist, I gave her a normal examination. I know she was only fifteen—'

'Hold it,' interrupted Frost. 'This is nothing to do with that . . . I wish it were, it sounds quite juicy. I'm enquiring about another patient of yours – Mrs Nancy Grover, Cresswell Street.'

In his relief, the doctor couldn't have been more helpful. He dragged a file from his filing cabinet and opened it up. 'Yes – those poor children. I had no idea she would do anything like that.'

'What were you treating her for?'

'Depression – paranoia. She imagined people were following her everywhere she went, watching her, staring at her through the windows of her bungalow at night when her husband wasn't there.'

'And the bastard rarely was there, was he? Shouldn't she have had specialized help?'

'Yes. I wanted to send her to a consultant psychiatrist, but she wouldn't go. I prescribed tranquillizers, but I don't think she took them.'

'You say she was imagining she was being watched . . . that a man was looking through her window. Could this really have happened?'

'It's possible. It's difficult to be certain with patients like her. They are convinced that things that only happen in their own minds are actually occurring. She was so upset because her husband didn't believe her.'

'What do you think brought it all on?'

The doctor gave a sad smile. 'Three children, another on the way. A husband who worked most of the day and was then out drinking most of the night. No relatives or close friends she could confide in. It was all getting too much for her.'

Frost stared at the desk in silence. He felt so sorry for the poor cow. He stood up. 'Thanks, doc.'

Angry faces sped him on his way out of the waiting-room. Outside in the darkened street, the first heavy drops of rain were splattering the pavement.

'Penny for the guy, mister?'

He froze. The small boy standing in front of him with his palm outstretched, a misshapen Guy Fawkes propped up in a pushchair at his side, was the spitting image of Bobby Kirby. But it wasn't Bobby, of course.

'You didn't ought to be out,' said Frost.

'You tight-fisted old sod,' said the boy, trundling off with the pushchair.

Frost watched him go and wondered if parents should be warned of the dangers. He'd have a word with Mullett when he got back.

As he turned the key in the ignition and his engine tried to cough itself into life, the radio called him. Burton sounding excited. At first Frost couldn't take in what he was saying, his mind was still on that poor woman and her kids, terrified because someone had been staring in the house. Her husband didn't believe her and had left her all alone. Could the face at the window, the face that everyone thought was only in her mind, have been the face of Sidney Snell? He shuddered, then realized Burton was still talking.

'Sorry, son – I didn't catch that.'

Burton told him again, slowly and clearly as if the poor old sod was going deaf. This time Frost was able to share the DC's delight. The first stroke of luck they had had in the Lemmy Hoxton case.

The television set bought posthumously with Lemmy's credit card had been registered for the guarantee.

They had a name and address.

11

'He registered the guarantee!' said Burton triumphantly. 'Douglas Cooper, 2a Merchant Street, Denton. And he's got form.' He handed the inspector a photostat of the form sheet.

Frost didn't need to read it. 'I know Duggie Cooper, son. I've nicked him a couple of times . . . breaking and entering, handling stolen goods, obtaining money under false pretences.'

He looked at his watch. Ten past two. He shook his wrist with annoyance. He must have forgotten to wind the damn thing last night. 'Have we got time to give Duggie a tug before the ransom caper?'

Burton checked his own watch. Six thirty-five. The ransom call was due to be made at eight. 'Not really,' he said.

'Let's do it anyway,' said Frost.

Merchant Street, a narrow side road to the north of Denton, was jam-packed with parked cars, most of them without a current tax disc. Burton had to double park at the end of the street and they walked back to the house. A dark grey Ford transit van stood outside Duggie's house and this reminded Frost that he should get someone to keep an eye on the boyfriend of Tracey Neal with the light brown van.

Cooper answered their ring. A thin-faced, shifty-eyed man in his late thirties, he had a little toothbrush moustache with dark, greasy hair brushed straight back. His face fell when he saw who his visitors were. 'Mr Frost!'

'Just passing,' said Frost. 'Knew you'd never forgive

us if we didn't drop in and say hello.' He pushed past Cooper and went straight into the lounge. There it was, in the corner, gleaming and dominating the room, a large screen Panasonic television set. Frost plonked himself down on the settee and pulled out his cigarettes.

Cooper hurried in after them looking very agitated. 'What do you want, Mr Frost?'

Frost tutted reproachfully. 'Since when do friends have to have a reason for calling on each other?'

'I ain't done nothing,' said Cooper.

Frost cupped a hand to his ear as if he had difficulty in hearing what Cooper was saying. 'You give us permission to search your house, did you say? That's damn decent of you, Duggie. It saves all that sodding about getting a warrant.' He nodded to Burton, who scuttled up the stairs before Cooper could stop him.

A woman bounded into the room. Duggie's wife Jean hadn't started out as a redhead and the various colour changes she had gone through before reaching her present shade had left their mark on the final result. 'There's a bloke going up our stairs,' she shouted, stopping abruptly in mid-protest when she saw Frost. She screwed up her face in annoyance. 'Oh no – just what we bloody need!' Hand on hips, she glowered at her husband, then spun back to Frost. 'Don't try and tell me he's done something, because he never does damn all. He sits on his arse in the house all day and never does a bloody stroke.' The thudding of Burton's feet across the ceiling made her look up. 'What's he looking for? There's nothing in the house that shouldn't be here . . .' And then she saw the expression on Duggie's face. 'At least, there bloody well had better not be!'

'Nice telly,' said Frost, nodding at the set in the corner. 'Must have cost a bomb.'

'It's all legitimate,' she snapped. 'We've got the receipt.' She darted across to the sideboard and pulled open a drawer. 'It's in here . . .'

Duggie sprang across and pushed the drawer shut. 'No, it isn't,' he said.

She frowned. 'What are you talking about? I saw it there this morning.'

'No, you didn't,' he hissed. 'I lost it . . . weeks ago.'

'But I saw . . .' And then the penny dropped. With an icy glare at her husband which said, I'll sort this out with you later, she turned to Frost, smiling sweetly. 'Duggie's right. We lost it.'

'Then it's lucky I called in,' said Frost. 'Because I've got a copy of the receipt here.' Humming to himself, he unfolded the photostat and pretended to check the details. 'Panasonic . . . Model No. TXT2228 . . . serial number . . . call out the serial number, would you, Duggie – it's on the back.'

He waited as Duggie moved the heavy set with difficulty and read it out. 'TXT2822311Y.'

'Check,' beamed Frost, folding the receipt and returning it to his inside jacket pocket. He stood up. 'Sorry I troubled you, Lemmy . . .' He frowned. 'Why did I call you Lemmy? Your name isn't Lemmy . . . I must be going bloody mad.' He took the receipt from his pocket again as if to check the name.

'All right, all right,' said Duggie. 'It was bought with Lemmy Hoxton's credit card. He owes me, so he let me use it.' He fumbled for a cigarette and lit up with a none too steady hand.

'Ah,' said Frost, sitting down again. 'I knew there was a rational explanation. When did he give you his card?'

'The same day I bought the telly.'

'You bought the telly and gave the card back to him?'

'Of course.'

'What deodorant does Lemmy use?' asked Frost.

'Eh?' frowned Duggie. 'What's that got to do with it?'

'It must be bloody strong stuff, because the day he lent you the card Lemmy would have been stinking the place out – he'd been dead for two months.'

'Dead?' Duggie's mouth gaped open, the lighted cigarette dangling from his lower lip.

Frost nodded cheerfully. 'Dead – the way Domestos kills ninety-nine per cent of known germs. You killed him and took his credit card.'

'Killed him?' echoed Duggie, his face now a chalky white.

'Him? Kill Lemmy?' screeched his wife. 'Don't make me laugh. He wouldn't kill a bloody fly.'

'A bloody fly hasn't got a credit card, has it?' asked Frost. He looked up as Burton returned carrying a drawer from a dressing-table.

'Found this upstairs,' said Burton. It was crammed with cheap jewellery, silver-plated photo frames, trinket boxes, tawdry stuff, most of which Frost recognized from the list of articles stolen by the phoney Water Board inspector.

'Dear, dear,' said Frost. 'I might have overlooked you murdering Lemmy, but stealing from old ladies . . . Douglas Cooper, I'm arresting you on suspicion of murder and robbery. Anything you say, etc. You know the rest off by heart.'

'I never damn well killed him,' cried Duggie.

'On being charged, the prisoner said, "It's a fair cop, guv'nor, you've got me to rights,"' chanted Frost. 'Come on, Duggie. We're off to the nick.'

Duggie's wife was boiling with rage. 'That bloody telly. You had to be clever and buy it. There was nothing wrong with the old one.'

'You said you wanted a big one,' answered Duggie, meekly.

'She didn't mean the telly,' said Frost, hustling him out. 'Come on – I'm running late.'

There was a sour, stale smell in the interview room. Someone had been sick in it recently and the lingering aroma was proving its superiority over the cheap pine disinfectant used to swab it out.

Burton fed a cassette into the recorder and announced who was present while Frost lowered himself carefully into the chair opposite Duggie.

'Right, Duggie,' said Frost. 'Time to make a clean breast of all your naughtiness. We found a quantity of items believed to be stolen in your house today. Would you like to tell us about them?'

'No comment,' said Duggie.

'We also found a television set known to have been purchased with Lemmy Hoxton's credit card some two months after his death. Would you like to tell us about that?'

'No comment,' said Duggie.

'Are you going to say "No comment" to everything I ask you?'

'No comment,' repeated Duggie, stubbornly.

'Switch the bleeding tape off,' said Frost. 'Interview terminated at whatever time it is.' He rammed a cigarette in his mouth. 'You're a prat, Duggie. We don't need your statement. I've got enough evidence to convict you without it. I don't think you killed Lemmy – you haven't got the bottle – but I need an arrest and you are tailor made. As long as I get a conviction, I score the Brownie points and the fact that you didn't do it is neither here nor there.' He jerked a thumb at Burton. 'Take him back to his cell.'

He wandered back to his office where Liz Maud was working diligently through a pile of returns, too busy to look up. He sat at his desk, trying to work out where he was with the cases they were handling. The dead Dean Anderson was connected with the Bobby Kirby kidnapping and, hopefully, this would be resolved tonight when they nabbed the kidnapper picking up the ransom. A message on his desk from Newcastle police stated there was no sign of Snell back at his flat, but they were keeping a close watch. So that case was in abeyance until they found him. Another sheet of paper on his desk detailed the findings of the lab who had analysed the contents of Lemmy Hoxton's stomach and were able to report that Lemmy had died within two hours of consuming a meal consisting of salmon fish cakes, chips and peas, washed down with a carbonated Coke drink.

He interrupted Liz and told her to check with Lemmy's wife and see if she had served up such a meal to Lemmy, remarking, 'The fizzy drink sounds more like a meal she'd serve to her toy boy.' He thought about it and liked the sound of it. 'You know, that could be it. She had the meal all ready for her toy boy when Lemmy arrived home unexpectedly, so she has to pretend it was for him. After dinner, he spots the kid hiding behind the curtains, his dick dragging on the floor. There's a fight and they split his skull open.'

'Then why did they cut the top of his fingers off?' asked Liz.

'It could have happened during the fight,' said Frost lamely. He sighed. 'I don't know.' He pushed himself back from the desk, his chair scraping the brown lino with a teeth-setting squeal. 'All this talk of stomach contents is making me hungry. I'm off to the canteen.'

Arthur Hanlon spotted Frost in the canteen and waddled over carrying his tray of food. He sat down opposite him and dolloped sauce on his egg and chips. 'Everything laid on for tonight, Jack?'

'I hope so, Arthur. The phones are tapped and the suitcase should be bugged.'

'How many men will you need?'

'Don't confuse me with numbers, Arthur,' said Frost, forking a chip from Hanlon's plate. 'One man watching the phone booths, one keeping an eye on Cordwell and tailing his car in case the homing device conks out, two area cars on call, the SAS, the United States Cavalry . . . two or three hundred should do it at a pinch. How many can I have?'

'Twelve if you're lucky.'

'As long as one of them is Arnold Schwarzenegger, we should manage.' He dipped one of his own chips in Hanlon's egg, then had to leave when the tannoy called him to the phone. Duggie Cooper had decided to make a statement.

On his way down to the interview room he spotted Cassidy and Mullett in cosy conversation, both frowning and nodding curtly to him as he passed. Cassidy had handed the superintendent a wad of completed progress reports and Mullett was beaming all over his face. 'You haven't done them already, Cassidy!' he exclaimed delightedly. 'Good man!'

'You wanted them, so I did them,' said Cassidy.

Frost squinted at the returns. They were the ones he had seen Liz Maud filling in earlier. Liz had done the work and Cassidy was unashamedly taking the praise. The man hadn't changed since he was last in the division.

Duggie Cooper was already in the interview room, waiting for him. 'I hope you're not going to waste my time, Duggie,' grunted Frost, settling down wearily in the same uncomfortable chair. 'I've got important things to do . . . I can always frame you later.'

'Look, Mr Frost. I didn't kill Lemmy. I'll cough for a few bits of nicking if it makes you happy, but I haven't killed anyone.'

Frost signalled for Burton to bung in a tape. 'You're on the air, Duggie, so sing.'

'Me and Lemmy Hoxton were working together. He was the brains. He had this idea about conning our way into people's houses, and while they were busy downstairs, nicking their stuff upstairs. Sometimes we got rubbish, but now and again we hit the jackpot.'

'So how did it work?' asked Frost.

'We'd pretend to be men from the Water Board. We'd case some likely places – mainly old dears living on their own – then one of us would put on overalls and pedal up to the house on an old bike. We had various scams. One was to turn the water off at the hydrant outside, then knock and say we'd had complaints about the water supply, and would they check their taps. So they'd do it and the tap would run dry. "Never mind," we'd say. "I'll fix it for you." We'd turn the hydrant back on again and give them another knock. "Try it now." And of course, now it works fine. "You watch the tap," we'd say, "and I'll go upstairs and flush the toilet. Let me know if it makes any difference to the flow." They were tickled pink to help. While we were upstairs, we'd nip in the bedroom for a quick rummage. You'd be surprised at the stuff people stow in their dressing-tables . . . some of them had hundreds of pounds in cash. Anyway, we'd stick the loot in our tool bag, toddle off downstairs, refuse the cup of tea the grateful old dear would offer and get the hell out of there on the bike. One of us would be waiting in the van. We'd stick the bike inside and rip off the overalls. If the cops are on the lookout, they're after a man on a bike in overalls, not two men in a van in suits.'

'Speed it up, Duggie,' said Frost. 'I want to get to the bit where you kill him.'

'I never killed him,' insisted Duggie, 'though the sod was swindling me left right and centre. Everything I found we'd split fifty-fifty. If Lemmy found anything good, he'd pocket it and say there was nothing there.'

'You should have complained to the police,' said Frost. 'That's what we're here for. All right, fast forward to the bit where you nick his credit card.'

'The last job we did together was back in August . . . 6th August I think. We had a few jobs lined up for that afternoon. The first was a cottage near Alderney Cross . . . two women living alone. Lemmy reckoned it was ideal . . . remote and looked as if there would be rich pickings. Before the job we had lunch in a pub.'

'What pub?'

'Forget its name – little country pub just off the main road.'

'What did you have to eat?'

'Bloody hell, Mr Frost, this was months ago. I can't even remember what I had for dinner last night.'

'Did Lemmy have anything to drink in the pub?'

'Nothing alcoholic. We made a point of it . . . these old dears get suspicious of workmen with beery breaths. We stuck to soft drinks.'

Frost exchanged glances with Burton. This tied in with the analysis of the stomach contents. 'Then what?'

'I parked down a side lane. Lemmy changed into his overalls and pedalled off. I read the paper, smoked a fag and waited . . . and bloody waited. He never came back. I waited over an hour then thought, bloody hell, he's been nicked, so I roared off back home and sat indoors in fear and bloody trembling expecting the Old Bill to knock any minute. But nothing. Nor the next day. I phoned his house, but his old lady said he'd gone away for a few days and she didn't know when he was coming back.'

'And . . . ?' asked Frost.

'That's it. I never saw him again.'

'You must have seen him to nick his credit card.'

'His suit jacket was in the van. He'd gone off in his overalls. I stuck the jacket in my wardrobe for when he came back, but he never did.'

'What did you think had happened to him?'

'I reckoned he'd probably struck bloody gold at the cottage he did over that day.'

'What do you mean by that?'

'I reckoned he'd found the old girl's life savings in the bedroom – a few thousand quid – and decided he wasn't going to share it, so he did a runner. So I thought to myself, "You lousy bastard, Lemmy," and I took the wallet from his jacket, helped myself to the few quid in it and bought myself a telly with his credit card.'

'You didn't buy anything else with it?'

'I wasn't going to push my luck any more. I chucked it away after that.'

Frost leant back and puffed a salvo of smoke rings up to the ceiling. 'Not a bad story, Duggie, but I prefer my version . . . that you quarrelled over the split-up of the loot and you killed him.'

'On my life, Mr Frost . . .'

'What was the address of that cottage he was going to do?'

'It was called Primrose Cottage – you can't miss it, it was painted yellow like custard.'

Frost flipped open his burglary file and checked. No-one had reported a robbery or an attempted robbery at that address. He snapped the file shut. 'I don't believe a word you've said, Duggie, but you know me – heart of gold – so I'll tell you what I'm going to do and you can abase yourself in gratitude later. I'll try and check out your story. But first, I want you to put your hand up to all the jobs you and Lemmy did – all of them.'

'Right, Mr Frost.' Duggie couldn't pour out the details quickly enough. 'First there was—'

Frost quickly restrained him. 'No – not to me, Duggie, I haven't got time. Hold on a minute . . .' He was out of his seat and looking up and down the passage. The unlucky passer-by was Arthur Hanlon.

'Congratulations, Arthur,' called Frost, grabbing him by the arm. 'You've just solved a whole batch of burglaries . . . Mr Mullett will pee himself with pleasure when you tell him.'

'Eh?' said Hanlon as Frost steered him into the interview room.

'You know how I hate paper work, Arthur. You can have all the credit and be Mr Mullett's blue-eyed boy.' He jabbed a finger at the prisoner. 'OK, Duggie – cough!'

PC Collier, wearing plain clothes, drove slowly to the end of the road where he parked silently and switched off the lights. Rain was bucketing down and visibility was limited, but the floodlit drive to Sir Richard Cordwell's front door made it easy to keep tabs on what was going on. As soon as Cordwell drove out, he would radio to let Frost know, then, at a discreet distance, follow.

In the crowded shopping mall leading to the Savalot supermarket, Burton jostled his way to a wooden bench that gave him an unrestricted view of the clump of four public telephone boxes. Syrupy music oozed from overhead speakers, interrupted from time to time by a chirpy voice advising shoppers of the latest bargains to be had in the store. The four kiosks all had 'Out Of Order' notices on their doors and the phones had been fixed so no outgoing calls could be made. This had been done by Cordwell's security officers to ensure the phones were not being used by the public when the kidnapper tried to make contact.

Burton eased the radio from the inside pocket of his jacket and made a call to the incident room to test that the scrambler was working as it should.

'I can hear you, and that bloody music, loud and clear,' Frost told him. He checked his watch. Coming up to a quarter to eight. Cordwell should be leaving the house any second.

'Can I have a word, inspector?'

Hopalong flaming Cassidy! And the edge to his voice meant he was going to have a moan about something. 'What is it, my son?'

'I'm not your son, I'm an inspector, if you don't mind,' corrected Cassidy. 'Could we go outside?'

'Call me if anything happens,' said Frost to Lambert as he followed Cassidy out to the corridor. 'So how can I help you, inspector?' He kept his eye on the door, ready to dash back any minute.

'You can help me by letting me handle my own cases,' snapped Cassidy. 'Lemmy Hoxton. Am I handling it or not!'

Oh shit! thought Frost. He's found out about Duggie Cooper, and I never told him about Mullett's mate, Mrs Roberts. 'Do you mean Cooper?'

'Yes, I damn well do. Not only have you questioned him without bringing me in on it, you've let that fat sergeant take all the credit for clearing up the robberies.'

'Sorry, son,' said Frost, 'but I knew you wouldn't want to take the credit for things you weren't entitled to.' Cassidy's eyes flickered at the shaft. 'Anyway, it's your case from now on.' Cassidy still wasn't satisfied and was ready with the next moan, but Frost was spared this by the door opening. 'Radio message, inspector,' called Lambert.

He dashed back inside. PC Collier was on the radio reporting that Cordwell had left the house.

'Which car was he in?' asked Frost, hoping it wasn't the inconspicuous pearl grey Rolls-Royce with the peronalized number plate. They'd have half of Fleet Street following if it was.

'It's a dark green Nissan,' reported Collier. He gave the registration number. 'Shall I follow?'

'Yes, but keep well back. We know he's coming to the store, so you needn't hug his tail. Once he's in the store, park in a side street off the Market Square. We'll contact you when he comes out.' He radioed through to Burton to let him know Cordwell was on his way. 'Should be with you in five minutes.'

'Right,' acknowledged Burton.

Frost was lighting up when Liz came in. 'We've located the pub where Cooper says he and Lemmy went to. It's the Green Dragon. They serve pub lunches. The menu changes every day, but every Friday it's salmon fish cakes, and 6th August was a Friday.'

'I used to like salmon fish cakes,' said Frost, 'but not since I saw them swimming around inside Lemmy's stomach. Funny how little things like that can put you off.' He spun his chair round as the radio speaker crackled, but it was only static. 'Did you check out Custard Cottage?'

'Primrose Cottage. Two sisters, one around forty, the other in her mid-thirties. I haven't spoken to them yet, though.'

'Good. We'll do it together – tomorrow morning. Remind me.' His smile died when he saw Bill Wells making his way over to him. The sergeant's face shouted 'Trouble.' Something had gone wrong.

'Were you going to get Tommy Dunn to plant that homing device, Jack?' Wells asked.

'Yes – why?'

'I wouldn't count on him doing it.'

'Why not?' asked Frost, very concerned.

'Tommy's got himself arrested.'

Frost's stomach screwed into a tight ball. 'Arrested?'

'PC Simms is bringing him in. He was caught nicking two bottles of whisky from Savalot's liquor store.'

Frost stared at Wells, hoping and praying he had misheard. 'Stealing?'

'Savalot want him charged. And they want his flat searched. They think he's been making a habit of taking their stock home and they'd like some of it back.'

Frost stared at the ceiling and swore softly. 'Bloody, bloody hell.' He punched his palm with his fist and thought quickly. 'All right – change of plan. Tell all cars engaged in the exercise that due to circumstances beyond our bleeding control, we won't have the homing signal, so it's vital we don't lose track of Cordwell's car. Circulate the description and registration number to all mobiles. If they sight it, let me know. And tell all mobiles not in the exercise to stand by. We might have to call them in as well if we lose him.' He groaned audibly as Mullett marched in. 'Oh no!' The bleeding vultures were descending.

'What's this I'm hearing about Tommy Dunn, Frost?'

He obviously knew all about it, so Frost was terse.

'He's been arrested for theft. We won't have the homing device.'

Mullett's eyes glinted and he smirked in self-justification. 'I warned you about using rubbish like him, but you wouldn't listen and now you must pay the consequences. Can we still go ahead with this without alerting the kidnapper? If that child is harmed because of your incompetence—'

'We can still do it. What I've done is—'

Mullett's hand shot up. He didn't want the details. Hearing them could imply his seal of approval and this would only be forthcoming if everything went off without a hitch. 'Just make sure nothing goes wrong.'

He turned on his heel and marched to the door, spurred on his way with a V sign, behind his back, from Frost who then tapped his desk to get everyone's attention. 'Just thought you'd like to know that Mr Mullett is one hundred per cent behind us, providing we pull it off. But if we fail then God help us!' He drummed his fingers impatiently and looked pleadingly at the speaker, waiting for the next radio report.

'Subject car in car-park,' radioed Collier. 'Cordwell getting out and entering the mall by the side entrance.'

A few minutes later Burton called in. 'I have Cordwell in sight. He is waiting outside the four phone kiosks.'

'Check the phone bugging devices again,' called Frost. If they were going to go wrong, then now was the time.

The officer with the earphones did a quick check and gave the thumbs-up signal. 'All working perfectly.'

'Right.' Frost kept the radio channel to Burton open. They could hear the bustle of shoppers in the mall. The Musak had stopped, no doubt by Cordwell's orders so he could hear the phone ringing. The wall clock in the incident room clunked away another minute. The kidnapper was already five minutes late.

'I don't think he's going to phone,' said Liz.

'Don't be a bloody pessimist,' said Frost. 'He's probably in the middle of a long wee-wee. You don't pick up ransom money with a full bladder.' Still only crowd noises from the monitor speaker.

Burton's voice suddenly made everyone sit up. But it was only to report that nothing was happening.

'For Pete's flaming sake!' yelled Frost. He hated people reporting there was nothing to report.

Cassidy came in and stood behind Frost. 'What's happening?'

'Sod all,' grunted Frost.

'Did I understand you were going to use Tommy Dunn?' Cassidy asked.

'Yes,' said Frost.

'I'd like to talk to you about it,' hissed Cassidy.

'Some other bloody time,' snarled Frost. Cassidy was really getting on his nerves tonight. He was relieved when the acting inspector left the room.

Twenty past eight.

'Are you sure the bloody phones in the kiosks are working?' asked Frost. 'What if Savalot's security men accidentally cut off incoming calls when they cut off the outgoing?'

'You could always try ringing one,' suggested Liz.

Frost dragged a phone towards him and dialled.

A yell over the speaker from Burton. 'Cordwell's moving towards a kiosk. The phone's ringing.'

Frost hastily banged the receiver down. 'I know – it was me. Just testing.' This is turning into a flaming farce, he told himself.

Almost immediately Burton was back on the radio. 'Something's happening. A manager from Savalot is running towards Cordwell . . . talking to him. Cordwell's leaving the kiosks. They're both running back towards the store.'

'Follow him,' hissed Frost. 'Don't let the sod out of your sight.'

Lots of rustling and roars from the radio as Burton barged his way through the crowd. 'Lost him . . . no, I see him. He's going to the Customer Service Desk. He's picking up their phone . . . I can't get too near, he'll spot me . . . He's listening. He's put the phone down . . . Now he's going through a Staff Only door. Do I follow?'

'No!' snapped Frost. 'He's probably gone to get the money. Has he got to come past you again to get to his car?'

'I don't know.'

Frost's mind raced. 'Right – get down to the car-park. Locate his car and let me know when he leaves.' He clicked to Collier. 'Collier, go to the car-park exit and get ready to follow when he leaves . . . All other units, stand by.'

'What's happening?' Sensing that something was going wrong and anxious to witness Frost's discomfiture when it did, Cassidy had returned.

'The sod's put one over on us,' Frost told him. 'He never intended using the kiosks – must have guessed we'd bug them. He phoned direct to the store.'

'So what are you going to do?'

'I'm hoping we can follow without Cordwell or the kidnapper spotting us. We might have to anticipate where he's making for and try and get there before him. We play it by ear.'

Cassidy smirked to himself. It seemed as if this whole operation could blow up in Frost's face. He was pleased he had expressed his doubts to Mullett when his views were sought. 'I foresee trouble, sir,' he'd said. 'It's too slapdash.' And Mullett had nodded grimly in agreement.

A muffled roar and some fragments of speech, totally incomprehensible, from the loudspeaker. 'Say again,' yelled Frost. 'Say again.' More gibberish. 'What's going on?'

PC Lambert jiggled some switches. 'It's the underground car-park – the radio can't work down there.'

'Tell him to move outside,' said Frost.

Lambert spoke into the mike then shook his head. 'It's no use. We can't hear him and he can't hear us.'

Frost snatched up his radio. 'Collier. Cordwell should be coming out any second. Get ready to follow.'

'Burton to Control – receiving? Over.'

A collective sigh of relief. Burton had moved to an area of better reception. 'Cordwell has put a canvas travel bag on the front seat of his car. He's got a couple of his security men with him, so it must be the money. He's getting in the car . . .'

'On his own or with the security men?'

'On his own . . . He's driving out now.'

Frost clicked on the other radio. 'Did you hear that, Collier?'

'Yes . . . I see him . . . I'm following.'

'Don't get too close,' pleaded Frost, 'but for God's sake, don't lose him.'

'I'll try.'

'Collier's not up to it,' said Cassidy.

'Neither am I,' said Frost, 'but we've got to use what we've got.' He could murder Tommy bloody Dunn. He'd been pinning all his hopes on being able to sit back and follow the homing device.

'Subject turning into Bath Road,' reported Collier.

Frost glanced across to Lambert who was marking up a map. Too soon yet to work out where Cordwell was making for.

'He's turning left . . . he's slowing down . . . I'm not sure, but I think he's spotted me.'

'Drive straight past him,' ordered Frost. 'Don't look at him as you do.' He ran across to consult Lambert's map. 'He can't turn off until he reaches Hilton Road, so go and wait for him there. Tell me when he passes you.'

He lit a cigarette before noticing he already had one smouldering away in the ashtray. He called Burton and told him to get ready to take over the tail from Collier.

The monitor speaker hummed softly to itself, now and again giving a little crackle as if it was going to speak, but nothing. Impatiently Frost snatched up the radio and jabbed the transmit button. 'He should have bloody reached you by now, Collier.'

'But he hasn't. I'm looking straight down the Bath Road . . . visibility's a bit hairy in this rain, but I should be able to see him. There's a couple of lorries, but that's all.'

'Damn!' Frost scrubbed his face with his hands, trying to work out what had happened. 'The bastard must have done a U turn. Collier – drive back. If you see him, swing round and follow . . . report to me when you reach where you last saw him.'

He stood up and paced around the room, swinging round abruptly as Collier's voice came over the radio.

'I've gone right back to the Bath Road turn-off. No sign of him.'

'Shit!' Frost pounded the desk in frustration. 'All units . . . you heard that. Look for the bugger . . . Report as soon as you get a sniff of him.'

The door clicked open and Mullett marched in. He had a genius for turning up at precisely the wrong time. 'How's it going?'

'The inspector seems to have lost him,' said Cassidy, barely concealing his delight, just as Frost was about to lie and say all was going to plan.

Mullett's face hardened. 'Is this correct?'

'Temporary set-back,' Frost assured. 'We'll find him.'

'You'd better,' snapped Mullett. 'You'd damn well better.' He marched out.

'He's got a foul tongue, hasn't he?' observed Frost. He suddenly felt he couldn't bear to be cooped up in the claustrophobic incident room any longer, just listening and not being a part of things. He grabbed his scarf. 'I'm going to join in the hunt. The more cars looking for him, the better.' He looked at Cassidy. 'Want to come?' He only asked because he was sure the acting inspector intended coming anyway.

Cassidy hesitated. If it all went wrong he wanted no part of it, but if Frost was successful, if he arrested the kidnapper and got the boy back, then Cassidy wanted to be there to share the glory. The thought of glory won. He snatched up his coat and followed Frost out.

They dashed, bent double through rain, to the Ford. Frost slipped behind the steering wheel and persuaded the engine to start at the third attempt. The car splashed through deep puddles as he manoeuvred out of the car-park.

'Where are we going?' asked Cassidy.

'I'm heading towards Denton Woods. If I was arranging a cash hand-over, that's where I'd choose.'

'That area is bloody big,' said Cassidy.

'So's my dick,' grunted Frost, 'but I usually manage to find the bit I want.' He radioed through to Lambert to ascertain the current position of all mobiles. Lambert reported straight back. As many cars as possible were scouring the town, but there were too many roads which Cordwell could have used and not enough vehicles to cover them. Again Frost cursed Tommy Dunn. With the homing device it would have been a doddle; without it they were flying blind in the thickest of fogs. Sod Tommy bloody Dunn.

'Tommy Dunn.' A voice sliced through his thoughts as if it could read his mind.

'Eh?' Frost's head swivelled round. Cassidy was staring hard at him, waiting for an answer. 'Sorry, son, I was miles away.'

'I'm not your damn son and I asked you for Tommy Dunn's address.'

'I don't know it,' muttered Frost, squinting through the windscreen at an approaching car that could have been green. But it wasn't.

'You're a bloody liar,' said Cassidy.

Frost didn't reply. Yes, he was lying. He knew Tommy's address but he wasn't going to let Cassidy go round there stirring everything up again. 'It happened a long time ago, son. Let the wounds heal.'

'You and Tommy made a great team, didn't you? One damned incompetent and the other always on the take.'

'I did my best to find the hit and run driver, son. We all did. We worked bloody hard, but we failed.'

'I don't doubt you did your best, inspector, but your best is inadequate and bloody pathetic.' Frost shrugged. Cassidy had idolized his daughter and his bitterness at the failure of the investigation, even after all these years, was understandable, if not excusable.

'That bastard hit my daughter at speed, and roared off without bothering to see if she was alive or dead. She was smashed to pieces. Fourteen years old. She hadn't lived. She hadn't bloody lived!'

'I know son. I know.'

'You know much more than you're damn well saying.'

'What do you mean?'

'You let me down four years ago, so I've been making my own enquiries. I've found a witness.'

'Oh?' A green car roared past them, but it was a hand-painted VW Beetle.

'He was in the car-park at the Coconut Grove when he saw this car speeding past. Then he heard it pumping its horn, and the smash as it hit my daughter.'

'He didn't actually see the accident?'

'No. He went running out to the road and there was a crowd of people and they were looking down at my daughter's body.'

'We know all this, son.' Frost would never forget that night . . . the flashing blue light of the ambulance reflected in the shiny pools of blood inside the chalked outline marked out by the traffic police. He had viewed the smashed and broken body in the morgue, the small fourteen-year-old body that had spilt so much blood on the road. He had tried to stop Cassidy from seeing her until they had tidied her up, but had been pushed aside . . . The memory of the man's grief and anger still hurt, a mental wound that would never heal. 'We know all this,' he repeated.

'Then here's something you apparently don't know. There was a BMW parked in the road outside the club. The driver was in it. Tommy Dunn was talking to him.'

'I've no knowledge of Tommy talking to anyone, son. If he had, there would have been a witness statement.'

'Depends on how much Tommy was paid to keep his mouth shut.'

Frost lit a cigarette. 'It depends on how reliable your witness is. Funny he never told anyone about this at the time.'

'He says he told you,' said Cassidy.

Frost slowed down. He was driving much too fast. 'He's mistaken.' Headlights of an approaching car dazzled the windscreen. A white Mercedes. 'Look, son, let's drop it for now. We're not concentrating on the job in hand.'

'I'd like to see the file on your investigation of Rebecca's death,' said Cassidy stubbornly.

'I'll dig it out and let you have it,' replied Frost. As soon as he got back to the station he would hide it where no-one could find it. There was no way he would let Cassidy see it. And he'd get Tommy Dunn to have a word with this mouthy witness. He knew who he was. He offered a cigarette to Cassidy which was curtly refused.

'What was Dunn doing at the Coconut Grove that night – collecting backhanders?'

'Checking on stolen credit cards,' said Frost, twisting his neck as another car sped past. 'I never realized there were so many damn green cars in Denton.' He sank back gloomily in his seat, squinting at the road ahead through the solid curtain of rain which his squealing windscreen wipers were making pathetic efforts to clear.

'Burton to Inspector Frost. I've found him. Back on the Bath Road, heading north. I'm following.'

'Exactly where on the Bath Road?' yelled Frost into the handset as he swung the car around, shooting up a shower of rainwater.

'Just passing Sandown Road.'

'Right – Frost to all mobiles. I want two of you to get ahead of him. Charlie Baker – you get to the motorway turn-off, and when he approaches, you take over from Burton. Charlie Abel – tail them both. If it looks as if he's spotted Charlie Baker, then you take over.' He began to whistle cheerfully. Action – this was more like it.

'Subject turning north into Forest Row,' reported Burton.

Frost nodded resignedly. It looked as if Cordwell was heading for Denton Woods where it would be bloody difficult to keep track of him once he left the car. It now needed lots more men than he had available. And yet again that evening he bitterly cursed Tommy Dunn for dropping him in it like this.

'He's slowing . . . he's slowing,' reported Burton. 'He's stopped.'

'Where?' yelled Frost. 'Just in case we might want to know.'

'Sorry. By the public call box, corner of Forest View. He's getting out of the car, making for the call box. He's waiting and checking his watch. The phone's ringing . . . he's answered it. Now he's hung up and he's dashing back to the Nissan.'

'It must be the final instructions for the drop,' said Frost. 'Don't lose him . . . we'll be with you soon.'

Burton braked. He was getting too close. A short way back he had lost sight of the Nissan and had jammed down on the accelerator only to have to slam on the brakes to avoid shooting up its backside. Luckily

Cordwell had other things on his mind and did not seem to notice.

The road wriggled into another sharp bend and again the rear lights of Cordwell's car slipped out of sight. Burton accelerated as much as he dared. The weather conditions were making the road surface treacherous. As he negotiated the bend, he cursed. The Nissan had stopped. Had Cordwell seen him? Was he, perhaps, checking to see if he was being followed? Burton drove straight past, avoiding turning his head as he passed, but at the very next bend, he slowed and bumped the car up on to the grass verge. Quickly, he stuffed the radio into the pocket of his raincoat, slung the night glasses round his neck and stepped out into torrential rain.

Running back towards the oak tree, he reported to Frost. 'He's stopped.'

'Where?' asked Frost.

'The big oak alongside Forest Common.'

'What's he doing now?'

Burton didn't know. He couldn't see a flaming thing. He couldn't even see the car. Cordwell had switched off the lights and the rain was making visibility very limited. 'Wait,' he panted, dropping the radio back in his pocket and getting out the night glasses.

He located the oak tree, then moved down to the car. It was empty. He panned the common. Bushes, trees . . . He'd lost him . . . he'd damn well lost him. He began swinging the glasses wildly from left to right, hoping to pick up something. What was that? Something white. He held the glasses steady on Cordwell in his white mac. Thank goodness it was a white raincoat otherwise he might never have spotted him. He adjusted the focus. Cordwell was carrying something. The money bag.

He became aware of squawkings from his pocket. The radio. Frost pleading for some news. He fished it out and reported breathlessly, 'Have subject in sight. Will report back.' He raised the night glasses again. Damn. Bushes, trees, but no sign of Cordwell. He panned quickly from left to right. Nothing. Where the hell was he? He almost shook with relief when he again picked up a blur of white. Cordwell emerging from a line of bushes and bramble. He was coming back . . . Returning to his car. Had he made the drop? At first Burton wasn't sure. Cordwell was at the wrong angle, but when he turned towards the oak, Burton could see that the supermarket chief no longer had the travel bag.

He pulled out the radio and brought the anxious Frost up to date. 'He's made the drop.'

A sigh of relief from Frost. 'Good boy. What's he doing now?'

The night glasses followed him. 'He's going back to his car.'

The sound of the Nissan's engine could just be heard over the drumming of the rain. 'He's reversing. He's heading back to Denton.'

Frost ducked his head as approaching headlights flared in the windscreen and Cordwell roared past them on his way back. He radioed Charlie Baker, the area car, to wait by Sandown Road and, as soon as Cordwell passed, to follow him at a discreet distance. 'If he goes anywhere but straight home, I want to know.' The kidnapper was such a wily bastard, all that had happened could have been a feint; the money could still be with Cordwell to be dumped elsewhere.

Looming ahead of them, creaking in the wind, was the large oak tree where Cordwell had parked. Frost slowed down, squinting through the windscreen for Burton's car. He spotted it just round the next bend and bumped up on the grass verge to park behind it. He and Cassidy climbed out and peered into rain and darkness. No sign of Burton. 'Where are you, son?' Frost whispered into his radio. Burton blinked his torch a few times and they homed in on his signal.

It was an uncomfortable walk in the dark over bumpy and puddle-ridden ground fighting against the wind and the rain, and it was making Cassidy's stomach hurt like hell. Was this why Frost had asked him along – to show up his damn weakness? If so, and he winced as a flame of pain rippled across his stomach, if so, Frost was going to be disappointed.

Burton was crouched behind the trunk of a stunted tree. Not much of a place to hide, but better than nothing. He pointed to a dark mass ahead and handed Frost the night glasses. 'The money is behind there somewhere.'

Frost shook off the rain and raised them to his eyes. 'I can't see a bleeding thing.'

Cassidy took the glasses. 'Those bushes?' he exclaimed. 'They're seventy yards away. Can't we get any closer?'

'It's all open ground,' said Burton. 'We'd be seen.'

'So where's the money?'

'Round the back somewhere,' Burton told him.

'Somewhere? Can't you be more precise?'

'I saw him go behind with the money and come back without it.'

'So it could be any of those flaming bushes and we're on the wrong side seventy yards away.'

Burton indicated the sprawling terrain. 'There's nowhere on the other side to hide. We'd be seen miles away.'

'What about those bushes there?' Cassidy pointed.

Frost gave them a glance, then shook his head. There was too much open ground between them. 'This is as good a place as any.'

The call light on the receiver flashed. Burton turned the volume down and listened. Charlie Baker reporting in. Cordwell had made one stop on the way back – at a phone box. As he approached it, it rang. He spoke briefly, then drove straight home.

'The kidnapper wanting confirmation the drop had been made,' said Frost. 'He must have phoned from a call box. Where's the nearest one from here?'

'The one in Forest Row,' said Burton.

'If that was the one he used, he should be here in less than ten minutes,' said Frost to Burton. 'Get back to your car and wait and be ready to tail him after he collects the money.'

'He might not have used that one,' objected Cassidy. 'He might have a mobile phone. For all we know he could be standing in those trees over there, watching.'

'If he had a mobile phone and was standing in those trees,' said Frost, 'he'd have seen Cordwell drop the money and wouldn't have needed to make the phone call.' He nodded Burton on his way.

Burton hurried off while Frost panned the area through the night glasses to see if he could spot anyone watching them. A radio call from Burton. He was back in his car awaiting further instructions.

Frost consulted his wrist-watch. Nine forty-six. His clothes were sodden and rain was beating down on them. Too wet to smoke and nothing to do but to wait.

They waited.

12

Cassidy wriggled and tried to make himself comfortable on the soaking wet grass. 'How long do you think we'll have to wait?'

'Not too long,' muttered Frost, scanning the far ground through the night glasses. 'There's too much money just lying around. He won't want to risk anyone else finding it.'

'Car coming,' reported Burton over the radio.

They held their breath and waited. But it sped past. And so did the next.

A lull in the traffic and Frost went back to his surveillance of the bleak-looking area. It was tricky using the night glasses and he hadn't got the hang of them. Every now and then his view would be completely obscured as a large bush or tree trunk took up the entire field of vision. He swung back to the bushes where the money was hidden.

A clap of thunder and the heavens opened, rain drumming on the ground so they had to shout to hear each other. Cassidy wiped stinging rain from his eyes and brushed back dripping wet hair. 'Bloody weather,' he snarled.

'It's perfect,' said Frost. 'No-one but kidnappers and prats of policemen would be out in this. Whoever turns up has got to be our man.' Again he raised the glasses and focused on some trees eighty yards or so away. Just before the downpour, he thought he had seen something move. The stair rods of rain were making it difficult to see anything and he was just convincing himself he was mistaken when . . . Yes, there it was. He nudged Cassidy. 'I spy, with my little eye, something that looks like a motor.'

'Where?' hissed Cassidy, straining his eyes into the blurred darkness.

Frost handed him the glasses and pointed. 'Behind the trees.'

Cassidy panned carefully. He located the trees and . . . yes. Frost was right. Half hidden . . . a car. He locked on to it, holding his breath and bracing himself to steady the night glasses. A Ford Escort. The glasses gave everything a green tinge, but it was a light colour . . . cream, brown or grey, perhaps. 'I see it. Its lights are out.'

'Most of the cars that come down here turn their lights out,' grunted Frost. 'They only turn them on if the girl can't find her knickers afterwards. Can you see anyone inside?'

Cassidy stared hard, trying to penetrate the curtain of blurring rain. 'No.'

'Let me have a go.' Frost took the glasses.

'Shall we pick him up?'

'No,' said Frost. 'Until he collects up the money, we've nothing on him . . . Hello . . .' He steadied the glasses and started to chuckle.

'What is it?' hissed Cassidy.

'You'd better see this.'

Cassidy snatched the glasses, then he snorted with disgust. The car was bouncing up and down on its springs and the windows were well steamed up.

'Not our kidnapper, I'm afraid,' said Frost ruefully. Then he remembered a poem he'd seen on a lavatory wall once and began to recite:

> 'You could tell he was a master,
> In the art of love.
> First the slight withdrawal
> Then the mighty shove.'

Cassidy snorted his disgust. Hadn't Frost got any damn taste? They were trying to catch the killer of a child, for Pete's sake!

The car gave a sudden lurch. 'Flaming heck,' said Frost with admiration. 'That was a mighty shove all right. I bet that brought the colour to her cheeks.'

'Bloody animals!' snarled Cassidy.

But Frost was lost in recollection. 'I used to come here and behave like a bloody animal . . . Long time ago of course . . .' It was when he was in his teens, young and lusty . . . Who was that dark girl . . . the little goer. What was her name . . . ? And then he remembered. Flaming heck, how could he have forgotten! It was his wife. Long before they were married. She was a little doll in those days . . . bouncy little figure, jet black hair, snub nose, and she thought the world of him . . . that showed how long ago it was! A time, before all the rows, when everything marvellous was going to happen. When they made plans about getting married, about him joining the police force and rising in the ranks to chief superintendent. It all came back . . . that night . . . that summer night when it was so hot you could have trampled through the grass in the nude at midnight and not feel cold. That was when it happened for the first time . . . when he undressed her and . . .

Someone was shaking his arm. 'Frost!'

'Eh?' It wasn't a summer night any more. It was peeing with rain and he was wet and cold. Cassidy was shaking his arm and pointing back to the road. 'What did you say?'

'Another car coming.'

All they could see at first were the headlights shining blearily through the rain. Then the car. A dark blue Austin Metro.

'He's slowing down,' said Cassidy in excitement. 'He's stopped . . . the bugger's stopped.'

Frost squinted through the glasses. He could just

about make out the figure at the wheel. There didn't appear to be anyone else in the car, which splashed to a stop, almost dead in line with the clump of bushes where the money was hidden.

'It's him!' hissed Frost. 'It's bloody got to be him.'

For some minutes the car just stood there, engine ticking, lights on. Then the lights went out, the engine was switched off and the only sound was the drumming rain.

'Keep down,' hissed Frost, tugging at Cassidy who was raising his head to get a better view.

They waited. Frost was able to wriggle through the long grass and pick out the registration number through the binoculars. Cassidy whispered it into the radio for Control to check. The reply came back in seconds. The registered owner was a Henry Finch, 2 Lincoln Road, Denton. It hadn't been reported stolen and nothing was known about the owner.

Frost grabbed the radio. 'The kidnapper would be a prat driving his own car. The owner might not realize his motor's gone. Phone Finch and ask where his car is. If he says it's parked in the street outside, then we know this one's been nicked. If there's no answer, send an area car round to his house to nose around. If Finch is the kidnapper the kid might be in the house. Get cracking.'

'Will do,' acknowledged Control. 'Don't switch off – Mr Mullett wants a word.'

'Over and out,' said Frost, dropping the radio back in his pocket.

Cassidy nudged him. 'Someone's getting out the car.'

The driver's door had swung open and a man in a dark blue raincoat, shortish and plump, got out, snapping open an umbrella before stepping gingerly over a puddle. For a while he stood still, head turning from side to side, like an animal checking for signs of danger. It was difficult to make out his features as rain streamed off the umbrella and curtained down to the ground. Frost guessed he would be somewhere in his late fifties.

There seemed to be no-one else in the car. Frost nodded his satisfaction. 'Not a courting couple and this is definitely not the weather for a peeping tom . . . This could be our bloke!' Then he frowned. 'Bloody hell . . . what's he doing now?' The man had turned and was leaning back inside the car and seemed to be taking something from the glove compartment and stuffing it into his pocket.

'Did you see what it was?' asked Cassidy. 'Could it have been a gun?'

'I flaming hope not,' said Frost. 'It looked too small for a gun.' He had the glasses firmly fixed on the man, who was now opening the rear passenger door and seemed to be talking to someone inside. His mouth was moving but the wind tore the words to shreds before they reached them.

'There's someone else in there!' said Cassidy.

'They must be bleeding small, then,' said Frost, 'because I can't see anyone.'

The man, huddling under the umbrella, took a few steps, then turned and called out something. A small, white and brown Jack Russell terrier, its tail docked far too short, jumped from the back seat, yapping excitedly. The man closed the car door, then took the object from his mac pocket – a well-chewed tennis ball, which he hurled across the waste ground, urging the dog to fetch it. Undeterred by the rain, the dog raced after it while the man stood by the car and watched.

Cassidy snorted his disappointment. 'He's exercising his dog. He's not our bloke after all.'

'Worse than that,' said Frost, glumly. 'Him and bloody Rin Tin Tin could drive the real kidnapper away.'

The radio in his pocket called him. Control reporting. As ordered they had rung Finch's number. No reply. An area car had been despatched and was at the house now. The house was in darkness and no-one answered their knocking. A neighbour said she had seen Mr Finch drive off with his dog about half an hour ago.

Frost grunted resignedly. It was just telling them what they already knew. This flaming clown had stumbled on the very spot the ransom money was to be collected from and was going to play ball with Fido all flaming night.

The cigarette he tugged from the packet was sodden before he could get his lighter to it and flopped limply in his hand. He shoved it into his top pocket to dry out for later. That damn man, seemingly oblivious to the belting rain, was huddled under the umbrella, calmly hurling the ball; no sooner had the dog retrieved it, than he would take it and fling it again. Bite the bastard, Frost silently urged the animal. He shrunk his neck down deeper into his mac in response to the cold trickle of rain running down the inside of his upturned collar. He was wet, and uncomfortable, and was getting that all too familiar feeling that, bad as things were, they were going to get a bloody sight worse. He could sense the smirk of satisfaction at his discomfiture on Cassidy's face.

Then, in a flash, his despair evaporated. The dog had returned with the ball which it dumped proudly at the man's feet, its stump of a tail wagging wildly. Scooping up the ball, the man suddenly turned at right angles and hurled it straight into the midst of the clump of bushes where the money was hidden, apparently unobserved by the dog which was still sniffing around in the grass. They could hear the man saying 'Fetch, fetch,' pointing to the bushes, but the dog just yapped its puzzlement and jumped up at him for the ball to be thrown again.

Finch bent down and picked up the dog, then carried it back to the car. With the waggle of a finger, telling the dog to 'Be good!', he turned and walked back towards the bushes, disappearing from view behind them.

'It was him all the time!' breathed Frost. 'He's putting on a bloody good act, but it's him!' He radioed through to Burton. 'Get ready to tail him, son. He's collecting the money now.' There was no denying the simple brilliance of Finch's ploy. If the police pounced, he could feign innocence – he was simply looking for his dog's ball – and if he had already collected the money he could claim he found it by accident. And there'd be no way we could prove otherwise, thought Frost . . . unless the bastard has got the kid in the boot of his car. He swung the binoculars over to the Austin. All he could see was the brown and white head of the Jack Russell, paws up at the window, waiting for its master.

Control radioed through. A further report from the area car at Finch's house. They had nosed around as much as they could without actually breaking in. Nothing obviously suspicious could be seen from the outside.

'Tell them to stay put,' said Frost. If Finch was arrested they could help search the premises. He clicked off and returned to his surveillance of the thicket. 'Hasn't he come out yet?'

Cassidy shook his head.

Frost wiped the rain from his eyes and raised the night glasses again. He stared at the thicket until his eyes hurt. No movement. Nothing. 'He's taking his damn time.' Worry started gnawing. 'Could he have come out and we didn't see him?'

'We'd see him going for his car,' said Cassidy. Then a thought struck him. 'Unless he's letting us watch the Austin and he's got another car parked further up the road for his getaway.'

'Shit!' Frost hadn't thought of this. He turned and looked again at the Austin. The dog was still staring out of the window and seemed to be whimpering. 'I can't see him abandoning his dog,' said Frost. 'The bastard might kill a kid, but he'd never leave his dog.' He hoped and prayed he was right and that the dog wasn't some poor stray Finch had collected from the gutter on the way over.

Cassidy came up with another depressing theory.

'We're not even certain this man is Finch. He could have pinched Finch's car and his dog and left Finch tied up somewhere.'

Frost checked his watch. 'How long has he been behind there?' It seemed like hours, but it was only six minutes. Finch might have grabbed the money: they might be sitting here like a couple of wallies, looking at a lousy bush. On the other hand, if they charged across now, they might find Finch doing a long pee and the real kidnapper could spot them and jag it in. He sighed. Whatever he did could be wrong. But he always believed that doing something was much better than doing nothing. He jerked his head at Cassidy and stood up. 'Come on – let's take a look.'

'I think we should wait,' said Cassidy, just to get it on record that he had his doubts. But Frost was already lumbering over the uneven ground. Cassidy pushed himself up, hissing in agony at the damp-aggravated pain from his scar. He hobbled along behind Frost, moving as quickly as he could while stamping his foot and muttering about 'Damn cramp'.

They split and went around each side of the thicket, Cassidy praying that Finch wouldn't break away in a run. There was no way he could run after him.

Their torches slashed through the darkness, the beams steaming in the rain. There was no-one there. A noise. 'What was that?' They listened. Just the drumming of the rain then . . . There it was again. A groan. Frost directed his torch downwards. Someone sprawled on the ground. It was Finch.

He was lying face down in the long grass. As they turned him over, the dog's ball rolled from the pocket of his raincoat. His eyes were closed and the blood trickling from a swelling lump on his forehead was diluted to a watery pink and spread over his face by the rain. He felt cold. As Cassidy radioed for an ambulance Frost looked everywhere, beating the grass flat, kicking aside the thick carpet of fallen leaves, looking for the travel bag. It had gone.

'The Ford Escort!' exclaimed Frost. 'The bloody Ford Escort!' He turned the glasses towards the trees. No sign of the damn thing. He fumbled for the radio and called up Control. 'Message for all mobiles. I'm anxious to interview the occupants of a Ford Escort, lightish colour, last seen on the outskirts of Denton Woods by Forest Row. Believe man and woman inside. Any vehicles answering this description to be stopped and held.'

'Do you have details of the registration number?' asked Control.

'If I had, I would have bloody well told you,' shouted Frost.

'It's not much to go on,' said Control.

'It had four wheels and two red lights at the back,' snarled Frost. 'Does that help?'

'Thank you,' said Lambert, his mildness tacitly rebuking Frost's outburst. 'Mr Mullett wants a word.'

'How did it go?' asked Mullett eagerly.

Frost stared at the radio, trying to think of a pithy reply that would shut Mullett up for all time. The bugger never asked how things had gone when they had gone off brilliantly. 'Couple of minor snags, super,' he said. 'I'll fill you in when I get back.'

'Snags?' roared Mullett. 'What snags?'

But Frost had switched off.

The junior house doctor, looking dead tired, came into the waiting-room. 'Inspector Frost?'

Frost stood up, pinching out the cigarette and dropping it into his mac pocket. 'How is he?'

'He's had a nasty knock. Mild concussion, nothing serious. We'll keep an eye on him tonight, but he can go home tomorrow.'

'Is he conscious?'

'Yes, but I'd prefer it if you didn't question him tonight.'

'Your preference noted, doc, but I've got a missing seven-year-old kid . . .'

The doctor shrugged and pointed to the end bed where a young nurse was twitching back the curtains. He yawned again. He was too tired to argue.

Frost shuffled over to the bed. He too was tired. It had been a long day and the adrenaline that had kept him hyped up while they were waiting for the money to be collected was now drained by failure and he felt ready to drop. The little nurse smiled. She recognized him. The number of visits he had made at night to the hospital. The times they had called him in because they hadn't thought his wife would last out until the morning, but she had hung on. There was an empty bed in the centre of the row, its clean white sheets folded back. He wished he could just climb in and go straight off to sleep. But Mullett was waiting for him back at the station. There was a bollocking to be got through before he could enjoy the luxury of sleep.

The clipboard at the foot of the bed read: 'Henry Alan Finch, aged 66.' There were figures for temperature and blood pressure and a scribbled prescription for pain killers.

Finch looked older than when he had climbed out of the car. His face was grey, his eyes were closed and his breathing heavy, almost a snore. A rectangle of plaster covered the wound on his forehead. Plumpish, with thinning, gingerish hair and a clipped, ginger moustache, he had the appearance of a retired army officer.

Frost dragged a chair up to the bed and dropped down into it. He loosened his scarf and unbuttoned his mac. The ward was hot and he had to fight off the urge to close his own eyes and drift off to sleep. 'Mr Finch?'

The eyes fluttered open and he winced as he swivelled his head to look at Frost. 'Who are you?'

Frost held up his warrant card. Finch blinked at it. 'Where's my dog?'

'At the station. He's being looked after. How do you feel?'

'I'm all right. I want to go home.' He squinted down the darkened ward. 'Where's the nurse?'

'A couple of questions first. What were you doing on the common at that time of night?'

'Taking the dog for a run.'

'In the peeing rain?'

'I do it every night. There's no law against it, is there?'

'Do you always go to the common?'

'Yes.' His eyes were still focused down the ward. 'Nurse!'

'What happened tonight?'

'Some bastard attacked me – knocked me out.'

'Let's take it step by step. We saw you pull up in your car.'

Finch's eyes narrowed. 'What were you doing there?'

'Never mind why we were there. You're lucky we were. You could have been lying unconscious all night and ended up with pneumonia. You pulled up in the car. You took your time getting out – why?'

'The rain suddenly came down heavily. I was wondering whether to give it a miss.'

'But you didn't?'

'The dog was all excited. I didn't want to disappoint him.'

'Did you see anyone else about?'

'No.'

'There was another car parked under the trees. Did you see that?'

'No.' He gritted his teeth as he wriggled his back and tried to make himself comfortable. 'Do you want me to tell you what happened?'

'Please.'

'I was throwing the ball for the dog when it went into those bushes. I tried to get him to fetch it, but he wasn't interested, so I put him in the car and went off to look for it.'

'In all that rain? A lot of trouble for a ball.' Frost fished the well-chewed, almost bald tennis ball from his pocket and placed it on the bedside locker.

'Have you got a dog?'

'No,' admitted Frost.

'Then you don't bloody know! It was his favourite ball. If you had a dog you'd understand.'

'OK. You went behind the clump of bushes . . .'

'I looked for the ball when I saw this travel bag. It looked new and felt heavy. It was still fairly dry so I guessed it hadn't been there long. I decided to lug it back to the car and hand it in to the police station in the morning.'

'Very commendable,' said Frost. 'You weren't at all curious as to what might have been inside?'

Finch sighed. 'All right. I was going to take it home and force the lock. If it was full of drugs, I'd take it to the police, but if it was money . . .' He twitched his shoulders. 'Well, I don't know. But I never had the chance to find out how honest I was. Suddenly this lout is there. He says, "Ah, you've found my bag . . . thanks very much," and tried to get it off me.'

'Did you give it to him?'

'No, I damn well didn't. So he threatened me. He said, "If you don't want to get hurt, grandad, just hand it over," and he balls his fists as if he's going to hit me. Me – I was in the war. I fought for bastards like him. "Just you try it, sonny," I said. So he shrugs as if to say "You win" and makes to go. Like a silly sod I turned my back on him and, wham!, he's belted me with a brick or something. I hit the ground with a thud. The next thing I knew I was in the ambulance.'

'Can you describe him?'

'About five foot nine, clean-shaven and a sneer on his bloody face.'

'How old, do you reckon?'

'I don't know – mid-twenties, I suppose.'

'Colour of hair?'

'Couldn't see – he wore one of those anorak things with the hood up.'

'What colour anorak?'

'Dark blue, red lining and sort of rabbit's fur round the hood.'

'Trousers?'

'Dark – darkish . . . didn't pay much attention to them. But I'll tell you something. I'd recognize him anywhere. Let me get near him when he hasn't got a brick in his hand, I'll show the little swine.'

Frost was now beaming. 'You'd recognize him?'

'Like a bloody shot!'

Frost jumped up. He wasn't tired now. 'Nurse – get this gentleman his clothes. He's coming with me.'

The dog, sensing its master was in the station, was yapping almost hysterically. Sergeant Wells let it into the interview room where it went mad, jumping up at Finch, its stumpy tail a blur. Finch was settled down at the table with a cup of tea from the vending machine and the books of photographs placed in front of him. 'Take your time,' said Frost. 'If you're not sure, just say so.'

'If he's in your books, I'll spot him,' said Finch, firmly. He took a swig at the tea, patted the dog which was now stretched out on the floor at his feet, and turned the first page. Frost left him with Burton and went into his office.

Another batch of paperwork had been heaped in his in-tray, most of it nagging rubbish from Mullett. Didn't the sod have anything better to do? He flopped heavily into his chair, lit up a cigarette and pulled the tray towards him, at the same time dragging the wastepaper basket over with his foot. The first three were Mullett memos beginning 'When may I expect . . . ?' 'You can expect whenever you flaming well like,' he muttered, 'but you're not going to get.' He screwed them into a ball and flipped them into the bin. The fourth was again from Mullett: 'I have repeatedly asked for . . .' It joined the others.

'Ah Frost, there you are! I've been waiting for you in my office.'

Heck! Hornrim flaming Harry! He had been putting off attending the old log cabin for his bollocking until he had some good news from Finch to take the edge off it.

'I was just coming, super.'

Mullett eyed the screwed-up balls of paper in the waste-paper bin. They looked suspiciously like the memos he had dictated earlier. 'I sent you some memos,' he said.

'Did you?' said Frost, all wide-eyed and innocent. 'I haven't come across them yet.' He jumped from his chair and footed the waste bin under his desk. 'What was it you wanted to see me about?' He followed Mullett to his office.

Mullett went on and on. Frost managed to shut most of it out, but the words 'fiasco', 'ill-conceived', 'sloppy', 'utter disgrace', kept filtering through. The old log cabin, like the hospital, was overheated and that, plus Mullett's droning, was sending him to sleep. His head began to droop, then snapped up as his auto-pilot told him Mullett was expecting an answer.

'Sorry, super . . . won't happen again,' he muttered, hoping it was the right response.

'Sorry! Sorry isn't good enough,' said Mullett, getting his second wind.

Isn't it, thought Frost, then what about 'balls'? How was this helping? He was just working himself up to the point where he was going to tell Mullett to stuff his flaming job when he was saved by the bell. The phone.

Annoyed at being interrupted, Mullett snatched at it. 'Mullett,' he barked. A look of alarm crossed his face. He clapped a hand over the mouthpiece. 'It's Sir Richard

Cordwell,' he hissed. Back to the phone. 'Hello, Sir Richard . . . Yes, I've just got into the office and I believe that what you say is correct. I know he gave his word . . . I shall look into it . . . I don't know the details . . . I wasn't involved, of course . . . No, disappointingly the man got away . . . No, regretfully we have no idea who he is . . .' He eased the phone away from his ear and the buzzing of angry invective crackled round the room. At a pause for breath from the other end, Mullett smiled ingratiatingly into the mouthpiece and asked, 'I suppose the kidnapper hasn't contacted you with news of the boy's release?' He winced and pulled the phone away again as another molten lava of abuse erupted from the earpiece. 'No contact from the kidnapper,' he hissed superfluously to Frost. Back to the phone. 'Yes, Sir Richard, but I don't really think you can blame us . . . Oh come . . . that's hardly fair . . .' His feeble interjections were receiving short shrift.

The internal phone buzzed and, at Mullett's signalling, Frost, who was wondering if this might not be a good opportunity to slip out, answered it. An excited Burton. 'Mr Finch has made an identification. We're checking it out now.'

'Is he sure?' said Frost, waving down Mullett who was signalling for him to be quiet.

'He says he's bloody positive.'

He put the phone down and waved to Mullett who again slapped his hand over the mouthpiece. 'We could have an identification. If so, we could make the arrest tonight.'

Mullett hesitated. 'Is he definite?'

'He says he's positive. I'm checking on it now.'

A deep sigh of relief from Mullett who conveyed this information to Cordwell. 'I'll be back to you very shortly,' he assured him. 'You'll be the first to know, Sir Richard.' He replaced the phone and gave it a little satisfied pat. 'I'll come with you,' he said.

He followed Frost back to the interview room where a smugly self-satisfied Finch was leaning back in his chair, his hand ruffling the neck of his dog. 'Definitely him,' he told Frost proudly. 'I'd know him anywhere. I never forget a face.'

Mullett beamed and gave the dog a couple of tentative pats while Frost studied the details under a photograph of a scowling youth. Richard Francis Hartley, aged twenty-four. Lots of petty offences, scaling up to robbery with violence for which he had served a two-year stretch. Not one of Frost's arrests, so he couldn't place him, but from his mug shot, he looked a real right charmer.

The door opened and Burton looked in. He caught Frost's eye and beckoned, at the same time giving the thumbs-down sign to signal it was not good news. A dismayed Frost went to sidle out but Mullett wanted to hear the good news first hand and called Burton in.

'A slight complication,' said Burton. 'The man Mr Finch positively identified is in the remand centre at Bister. He's been there for the past two weeks.'

Mullett glared at Frost whose fault this clearly was. 'Typical,' he snapped. 'Damn typical!'

'I could have sworn it was him,' said Finch, completely unabashed. 'If it wasn't him, it was someone very much like him.'

'The courts don't go much on look-alikes,' said Frost. 'They insist on the real thing.'

'Sorry,' shrugged Finch, taking the dog's lead.

'Never mind,' smiled Frost through clenched teeth. 'We'll catch him.'

'When you do,' said Finch, 'just give me a shout. I'll identify him.'

'Or someone very much like him,' added Frost as the door closed. 'Stupid old sod.' He dropped into the chair vacated by Finch. The tiredness was back.

'Tonight's stupidity was not confined to him,' said Mullett significantly.

Frost was too tired to come up with an answer. He could barely make the V sign as Mullett left. From outside he could hear Finch's dog yapping. Bloody dog. It had the chance to bite Mullett and didn't do so. He took another look at the photograph Finch had identified. 'I suppose he hasn't got a twin brother who's done time for kidnapping?'

Burton grinned and shook his head. 'A sister on the game, that's all.'

A match flared as Frost scratched it down the side of the table and lit up. 'Not one of my better days, son. We don't know who the kidnapper is, we've lost the money and the kid isn't back. On the credit side, Mullett isn't very happy, but even that doesn't entirely cheer me up.' The interview door opened and Cassidy came in. Frost forced a smile of welcome. 'You've heard about Finch's identification?'

'Yes, rotten luck,' said Cassidy, in a tone completely devoid of sympathy. 'We've got Snell.'

'Good,' said Frost. He was too bloody tired to care. 'Where was he?'

'PC Jordan spotted him driving away from his mother's place. He went back to collect his things. They're bringing him in now.'

'Terrific!'

'I'd like to do the questioning.'

'Sure.' He wasn't going to fight over the questioning. All he wanted to do was go to bed. In any event, he wasn't sold on the idea that Snell had killed the woman and the kids. He stood up and wound his scarf round his neck. 'See you in the morning.'

'Yes,' agreed Cassidy. 'In the morning.'

A tap at the door. 'Do you want Snell in here?' asked Wells.

Cassidy nodded. He decided to ignore the lack of a 'sir' or 'inspector'. 'Yes, sergeant. Bring him in.' He quickly sat down in the chair vacated by Frost in case the inspector decided to stay after all, then smiled in anticipation as Jordan and Simms ushered in Snell. He looked frightened. None of his cockiness from the previous day remained. It was Frost he turned to.

'I didn't do it, Mr Frost. I never touched them.'

Frost pointed to Cassidy. 'This is the gentleman you tell your lies to tonight, Sidney.'

Cassidy indicated the chair opposite him. 'Sit down.'

As Snell dragged out the chair, his coat sleeve rode up showing the edge of the bandage round his wrist. Frost grabbed his arm and pulled the sleeve back further. 'Hurt yourself, Sidney?'

Snell snatched his arm away. 'Cut myself,' he muttered.

'What with – the edge of a sharp bible?'

Cassidy showed concern as Frost started to unwind his scarf as if he had decided to stay. There was no way he was going to let Frost elbow his way in for a share of the limelight. 'I'll see you in the morning, then, inspector.'

Frost took the hint and, with a brief nod, wandered out to the car-park. He heard hurrying footsteps clattering down the corridor behind: a grim-faced Mullett in his tailored overcoat was determined to get out of the station before Cordwell rang back to ask about the promised arrest of the kidnapper.

'Mr Mullett!'

Mullett's brow creased with annoyance as Wells hurried after him. 'Sir Richard Cordwell on the phone. Wants to know if we've made the arrest.'

'Tell him I've left,' said Mullett, pushing open the doors to the car-park. 'Tell him you can't contact me.'

Wells stood by Frost, staring at the undignified sight of the Divisional Commander, overcoat flapping, running to his car. 'Then he wants to speak to you, Jack.'

'Tell him I'm with Mr Mullett,' said Frost.

Now that there was no need to lie in the open on wet grass, the rain had eased off. He didn't drive straight home. For some reason he detoured and took the road by the golf course, finding himself coasting down Cresswell Street where he stopped outside the house and switched off the engine. The murder house, dark and silent like the other houses in the street, but a different dark, a different silence. A creaking sound. The front gate swinging in the wind, the way it was swinging when Mark Grover came home in the early hours of the morning. Frost climbed out of the car to click it shut, then decided to take a quick look around.

His footsteps crunched up the path. The evening paper was poking from the letter box. No-one had stopped it. It signalled that the house was empty, an open invitation to burglars. He pushed it through and heard it plop on the door mat. On impulse he took the key from his pocket and let himself in. Still the lingering smell of Johnson's baby powder. Still that terrible silence. Not a rustle, not a creak. He dug down deep in his mac pocket for a torch and let the beam creep along the passage. He hesitated outside the nursery blue door, but didn't want to go in that empty bedroom with its row of sad-faced dolls.

On to the kitchen. All the mugs and plates the police had used had now been washed up and the place looked neat and tidy. Crossing to the back door, he undid the bolts and stepped outside to the garden. The original sheet of plywood covering the broken glass panel had been removed by Forensic for tests on the traces of blood and skin tissue. A new square of ply had been nailed securely in place. Was he standing where Snell had stood, where Snell had poked his hand through and let himself in? The same Snell he could have arrested, but had let off with a caution because he was too damn lazy and wanted someone else to do all the paper work.

He stepped back into the kitchen and bolted the door. An involuntary shiver shook his body, so strong was the aura of tragedy that pervaded the whole house. What the hell was he doing here? He pocketed the torch and hurried back to his car where Cassidy, oozing smugness, was calling on the radio, anxious to impart his news.

'Thought you'd like to know, inspector. Forensic have done a quick test. Every indication that the blood and skin on the plywood panel definitely came from Snell. They also found small splinters of plywood on his wrist. So we've got our killer.'

'Terrific!' said Frost, trying to sound pleased.

'I've phoned Mr Mullett. He's over the moon, although he feels it's a great pity Snell wasn't arrested yesterday. He says he would like to have a word with you about it tomorrow.'

'I can't wait,' said Frost. He clicked off and chucked the radio down on the passenger seat alongside him. Three kids and their mother. Would they still be alive if he had locked Snell up? He had never felt more guilt-ridden, more inadequate and more bloody useless as a policeman than he did right now. He reached into the glove compartment for the bottle of duty frees Shirley had given him.

He shouldn't have drunk the whisky. He tried to work out how long it had been since he had had anything substantial to eat, but gave it up. It was too far back. Too much spirit on an empty stomach. He yawned, but fought off sleep although the urge to close his eyes, just for a few minutes, was almost irresistible. He would drive home and go straight to bed. It required a lot of concentration to start up the engine. Very, very carefully he eased the car from the kerb and turned back towards the town. It was so hot inside the car. He loosened his scarf as he turned on to the ring road.

At first he drove slowly, but gradually, so gradually he was hardly aware of it, the car gathered speed. Huddles of trees and houses swished past and then he was racing down the main road to the town.

Not another car in sight. Ahead of him he could see, in

diminishing dots of colour, all the approaching traffic lights pinpricking into the distance like a string of tiny fairy lamps. He wound down the window and let the cold slap of the slip stream cool his head. That whisky was a mistake, a bloody mistake. He was feeling lightheaded. He fought off the urge to drive straight round to Mullett's house, throw stones at his bedroom window and demand, 'If you've anything to say to me, bloody say it now.'

At the junction of Bath Road the traffic lights had changed to red, but he took a chance. As the car floated across the junction the vibrating clang of a sudden hammer blow made him jerk forward, snapping against the restraint of the seat belt. Then a splintering and a shattering of glass and the furious blasting of a horn. He slammed on his brakes and stared through the windscreen in dismay. He had shunted a dirty great expensive-looking motor that had suddenly appeared out of nowhere.

He climbed out of his car, leaning against it for support. The other driver, an indignant woman in her late fifties wearing a full-length mink coat, came striding over to confront him. The coat looked as expensive as her car, a Bentley, all gleaming paintwork and stainless steel. It couldn't have been more than a few months old, but now the front wing was crumpled and the headlight smashed.

She looked ready to scratch his eyes out before getting down to more savage violence. 'You stupid, silly bastard. What's your flaming game? Are you blind or something – didn't you see the bleeding traffic lights?'

The woman and the Bentley blurred out of focus, suddenly clicking back sharp and clear, with every detail of the damage screaming at him. The cold air and the shock of what he had done served to sober him up. 'I'm sorry, love,' he mumbled. 'All my fault.'

'You bet it's all your fault. You could have killed me!'

Her nose quivered. She leant forward and sniffed. 'You're drunk! You're bloody drunk! No wonder you drove straight past the red light. I'm calling the police.' She fished a mobile phone from inside the Bentley. 'Bastards like you ought to be locked up.'

His dejection was complete. As if he wasn't in enough trouble! His medal wasn't going to get him out of this little lot. Mullett would have a field day. But why was the woman studying him, staring at his face? He stared back. Something about her pressed a buzzer, but not loudly enough.

She poked an accusing finger at him. 'I know you, don't I? You're a cop. A bloody cop!' She snapped her fingers as a name came up. 'Frost . . . Sergeant Jack Frost.'

'You'll never believe this, madam,' he said, leaning heavily against his car as his legs didn't seem to want to support him, 'but it's now Detective Inspector Jack Frost.' He focused his eyes on her. A faint ripple of recollection. 'Do I know you?'

'You ought to, you old sod, the number of times you've run me in for soliciting.'

'Soliciting?' It was difficult to say the word without slurring. He closed his eyes. A mental picture of a thinner, much younger version of the woman, this time wearing a cheap, imitation leopard skin coat. He opened his eyes as the filing index of his mind obliged with a name. 'Kitty – Kitty Reynolds. And you haven't changed a bit. Are you still on the game?'

She grinned. 'A different branch of the business. I'm in management now. I run a little specialized house – four girls. I won't tell you where, though.'

'I don't want to know, love,' said Frost, holding up his hand. 'I can't even cope with the cases I've got.' He took a squint at the Bentley and walked as steadily as he could over to it. Now he could see it properly the damage looked even worse. 'I seem to have put a tiny dent in your motor.' He wet a finger and rubbed it over the wing as if that would put it right.

'A tiny dent, you drunken pig? There's nearly a thousand quid's worth of damage there.' She gave a conspiratorial grin. 'But have it on me. I'll tell the insurance company the other motor didn't stop and I couldn't get its number.'

The wind wasn't so cold. The night wasn't so dark. His guardian angel had come back from holiday just in time. 'You're a saint, Kitty, a bloody saint.'

She grinned again. 'I owe you a few favours, Jack – that blind eye you turned when I could have got into serious trouble.'

Frost tried to recall the circumstances, but couldn't. There had been so many blind eyes. 'Don't remember it, Kitty, but whatever I did, it was a pleasure.' He gave her a wave. 'I'd better get off back home before the filth start sniffing around.' He tried to walk back to his own car, but found his legs weren't interested in taking his orders and he had to grab the Bentley for support.

Kitty threw back her head and laughed. 'You're too bloody drunk to drive. Hop in my car. I'll park your heap down that side street, then I'll take you back to my place and try to sober you up.'

Her place was down a murky side road leading off Vicarage Terrace. From the outside it looked down at heel and scruffy, just like Frost, but the front door was fitted with the most sophisticated security lock, a lock which looked as if it cost more than the house.

'Through here, Jack.' The hall light was on and the inside was a revelation, everything new and expensive . . . very expensive. She took his arm and steered him through to the lounge where she sat him down on a deeply cushioned chesterfield and pushed a solid silver cigarette box towards him. She retired to the kitchen while he sat, feeling warm and happy, savouring the rich coffee smell that floated through the open door. Kitty emerged carrying a tray holding cups, saucers and a percolator. Two cups of hot, steaming black coffee were poured and then she settled down in the armchair opposite him, sipping from her cup and watching him drink.

'It's flaming hot,' said Frost.

'Stop your bloody moaning – just drink it.'

He spooned in a shovelful of sugar and stirred. He hated black coffee. 'So you packed the old game in then, Kitty?'

'I had to, Jack. I was getting past it.'

He sipped and swallowed. 'I'm well past it, but I'm still carrying on.'

'My,' she said, pulling a face, 'we are feeling sorry for ourselves, aren't we?'

A wry grin. 'I was, but not any more.' He unwound his scarf and unbuttoned his mac, then drained his cup in one gulp and shuddered as if he had taken a dose of medicine. To his dismay she leant over and immediately refilled his cup. He ladled in more sugar and took a sample sip. 'Whatever men found irresistible about you, Kitty, it certainly wasn't your lousy coffee . . . It tastes like horse pee.'

'You're always moaning. Just drink it down and sober up. I'm not sending you back to your wife in that state.'

'My wife's dead.'

Her expression changed. 'Oh Jack, I am sorry. It must be lonely for you without her.'

'I was lonely with her, love. We didn't get on too well, I'm afraid.' He loosened his tie and tugged at the tight, petrified knot. The heat was counteracting the sobering effects of the coffee.

She shook her head sadly. 'You poor old sod. You can stay here tonight if you like.'

'Eh?' said Frost, feeling everything coming back to life again.

'If you're going deaf, Jack, forget it. I don't sleep with

deaf men.' Rising from the armchair she collected the coffee cups and carried them back to the kitchen. When she returned, she studied him, her head to one side, hands on well-padded hips. 'You wouldn't look so bad if you got yourself a decent suit.'

Frost looked down at his jacket and scrubbed away a patch of spilt coffee. 'I thought this was a decent suit. I paid a bomb for it.'

'When – before the First World War? Look at it – frayed cuffs, your trousers all shiny. And there's a button coming off your sleeve. I'll sew it on for you if you like.'

He fingered the loose button. 'You sew as well?'

She gave a smile full of meaning. 'You'd be surprised at the little services I can perform.'

He was in the mood for being surprised. Sod the kidnapper. Sod Mullett. Sod everything. He stood up and moved towards her and that was the moment Control chose to page him.

'Control to Inspector Frost. Come in, please.'

The sudden strange voice made Kitty start. 'What the hell is that?'

Frost fished the radio from his pocket and sighed deeply. 'It's an electronic chastity belt.' He pressed the transmit button. 'Frost here, over.'

'Can you come back right away, inspector. We've got a man on the phone claiming to be the kidnapper. He's demanding to speak to the investigating officer . . . Hold on.' There was a brief pause, then Lambert was back sounding excited. 'We've traced the call to the public phone box outside the main post office. He's still on the line. Jordan and Simms are investigating.'

'I'm on my way,' said Frost. He stuffed the radio back in his pocket, then looked regretfully at the woman. 'Sorry, love. It's not only my button that's going to be left dangling. Duty calls.'

'Well, you know where I am,' she said, helping him on with his mac and brushing cigarette ash from the collar.

But as the front door closed behind him, she knew he wouldn't be back.

The kidnapper call was a hoax. The caller was blind drunk and was being egged on by his equally drunk mate. They were both brought back to the station and charged with wasting police time.

A disappointed Frost drove back home and tried to get some sleep, but Kitty's black coffee kept him awake until just before the alarm went off.

13

He arrived at the station early, anxious to check progress and then get well out of the way before Mullett arrived. Liz had beaten him to it and was already at her desk, hunched up over a stack of reports and a complicated-looking form which she was meticulously filling in. The office smouldered with her resentment.

Frost peeked over her shoulder. She was doing the quarterly crime clear-up rate statistical return. 'I thought Mr Cassidy was doing this?'

'No,' she snapped. 'I've been ordered to do them.'

Frost rasped a match down the front of the filing cabinet. He offered a cigarette to Liz, who refused. 'Too much to hope the boy's been returned?'

'I wouldn't know – I'm only the clerical assistant.' She fanned away the smoke which was drifting over her figures.

He thought he'd better take a chance and give Cordwell a ring in case the kidnapper had made contact, but at that hour of the morning, all he got was the answerphone. He hung up, frowned and then yelled, 'The answerphone! Of course – the bloody answerphone!'

'Eh?' said Liz tetchily. She'd hoped that by coming in early she could get the return done without interruption.

'The answerphone!' repeated Frost. 'Something's been bugging me about Grover's alibi and I've just realized what it was.'

'Oh yes?' she said, flatly. He should be telling Cassidy,

not her. She was only fit to fill in forms. 'Don't forget we're going to see the woman in the cottage this morning.'

'What woman?' frowned Frost.

'Primrose Cottage – where Lemmy Hoxton was supposed to have pulled his last job.'

'Later,' said Frost, impatiently. 'One case at a time. You spoke to their boss about his phone call to the store that night, didn't you? What did he say?'

She paused, pen hovering over a column of figures, and sighed. How many more times was he going to go over the same ground? She put the pen down and checked her notebook. 'He spoke to Mark Grover just before midnight, which was round about the time his wife was killed and round about the time the neighbours heard the sounds of a quarrel.' She snapped the notebook shut and went back to the return where she was trying to transfer some of Frost's figures to the main sheet. 'Is this a three or a five?'

Frost squinted at it and shook his head. 'Could be either. Does it really matter?'

Another sigh. Frost's figures were probably spurious anyway, so what the hell did it matter. She made it a five.

'The point is,' Frost continued stubbornly, 'on the night the kids were killed I asked young Collier to phone the store to check with the security guard. But all he got was the answerphone. The phones are switched off at night. So how could their boss phone them?'

Liz tapped her teeth with her pen. 'But why should he lie?'

'I thought we might go and ask him.'

She looked down at the mass of papers on her desk, most of them with Frost's scrawled, indecipherable and mainly fictitious figures, and decided anything was better than this. She reached for her coat. 'Why not?'

* * *

Frank Maltby, the owner of Denton Shopfitters, was not at home. His wife told them he was over at Bonley's department store supervising the counter fittings. Which is where they found him, a pugnacious little man with a loud voice, standing in the centre of acres of brand new red and blue carpeting which had been laid by Grover and Collard on the night the children were killed. Workmen on piece rates were hammering and sawing. Liz showed her warrant card while Frost was still digging down in his pocket amongst the cigarette ends for his.

Maltby scowled. 'Now what?' His face went angry and he yelled over Frost's shoulder at a workman wielding a saw. 'Mind what you're doing – that's solid bloody mahogany you're ruining, not plywood.' Back to Frost. 'What is it now?'

Frost had to shout over the clatter of the hammering. 'Just checking. Are you sure you phoned Mark Grover just before midnight?'

'Of course I'm sure. I told the tart – the lady – her!' He jabbed a thumb at Liz.

'Well,' yelled Frost, 'in spite of what you told the tart, the lady, her, we seem to have a problem.'

'And what's that?'

'The store switchboard shuts down at eight and all calls go to the answerphone.'

Maltby gave a smug smile. 'I didn't use the store's line. I called him on his mobile phone.'

'His mobile phone?' echoed Liz in dismay. 'I assumed you used the normal phone.'

'Then you assumed wrong, darling, didn't you?'

'You told me he was definitely at the store.'

'And so he was. Where else would he be?'

'Any bloody where he liked,' said Frost. 'He could have been having it away in bed with the tart, the lady, her, or he could have been back at home.'

'Well, he wasn't, smart-arse. He was here working.'

'And how can you be so bloody positive?'

'Because he bloody told me, that's why. Now if you'll excuse me, some of us have got work to do.'

'All right,' said Liz defensively as they walked back to the car. 'It no longer proves he was at the store, but that doesn't mean he wasn't. We've got two other people who confirm he was there.'

'You're too negative,' said Frost. 'He started off with three people supporting his alibi, and now there's only two. Let's go and see the night security guard.'

They heard the radio squawking away as they neared the car. It was Cassidy at his smuggest. 'Thought you'd like to know, inspector, I've got the case all tied up. Snell has confessed.'

At first Frost couldn't take it in and stared at the handset in disbelief. 'Confessed?'

'Coughed the lot – the mother and the kids. Said it all happened in a haze – he didn't know what came over him.' There was a long pause. Frost, so sure Snell didn't do it, so bloody sure, couldn't think of a thing to say. 'Are you still there?' asked Cassidy.

'Yes,' said Frost hastily. 'Sorry. Congratulations . . . good work.' He did his utmost to sound sincere, but knew he hadn't succeeded. A rustling over the speaker as someone else took the microphone. It was Mullett.

'Whatever you are doing, Frost, I want you here, now – no excuses.'

Frost switched off. 'The bugger's confessed,' he told Liz, still unable to believe it. 'Which rather tends to shoot my theory that the father did it right up the arse.'

She felt sorry for him. 'You spotted an inconsistency that no-one else did, inspector . . . even Mr Cassidy. You checked it out.'

He flashed her a wry grin. 'For a tart, a woman, a what's it, you're not at all bad, sergeant. Ah well, it's bollock-chewing time, folks. Back to the ranch.'

Mullett was waiting for him and managed a quick jab

with his finger at the chair just before Frost decided to sit anyway.

'Two things, Frost. The press have somehow got hold of the fact that you suspected Snell before the killings but did nothing about it. They're clamouring for a statement. Secondly, I've had Sir Richard Cordwell on the phone. May I take it you have not yet been in touch with him?'

'Not yet,' said Frost.

'Not yet?' echoed Mullett in a tone of exaggerated disbelief. 'You're telling me that you haven't even phoned to ask if, by some remote chance after last night's fiasco, the kidnapper had kept his side of the bargain?'

'I'm sure Sir Richard would have told us if he had,' replied Frost.

'Pathetic!' snapped Mullett.

Frost nodded wryly. This time Hornrim Harry was right.

'You will not, I am sure,' continued Mullett, 'be surprised to learn that there has been no such contact. Cordwell is convinced it is because of your clumsy intervention after promising to stay out of it.' He leant forward. 'You assured me nothing could go wrong. You gave me a categorical undertaking.'

Frost did a mental playback of his conversations with the superintendent and was damn sure he had given no such assurance.

Mullett removed his glasses and polished them sadly. 'I can't save you from the wolves this time, inspector.' He oozed insincerity.

When have you ever? thought Frost.

'Now that he's laid out the money, Cordwell wants his pound of flesh. He was hoping to be fêted as the saviour who paid the ransom and saved the child, but now that is no longer possible, he is settling for the benefactor whose excellent intentions were thwarted by police bungling. He has called a press conference for ten o'clock to tell everyone about the fiasco.'

'There was no fiasco last night,' said Frost. 'We didn't show ourselves until long after the kidnapper had left with the money. The fact that the old boy Finch turned up on the scene with his fleabag of a dog had nothing at all to do with us.'

A thin wintery smile from Mullett. 'I imagine Sir Richard will tell the story slightly differently. But hear this, Frost,' and he jabbed his finger at the inspector. 'You are not dragging me down into the mire of your foul-ups.' He waved a sheet of paper filled with his neat handwriting. 'I am already drafting my report to the Chief Constable.'

Frost nodded curtly as he stood up. 'Don't take too much of the blame on yourself, sir, just to get me out of trouble . . . and don't overpraise me – you know how embarrassed I get.'

Mullett shrugged as he pulled the cap from his Parker fountain pen. He would let it go. With luck, the inspector wouldn't be with Denton Division much longer.

In the outer office the clatter of the typewriter suddenly started up as Ida Smith, Mullett's devoted private secretary, quickly returned to her typing after straining her ears to hear the music of her boss giving Frost a dressing down. She was loyal to Mullett and if he didn't like the inspector, then neither did she. In any case, the man was uncouth. That filthy seaside postcard! And she certainly wasn't bending down anywhere within jabbing range of that stubby finger. If it wasn't so embarrassing she would have put in an official complaint. She gave a malevolent smirk as Frost ambled past her. To her surprise he stopped and put a hand on her shoulder. 'It's good to know I've got at least one friend in this place, Ida,' he said, giving her a little squeeze.

Like her boss, it took her a little time to recognize sarcasm. She returned to her typing, hammering the keys as if they were nails to be driven into Frost's coffin.

Sergeant Johnnie Johnson waylaid him as he was on his way to his office. 'Jack – guess who's here to see you?'

Frost furrowed his brow as if giving this serious consideration. 'Not Princess Di again – I told her never to bother me at work.'

'No.'

'Then I give up.' He was in no mood for guessing games.

'Tommy Dunn. He wants to see you.'

'Well, I don't want to see him. He's dropped me right in it thanks to his bloody sticky fingers.'

'He says it's urgent,' insisted Johnnie, trotting behind him into the office.

Frost dropped into his chair, flicked through his in-tray and weeded out the two latest memos from Mullett, which he consigned to the rubbish bin. 'What does he want?'

'He was charged with stealing last night. He wants you to get him off the hook.'

'I want someone to get me off the bleeding hook. Tommy knows damn well I can't help him.' He sighed. Dunn was a shit and a bastard, but he had done Frost one or two good turns in the past. 'All right – wheel him in . . . but for Pete's sake don't let Cassidy know he's here.'

Dunn was an overweight, useless-looking man. A red-faced Oliver Hardy without the little moustache, and in his late forties. He waited for Johnnie Johnson to leave before sitting down. 'Sorry about last night, Jack.'

'You dropped me right in it, Tommy. Right flaming in it!'

'Wouldn't have had it happen for the world, Jack,' mumbled Dunn. 'Look – you've got to help me. I don't want to go to prison. You know how they love ex-cops inside.'

'You won't go to prison for a first offence.'

'It's not a first offence, Jack. I had a similar unhappy

experience when I was security guard over at Casheasy's in Lexton, then there was—'

Frost cut him short. 'Then how did you get a job with Savalot? I thought they vetted their security staff?'

'I fiddled my reference. I got some of their letter heading.'

Frost held up a hand. 'Spare me the details, Tommy. So what happened this time?'

'Silly mistake. I came out without any money so I took a couple of bottles from their spirits store. It wasn't pinching – I intended buying two bottles to replace them, but they caught me before I could do it.'

'And what happened when they searched your house?'

'Another misunderstanding. They found some bottles of spirits and tried to make out I'd nicked them. But I'd bought them, Jack – days ago.'

'If you had bottles in the house, then why did you have to take two more without paying? I'm sorry, Tommy. You're not only a silly sod, you're a lying bastard as well. I'm pretty gullible, but even I can't swallow that.'

Dunn pulled a handkerchief from his pocket and mopped his brow. 'I can't go inside, Jack. I couldn't face it. You're in with Cordwell. You've got to get him to drop these charges.'

Frost gave a scoffing laugh. 'Me in with Cordwell? He wants my head and my private parts on a platter, and with Mullett's help he's probably going to get them.'

Dunn looked round to make sure the door was shut, then leant across the desk to Frost, his voice lowered. 'A deal, Jack. I've got some dirt against him that you can use as a lever.'

'I'm not getting involved in your bloody blackmailing capers,' said Frost. 'Forget it, Tommy. I can't help.'

'At least listen to what it is, Jack.'

Frost chucked him a cigarette and poked one in his own mouth. 'All right, but make it quick.'

Dunn took a long drag at the cigarette, squirted a

stream of smoke then perched it on the edge of Frost's ashtray. 'Do you remember that spate of forged ten and twenty pound notes we had in the town about eighteen months ago?'

Frost nodded. Some £30,000 worth had been passed before the bank twigged and the shops were put on the alert. They had never caught the gang, who had moved on to somewhere else and were eventually arrested in Manchester. 'Mr Allen's case. What about it?'

'Savalot got lumbered with about twenty thousand quid's worth of the forgeries.'

'Too bad,' said Frost, not giving a damn.

'If you remember, the gang started passing on a Friday – Savalot's big shopping day. We whammed the takings into the bank on the Saturday morning. Monday was a bank holiday and we were open on the Sunday as well – three days of peak trading. Tuesday morning, first thing, the bank phones us – the money we paid in on Saturday morning included four thousand quid's worth of forgeries. They told us how to spot them so we wouldn't take any more, but it was a bit bleeding late. We'd another three days' worth in the safe ready to pay in. Cordwell did his nut.'

'I'm glad it had a happy ending,' said Frost.

'You haven't heard the punch line yet, Jack. We didn't even get the forged notes back – they were confiscated. So we checked the weekend's takings and there it was – another fifteen thousand quid's worth of phoney tens and twenties.'

'There's going to be some point to all this, I hope,' said Frost.

'Patience, Jack, patience. Anyway, once Cordwell realized we had all this duff cash and if he tried to pay it into the bank he would lose the lot, he went berserk, so he packed it all away in his safe. He's been hoping for a robbery or a fire so he can claim it off the insurance as genuine. And over the months he's been passing small amounts of it out to all his branches. It goes in the tills and gets handed out to customers in change. He's got rid of nearly two thousand quid that way and has only had a couple of come-backs. Anyway, let's jump to the ransom . . .'

A gleam flashed in Frost's eye. He was way ahead of Dunn now. 'You're not trying to tell me he used the forged notes to help make up the ransom money?'

'Getting on for £13,000 worth. I don't suppose it's a crime to pay off a kidnapper in forged currency, but I bet he wouldn't want the public to know.'

Frost leant back in his chair and beamed up at the ceiling. 'Tommy, if you're telling me the truth . . .'

'I am, Jack, I am.'

'Then not only are you off the hook, I might be as well.' He opened the door and ushered Tommy out. 'I'll be in touch – but bake a cake with a file in it just in case.' As Dunn turned the corridor, Frost was yelling for Burton. 'Keep an eye on the shop, son. I'm off to see Cordwell.'

Cordwell looked at Frost, his eyes glinting malevolently. 'You've got two minutes, then the press conference. Have you caught the kidnapper or got the kid back?'

'No,' said Frost.

'Then start scouring the Help Wanted ads, because you'll be out of a bloody job after today.'

'I don't think so,' said Frost.

'You sodded it up. You mounted an inadequate surveillance after assuring me you would not get involved. You let the kidnapper get away with my money and because the police were there, he won't release the kid, so you've got that on your bloody conscience.'

'There's a rumour going around—' began Frost.

Cordwell banged his fist on his desk. 'I am not interested in bloody rumours.'

'You'll be interested in this one. The very strong

whisper is that the reason the kidnapper hasn't kept his side of the bargain is because he didn't appreciate being paid out with forged banknotes.'

Cordwell jerked back, wincing as if he had been hit, but quickly composed himself and picked up a paper knife which he gently tapped on his desk. He spoke quietly, looking at something behind Frost as if the matter was of no importance. 'And who has been putting about these malicious rumours?'

Frost gave him a sweet smile. 'A couple of nasty bastards – me for one, Tommy Dunn for the other.'

'Dunn? My crooked security man? The guy who's been emptying out my spirit warehouse? Is this where you got your information from?'

'We never reveal our sources,' said Frost. He stood up. 'I'll see you at the press conference.'

Cordwell's eyes narrowed. 'The press conference?'

'I want to suggest a few headlines for them,' said Frost. 'How about "Supermarket Chief's Swindle Costs Child His Life"? It would take more than a penny off a tin of beans to make the public forget that . . . Then, of course, the press will want to know about possible criminal charges, like being in possession of forged banknotes, withholding information from the police.' He looked at his watch. 'Better not keep them waiting.'

Cordwell stabbed the paperknife into the desk top and left it quivering. 'You're a bastard, Frost.'

'It takes one to know one,' smiled Frost.

'I presume I can buy my way out?' He brought out his cheque book and tapped it suggestively with a gold-cased fountain pen.

'A lot cheaper than you deserve,' said Frost. 'Forget the press conference and drop the charges against Tommy Dunn.'

'Dunn's an ex-copper, isn't he? You bastards certainly look after your own.'

'No-one else looks after us,' explained Frost. 'Lastly, I

want full details of the duff notes . . . denominations, numbers, the lot . . . and I want them now. And warn your staff to be on extra alert for the forgeries. If our luck's in, he might try to start passing them.' He slid the antique phone across the desk. 'Do it now, please.'

Cordwell picked up the phone. A tap at the door and his secretary looked in, cringing as she received the full force of his laser-beam scowl. 'Sorry to disturb you Sir Richard, but the press conference is in two minutes.'

'Get out of here, you cow. Tell them it's cancelled,' yelled Cordwell.

As he breezed through the lobby, he was beckoned over by Johnnie Johnson. 'What have you done to Mr Mullett, Jack? He's been in a foul mood ever since you phoned him.'

'It's relief coupled with joy,' explained Frost. 'He was heart-broken because he thought he was going to lose me and now he's over the moon because he isn't.' He pulled the list of forged notes from his pocket. 'Have this photostated then taken round by hand to all banks, stores, garages, discount warehouses, public toilets, the lot. Get them to pay particular attention to anyone paying cash for large purchases, even in genuine notes. If anyone passes any of the duds we want to know right away.'

Johnson took the list and, in return, passed over a thick wad of computer print-outs. 'And this is for you, Jack. Details of all registered owners of Ford Escorts in Denton and the surrounding area.'

Frost flicked over the pages. It went on and on and on . . . There were hundreds of names and addresses. 'What silly sod asked for this?'

'You did, Jack. You're looking for the Ford Escort you saw just before the ransom money was taken.'

Frost stuck the print-out under his arm. 'I must have been bloody mad. Still, I won't be short of toilet paper this week – it'll make a change from Mullett's memos.'

Liz, her coat buttoned, was waiting for him in the office. 'Ready when you are, inspector,' she said.

'Ready for what?' asked Frost. 'If it's sex, then shut the door – I'm sorry I kept you waiting.'

She didn't even flicker a grin. The return she had so meticulously prepared had been snatched from her without a word of thanks by Cassidy and she had heard Mullett praising him for such a good job. 'You said we were going to Primrose Cottage – where Lemmy Hoxton was supposed to have pulled his last job.'

He hesitated. It was Cassidy's case, but Cassidy would have enough on his hands with Sidney Snell. He looked at the computer print-out and wondered if he should get people checking. But they didn't have the manpower and the list was too bloody long. 'Primrose Cottage? Right, let's do it now.'

Primrose Cottage, standing on its own at the end of a long winding lane, was a detached two-storey building erected in the sixties, but tarted up to look as if it dated from the seventeen hundreds. The doors were oak, stained black to give the appearance of age, the tiny bow windows were chintz-curtained and the walls were painted a fading buttercup colour. A white wooden gate opened on to a path to the front porch. Frost ducked to miss the hanging flower basket and rapped at the well-polished brass knocker.

'Who is it?' called a woman's voice, raised over the sound of a dog yapping.

'Police, Miss Fleming,' answered Frost. 'Nothing to worry about – just checking.'

The door opened slightly on a length of stout chain and the proffered warrant cards were studied. Then, reluctantly, she let them in. Millie Fleming was in her early forties, slightly plump, dark brown hair, and wearing a pink woollen cardigan over a floral dress. The dog was a small spaniel which hid under a chair the minute they walked in. 'Not a very good house dog, I'm afraid,' she smiled, 'but we hope his barking might frighten any burglars away.' They were in the living-room with its dark oak and chintzy furniture.

Frost patted the dog, which looked at him with big brown eyes filled with apology for its cowardice and licked his hand. 'Seems friendly enough,' he said. 'How old is he?'

'About four months. We haven't had him long.'

'You're pretty remote up here,' said Frost. 'You need a dog. Is it just you and your sister?'

'Yes. How can I help you, inspector?'

'Won't take up too much of your time. Did you have a visit from a man from the Water Board – or someone who said he was from the Water Board?'

'A long time ago,' she said. 'About five years – when we first moved in here. He turned on the water for us.'

'This would have been a bit more recent than that – about three months ago – early August?'

She shook her head. 'I don't think so.'

'He might have called when your sister was here,' suggested Frost. 'Is she in?'

'No. She works at the hospital – she's a nurse. She should be back soon, though.' She turned to Liz. 'Can you tell me what this is about?'

'We had complaints of a man preying on women like yourself,' said Liz. 'He claimed to be from the Water Board. Got the woman to turn on the kitchen taps while he stole jewellery and money from the bedroom.'

'Oh dear,' tutted Miss Fleming. 'How awful! If anyone comes here saying they are from the Water Board, I'll phone the police right away.'

Frost fished in his pocket for the photograph of Lemmy Hoxton. 'This might refresh your memory. Has this man ever called here?'

She took it to the window and studied it carefully, returning it with a shake of her head. 'I'm pretty certain I haven't seen him before. Can I ask why this is considered so important that an inspector and a sergeant have called on me?'

'He was found dead,' said Frost.

She clutched her dress. 'Dead?'

'We're trying to trace his movements. We believe he intended to call here on the day he died.'

'To rob us? Well, he didn't, I'm relieved to say.'

A car drew up outside, then the sound of a key turning in the front door. The dog emerged from under the chair and raced out of the room, barking joyously. Millie Fleming stood up. 'That will be my sister. Perhaps she might remember him.'

She left them and went to the passage. A brief murmur of conversation, then she returned, followed by a dark-haired, vivacious-looking woman in her mid-thirties wearing a nurse's uniform. Her hair gleamed and her face had a well-scrubbed look. She wore black tights which, as Frost was pleased to observe, showed off terrific legs.

The two women sat side by side on the settee opposite him. 'This is my sister, Julie,' said Millie.

The nurse smiled, showing perfect teeth. I'd love to have them nibbling round my ear-hole, thought Frost. 'Millie says it's something about a man calling here?' she asked.

Frost quickly filled her in and showed her the photograph, but her response was the same as her sister's. 'I'm pretty good at faces, but I can't recall seeing this man before.'

'Is it possible he called, but you were both out?' asked Frost. 'The afternoon of Friday, 6th August. Any way of checking if you were here?'

The nurse moved a stray wisp of hair from over her eyes. Frost was finding her disturbingly sexy and he wriggled uncomfortably in his chair. 'Depending on what shift I was on, I would either be at the hospital or in bed asleep.' She consulted a diary from her pocket. 'Nights that week. I'd have been at home.'

'And I'd probably be doing some gardening,' said her sister. 'I certainly didn't go out.'

Frost exchanged shrugs with Liz. It didn't look as if Lemmy made it to Primrose Cottage that day.

They took their leave. 'I didn't half fancy that little nurse,' said Frost, settling himself in the car. 'She can give me a blanket bath any time she likes.'

Liz gave a knowing smile as she jerked the car into gear. 'I don't think she would be very interested in you, inspector.'

'Oh?' said Frost, deflated.

'I think she might be more interested in me.'

'Eh?' It took a few minutes for the penny to drop, but he wasn't prepared to accept the insinuation. 'Oh, come off it. How can you tell?'

'Women have a way of knowing.'

He pictured the nurse again in his mind, then firmly shook his head. No way! He looked out of the window as they took a bend. 'Stop the car!'

They were at a turn-off where a rut-ridden lane meandered down to a small farm. This was the spot where Duggie Cooper claimed he parked the van when Lemmy went cycling off into the sunset to Primrose Cottage. Frost peered down the lane, then looked back the way they had come. 'If Duggie is telling the truth, Lemmy would have to come back this way. There's nowhere else for him to go.' He scratched his chin. 'The two women say he never arrived and Duggie says he never came back, so who is lying?' He signalled for her to drive on. 'I think we had better talk to Duggie again.'

Duggie was adamant. 'I'm telling you, Mr Frost, he pedalled up to the cottage on the bike and he never came back while I was there. Why should I lie?'

Before Frost could come up with his reasons, there was

an urgent tap at the door of the interview room. An excited DC Burton beckoned him over.

'Some of that funny money's turned up.'

'Already?' asked Frost. This was bloody marvellous. He thought they might have to wait days.

'The bank phoned. They've just had over £6000 paid in, over a thousand of it in forged notes.'

'Who paid it in?'

'Someone called Philip Mayhew, 47 Haig Avenue, Denton. I've checked with records. Nothing known about him.'

'Then let's make the sod's acquaintance,' said Frost, twisting his head back into the room and yelling, 'Interview suspended.'

It was a semi-detached house, newly pebble-dashed. Two cars, a Jaguar and a Ford Sierra, were parked in the road outside and there was a Range Rover in a driveway leading to closed garage doors.

'A lot of motors for one house,' commented Frost as they cruised slowly past, surveying the situation. The curtains to one of the upstairs rooms were drawn. He wondered if the boy was up there. They drove round the block. There seemed to be no rear exit from the property, except by clambering over about six garden fences to reach the side road. In one of the gardens a large, rippling-muscled rottweiler paced up and down, looking ready to tear any intruders to shreds. Little chance anyone would risk that, but to be on the safe side Frost posted a couple of men in the side road. His mind raced over all the things that might go wrong, but there were too many of them to worry about. They stopped outside the front of the house. 'All right. Let's go, go, go.'

Followed by Liz, Burton and two uniformed officers, he trotted up the path and hammered on the knocker. The door was no sooner opened when he slammed it back and the others raced inside.

'Police!' yelled Frost as the man, a brawny individual in his mid-forties, sporting a beard, and brandishing a baseball bat, tried to push the door shut, shouting for someone inside the house to call the police.

He swung the bat at Frost, but Liz, leaping on him from the back, managed to grab his arm and twist it. 'Drop it!' The bat clattered to the floor.

'Police,' repeated Frost, showing the man his warrant card. 'And we've got a warrant to search these premises.'

'You've got the wrong house,' bawled the man.

'Are you Philip Kenneth Mayhew? Then we've got the right house. Let's go inside.'

He pushed Mayhew through the first door leading off the hall which took them into a spacious lounge with an enormous five-speaker, cinema-sound television set that made the one Duggie had bought on Lemmy's card look like a portable. Suddenly, a woman in a tight-fitting black dress charged in, swinging an iron bar. Her long fingernails were painted silver. She looked as if she would happily use them to scratch Frost's eyes out. 'I've called the police, you bastards,' she screamed.

'We are the police,' said Frost.

She lowered the iron bar, but kept it swinging in her hand, warily. This scruff looked nothing like a policeman. She was only half convinced when she studied his warrant card. 'What's this all about?'

'That's what I want to know,' said the man. 'They claim to have a warrant.'

'We have got a warrant,' said Frost.

He gave it to Mayhew who skimmed through it and passed it over to the woman. 'Call our solicitor,' he said.

'You paid a large sum of money into the bank today,' said Frost.

'No, I didn't. I haven't left the bloody house all day.' He jammed a cigarette into his mouth and lit it with a table lighter in the shape of a vintage Rolls-Royce Silver Ghost.

'I'm telling you that you paid £6495 into Bennington's Bank in the High Street at 10.54 a.m. today,' insisted Frost.

'And I'm telling you I did not,' spat the man.

'If you must know, I paid it in,' shouted the woman. 'Why don't you get your bloody facts straight? No wonder innocent people get sent to prison.' The sound of thuds and bangs from upstairs suddenly intensified and sent her head jerking up. 'What are those buggers doing?' She went to charge out, only to be stopped by Liz. 'Let me go, you cow.'

Frost borrowed the Silver Ghost lighter for his own cigarette. He smiled sweetly at the woman, whose eyes were spitting bullets. 'I don't give a sod who actually paid it in,' he said. 'All I'm concerned with is that over £1000 of it was counterfeit.'

This stopped the woman in her tracks. She stared wide-eyed at her husband, whose jaw had sagged, showing his gold fillings. 'Counterfeit?'

Frost nodded.

The man smashed his cigarette out in a round glass ashtray which was enclosed in a miniature rubber car tyre. 'The bastard. The lousy rotten bastard. I'll break every bone in his body.'

'What particular bastard are we talking about?' asked Frost.

'The bastard I sold the car to.'

Frost frowned. 'What car?'

'The Honda Accord. He paid six and a half grand in cash and drove it away this morning.'

'You sold him a car?'

'Hoo-bloody-ray,' said the man, giving a mock clap. 'A brilliant deduction. Yes, I sold him a car. That's what I do. I sell used cars – didn't you damn well know?'

Frost didn't damn well know. Mayhew pushed a copy of the local free paper over to him. There was a block of cars for sale ringed round in the classified section. One of them was a Honda Accord priced at £6750.

The clatter of footsteps down the stairs and Burton looked in. His face told Frost they had found nothing, neither the ransom money nor any trace of the boy. 'You'd better do this room,' he told Burton. 'The other two can do the garden and the shed.'

He ushered Mayhew and his wife into the kitchen, a beautifully fitted room with expensive units, but empty bottles and unwashed crockery sprawled all over the place.

'It might speed things up if you told us what you were looking for,' said Mayhew. 'We might even be able to tell you where it is.'

'We're looking for the rest of the money.'

'What money? That's all he gave me. I paid it all into the bank.'

Frost leant against the dishwasher. 'Let's get this straight. You sell second-hand cars. So why did you try and attack us with a baseball bat?'

'Some people are dissatisfied with their purchase. Some come back very stroppy. We have to defend ourselves.'

'So this has happened before?'

He shrugged. 'Now and again. Some niggling little thing goes wrong and they want their money back.'

'Niggling little things? Like the wheels falling off or sawdust leaking from the gearbox?'

'The condition of the cars we sell is reflected in the price. You can't expect an ex-showroom Mercedes for three hundred quid.'

'Tell me about the Honda Accord,' said Frost.

'This bloke phoned me.'

'When?'

'This morning. Said he'd seen my ad in the local rag for the Honda. If it wasn't sold, he wanted to come round and have a look at it. I told him it hadn't been sold, but it was such a snip, he'd better get round quick before someone else snapped it up. He said he'd be round in half an hour.'

'And was he?'

'Half an hour – forty-five minutes . . . not long, anyway.'

'And how did he come – on foot?'

'No, in a grey Ford Escort. There was a girl with him. She drove.'

'Did she come in with him?'

'No, she waited outside.'

'Then what?'

'I showed him the motor – it was parked where the Rover is now – and I gave him a test drive round the block. He had a look at the engine and gave the tyres a kick. He asked how much I'd knock off for cash – as if I'd take a bleeding cheque! He told me he'd had a win on the horses. I said, Then it's your double lucky day because I'll let it go for six-five. He said, "Done". We shook hands and he fetched a plastic carrier bag from the Ford. I brought him in the house to give him the log-book and his receipt, while the wife tipped the money out and counted it. There was a fiver short, but I wasn't going to quibble over a lousy fiver. He took the log-book and his receipt, then drove off, followed by the tart in the Ford. End of story.'

The two uniformed men came in from the garden. 'Nothing,' they reported.

'You come back in a couple of days' time,' Mayhew told them. 'If I lay my hands on the bastard you'll find his body buried there.'

Burton also reported he had found nothing in the lounge, but Frost didn't seem too worried. 'If you gave him a receipt, you'll have his name and address?'

They followed Mayhew back to the lounge where he tugged open a sideboard drawer overflowing with papers. He gave Frost the carbon copy. 'Jack Roberts, 187 Kitchener Street, Denton.'

Frost passed it to Burton. 'See if we know him.'

Burton moved to the back of the room and whispered into his radio while Frost stubbed out his cigarette in the motor tyre ashtray. 'Describe him,' he said.

Mayhew thought for a moment. 'Twenty-five, twenty-six. Hair in a pony tail. Not much meat on him . . . slim build, about five feet eleven. He was wearing jeans . . . frayed cuffs, dirty trainers.'

'A bloody Beau Brummell,' said Frost. 'You weren't surprised he had six and a half grand on him?'

'Nothing surprises me in this game.'

'When we pick him up, I'll want you to identify him.'

'If I get to him first, he'll be the man with his dick ripped off.'

Frost grinned. Things were going right for a change. With luck they could make their arrest and have the kid back within the hour. He looked up expectantly as Burton clicked off the radio. But the expression on the constable's face sent his hopes nosediving to the ground.

'House numbers in Kitchener Street only go up to 92,' reported Burton. 'That name and address are as phoney as his money.'

14

Frost sat on the corner of the desk in the briefing room, an unlit cigarette dangling from his mouth. He filled everyone in on the latest position with the kidnapping. 'I'm getting worried,' he told them. 'He's got the ransom money, he's spending it, but he hasn't returned the boy. This could mean that Bobby is dead.' There were nods of agreement. Most of the team were beginning to share this view.

He lit the cigarette and took a deep drag. 'We've got one bit of luck on our side. The kidnapper has no idea that some of the money is dodgy, so he's got no qualms about spending it. He's bought himself a red Honda Accord and we've got its registration number. He's local, and he's going to be driving it around, so everyone keeps their bloody eyes open.' He nodded at Arthur Hanlon who had his hand up to ask a question. 'Yes, Arthur?'

'How do we know he's local?'

'He spotted the ad for the Honda in the *Denton Free Advertiser*, which is only distributed locally. It only took him half an hour to reach the bloke who was selling it. We know a bit more about him. He's got a girlfriend who drives a grey Ford Escort, in which she is not averse to having it away, although, sadly, that probably applies to half the female population of Denton. Unless he's got a garage, the Honda could be parked out in the street, so go over every bloody street and back alley. Find the bastard. But remember, as much as we want him, more importantly we want to find the kid. If we spot him, don't pick him up . . . follow and keep me informed. Off you go . . .'

He watched them file out, then winced as Mullett came bowling in. 'Another lead fizzled out, then, inspector?'

'Yes,' grunted Frost. Go and gloat somewhere else, you vindictive sod.

'Pity you don't have the success Mr Cassidy seems to be enjoying. It might not be a bad idea if you let him take over this case.'

Frost tightened his lips, but said nothing. He stood up and squeezed past Mullett. 'I think that's my phone ringing,' he said.

He barged past Mullett who strained his ears, but couldn't hear a phone.

Bill Wells grabbed him just as he was going out for a drive around. Anything to get away from Mullett. 'Sidney Snell wants to talk to you, Jack.'

'Not my case,' grunted Frost.

'He says it's very important.'

'Where's Cassidy?'

'Out somewhere.'

Frost shrugged. What the hell – it wouldn't hurt to find out what Snell had to say. He followed Wells down to the cells and waited while the door was unlocked. Snell, sitting on the bunk bed, hugging his knees, looked up plaintively.

'I didn't do it, Mr Frost.'

'You haven't dragged me down here just to hear that same old cracked record, I hope, Sidney. I know it off by heart. *"I didn't do it, Mr Frost, honest, on my mother's grave."*'

'Well, this time it happens to be true.'

'Even if it is, so what? You're a scumbag, Sidney . . . for that alone you deserve to be banged up.'

'But not for something I didn't do. I don't kill kids and I don't kill women.'

'But you do sign bleeding confessions,' said Frost.

'He made me, Mr Frost. Mr Cassidy kept on and on telling me I did it, and that I'd feel better if I got it off my chest. In the end I just signed the confession to get a bit of peace.'

'I reckon you'll get twenty-five years' worth of peace, Sidney – perhaps a couple of days less for good behaviour.'

'I confessed, but I didn't do it,' Snell insisted.

'The Guildford Four, the Birmingham Six and now the Denton One. Face up to the facts, Sidney. One of the dead kids was stabbed, the way you stab little kiddies, your blood and chunks of flesh are over the plywood on the back door panel. You were seen running away afterwards. And if that wasn't enough, you're a slimy little bastard, and I hate the sight of you.'

'I was there that night, Mr Frost, I don't deny that. I followed her about when she took the kids out to the park, and I used to stare at her through the windows . . . but I never killed her or the kids.'

'So why did you break in at one o'clock in the morning? To apologize?'

'All I intended to do was look through the window. As God is my witness, Mr Frost, that's all I intended doing, but sometimes I can't control myself . . . The devil talks to me.'

'And what did the devil say – "Kill them all, just to spite that silly sod Mr Frost who should have had you arrested, but was too bleeding lazy"?'

'He drew my attention to that loose sheet of plywood. He said I should push my hand through and unbolt the door.' Snell rubbed his bandaged hand. 'I just meant to look at them . . . I like looking at kiddies asleep in their cots.'

'I like looking at naked nymphomaniacs, but I couldn't promise I'd just look at them. You had your stabbing knife with you, and you bloody used it.'

Snell buried his face in his hands. 'Just enough to break the skin, Mr Frost. I can't help myself. I don't know why, but I like it when I see the blood . . . tiny drops of red on their little arms.'

'Look out, Sidney, you're dribbling,' said Frost.

Snell wiped his mouth. 'I get a sexual kick out of it, but I don't kill – I couldn't.'

Frost sat down on the bunk beside him and lit up a cigarette. 'According to your statement, the kids woke up and started screaming . . . all three of them. You had to silence them, so you used the pillow . . . and then their mother came running in and you had to kill her as well.'

'No!' Snell was almost shouting now. 'Mr Cassidy put the words in my mouth. I couldn't kill anyone. I'm terrified of death and dead bodies.' He waved away the cigarette Frost was offering. 'They made me look at my mother's dead body in the hospital. She was all shrivelled up. She looked horrible.'

'She looked pretty bleeding horrible when she was alive,' said Frost.

'I thought they were showing me the wrong body . . . but it was her. I ran out and never went back. Do you think I'd want to see any more dead bodies after that, Mr Frost?' He shook his head firmly. 'No way . . . no way!'

'If you want to withdraw your confession,' said Frost, 'then tell Mr Cassidy. This isn't my case.'

Snell ignored him, eyes glazed in recollection. He was back in the house that cold, frosty night. 'I tiptoed over to the kids' room. I pushed open the door and held my breath. It was so quiet – that should have warned me something was wrong. You can usually hear kids . . . they make a hell of a row when they're asleep, snorting and snuffling. But I was too excited to worry. There was this little boy. He had little podgy arms lying on top of the eiderdown. I pulled back the sleeve of his pyjamas and pricked him, very quickly. It doesn't hurt them, Mr Frost. They get frightened when they wake, but it doesn't hurt them. I broke the skin, but he didn't murmur or wake up. I let go of his arm and it just dropped down. And when I touched his face, he didn't move, and I couldn't hear him breathing. None of them were breathing. Then I realized he was dead . . . they were all dead. I was in a room with three dead kids. I panicked. I charged straight out through the front door and into the street.'

'Was there anyone about in the street at the time?'

'An old boy with a dog. I nearly sent him flying.'

'We know about him. Anyone else?'

'I didn't see anyone. I just raced for the car and got the hell out of there. You've got to help me, Mr Frost. I'm innocent.'

Frost dropped his cigarette end and stamped it to death on the cell floor. 'You're not innocent, Sidney. You're a perverted little bastard who interferes with kids. We might have got you for the wrong crime, but so what – the end result's the same. You get put away and everyone's happy.'

'But if I'm banged up for this, Mr Frost, it means the real killer gets away with it.'

Frost sighed. 'All right, Sidney, I'll have a sniff around and see what I come up with – but don't hold your breath.' He yelled for Bill Wells to let him out. 'Gross miscarriage of justice,' he told the sergeant.

'The only miscarriage of justice would be if they ever let the sod out,' said Wells.

The tottering heap in his in-tray looked ready to fall over at any minute. He skimmed through it to see what he could throw away. A thick wad turned out to be the Crime Rate Detection Statistical Analysis that Liz had prepared with the request that he should check through it and sign it as correct. He signed it unread and hurled it into his out-tray. Then all the papers on his desk fluttered as Cassidy, his face distorted in anger, burst in and jabbed an accusing finger. 'You've been talking to Snell?'

'He asked to see me.'

'Whether he asked to see you or not, he is my prisoner and this is *my* case. You ask me first – understand?'

'All right,' shrugged Frost. 'Keep your hair on.' He was getting more and more fed up with Cassidy.

'What did he want to see you about – or did you intend keeping that to yourself?'

'He said he didn't do it.'

Cassidy fluttered pages of stapled typescript in Frost's face. 'He has signed a confession!'

'He wants to withdraw it.'

Cassidy's face went a dirty brick red. His fists clenched and unclenched as if he was ready to punch Frost on the chin. 'It may not fit in with your crack-pot theories but Snell, the man you refused to arrest, has admitted everything. He did it – the kids and the mother. So stay away from him. This is my case and I don't want you ruining it to satisfy your own personal ego.' With one last sizzling death-ray of a glare, he spun round and stamped out of the office, nearly sending Burton flying as he did so.

Burton had to clear his throat to attract Frost's attention. 'Mr Cassidy sounded a bit upset?' He tried hard to keep the pleasure out of his voice.

'You noticed it too?' said Frost in mock surprise. 'I thought it was just me. What can I do for you?'

'You told us to keep an eye on Ian Grafton's place.'

Frost frowned. 'Then I'm sure I had a good reason for it – but who the hell is Ian Grafton?'

'The bloke who took Tracey Neal to the bank when Carol Stanfield was abducted.'

'Ah – the bloke with the pigtail. What about him?'

'A lot of expensive hi-fi equipment was delivered there this morning. Nine hundred and ninety-five quid's worth.'

He now had Frost's full attention. 'Right – check with the shop. Find out how he paid for it.'

'I did,' said Burton, sounding hurt. It was the first thing he had done. 'Cash. Spot cash.'

Frost unhitched his scarf from the hat-stand. 'I think he's worth another visit, son.'

'What – now?' asked Burton.

Frost paused. His mind was still on Snell and the three dead kiddies. 'No. There's something I want to do first. That security guard who said Grover and his mate never left the store. I want to talk to him.'

'But that's Mr Cassidy's case,' Burton pointed out. 'Didn't he just say—'

Frost's hand flashed up to cut him short. 'I didn't quite catch what Mr Cassidy said, son. He was shouting so much. But I'll check with him when we get back.'

The security guard, Paul Milton, lived in a small, three-bedroomed terraced house on the far side of the golf course. If it wasn't for the swirl of damp mist clinging to the green, the bungalow where the tragedy took place could just about be seen from his upstairs window. Milton's wife, a six-month-old baby in her arms, let them in. 'He's just gone up to bed,' she told them. 'He's on nights this week.'

They followed her into the dining-room where a chubby boy of two was sitting in a high chair chewing solemnly on a slice of bread and jam.

'We would like to see him,' smiled Frost. 'It won't take a minute.'

'Paul!' she yelled, as she plonked herself down next to the high chair and started shovelling Heinz baby food down the infant's throat.

'What is it now?' replied an irritated voice from above. 'I've only just this bloody minute gone up.'

'Police!'

'What do they bloody want?'

'If you bloody come down you'll find out.'

Paul Milton, tucking his shirt inside his trousers,

staggered into the room. He was bleary-eyed and unshaven. 'I should be asleep,' he moaned to Frost. 'I'm on duty tonight.' He sat in a chair next to his wife. 'What can I do for . . . Shit!' The expletive because the baby had spat a mouthful of food all over him. The little boy in the high chair dropped his bread and jam on the floor and started to cry. 'It's like a flaming madhouse in here,' he yelled as his wife placidly retrieved the slice of bread, picked off the worst of the fluff and returned it to the child. He stood up and buttoned his shirt collar. 'We'll go in the lounge.'

He led them out into the passage, but as his hand reached for the door handle to the lounge, he hesitated and did a U turn. 'Perhaps the kitchen would be better.'

But nothing could have been worse than the kitchen which was a tip, even by Frost's low standards. Unwashed plates and saucepans piled high on the draining board, bits of food on the floor alongside a long-unemptied cat's litter tray. A nappy bucket, filled to overflowing, was parked alongside the washing machine. Milton shook a chair to dislodge a heap of mucky bibs and nappies and waved a hand for Frost to sit. The invitation was hastily declined, as was the offer of a cup of tea.

Frost lit up a cigarette. He wasn't sure if it was the cat's litter tray or the nappy bucket that was getting to him, but hoped his cigarette smoke might improve the atmosphere. 'Couple of questions to ask you, Mr Milton. I know you've covered all this ground already, but I just want to be absolutely sure. It's about Mark Grover.'

Milton sighed and shook his head in sad disbelief. 'Those poor kids. His wife must have been right round the bend.' He pulled a face at the howls from the dining-room. 'I often feel like wringing my own kids' necks, but I'd never actually do it.'

Frost gritted his teeth against the noise. 'If you feel like doing it now, Mr Milton, don't let us stop you.' He consulted his notes. 'Grover told one of my officers that he and Phil Collard arrived at the store around eight to do the carpet and didn't leave until around ten to two in the morning. Is that correct?'

He yawned, not bothering to cover his mouth. 'Quite correct.'

'Any chance either of them could have left the building without you knowing?'

'No way. It's all electronically controlled. I'd have to operate the switch.'

'They were working on the top floor. Where were you?'

'Either in my cubicle by the back entrance, or doing my rounds. I have to cover every floor at half-hourly intervals and click a key into time locks.'

'While you were on your rounds, could they have got out?'

'Not without setting off the alarms when the door opened – and they'd have to have the master key and that was with me all the time. If they wanted to go out, they only had to ask – it's not a flaming prison.'

'And they didn't ask?'

'No.' Another yawn.

Frost accepted this gloomily. He was convinced Mark Grover had found a way to leave the store without anyone knowing, but he couldn't see how he could prove it. 'Thanks for your trouble, Mr Milton. We'll let you get some sleep.'

At the door to the lounge he stopped. Why didn't Milton want to take them in there? What was he hiding? Stuff nicked from the store perhaps? He reached for the door handle. 'Is this the way out?' he asked innocently.

'No, not in there,' called Milton, running forward, but he was too late. Frost was already inside.

The strong aroma of expensive new wool filled the room, a smell Frost had noted earlier in Bonley's department store. Woollen carpeting. He switched on the light. And there it was, on the floor, red, blue and expensive, stretching from wall to wall. The pattern was very familiar. It was the design for Bonley's new restaurant, an exclusive design, specially made and imported for them.

'I spy,' said Frost, 'with my little eye, something that has been nicked.'

'An odd remnant that was left over,' spluttered Milton. 'It would only have gone to waste.'

Frost sat down on the settee and prodded the carpet's springiness with his foot. 'Tell me about it.'

'Someone must have made a mistake with the measurements because there was this great chunk of carpet left over . . . so me and the fitters had half each.'

'How did it manage to find its way from the store to here?'

Milton shuffled his feet and wouldn't meet Frost's eye. 'They dropped it in for me.'

'So Grover and Collard did leave the store that night?'

'Well – yes. But not for long . . . hour or so at the most.'

'And you lied to us?'

'A white lie. I'm supposed to be the security guard. If Bonley's ever found out I was party to sneaking out a thousand quid's worth of top quality carpeting, I'd have been for the high jump.'

'You still might be for the flaming high jump. We're investigating a murder and you are making false statements to the police. Unless you want to get deeper into the mire than you already are, you'd better tell me everything . . . right from the start . . . and the bloody truth this time.'

'All right. They turned up just after eight, like I said, and they worked like the clappers – didn't even stop for anything to eat. By midnight they were well on the way to finishing and they find there's a dirty great chunk of carpeting left over . . . worth around a thousand quid, so

Mark Grover reckoned. We made a deal. They'd lay it in my lounge for me and they'd keep the rest. Just before midnight I let them out. They dropped off my bit and took their own piece. They were back again around half-past one and finished off at the store . . . Yesterday afternoon the fat one – Phil Collard – called here to lay it for me. He stressed we should all keep our mouths shut about the other night, in case we got found out.'

Frost gnawed away at his thumb knuckle. 'How did they seem when they came back?'

'Same as always. I didn't pay them too much attention as I was due for my next round of clocking on. I could hear them working away up there and just before two they came down and went off home. You won't tell my firm, will you?'

Before Frost could reply, Burton was hammering at the front door. 'Control have radioed through. The red Honda – Jordan and Simms have found it parked in Whitmore Avenue.'

As the car sped through the traffic, Frost brought Burton up to date regarding his talk with the security guard. 'So that's Mark Grover's alibi shot right up the fundamental orifice.'

'So he could have done it,' said Burton grudgingly, inching the car forward in anticipation of the traffic lights changing, 'but that doesn't prove that he did do it.'

'You're too bloody finicky,' grunted Frost. 'Mr Cassidy won't like it but I'm having Grover and his fat mate in for more questioning.' They turned a corner and Frost pointed. 'There's the area car . . .'

PC Jordan, in Charlie Bravo, was waiting for them down the side street while PC Simms, a mac over his uniform, was in Whitmore Avenue keeping an eye on the Honda. 'Let's take a look,' said Frost.

He went with Jordan and cautiously peered round the corner. Whitmore Avenue was a broken-down terrace of three-storey houses, some of them with basements. Many of the buildings had been split up into flats, others, beyond repair, were boarded up and empty. The road was jam-packed with cars, mostly old bangers, but the nearly new red Honda, gleaming under the light of a nearby lamp post, screamed at them as the odd man out.

'About as inconspicuous as a topless tart in a monastery,' commented Frost.

Simms wandered down to join them. 'We're presuming the kidnapper is in one of the houses,' he told Frost, 'but we don't know which one. He's probably stuck it where there was a vacant space and not necessarily outside where he lives.'

'He may not even live in this street,' said Burton. 'He could have parked it well away from his own place.'

'No,' said Frost. 'A shiny new motor in this bloody neighbourhood. He'll park it where he can keep an eye on it. A fiver says he lives in one of these houses.'

They went back to the side street to await reinforcements. In a couple of minutes another car shuddered to a stop behind Frost's Ford and Liz Maud, accompanied by two other officers in plain clothes, got out. A burst from the radio. Another car with four more officers was on its way. Frost directed them to go round the block and wait at the opposite end of Whitmore Avenue. It might be over-kill, but he was taking no chances this time.

Back with Burton to take another look. There were some twenty three-storeyed houses on each side. 'Damn,' muttered Frost. 'We can't go knocking at bloody doors asking for the owner of the red Honda to come out. If he's got the kid holed up here, we could end up with a hostage situation.'

'So how do we get him out?' asked Burton.

Frost thought for a moment, then he walked over to a ramshackle waist-high brick wall that protected the basement area of a boarded-up property. The cement was crumbling and most of the bricks were loose. He worked a brick free and walked casually over to the red Honda. A quick look up and down the street, then with a hefty blow he smashed the brick down on the driver's window, shattering the glass.

Immediately the car alarm system screamed out and the car lights flashed on and off. Frost stuck his hand through the broken window and tried to reach the cassette player on the dash.

A shaft of light sliced across the street as an upstairs window shot up. A man leant out. 'Get away from my car, you bastard.' Frost ignored him, still reaching for the cassette player.

The head disappeared and a few seconds later the street door opened and the man burst out, charging across the road, his pony tail flying. 'Go, go, go!' yelled Frost into his radio, realizing even as he said it that he hadn't positioned his team properly.

The police thudded down from each end of the street. Half-way across the road, the man hesitated, spotted the stampede and turned to run back to the house.

'Shit!' snarled Frost. He hadn't made certain someone was near to cut off his escape. If the man got back inside and slammed the door they could be faced with the very hostage situation he had tried to avoid. He started to chase after the man, but quickly realized he was not going to make it in time. To his relief, he saw that Liz had had the foresight to run down the other side of the road, ready to block his path.

'Stop . . . Police!' she yelled.

'Out of my way, you bitch,' screamed the man, his fists flailing. It wasn't quite clear what happened next. Like a terrier after a rat, Liz darted forward, grabbed the man's arm. Her knee came up, the man yelped with pain and collapsed to the ground, clutching his groin. Before he had time to recover, Liz had him face down and was pinning his arms behind his back. Then Burton and Frost were with her.

'Get this fat cow off of me,' yelled the man.

Burton leant down and snapped the cuffs on his wrist. 'You're nicked,' he said, rather redundantly. Liz stood up, dusting herself down, while Burton hauled the man to his feet and went through his pockets. He found a driving licence and flipped it open, then handed it to Frost.

'Craig Hudson. Is this you?'

The man, white-faced, nodded.

'And is this your car?'

'Yes – and you'll pay for the damage, you bastard.' Then the pain gave him a jab making him hiss through clenched teeth. 'That bloody cow – I need a doctor.'

'Play your cards right and she might kiss it better,' said Frost, grabbing him by the arm. 'Let's go inside and have a talk.'

They marched him back into the house and up a flight of stairs covered in dark green lino. The door to the first-floor flat was wide open and they walked into a largish room, barely furnished with a TV set and a three-piece suite in a faded floral moquette. The floor was littered with empty foil takeaway food containers and the spicy reek of takeaway curry battled with marijuana for supremacy. At first they thought the room was empty, but a puff of thick smoke billowed above the back of the settee. Lying full length, a dark-haired girl in her early twenties, eyes half closed and a look of utter euphoria on her face, was dragging at the fat parcel of a hand-rolled joint. She had on a grey sweater which had been rolled up to her neck, exposing gorgeous bare breasts and a flat stomach. Her jeans and black knickers were round her ankles. 'I hope we haven't interrupted your meal,' murmured Frost politely, his eyes bulging.

The girl smiled blissfully and offered Frost a drag on her joint.

'Get yourself covered up,' hissed Liz.

'Leave her,' said Frost. There had been too few perks with the job recently. He dragged his eyes away and turned his attention to the man. 'Sit!' he commanded. Burton pushed him down into the chair.

Sounds of a commotion from downstairs, then heavy footsteps and Cassidy came barging in. 'Mr Mullett thought I should be in on this,' he announced.

'Great,' said Frost, flatly. Cassidy was Mullett's blue-eyed boy at the moment. Quickly, he filled him in, then got Jordan and Burton to thoroughly search every room in the house. And next they would have to check every house in the street. The boy could be bound and gagged in any of the derelict boarded-up properties. Back to the man. 'Where is he?'

'Who?'

'Don't sod us about,' shouted Cassidy. 'You know damn well who we mean. Where is the boy?'

'Boy? What boy?'

The girl on the settee had let her cigarette go out and was now humming a little song to herself as her hands rubbed up and down her body. Frost was finding it increasingly difficult to concentrate on the matter in hand.

'Bobby Kirby,' said Cassidy. 'Where is he?'

'Never heard of him,' said the man. 'Can I have these handcuffs off now, please.'

'When we're ready,' said Cassidy.

'Take them off,' said Frost. Hudson wasn't going to try anything now.

Burton unlocked them, watched by a scowling Cassidy, angry that Frost had undermined him.

Hudson rubbed his wrists to restore the circulation. 'I demand to know what this is about.'

'Shut up!' snarled Cassidy. 'I do the bloody demanding, not you.'

Jordan signalled to Frost from the door. He'd done a

quick check through the flats in this house. No sign of the kid. He was moving on to the other houses.

Cassidy was about to interrogate Hudson further when Frost suddenly came out with the stupid question, 'Where did you get the takeaway?'

Cassidy gaped and stared in disbelief. What the hell did that matter? They were looking for a missing kid, for Pete's sake!

Seeing Cassidy's annoyance, the man grinned. 'The Taj Mahal round the corner. Why – do you want some?'

'Did you collect it, or was it delivered?'

'Delivered. What the bloody hell is this about?'

Frost took Liz to one side. 'Nip round the Indian and find out what was delivered.'

She looked at him the same way Cassidy did. 'Why?'

'If they've got the kid here somewhere, I'm hoping they'll feed him. Miss Curry-tits on the settee doesn't look as if she could butter a slice of bread without getting it all over her nipples, so I'm hoping they might have got three meals in from the takeaway.'

Begrudgingly, she acknowledged the sense of this and went out to make her enquiries.

Cassidy went back to his questioning. 'You paid six and a half grand for a car. Where did a scumbag like you get that sort of money?'

'I had a win on a horse.'

'What horse?' barked Cassidy.

Hudson fired the answer straight back. 'Dancing Foam, two o'clock race, yesterday.'

There was a morning paper on the floor by the settee. Frost opened it at the racing page and checked. 'He's right. Dancing Foam won five to one.'

'You see!' smirked Hudson.

'But at five to one,' pointed out Frost, 'you'd have to stake over a thousand quid to win your motor money. To quote my good friend Mr Cassidy, where did a scumbag like you get a thousand quid?'

'I saved it up.'

'I knew there was a logical explanation,' said Frost.

Burton came into the room triumphantly brandishing the travel bag. 'Look what I found stuffed behind the wardrobe,' he said.

Frost unzipped it. It was packed tight with ten and twenty pound notes. 'Did you save this up as well?'

Hudson stared at it, then jerked his head away. 'Nothing to say,' he mumbled.

'You'd better bloody say something,' snarled Cassidy. 'This money was used to pay the ransom for Bobby Kirby. You're in serious trouble, my friend. So where is the boy?'

'I don't know anything about the boy.' He slumped back in the chair.

Frost leant over him and pointed to the near-naked girl on the settee, who was stroking her breasts with feathery fingers and grinning inanely. 'Take a good look, son. You won't get any more of that if you're doing twenty years in the nick. I'd start answering a few questions if I were you.'

Hudson looked over at the girl, who grinned back at him and wriggled her body provocatively. 'All right. I found that money.'

'Where?'

'Dumped by a rubbish bin, just outside the car-park in the town centre.'

'You're a bloody liar,' yelled Cassidy. 'Where is the boy?'

'How many more times? I don't know anything about the damn kid.'

The girl on the settee had now decided to try and sit up. The effort made her giggle. Frost went over to her and shook her by the shoulders roughly. Her head snapped from side to side and her hair fell all over her eyes. A bonus was her breasts which swayed delightfully from side to side like the head of a questing snake.

Frost found a part of him enjoying the view, the other deeply concerned about the boy. 'Where is he?'

She gaped up at him, trying to focus through wisps of stray hair, her expression one of bemused delight. 'I love it when you get rough . . .'

'I haven't started getting rough yet,' snapped Frost. 'Where is the kid?'

'I haven't got a kid,' she giggled. 'I'm on the pill.'

Frost let her drop. This was useless. He beckoned Burton over. 'Get SOCO and Forensic . . . and tell Sergeant Wells I need a lot more men down here.' He turned to Cassidy. 'Take Hudson and Miss Curry-belly down to the station and try and get them to tell us where the kid is. I'll follow on as soon as we've got things organized here.'

Blankets from the bedroom were draped over the girl and she was hustled out with Hudson.

Frost smoked and watched and tried not to get in anyone's way as he waited for Forensic and SOCO. 'Go over every inch of this place,' he told them. 'We want to know if the kid has been here.' Slamming of car doors outside as more men arrived. He went down to meet them. 'Search every building in the street. Search every flat, every basement, occupied or not – kick in doors if necessary, I'll carry the can if anyone complains.' He waited while Burton organized them into search groups, then drove back to the station.

Hudson, in the white one-piece boiler suit they had forced him to put on while his clothes were taken away for forensic examination, sat in the interview room rubbing his wrists and his groin. If he ever met up with that cow of a policewoman on a dark night . . . He stared moodily at the uniformed officer leaning against the green-painted walls. 'How much longer?'

The officer shrugged.

'Where's Cindy, my girlfriend?'

Again the officer shrugged.

'Can I have a fag?'

'I don't smoke,' said the officer, sounding pleased he was able to deny this to the prisoner.

Hudson looked up as Cassidy, followed by Detective Sergeant Hanlon, came in. 'About bloody time.'

Cassidy gave the prisoner his long, hard stare and waited for Hanlon to load up the cassette recorder. 'My name is Cassidy, Acting Detective Inspector Cassidy. Also present is Detective Sergeant Hanlon. Where is the boy?'

'You don't bloody listen, do you? Watch my lips – I know nothing about no boy.'

'You demanded a ransom. You paid for a Honda Accord vehicle with part of that ransom money.'

'I told you, I found it!'

'You are lying.'

'Prove it!'

'Where's the kid?'

'I don't know anything about any kid . . .'

Frost waited impatiently in his office for the result of the search, a cigarette smouldering away in a disgusting-looking ashtray, piled high with grey ash. Liz had phoned through to report that the Indian takeaway had delivered a meal for two, not three. If they had the kid, surely they would feed him . . . or perhaps the kid was dead, so they didn't have to. Hudson wasn't intelligent enough to have organized the kidnap. Perhaps someone else was behind it . . . the girl? She was still in no state to be interviewed, so it was up to Cassidy to try and get something from the man.

'Any news?'

It was flaming Mullett in his smart, TV interview uniform. He'd been sticking his head round the door every five minutes.

'Nothing yet,' Frost told him.

Mullett scowled as if the lack of progress was Frost's fault. 'I want a quick result on this one.'

'I believe you have mentioned it, sir,' muttered Frost. The phone rang. He snatched it up. Burton calling from the flat. 'Forensic have crawled over every inch of the place. Not a damn thing to link Hudson with the kidnapping – apart from the ransom money, of course.'

'And how is the search of the other properties going?'

'No joy so far. A couple of people have refused permission to let us in to their premises.'

'Sod their permission. Go in anyway. We can always apologize afterwards.' He hung up. Mullett pretended not to have heard Frost's instructions so he could absolve himself from any involvement in the event of a comeback.

Frost glanced at his watch. What the hell was Cassidy playing at? He'd been questioning Hudson for well over an hour. A clatter of footsteps down the corridor and Cassidy came in, looking angry and frustrated.

'I can't get anywhere with him. He denies any knowledge of the kidnapping and repeats over and over again that he found the bag of money dumped in the car-park.'

'Why don't we set up an identity parade – get Finch to identify him?' Mullett suggested.

'I'd prefer to avoid that if possible,' replied Frost. 'Finch has already identified the wrong man. His defence would pull any subsequent identification to shreds . . . and the silly sod could well pick out another flaming look-alike.'

'What have Forensic turned up?' asked Mullett.

'Slightly less than sod all.' Frost picked up his ashtray and emptied it into the waste bin. 'Right. Back to Hudson. We forget the niceties and scare the shit out of the bastard.'

'Wait,' called Mullett. 'We don't want any of your famous short-cuts and corner cutting, Frost – things that won't stand up in a court. The important thing is to secure a conviction.'

'No,' said Frost. 'The important thing is to find the kid . . . and that's what I intend to do.'

'I'm warning you,' said Mullett. 'If we lose a conviction because of your underhand methods . . .'

'If my underhand methods result in us finding the kid, then we'll get a conviction anyway. Don't worry, sir, I'll be taking all the blame if things go wrong.' He knew he'd get the blame anyway.

'On your own head be it,' said Mullett as Frost brushed past him on his way to the interview room. 'If this blows up in your face I shall deny all knowledge of this conversation.'

Cassidy gave a sympathetic smile to Mullett as he followed Frost out, his smile saying, 'I'm with you all the way, sir, if things go wrong . . .' But if they went right, he was determined to grab his share of the glory.

'Now what?' asked Hudson as Frost entered the interview room with Cassidy.

Frost dropped into the chair opposite him and banged a folder on the table. Cassidy had the cassette ready to insert into the machine, but Frost stopped him. 'I don't want this recorded.' He smiled sweetly at Hudson. 'Where is Bobby Kirby?'

'I'm not wasting my breath answering this same question any more. For the last time, I know nothing about no kid.'

'Right,' said Frost. 'I haven't got time to sod about.' He swung round to the uniformed man. 'Would you wait outside, please, constable.'

The constable hesitated, but did what he was told, closing the door firmly behind him.

Frost beamed at Hudson. 'Isn't this cosy? Just the three of us.'

Hudson's eyes flickered apprehensively between the two detectives. 'What's going on?'

Frost beamed at him and pulled two photographs from the folder. He slid them across to Hudson.

'Recognize them?'

Hudson gave them a half-hearted glance. 'No.'

'That's funny,' said Frost, as he tapped the photograph of Bobby Kirby. 'This is the boy you kidnapped.'

'I've already told—'

'Shut up!' Frost's voice rose to a bellow. 'I'm tired, I've been up half the night and I'm not in the mood for any more sodding around. I don't give a toss what you say, I'm telling you what happened.' He banged a finger on Bobby Kirby's photograph. 'You kidnapped this kid and you killed the other one. You sent the ransom demand and you went with your slut of a girlfriend to the common to collect it. You knocked the old boy out and snatched the cash. You thought you would get away with it. You thought the money would be untraceable . . . but it wasn't. We've got you to rights so we don't give a sod about all your lies that you know nothing about it. We're not even bothering to record them any more.'

'Look, I don't know what you're talking about. I found that money. If you think you can prove otherwise—'

'Shut up!' roared Frost again. 'You won't know me, sonny. My name is Jack Frost. I'm not a very good cop and I'm not a very smart cop, so I have to cut corners. Sometimes I might even have to lie to secure a conviction, so I'm prepared to tell all the lies going about you, you toe-rag. I've got no compunction because I know you are guilty.'

To show his lack of concern, Hudson pulled a comb from his pocket and flicked it through his hair. Frost stretched out a hand. 'Can I borrow that?'

With a bemused smile, Hudson handed it over then watched in bewilderment as Frost tugged a few hairs from the comb and slipped them into a small transparent envelope which he tucked inside the folder. 'What's that for?'

'We've asked our Forensic Lab to do a thorough check of the dead kid's clothes to see if there is anything on them that would help us identify the killer . . . like hairs, for example.' He patted the folder.

The smirk had slid from Hudson's face. 'You are going to fit me up, you bastard.'

Frost looked apologetic. 'Only if I have to, son. You're guilty anyway, so I wouldn't lose any sleep over it.'

'You wouldn't dare.'

Frost smiled sweetly. 'Just watch me.'

Hudson spun round to Cassidy, hoping for support. He sensed the antagonism between the two men. 'You heard what he said. You're my witness!'

Cassidy stared straight ahead, saying nothing. If this thing blew up, he would drop Frost right in it.

Hudson's face was ugly. 'You bastards!'

'Sticks and stones,' reproved Frost. 'Where's the kid?'

The man folded his arms and leant back in his chair. 'All right. I'll tell you the truth. Yes, I nicked the money. I was with Cindy . . . she loves having it away out in the open. We see this green Nissan car pull up and a bloke nips out with a travel bag and hides it in the bushes. I thought I'd take a look-see, so after about a quarter of an hour—'

'Why did you wait so long?'

'First, because it was peeing down with rain and I was hoping it might ease up, two I had no trousers on at the time and three, Cindy was demanding seconds. By the time I got over there, this old boy was ferreting about. He pounces on the bag, so I nipped in quick and tried to grab it from him. He puts up a bit of a fight. I don't want no aggro so I welt him with a chunk of wood, grab the bag, nip back to the car and we sodded off back home. When I saw all that money inside, I just couldn't believe my rotten luck. That is all I am admitting to and I know nothing about no bleeding kids . . .'

15

Frost was in his office gloomily staring at his ashtray with its mountain of fluffy grey ash studded with cigarette ends. The room was fogged with smoke, his mouth tasted horrible and his fingers glistened with oily nicotine. He had smoked himself sick and didn't want another cigarette, but the urge to punish himself for his lack of progress was overwhelming, so he lit up yet another of Mullett's specials as he waited for Liz to return from questioning Hudson's girlfriend. He just knew she would confirm Hudson's alibi and absolve him from any connection with the kidnapping and that yet another lead would come to a dead end.

It hadn't been a good day so far. Mullett had finally stamped off home in high dudgeon when he realized he wouldn't be able to make his television announcement that the boy had been found safe and well, and the kidnapper had been arrested. On top of that, Snell had got himself a solicitor and had withdrawn his confession, saying it was obtained under duress, and for that Mullett and Cassidy definitely blamed Frost and had lost no time in telling him so.

Liz came in, coughing and fanning the air with her hand against the smoke. 'She's told you where the kid is?' asked Frost hopefully.

Liz shook her head and sat at her desk. 'No. She bears out everything Hudson said. They were both having it away when they saw the money being dropped. They nicked the money, but that's as far as they were involved.

She also confirms that the night the boy was taken, she and Hudson were at a disco in Levington until gone midnight. She's given me a string of names who can confirm this.' Liz offered him the list, but he wasn't interested. 'Check it out,' he said, but he knew it would confirm their statements.

Frost yawned. He felt deflated. The third day of the investigation and they were exactly nowhere. He tossed a screwed-up Mullett memo in the air and headed it into the wastepaper bin. 'Do you like fish and chips?' he asked.

She blinked her surprise. 'Yes – why?'

He pulled his scarf from its hook. 'Let's go and get some.'

The door to the incident room crashed open and Frost came in clutching a greasy brown paper carrier bag to his chest. He pulled packages from it and tossed them around the room . . . 'Cod and chips . . . plaice and chips . . .'

Bill Wells, who had wandered in for a chat, was appalled. 'Fish and chips? You know Mullett has forbidden them in the station. They stink the place out.'

'No more than his poncey after-shave.' He held up a package. 'I take it you don't want this – it's cod and chips.'

Wells hesitated, then grabbed it. 'As you've bought it – but open the windows afterwards.'

Frost perched himself on the edge of a desk and began eating with his fingers as he addressed his team. 'Fish is supposed to be brain food, so let's see if it does anything for us. Now, we're checking their alibi, but it looks as if Hudson and Miss Twin Peaks are out of the frame.'

'Which puts us right back in square one,' said Cassidy who had been staring sullenly out of the window. Thanks to Frost his case against Snell wasn't looking as strong as it did, and he was now being associated with another of

Frost's abysmal failures. He hadn't demeaned himself by ordering fish and chips and now regretted it. His stomach was rumbling and the heady bouquet of chips and vinegar was making him drool.

'More or less,' grunted Frost, spitting out a fish bone. 'Just in case we have missed something, let's go over it again. The kid was snatched for the sole purpose of obtaining the ransom money. Dean Anderson, the first kid he snatches, dies, so he calmly goes out and grabs another one. Why didn't he pretend Dean was still alive? He would still have got the ransom money. Don't tell me he was worried about contravening the Trades Descriptions Act.'

'The kid had to be alive to make the taped message for the press,' said Burton.

Frost nodded. 'I'll buy that. Which convinces me we are dealing with a methodical sod, not a tearaway like Hudson. His plan demanded a taped message, so there had to be one, even if it meant going after a second kid.' He opened his mouth and tipped in the crumbs from the chip bag, then threw away the greasy paper and wiped his hands down the front of his jacket. 'OK. Puzzle number two. Everything proceeds as planned, all his demands are met. But he doesn't turn up to collect the money – why?' He scratched his chin in thought as he sent his cigarettes on the rounds.

'Something must have happened that prevented him?' suggested Liz.

'It must have been at the last flaming minute,' said Frost, 'because he was on the phone to Cordwell almost as soon as the money was dropped.'

'A heart attack?' offered Burton.

'Don't be a fool!' snarled Cassidy.

'Hold on,' said Frost. 'That could be it. You get a phone call telling you there's a quarter of a million quid waiting to be picked up . . . you could either wee yourself of have a heart attack.' He pointed to Burton. 'Phone

Denton General and find out if anyone suffering from a heart attack was admitted last night.'

'Why just a heart attack?' said Cassidy, sourly. 'He might have got run over – or broken his leg.'

'Or had his dick cut off.' Frost nodded his agreement and told Burton to check with the hospital for details of everyone admitted as an emergency last night. Collier came in and handed Frost a sheaf of papers. They included carbon copies of the statements made by Hudson and his girlfriend. He shuffled through them. There was a list supplied by Denton Council of the people who used to live in the old shacks where Lemmy Hoxton's body was found. A name on it screamed out at him. He jabbed it with his finger and showed it to Liz.

Liz whistled softly. 'Millicent Fleming? The woman from Primrose Cottage.'

'It's a small world, isn't it!' commented Frost. 'Strange she never mentioned this when we called on her. We'll pay her another visit tomorrow.'

The phone rang. Hanlon answered it and relayed the message to Frost. 'Jordan and Simms have contacted three of the people who were at the disco. They all confirm that Hudson and Cindy were there until gone midnight. The girl threw up on the lobby so it rather sticks in their mind.'

Frost shrugged philosophically. He had written them off as suspects anyway. He took a quick look through Hudson's statement before deciding to call it a day when he suddenly straightened up. He flapped his hand for silence as he read it through again, then he beamed. 'Our unanswered question was, why didn't the kidnapper pick up the ransom money?' He slid off the desk top and started striding around the room. 'The answer is so bloody obvious, even Mullett could have spotted it, but we've all missed it!'

'And what have we missed?' asked Cassidy, his tone implying that whatever it was, it was a load of rubbish.

'The kidnapper did pick it up,' said Frost. He paused dramatically. 'But it was taken from him.'

He was met with blank stares, everyone trying to work out what he meant.

The penny dropped for Burton first. 'You mean Finch – the old boy with the dog?'

Frost nodded.

'Just because he happened to be there,' scoffed Cassidy.

'It was peeing down with rain. No-one with any sense would have been out in it, but he was chucking a ball for his dog.'

'I checked with his neighbours,' said Burton. 'They confirm he's been taking the dog out for a run every night, come rain, hail or shine.'

'Building up a pattern,' said Frost. 'We know the kidnapper is methodical.'

'Thousands of people are methodical,' said Cassidy. 'That doesn't make them kidnappers.'

'Thousands of people don't chuck the dog's ball at the very spot where a quarter of a million quid is stashed.'

'Coincidence!' said Cassidy dismissively.

'I don't believe in coincidences,' said Frost, 'not unless it suits me . . . and this time it doesn't suit me. Finch is our man!'

'You'll have to come up with something a lot more than this to convince me,' said Cassidy. He was looking at the cigarette Frost had given him. It was not the inspector's usual brand. It was the expensive brand Mullett reserved for special visitors.

'Then how about this?' said Frost, and he read aloud part of Hudson's statement: '"I saw this bloke wandering around to where the bag had been dumped, so I nipped across there smartish. He was kicking at the grass, looking for something. He picks up this bag from out of the long grass. He hadn't heard me coming, so I tried to grab it . . ."' He looked up at blank faces and frowned.

'I'm supposed to be the dim twat here. How come I'm the only one to spot it?'

'To spot what?' asked Cassidy.

'Hudson says he saw Finch kicking at the long grass, looking for something.'

'The dog's ball,' said Cassidy, as if explaining to a child.

'But when we found poor Mr Finch, knocked out cold, he already had the dog's ball in his pocket. So if he'd already found the ball, what the hell was he still looking for?'

'The money!' exclaimed Burton.

'Yes, son,' agreed Frost. 'He was looking for the money.'

Cassidy chewed this over, testing it for weaknesses, but he grudgingly had to agree it held water.

'It was bloody clever,' continued Frost. 'If the police weren't watching, he'd pick up the money and no-one would be any the wiser. But if the Old Bill was there, he could claim he found it by accident and who the hell could prove otherwise?' He turned to Burton. 'You chatted up the neighbours. What do we know about him?'

'He's a self-employed accountant – does the books for some small businesses in and around Denton. His late wife used to work for Savalot on the check-out. She was with them for fifteen years, but when they moved to the big new super-store, they sacked all the old check-out girls.'

'Why?' Frost asked.

'They wanted youngsters they could train to the new system from scratch. The neighbour said her job was her life. She got depressed and eventually took an overdose about eighteen months ago.'

'So Finch would have a very good reason for hating Cordwell?'

Cassidy shook his head. He couldn't accept this.

'You're not suggesting this whole kidnap was done for revenge? She died over eighteen months ago.'

'Revenge has to smoulder before it bursts into flame,' said Frost. 'It's all coming together.'

'All you've got at the moment,' objected Cassidy, 'is a theory – and you're bending the facts to support it.'

'That's the way I always work,' said Frost. 'And if Finch isn't our man, then it's hard bleeding luck, because I am going to give him the works.' Back to Burton. 'What else do we know about him?'

'Not much . . . He keeps himself to himself and he hasn't had the dog long.'

Frost's eyebrows shot up. 'How long?'

'Two . . . three weeks.'

Frost chewed this over then pounded his fist into his palm. 'I said he was a calculating bastard. I bet he got the dog as part of his plan. It's all been worked out to the smallest details.' He chewed his knuckle, then waggled a finger at the team. 'And that's why Dean Anderson had been stripped naked. Finch is not going to leave us with a single clue. I bet there were dog's hairs on the kid's clothes . . . so off come the clothes.' He was now warming to his theme, getting more and more excited. 'And the indentation the pathologist noticed on Dean's forehead. I bet that was the marks of an elasticated shower cap. He was covering up the kid's hair so it wouldn't pick up traces of anything that could lead us back to him.'

'I can't believe Finch is such a calculating bastard,' said Liz. 'He doesn't look it.'

'Don't go by appearances,' said Frost. 'Mullett doesn't look like a prat.'

Cassidy compressed his lips. This was not the way one should speak of senior officers to the lower ranks.

'We know it's Finch,' continued Frost. 'So how do we play it?'

'Slowly and carefully,' urged Liz.

'We can't go slowly,' said Frost. 'Time isn't on our side. He's killed one kid, so he's got nothing to lose by killing the other.' The phone rang again. He paused as Cassidy answered it.

It was the Casualty Officer from Denton hospital. Apart from a pregnant woman who had fallen down a flight of stairs, no-one came into Casualty between nine and ten thirty the previous night with anything serious enough to keep them away from a quarter of a million pound ransom. Cassidy relayed this to Frost, then stood up and flexed his leg which was stiffening up. He wanted to go home, but was determined not to leave before Frost.

'What is this terrible smell?'

Flaming hell! groaned Frost. Where had bloody Mullett sprung from? 'I noticed it the minute you came in, sir – have you trod in something?' He signalled for Burton to open up the window, then took Mullett by the arm and led him outside. 'I'd like a quick word.'

'And I want a word with you, Frost.' He said nothing more until they reached his office. 'I've had a phone call from the Chief Constable and he is very concerned about our lack of progress with this kidnapping. He understands the boy's mother has given an interview to one of the papers complaining the police are doing nothing.'

'We're not doing nothing, sir, we just haven't come up with anything . . . until now.'

'Until now?' Mullett's head came up and his eyes gleamed. 'You've got a lead?' If this was true, he'd get straight back to the Chief Constable.

'A good one.' He quickly told Mullett about Finch.

'Finch? The man who was attacked?'

'Yes, sir.'

Mullett scratched his chin thoughtfully. 'The boy could be at Finch's house? We could get him back to his mother tonight?' That would be a triumph. It would make the papers look absolute fools in the morning.

'It's possible, super,' said Frost. 'I doubt if the boy is hidden in the house, but we should find something that would lead us to him.'

'So what do you suggest?' He consulted his watch. 'It could take some time getting a search warrant.'

Frost gave him a knowing wink. 'Just leave that to me, sir.'

Mullett stared at Frost. He had no wish to know about the underhand methods Frost intended to use. 'Stick to the rules, Frost,' he said, 'and let me know how you get on.' When Frost had left, he smiled a smug smile of satisfaction as he practised what he would say to the Chief Constable if Frost pulled it off. 'I know it was bending the rules, sir, but the child came first . . . I realized my career would be on the line, but that wasn't a consideration . . .' He practised saying it silently, but with the right degree of modesty. Then his expression changed and his eyes narrowed as he rehearsed what he would say if things went wrong. 'I specifically told Frost to play it by the book . . . there was a child's life at stake and no reason for taking chances . . .' He congratulated himself. This was the sort of situation he liked. Either way, he couldn't lose.

In the incident room, Frost was briefing his team. His cigarette packet was empty, but he found a fair-sized stub in his top jacket pocket and poked it in his mouth. 'Finch mustn't know we suspect him. If we don't find the kid in the house, then we'll put him under constant surveillance in the hope he leads us to him.'

'You don't want him to know we suspect him?' said Cassidy. 'But the minute we turn up with a search warrant, of course he'll flaming well know.'

'We don't turn up with a search warrant,' said Frost. He puffed a mouthful of smoke up to the ceiling and watched it get sucked out of the open window into the cold night air. 'We use a bit of the tact and subtlety for which I am world famous.'

* * *

The dog barked incessantly at the knocking at the door and wouldn't be hushed as Finch switched on the passage light and demanded, 'Who's there?'

'Police,' replied Frost. 'Can you spare us a moment?'

Finch opened the door and there was that scruffy man with the mac and the trailing scarf. 'Mr Frost, isn't it?'

'That's right, sir. Sorry to bother you, but we've had a bit of luck. We've caught the man who attacked you and stole the money.'

Finch's face lit up. 'Good work, inspector.' He led them into a living-room, all neat, tidy and polished, the room of a methodical man. He had his jacket on.

'Going out, sir?' asked Frost.

'Just taking the dog for a run. I do it every night. So how can I help you?'

'We need formal identification of the travel bag and we'd like you to identify the man.'

'Does he admit to kidnapping that poor boy?'

'He's lying his head off, sir. He says he found the money by chance and you tried to take it away from him.'

'That is ridiculous. He put me in hospital. Of course I'll identify him. If you could hand me my overcoat.'

It was hanging neatly over the back of a chair. Frost passed it across. Seeing his master getting ready to go out, the dog began yapping its excitement and leaping up and down at the prospect of an outing.

'Take him with you, sir,' suggested Frost. He wanted the dog out of the way. 'There is just one more thing, sir . . .' He smiled his most frank and open smile. 'You're probably going to think it a bloody cheek, but do you think I could do a quick search of your premises?'

Finch's eyebrows shot up. 'Why?'

'Once you've identified this man, he is going to deny all knowledge of the kidnapping and try and involve you in it. He'll claim you were there for the sole purpose of collecting the ransom.'

'But this is preposterous,' spluttered Finch. 'I found the bag simply by chance.'

Frost nodded sympathetically. 'Of course you did, sir. But he's going to say you've got the boy hidden away. What I'd like to do – with your permission of course – is do a token search of the premises, so we can refute his allegations right from the start.'

'Do you have a warrant?'

'It hardly justifies a warrant, sir. I'm not really taking it seriously. I can get one if you like, but it won't take more than a couple of minutes.' He opened a door and clicked on the light. 'Is this the lounge?' He peeked inside. 'Well, he's obviously not in here.' He pulled the door shut. 'I'd better see the kitchen in case you've got him hidden in the bread bin.'

A knock at the front door. The dog went haring up the passage, barking again. Jordan stood on the doorstep. 'The station have radioed through. They've moved the time of the identity parade – they want us there now.'

'Damn!' said Frost. 'I want to get this finished. Can it wait five minutes?'

'Sorry, sir,' said Jordan, 'but they say it's got to be now. They've got everyone lined up.'

Frost turned to Finch who was trying to calm the dog. 'Do you think you could go with the officer, sir? I'll finish off here and follow on in a couple of minutes.'

Finch hesitated, then shrugged and hurried out to the car. 'Don't forget to close the front door.'

'I won't, sir. Don't worry.'

He watched Finch, followed by the dog, climb into the back seat of the area car. As soon as it turned the corner he was whispering urgently into his radio. 'He's gone. Let's have you!'

Two cars that had been waiting round the corner disgorged eight men, mostly from Forensic, who quietly entered the house.

He gave them a quick briefing. 'Be bloody thorough, but put everything back where you found it, because Finch mustn't know. We are looking for anything that could prove the kid was here . . . hairs, fibers, blood. And look for a cassette recorder, a dot matrix printer, bottles that could have contained chloroform. If you find the kid, tied to a chair, watching the telly, I'd even settle for that.'

They went about their task with practised efficiency while he mooched about, opening and closing cupboard doors, trying not to get in anyone's way. Finch was a very methodical man with everything in its proper place and this made the search relatively simple.

On the wall of the living-room was a framed photograph of a younger Finch and a fair-haired woman taken at a dance of some sort. Frost studied it. They both looked very happy.

'Sir!' Burton was calling from the hall where he had found a door under the stairs. His torch revealed stone steps leading to a cellar which exuded a musty smell of long disuse. 'There's nothing there,' said Frost, 'but look anyway.' He stayed at the top, watching half-heartedly as Burton slowly descended, his torch beam bouncing off heaps of stored junk. Jordan was called in to help and together they shifted as much as was necessary to ascertain there was no child, alive or dead, hidden there. Carefully, they moved everything back to where it was. Burton's foot kicked a blue fluted bottle which rolled across the stone floor. Burton pulled out the stopper and sniffed it hopefully. It was turpentine substitute.

'Jack!' Arthur Hanlon calling him from a first-floor room. He thudded up the stairs.

One of the bedrooms had been converted into a small office and Arthur Hanlon was excitedly indicating an Amstrad word processor on a wooden desk with a dot matrix printer alongside it. Hopes were quickly dashed by Harding who pointed out it was a nine pin machine and the ransom demand had been printed out by a twenty-four pin model.

Frost mouthed a silent expletive and looked through some of the print-outs at the side of the machine. Stock records and account details. The wastepaper bin had been recently emptied and contained only a torn window envelope. He peeked through the curtains to the darkened street below. Just inside the front gate a rubbish sack awaited its morning collection by the refuse van. Frost pointed it out to Hanlon. 'Get someone to pick it up and take it to the station.' He pulled a desk drawer open. Neat clipped stacks of bills and statements. A quick riffle through, but nothing of interest.

He was hindering Hanlon, so went downstairs to the kitchen where two men from Forensic, on their hands and knees, were painstakingly checking for prints and fibres. 'Mainly dog hairs so far,' they told him.

'Probably from the dog,' said Frost, ever anxious to help.

The kitchen table bore further testimony to Finch's methodical habits. One cup, one saucer and one spoon laid out alongside a cereal bowl and a bread and butter plate, all ready for the next morning's breakfast. 'I bet there's one senna pod and one sheet of toilet paper in the loo,' grunted Frost, who was never impressed by neatness.

He consulted his watch. Nearly ten minutes had passed since Finch had left. 'I'd better get down to the station before he gets suspicious. Let me know the minute you find anything, but please, put everything back exactly where you found it.'

Finch was becoming impatient. He knocked back the dregs of the cup of tea Liz had brought him and gave the custard cream to his dog. 'I thought it was all ready.'

'Last-minute hitch,' Liz told him, and was so relieved when Frost walked in.

'Sorry I'm late,' said Frost. 'Got another call on the way back. Have you identified him yet?'

'It still hasn't started,' snapped Finch. 'I'm not very impressed at police efficiency.'

'Go and see what the delay is,' Frost said to Liz.

'Did you find anything?' said Finch.

'Eh?' said Frost vaguely, as if he didn't know what Finch was on about.

'The search.'

'Oh, that?' He gave a short laugh. 'I found six boys in the fridge, but none of them was the one we wanted.' He was relieved when Finch grinned back. 'I shut the front door as you asked.'

Liz returned. 'Hudson has signed a statement admitting taking the money and assaulting Mr Finch,' she said. 'So there's no need for an identity parade.'

'What about the kidnapping?' asked Frost.

'He strongly denies that.'

'Let's see if he still denies it after I've finished with him,' said Frost, grimly. 'Get Mr Finch to formally identify the travel bag. It's in the Exhibits Stores.'

'Won't take long, sir,' said Liz, leading Finch out. As soon as he had gone, Frost was on the radio to Burton at the house.

'We've found nothing that would tie him to the kidnapping and nothing that would suggest the boy was ever in the house,' reported Burton.

'The car . . . did you check his car?'

'Forensic gave it a proper going over – nothing.'

'Right.' It was a sod, but what the hell. He'd have to think out his next move. 'Get out of there. He'll be back soon.'

Cassidy walked in on the tail end of the conversation, taking secret delight at Frost's downcast expression. 'Doesn't look as if your theory was right then, inspector.'

'I'm not wrong on this one,' said Frost stubbornly. He bent to pat the dog which was asleep under the table. 'It's your bloody master, Fido, and I'm going to get the bastard.' The dog opened one eye and licked his hand.

Finch returned. 'All right for me to go now?'

'Yes, sir. Thank you very much for your help. Our lady sergeant will drive you back.' Frost tried to sound as if his mind was on other, more important, matters.

Mullett waylaid him on his way to the incident room. 'Frost!' He sounded angry. Very angry. He had been sitting in his office, the phone in the centre of his desk, ready to ring the Chief Constable with the good news. 'The Denton team have done it again, sir,' he would announce. 'No, no,' he would add modestly after the Chief had congratulated him. 'I can't claim all the credit.' But his speech would remain unspoken. He had seen Finch come and long faces all round but no-one had bothered to tell him what had happened.

Bloody hell, thought Frost. I was supposed to keep him informed. 'Just on my way to see you, sir,' he said.

'You've let Finch go? Do I take it you found nothing?'

'Not a bleeding thing,' said Frost.

'Nothing at all?' persisted Mullett.

'That's what "not a bleeding thing" means,' said Frost.

'All this time and effort,' snapped Mullett. 'All those men – a full Forensic team – all on overtime. Do you know how much this little jaunt has cost?'

'I neither know, nor care,' Frost snapped back. 'If there's a cash limit on the amount we must spend to find the kid, then let me know.'

'An expensive success I can accept, Frost, but not an expensive failure.' He stamped back to his office.

Frost joined his dispirited team in the incident room. 'All right, so we found nothing, but that doesn't mean we're on the wrong track. Finch is our man.' He ignored the scoffing snort from Cassidy. 'Take it from me. Finch has got the kid. The only queston is, where the hell is he? Can anyone come up with some bright idea, beause I'm blowed if I can.'

'Assuming Finch is the kidnapper,' said Burton, 'why hasn't he come up with a second ransom demand?'

'He's probably got to work out another way of collecting the money. He's been seen at the collection point once, a second time would be too much of a coincidence even for dim twats like us.'

Lambert raised a hand. 'Do you think he's got an accomplice looking after the kid?'

'No,' said Frost. 'Finch is a loner. He's in this absolutely on his own. He's got the kid gagged, blindfolded and trussed up somewhere, so how do we find him?'

'We tail him,' suggested Hanlon. 'Twenty-four hour surveillance. Let him lead us to the kid.'

'Why should he go to the kid?' asked Frost. 'It would be too dangerous.'

'He's got to feed him – see if he is all right. The poor little sod is only seven.'

'Finch is a callous bastard. I don't think he gives a toss about the kid,' said Frost.

'If there's nothing to connect him to the kid and he doesn't lead us to him, then what do we do?' said Liz.

'We worry ourselves bleeding sick,' said Frost. Then he stopped dead. 'I think I know where the boy might be.'

'Where?' asked Cassidy, without enthusiasm. Nearly all Frosts bright ideas had fallen flat on their face up to now.

'I was looking through some invoices and bills in his office. One bill was for the ground rent for the parking of a holiday caravan. A holiday caravan in the autumn . . . what better place?'

'Worth a look,' said Cassidy begrudgingly. 'So where is it?'

Frost spread his palms. 'I don't know. I wasn't paying that much attention at the time.'

Cassidy shook his head in exasperation. 'So how do we find out, short of asking Finch?'

'Leave it to me.' Frost glanced up at the wall clock. Liz should still be driving Finch back. He snatched up the internal phone and told Control to radio through to her in the car. She was to phone Inspector Frost urgently as soon as she reached the house. He hoped she would twig that this was something he didn't want mentioned over the radio in Finch's hearing.

The next few minutes crept by as he waited for her to ring back. It was a few minutes to midnight. The phone rang. Liz.

'Can Finch hear us?' He found himself whispering although there was no need.

'No. He's in the kitchen feeding the dog.'

'If he asks, tell him it's about a rape case. This is what I want you to do. There's a room upstairs he uses as an office. In the left-hand desk drawer there's a bulldog clip of bills waiting to be paid. One is from a caravan site. I want the address of that site.'

'How do I get it?'

'Tell him you want to do a Jimmy Riddle – the bathroom's upstairs next to his office. If he offers you a bucket we'll have to think again. Do your best, love. It's bloody important.'

'I'll try.'

'Good girl! Don't forget to pull the chain afterwards – he's a suspicious sod.'

She radioed back from her car in eight minutes. The invoice was for the ground rent of a caravan at the East Seaton Holiday Caravan Park.

'That's nearly forty miles away!' protested Cassidy.

'So?' replied Frost. 'About an hour's drive. He could get there and back to Denton in good time to take the dog out for a walk.' He walked over to the regional map and marked it with his finger. 'There it is! Forty miles from Denton, remote and no-one staying there in the autumn. If I wanted to hide a kidnap victim, I couldn't think of a better place.'

Cassidy studied the map. The caravan parking site was tucked away well off the beaten track. 'We'll need a search warrant,' he said.

'No time for that,' said Frost, already winding his scarf round his neck.

'Then Mr Mullett will have to be told.'

'No time for that, either.' Mullett would only say no.

'Seaton is in Felford Division. Shouldn't we let them handle it?' asked Burton.

It was Cassidy who answered. If the boy was there, no other division was going to steal the glory for finding him. 'It's our case,' he said firmly.

'There could be trouble,' said Burton, shaking his head doubtfully.

'Not if we play our cards right,' said Frost.

But Frost rarely played his cards right.

Burton coasted the car up the bumping approach to the caravan site and switched off the lights. A high, chain-link fence enclosed a field, its grass overgrown and sagging with the weight of rain water. Huddling under the shelter of a group of trees to the rear of the site was a line of caravans of all shapes and sizes. The wind rattled the fencing and caused the trees to groan in protest. In this weather the caravan park was a cheerless, desolate place.

There were four of them, Frost, Burton, Cassidy and Liz. He had considered bringing at least another four in a second car, but Mullett's dire threats about overtime payments decided him against it. In any case, for this clandestine operation, the fewer people involved, the better. 'What a dump!' he grunted, holding out his hand for the night glasses. Burton gripped his arm and pointed. A light had come on in one of the caravans. But he'd already seen it.

He fumbled at the focusing control and panned across the front of the caravan. The curtains were tightly drawn, but a thin crack of light seeped out into the night. He located the door and the number shimmered into focus: 12. It was Finch's caravan. He grinned to the others. 'I think our luck's changed.'

The chain link fence was too high for them to scale and the heavy padlock on the main gates refused to yield to any of Frost's skeleton keys, so they watched impatiently as Burton, his face contorted with the effort, clamped the cutters across the chain and squeezed. The jaws bit through the chain and the padlock dropped on the mud. The gate creaked and ploughed a groove in the muddy ground as they pushed it open.

Crouching low, the long, wet grass slapping at their legs, they squelched past the silent row of dark caravans on to number 12.

Frost checked to make sure the only exit from the caravan was by the main door, then he mounted its two wooden steps. From inside they could hear a voice babbling, then music. A radio playing. He banged the door with his fist. 'Police. Open up!'

Almost immediately, the light went out and the radio was silenced. 'Don't sod us about. We know you are in there.' He waited. Silence. He stepped to one side so Burton could smash the glass of the door panel with the heavy duty cutters and slip his hand inside to turn the catch. The door swung open. A stale, empty smell. They stepped gingerly into darkness and silence.

'Torch!'

Burton's torch beam sliced through the darkness and picked out a light switch. Frost tried it. It worked, the dim bulb revealing a plastic-topped table that could be folded back and two bunk beds stripped of clothing. There was a lamp and a small mains radio on the table, both connected to an electronic control programmed to come on at different times during the night. Frost pressed the manual button. The lamp lit up and the radio came on. A burglar deterrent.

The bottom bunk was over a storage area. They opened the doors to reveal bedding and table linen jam-packed. A partitioned section was the kitchen, its oven powered by propane gas. Opposite the cooker was the sink. Frost spun the tap and a jet of rust-coloured water hammered out, bouncing off the sink and splashing everywhere. He quickly turned it off and wiped water from the front of his mac. The carpeting on the floor was sodden. 'I don't know why I did that,' he said.

'It doesn't look as if anyone's here,' observed Liz, rather redundantly.

'I was beginning to come to that conclusion myself,' sighed Frost. 'Let's get the hell out of here.'

'What about the broken door glass?' asked Cassidy.

'It was already broken when we got here,' said Frost. 'Bloody kids!' It had been a long day. A fruitless day. He wanted to get home and put an end to it and hope that the morning would bring something marginally better.

He switched off the light and closed the door behind them as they descended the wooden steps. Then he stopped dead, a finger to his lips. 'I heard something,' he whispered.

A rustling in the grass. Someone moving about. Burton's head turned from left to right, trying to locate the source, then he nudged Frost and pointed. 'There!'

A dark shape loomed, then another. A white, blinding glare as torches were shone straight into their eyes.

'Hold it! None of you move. Police!'

'Oh shit!' groaned Frost.

Mullett was almost foaming at the mouth. 'You went into another division's area and you neither sought my permission, nor did you have the common courtesy to let them know!'

'I forgot,' said Frost, edging towards the door. He was too tired and fed up to think of a decent excuse and, in any case, this sort of escapade was excusable only if it produced results. They had been dragged off to Seaton station by the uniformed men who ignored all their protests, but luckily their Station Sergeant recognized Frost. 'Why didn't you let us know, Jack? We've had a spate of break-ins on those caravans, so when someone phoned to report four suspicious-looking thugs creeping about and we find the padlock cut off . . .'

'I have been dragged out of bed in the middle of the night, phoned personally by the Seaton Divisional Commander,' continued Mullett. 'He was absolutely furious – and justifiably so. Fortunately he is a personal friend of mine, so I apologized profusely on your behalf.'

'Good,' grunted Frost, reaching for the door handle. 'No harm done, then.'

'No harm done?' Mullett's voice had soared to a screech. He pointed to a chair. 'Sit!' He was getting his second wind. 'You've done lasting harm, Frost. There are certain basic procedures, procedures that even the rawest recruit would automatically follow. You do not leave your own division without telling me. You do not enter another division without permission and you do not break into other people's property without a search warrant.'

'I was sure the kid was there. There wasn't time to get a warrant.'

'There was plenty of time. You just couldn't be bothered. In my division you do things by the book – understand?'

'Yes, I'll bear it in mind,' said Frost vaguely. His mind was elsewhere and he was only giving the superintendent a small part of his attention. He stood up.

'And what is worse, you dragged Cassidy along with you, giving him the impression you had my permission.'

Frost's lips tightened. Cassidy knew what the score was and had obviously got his own version of events in first. 'That was unforgivable of me, sir,' he said flatly.

Mullett glared. He never knew how to take it when

Frost agreed with him. The sooner he could find a way of replacing him with Cassidy, the better. 'There are going to be some changes in this division,' he warned grimly.

Frost visibly brightened up at this. 'They're not moving you on, are they, sir? It's not fair, you're doing your best . . .'

'No, Frost,' snapped Mullett icily. 'They are not moving me on.'

'Oh!' Frost tried not to sound disappointed, but didn't succeed. He pushed himself up from the chair. 'Well, if there's nothing else . . .'

Mullett sighed. What was the point? 'No, inspector. There is nothing else.' The man was impossible, but this strengthened his resolve. Frost would have to be transferred.

Frost climbed into his car, his mind churning over the events in the caravan park. Something in the caravan had flashed the briefest, subliminal message . . . something important. He yawned. Whatever it was, it would have to wait. Three o'clock in the morning and he was deadbeat. Sod everything.

He dug into his pocket for a cigarette. The packet was empty. Panic broke in as he searched deep into every pocket and scrabbled through the glove compartment. The ashtray held only ash. Sod it. He couldn't get through the night without a cigarette and the knowledge that he didn't have any made the craving almost unbearable. No shops open in Denton at this hour of the morning. Nothing else for it then. He spun the wheel and took a detour.

She hadn't been able to sleep and was in bed reading when she heard the car draw up outside. She picked up the bedside clock. Sixteen minutes past three in the morning. Footsteps up the path, then the ringing of her door bell. She slipped on her dressing-gown and cautiously made her way down the stairs.

A quick peek through the spy-hole and a deep sigh as she opened the door. A scruffy, apologetic-looking individual stood on the doorstep, shuffling his feet and grinning hopefully.

'Jack flaming Frost!'

'Hello, Shirl. Sorry I'm so late.'

'Late? Only thirty-six flaming hours late. You were supposed to be taking me out for dinner.'

He clapped a hand to his forehead. 'So I bloody was! Sorry, Shirl – this missing kid . . .'

'You could have phoned. I was all dressed up, sitting, waiting, stomach rumbling . . .'

He hung his head in contrition. 'I'm truly sorry, Shirl. I've been on the go non-stop ever since that kid went missing. I had no sleep at all last night.'

She shook her head in mock sympathy. 'You poor old git. You'd better come in then.'

He shuffled in after her into the lounge and took off his coat. She switched on the electric fire with its flickering flame log effect. He felt warmer, happier, and perhaps a little less tired as he dropped down on the settee. 'Better late than never,' he murmured. 'I just had to come and see you.'

Her expression softened. She sat down on the settee beside him and snuggled in closer. 'Perhaps you're not such a rotten old sod after all.'

He silently counted up to ten, then nuzzled her soft, warm cheek. 'You wouldn't have a packet of fags on you by any chance?'

She jerked upright. 'You bastard!' she said.

The bed was hard and uncomfortable and as he lay there a thousand thoughts hurtled around his brain making sleep impossible. Wearily, he clicked on the bedside lamp and lit up one of the cigarettes from the packet Shirley had hurled at him and lay back, watching the smoke curl to the ceiling.

His mind was replaying the abortive visit to the caravan. There was something there, something that tried to jog his memory, but his thoughts just kept going endlessly round and round, getting him nowhere. He tried to switch to something else, but again his mind insisted on replaying the search . . . the stripped bunk beds with the thin mattresses, about as uncomfortable as the one he was lying on . . . the cupboards full of bedding . . . the kitchen . . . the rusty water belting out and soaking the carpet . . .

At last tiredness began to envelop him and the bed suddenly became warm and comfortable and the outside cold and unfriendly. He stubbed out his cigarette and sank back, sinking down, down, down into a deep sleep, his brain fading on the picture of the caravan . . . the tap . . . the sodden carpet . . .

He sat up with a start. The carpet! The bloody carpet . . . That's what his mind was scratching and nagging away at, trying to nudge him into action. The right clue for the wrong bloody case . . .

Out of bed, and he was in the car within minutes and back at the station in a quarter of an hour. As he pushed open the door into the lobby the siren smell of frying bacon lured him up to the canteen where he was pleased to see Bill Wells and Burton sitting together, polishing off the standard fry-up breakfast before they finished their shift. He joined them, dumping his loaded tray on the empty chair.

Wells looked at his watch. Half-past five. 'What's the matter, Jack? Did she kick you out of bed?'

'She kicked me out before I got in,' said Frost, dipping his piece of bread into Wells's fried egg. He turned to Burton. 'I've got a job for you, son.'

'I'm just going home,' said Burton.

'No, you're not,' said Frost. 'You're on extended overtime.' A clatter of trays made him spin round. Jordan and Collier from the night shift, stoking up with food before going back to the Police House. He called them over. 'Job for you . . . overtime.'

'Mr Mullett's got to authorize overtime, Jack,' protested Wells.

'Sod Mr Mullett. It can't wait.' He dragged his chair back so he could include Jordan and Collier at the adjoining table in the conversation. 'Remember when you were dragging the canal for the kid – all that junk we found and chucked back? I want some of it out again.'

'Not the dead goat?' said Jordan.

'No – that roll of carpeting.'

'It'll never fit your lounge, Jack,' said Wells. 'And it will be stinking to high heaven by now.'

'Especially if that bag of offal has leaked over it,' added Jordan.

Frost ignored the wisecracks. 'Go and hire a rowing boat.'

'We need Mullett's authorization for that as well,' objected Wells.

'Or that of the senior officer, which is me,' replied Frost, 'so let's get cracking before he comes in and says no.'

It was still dark. Lights from the road bridge reflected off the oily black velvet of the canal and broke up into tiny shimmering dots as the oar blades cut through.

'I think we've got it,' called Burton to Frost who was standing on the towpath, watching. Collier stuck his pole down alongside Burton's and they heaved up a dripping bundle.

Frost's heart started to hammer. Not another bleeding body, he pleaded. If so, they can chuck the bugger back. The smell of decay seemed to confirm his worst fears but they had dredged up the bag of butcher's offal. 'Dump it,' yelled Frost. 'I've had breakfast.' They let it slither back into the depths where it belched evil-smelling bubbles.

'It was more to your left,' said Frost.

They followed his pointing finger and tried again. Half an hour later they found it, nowhere near where Frost had said. They had to remove the putrefying goat carcass to get to it, but managed to drag up into the boat a sodden bundle of folded carpeting, about four feet square, tied with string and stained with stinking black mud.

'Now what?' called Burton.

'Let's have a look at it.'

They rowed to the bank and heaved the squelchy bundle on to the towpath. It had been too near the goat and stunk to high heaven. Holding his breath, Frost bent over and teased out a corner of the carpet material so he could see the pattern. At first he was disappointed. It was far too dark, almost black, and the sodium lights from the bridge distorted the colour. He illuminated it with his torch and this time, he knew he was right. He straightened up and beckoned to Burton who was climbing from the rowing boat. 'Recognize it, son?'

Filthy, sodden red and blue carpeting. What was he on about? Then Burton frowned. A frown of puzzled recognition. Yes, he did recognize it. 'This is the carpet they laid at Bonley's?'

'Top of the class, my son. The special, exclusive pattern obtainable nowhere else.' His penknife slashed at the string. The bundle fell open and disgorged a flood of stinking water all over his shoes. 'Knickers!' The expletive would have been stronger, but his attention was snatched by a couple of large chunks of coloured paving slabs used to weigh the bundle down.

'They wanted it to sink. Brand spanking new carpeting worth about twenty quid a square metre.' He looked across at Jordan and Collier who were manhandling the rowing boat up to the towpath. 'Your luck's in, lads . . . another lovely job for you.' He prodded the bundle with his foot. 'Get this over to Forensic. If there's no-one on duty get someone in . . . sod the overtime bill. I want them to go over this with a tooth comb . . . stains, marks, dribble, jam, wee-wee or even bloodstains . . . Tell them it's urgent.'

Jordan regarded the waterlogged bale with a marked lack of enthusiasm. 'It's wringing wet, sir, and it will stink the car out . . . couldn't we get a van or something?'

'No,' said Frost. 'And when you've done that, another job for you. Go to the house where the kiddies were killed . . . take the bits of slab with you. Check if it's the same as their new patio and see if you can spot where in the garden it came from.' He yawned. A quick check on his watch. Quarter to seven. No point in trying to get any sleep now. 'I'm off to the station,' he announced.

'Shall we drop you off?' asked Jordan.

Frost backed away from the smelly carpet. 'No thanks. I'll go in Burton's car.'

16

He sat in the incident room smoking the cigarettes Shirley had flung at him and waiting for Forensic to come back to him with their report on the carpeting. They were taking their flaming time. He reached for the phone, but hesitated. They had given him a right mouthful the last time he rang them – 'We're going as fast as we can and we'd go a damn sight faster if we didn't have to keep answering these stupid phone calls every five minutes. Don't call us – we'll call you.'

A rattle of buckets from outside. The cleaners had arrived. Through the grimy windows dawn was giving the sky an orange glow to start off another cold day. He extended his arms and yawned, a long drawn out yawn, almost hurting his mouth as it stretched open. He felt sticky and grubby. His eyelids were scratching his eyes. He was so damn tired. If he hadn't asked Shirley for those fags he would be tucked up alongside her, warm and happy, not sitting all on his own in this cheerless incident room. He raised his wrist and tried to focus on his watch. Just gone seven. Mullett would be here in a couple of hours, all clean shaven and gleaming, ready to start the day off with a moan about the boat being used and the overtime agreed without his authority. And he'd moan even more if there were nothing to show for it. He shook his head and looked pleadingly at the phone. Come on, Forensic. Do your bloody stuff.

As he poked another one of Shirley's cigarettes into his mouth, his nose wrinkled. He couldn't get rid of the smell of that flaming goat which was almost as bad as one of Drysdale's choicest autopsies. Even the cigarettes tasted of it, but he persevered.

Bill Wells brought in the local paper. 'Thought you'd like to see this, Jack.' A large photograph of Bobby Kirby's tear-stained mother took up most of the front page, with an insert of Bobby. Above it, the caption read 'Police Dragging Heels In Search For Little Bobby Claims Weeping Mother'. Further down a sub-heading read 'Millionaire Supermarket Chief Offers Reward For Boy's Return'. A publicity photograph of a grinning Sir Richard Cordwell headed the story that he was offering a reward of £10,000 for information leading to the return of the boy. 'Thanks,' grunted Frost, consigning it to the rubbish bin. 'I needed cheering up.' He turned his attention back to the phone. 'Ring, you sod, ring . . . I haven't got all day.' As if answering his plea, the phone gave a throat-clearing cough. He snatched it up even before it rang properly, but it wasn't Forensic. Jordan reporting that he and Collier had searched the Grovers' garden and had found a heap of broken patio slabs, a couple of which matched those used to weigh down the carpet. 'You did say we were on official overtime?' asked Jordan, sounding worried. 'Yes, yes,' Frost assured him. He thanked them and told them to go to bed. Again he yawned and wished someone would tell him to go to bed.

He banged the phone down, almost jumping from his seat as the sudden, immediate ringing caught him off guard. This time it was Forensic.

'Bloodstains,' reported Harding cheerfully. 'Quite a lot of blood.'

Suddenly the cigarette tasted fine. 'I'm all ears.'

'Blood group A.'

He exhaled a stream of smoke in a long sigh of relief. 'The same as the dead mother! Don't let anyone call you a load of useless twats again.'

'The overtime has been authorized on this?' queried Harding. 'Only I've had to get a couple of men in.'

'Of course it is,' he said, wondering how the hell he was going to get Mullett to agree. He picked up a pencil and practised writing Mullett's signature on a scrap of paper. A little judicious forgery might be required. Then he hurled the pencil up in the air with a whoop of delight. He didn't give a damn if Mullett moaned about the overtime, or not. It had paid off. Blood, the same group as Nancy Grover, on the carpet retrieved from the canal. He looked again through the window at the lightening sky. It wasn't going to be such a lousy day after all, although Mark Grover wasn't going to enjoy it.

He no longer felt tired, but wished there was someone with whom he could share his triumph. He grinned delightedly as Burton came in with two steaming mugs of tea. 'You're early, my son. I'm afraid your lady love isn't in yet.'

Burton smiled and placed one of the mugs on Frost's desk.

'Did you see the way she kneed that bloke in the goolies yesterday?' asked Frost, stirring his tea with a pencil. 'You'd better watch it if you take her out – that could have been you squirming on the floor.'

'If my luck's in,' said Burton.

Frost laughed and took a sip at the tea. 'Talking of luck, we've had a break with the Grover case.' He told Burton about Forensic's examination of the carpet.

'So Grover's involved?'

'Right up to his bloody neck, son. Let's start the day off by arresting him.'

He phoned the hospital, but was told by the staff nurse that Mark Grover had discharged himself last night and was staying with his sister. Yes, she did have the address . . . He sent Burton to the Forensic Lab to bring back the carpet, then sauntered out into the car-park.

* * *

A plump little woman answered the door to his knock. Mark Grover's sister was some ten years older than her brother and her face was full of concern when Frost announced himself. 'I don't think he's up to answering any questions. The poor boy is absolutely shattered.' She took him through to the kitchen. 'He loved those children . . . just idolized them.'

Frost nodded in sympathy. 'I know, love . . . I know . . . If it wasn't important I wouldn't bother him.'

Mark Grover didn't look well, the pallor of his face emphasizing the dark, bruise-like rings round his eyes. He recognized Frost and greeted him without enthusiasm. 'Any news?'

'Couple of promising leads,' said Frost. 'I know you don't feel up to it, but it would help if you could come down to the station and look at some of the things we've found and tell me if they came from your house.'

Glover hesitated. 'I don't know . . .'

'Go with the man,' urged his sister. 'The fresh air will do you good.' When he went off to fetch his coat, she whispered to Frost, 'Mark could do with cheering up.'

'I'll see what I can do,' promised Frost, leaving her thinking what a nice man he was.

Grover kept fidgeting in the car, gazing blankly out of the window, not listening to Frost's aimless chatter. He frowned and turned to the inspector. 'Are we going the right way?'

Frost had deliberately detoured to go down Cresswell Street. 'Just wanted to take a look,' said Frost. He drove slowly past the house, where a mass of wreaths and floral tributes from neighbours were laid out in the front garden. One wreath was in the heart-rending shape of a teddy bear. Grover swallowed hard, then snatched his eyes away and shuddered. 'I'm never going back in there again. I couldn't.'

Frost nodded sympathetically, but he'd achieved what

he wanted – Grover to be emotional and unprepared for the little surprise he had in store for him.

'What exactly do you want me to identify?' Grover asked.

'Won't take long,' said Frost vaguely as he turned the car into the station car-park, pulling up by the large storage shed at the rear. He opened the shed doors and ushered Grover in. 'This way,' he said. The smell greeted them as he switched on the fluorescent lights. They flickered on and Grover stepped in to face the large section of exclusive Bonley's carpeting hanging to dry by the end wall, covered with chalked circles to outline the siting of the bloodstains located by Forensic. Grover stood stock still, his mouth gaping open, then he turned, shouldering Frost out of the way as he charged out of the shed and into the car-park.

'Don't be a twat,' yelled Frost making no move to follow. 'Where can you go . . . where would you hide?'

Grover faltered, then stopped and slowly turned, shoulders slumped, his face the picture of despair. He was trembling violently. 'My God,' he said. 'Oh my God!'

Frost ambled over and took his arm. 'Let's talk about it, son. It'll make you feel better.'

Mullett, who had seen Frost arrive and had learned of the unauthorized overtime, met Frost in the corridor. 'I want to see you,' he snapped.

'Later,' said Frost, moving him to one side so Grover could pass.

'Now!' shouted Mullett, quivering with rage.

'Later!' snarled Frost. 'Bloody later!'

He sat Grover down in the small interview room which smelt stalely of sweat and unwashed socks. Burton brought in mugs of tea, then started up the recorder while Frost lit up a cigarette and shook out the match. 'Right, Mr Grover. You've been cautioned. You know you don't have to say anything, but let me tell you how I see it. You had a row with your wife. You were sick and tired of her and the kids. You went off to Bonley's, but returned later with the chunk of carpet you had nicked and your wife was waiting, ready to start the row again. Something snapped. You grabbed up a knife and you killed her. The kids saw you do it and started screaming, so you had to silence them, so you killed them as well.'

Frost knew this fitted few of the facts, but his intention was to stir the suspect up and it worked.

'No!' Grover was standing up and shouting at Frost. 'I wouldn't harm my kids. I loved them.'

Frost took another deep drag and continued doggedly. 'Her blood was all over the nice carpeting you'd brought, so you had to get rid of it. You dumped it in the canal on the way to the railway tunnel where you chucked your wife's body in front of a train to make it look like suicide. Then you went back to work to earn an honest crust and establish your alibi.'

'No!'

Frost beamed up at him. 'Sit down, son, you'll be more comfortable.' He waited for Grover to sit. 'I'm open-minded. If you've got a better story, I'm willing to listen, but if not, I'm perfectly happy with my own version.'

'It didn't happen like that,' Grover turned to Burton, who seemed to have a more sympathetic face. 'It didn't happen like that.'

'Then tell us how it did happen,' said Burton.

Grover wiped hair away from his forehead. 'Yes – we'd been rowing. We were always bloody rowing – that was our life, one long bleeding row! She said the kids were getting her down and I was never there when she wanted me. I told her I had to earn the bloody money for her to spend and I couldn't do that sitting at home all day. Then we had this rush job at Bonley's. That really got her going. She said that if I went out and left her on her own, she'd kill herself. I said, "Good – then we'll have a bit of peace and bloody quiet." I stormed out, slamming the door.'

'Had she threatened to kill herself before?' asked Frost.

'It was her bleeding theme song. She'd get hysterical . . . the kids would cry . . . she'd shout at the kids and I'd shout at her. Happy bloody Families! It used to end up with me saying, "Kill your bloody self then – it'll do me and the kids a big favour."'

Frost's expression must have registered. Grover lowered his head and stared into his empty tea mug. 'I know. I was a bastard. She hadn't been well. She'd go to the doctor's, then she wouldn't take his bleeding pills – said he was trying to poison her. I suppose I should have felt sorry for the poor cow.'

'I don't suppose she got many kind words,' said Frost.

A door slammed outside somewhere. Footsteps clattered up the passage. The motor of the cassette deck whirred as Frost shot smoke up to the ceiling and waited for Grover to continue.

'There was this chunk of carpet over. Some silly sod had messed up the measurements. It was good quality stuff and would only go to waste, so we did a deal with the security guard. Half for him and we would keep the rest. Phil Collard didn't want his share, but the kids had messed up our old lounge carpet so we were going to drop it into my place. Just before midnight we took one piece round to the security bloke's place, then went on to my house. I didn't want any nosy gits to see us, so we went in round the back way. The house was all dark so I thought Nancy was in bed. I got a knife from the kitchen to cut the string and me and Phil carried the carpet through to the lounge. I switched on the light and spread it on the floor to see how it looked. Then I realized Nancy was there. She'd been sitting in the dark. She had a smug, sort of self-satisfied expression on her face and she was giggling away as if she knew something funny that I didn't. I said, "What's the joke?" She said it was a very funny joke. She said, "We won't have to shout at the children any more because they are all dead."' He shook his head, registering the disbelief he felt that night. 'I said, "What are you talking about, you silly cow?" And she pointed to the kids' room and giggled. I charged into their bedroom . . .' He stopped. He couldn't go on. He buried his face in his hands and his body shook convulsively.

Frost waited. The cassette recorder counter clicked to its next number. Burton raised his eyebrows, tacitly suggesting they should break off the interview at this point. Frost shook his head. A break could give Grover a chance to compose himself, to change his story. He lit up another cigarette and waited. The shuddering subsided. Frost pushed a cigarette across to Grover who snatched it up gratefully, dabbing at his eyes with a handkerchief.

'Thanks.' He leant across to receive a light.

'You went to the kiddies' room,' prompted Frost.

Grover knuckled his eyes and nodded.

Frost waited.

Grover stared at the glowing end of his cigarette, swallowing hard.

'And . . . ?' prompted Frost again.

Grover glared angrily. Then he was shouting. 'You know bloody well what I saw . . .' He sniffed back the tears.

'The children?' said Frost softly.

Grover nodded, suddenly calmer. 'They were lying in their cots, still and quiet. I thought they were sleeping. I prayed that they were sleeping. But . . .' Again he couldn't go on. His body shook and he screwed up his face as if in intense pain. 'It was a bloody nightmare.'

'They were dead?' asked Frost.

'Of course they were. She killed them. That bitch had killed them. Aren't you listening?'

'I'm listening,' said Frost.

'I could hear her in the lounge, laughing. I charged in there. She was sitting in the chair, rocking from side to side and sniggering. She said, "I told you I would do it . . . you wouldn't believe me." She said it as if it was something to be proud of. I still had the knife in my hand. I went berserk.'

'You stabbed her?'

'Yes. The next thing I knew, Phil was dragging at my arm, yelling at me to stop. But it was too late. She was dead.'

'Where had he been all this time?'

'Out in the kitchen. He saw there was going to be a row and didn't want to get involved.'

'He went out there, when?'

'Immediately after we brought the carpet in. When he heard her screaming he came running back.'

'And she was already dead?'

'Yes. There was no pulse . . . nothing. I said call the police. He told me not to be a bloody fool. He said they'd bang me inside for murder. She kills my kids and I end up in the nick for life. He brought me some clean clothes and made me wash and change. He said if we dumped her in front of a train it would look like suicide.'

'And the carpet?'

'It had her blood all over it. He said we should chuck it in the canal.'

'And you did what he said?'

'I was in no state to argue. He poured me a couple of brandies and we manhandled her out to the van. Then we rolled up the carpet and Phil put some bits of patio slab in to make sure it sunk. We dropped it in the canal on the way to the railway cutting.'

'What happened to your bloodstained clothes?'

'Phil burnt them. He's got a coal-fired boiler.'

Frost scratched his chin. 'Good old Phil.'

'She killed my kids,' said Grover defiantly.

'I know,' said Frost.

'She was pregnant. She wanted an abortion. I said no. I didn't want an unborn child killed.' The irony of this made him bow his head and sniff back more tears.

Frost said nothing. Whatever the reason, whoever was to blame, the poor sod had lost his wife and his children. 'We'll get this typed up, then you can sign it.'

Suddenly Grover looked small and helpless. 'Will I be let out for the funeral? The kids – not her. I want them buried with their favourite toys.'

'I'm sure that can be arranged.' Frost stood up. This was a mucky case. Nothing would bring the kids back and there was no satisfaction in cracking it.

'What happens now?' asked Grover as Burton took his arm to lead him out.

'I think you'd better get yourself a solicitor,' said Frost. 'You're going to need one . . . and so is good old Phil.'

In the corridor outside the interview room Cassidy was pacing up and down. He watched Grover being led out, then angrily marched over to meet Frost. 'Do you mind telling me what the hell is going on? This is supposed to be my damn case, don't forget.'

'It's still your damn case,' said Frost. 'He's confessed. She killed the kids and he killed her. His mate Phil Collard is an accessory after the fact.' He handed Cassidy the cassette. 'It's all on tape – get it typed.'

He never made it back to his office. Bill Wells came running up to him. 'Jack. We've got a couple in the front office who reckon they know where the kidnapped boy is being held.'

Frost was unimpressed. They'd had so many false leads from people absolutely positive they had seen Bobby.

'These two sound genuine,' Wells assured him.

'All bloody nutters sound genuine,' grunted Frost. Sod it. It was probably another time-waster, but he daren't ignore it. 'All right, I'll see them.'

They were eagerly waiting for him in the spare interview room. The man, in his late fifties, was small and sharp-featured, his head constantly moving from side to side like a terrier looking for a rat. His wife, a few years younger, was short and plump; her light brown hair, worn with a little girl's fringe, and her short-skirted dress revealing tubby legs, made her look like a retarded schoolgirl. Frost introduced himself and sat down. He glanced at the information sheet Wells had given him. 'Mr and Mrs Mason, 18 Fullers Lane. You reckon you have information about this missing boy.'

'It's not the reward,' said Mason. 'I want you to understand it's not the reward.'

'Of course it isn't,' said Frost, thinking, I bet it is, you bastard.

'We should have come sooner, but one hates sneaking on one's neighbours . . . and they used to be so good to me.'

'When were they ever good to us?' asked his wife.

'Well, he lent me his lawn mower.'

'His old rusty one – he wouldn't let you have his precious new one. And those tight clothes his wife wears . . . you can see her nipples.'

Frost cleared his throat. 'If you could get to the point . . .'

'Yes, of course,' said the man. 'This missing boy.' He looked from side to side, as if checking on eavesdroppers, then leant over the table, lowering his voice. 'They'd be the last people on earth I'd suspect of doing anything like this, but—'

'Who are "they"?' asked Frost.

'Oh – sorry. I'm talking about Mr and Mrs Younger . . . 20 Fullers Lane.'

'Mrs Younger – she's the one with the nipples?' asked Frost, wishing it was her who was sitting opposite him.

'That's right. We live at number 18 – they live next door,' explained the woman. 'They've got this shed . . .'

'Let me tell it, dear,' said her husband, glaring her to silence. Back to Frost. 'It's a shed at the end of their garden. Nice little shed – he keeps his lawn mower and stuff in it.' He hesitated and looked at his wife. 'No dear, we must be wrong . . . They're such a nice couple. They wouldn't hurt a fly.'

'All right,' snapped Frost. 'They're living bloody saints and she's got terrific nipples. Now, for Pete's sake tell me why you think they've got the boy.'

Mason exchanged hurt glances with his wife, but decided to overlook Frost's outburst.

'This shed. Last week he ran an extension lead from the house so he can have electric light in it. And yesterday I noticed they'd put curtains up.'

'It was me that noticed it,' corrected his wife. 'I told you about it.' She turned to Frost. 'Curtains in their shed! And they're kept drawn so you can't see inside. So what I want to know is, what has he got to hide?'

An enormous dick, thought Frost wearily, slumping down in his chair.

'The light comes on at all hours of the day and night,' added her husband.

'So?' asked Frost, getting fidgety. This all seemed a waste of time.

'I've seen him taking food down there,' said the woman. 'Hot food on a tray.'

'Food?' Now Frost was interested. He sat up straight and gave them his full attention. 'Go on.'

'The last couple of days, just before he goes to work and just after he comes home at night, he sticks his head out of the back door checking that no-one's watching, then he scurries off down the garden as fast as he can with a tray of food and he's inside that shed with the doors shut and the curtains drawn.'

'And you reckon he's taking food there for the boy?' asked Frost.

'Well, he's not feeding his bloody rusty lawn mower,'

said the man. 'And apart from the food, he's taken bedding down there . . . a big heap of bedding, I saw him.'

Gleefully, Frost rubbed his hands. This was getting more and more promising. 'And what does Mr Younger do for a living?'

'He's a paramedic . . . drives around in an ambulance treating people for strokes and helping girls who have babies on buses.'

'If you swallow your false teeth, he's the man to call on,' added his wife. 'There was that woman round the corner – the one who had her womb scraped . . .'

Frost winced and held up a hand in protest. It was too early in the morning for scraped wombs. 'You've actually seen him taking food down to the shed?'

'Come down to our house now and you can see for yourself,' said the man. 'He does it half-past eight on the dot.'

Frost checked the time. Quarter past eight. He drummed his fingers on the table with excitement. Bedding, food, drawn curtains, and, as an ambulance driver, Younger would have access to chloroform or ether. Knock out the kid and bung him in the back. Who would suspect an ambulance?

Frost smiled at the couple. The dislike he had felt when he first met them had almost gone. 'Hold on a moment – be right back.'

He raced off to the incident room. 'Got a strong lead on the kid. A couple of nosy neighbours reckon he's hidden in a shed in the garden of 20 Fullers Lane.' He gave them the details.

'So it looks as if you were wrong about Finch?' said Liz.

'Infallibility is not my strong point,' answered Frost. 'I've been wrong before and I'll be wrong again.' He moved over to the wall map. 'Where the hell is Fullers Lane?'

Burton showed him.

'Right.' He studied the location. 'One car round the front and one round the back ought to do it. Burton – you take the back-up car. Liz, Collier – you come with me.'

They were in the Masons' bedroom with its cute pictures of puppies on the wall and zip-up pussy cat pyjama cases on both pillows of the bed. Two large windows overlooked the rear gardens and a comfortable chair was already in position at each. Hanging from the back of each chair was a pair of field glasses in a case. Between the chairs was a coffee table holding fruit, snacks and a thermos flask. 'The complete nosy bastard's outfit,' commented Frost, picturing the Masons, side by side each night, spying on the neighbours through the Terylene curtains, chomping away at their snacks and nudging each other when something tasty clicked into focus. Frost sat in one of the chairs and picked up the field glasses. Liz sat in the other.

A creaking of stairs and the chinking of crockery as Mr Mason came in with mugs of tea on a tray and a plate of chocolate digestive biscuits. 'Thought you might like this.' He peered through the curtains and pointed. 'That's the shed, there!'

At the end of the next garden, a shed about eight feet by six, in creosoted wood with a green felt roof. The drawn, thick red curtains looked incongruous. Frost swung the glasses to the door. It was fitted with a heavy padlock which looked new and far too hefty for a garden shed.

'How long has that padlock been there?'

'We saw him putting it up last week,' said Mason. 'Probably frightened someone will steal his lousy lawn mower that's too good to lend people.'

Frost slowly panned across the window, but nothing at all could be seen through the curtaining.

'Look out! He'll see you.' Mason jerked Frost back, letting the lace curtain drop into place. 'He's coming out.'

By pressing his face close to the window pane Frost was able to see the back door of the adjoining house open and a man's head emerge to look furtively around. The man stared up suspiciously at the window of the Masons' bedroom and Frost jerked back. Younger must know what a pair of nosy bastards he had as neighbours. He hesitated, then came out carrying a tray covered with a cloth. He hurried to the shed, unlocked it and was inside in a couple of seconds. The light came on, but the curtains remained drawn.

'Good enough for me,' grunted Frost. He clicked on his radio and told Burton to hold his position at the rear of the property. He jerked his head to Liz. 'Come on. We're going in.'

The woman who opened the door was in her mid-thirties, a hard-faced blonde in an electric blue dress. 'Yes?' Her expression changed to anger as Frost and Liz barged past her, Collier following behind. 'What the bloody—'

'Police!' snapped Frost, flashing his warrant card. 'We're going to search your premises.'

'You are bloody not.' She parked herself in front of Frost, blocking his way, but was yanked off by Liz.

'Calm down or I'm putting the cuffs on you,' she threatened.

'Cuffs? In my own flaming house? Where's your search warrant?'

'We don't need a warrant if we believe there's a life in danger,' Liz told her.

'Danger? What bloody danger?'

'Look after the lady,' Frost told Collier. 'We're going to take a look in their shed.'

As he and Liz went out to the garden, the blonde yelled after them. 'Arrest the bastard. Lock him up. It's nothing to do with me.'

They charged up the garden and burst into the shed. A man was sitting inside eating beans on toast from a tray. A portable radio was playing. As they burst in, he leapt up, sending the tray on his lap clattering to the floor.

'Police!' yelled Frost.

'Oh, shit!' said the man.

Along one wall was a camp bed. Stacked at the rear was a pile of hospital sheets, blankets and medical supplies. There was no-one else.

'Where's the boy?' demanded Frost.

'What boy?'

Frost radioed Burton who scrambled over the rear fence. 'Bring him into the house.'

The blonde was at the back door, trying to get past Collier. 'Keep that bastard out of my house,' she yelled. 'I'm having nothing to do with him.'

'Isn't this your husband?' asked Frost.

'Until I divorce the sod, yes. Until then, he cooks his own meals and has them in the shed and he sleeps in the shed. I am not having him in the house.'

'Why?' Frost added.

'The bugger's only been having it away with a tart in the back of his ambulance.'

'Once – it happened once,' moaned the man.

'You were only found out bloody once,' she snapped back. She turned to Frost. 'Do me a favour. Arrest him. Lock him up. Throw away the flaming key.'

'On what charge?'

'You've seen that stuff in the shed. All the gear he's nicked from the hospital. It's no bloody use to anyone, but he nicks it.'

Frost's shoulders slumped. Another false lead. 'You can have this one,' he told Liz. 'I'm sure the hospital will want to press charges.'

Liz radioed for a van to collect the loot, then marched Younger out to the car. 'I suppose it was those two nosy bastards next door who shopped me?' he said, glaring up at their bedroom window where the curtains suddenly twitched and sunlight flashed on the lenses of two pairs of field glasses. 'I'll get you, you sods,' he yelled. 'I'll bloody get you.'

'Another false lead, Frost?' said Mullett, striding into Frost's office and pulling a face to show his disapproval of its untidiness. He had the local paper in his hand.

'Yes, another false lead,' agreed Frost, swinging his legs off the desk. Why did the bloody man always have to state the obvious?

'You probably haven't heard,' continued Mullett with a sadistic smirk, 'but Cassidy has obtained a confession from the husband in the child-killing case.'

'Yes, I had heard,' muttered Frost.

'The wife killed the children and the husband murdered the wife.'

'Something like that.'

He's jealous, thought Mullett, jealous of Cassidy's success in the face of his own failures. Well, let's twist the knife a little more. 'And this clears Snell – the man you refused to arrest?'

Frost nodded and started patting the layer of papers on his desk to locate his cigarette packet.

'Cassidy got you off the hook with this one, Frost. You should be eternally grateful.'

'I am,' said Frost, lighting up. 'Anything else?'

Mullett frowned. He produced the local paper and dropped it on Frost's desk. He tapped the front page item – 'Police Dragging Heels In Search For Little Bobby'. 'Have you seen this?'

Frost picked up the paper. '"Flasher At Pensioners' Tea Party",' he read. He frowned in pretended puzzlement. 'Is he a friend of yours, sir?'

Mullett banged his finger on the correct news item. He knew Frost was just trying to be aggravating. 'That is what I mean, Frost. Police dragging their heels. Not the sort of thing I want to read about my division. So what is the position on the kidnapping?'

Frost rubbed his face wearily. 'After Cordwell's magnanimous offer, we're being flooded out with more sightings and leads from the public who hadn't said a word before the reward was offered. We're following them all through, but I don't expect they will lead anywhere.'

'We can't waste time or money or manpower on false leads,' said Mullett, 'but if it transpires we ignored one that would have led us to the boy . . .' A typical Mullett instruction making sure he was covered whatever happened.

'And I'm going to have Finch followed,' said Frost.

'Finch? You've gone over every inch of his house, his caravan, his car . . . you've found nothing.'

'He's our man.' Even as he said it, he had his doubts. Earlier today he was damn sure Younger was the kidnapper. He took a drag at the cigarette. 'He'd better be our man . . . he's all we've bloody got.'

'And what do you hope to achieve by following him?'

'I'm hoping he'll lead us to the kid.'

'And if he doesn't?'

'Then we're in trouble.'

'You will be in trouble,' said Mullett grimly. 'Make no mistake about it, inspector. You will be in serious trouble.' He made no attempt to suppress his smile of satisfaction as he turned and marched out of the office.

'When am I never in trouble?' sighed Frost, swinging his feet up on the desk again.

Liz Maud led Harold Younger out of the charge room and walked him to the main entrance. He had been charged and released on police bail and was free to return to his shed at the bottom of the garden. He had been warned that if he tried to make trouble with his neighbours his bail would be revoked.

Harold Younger was a toe-rag. He thought he was God's gift to women. He kept calling her sweetheart and in the car on the way to the station had slyly rested his hand on her knee. She had given him a sweet, encouraging smile, then stubbed her cigarette out on the back of his hand. He had sucked the burn and sworn at her, but didn't try anything else.

She ushered him out of the door, then returned to the incident room. Liz was not very happy. Cassidy, the same rank as her in spite of his temporary promotion, was tidying up on a murder investigation, while she was stuck with the petty theft of items from the hospital storeroom.

She found Frost in the incident room, seated at a desk, holding the phone away from his ear while a stream of angry abuse buzzed and crackled into empty air. When the noise stopped, he put the phone back to his ear. 'I appreciate your concern, Mr Stanfield. The enquiries into the abduction of your daughter are proceeding. I have every hope we will be able to make an early arrest.' More angry buzzing, so he put the phone down on the desk and lit up a cigarette, then when it went quiet, picked the phone up again. 'Got to go now, sir . . . urgent call.' He hung up and swung round to Liz. 'That was Mr Stanfield. He read in the paper how we're dragging our heels over the kidnapping and intends telling the paper how we're dragging our heels over his daughter's abduction.' He stood up and stretched. 'So I suppose we had better do something about it. Let's find out how . . .' He clicked his fingers. 'What was his name – the one with the pigtail?'

'Ian Grafton?' suggested Liz.

'Yes . . . how an out-of-work layabout can afford an expensive hi-fi.'

'We were going to call on those two women at Primrose Cottage,' Liz reminded him.

'Primrose Cottage?' frowned Frost, trying to recall what it was about.

'Lemmy Hoxton. They lived in the area where he was found.'

'Oh, flip, yes.' He had completely forgotten about that case. Too much happening at once. He couldn't keep up with it.

Jordan came in with PC Collier trailing behind. 'You wanted to see us, inspector?'

'Did I?' asked Frost. 'What the hell for?' Then he remembered. 'Finch . . . I've promoted him to my number one suspect in the kidnapping case again.' Noting their surprise, he added, 'All right – so he's my only bleeding suspect. I want him tailed. I'm hoping he'll lead us to where the kid is, but for Pete's sake don't let him know you're following him. If he suspects anything he'll probably sit tight, stay indoors and let the kid die of starvation. You can call on other cars to help if necessary.'

He sat down again at the desk, then realized Liz was still standing there. 'Primose Cottage?' she said.

'No.' He shook his head. 'Lemmy's been dead for months, another couple of hours won't make any difference. We'll go and see Ian Grafton.'

He was feeling too fragile to let Liz drive, so he took the wheel himself. She glanced at him out of the corner of her eye. The poor old sod looked dead tired and much older than when she had first seen him when he turned up out of the blue at Patriot Street. 'Do you mind if I ask you a question?' she said.

'As long as it's not rude,' said Frost.

'It's about Mr Cassidy's daughter.'

'Oh yes?' said Frost, guardedly.

'He seems to blame you for the failure of the investigation.'

'Yes,' agreed Frost. 'He thought I should have tried harder.'

'Can you tell me what happened?'

'He idolized his daughter,' said Frost, 'but he was always very busy in those days. He was never able to spend much time with her. That night he'd arranged to take her out for a treat or something – I think his wife was away. Anyway, he had to call it off at the last minute as something boiled over on a case he was working on. The next thing we know is a call from Tommy Dunn that she'd been knocked down and killed by a hit and run driver outside the Coconut Grove.'

'The Coconut Grove? What was she doing there?'

Frost shrugged. 'God knows! She might have tried to get inside the club – you know what kids are like – but Baskin would never allow that: he knows how keen we are to take his licence away. I went straight down there. Plenty of people who heard the car hitting her, not a soul who saw it.' He sighed. 'So – another of my failures. We never caught the driver and Mr Cassidy has never forgiven me.'

'Mr Cassidy suggests you didn't follow up the case with your customary vigour,' persisted Liz.

'I bet he didn't put it that politely,' said Frost. 'Let's drop the subject.' He turned the car into Fairfield Road. He couldn't park outside Ian Grafton's house. The battered old van was missing. In its place was a gleaming black Porsche.

'When they come into money, they buy fast cars,' said Frost with a smirk of satisfaction. He had no doubt now who had abducted Carol Stanfield. Grafton answered their ring. He was disconcerted to see them and had to shout over the sound of heavy metal music rolling down the stairs. 'You can't come up – I've got someone with me.'

'Only take a couple of minutes,' breezed Frost, barging past him.

As he opened the door the blast of noise from the massive floor-standing tannoy speakers almost hit him in the face. The speakers and the state of the art hi-fi unit almost filled the room. But there was still room for the bed. And sitting on the bed, her expression changing from delight to utter dismay when she saw it was Frost and not Ian, was Carol Stanfield. Spread on the bed next to her were heaps and heaps of banknotes. She said something, but he couldn't hear. The noise from the hi-fi was deafening and when he struggled to turn it off he only succeeded in turning up the volume. Liz pushed past him and cut the power off from the mains. In the sudden, stunning silence they were slow to hear the sound of running feet taking the stairs two at a time. Ian and Carol were dashing for the front door.

By the time Frost and Liz reached the street, the Porsche was roaring round the corner.

Liz started to run for the Ford, but Frost stopped her. 'We'll never catch them in that, love. They've got no money and nowhere to go. They'll be back.'

They went back inside the flat to gather up the banknotes. He radioed the station to ask all units to keep an eye out for the Porsche and report its position. 'Apprehend the occupants if possible, but I want no Brands Hatch speed chase.'

He dropped Liz off at the station with the money, then went on his own to Primrose Cottage.

17

It was the younger sister, the bubbly nurse, who opened the door. She blinked her surprise at seeing Frost back again so soon.

'Trivial matter,' he said, following her into the chintzy lounge where her sister, Millicent, was watching the television. She pressed the remote control to switch it off, then turned to greet their visitor. She did not seem at all happy when she realized who it was. 'Sorry to bother you both,' said Frost, lowering himself down into an armchair and loosening his scarf. He started patting his pockets, smiling apologetically. 'Now where did I put it? Ah!' He produced the typed list of names, which he unfolded and studied. 'You used to live at Woodside Lane?' The nurse kept her face impassive, but from the corner of his eye he saw the older woman visibly start: she snatched up some knitting then pushed it away.

'That's right,' said Julie. 'A long time ago.' She sounded almost too casual.

'I'm a bit puzzled as to why you didn't tell me you used to live there.'

Julie frowned. 'Why on earth should we?'

Still watching the older woman, whose hands appeared to be shaking vigorously, Frost said, 'Because that's where we found the body, right near where you used to live . . . the man you said never called here.'

'Good Lord!' exclaimed Julie, wide-eyed and incredulous. 'He was found there?'

'You know damn well he was,' snapped Frost. 'In a coal bunker, right opposite your old garden.'

'How on earth were we to know that?' replied Julie. 'You never told us where he was found.'

He tried to hide his dismay as his mind raced over their previous conversation. She was right. He hadn't told them. Damn, damn and bloody double damn! His one ace trumped.

Julie sat on the settee next to her sister and took her hand. 'Millie isn't very well, inspector. We've told you we know nothing about this man, so unless there is any other way we can help . . . ?' She stared at him, her expression frank and open, but somehow, he knew she was lying. All right, he thought, if it's lies you want . . .

'I hate to suggest you're not telling me the truth, Miss Fleming, but we have a witness . . .' He looked again at the sheet of paper as if confirming details. 'A witness who saw the dead man, Lemmy Hoxton, come into this house on the day in question. And he never saw him come out again.'

The nurse flushed angrily. 'I resent the implication. If this man called here, why on earth would we try to pretend he hadn't?'

'Why indeed?' Frost gave his enigmatic smile which implied he knew everything. But he knew damn all. He was floundering. He stared at Julie, a long, hard stare. She returned it, her gaze unwavering. Game, set and match to her. His bluff had failed.

But he hadn't been watching her sister.

'Tell him, Julie. For God's sake tell him and get it over with.'

She was standing, shaking, her face white.

'Tell me what?' asked Frost.

Julie moved protectively in front of Millie, and tried to get her to sit down. 'You can see she's not well. Would you please leave now.'

'What does she want to tell me?' repeated Frost.

Julie signalled her sister to keep silent, then glared defiantly at the inspector. 'It's nothing. She doesn't know what she is saying.'

Frost stood up and sighed wearily. 'It might be better if we all went down to the station.'

'All right,' said the nurse, patting her sister's hand and gently pushing her back on to the settee. She sat down beside her. 'Yes, that man came here. Yes, he robbed us, and then he left.'

'He robbed you?' said Frost. 'And you did nothing about it?'

She stared at the floor. 'We didn't want anyone to know what he had taken.'

'Which was . . . ?'

She hesitated, drew a breath, and put an arm round her sister who was starting to sob quietly. 'Photographs.'

'What sort of photographs?'

'Explicit photographs. Photographs of . . .' She looked at her sister. 'Photographs of us doing things . . .' She lowered her eyes and her voice was a whisper. '. . . using things.'

Frost's jaw dropped. He wasn't sure he had heard correctly, then he remembered what Liz had said about them. 'What sort of things?'

She flushed brick red. 'Do we have to go into details?'

'You use them on each other?'

'Yes.' She was now staring straight through him to the far wall.

'But you are sisters?'

'No. We live together. We have a circle of friends, we go to the church . . . We thought it best to give the impression that we were sisters, but that isn't the case.'

'So Lemmy discovered your secret?'

'Yes. He took the photographs and jewellery and money. He threatened to blackmail us if we told the police.'

'And where were the photos and jewellery and stuff kept?'

'In the bedroom.'

'The connubial bedroom?'

An angry frown. 'Of course.'

Frost pushed himself out of his chair. 'Show me.'

'I protest. Surely this isn't necessary . . . ?'

But Frost was already half-way up the stairs. Still protesting, she followed him, leaving Millie, face tear-stained, on the settee. He opened a door to a daintily furnished room with a double bed. He felt disappointed. He had expected mirrors on the ceiling, black sheets, whips and leather knickers. It was chintzy like the lounge. He tugged at the top drawer of a mahogany dressing-table. 'He took the jewellery from here?'

She was standing by the door. She nodded. 'Yes.'

He looked in another drawer. Tucked away under a pile of neatly folded underwear was a grey plush-covered box with a gold clasp. He opened it. Inside were gold neck chains, a locket, two jewelled brooches, a cameo watch and a heavy gold and ruby bangle. He showed it to her. 'How come he missed these?'

She looked away and said nothing.

'I'm waiting for an answer,' said Frost. 'You said he took your jewellery, but your jewellery is still here.' He smiled at her. 'Perhaps you then went out and bought some more, in which case just show me the receipts and I'll slink away with my tail between my legs.'

She was engrossed in the pattern on the carpet.

He pulled open other drawers. In the bottom one he found a wad of coloured Polaroids bound with elastic bands. He flicked through them. The two women naked and intertwined. The nurse, wide-eyed and panting, had a stunning figure. 'You take a good picture,' said Frost. At the back of the drawer, the sex aids. The object he brought out and held aloft was obscenely realistic. 'Alas poor Yorrick,' he declaimed. 'I knew him well.'

She winced. 'Must you be so unpleasant, inspector?'

'If I'm pleasant, people lie to me,' he said. He didn't

take your jewellery, he didn't take your family snapshots and I'm damn sure he didn't take your money. Lemmy would never leave without them . . . not unless he was dead.' He picked up the pink and red tipped appliance, waggled it, then slapped his palm with it. 'This wasn't the murder weapon, I hope?'

She looked away, screwing up her face. 'You're quite disgusting, inspector.'

'Lemmy's body was pretty disgusting when we fished it out of that coal bunker. You know the one I mean . . . next to your old house.'

'We've got to tell him, Julie.'

They hadn't heard her come in. Millie was holding tightly on to the door frame as if she was ready to collapse.

'Yes,' said Frost. 'You've got to tell me.' He waited while the nurse took the other woman's arm and gently led her over to the bed, then sat beside her, tightly gripping and patting her hand. Frost nodded for Millie to begin, but it was the nurse who spoke.

'I was home when he called. He must have thought it was only Millie in the house, but I had a migraine and was lying down in the back bedroom where it was cooler. It was so hot that day. All I had on was a nightdress and I was lying on top of the bed. Millie let him in. He did all the things you said . . . got her to turn on the kitchen taps while he came upstairs to the bathroom, ostensibly to flush the toilet. I heard him in our bedroom, opening drawers, so I got up and went to see what he was up to. He was at the dressing-table, his back to me.'

'This dressing-table?' pointed Frost.

'Yes. He'd opened the bottom drawer and found the photographs and the other things. When I shouted at him, he spun round, a dirty grin on his face. He wouldn't hand over the photographs. He said if I wanted them back, I would have to pay. He said . . .' Her voice dropped and Frost had to lean forward to catch what she was saying. 'He said, "Why not try the real thing?" Then he grabbed me and tore off my nightdress. I struggled and tried to get away, but he was too strong. He pushed me over to the bed. He was going to rape me. Thank God Millie heard the noise and came running in.' She turned and smiled at the other woman who took up the story.

'I heard Julie screaming so I grabbed the rolling pin and ran up. His trousers were gaping open and he was forcing Julie back on to the bed. I hit him . . . hit him . . . again and again. He turned and stared at me, then he collapsed on the floor. I prayed he was unconscious, but Julie said he was dead.'

'You didn't call an ambulance, or a doctor?' asked Frost.

Julie looked up. 'There was no point. I'm a nurse. I know when someone is dead.'

'And you didn't consider calling the police?'

'No.'

'You were being attacked . . . he was trying to rape you . . . you were screaming in fear of your life. I can't see any jury convicting you, especially when they learnt what a bastard Lemmy was.'

Julie shook her head hopelessly. 'Too much personal detail would have come out.'

'But it's all going to come out now, isn't it?' said Frost. 'All the lip-smacking details.' He put a cigarette in his mouth, but didn't light it. 'You hid the body?'

'We wanted to put him somewhere where he wouldn't be found for a long time. Millie thought of the coal bunker near the old house.'

'A good place,' said Frost. 'If we hadn't been looking for a missing boy, we might never have found him.' He lit the cigarette. 'You did something else to him. His fingers?'

The nurse shuddered. 'Yes.'

He dribbled out a stream of smoke. 'Why did you do it?'

'We'd just painted the bathroom. He must have touched the paint. It was all over his fingers. We tried to get it off, but we couldn't.'

'Why was it important you got it off?'

'It was our own special colour. The shop mixed it for us to match the bathroom curtains.' She saw Frost still looked mystified. 'The shop keeps all the details of these special mixes in case you want a repeat order. If the body was found, we thought you could have traced the paint back to us.'

Frost gave a wry smile. 'You wasted your time, love. I wouldn't have been that bleeding clever.'

'We scrubbed and scrubbed, but it wouldn't shift,' said Millie. 'Then Julie said we would have to . . .' She left it unsaid. 'We waited until it was dark, then took the body to our old place. Every day from then was a nightmare. We kept expecting to read in the papers of someone who hadn't returned home. Nothing. So we thought he had no relatives . . . no-one who would miss him. We were lulled into a sense of false security. We even began to fantasize that it never really happened. And then you came . . .'

'Yes,' nodded Frost in sad agreement, 'and then I came.' He pinched out the cigarette and dropped it in his pocket. 'Grab your coats, ladies. Let's go to the station.' He kneed shut the drawer with the photographs. Bloody hell, he thought. The press are going to have a field day with this one.

In the car the older woman was sobbing bitterly, tenderly comforted by her companion. Frost said nothing. There were occasions when it gave him great satisfaction to bring a case to a conclusion, but plenty, like now, when he wished he hadn't been so bloody efficient or lucky.

'What will happen?' Julie asked.

'We'll take statements,' he said. 'You'll be charged and you'll more than likely be granted bail.'

'And then?'

'A half-decent lawyer and you'll probably get a suspended sentence.'

'The trial,' sobbed Millie. 'It will all come out.'

'It doesn't matter,' said Julie. 'It doesn't matter.'

Poor cows, thought Frost. The photographs as exhibits and all the details of their relationship . . . he could see the tabloid headlines now . . . Of course it bloody mattered.

They were on the main Denton road. The line of traffic seemed to be moving very slowly and they were just crawling along. The car in front of Frost showed its brake lights and stopped. There was a hold-up ahead. He wound down the window and stuck his head out, but all he could see over the long line of vehicles ahead was flashing blue lights. He wound the window down, resigned to a long wait. 'Don't know how long this will take, ladies,' he said. 'Looks like an accident.'

It took nearly three-quarters of an hour for the traffic to start moving again. The older woman had stopped sobbing and sat, head bowed and red-eyed, staring blankly through the car window, while the nurse, deep in her own thoughts, absently patted her hand. Vehicles slowed down again as they reached the cordoned-off scene of the accident. A large chemical-carrying tanker had slewed across the road and was lying on its side. There didn't appear to be any leakage of fuel, but firemen were standing by. An ambulance was parked on the hard shoulder to the rear. In front of it, another group of firemen with a mobile crane were trying to raise the tanker so they could get to the crushed car underneath. It was a Porsche. A black Porsche. Hovering alongside the firemen, a team of paramedics waited, ready to dash in.

Frost braked abruptly and got out, ignoring the angry blast of car horns behind him.

A traffic policeman hurried over. 'Please get back in your car,' he ordered. 'There's nothing to see here.'

Frost flashed his warrant card. 'What happened?'

The traffic policeman shrugged. 'We don't know yet, inspector. It looks as if the Porsche was going too fast and crashed over the central barrier smack in the path of the tanker coming the other way.'

'Couple of teenagers – a chap and a girl – in the Porsche?'

'Yes.' The traffic policeman was looking over Frost's shoulder where the firemen had managed to raise the tanker and were now using cutting gear on the Porsche.

'Alive or dead?'

A screaming of metal as the roof of the Porsche was torn off. Two of the paramedics pushed forward and looked inside, then moved back, shaking their heads and signalling for the firemen to carry on.

'I think they are dead, sir,' said the policeman.

Frost sat them in separate interview rooms and asked a WPC to bring them mugs of tea which they looked at with obvious distaste and pushed away after the first sip. 'I'll be back soon,' he said and went off to find Liz to tell her about the Porsche. He hoped she would be in his office, but it was Cassidy who was waiting for him, pacing up and down to work off his anger. Frost wasn't in the mood for Cassidy, but he masked his feelings and gave an enquiring smile.

'The Lemmy Hoxton case is mine,' hissed Cassidy. 'You told me you wouldn't interfere and yet you've been off to see those women, without a damn word to me. You're deliberately keeping me out of it . . .'

Frost thudded down into his chair and rested his chin on his palm. Cassidy was chuntering away with his moan, non-stop, just like Mullett. So Frost applied his anti-Mullett technique, switching off his ears until Cassidy ran out of breath.

A pause, so he got in quick. 'I'm sorry, son. I forgot.'

'Forgot?' echoed Cassidy incredulously. 'How the hell could you forget?'

'Because I'm stupid,' said Frost. 'I shouldn't have done it. The women are in the interview rooms and they're ready to make statements confessing to the killing.' He told Cassidy the details. 'So it's all yours.'

Not in the least mollified, Cassidy marched to the door, turning for one final snarl. 'You haven't heard the last of this,' he said.

'I'm sure I haven't,' murmured Frost wearily.

PC Collier yawned. He liked working for Frost and he welcomed the overtime money, but the inspector always kept everyone up late, then expected them to be bright-eyed and bushy-tailed, with hardly any sleep, the next day. The succession of late nights were taking their toll and the warm interior of the car was whispering how great it would be to close his eyes, just for a few minutes, and drift off. He jerked his head up and wound down the window. They were parked at the end of Finch's turning, tucked away well out of sight, but from where they could just see the blue Austin Metro.

At his side, Ken Jordan was slumped in the driving seat, eyes closed, breathing heavily in a deep sleep. It wasn't fair. There should be two of them watching. They'd nearly missed Finch before when he had slipped out of the house, but didn't take the car. Collier had followed him on foot to the supermarket where Finch bought some food and returned home. If he sneaked out again . . . Collier stiffened and nudged Jordan sharply. 'He's coming out!' Immediately, Jordan was awake and alert. He snatched up the radio to report to Control, then slipped out of the car, his turn to follow on foot if Finch didn't use the Metro.

The front door slammed as Finch and an excited yapping dog walked to the car. Finch was carrying a carrier bag which he slung on to the back seat. It looked like the food he had bought earlier at the Savalot supermarket. When it was clear Finch was taking the car, Jordan slid back into the driving seat and picked up the radio. 'Subject in car driving south into Market Street. We are following . . .'

Frost located Liz in the main interview room. She had Tracey Neal with her, the travel bag with the money between them on the table. Tracey didn't look so cocky as when they had last seen her.

'Tracey's told us about the abduction,' said Liz.

'It was Carol's idea,' insisted Tracey. 'I just went along with her. I haven't had any of the money.'

Frost sat next to Liz. 'Stealing from her own parents. Why?'

'They're not both Carol's parents,' said Tracey. 'Her father divorced her real mother and married again. He spends all his money on her – furs, expensive clothes, jewellery. Carol said she'd only married him for his money.'

'So Carol was jealous?'

'The new wife would get his money when he died. Carol didn't think that was fair.'

'So you staged the fake abduction?'

'Yes.'

'Why did you dump the jewellery and furs and stuff?'

'We didn't know what to do with it. Ian thought we'd be bound to be found out if we tried to sell them.'

'So why take them in the first place?'

'It was Carol's idea. To spite her new mother, I suppose.'

Frost intertwined his fingers behind his head and studied the ceiling. 'All right, love, you can go,' he said at last.

Liz looked at him as if he had gone out of his mind? 'Go?'

'I don't think Carol's father will be pressing charges,' he said. 'If he does, we'll think again.'

Liz showed the girl out, then came back, clearly piqued and ready for a row. She wanted to tie this one up herself. Cassidy seemed to be getting all the successful cases and she was getting nothing. But when Frost told her about the accident she was stunned.

'We'll have to break the news to her father,' said Frost. 'Double bad bloody news. It was his daughter who stole his money and now she's dead.' He sighed. 'I wish Cassidy had snaffled this flaming case as well.'

Burton chased after them in the corridor and called them into the incident room. 'Finch is on the move. He's got a carrier bag of food with him. He could be on his way to the kid.'

'Let's hope he's not on his way to the park to feed the bloody ducks,' said Frost, glad of the chance to put off calling on Stanfield.

In the incident room he snatched up someone's mug of tea and settled down in a chair in front of the speaker.

'Jordan to Simms. Subject heading north to Bath Road. Can you take over?'

'Simms, receiving. Affirmative. We are at first turn-off in Bath Road.' A pause, then, 'We see him. Taking over now.'

'Right. We'll move ahead of him and wait at the Lexton turn-off.'

Jordan pressed down the accelerator and the car shot forward, flashing past Finch's Metro. They resisted the temptation to turn their heads as they passed, not wanting there to be any hint they were interested in him. No side roads for the next ten miles or so and the first possible diversion was just past the Fina service station near the Lexton turn-off. When they reached the service station Jordan drove up on to the forecourt and waited.

* * *

'Am following,' reported Simms. 'Not much traffic about and road fairly straight, so I'm having to keep well back.'

'Be careful,' urged Frost. 'He mustn't know he's being followed.'

'He's putting on some speed,' reported Simms. 'He's roaring ahead.'

Frost frowned anxiously. 'He hasn't spotted you?'

'I don't think so.'

A quick glance at the road map. 'He can't go anywhere but straight ahead. Drop well back and let Jordan take over when Finch reaches the service station.'

'Roger,' said Simms.

'Roger,' said Jordan.

The radio went quiet. Frost scrabbled at the cellophane on a fresh pack of cigarettes, cursing when the damn stuff refused to tear. At last he ripped it off in several pieces, stuffed a cigarette in his mouth and passed the pack around. Another check with the wall map. No way yet of knowing where Finch was heading, but it was clearly well outside Denton. Back to the speaker, which was making little crackling sounds. 'Come on, come on,' he muttered, 'Finch ought to be with you by now.' He clicked on the mike. 'I haven't bloody offended you, have I, Jordan? Talk to me.'

'No sign of Finch yet,' reported Jordan. 'I . . .' A pause, then, 'Oh shit!'

'What is it?' roared Frost.

'I can see Simms . . . but Finch hasn't reached us.'

'He must have flaming well reached you. Simms was behind him. He can't have bloody vanished!'

'He was ahead of me,' said Simms.

'Well, he hasn't passed us,' said Jordan.

Frost killed his cigarette in the ashtray. 'The bastard's got to be somewhere. Jordan – stay put. Simms – double back and see if you can spot him.' Another cigarette. He dragged smoke deep into his lungs and waited. A burst of static.

'Simms to Control. I see him!'

'Where?' pleaded Frost. 'Share it with us!'

'He's parked up on the grass verge where the road bends.'

'Is he in the car?' Frost was concerned that Finch might have parked the car and gone on foot to where the boy was.

'Yes . . . him and the dog. Just sitting, doing nothing. What do I do?'

'Drive on,' said Frost. 'When you're out of his sight, do what he's done – get up on the verge and wait.' He changed channels. 'Jordan. Stay put. He's in between the two of you. Unless the sod's got a helicopter in his boot, he must go one way or the other.'

He stood up and stamped around the room. The tension was getting to him.

'Finch has just passed me,' called Simms. 'He's done a U turn. He's heading back to town.'

Frost's shoulders slumped. He knew where Finch was heading. 'Follow him.'

'What's he up to?' asked Burton.

'I hope I'm wrong, son, but I reckon he spotted us.'

A few minutes later Simms reported, 'He's gone back to his house. I'm parked at the end of the road. Finch is getting out . . . and the dog. He's picking up the carrier bag of food . . . now he's gone inside.'

'Bum-holes!' said Frost mildly. This confirmed what he suspected. 'Tuck yourself somewhere at the end of the road and keep watch. A hundred to one he won't be coming out again today, but we can't take any chances.'

'What happened?' Liz asked.

'Finch was testing us,' said Frost. 'He wanted to find out if he was being tailed and we screamed out to him that he was. Damn! I've blown it.'

'I don't see what else you could have done,' said Burton.

'I should have had more bloody cars. Sod Mullett and

his economy drive. Finch notices a car behind him. He gets off the road and waits. The same car does a U turn and comes back again. You'd have to be as dim as flaming Mullett not to know you were being followed.' He knuckled his eyes. 'Come on, Liz. More job satisfaction. Let's break the news to Stanfield about his daughter.'

Stanfield opened the door to them. 'Why – it's PC Plod,' he sneered. 'I bet you haven't come here to tell me you've got my money back?'

'We have got it back, as it happens—' began Frost.

Stanfield wouldn't let him finish. 'What?' he shouted. 'That's bloody marvellous!' He jerked his head round and yelled back into the house. 'It's the police. Marvellous news! They've got the money back.' Almost dancing with delight he ushered them in. 'Come in, come in . . .'

In the lounge his wife, all smiles, came to meet them. 'This is wonderful,' she said. 'First the jewellery, now the money . . .'

'It's a bit early in the day,' said Stanfield, opening up the cocktail cabinet, 'but this definitely calls for a drink.'

But his wife, looking over his shoulder, saw the expression on Frost's face. An expression which said something was terribly wrong. She went white. 'What is it?' she whispered. 'For God's sake, what is it?'

They saw themselves out, quietly closing the front door on the bitter sound of sobbing. 'I properly sodded that up,' said Frost. He felt shattered. Another of his complete and utter shambles. He radioed Control in the hope that Finch had thrown caution to the wind and driven off to feed the boy. But Finch was staying put in the house. Frost drummed the steering wheel with his fingers, then came to a decision. 'No use pussy-footing around. Finch knows we're on to him, so let's bring the bastard in.'

* * *

Frost pulled out a chair and shook off some loose papers which fluttered to the floor. He waved a hand for the man to sit. 'Good of you to come, Mr Finch.'

Finch sniffed, and sat down. 'The way your officer spoke, it seemed as if I had little choice.'

Frost frowned and tutted. 'I'm sure he didn't mean to give that impression.'

'Well, that's the impression he conveyed.'

'Then I apologize on his behalf. Just a couple of things I want to get clear. Back to the other night, when you found the money. Did you see anyone else in the vicinity?'

'Yes – the thug who attacked me and sent me to hospital.'

'Anyone else?'

Finch folded his arms. 'If there had been anyone else, inspector, don't you think I would have mentioned it?'

Frost switched on his disarming smile. 'Forgive me for asking apparently stupid questions. Our difficulty is that the kidnapper went to a lot of trouble to ensure the money was dropped where he wanted it, but then – unless we consider two strong possibilities – completely failed to collect it.'

Finch smoothed his moustache. 'And those two, strong, possibilities are . . . ?'

'We were watching the money. Only two people turned up in the appointed spot – you and the man who assaulted you. Hudson has got a cast-iron alibi for the kidnapping, so we've cleared him. Now we'd like to clear you.'

'I see.' Finch gave a curt nod. He didn't seem at all worried.

Frost leant back in his chair. 'Your wife worked for Savalot supermarkets?'

Finch frowned. 'What has that got to do with it?'

'The supermarket provided the ransom money. We're just wondering if there could be any link.'

'My late wife worked for them – for more than fifteen years.'

'Why did she leave?'

'The new supermarket opened and her smaller shop was closed down.'

'Did she want to leave?'

'No.'

'Why didn't she move to the new supermarket?'

'The new store was fully computerized. They needed computer trained staff and considered my wife was too old to learn new methods.'

'And this upset her?'

'Yes.'

'She ended up by taking her own life?'

'Yes.' Finch stared straight ahead.

'How long after she lost her job?'

'Eighteen months. She became very depressed at being thrown on the scrap heap after fifteen years of loyal service. The job was her life.'

'She took an overdose?'

'Yes.' His face was tight, trying to suppress emotion.

'Did you blame Sir Richard Cordwell for her death?'

'Yes.'

'Enough to want revenge?'

'Yes.'

'Was that why you chose Savalot to provide the ransom?'

'No.' He stared up at the ceiling then took his glasses off and polished them carefully. 'I loved my wife, inspector, and I hated Cordwell as being the root cause for her death. It was an intense hatred and not one that could be satisfied by getting them to pay £250,000. It was a hatred that made me feel like setting fire to all their stores . . . running Cordwell down in my car . . . A hatred that, to my eternal shame, I did nothing about. The pain is still there, but time has numbed it. I did not kidnap the child.'

'We know the kidnapper used chloroform. You do the accounts for a couple of chemists. You could have helped yourself to the odd bottle.'

'I could have, but I didn't.'

'Do you possess a cassette recorder, Mr Finch?'

'My wife had one a long time ago. I don't think I still have it.'

Frost offered a cigarette which Finch waved away. 'There's another point that puzzles me. Hudson says that when he charged across to grab the money, he saw you kicking the long grass as if you were looking for something.'

'That's right – the dog's ball.'

'But that was already back in your pocket, sir.'

Finch creased a puzzled frown. Then his brow unfurrowed and he smiled as if the explanation was so simple. 'Of course – I'd forgotten. My foot touched something hard in the grass. I was looking to see what it was, and that's when I discovered the travel bag.'

'I see, sir,' said Frost, trying not to show his disappointment. Either Finch was innocent, or he was bloody clever, and he was sure Finch wasn't innocent. He shook two photographs from the folder and slid them across the desk. 'Seen either of these boys before, sir?'

Finch adjusted his glasses and studied them. 'No.'

Frost tapped one of the photos. 'This little boy choked to death on his own vomit. I'm sure the kidnapper did not intend his death. When it comes to a charge, we probably would not be talking murder.'

Finch nodded vaguely as if this was of no interest to him.

'If we got the other boy back safe and sound, I think we might be able to say a few kind words on the kidnapper's behalf to the judge.'

'You should be telling this to the kidnapper,' said Finch, 'not to me. Are you accusing me?'

'We have to keep an open mind, sir,' said Frost. 'Explore all possibilities.'

Finch stood up. 'You've searched my house, you've searched my car and you've found nothing. If you have anything at all to tie me to this crime, then please charge me. If not, I take it I am free to go?'

'Of course you're free to go,' said Frost. 'I'll get someone to drive you home.'

'I can find my own way back, thank you,' snapped Finch. He strode out of the office.

Frost hurried back to the incident room where Burton was waiting. 'Well, sir?' he asked.

'Guilty as hell,' said Frost. 'I only need two things now to make an arrest – proof and the kid.' He gratefully took the cup of tea Burton offered. 'He's a glib bastard. Always comes up with a clever answer for everything.'

'Perhaps it's because it's the right answer?' suggested Cassidy, who was feeling pleased with himself now that he had taken the confessions from the two women which tied up the Lemmy Hoxton case.

'He's guilty!' said Frost firmly. But even he was beginning to have doubts.

Collier nudged Jordan. They were back at the end of the road, watching Finch's house. Jordan yawned and opened his eyes. 'What is it?'

'How much longer are we supposed to be stuck here?'

Jordan shrugged. 'Until we're relieved, I suppose.' He was glad to have a nice easy job for a change where he could catch up on lost sleep.

'For all we know they've arrested him. It's been more than three hours since they took him in. No-one would think of telling us.'

'I'll check,' said Jordan. He radioed Control.

'What do you mean, what's happening with Finch?' demanded Control. 'Isn't he back?'

'If he was back, I wouldn't be asking,' said Jordan.

* * *

Frost had returned to his office where he slumped down in a chair and closed his eyes for a couple of seconds. He had plunged instantly into a deep sleep, a sleep boiling with jagged dreams involving Finch and the body of Bobby Kirby, hand flopping limply, the severed finger dripping blood. The phone woke him. He jerked up with a start, trying to work out where he was, groping for an alarm clock that wasn't there. Of course . . . he was in the office. He hooked the cord round his finger and bumped the phone off its rest and across the desk. 'Frost.'

Lambert in Control. He had Jordan on the radio and he wanted to know what was happening with Finch?

Frost yawned and shook his head to try and wake himself up. What was Jordan on about? He and Collier were supposed to be watching the house and Finch should have been back long ago. 'I'm coming,' he yawned into the phone and made his way to the incident room.

'What do you mean, he never came back to the house?' he asked Jordan over the radio. 'He left here hours ago.'

'I don't know about him leaving you, inspector,' replied Jordan. 'All I know is, he certainly hasn't come back here.'

Frost creased his brow, trying to remember what had happened when he let Finch go. He couldn't remember allocating anyone to drive him back. Then he went cold. Finch had turned down the offer of a lift and he had let his number one suspect, his only bloody suspect, wander out of the station on his own. 'You're sure he hasn't returned to the house?'

'Positive,' said Jordan. 'We've been watching.' Collier, at his side, reacted to the 'we'.

'Then be even more bleeding positive,' said Frost. 'Go and bang on his door. That should set the dog barking. See if someone who isn't there tells the flaming thing to keep quiet.'

'I know he isn't there,' said Jordan.

'Just do it!' barked Frost. He waited impatiently, listening to little bursts of static from the speaker until Jordan returned.

'He's definitely not in the house,' reported Jordan with an air of 'I told you so'.

'You needn't sound so bloody pleased about it,' said Frost. 'What happened?'

'I knocked. The dog inside went mad . . . yapping and whining. I can still hear it barking from here. No-one told it to be quiet, no-one came to the door.'

'Is his car still there?'

'Yes.'

Frost sighed. What else could go bloody wrong? 'Stay put. I'll get back to you.' He clicked off the radio, conscious of everyone watching him, waiting to be told what to do. Control was instructed to order all patrols and mobiles to actively search for Finch. Bill Wells was to send every available man out to scour the town . . . pubs . . . cinemas . . . everywhere. He got one of the WPCs to phone all the firms Finch did accounts for, in the hope he was with one of them. Then he contacted Felford Division for someone to keep an eye on the caravan, should Finch decide to return there.

He briefed his team in the incident room, stressing how important it was to find him. 'He's a calculating sod. If he's gone missing, there's a reason. If he's done a bunk, we'll never know where the kid is so we've got to find him. Someone check buses and the railway station.' He paused, trying to think of anything he might have missed out. 'And if anyone thinks of anywhere else he might be – public lavatories, knocking shops, sex change clinics, Toys R Us – don't tell me, just go and look.'

They bustled out, passing the Divisional Commander on his way in. Mullett always managed to appear when things were going wrong. 'What's the position with Finch?'

Frost told him.

'You just let him walk out of here?' said Mullett, his voice shrill with incredulity. 'You said you were having him followed. You said he would lead us to the boy.'

'I know I said that!' snapped Frost. 'But I sodded it up.'

'Something you seem to be doing a lot of lately,' said Mullett. 'Strange that Cassidy seems to be having all the success while you have all the failures.' He marched to the door, where he turned to fire one last bullet. 'If you mess this one up, Frost . . .' The slamming of the door punctuated the threat.

'Thank you for your encouraging words,' Frost muttered to the closed door.

He waited impatiently by the radio. Nothing. He got Control to radio out to everyone in case their radios had failed. Everything in order. Then the negative reports began flooding in. No sign of Finch anywhere.

Another half an hour passed. No news. He radioed through to Jordan. 'Please,' he pleaded, 'say Finch has come home, he's safe indoors, but you forgot to tell me.'

'Sorry, inspector,' said Jordan.

Burton and Liz returned, tired and unhappy. 'Sorry, inspector,' said Liz. 'I don't know where else we can look.'

Frost stood up. 'You and Burton, come with me.'

'Where are we going?' she asked.

'To Finch's house. Let's go over the place again.'

'But we didn't find anything before.'

'Then let's hope we bloody well find something this time.'

18

The dog began barking again the minute they walked up the path. They could hear it scratching furiously at the kitchen door, trying to get out. Frost rang the bell and hammered on the door, just in case. He waited a couple of seconds then gave the nod to Burton, who moved forward with the heavy hammer. Two blows were enough. The door shuddered and screws squealed as they were wrenched from the woodwork. Burton kicked it open and they entered the house. The dog was barking itself into a state of hysteria and Frost had to raise his voice to make himself heard.

'This is make or break,' Frost told his team. 'Strip the place bare, peel the bleeding wallpaper off if you have to, but find me something that leads us to the kid.'

He left them to it and wandered out to the Metro in the drive. Burton, with the help of an enormous bunch of keys borrowed from Traffic, had got the door open and was sitting in the front seat, going through the contents of the glove compartment. Car handbook, road map, old parking tickets . . . Frost took the road map, which was of Denton and the surrounding area. His pulse quickened when he saw a section carefully ringed, but it was simply showing the location of the caravan that Felford Division were keeping an eye on. Burton rummaged through the dash compartments. They yielded nothing. Frost left him to it and returned to the house and the barking dog. He told Collier to try and get the animal to keep quiet.

Collier wasn't too happy about this. It was yapping non-stop and scratching frenziedly at the door, sounding ready to tear the intruders' throats out. Gingerly, he opened the kitchen door inch by inch. The barking stopped. Collier froze. A danger signal. He had been told that when the barking stopped, the animal attacked. The dog waddled towards him, growling menacingly, then leapt up and licked his hand. He gave it a pat, and fed it some tinned dog food from the larder. It gulped the food down, then went off to sleep oblivious to the houseful of strangers. 'Bloody good house dog,' commented Frost.

In the lounge Jordan was on his knees by the magazine rack, taking each magazine out in turn, shaking it, then leafing through the pages. Frost wanted to tell him not to bother – Finch wasn't going to hide the boy's location in a magazine – but he didn't want to discourage enthusiasm, no matter how misplaced.

Everyone was bustling with their own search areas. No need now to put everything back exactly as it was. Upstairs, in Finch's office, Burton was studying the items on the cork-based pinboard, taking each off and checking the backs. Nothing very exciting. A few business cards . . . a hand-written list of his premium bonds, a picture postcard from Spain . . . the telephone number of a plumber. In the bedroom Liz was going through the pockets of all the clothes in the wardrobe.

Frost was in the lounge. On a coffee table was an answerphone, its little green light flashing to signal that a message had been left. He played it through . . . it was a call from a firm asking if Finch could do their accounts a week earlier than planned. He switched it off. The phone had several numbers stored in its memory so he tried them all, only to get other people's answerphones. They were all to do with Finch's accounting business. The man didn't seem to have much of a private life.

Bill Wells called him on the radio. 'We've just had a

complaint from the woman who lives next door. She says there's a gang of scruffs in Finch's house acting suspiciously.'

'OK,' said Frost. 'I'll see to her.' Everyone else was busy, so he ambled over to the next house himself and charmed his way into a cup of tea.

'Knock the dog off the chair,' said the little grey-haired woman, pouring hot water into a cup and adding a tea-bag. As soon as Frost sat down, the animal, a fat, snuffling bulldog, was up on his lap dribbling all over his trousers.

'You're honoured,' said the woman. 'He doesn't take to everyone.' She added milk and passed the cup, with its floating tea-bag, to Frost. 'Why are the police here?' she asked. 'Mr Finch isn't in any sort of trouble, is he?' She said it as if she hoped he was.

'Good Lord no!' said Frost. 'He kindly gave us permission to search his house in case we overlooked something.' He didn't elaborate further.

'I saw him go out earlier,' said the woman, 'but I didn't see him come back . . . and I usually notice.'

I bet you do, you nosy cow, thought Frost. 'Any idea where he might be?'

She shook her head. 'Hardly know anything about him. I used to chat with his wife, but that stopped when she died.'

'Yes, I suppose it would,' said Frost.

'Killed herself,' she said confidentially. 'He never got over it.' Frost nodded sympathetically, then his nose began to twitch. A most foul aroma. He hated to suspect the woman, but the dog was looking very innocent.

'Oh dear,' said the woman, catching a whiff. 'He's not being naughty, is he? He suffers from the odd touch of flatulence.'

'He's not selfish. He shares it around,' said Frost. He lifted the dog off and stood up. 'I'd better make a move.' The woman followed him to the front door where he bent and gave the dog a pat to show he bore it no grudge. 'How does he get on with Mr Finch's Jack Russell?'

'That's not Mr Finch's dog,' she said. 'He's looking after it for someone while they're on holiday.'

He gave her a wave and returned to Finch's house. A glum-faced team awaited him. 'Nothing,' reported Burton. 'Not a damn thing.'

He sat on one of the bottom stairs and fumbled in his pocket for a cigarette to give him time to think. This was his last hope. There just had to be something here.

'I hate to say it,' said Burton, 'but it could be you've made a mistake about Finch.'

He shook his head. 'It's him,' he said, stubbornly. He was at his lowest ebb. The investigation had come to a dead end, it was peeing with rain and a seven-year-old was out there somewhere and he hadn't the slightest hope of doing anything about it.

'It's all a mess here,' said Liz. 'Shall we tidy up?'

'No,' he said. 'Leave it . . . Let's all go to the pub and get pissed.'

From the kitchen a salvo of barks. Something must have disturbed the dog. Frost stopped dead. The barking triggered the memory of what the next-door neighbour had said, something that didn't seem important at the time. 'It's not his dog!' he exclaimed. 'It's not Finch's bloody dog!'

They looked at him as if he was mad. 'Have I missed something?' asked Liz.

'No, but I nearly did,' said Frost, beckoning to Burton. 'Up on that pinboard in his office there's a holiday postcard from Spain. Go and get it.'

With a puzzled shrug to the others, Burton galloped up the stairs and brought down the card which he handed to Frost. A highly coloured beach scene with towering hotel blocks in the background. He turned it over and read the message. '"Dear Henry: Very hot here. We pity you shivering in Denton. Yes, please pay the phone bill for us and I'll settle up when we get back next week. Ethel & Wilf."'

He looked up at them expectantly, only to be greeted by a wall of blank stares. 'Flaming hell!' he moaned. 'I'm supposed to be the dim one.' He jabbed his finger on the card. '". . . please pay the phone bill for us . . ." Doesn't that suggest anything?'

They looked at each other, eyebrows raised in bewilderment. 'It means they want him to pay their phone bill,' said Jordan as if answering a stupid, self-evident question.

'So how would Finch know about their phone bill?'

It was Liz who saw what he was getting at. 'Finch is keeping an eye on their place while they're on holiday. He's checking their post for them.'

'Which means he's got the key . . . to an empty house. A perfect place to hide a kid.'

'Possible, I suppose,' said Liz, grudgingly.

'It's all we've got, so it had better be bloody probable. So let's find out where Wilf and Ethel live. Did anyone spot an address book?'

They all shook their heads.

'His computer!' said Frost. 'People keep names and addresses in their computers.'

'I tried to access it,' said Burton, 'but it's password-protected.'

'What does that mean?' frowned Frost.

'It means you've got to key in the password to gain access to the information. We could probably crack it, but it would take time.'

'Time is what we haven't bloody got!' He paced up and down pounding his palm with his fist. 'They must live in or near to Denton otherwise Finch couldn't keep popping in to check all was well.'

'If we knew their surname it would help,' said Burton.

'So would their bloody address,' said Frost, 'but we haven't got it.' Then his head came up slowly and he smiled. 'I know how we can find them. The electoral register.'

'How would that help?' Liz asked.

'The electoral register lists everyone living in the Denton area eligible to vote and I'm damn sure that anyone called Ethel and Wilf have got to be of voting age. All we've got to do is look through it until we find an Ethel and a Wilf living at the same address.'

'But there's thousands of names on the register,' moaned Burton.

'Then the sooner we start checking, the better. Let's go.'

A blue haze of cigarette smoke was rolling around the incident room, the silence broken only by the drumming of rain from outside and the rustle of turned pages from within. Everyone available had been dragged in to help, even patrols dropping in for their meal break had to take sections of the register up to the canteen with them.

'I've got a Wilfred and Elizabeth Markham,' called Jordan.

'Check it out,' said Frost, blowing cigarette ash from his sheet. 'People sometimes use a different name from that on their birth certificate.' But he wasn't optimistic. No-one changed their name to Ethel from choice.

'What is going on?'

Frost raised his eyes from the page and groaned. Mullett again, scavenging around, trying to find something to complain about. Still, he was an extra pair of hands. He quickly explained and pushed a section of the register across to the Divisional Commander.

'Delighted to help,' boomed Mullett. 'We are, after all, a team.' He settled himself down at an empty desk, which made Frost's heart sink as his stomach was rumbling and he was hoping to send out for another feast of fish and chips. 'You'd be more comfortable in your own office, sir,' he suggested hopefully.

'I'm quite happy here,' smiled Mullett. 'What were those names we were looking for . . . George and Mildred?'

'Wilf and Ethel.'

'Of course, of course.' Mullett coughed pointedly. 'I'm sure we'd all work a lot better if people didn't smoke.'

They had three false dawns. Two 'Wilfred and Ethel's that seemed promising, but were at home watching television when the car called to check. At the third, the house was empty, but the next-door neighbour said they were at the pub and would be back in half an hour.

Frost rubbed a weary hand over his face. The names were beginning to blur and wriggle in front of his eyes. At one stage he suddenly realized he had turned a page but hadn't consciously read any of the names on it. There must be an easier way.

'What names did you say again?' asked Mullett.

Bloody hell. The man had a memory like a bleeding sieve – and how could he have been checking away for half an hour without knowing the names he was looking for? 'Wilf and Ethel,' said Frost patiently.

'I've got a Wilfred and Ethel here,' said Mullett, tapping the page with his finger. Frost dashed across and snatched it from him. 'Wilfred Percival Watkins and Ethel Maureen Watkins, 2 Wrights Lane, Denton.' He checked the map. Wrights Lane was a fairly exclusive area with a few detached Victorian houses in extensive grounds on the outskirts of Denton, not too far from the woods and the river.

After three disappointments, no-one got too excited; they plodded on with their own lists while Frost sent an area car to check this one out.

Within five minutes an excited radio message. 'Charlie Baker to Mr Frost. Checked the Wrights Lane address. Lights are showing, but as you instructed we did not approach. Neighbours say the owners are a retired pharmacist and his wife, holidaying in Spain. They also confirm they have a Jack Russell terrier which is being looked after by a friend.'

'Bingo!' yelled Frost, throwing his list up in the air where the papers fluttered and autumn-leafed to the ground. He grinned broadly at Mullett. 'Thank you, super. I always said you weren't entirely useless.'

By the time Mullett had worked out that this wasn't the whole-hearted compliment he had assumed, Frost and his team were racing across the rain-swept car-park, leaving empty desks and sheaves and sheaves of printed lists.

The car slithered and bumped up the unmade road that led them to Wrights Lane. Rain bounced and drained off the road into an overflowing ditch which ran along its length. The road dipped sharply as the car went beneath a small, iron railway bridge and churned its way through a deep puddle; a slight bend and there was the house, just to their left behind a fringe of trees. Its lights were on.

They turned into the drive, skidding to a splashing halt by the front door, the second car with the rest of the team having to brake sharply to avoid running into the back of them. Out of the car, heads down against the driving rain, and Frost was hammering at the front door after sending Burton and Jordan round to the back. No answer but he could see someone moving about inside the hall through the frosted glass of the door.

He was about to knock again when Finch's voice called, 'Who is it?'

'Police – open up.'

'Just a minute.'

A brief pause, then the door was opened by Finch, his jacket off, a sponge mop in his hand. He raised his eyebrows in pretended surprise. 'Inspector Frost! Twice in one day – what an unexpected pleasure!'

'We want to search these premises,' said Frost.

'Do you have a warrant?'

'No, but it won't take long to get one.'

'Is it about the missing boy?'

'Yes.'

'Then I waive my right to demand a warrant. Please search where you like.' He moved back so they could pass. 'Do wipe your feet . . . and don't make a mess. This isn't my house.'

He's too cocky, thought Frost, hoping and praying this wasn't going to turn out yet another wasted exercise. He's too bloody cocky.

They thudded past him. Liz went straight through to the back door to let in Burton and Jordan who were shivering in the rain. They stepped thankfully into the dry and on to gleaming chequer-board linoleum tiles, dripping pools of water which Finch hastily sponged up with the mop. 'Please,' he admonished. 'I've gone to a great deal of trouble to tidy this place up. It belongs to friends of mine who return from Spain tomorrow.' He checked the washing machine which was churning away. 'I've got so much to do before then.'

Liz allocated areas of search, while Frost sat with Finch in the lounge, a large, high-ceilinged room, its gleaming furniture reeking of polish.

'How did you find me here?' asked Finch, slipping on his jacket. Then he smiled. 'Of course – the address on the dog's name tag. How clever of you!'

Bloody hell, thought Frost. Don't tell me it was on the flaming dog's name tag all the time! He smiled back modestly as if pleased at his cleverness. 'That's right.'

'Why do you think the boy is here, inspector?'

'Because you are here, Mr Finch.' He took a cigarette from the packet and lit up.

Finch grabbed at a heavy glass ashtray and pushed it over to him. 'This smacks of harassment. I have already told you I know nothing about the boy. You have nothing to suggest otherwise, yet I am constantly having to put up with this cavalier treatment.'

'Where is he?' asked Frost.

'I wish I knew,' said Finch. 'The poor little mite, away from his parents . . .'

An urgent call from upstairs. 'Sir – here!'

Burton had found something. Frost shot a glance across to Finch, who remained impassive and was carefully blowing flakes of cigarette ash from the polished top of the table.

'In here, sir.' Burton was waiting on the landing outside a grey-painted door. 'Put your cigarette out, please.' Frost, puzzled, did as the DC requested. He exhaled smoke which Burton fanned away before opening the door a fraction, pushing Frost in, then quickly closing it behind them both.

They were in a small bedroom at the back of the house. An oak wardrobe, a small matching dressing-table and a single bed which was pushed tight against the wall. The bed had been stripped down to the ticking on the mattress and pillows. A smell of wet wool from the carpet which had been shampooed recently and was still slightly damp.

'Take a sniff, sir,' said Burton.

Frost sniffed. 'Polish? Carpet shampoo?'

Burton looked disappointed. 'Nothing else?'

Frost tried again, then frowned. A sickly, sweet smell. Very faint, but it was there. 'Chloroform?'

Burton nodded in agreement. 'That's what I think.'

'The kid's been in this room,' said Frost. 'On that bed!' He lowered his nose to the mattress and sniffed, but could detect nothing. He went to the door, opened it briefly and called for Liz to bring Finch up.

Finch came in and stood in the middle of the bedroom. 'Smell anything?' Frost asked him.

With a cocky smile, Finch took a deep breath, his nose twitching delicately as if he was savouring the bouquet of a rare wine. 'Furniture polish . . . carpet shampoo . . . ?' he suggested. His nose wrinkled in distaste. 'And stale tobacco smoke which I imagine is coming from you. May I open the window?'

'No,' snapped Frost. He gave a tentative sniff, but by now the dying linger of the anaesthetic had expired. 'We could smell chloroform!'

Finch gave a knowing smirk and shook his head. 'Dry cleaning fluid. There was a stain on the carpet – the dog. I cleaned it off and shampooed it.' He bent over and peered. 'It's completely gone now.'

Frost pointed to the stripped bed. 'Where's the bedding?'

'In the washing machine. The dog again – he was sick over the pillow.'

Liz was told to dash down to the kitchen and rescue the bedding from the washing machine in the hope Forensic could do their stuff on it.

'Inspector!' Jordan calling from below. It sounded important. Frost scuttled down the stairs, two at a time, hoping and praying that it was something that would wipe the supercilious smile from Finch's face. Under the stairs an open door led to steps to the cellar. Jordan was calling from there.

A large cellar, its floor of flagstones, the bare brick walls white-washed. An unshaded 75-watt bulb swung in a holder, flickering grotesque shadows on the walls, along which ran metal shelving stacked high with cardboard boxes, bottles, carboys, drums, stock left over from when Finch's friend sold his chemist shop.

'I found this,' said Jordan, handing the inspector a large bottle in blue, fluted glass with a label that read 'Trichloromethane $CHCI_3$ – Chloroform'.

Frost held it up to the light. It was about a third full. Removing the stopper, he lifted it to his nose. Not white spirit this time. Definitely chloroform. He nodded grimly, then looked down at the floor, stamping his foot down on the flagstones, pointing out a couple that appeared loose. Where better to bury a body? 'Have them up, son. All of them . . . especially the ones that don't look as if they have been moved.'

Back up the cellar steps, squeezing tight against the wall to get out of the way of the Forensic team who were crawling everywhere. Harding didn't look very optimistic even when he told him about the chloroform. 'You'd expect to find it amongst a chemist's stock. It doesn't really prove anything.'

'How's the search going?' Frost asked.

'He seems to have made sure there's nothing for us to find. This place has been scrubbed, sponged, polished and vacuumed. The vacuum cleaner is a wet and dry model, so it's had water through it which has removed nearly all traces of dust and fibre.'

'What about the bedding from the washing machine?'

'We'll have a go at it over the lab, but I reckon it's been too well washed to yield anything.'

'The kid was here,' said Frost firmly. 'I'm pretty certain he was here up to a couple of hours ago.'

'Would he have had the run of the place?' asked Harding.

'Hardly,' replied Frost. 'I reckon the poor little sod was trussed like a chicken on that bed.'

Harding shrugged. 'Then he wouldn't have left much trace in the rest of the house, would he?'

'Inspector!' Liz, this time calling him from the landing. Another bloody clue that would probably lead nowhere. Harding followed up the stairs. She took them into a small boxroom which had been converted to an office. It was very similar to the one in Finch's house. A small desk had been jammed up against one wall. On the desk was an IBM 286 PC connected to a printer. Liz pointed. 'A twenty-four pin dot matrix printer, the same type as the one used for the ransom demand.'

Frost grinned with delight. 'Then we've got him.' He turned to Harding. 'Can we prove the ransom note was written on this machine?'

Harding swiftly disillusioned him. 'All we can say is that the note was printed on a machine of the same type. There is no way we can prove this was the actual machine used.'

Yet again Frost was deflated. 'There must be some way.'

'I don't think so.' Harding sat himself down at the desk and peered at the printer. It was a Star 24–10, some five years old. 'There's no typeface, only little pins.'

'The ribbon,' suggested Frost. 'Wouldn't it leave an imprint on the ribbon?'

Harding sniffed his doubts. 'The ribbons are a continuous loop. They go round and round with subsequent letters printed on top of earlier ones. It would be almost impossible to separate them out.'

'Try anyway,' said Frost.

Harding lifted the printer cover. 'If it was a fairly new ribbon I suppose there might be a chance.' He took out the cassette and examined it, before shaking his head and passing it across to Frost. 'Out of luck again, inspector. It's too damn new. It hasn't been used. The old one has been replaced. As I said, your Mr Finch is determined not to give us anything to go on.'

Frost thudded down the stairs with the cassette and held it aloft. 'We're looking for a used printer ribbon, just like this one. Check waste bins, rubbish bags, dustbin sacks. We've got to find it.' But he knew Finch was too damn clever to replace the ribbon without making sure there was no way they could get at the old one.

In the living-room Finch was sitting, watching the proceedings with a cynical smile, a smile which said, all too clearly, There's no way you dumb policemen are going to find anything that would incriminate me.

'We found chloroform downstairs,' said Frost.

'That's hardly surprising. My friend used to run a chemist shop. Old stock, I imagine.'

'Chloroform was used on the first boy.'

'So you said.' He looked at Frost in mock reproach. 'You are surely not suggesting my friend had anything to do with it? I think you will find he was in Spain at the time.'

'You seem to be finding this all very amusing, Mr Finch. A boy of seven kidnapped, mutilated, frightened . . . a boy who might even be dead.'

'I don't find it remotely amusing, inspector. What I do find amusing – although I suppose "pathetic" is the right word – is that you should be wasting your time here . . . all these men . . . all these resources.' He stared at Frost. 'Can you tell me one thing, one single thing, you've found that proves I had anything to do with it . . . just one . . . ?' He gave a superior smile that made Frost fight hard to control the urge to smash his face in. 'You can't, because there isn't anything.'

'We'll find it,' said Frost, trying to believe it himself. He jerked his head at Liz and told her to take Finch to the station. 'We'll question him again there.'

Clanging noises echoing from the cellar drew him down the stairs to investigate. Jordan and Collier, both sweating profusely, were levering up flagstones. It was a tiring job. The flagstones were big and heavy, needing all their efforts to lift and move without crushing their fingers. Two stacks of removed flagstones stood in one corner. A large rectangle of earth was exposed. Dry earth, untouched since the floor was laid. Jordan wiped sweat from his brow. 'Nothing yet, inspector.'

Frost went over to the stacks. The flags were nearly three inches thick. He thought for a second. 'Pack it in – forget it. If it's taking two of you to lift one of them, he could never had done it on his own.' The smug look on Finch's face had convinced him they could tear the place apart and not find anything. They would have to look elsewhere. But where . . . where?

When he went back into the lounge to check progress,

one of the Forensic team going over the upholstery with a hand-held vacuum cleaner kept moving him on from wherever he tried to settle. He took the hint he was in the way and yelled that he was going back to the station.

He was standing in the shelter of the porch, turning up his mac collar ready for the plunge through the rain to his car, when he noticed the garage door was slightly ajar. It had already been searched, but on impulse he splashed across and went inside. A chocolate brown Renault took up most of the space. He squeezed through and checked the boot in the remote hope that the original searcher had been as slapdash as he usually was and that he would find Bobby curled up, fast asleep, happy to be rescued. All the boot yielded was a spare tyre, some tools, a metal petrol can and a towing rope. He flashed his torch to the ceiling and the beam caught a shelf high up on the wall. On the shelf were a couple of bulging blue plastic bags which didn't look as if anyone had had them down to check. He reached up and managed to grab the corner of one bag. He tugged, then a bit harder. The entire shelf tipped up and the bags slithered off and thudded to the ground, bouncing off his head on the way. Hitting the cement floor, they burst open, spewing out tins of slimming foods which rolled and clattered everywhere, and packs of cotton wool. More junk from the chemist's shop.

He rubbed his head ruefully, then booted one of the tins to relieve his feelings. It rolled underneath the car. He dropped on his hands and knees to retrieve it and it was then he noticed there was mud in the tread of the tyres. Fresh mud, still wet. Finch had been out in the car, very recently, and then must have dried off the bodywork to disguise the fact. Frost stood up. The kid. Finch had used the car to move the kid. That was why he was so smug and unconcerned when they were searching the house.

He yelled for Harding, who was annoyed at having to

run through the rain and glared at Frost with his hair streaming and his jacket soaking. Frost indicated the mud and asked if there was any way of determining where it came from . . . 'Some little six-inch square of Denton which had this unique type of mud, found nowhere else in the universe?'

Harding squatted and studied it, then he stood up. 'I can tell you exactly where this came from, inspector.' He pointed. 'From the lane just outside the front gate. Wherever he went, he picked that up on the way back but I don't suppose that is much help.'

'About as good as the sort of help Forensic have been giving me all bloody day,' snarled Frost, plunging out through the heavy curtain of rain back to the house. He went to the bedroom. The smell of chloroform had completely gone. He wondered how long it would have lingered. He was guessing that Finch had chloroformed and removed Bobby not too long before the police turned up. Burton came in to join him. He told the DC of his theory.

'You're saying that wherever he took the kid, it isn't very far away from here?' said Burton.

'That's exactly what I'm saying,' said Frost. 'Otherwise we wouldn't still have been able to smell chloroform.' He went to the window and looked out. The wind was blowing the rain almost horizontal. A few dotted lights of houses could be seen, but beyond them, just visible, was the dark, sprawling mass of Denton Woods. The woods! That had to be it. That's where the boy was. 'He's dumped the kid in the woods, somewhere,' said Frost.

Burton joined him at the window. The woods stretched on and on. 'If you're right, he could be anywhere.'

'I know,' said Frost.

'We'll have to wait until morning,' said Burton. 'We'll never find him in the dark in this weather.'

'By the morning the poor little sod could be dead,' said

Frost. He tugged his radio from his pocket and called Mullett.

Mullett wanted an almost cast-iron guarantee from Frost that they would find the boy before he agreed to authorize a full-scale search party.

Frost gave it to him.

'Two hours,' added Mullett, quickly checking the balance of the overtime account. 'If they haven't found anything in two hours, call it off.'

'Of course, sir,' said Frost.

In the interview room Finch had been reunited with the dog, which was stretched out on the floor at his feet. 'Where did you go in the Renault?' demanded Frost.

'Out to the lane and back. I wanted to check if it was functioning all right. If so, I would drive back home in it, if not, I would call a cab.'

'And?'

'It spluttered a bit – water in the carburettor, I think – so I decided I would take a cab when the time came. I didn't anticipate you would kindly provide me with transport.'

'Why did you dry the car off to conceal the fact you had been out in it?'

Finch waggled a reproving finger. 'You attribute the basest motives to me, inspector. It is my friend's car. When I borrow things, I return them in the state in which I receive them. The car was clean when I drove out. I made certain it would be clean when my friend returns from Spain tomorrow.' He smiled. 'Satisfied?'

Frost concealed his irritation. The bastard had a glib answer to everything, all delivered with that snide, unconcealed smile which showed his satisfaction in putting one over on the police. 'You took the kid to the woods, didn't you?'

Finch raised his eyebrows in mocking query. 'Did I? That's news to me.'

'We've got teams with dogs searching the woods now,' said Frost. 'It won't be so bloody funny when we find him.'

'I hope you do find him,' said Finch, 'but if you think I put him there, you are wasting your time.'

Frost saw no point in pushing it further. 'Interview suspended.' He marched out to his office. Forensic must have turned something up by now, something that would wipe the smile off the face of this smug bastard.

He pulled the phone towards him, then hesitated. If they had anything they would have been through to him. He stared moodily at the rain cascading down the window, blurring the view of the car-park.

The phone rang. He grabbed it. It wasn't Forensic, it was Arthur Hanlon.

'Radio message from Johnnie Johnson,' reported Hanlon. Johnson was leading the search team in Denton Woods. 'He says it's absolutely hopeless. The dogs are useless in this weather, the team can hardly see a hand in front of their faces and they're slithering and sliding all over the place. Unless we can pin-point a precise search area, they want to pack it in.'

Frost looked out again at the atrocious weather. He could sympathize. Soaking wet, stumbling through sodden undergrowth in the dark, brambles snagging and slashing, visibility down to a few feet. They'd have to stumble over the poor little sod to locate him. Hardly any chance of finding him in those conditions, but no chance at all if they packed it in. 'Tell them to give it another couple of hours,' he told Hanlon, completely forgetting Mullett's limit of two. 'Tell them I am sure the kid is there.' But don't tell them I'm equally sure the poor little bugger is dead, he muttered after he had hung up.

He steeled himself to phone Forensic. Let's get the bad news over. Harding answered the phone. He was most apologetic.

'That house has been cleaned so thoroughly, we've

found nothing that would help, but there were a few fibres that could have come from the child's clothing.'

Frost gripped the phone tightly. His luck had changed at last. 'Then we've got him.'

'I'm afraid not, inspector. The fibres mean nothing on their own. Find the child and from his clothing we can prove he's been in the house . . . but we need the child.'

'If I had the child I wouldn't bleeding need you,' growled Frost.

'We can't find what isn't there, inspector.'

He banged the phone down, but Harding was right. Finch was being too clever for all of them. He had stripped Dean of his clothing to avoid leaving any clues and had probably done the same with Bobby.

'How is it going, Frost?'

Bloody hell! Bang on cue when things were going wrong, there was Mullett ready to twist the knife in the wound.

'Not too brilliant,' he replied. 'Without proof it looks as if the bastard is going to get away with it.'

'Have you heard from Forensic yet?'

'Yes. They haven't come up with a flaming thing.'

Mullett stared at Frost, his lips tightening. This, of course, was all Frost's fault. 'So tonight's expensive exercise has achieved precisely nothing. In fact you've achieved nothing right from the moment you took on this case.'

Frost smiled sweetly. 'Thank you, super. You have the God-sent gift of stopping me from feeling big-headed.' He barged past him out of the office. He'd had all he could stomach of Mullett for one night.

Back to the interview room for another crack at Finch, but he found Liz there on her own, patting the dog. 'Toilet break for Mr Finch,' she explained.

'Let's hope the seat falls down on his dick,' he grunted. He sat down and immediately the dog leapt up on his lap. He patted it and it licked his hand. 'Friendly little sod, isn't he?' His eyes narrowed. He wondered if the dog had been friendly with the boy. If it had got on the boy's lap . . . nuzzled against him, licked him . . . could some hairs from the boy have got on to the dog? He scooped the animal up and dashed off to the incident room where he phoned Harding, catching him as he was just ready to go home.

'Worth a try, inspector,' agreed Harding. 'Extra overtime, of course.'

'Of course,' said Frost. An area car was called in to rush the dog off to the laboratory.

Finch, escorted by Burton, was led back into the interview room. He looked around. 'Where's the dog?'

'He's helping us with our enquiries,' Frost told him.

Finch stood up. 'I want him here – now!'

'Sit down,' snapped Frost. He shook a cigarette from the packet and offered one to Finch who waved it away in annoyance.

Frost lit up and grinned. 'Friendly little dog, isn't he? Did he jump up to the kid . . . was he the only friend the poor little sod had?'

'I've already told you—'

'That you don't know anything about the kid. Well, you've been bloody clever with your sweeping and scrubbing and vacuuming, but I bet you didn't give Rin Tin Tin a bath. Our Forensic Lab are checking the dog over now. Want to bet they find the odd hair or two from the kid . . . the poor little kid whose finger you chopped off? Come on – I'll give you ten to one we find something.'

The briefest flicker of concern blinked on Finch's face, but was quickly suppressed. He stared at Frost, expressionless. 'You won't find anything, because I know nothing about the kidnapping. I have already made a statement to that effect. I have no intention of saying the same thing over and over again. Unless you intend to charge me, I take it I am free to go?'

'Give my colleague another statement explaining your movements tonight,' said Frost. 'We'll get it typed up and you can sign it . . . but it might be best to wait until we get the results from the dog first in case you want to change it to a confession.'

If this was meant to ruffle Finch, it failed. I'd hate to play poker with you, thought Frost, making his way back to the incident room.

Burton sat by the old Underwood manual typewriter on the end desk in the incident room pecking out the statement for Finch to sign. Frost had told him to take his time so they could hold on to Finch until the results from Forensic came through. Burton didn't need telling. He was a very slow typist at the best of times and this snail's progress was his top speed. Frost came in and looked hopefully at Hanlon who had just put down the phone.

'They're still looking, Jack . . . It's the wrong sort of weather for a search.'

'It's the wrong sort of weather to be on holiday, but that's where I ought to flaming well be, not here.' He hurled himself down into a chair and realized one of their party was missing. 'Anyone seen Mr Cassidy?'

'No, thank God,' muttered Burton.

The external phone rang. Hanlon answered it, listening, then putting his hand over the mouthpiece. 'For you, Jack – Forensic.'

He took the phone, pausing before he raised it to his ear. He didn't think he could take much more bad news without something to cheer him up, like Mullett falling over and breaking his neck. 'Frost.'

'We've taken samples from the dog's fur,' reported the lab technician flatly. 'We've found three hairs that could have come from a young boy . . .' Frost's elation flared, but was instantly doused. '. . . but they do not come from Bobby Kirby. Sorry, inspector.'

He held the phone and stared blankly as waves of despair washed over him. Then his head snapped up. They'd only tried to match it with Bobby. 'The other boy – Dean – the dead boy. See if they come from him,' he roared into the mouthpiece. 'No – don't ring back. I'll hold.'

The phone at the other end went down with a bang and he could hear mutterings and echoing footsteps and then silence. He thought they had forgotten him and started whistling into the mouthpiece. Someone picked up the phone, said, 'Be with you in a minute,' and immediately put it down again.

He hunched up a shoulder to hold the phone to his ear while he fished out his cigarette packet. Before he could light up, Harding was back. This time he wasn't apologetic. He was downright jubilant. 'You were right, inspector. Those hairs come from the dead boy, Dean Anderson.'

It was so long since he had heard good news, he didn't know how to take it. 'Are you sure? Lie to me if you're not . . . but please say you're sure.'

'Positive. Absolutely positive.'

A hot surge of relief flooded his body. 'You're not so bloody useless as I thought.' He spun round in his chair and yelled in triumph. 'We've got the bastard! We've got him!'

He bumped into Mullett, nearly spinning him round, as he sprinted down the corridor to the interview room. 'You look absolutely ravishing tonight, super,' he cooed to a puzzled and gaping superintendent. 'We've got the bastard!' he explained. 'I'm going to charge him now.'

Finch was sitting, looking bored, as he waited to sign his statement, when Frost burst in. Right, thought Frost, now we wipe the smile off your face, you supercilious sneering sod.

He crashed down in the chair opposite Finch and leaned forward. 'It's the end of the line, you sod. Man's best friend has let you down. There are hairs from the dead boy all over it.'

Finch flinched as if he had been hit. He struggled to keep his face impassive, but he was clearly shaken. 'I don't think I want to say anything,' he said.

'Is Bobby still alive?'

Finch didn't answer.

'Don't sod about,' said Frost. 'It's all over. We've got you. Where is the boy?'

Finch sank his head and squeezed his chin in thought. Then he straightened up. 'I want the tape recorder switched off.'

'Why?' asked Frost.

'Turn it off and I'll tell you.'

Frost nodded to Liz who stopped the recording and removed the cassette tapes.

'I would now like the young lady to leave,' said Finch. 'What I have to say is for your ears only.'

Frost nodded and waited until Liz went out. 'Well?'

'You believe me to be the kidnapper.'

'I bloody know you are!'

'But your first concern is for the boy.'

'So?'

'Only the kidnapper would know where the boy was, and in telling you, he would be sealing his guilt.'

'Go on,' urged Frost.

'If I were the kidnapper, I would want a deal. An assurance, in writing, that if I reveal the boy's whereabouts, all charges would be dropped and any evidence you might have against me would be destroyed.'

'We don't make deals,' said Frost.

Finch shrugged. 'Well, in that case the boy will most certainly die.' He looked up to the ceiling, through which the rain bucketing down on the roof could be heard. 'Such shocking weather. If that poor boy is out in it, he'll be dead by the morning.'

'You're telling me he is still alive?'

A thin mirthless smile from Finch. 'Only the kidnapper would know that, inspector.' He moved his chair closer to the table. 'You've got nothing on the kidnapper. If he kept his mouth shut, the boy would die and the kidnapper would walk free. Do a deal and the kidnapper would still walk free, but the boy would live. As they said in *The Godfather*, surely an offer you can't refuse?'

'But you wouldn't walk free,' said Frost. 'We have evidence.'

The supercilious sneer returned and Frost began to worry again. What had the swine up his sleeve? 'Are you talking about the hairs from the boy you say you've found on the dog? I hardly think that would stand up in court.'

'It's good, solid, forensic evidence.' But even as he said it, he saw the flaw, the gaping hole in the evidence that he realized Finch had spotted first.

'It is only evidence that the hairs taken from the dog came from the dead boy. But how did they get there? You were at the scene of the crime when the boy's body was found . . . You could have picked up the hairs and when the dog jumped up on your lap, they could have been transferred. I wouldn't be at all surprised if many of the constables who have been in contact with the dog were also at the crime scene. The hairs could even have been picked up from the car that took the dog to your laboratory. Hardly good, solid evidence against me, inspector, especially as it is all you have.'

'You bastard!' said Frost.

'Do we have a deal?' asked Finch.

'I'll see,' said Frost.

He went out to find Mullett.

19

He barged out of the interview room, crashing into Cassidy who was hovering outside and moved to block him. 'I want a word,' he said.

'Later,' said Frost.

'It's about my daughter,' hissed Cassidy, 'and it's got to be now!'

'Your daughter's dead,' Frost snapped. 'Bobby Kirby might still be alive.' He pushed Cassidy out of the way and almost ran down the corridor to the incident room. Cassidy, his eyes spitting venom, followed him.

Hanlon was hanging up the phone. He didn't look very happy. 'The other search party, Jack. They want to pack it in. In this weather it's hopeless.'

'The kid's still alive,' said Frost. 'They've got to carry on. I'll talk to them.'

Before he could do anything about it, Mullett charged in, his tongue hanging out for the good news about Finch. Frost told him.

Mullett felt for a chair and dropped into it. 'He admitted he had taken the boy?'

'Off the record, no witnesses, with the tape switched off. He'd deny it in open court.'

'And he said the boy was alive?'

'Yes, but probably wouldn't last the night.'

'Do you believe him?'

'Yes.'

Mullett knuckled his forehead, trying to think. 'You haven't enough evidence to charge him?'

'Nothing that would stand up in court. The choice is that we do a deal, let him go and the boy lives, or no deal, we still have to let him go, but the boy dies.'

Mullett turned to Cassidy. 'What would you do?'

Cassidy was only too eager to tell him. 'I wouldn't have got myself in this position in the first place.'

'Quite,' said Mullett before turning angrily on Frost. 'This is all down to you. I absolve myself from all responsibility for this mess.'

'I'll take all the bloody blame if it makes you happy,' snarled Frost, 'but what are we going to do about the kid?'

'I've no authority to do deals,' said Mullett. 'That's a matter for the Chief Constable.'

'Then ask the flaming Chief Constable.' Frost picked up the phone and banged it down in front of the superintendent.

Mullett looked at the phone as if it was a live bomb, then, steeling himself, stretched out his hand. Then he flinched, anticipating what the Chief Constable would say. He snatched his hand back. 'No, Frost. You got us into this mess. You get us out of it.' He strode to the door, then spun round, pointing a finger at the inspector. 'I want a result on this, Frost. I want a watertight case against Finch and the boy returned safe and sound. The boy's safety is paramount. I don't care how you do it . . . but stick to the rules.'

'Thanks for sod all,' muttered Frost. He stood up and stretched wearily. He'd have to have another word with Finch . . . try a bit of subtlety like threatening to tear his dick off.

His path was again blocked by Cassidy.

'Whatever it is, it can wait,' said Frost.

'It can't wait,' said Cassidy, 'and it won't take more than a second of your valuable time.' He unfolded a small sheet of paper and waved it at Frost. 'Something you might recognize.'

Frost bent forward to read it. A car registration number. His stomach tightened. He knew what it was.

'This,' said Cassidy, waving it in front of Frost's face, 'is the registration number of the car that killed my daughter. The BMW, the car you said didn't exist. The car where Tommy Dunn was seen talking to the driver.'

'How did you get it?' asked Frost.

'Never mind how I got it. You were given this registration number at the time. You conveniently lost it.' He pushed his face right up to Frost. 'How much did the drunken sod of a driver pay you and Tommy to keep him out of it, you bastard?'

Frost said nothing.

'I'm going to trace the driver and I'm having the case reopened,' said Cassidy, his face a mask of disgust. 'See if your damn medal can get you out of this!'

'Hold it, Cassidy!' Heads jerked round. Arthur Hanlon, who had been sitting quietly by the radio, was coming over. Normally placid, his face was as flushed and angry as Cassidy's. 'You don't know the facts.'

'Facts?' echoed Cassidy. 'Frost lied his bloody head off and a drunken pig of a motorist was let free. Those are the facts.'

'If he lied,' said Hanlon, pushing between Cassidy and Frost, 'then he did it for you, you bastard.'

'For me? What are you bloody talking about?'

'How well did you know your daughter?'

'How well? I was her father, for Christ's sake!'

Frost tugged at Hanlon's sleeve. 'Leave it, Arthur.' But he was shaken off.

'You were her father,' said Hanlon, 'but how often did you see her? You were career mad. The job came first, seven days a week, twenty-four hours a day – sod your family, you hardly ever went home. You didn't know what she was getting up to.'

'Getting up to? She was fourteen bloody years old. What the hell could she get up to?' shouted Cassidy.

'What are you daring to say about my daughter?'

'Your daughter was on drugs. Your lovely, pure, fourteen-year-old daughter was on hard drugs.'

Cassidy's knuckles whitened as he clenched his fists tight. 'You're lying!'

'And to support her habit,' continued Hanlon doggedly, 'your fourteen-year-old daughter turned to prostitution.'

'You take that back, you bastard.' Cassidy had grabbed the front of Hanlon's jacket.

For a short man, Hanlon showed unusual strength. He pulled Cassidy's hand away. 'What do you think she was doing at the Coconut Grove that night? She was stoned to the eyeballs and plying for trade to pay for her next fix. Tommy Dunn saw her and hustled her out. He put her into his car and was about to drive off when she opened the door and flung herself out, right into the path of an oncoming car. The driver had had a few drinks, but there was no way he could have avoided her.'

Cassidy stared straight ahead as if he wasn't listening, but the muscle on the side of his face was twitching uncontrollably.

'She was killed instantly. Nothing could bring her back, but Jack Frost wanted to spare your feelings. He didn't want the facts to come out in court, so he let the driver go. Then he got the doctor at the hospital to do a very cursory post-mortem, ignoring the drugs abuse, the sexual activity, the disease. He wanted you to have the pure fourteen-year-old daughter you had always boasted about, so he lied and he covered up.'

Cassidy stared blankly and shook his head as if it would shake away everything he had heard. He turned to Frost. 'He's lying, isn't he?' Then back to Hanlon. 'You're lying! The old pals act. Everyone cover up for everyone else . . . just like Mullett and his mates lied when Chief Inspector Formby wrapped his car round that lamp post.'

He walked to the door. 'Sod you all!' he yelled, almost in tears. A flutter of paper as he tore up the registration number and hurled it to the floor. 'Sod you all!'

The door swung shut behind him.

'I wish you hadn't done that, Arthur,' said Frost. 'But thanks, anyway.' He poked a cigarette in his mouth and tried to think. What was he going to do before Cassidy sounded off? Oh yes. Have another word with Finch.

Liz looked tired and washed out so he sent her home. 'Burton will drive you,' he said. Burton seemed pleased at this. He kicked the door of the interview room shut. Just him and Finch.

'No deal,' he said tersely.

Finch shrugged. 'A pity, but I gave you a chance.'

Frost scraped a chair across the brown linoleum and sat down. 'I might be able to get the court to go lenient with you. The first boy's death wasn't intended and you co-operated in letting us recover Bobby. You could be out in five years.'

'According to my consultant, I haven't got five years,' said Finch. 'Any prison term, no matter how short, would be a life sentence, so you've got no carrots to offer me.'

'Tell us where he is,' said Frost.

'Only the kidnapper would know that,' replied Finch.

Frost stood up. 'I'll make you a promise,' he said. 'Whether we find that boy alive, or dead, or never, I'm going to nail you. I hope your consultant is right, because you are going to die in prison.'

He called for a uniformed constable to take Finch back to the cell. Fine bleeding words, he told himself, but how the hell am I going to do it?

Frost helped himself to a mug of tea from Bill Wells's thermos flask, then paid for it by having to listen to the sergeant's moans about the way Mullett kept blocking his chances of promotion and kept putting him down for duty on Christmas Day. He was only half listening. The kid was out there somewhere in the cold, torrential rain, and teams of men were looking for him. He was toying with the idea of driving over there to help, if only to be doing something constructive, but knew he'd just be getting in the way. He looked up as Burton returned from driving Liz back to her digs.

'Get your leg over, son?' he asked.

Burton grinned. 'Never had the nerve to ask her.'

'Did you hear about the bus conductress who married a bus driver?' asked Frost. 'On their wedding night she stripped off and said, "Room for one on top." When he'd finished he said, "But you didn't tell me there was room for five standing inside."' He cackled the loudest at his own joke, then stopped abruptly. It didn't seem right to be laughing while that poor little sod . . . He wryly recalled the empty threat he had made to Finch. Well, there was no way he was going to find the kid, drinking tea and telling dirty jokes. He swilled down the dregs and banged down the mug. 'Come on, son,' he said to Burton. 'Let's go for a drive.'

He sometimes thought better in the car so he lay back in his seat, smoking, eyes half closed, letting Burton drive through the stair rods of rain. The little buzzer in his brain started to sound off again. The house. There was something that had puzzled him when they went into the house in Wrights Lane. But what the hell was it?

'What happened when we banged on the door to get in there, son?' he asked Burton.

Burton couldn't help. 'You sent me and Jordan round the back.'

Frost leant back and gazed up at the roof of the car for inspiration, but none came. 'Drive me to her digs,' he told Burton. 'I want to talk to Liz.'

'She'll be in bed,' said Burton.

'Then she can get out of it again,' said Frost. 'I've got to talk to her.'

* * *

He banged on the door and kept his thumb jammed in the bell push. At last a light came on in an upstairs window, then the sound of footsteps descending the stairs. Bolts slid back and there was Liz, an unfastened dressing-gown over her nightdress, a police truncheon swinging menacingly in her hand.

'Bloody hell!' gawped Frost. This was a transformed Liz. Her hair, usually screwed back tightly, was now free-flowing down her back. It was gorgeous hair and she had a lot of it.

She had scrubbed off her make-up and her skin looked fresh and dewy. Her flimsy nightdress didn't conceal very much. 'What do you want?' she hissed to the dark shape standing in the doorway.

I'd love to tell you, thought Frost. 'It's me, Liz. Sorry it's so late.' He told her what was worrying him.

Liz shook her head. 'We knocked at the door, Finch let us in and then we searched the house.'

'All right, love,' he said. 'You go back to bed. I'm going to take another look around that house.'

'Wait,' she said. 'I'm coming with you.'

He waited in the car with Burton, who wanted all the tantalizing detail.

'She had a dressing-gown on,' said Frost, embroidering the facts to suit his audience. 'Nothing on underneath . . . she must sleep in the nude . . . and it kept flapping open.'

'Flaming heck!' breathed Burton.

'And her Bristols,' he added. 'Wow . . . I've never seen such nipples.'

'Tell me, tell me!' pleaded Burton.

'Have you ever seen ripe, Royal Sovereign strawberries, warm from the sun with the dew still on them?' said Frost, getting excited at his own fantasy.

'No, but I can imagine it,' said Burton, wriggling in his seat.

'Well . . . !' His expression changed abruptly. 'Look out, she's coming.' Burton leant back and opened the door for her.

Liz sat in the back seat. Burton kept eyeing her with renewed interest. She certainly looked different with her hair hanging loosely. As they paused at the traffic lights he turned and gave her a smile. 'You look smashing with your hair like that.'

'Keep your eyes on the road, constable,' she said icily.

The house was unguarded. With the search party out in force they didn't have enough men for that luxury. They went inside with Frost mooching from room to room, not knowing what the hell he was doing there or what he was looking for. Fingerprint powder was everywhere, but the only prints found were those of Finch and a few of the householder and his wife which had survived Finch's vigorous polishing and cleaning operation. In the bathroom and the kitchen, the sink traps had been removed and the contents taken away by Forensic for examination. The couple returning from Spain were going to have a shock when they arrived home tomorrow.

Frost opened and closed closet doors aimlessly and dug through pockets of clothing swinging from hangers. From the back bedroom he stared through the rain-shimmering windows to the garden, an enormous rain puddle making the lawn a lake. In the distance, a few smears of lights flickered intermittently as the poor sods in the search teams floundered about in the woods. He wondered if the little boy was under cover. A mental picture of the seven-year-old, bound, gagged, probably with masking tape over his eyes, made him shudder. And they were nowhere near to finding where he was.

Downstairs, in the kitchen, Liz was rummaging through drawers that had already been thoroughly searched. 'I wish I knew what we were looking for,' she said.

'You and me both, love,' he muttered, pulling open a

drawer next to the sink. It held cutlery and a bread board. He took out the board and a long, razor-sharp carving knife and wondered if this was what Finch had used to cut off the finger for the ransom demand. The board, well grooved with knife cuts, had been scrubbed white. He dropped them back, nudging shut the drawer.

Burton came in, dusting himself down. He had been up in the loft, crawling behind water tanks. 'We did a thorough job on the search first time,' he said. 'I don't see how they missed anything.'

Frost stared into space. 'It was right at the start,' he said. 'Right at the start. We banged at the door.' He looked at Liz. 'Then what?'

She frowned as she tried to remember. 'We knocked . . . he opened the door . . . we all charged in.'

Frost chewed his knuckle. There was something else. But what? 'We knocked. Finch was already in the hall. He said, "Who is it?" I said, "Police" and then . . .' He snapped his fingers in triumph. 'I've got it. He said, "Just a minute." He made us wait before he opened the door . . . only a few seconds, but he made us wait . . . Why?' He hurried out into the hall, Liz and Burton following. A pile of letters stood on the hall table awaiting the return of the holiday-makers; some of them, the ones that looked like bills, Finch had opened. He checked through the envelopes carefully, then pulled the table away from the wall in case anything had been jammed behind it. Nothing.

A door under the stairs led to the cellar, but there hadn't been time for Finch to nip down there. The only other things in the hall were the clothes hanging from the coat rack.

'Did we go through the pockets?'

'Yes,' said Liz.

'The women's clothes as well as the men's?'

'We went through them all,' said Liz. 'Nothing there that shouldn't be there.'

'Unless his dick was hanging out and he tucked it away before coming to the door, I reckon he hid something.' He looked again at the clothes on the rack. 'Let's go through these. Take everything out of the pockets and check the lining.'

The pile of odds and ends from the pockets mounted. Old receipts, bus tickets, scribbled shopping lists . . .

'What's this?' Frost had found something in the inside pocket of a woman's grey and white woollen coat. A black plastic credit card holder.

'Her credit cards,' said Burton. 'I checked them earlier.'

Frost was about to add it to the heap when an impulse made him look inside. He smiled grimly at Burton. 'You didn't check it thoroughly enough, my son.' He showed him the credit cards inside. They were all in the name of H. A. Finch.

Burton stared, shamefaced. 'I don't know how I missed that.'

'It doesn't matter, son,' said Frost. 'If you had found it earlier we wouldn't have attached any importance to it.' He went through it. 'So why was Finch so anxious to hide this?' Tucked in the end pocket were two Visa receipts. The first was for Finch's shopping the previous day at the supermarket. But the other bore today's date . . . 'Hatter's Garage, River Road, Denton . . . Petrol £12.74'.

He phoned the garage. 'Can you tell me what time this receipt was issued?'

'Some time this evening,' said the garage man. 'Latish.'

'Can't you be more precise . . . it's important.'

'If you can give me the registration number, I might be able to pinpoint it precisely. We've got a security video camera running all the time . . . too many people driving off without paying.'

Burton was sent off to get the number. Frost relayed it.

'Just a minute.' The sound of the phone being put down . . . noises off while the man dealt with a customer, then the clicking of controls as the video was wound back . . . 'Hello . . . Is it a Renault?'

'Yes.'

'Ten twenty-three this evening.'

'Thanks,' said Frost. 'Don't erase that tape. We're on our way now to pick it up.'

It took just over twenty minutes to reach the garage, where they sat in the manager's office as the garage man loaded up the tape. 'We get all sorts of things recorded on these,' he said chattily. 'Caught a bloke doing a number two behind the Derv pump last week. Want to see it?'

'No thanks,' said Frost. 'It might be me.'

'There you go!' The man found the approximate place and pressed the play button. Black and white images of single shots jerked across the screen like old silent films. The man pressed the pause button and there, quivering on the screen, was Finch using the pump. Frost rose from his chair and almost pressed his nose on the screen as he studied the car. If he was hoping to see the missing boy grinning out of a window, he was disappointed. The running time was shown on the corner of each frame. Finch arrived at ten twenty-three and left at ten twenty-seven. They commandeered the tape.

'So what does it all mean?' asked Liz when they were back in the car.

'He hid the receipt,' said Frost, 'which means he didn't want us to know he'd bought petrol here. Why not? Because he had Bobby Kirby in the boot. Finch was taking him to where he was going to hide him.'

'And where was that?' asked Liz.

'Definitely not in the woods,' replied Frost. 'There's plenty of filling stations he would have passed going there. Hatter's Garage is in the opposite direction.'

'He could have gone on to the woods afterwards,' said Burton.

'So why go to great lengths to hide the petrol receipt? No, son. All those poor sods falling over each other searching the woods and running up our overtime bill have been wasting their time. The kid isn't there.'

'Then where is he?' asked Liz.

Frost sighed. 'All we can do is guess. The road past the filling station leads straight down to the river.'

Liz paled. 'You believe he's dumped the boy in the river?'

'Alive or dead, I reckon that's where he is.' He told Burton to drive down there while he fished his radio out of the glove compartment. 'Frost to Control . . . over.'

'We've been trying to get hold of you, inspector,' said Lambert. 'Message from Mr Mullett. He wants to see you in his office right away.'

'Message for Mr Mullett,' said Frost. 'Tell him to get stuffed. This is urgent. Contact the search team in the woods. Tell them to stop immediately and get over to the top of River Road bloody quickly. I'll meet them there. And try and rustle up a couple of frogmen. We could be fishing for a body.'

'Right,' said Lambert. 'Mr Cassidy wants a word.'

A rustle as Cassidy took over the microphone. 'What's happening?'

Frost gave him the details. 'I'm getting a team over to search the river area in case he's still alive.'

'I'm on my way,' said Cassidy. If there was a chance of a successful outcome to this case with the boy still alive, he wanted to be part of the winning team.

'Great,' said Frost, trying to sound enthusiastic. 'The more the merrier.'

The river, some twenty feet across at this point, was little more than an open sewer, receiving the effluent from the various factories on the far side who found it cheaper to pay fines than conform to the stringent requirements of the Rivers Authority. Its surface was usually a sluggish mass of discoloured foam and oil-rainbowed scum, but the heavy rain of the past few days had made it overflow the sluice gates and now the flow was galloping past.

The road ran alongside the river for about a quarter of a mile and it was in this section that Frost intended to concentrate his search. He stood, watching the boiling river, drenched to the skin, while Burton and Liz, heads down, almost blinded by the torrential rain, looked for places where a tiny body might be concealed. He shouted Bobby's name in the forlorn hope the boy might be able to answer him, but all he could hear was the machine gun bullets of rain making snapping noises, almost like the crackling twig sound of a forest fire, as they pock-marked the river.

Headlights reflected off the water and he turned to see cars approaching. The search parties from the woods. From the first car, Arthur Hanlon, his hair plastered and dripping, squelched over to Frost. He eyed the current tearing past carrying broken branches and floating debris. 'Don't like the look of that, Jack.'

Frost nodded gloomily. 'All it needs is bleeding Lilian Gish on an ice floe.'

'You reckon Bobby's somewhere near here?' Hanlon had to shout over the noise of rushing water.

'Yet another one of my inspired guesses,' said Frost. 'If he's dead,' he hurled a stone into the water, 'he'll be on the bottom, sharing a sack with some bricks.'

He went over with Hanlon to the members of the search party, most of them still sitting inside their cars, not wanting to get any wetter or colder until they had to. All of them looked tired and dispirited, but they climbed out of the cars to huddle round him. 'Isn't this better than being stuck inside a stuffy office?' he asked, which produced a few laughs. 'All right. I've sodded you about up to now, but this has got to be our best lead yet. I know you're tired and fed up and hate my guts, but the poor little sod we're looking for is seven years old, shit-scared and could die if we don't find him quickly. Search everywhere, even the most unlikely places. If you're not sure, search again. So good luck.'

Hanlon split them into groups and directed them to various search areas while Frost made his way back to the bank. More voices and car door slammings. The mobile lighting unit and the frogmen. Hanlon sent a couple of men over to help them unload their gear and get the lights set up.

Frost walked up and down the bank, the rain beating down heavily on his bare head and soaking through his showerproof, water-blackened mac. The lights had been rigged and shone down on the river making it look like black velvet and bounced off the oilskins most of the men were wearing. False alarms as debris floating past looked just like a tiny body, but when it hit the lighted area turned out to be clumps of vegetation and earth from where the bank had collapsed into the river.

Jordan, in the small rowing boat with Collier at the oars, was prodding the muddy bottom with a pole. The monotonous, grating creak of the rowlocks as Collier fought to keep the boat steady against the drag of the current was setting Frost's teeth on edge.

'Something here, inspector!' Jordan calling from the boat, leaning over the side, dragging something from the water.

Frost's heart stumbled and skipped a couple of beats as an ominous-looking black plastic dustbin sack was hauled up and brought over to him. Don't let it be the boy, he pleaded silently. Please, don't let it be the boy. His knife slashed it open and it spewed stinking river water all over his feet. A long, low sigh of relief. Rotting household rubbish, dumped a long time ago.

Frost wiped the rain from his face and eyes and tried to concentrate to see if he got any feeling that the boy was somewhere near . . . that he was alive.

'Any luck?' called a familiar voice.

Bleeding Cassidy. He hoped he wasn't going to go on again about his daughter. 'We haven't found a dead body yet . . . that's about as lucky as we've got.'

'I had another word with Finch,' said Cassidy.

Did you? thought Frost. He's supposed to be my bloody prisoner, but be my guest . . .

'Mr Mullett thought I might be more successful than you.'

'Mr Mullett isn't questioning my infallibility, I hope?' muttered Frost.

'Finch is keeping shtum. I told him you were searching the river. He didn't seem at all worried.'

'He's hardly going to say "Oh my God, not the river!" is he? If he looks blank and acts dumb, we can't pin anything on him.'

'But if we find the boy—'

'There'll still be no proof Finch put him here. The fact he filled up at a garage in the vicinity is hardly bloody conclusive.' He pulled off his scarf, which was soaking wet and making him uncomfortable. 'I'll be happy if we find the kid alive, even if it means letting Finch go.'

The area was adazzle with all of the floodlights working and the generator throbbed away out of sight somewhere. Oars creaked, rain drummed and one of the floodlights sizzled and flashed intermittently as rain found a faulty connection. Searchers on the bank, in oilskins, bent low as they prodded the long wet grass.

'Put some bloody beef into it,' roared Cassidy, walking over to one of the groups who had been out in the rain and cold all night. Backs stiffened, but no-one said anything. They were too tired.

'Looking for the boy, Jack?'

Frost groaned. Sandy Lane from the *Denton Echo* with one of his photographers ready for one of his 'Police Fail Again' stories.

'Hello, Sandy,' he grunted. 'Been listening in to the police wavebands?'

The reporter grinned. 'No, Jack. We just happened to be driving past and we spotted all the lights.'

'Oh,' sniffed Frost. 'I thought there was an innocent explanation. Yes, we're looking for the boy.'

'Any reason why you chose this particular spot?'

'No. We just happened to see the lights and we thought we'd have a look. Now leave me alone, Sandy, there's a good boy. We're busy.'

The photographer took a couple of pictures of the searchers, then retired to the car with Sandy to wait for the body to be fished up, or the boy to be found alive. The reporter began working out alternative headlines to cover either eventuality.

The search had moved further down, leaving in its wake a trail of flattened grass and odd heaps of rubbish dredged from the river. Frost threw away the sodden cigarette that dangled from his mouth and tried to light up a fresh one from the damp pack in his pocket. He managed a couple of drags of bitter-tasting smoke before it sizzled and died. The feeling that the kid was here, almost within reach, was strong, but only as strong as the feeling they probably wouldn't find him. He felt like hurling himself in the car, tearing back to the station and doing a deal with Finch. Tell us where he is and we will drop all charges, give you a pension for life and all the Cup Final tickets you want.

He pulled back a sodden cuff to consult his watch. One o'clock in the morning. He could hear Cassidy shouting, redirecting one of the teams back to an area they had already searched. He thought of Finch in his nice, dry cell, snug and warm, and probably working out how much he could sue the police for harassment and wrongful arrest.

'Frost!'

A shudder quivered through him. Just what he wanted to make his misery complete. Mullett, immaculately turned out in his tailored raincoat which, in some mysterious way, seemed to repel the rain. He forced a smile. 'Hello, super.'

Mullett gaped at the floodlights, the frogmen, the teams of off-duty men, and tried to work out the cost. He transferred his glare to the drenched, drowned rat figure of Frost. 'Who authorized this?'

'I tried to get you,' said Frost, 'I rang your house – no-one answered.'

'I haven't been more than six feet away from the phone all night,' snapped Mullett.

'I must have got a wrong number, then,' said Frost. 'It rang and rang . . . and I knew you would have authorized it.'

'So Finch told you where the boy was?'

'Not exactly, sir.' He told Mullett about the petrol receipt.

Mullett stared at him in open-mouthed incredulity. 'And on the basis of that flimsy piece of so-called evidence you have committed us to an overtime bill far in excess of our resources, even after I had specifically told you . . .' His lips tightened. 'You deliberately didn't phone me, Frost, because you knew I would say no.'

You clever bastard, thought Frost. That's exactly why I didn't phone you.

'Inspector! Over here.'

A welcome diversion. Arthur Hanlon, Jordan by his side, was bending over something fished out of the river. He was waving. 'Excuse me, super.' He brushed past Mullett and hurried down.

Another dustbin sack. Hanlon had cut the white plastic tie. He tipped out the contents. A pair of fisherman's waders, plus a muddy stone to ensure the bag sunk. Frost lifted them up and examined the heavy rubber soles. No sign of any wear – they could have been brand-new.

Cassidy, determined not to be left out, came running over. 'What have we got?' Frost showed him. Cassidy shrugged. 'So what does it mean?'

'Why would anyone want to chuck away a pair of brand-new waders?' asked Hanlon.

'A fisherman could have dropped them in by accident,' suggested Cassidy.

'With a flaming brick inside to make sure it sunk?' snorted Frost. 'Besides, fishermen don't come here. Any fish that survived through the chemicals being shunted in the river would be purple and shine in the dark.' He shook his head. 'I'll lay odds Finch dumped these.'

'Why?'

'Because he didn't want us to know he'd been paddling in the bleeding river.' He was getting excited now. 'He's found a place to hide the boy, but had to get in the river to reach it.'

'Another possibility is that he waded in the river to dump the body in the deepest part,' said Cassidy.

'My brain can only deal with one possibility at a time,' said Frost. He looked over to the far bank. 'Could anyone wade across to that bank?' he asked Jordan.

Jordan shook his head. 'Far too deep.'

'Then we concentrate on this side.' He looked down at the cold swirl, steeled himself then stepped into the river which came well above his knees. He didn't believe in asking people to do things he wouldn't do himself. 'We need to search the bank from the river,' he told Hanlon. 'Get all the volunteers you can. Tell them they'll have to get their feet wet . . . their dicks too if it gets any deeper.' The water was icy and the current threatened to knock him off his feet, but, unsteadily, he pressed on, pushing aside the overhang of vegetation from the bank which was now bobbing in the raised water level. Behind came a splash as Jordan joined him. Cassidy stayed on the bank, keeping pace with them.

At one point Frost got his foot stuck deep in the mud and in pulling it free lost his shoe, but no time to retrieve it, only to curse softly and limp on.

He nearly missed it. It was at the point where the river

curved and the current was at its strongest and nearly kicked his feet from under him. He clutched at a clump of reeds to stop himself falling. And there it was, no longer hidden. An opening in the bank. Water was lapping almost half-way up a brown, glazed pipe, some eighteen inches in diameter. 'Jordan!'

Jordan splashed over to him. 'It's part of an old drainage system to run off rain water from some of these fields at back of us. They're blocked off now.' He pulled back the overhang of long, dank grass so Frost could look inside.

'Torch!' called Frost. Cassidy, from the bank, handed one down.

The beam ricocheted off something drably white. Passing the torch back to Cassidy, Frost squeezed his arm through and touched it. Cloth of some kind. Woollen cloth. He managed to get a grip on it and tugged. At first it didn't want to move, then it slid forward. The weight was right. His heart pounded. He now had it out and raised it out of the water. It was a child, cocooned in a sodden blanket which was bound round with cord. Brown plastic tape sealed the mouth and eyes. The flesh was cold. As cold as the river water. 'I've got him,' he yelled and could hear excited voices and people running towards him.

'Give him to me.' Cassidy, bending over, held out his arms for the bundle. Frost passed it up.

Helped by Burton, Frost managed to clamber up on the bank, and was still on his hands and knees, shivering with cold, as Cassidy was cutting the cord and stripping off the sodden blanket. Under it the child was naked. Cassidy shrugged off his greatcoat and swaddled the boy. Then he carefully peeled off the plastic tape. The eyes were tightly closed. He could detect no sign of breathing.

He's dead, thought Frost, hugging himself for warmth. The poor little sod is dead.

Liz pushed through the huddle and bent her ear to

the child's mouth. Her eyes narrowed as she listened. 'He's breathing,' she announced. 'Just about, but he's breathing.'

'Ambulance,' yelled Mullett. 'Get an ambulance.'

Frost took charge. 'No!' He grabbed Cassidy. 'It will be quicker to get him straight to the hospital. Take him in an area car. Radio ahead and let them know you are coming.'

Cassidy nodded and, clutching the child tight to his chest, pushed through to the area car. Electronic flash guns crackled as Sandy's man took photographs.

Mullett was beaming. He couldn't wait to get back to phone the Chief Constable. 'A most satisfactory ending,' he told Frost.

'Thanks, super.' The wind on his wet clothes was chilling him to the bone. 'Pass me the blanket . . . I'll get it over to Forensic.'

Mullett bent and picked it up. He frowned. He was looking at something caught up in the folds. 'Seems to be a receipt of some kind.'

'Show me,' said Frost excitedly. Soaking wet, but still readable, it was a till receipt for the purchase of petrol. Hatter's Garage. That day's date and paid for by credit card. Finch's credit card.

He looked up at Mullett and smiled. 'You clever old sod,' he said. 'We've got him. Thanks to you, we've got him.'

A doubtful smile flickered on and off Mullett's lips. He wasn't quite sure what it was he had done.

'The evidence we wanted,' explained Frost, slipping the receipt between the pages of his notebook to dry it. 'We can now tie Finch to the kid.' He looked round for Liz and beckoned her over. 'Ever charged a man with murder and kidnapping?'

She shook her head.

'Then here's your chance. Get that bastard Finch banged up.'

'Aren't you going to do it?' asked Mullett.

'I'm soaking wet,' answered Frost. 'I'm going home to change.' At the car he yelled his thanks to the search team. 'Booze-up in the incident room in an hour. I'll bring some bottles, but don't let that stop any of you from bringing your own!'

Clutching tightly to his chest bottles which clinked and threatened to slip from his grasp, he backed through the swing doors and into the lobby. From the raucous sounds seeping from the incident room the celebration party was already in progress. Bill Wells on the front desk beckoned him over.

'Finch wants to see you.'

'What about?'

'He didn't say,' said Wells. 'No-one takes me into their confidence.'

He left the bottles on the front desk, reminded Wells he had counted them, then went down to the cells.

Finch was lying on his bunk. He got up when Frost entered. 'You bastard!' he hissed.

'Sticks and stones . . .' said Frost, waggling a finger.

'You framed me. You fitted me up!'

'Fitted you up?' said Frost, his face a picture of injured bewilderment.

'That petrol receipt.'

'What about it?'

'You planted it. You found it with my credit card and you planted it.'

'My Divisional Commander found it – not me.'

Finch stood up and pushed his face close to Frost's. 'I don't care who found it – you planted it to be found.'

Frost shook his head. 'I know you like to think of yourself as infallible, Mr Finch, but you slipped up this time. The receipt must have fallen from your pocket as you were stuffing the poor little git up that drainage pipe.'

'There's a flaw in your reasoning, inspector, an insurmountable flaw. I drove to the river, I hid the child and I filled up with petrol on the way back. So how on earth could that receipt have got there?'

Frost shrugged and gave an enigmatic smile. 'One of life's little mysteries.' He paused. 'Do you want to make an official complaint?'

Finch barked a scornful laugh and sat down again. 'What use would it be? You'd lie your head off.'

'How well you know me,' said Frost.

20

He woke with a raging headache, feeling stiff, cold and uncomfortable. The alarm was shrieking, chewing through his brain like a rip saw. He fumbled to switch it off, but his hand floundered about in empty space. One eye creaked open to a confusion of images. He wasn't in his bedroom. The window was in the wrong place. And he wasn't in his bed, he was curled up on a hard, rigid-backed chair. Slowly, realization filtered through to his alcohol-deadened brain. The party last night. He was in the incident room and the ringing was the phone. He squinted at his watch, moving his arm to bring it into focus. 8.30 a.m. Reaching for the phone sent his headache throbbing anew. 'Frost,' he winced into the mouthpiece.

'Wakey wakey campers,' chirped a disgustingly cheerful Bill Wells.

'What do you want?' growled Frost, his eyes crawling round the incident room. Ashtrays overflowed with half-smoked broken-backed cheroots, empty glasses and bottles everywhere, on desks, rolling about the floor. Jordan and Arthur Hanlon were asleep on separate desks, snoring loudly. The atmosphere was thick with stale tobacco smoke and whisky and . . . God, his stomach churned at the thought of it . . . jellied eels. At five in the morning someone was sent to an all-night stall which sold sea food and came back with containers of cockles, whelks, winkles . . . jellied eels.

A fourteen-inch colour television set in the corner was

playing with the sound off. It was the early morning news and, in eerie silence, Cassidy, carrying the child, was seen dashing into the hospital . . . being hugged by the mother . . . making modest speeches to the press.

He snatched his attention back to the telephone. 'Sorry, Bill . . . what was that?'

'I said the good news is that the kid is pulling through. The bad news is that Mullett is in.'

'You haven't woken me up just to tell me that?'

'No, Jack. The solicitor for those two women who killed Lemmy Hoxton is here. He wants to see you.'

'It's Cassidy's case, not mine.'

'But it's you he wants to see.'

Frost sighed. 'Right. I'll be along.'

He staggered into the washroom, kicking aside an empty jellied eel tub on the way, and splashed cold water on his face. His rumpled hair was smoothed back, a cigarette stuck in his mouth and lit. His first cough of the morning, then he ambled out into the corridor.

The door to Mullett's office was swinging open. He could hear the Divisional Commander, oozing false modesty as he spoke on the phone to the Chief Constable, so he paused, ears cocked, hoping to pick up some titbits to pass on to Bill Wells.

'. . . I know the overtime level had been exceeded, sir, but my only concern was for the missing boy, so I took the risk in the belief that a human life was worth it, no matter what the outcome might be for me . . . You're too kind, sir, I was just doing my duty . . . Thank you, sir . . . Thank you very much.' A click as the phone was replaced.

Frost tiptoed a few steps back the way he had come, then, rather noisily, resumed his walk.

Mullett called him in as he was passing. 'Frost!'

He shuffled in and dropped into a chair.

'Take a seat,' said Mullett, too late as usual. He gave an ingratiating smile. 'You'll be pleased to learn that I've managed to get you off the hook regarding the excessive unauthorized overtime.'

'Thank you very much, super,' mumbled Frost. 'I don't deserve you.'

He said this with such sincerity that Mullett saw no double meaning and beamed happily. 'Cassidy did well.' He tapped the *Denton Echo* on his desk. A large picture of Cassidy, the boy in his arms, under the headline 'Policeman Hero Saves Child From River'.

'Didn't he just?' said Frost.

'Unfortunately, Lexford Division want him back again.'

'Tough,' grunted Frost.

'So I might have some good news for DS Maud regarding a temporary promotion.'

'She deserves it,' said Frost.

George Perry, the solicitor for the two women, was white-haired and stooped. He looked benign, but he was shrewd. Very shrewd.

Frost led him to his office. As he opened the door he nearly tripped over a heap of clothes. Liz and Burton were asleep on the floor near the radiator, locked in each other's arms. Neither was wearing very much. Frost backed out, closing the door firmly. 'We'll try next door,' he said.

They went into the office Cassidy was using. Frost sat at the empty desk and offered Perry a chair. 'So what can I do for you?'

Perry unzipped his solid leather briefcase and pulled out two typed statements. 'I am acting for Miss Millicent Fleming and Miss Julie Adams. You took statements from them yesterday?'

'Not me,' said Frost. 'My colleague Inspector Cassidy.'

'The statements were taken without a solicitor being present.'

'They were asked if they wanted one. They both declined.'

Perry smiled. 'I am sure everything was explained to them. The thing is, my clients would like to withdraw their statements.'

'Can't be done,' said Frost.

Another smile. 'Come now, inspector. All things are possible. They admit the crime but the prurient details . . . the sexual relationship . . . the photographs . . . They are going to cause such a stir.'

'I'm afraid so,' nodded Frost.

'They have families . . . friends. They are respected members of the church. They would much prefer that these details were not part of the case against them.'

'So what are you suggesting?'

'Hoxton came to rob them. He tried to rape Julie. Millicent hit him to stop him and he died. That is not in dispute. But surely there is no need for the sexual aspect to come out. They are both most concerned – almost suicidal about this.'

'Their statements will have to be read out in court.'

'I'm suggesting we tear up the original statements and destroy the tapings of the interviews. They will give you fresh statements that will omit the sexual aspect.'

'I don't see why we can't do that,' began Frost. 'I'll have a word with my colleague, it's his case.'

As if on cue, Cassidy came in, scowling his annoyance to find his office being used by Frost. 'Can I ask what's going on?'

Frost explained.

'No way,' said Cassidy emphatically. 'No flaming way.'

'It wouldn't harm our case,' said Frost.

'It would be bending the rules,' said Cassidy, 'and I don't bend rules for anyone.' He stood pointedly by his desk, waiting for Frost to give up his chair.

Frost pushed himself up. 'Sorry, Mr Perry.'

Perry gave a sad smile. 'I tried,' he said. 'They'll be terribly disappointed, but I tried.'

In the corridor outside, Frost watched Perry, shoulders sagging, walking towards the custody area. He chased after him. 'Mr Perry!'

The solicitor paused and turned.

'I shouldn't be surprised if the original tapes and statements get lost,' whispered Frost. 'I'm well known for losing things. Give me a call later today. We might need your clients to give us fresh statements.'

Perry twisted his head up and down, making sure no-one could hear. He lowered his voice. 'Your colleague is dead against it. I wouldn't want to get you into trouble, inspector.'

'I don't need outside help to get me into trouble,' said Frost. 'I can do that very well on my own.'

He sailed past Perry and out into the lobby.

'Have you seen Wonder Woman this morning?' called Wells. 'Mullett wants her.'

'She might be taking things easy this morning,' said Frost. 'She had one winkle too many last night.'

He turned up the collar of his mac and stepped out into the pouring rain. There was a dead firework on the pavement. He kicked it away.

THE END

NIGHT FROST

Sunday

The old lady's name was Mrs Haynes – Mary Haynes, but no-one had called her Mary for years, not since her husband died. She was seventy-eight years old and she stood on the doorstep trembling with fear.

She had just come back from the churchyard. She went there every Sunday, weather permitting, to tidy up her husband's grave and put fresh flowers in the cut glass vase that had once stood on the dark oak sideboard they had bought the first year they were married and which was now in the unused back room. Today, when she reached the churchyard the vicar was waiting for her, his face grim. 'I'm afraid you must prepare yourself for a shock, Mrs Haynes.'

When she saw what they had done to the grave she thought she was going to pass out. The headstone she had saved for so carefully was desecrated with purple painted graffiti. A crudely drawn skull and crossbones and words she couldn't bring herself to repeat defaced her husband's name. The vase had been hurled against the headstone and smashed to pieces.

The vicar was most sympathetic. He and his curate had been comforting distraught mourners all day. Vandals had left a trail of broken headstones, graffiti and strewn wreaths in a mindless moronic orgy of destruction. The police had been informed, he assured her, and had promised that the cemetery would be kept under constant observation in the hope of catching the perpetrators in the act.

She couldn't remember the journey home, her mind in a whirl at what had happened. Such a relief to creak open the front gate. But at the tiny porch another shock. As she fumbled in her purse for the key she noticed that the porch doormat had been moved. She was ever so careful how she replaced it when she hid the spare door key and there was no doubt it had been moved.

Hands shaking, she lifted the corner of the mat. The key wasn't there. Someone had taken it. Perhaps even used it to get inside. She stepped back and looked up at the house. Was it her imagination, or had the bedroom curtains shivered as if someone had just twitched them shut?

Her gloved hand clutched her chest to hold the hurt of her fluttering heart. She needed help. Anyone's help. A light was on next door where that awful young man with the motor bike lived. She staggered across and pressed the door bell. She could hear it ringing inside the house. No-one came. She pressed it again.

Upstairs in the bedroom, the man with the knife smiled to himself and patiently waited.

Monday morning shift

Rain slashed across the windows blurring the view of the dreary houses on the opposite side of the street. Liz Gilmore, kneeling on the settee, stared out moodily. It hadn't stopped raining since they moved into this poky little house two days ago. Married three years and all they'd ever lived in was a succession of rented police accommodation. 'I hate this lousy town,' she announced.

She had never wanted to come to Denton. When the promotion came through she was hoping he'd be posted to somewhere exciting, somewhere with a bit of life – theatres, clubs, decent shops . . . not this boring little backwater.

Her husband, Detective Sergeant Frank Gilmore, twenty-four, stockily built with dark, close-cropped hair, checked his watch for the eighth time. He wished Liz would stop her moaning. He had so much on his mind. 8.45. In a quarter of an hour he would be meeting his new Divisional Commander to take up his first assignment as a newly promoted detective sergeant. He wanted to keep his mind clear. First impressions were important. Denton was a one-eyed town, but it was the first step on the ladder leading to dizzy heights. 'It won't be for long, Liz.'

She flicked back her blonde hair and picked up the local newspaper, the Denton *Echo.* The front page was dominated by a photograph of upturned, smashed and graffiti-desecrated headstones. *Graveyard Vandals Strike Again,* screamed the headline. *Vicar Suspects Black Magic Coven.* 'Black magic coven,' she muttered. 'If I knew where it was, I'd join it. Probably the only bit of excitement in this dead-and-alive hole.'

He faked a smile. Liz seemed to delight in shocking people with her outrageous remarks. 'Any other news?'

'"Denton crippled by flu epidemic",' she read, then tossed the paper to one side. 'Graveyards, flu, poky rooms and non-stop rain. This town is just one bag of laughs!'

Again he consulted his watch. Timing was important. He didn't want to turn up too early. That smacked of insecurity. A newly promoted detective sergeant shouldn't appear insecure. He wanted to breeze in at a minute to nine and be shown directly to the Divisional Commander's office. 'I'll have to leave soon.'

'Let's have a look at you.' She stood up and studied him, removing an imaginary speck of fluff from his new charcoal grey Marks and Spencer's suit. An approving nod. 'You'll pass.' And then she was the old Liz, pressing close to him, her arms holding him tight. 'I'm sorry I'm such a bitch sometimes.'

'You're not!' he assured her, his arms round her.

She winced. 'Your pen is sticking in me.' She unbuttoned his jacket and he could feel her hot, burning body and the arousing smell of her perfume. Good old Liz. Her timing lousy as always.

'You smell nice,' she purred, nuzzling her nose against his chin.

He frowned uneasily. At her insistence he had put on that expensive Chanel aftershave she had bought him for Christmas, but he knew it was the wrong thing. He pulled away. 'I really must go. I'll be late.'

'And you will be back at six? None of this working all the hours God sends stuff?'

He smiled. He was now on surer ground. The Denton Divisional Commander's office had sent him an itemized timetable, detailing almost minute by minute his itinerary for the coming week. Denton was clearly a well organized, efficiently run station. Today, after his meeting with the Divisional Commander, he was to be taken around the station and introduced to the personnel and the various departments. Then his new boss, Detective Inspector Allen, was taking him on a tour of the district to familiarize him with the area. After lunch in the canteen (1.15-2.15) he was off to visit the local Forensic Laboratory. At 5.30 precisely, a car would collect him up and return him to his home (e.t.a. 5.55 p.m.). 'I'll be back by six,' he assured her.

One last lingering kiss and he put on his mac and

dashed through the rain to his car. Liz flopped back on the settee and flicked through the paper again. She barely gave a glance to the item at the bottom of the front page: *Hope Dies For Missing News Girl.*

Denton Police Station didn't look the model of efficiency Gilmore had been led to expect. The lobby was unattended, the floor wet from a hasty mopping and reeking of disinfectant. Somewhere a phone was ringing and no-one answered it. Leaning against the counter, snorting with impatience, a middle-aged man waited. He raised his eyebrows to the ceiling as Gilmore entered, inviting him to share his disgust at the treatment meted out to rate-paying members of the public. 'My car's been pinched. They won't accept details over the phone – that's too bloody easy. You have to take time off from flaming work, hire a cab because you've got no car and come down in person and fill in a damn form.'

A balding, uniformed sergeant with a mournful face came in. This was Bill Wells, pushing forty, tired and fed up. Today should have been his rest day. 'Right, Mr Wilkins. Details have been circulated.'

'So what happens now?'

The sergeant shrugged. 'It was probably taken by joyriders. If a member of the public reports it abandoned somewhere, we'll let you know so you can collect it.'

'And that's the limit of the help I get from the police? If someone happens to spot it, you'll pass on the message. Brilliant. Aren't the police going to look for it?'

'Of course we are,' the sergeant told him, 'but we do have more important things on our plate.' He nodded towards the poster on the wall behind him. The poster displayed a black and white photograph of a child in school uniform standing by a bike. The heading read: *Missing – have you seen this girl?*

The man snorted his contempt as he stamped out. 'If I've got to wait for you to find that poor little cow, I'll wait for ever.'

Wells stared stony-faced at the man's retreating back, then opened a door to yell, 'Can't someone answer that damn phone,' before turning his attention to Gilmore. 'Can I help you, sir?'

'Detective Sergeant Gilmore to see Mr Mullett.'

Behind Gilmore the lobby door opened again and two men and a woman came in, shaking umbrellas. One of the men unbuttoned his raincoat to reveal a clerical collar. 'Appointment with Mr Mullett,' he announced.

'Yes, vicar. He's expecting you,' Wells told him.

'My appointment's at nine,' hissed Gilmore, waving his itinerary as proof.

'Then you'll have to wait.' The sergeant brushed past him to escort the trio through the swing doors to the Divisional Commander's office.

Fuming, Gilmore checked his watch. A minute to nine. The one thing he knew about his new Divisional Commander was that Mullett was a stickler for punctuality and, because that fool of a sergeant had let the newcomers through first, he was going to be late reporting for duty on his very first day.

He slumped down on the hard wooden bench and prodded a puddle of disinfectant-smelling water with his shoe. The hands of the wall clock clunked round with monotonous regularity, marking out the number of minutes he was going to be late. He shifted his gaze to the missing girl poster. *Paula Bartlett, aged 15, dark hair, pale complexion, height 5′3″. Last seen September 14th, in the Forest Lane area.* September 14th! Some two months ago!

She wasn't a particularly pretty-looking kid, but perhaps the photograph didn't do her justice.

The swing doors clicked together as the sergeant returned. Gilmore sprang to his feet. 'My appointment with Mr Mullett . . .'

'You'll have to wait.' Wells had no time for jumped-up newly promoted constables.

Gilmore felt he had to report to someone. He consulted his itinerary. 'Tell Inspector Allen I'm here.'

'He's off sick. Everyone's off flaming sick.' The internal phone buzzed. 'No, Mr Mullett, Mr Frost isn't in yet. Yes, I did tell him nine o'clock. Yes, sir.' He hung up.

Rain blew in from the lobby doors as a scruffy figure in a dripping mac pushed through. He peeled a sodden maroon scarf from his neck and wrung it out. 'It's peeing down out there,' he announced, then his nose twitched. 'Disinfectant and perfume. This place stinks like a tart's slop-bucket.'

'The disinfectant is from the cleaners,' the sergeant informed him. 'We had drunks throwing up all over the place last night. And the poncey scent is from the new boy's aftershave.' He jerked his head at Gilmore, who scowled back. 'Mr Mullett's been asking for you.'

'He's always asking for me. I think he fancies me. He likes a bit of rough.' He unbuttoned his mac to expose a crumpled blue suit with two buttons missing. The red tie beneath the frayed shirt collar had a tight, greasy knot and looked as if it had been put on by being pulled over his neck like a noose. He turned to Gilmore and held out a nicotine-stained hand. 'I'm Detective Inspector Jack Frost.'

Gilmore shook the proffered hand, his mind racing. A detective inspector! This rag-bag was a detective inspector? A joke, surely? But no-one seemed to be laughing. 'You'll be working with me,' continued Frost.

Now that just had to be a joke. He waved his itinerary. 'I've been assigned to Mr Allen.'

'All been changed – Allen's got the pox,' said Frost.

'He's down with flu,' corrected the station sergeant. 'Half the damn station's down with it, most of the others are on sick leave following Friday's punch-up and the rest of us silly sods are dragged in on their rest day and working double shifts.' The internal phone buzzed.

'If it's Mullett . . .' said Frost, backing towards the exit doors.

It wasn't Mullett. It was Control for the inspector. 'The Comptons – the couple receiving the hate mail. They've had a fire – someone's tried to burn their summer house down.'

'On my way,' said Frost, banging down the phone. He jerked his head at Gilmore. 'Come on, son. If you like rigid nipples you're in for a treat – the lady of the house is a cracker.'

'But I'm supposed to report to the Divisional Commander,' Gilmore protested.

'You can do that when we get back.'

The internal phone rang. This time it was Mullett.

Frost grabbed Gilmore's arm and hurried him out into the rain.

Frost's old Ford Cortina was tucked out of sight, round the corner from the station car-park where, hopefully, Mullett wouldn't spot it. While Gilmore waited in the pouring rain which was finding its way through his new raincoat, Frost cleared the junk from the passenger seat, including two mud-encrusted wellington boots which he tossed into the back of the car. 'In you get, son.'

Gilmore scrubbed pointedly at the seat with his handkerchief before risking its contact with his brand new suit. His head nearly hit the windscreen as Frost suddenly slammed the car into gear and they were away.

'Where are we going?' he asked, hastily clicking the buckle of his seat belt as the car squealed into Market Square, shooting up spray as it ploughed through an unexpectedly deep puddle.

'A little village called Lexing – about four miles outside Denton.' A blur of shops zipped past then the engine was labouring and coughing as it clawed up a steep hill and there was a smell of burning oil. Frost sniffed and frowned. 'Do you know anything about engines, son?'

'No,' said Gilmore, firmly. There was no way he was going to mess up his new suit poking under the bonnet of Frost's filthy car. They were now passing a heavily wooded area, with sagging, rain-heavy bushes.

Frost jerked a thumb. 'Denton Woods. Right over the far side is where that schoolgirl went missing. She was doing a newspaper round, but never finished it. Her bike and her undelivered papers turned up in a ditch, but no trace of the kid.'

'Had there been trouble at home? Could she have run away?'

'Don't know, son. It was Mr Allen's case until he conveniently got the bloody flu. Now I'm lumbered. We'll have to start reading through the file when we get back.' He scratched a match down the dashboard and lit up, then remembered he hadn't told Gilmore about the case they were driving to. 'Married couple, in their mid-twenties, live in a converted windmill. Some joker's been frightening the life out of them.'

'How?' Gilmore asked.

'Lots of charming ways. Sending fake obituary notices

– tombstone catalogues and things like that. They even had an undertaker call on them last week to collect the husband's body. His poor cow of a wife went into hysterics.'

The car was now jolting and squelching down a muddied lane and the smell of burning oil was getting stronger. Frost wound down the window to let in some air, then pointed. 'There it is!' Looming up before them, imperfectly seen through the Cortina's mud-grimed windscreen, was a genuine old wooden windmill, its sails removed, and painted a smart designer black and white.

Gilmore leant forward and craned his neck to take it all in. He was impressed. 'That must have cost a few bob?'

Frost nodded. 'Rumour has it that the Comptons paid close on a quarter of a million for the place. With the slump in the housing market it's worth a lot less now.'

The car scrunched up the gravel driveway which led to a white-framed, black front door outside which a police car was already parked. Alongside the drive ran a lawn, once immaculate, but now a muddy, churned-up, tyre-grooved mess a-slosh with dirty water. Their job done, firemen were clambering into a fire engine ready to drive off. In the middle of the lawn the Fire Investigations Officer, rain bouncing off his yellow sou'wester, was gloomily poking through a jumble of sodden ashes and burnt, paint-blistered wood, all that was left of the summer house. Frost paddled over to him, cursing as water found the holes in his shoes and ruefully remembering his wellington boots snug and dry in the back of the car. Gilmore stayed put on the path. He wasn't ruining his shoes for a lousy burnt-out summer house.

Frost flicked his eye over the smouldering remains. 'I could have made a better job of putting it out by peeing on it.'

The fire officer straightened up and grinned. 'We didn't stand a chance, Jack. The wood was soaked with petrol. We got here twelve minutes after the call, but it had almost burnt itself out by then.'

'Petrol?' Frost picked up a chunk of wet burnt wood and sniffed it. It smelled just like wet burnt wood. He tossed it back on the pile and watched the fire engine drive away.

'No doubt about it. I'm still checking, but it was probably set off by some crude form of fuse – a candle or something. I'll be able to tell you more when I find it.'

'You know me,' said Frost. 'If it's crude, I'm interested.' He squelched back to the drive.

Gilmore hammered at the front door while Frost scuffed moodily at the gravel path and tried out the rusty bell on an old-fashioned, woman's bicycle which leant against the wall. The door creaked open on heavy, black, wrought iron hinges and a scrawny, leathery-skinned woman in her late sixties, carrying a mop and bucket, scowled out at them. She wore a man's cap, pulled right down over her hair, and a drab brown shapeless dress, tied at the waist with string.

Frost nodded towards the bucket. 'No thanks, Ada – I went before I came out.' He introduced her to Gilmore. 'This is Ada Perkins, the Swedish au pair.'

The woman grunted. 'You're not half as funny as you think you are, Jack Frost.' She jerked a bony thumb towards a door at the end of the passage. 'There's a policeman in the kitchen drinking tea.'

'Then let's start in the kitchen,' said Frost.

It was a spacious, no-expense-spared kitchen, fitted out in solid oak with marble worktops, burnished copper cookware on the walls and miniature hand-operated water pumps instead of taps over the sink. A black Aga disguised to look like an old coal-fired cooking range breathed the warm crunchy smell of baking bread. Black-moustached PC Jordan, twenty-six, his tunic unbuttoned, was seated at a scrubbed pine designer table drinking tea from a thick designer mug. He jumped up to attention as the detectives entered, but Frost waved him to sit and dragged up a chair alongside him. Gilmore did the same.

'I suppose you want some tea?' said Ada and, without waiting for their reply, poured two teas from a brown teapot, pushed the sugar bowl across, then shuffled out, muttering something about having work to do.

Frost found a tea towel and dried his wet hair. 'This is Frank Gilmore.'

'Hi, Frank,' said Jordan, offering his hand.

The hand was ignored. 'Detective *Sergeant* Gilmore,' came the icy correction. 'And button up that jacket.' Start as you mean to go on. Don't let the lower ranks get too familiar or they'll walk all over you.

Frost passed round his cigarettes, then asked for a report. Jordan, stifling his resentment at Gilmore's snub, flipped open his notebook. 'I got the call from Control at 9.23. I arrived at 9.34. The fire brigade was already here so I left them to it and went straight in to Mrs Compton.'

'Mrs Compton?' interrupted Frost. 'Not the husband?'

'He's away on business,' said Jordan.

A smile traversed Frost's face. 'Good. Then I won't have to watch him fondling her bloody body . . . What's she wearing this morning?'

'That pink shortie nightie,' said Jordan. 'The one she wore the first time.'

Frost whooped with delight. 'The shortie – wow!

That's the one that barely covers her bum. I must try and drop something on the floor for her to pick up.' Then he remembered the serious business of the day and nodded for Jordan to continue.

'She got up just after nine, picked the post up from the mat, made herself a cup of tea and went into the lounge. The first letter she opened was this.' Jordan pushed across a transparent plastic bag. Inside it was a sheet of cheap quality A4 paper on which were pasted letters cut from a glossy magazine to form words.

Frost read it, his face grim, then passed it across to Gilmore. The message was short and chillingly to the point. THE NEXT THING TO BURN WILL BE YOU, YOU BITCH.

'Where's the envelope?' demanded Gilmore. This case was looking a little more worthy of his attention now. Jordan handed over another plastic bag containing a manila envelope, 9 inches by 4 inches. The address, typed in capitals, read: MRS COMPTON, THE OLD MILL, LEXING. It bore a first-class stamp and had been posted in Denton the previous evening. He motioned for Jordan to continue.

'Next she heard this roaring sound from outside. She opened the lounge curtains and saw the summer house on fire, so she dialled 999.' He closed his notebook.

Frost drained his mug and dropped his cigarette end in it. 'This is getting nastier and nastier. It started off with heavy-breathing phone calls, now it's death threats. Right, Jordan. Nip down to the village and ask around. Did anyone see anything . . . any strange cars lurking about . . . someone stinking of petrol.' As the constable left, he stood up. 'Buttock-viewing time,' he told Gilmore. 'We're going to chat up Mrs Compton.'

Gilmore followed him out of the kitchen, along the waxed wooden-floored passage and into the lounge, a large, high-ceilinged room which had a rich, rustic, new-sacking smell from the dark chocolate-coloured hessian covering its walls.

Jill Compton, standing to receive them, looked much younger than her twenty-three years. She wore a gauzy cobweb of a baby doll nightdress which hid nothing, and over it a silken house-coat which flapped open so as not to spoil the view through the nightdress. Her hair, fringed over wide blue eyes and free-flowing down her back, was a light, golden corn colour. She wore no make-up and the pale, china doll face with a hint of dark rings around the eyes gave her a look of vulnerability. She smiled bravely. 'I'm sorry I'm not dressed.'

'That's quite all right, Mrs Compton,' said Frost, and there was no doubting the sincerity in his voice. 'It's a sod about your summer house.'

'It could have been the house,' she said, her voice unsteady. 'Did you see that letter?'

Before Frost could answer the front door slammed and a man's voice called, 'Jill – I'm home! Where are you?'

'Mark!' She ran out to meet her husband.

'Damn!' grunted Frost. 'The buttock-squeezer's back!'

Mark Compton was twenty-nine and flashily good-looking. Fair-haired, a bronzed complexion, although slightly overweight from good living, he looked like a retired life-guard out of *Neighbours*. Gilmore hated him instantly for his looks, his money, his perfectly fitting silver-grey suit, his arm around Mrs Compton, but most of all for his hand caressing her bare arm.

'A letter? My wife said there was a letter threatening to kill her.'

Frost showed it to him. His face went white. 'Why are we being persecuted like this?' He sank down into a leather armchair. His wife dropped down on his lap and snuggled up to him.

'That's what I want to know,' said Frost. 'Why?' He and Gilmore were sitting, facing the Comptons, in a large leather settee. He fumbled for his cigarettes. 'Whoever's doing this must have a reason.'

'Reason?' said Compton 'There's no bloody reason. It's the work of a maniac.'

'We've been receiving a spate of complaints about poison pen letters. "Did you know your wife's been having it off with the milkman?" – that sort of thing. I'm wondering if it could be the same bloke.'

'We've had death threats, Inspector, not stupid poison pen letters.'

'Run through the main course of events again,' said Frost. 'Just for the benefit of my new colleague here.'

Mark Compton slipped his hand under Jill's house-coat and gently stroked her bare back. 'OK. As you know, we run a business from this place . . . Jill was on her own one night when this bugger phoned.'

'What sort of business is it?' interrupted Gilmore.

'Dirty books,' said Frost.

Compton glowered. 'We're fine art dealers,' he corrected. 'Mainly rare books and prints, a small proportion of which might be termed erotica, and manuscripts, but not many. There's over a quarter of a million pounds' worth of stock upstairs.'

Gilmore whistled softly to show he was impressed. 'Safely locked up, I hope?'

'We couldn't get insurance if it wasn't,' Compton replied icily. 'Your Crime Prevention Officer has given us the once-over and was quite satisfied. We've got a sophisticated alarm system with automatic 999 dialling. If anyone tried to break in, they'd set off the alarm at your police station.'

'Books and manuscripts,' said Gilmore, 'and a wooden building. I shouldn't think the insurance company were too happy about that?'

Mark Compton pointed to metal roses dotting the ceiling. 'Automatic sprinklers in every room, a condition of the policy.'

'So not too much danger from fire?'

'An ordinary fire, perhaps, but if some stupid bastard starts pouring petrol all over the place like they apparently did with our summer house . . .'

Frost's head came up sharply. 'How did you know that, sir?'

'The fireman outside told me. It's not a state secret, is it? I am entitled to know the methods maniacs use to destroy my property.'

Frost smiled and switched his attention to the woman. 'Tell us about the phone calls.'

The recollection made her shudder. 'It started about two weeks ago. The phone kept ringing in the middle of the night. Every time I answered it, the caller hung up. It was frightening. This place is so isolated. I was terrified.' Again she shuddered. Her husband moved his hand up to cup and squeeze her breast in reassurance. In case Gilmore hadn't spotted this, Frost drew it to his attention by a sharp dig in the ribs with his elbow. Gilmore pretended not to notice and, trying to keep his eyes well above breast level, he asked Jill to continue.

'The next morning a black Rolls Royce came up the drive. It was a hearse, with a coffin in the back!' She was shaking uncontrollably. Mark squeezed her tighter and she clung to him. At last she was able to continue. 'Two men dressed all in black got out and knocked. They said they were undertakers and had come to collect the body of my husband. I think I screamed.'

'Some stupid, sick bastard's idea of a joke,' cut in Compton angrily. 'Fortunately I came home a couple of minutes later. Jill was having hysterics. Then the phone rang. The Classified Ads section of the local paper checking details of my obituary notice which had just been phoned in. Apparently I had died suddenly as the result of a tragic accident. Just imagine if Jill had taken that call.' She blinked up at him and buried her face in his chest. 'Later that day, just to complete this hilariously funny sick joke, a firm of monumental masons sent me a quotation for my headstone. That was when I called in the police . . . not that it did us any damn good. The next day our ornamental pond was full of dead fish. They'd been poisoned. The maniac had poured bleach in. Then he phoned me.'

Gilmore's head shot up. 'Phoned you?'

'He said, "Dead fish first, dead people next." Then he hung up.'

'Did you recognize the voice?' asked Gilmore.

'Of course I didn't recognize it. Would we be sitting here wondering who it was if I did?'

Gilmore flushed. It would almost be worth his job to smack the smug bastard one in the mouth. 'Can you describe the voice, sir?'

'It was obviously disguised. Very soft, almost a whisper. You couldn't tell if it was a man or a woman.'

'Anything else?'

'Things came through the post – newspaper cuttings, obituaries of people called Compton, or reports of killings or sudden deaths with the victim's name crossed out and our name written in. Charming little things like that.'

'Right,' said Gilmore. 'Whoever is doing this must hate you. Any suggestions?'

'Don't you think we've racked our brains, trying to think of something?' barked Compton. 'There's no rhyme nor reason behind this. I keep telling you, this is the work of someone with a sick mind.'

'Sick minds or not, sir, they've got to have a reason for picking on you in the first place.'

Jill Compton caught her breath and her eyes widened as if a thought had suddenly struck her. 'Mark . . . that man who tried to pick a fight with you!' She rose from his lap and sat on the arm of the chair.

Her husband frowned. 'What man?'

'In London – the security system exhibition.'

A scoffing laugh. 'That was over a month ago.' To the detectives he said, 'A bit of nonsense. It's got nothing to do with this.'

Then why did you look guilty when she mentioned it? thought Frost. 'Let's hear about it anyway, sir. Suspects are pretty thin on the ground at the moment.'

'It's got nothing to do with this,' insisted Compton. 'We'd gone up to London for an antiques fair at the Russell Hotel. This security system exhibition was on at the same time at a different hotel – I forget the name . . .'

'The Griffin,' his wife reminded him.

'That's right . . . Anyway, Guardtech, the firm that fitted up the alarm systems here, had sent us an invitation, so we looked in for a couple of hours. I was in the bar. Jill had gone off somewhere.'

'I was powdering my nose,' she told him.

'Well – whatever. This woman comes up to me and asks for a light. Suddenly, her drunken lout of a husband staggers over and accuses me of trying to take his wife away from him. I didn't want any trouble, so I turned to go. He swings a punch at me, misses by miles and falls flat on his face. It turned out he was a salesman for Guardtech security systems. Their sales manager came over and apologized. Said this chap was insanely jealous of his wife and had been knocking back the free booze all day, just spoiling for a fight with anyone.'

'Do you remember his name?' asked Gilmore, hopefully.

Compton shook his head.

'His name was Bradbury, darling,' said his wife, looking proud that she could supply important information. 'Simon Bradbury.'

'Something like that,' grunted Compton begrudgingly. 'But you're wasting your time going after him. He lives in London.'

While Gilmore scribbled the name in his notebook, Frost stood up and wound his scarf round his neck. 'We'll check him out, anyway. If anything else happens, phone the station right away.'

Mark Compton's mouth dropped open in disbelief. 'You're just walking away? For God's sake, man, my wife's life has been threatened. I want round-the-clock protection.'

Frost shrugged apologetically. 'I'll get an area car to make a detour from time to time, just to keep an eye on the place, but we haven't got the resources for twenty-four-hour surveillance.'

Compton's voice rose to a shout. 'Bloody marvellous! Well, let's make one thing clear. If the police won't do anything, then I will. If he lays one finger on my wife, and I catch the bastard, I'll kill him with my bare hands, and that's a bloody promise.'

The Fire Investigations Officer was sitting in the back seat of the Cortina waiting for them. He declined a cigarette, pleading a sore throat. 'I think I'm coming down with flu, Jack. Half the watch are off with it.'

'Tell me what you've found and then push off,' said Frost. 'I don't want to catch it from you.'

The fireman passed across a plastic envelope. Inside was a chunk of burnt wood with a snail's trail of a dirty grey waxy substance dribbled over it. 'Candle grease from an ordinary household candle. And I've found several scraps of burnt cloth. My guess is that the fire was set off by a stump of candle burning down to some inflammable material – possibly rags soaked in petrol.'

Frost handed the envelope back. 'How long would a fuse like that take to burn down?'

The fireman scratched his chin. 'Depends on the length of the candle, but I shouldn't think they'd use a full one, not in that situation. Too much risk of it toppling over or getting blown out. The more reliable way is just to use a stump, the shorter the better and then you're talking an hour – maybe a lot less.'

'But if they did use a full-length one?'

'Four and a half hours top whack.'

Frost chewed this over and stared up at the black-clouded sky through the windscreen. 'How good is that sprinkler system in The Mill?'

'Damn good.'

'Even if petrol was used again?'

'It would definitely keep it under control until we got here.' His nose wrinkled and his eyes widened as he dived into his pocket for his handkerchief, but too late. His violent sneeze rocked the car.

'Thanks a bunch,' grunted Frost. 'Flu germs are all we bleeding need.'

* * *

The Cortina bumped down the puddled lane on its way back to Denton. An agitated Gilmore, concerned about his delayed meeting with the Divisional Commander, was fidgeting impatiently, willing the inspector to drive faster. Frost seemed to be driving by remote control, his mind elsewhere, his cigarette burning dangerously close to his lip. They were approaching the gloomy Denton Woods before Frost spoke. 'What did you think of Jill Compton?'

'A knock-out,' admitted Gilmore.

Frost wound down the window and spat out his cigarette. 'Did you see how he was groping her? I thought she was going to get his dick out any minute.' He shook another cigarette from the packet straight into his mouth. 'When you get a chance, son, find out where Compton was last night and if there's any way he could have started that fire.'

'Compton?' Gilmore was incredulous. 'Why should he destroy his own property?'

'I don't know, son. I don't like the sod. He's a bit too bloody lovey-dovey with Miss Wonder-bum for my taste – almost as if he wants to shout out for our benefit how devoted he is.'

Gilmore was unimpressed. 'I thought he was genuinely devoted.'

'Maybe so, son. I'm probably way off course as usual, but check anyway.' The car was now speeding down the hill leading to the Market Square. 'I'll drop you off at the station. If Mullett asks, you don't know where I am.'

The radio belched static, then Control asked for Mr Frost to come in please. 'What's your position, Inspector?'

Frost looked through the window at the row of shops and the turning just ahead leading to the police station.

A bit too close to Mullett for comfort. 'Still at The Mill, Lexing, investigating arson attack.'

'Would you call on Dr Maltby, The Surgery, Lexing. One of his patients received a poison pen letter this morning and tried to kill himself.'

'On my way,' replied Frost, spinning the car into a U-turn.

'Is Detective Sergeant Gilmore with you?' asked Control. 'Mr Mullett wants to see him right away.'

'Roger,' said Frost.

'He also wants to see you this morning without fail,' added Control.

'Didn't get that last bit,' said Frost. 'Over and out.' He slammed down the handset and turned off the radio.

Lexing was a small cluster of unspoilt houses and cottages, nothing later than Victorian. Perched on the hill to the north was the mill they had just visited and leaning against the front door of Dr Maltby's cottage was the same bike they had seen outside the Comptons'. And, sure enough, it was Ada Perkins who let them in.

'What did the doctor say, Ada?' asked Frost confidentially. 'Are you pregnant or is it just wind?'

'Not funny,' she snapped. 'I've just done the hall so wipe your muddy boots.'

She ushered them into the surgery. Maltby, a grey-haired, tired-looking man in his late sixties, wearing a crumpled brown suit, was seated at an old-fashioned desk and was furtively stuffing something that chinked into his top drawer and slamming it shut as he popped a Polo mint in his mouth. The waft of peppermint-tinted whisky fumes hit Gilmore as Frost introduced him.

'This is Dr Maltby, son. He's got the steadiest hands in the business. He can take a urine sample and hardly spill a drop.' In spite of this build-up the hand that Gilmore shook didn't seem at all steady.

Maltby squeezed out a token smile. 'I'm not much fun this morning, Jack. I've been up half the night – patients are dropping like flies from this damned flu epidemic. And now this. I said someone would kill themselves if you didn't stop these poison pen letters and now it's happened.'

'Calm down, doc,' said Frost, scraping a match down the wooden wall panelling. 'Just give me the facts, and slowly – you know what a dim old sod I am.' He slumped down in the lumpy chair reserved for patients and wearily stretched his legs, puffing smoke at the *'Smoking Can Kill'* poster.

'Ada found him,' said Maltby.

'Found who, doc? Don't forget I've come in in the middle of the picture.'

'Old Mr Wardley,' said Ada. 'He lives next door to me. I do his cleaning once a week when I've finished at The Mill. I got no reply when I knocked so I used the spare key he gave me. No sign of him downstairs. "That's strange," I thought. "That's very strange." So I called out, "Mr Wardley, are you there?" No answer.'

'Get to the punchline, Ada,' prompted Frost, impatiently.

'I went upstairs and there he was on the bed, fully dressed.'

'I'm glad his dick wasn't exposed,' said Frost.

She glowered, but carried on doggedly. 'His face was deadly white, his flesh icy cold, just like a corpse. So I dashed straight over to the doctor's and he came back with me.'

Frost cut in quickly and poked a finger at Maltby. 'Now your big scene, doc.'

The doctor rubbed his eyes and took over the narrative. 'He'd swallowed all the sleeping tablets in his bottle. He was unconscious, but still alive. I phoned for an ambulance and got him into Denton General Hospital. I think he'll pull through.'

'Good,' nodded Frost. 'I like happy endings. So, in spite of your big build-up, no one's actually killed themselves?'

'Not for the want of trying,' said Maltby.

'Was there a suicide note?' asked Gilmore.

'I didn't see one,' said the doctor.

'So why did you say it was suicide? It could have been accidental.'

'You don't accidentally take an overdose of sleeping tablets at nine o'clock in the morning with all your clothes on,' Maltby snapped irritably.

'All right,' murmured Frost. 'Show me the poison pen letter that made him do it.'

'We couldn't find the letter,' said Maltby, 'but this was on his kitchen table.'

He handed the inspector a light blue envelope bearing a first-class stamp which had missed the franking machine and had been hand-cancelled by the postman. The name and address were typewritten. Frost checked that the envelope was empty before passing it over to Gilmore who compared the typing with that on the envelope received that morning by Mrs Compton. Gilmore shook his head. 'Different typewriter.' Frost nodded. He knew that already. He also knew that the envelope and the typing were identical to the two poison pen letters in the file in his office. 'An empty envelope, doc. Why should you think it was a poison pen letter? Why not a letter from the sanitary inspector about the smell on the landing?'

A pause. But it was Ada who broke the silence. 'If you

don't want me any more, doctor, I've got lots to do.' She clomped out of the room.

As the door closed behind her, Maltby unlocked the middle drawer of his desk and took out a sheet of white A4 typescript. 'This came in an identical envelope.'

He handed it to Frost who read it aloud. '"Dear Lecher. Does your sweet wife know what filthy and perverted practices you and that shameless bitch in Denton get up to? I was watching again last Wednesday. I saw every disgusting perversion. She didn't even draw the bedroom curtains . . ." Bleeding hell, this is sizzling stuff,' gasped Frost. He read the rest to himself before chucking the letter across to Gilmore. 'What's cunnilinctus, doc – sounds like a patent cough syrup.'

'You know damn well what it is,' grunted the doctor. He looked across at Gilmore who was comparing the typing with that on the envelope addressed to Wardley. 'The same typewriter, isn't it, Sergeant.'

'Yes,' agreed Gilmore. 'The "a" and the "s" are both out of alignment. How did you come by it, doctor? It wasn't addressed to you, was it?'

'I should be so bloody lucky,' said Maltby. 'One of the villagers received it and asked me to pass it on to the police. For obvious reasons he doesn't want me to tell you his name.'

'We've got to talk to him,' insisted Frost. 'We need to find out how the letter writer discovered these details.'

Maltby shook his head. 'I'm sorry, Jack. There's no way I can tell you.'

Frost stood up and adjusted his scarf. 'Well, we'll let our Forensic whizz kids have a sniff at the letter and envelope, but unless people are prepared to co-operate, there's not a lot we can do.'

'You're going to do something, though?' insisted Maltby.

'We'll have a look through Wardley's cottage and try and find the letter. I'll have a word with him in the hospital. How old is he?'

Maltby flicked through some dog-eared record cards. 'Seventy-two.'

'I wonder what he's been up to that made him try to kill himself.' At the door he paused. 'What do you know about the Comptons, doc?'

'Seem a loving couple,' said Maltby, guardedly.

'Yes,' agreed Frost, 'too bloody loving. They were nearly having it away on the dining table while we were there. Know anyone who might have a grudge against them?'

Maltby shook his head. 'Ada told me what's been happening. I can't think of anyone.' The phone rang. He lifted the receiver and listened, wearily. 'Right,' he said. 'Keep her in bed. I'll be right over.'

Back in the car Frost gave the volume control on the radio a tentative tweak. '. . . Mr Frost report to Mr Mullett urgently.' Hastily he turned it down again. 'I get the feeling its going to be a sod of a day, son.'

Monday afternoon shift

Police Superintendent Mullett, Commander of Denton Division, gave his welcoming smile and nodded towards a chair for Gilmore to sit down. They were in Mullett's spacious office with its blue Wilton carpet and the walls, with their concealed cupboards, panelled in real wood veneer. A striking contrast to the dark green paint and beige emulsion decor of the rest of the station.

He turned the pages of Gilmore's personal file and nodded his approval. This was exactly the sort of man they wanted in the division, young, efficient and ambitious. He looked up as Station Sergeant Bill Wells tapped on the door and walked briskly in.

'Mr Frost has gone home, sir,' Wells announced. 'I phoned his house, but there was no answer.'

Mullett tugged the duty roster from his middle drawer. Just as he thought, Frost was clearly marked down for afternoon duty.

'He was on duty all last night and most of this morning, sir,' explained Wells. 'He's probably grabbing some sleep.'

Mullett sniffed his disapproval. What was the point of having duty rosters if they were blatantly ignored? The envelope from County marked *Strictly Confidential* glowered up at him from his drawer as he replaced the roster. Frost was really in trouble this time.

'I want to see the inspector the minute he gets in, Sergeant . . . the very minute.' Let Frost try to wriggle out of this one.

'I've left instructions, sir. I'm off home myself now.' Wells yawned loudly and rubbed his eyes to show how tired he was.

Again Mullett snatched up the roster and jabbed his finger on the afternoon shift which showed that Wells was the station sergeant on duty until six o'clock. He studiously consulted his gold Rolex wrist-watch. Half-past three!

'I'm on again at eight o'clock tonight, sir,' explained Wells. 'I'm filling in for Sergeant Mason. He's down with the flu.'

Mullett flapped a hand impatiently. He didn't want all

the fiddling details. 'If you must alter all the shifts around, Sergeant, do me the courtesy of letting me know.' He grunted peevishly as his red biro neatly amended the roster. 'I can't run a station in this slipshod fashion.'

Wells bristled. There he was, working all the hours God sent, doing double shifts, and all this idiot was concerned with was his lousy duty roster. 'This virus thing is making it impossible, sir. We need more men.'

'We have one extra man,' beamed Mullett, nodding towards Gilmore. 'And I'm sure, like me, he would like a cup of tea.' He flashed his teeth expectantly.

'Tea?' spluttered Wells. 'I've got no-one I can spare to make tea, sir. As you know, the canteen's closed . . .'

Mullett didn't know the canteen was closed and he wasn't interested. 'Two teas,' he said firmly, 'and if you can find some biscuits . . . custard creams would be nice.' What a sullen look the man gave him as he left. He would have to speak to him about it. He swivelled his chair to face Gilmore. 'I'm having to plunge you straight in at the deep end, Sergeant. You'll be working split shifts with Mr Frost, so you're on again tonight.'

'Tonight?' echoed Gilmore in dismay.

'That presents no difficulties, I hope?'

'No, sir. Of course not.' God, Liz would raise hell over this.

'Good. One other thing.' Mullett cleared his throat nervously and hesitated as he carefully picked his words. 'If, when you are working under Mr Frost, you notice anything that you feel should be brought to my attention, you will find I have a very receptive ear.' He lowered his eyes and began fiddling with his fountain pen.

Gilmore pulled himself up straight in his chair. 'Are you asking me to spy on the inspector, sir?'

Mullett looked pained. 'If you consider that what I

have suggested constitutes spying, Sergeant, then of course you will forget I ever said it.' He closed the green cover of the detective sergeant's personal file. 'You are promotion material, Sergeant, but to promote you, I need a vacancy.'

He stared hard at Gilmore. Gilmore stared back, holding Mullett's gaze, then gave a tight smile and nodded.

They understood each other.

They were still smiling smugly at each other when Wells crashed in with the tea.

'This will be your office.' Detective Constable Joe Burton, stocky, twenty-five years old and ambitious, tried to keep the resentment out of his voice as he showed the new detective sergeant around. Gilmore stared in amazement. The poky room he was expected to share with that scarecrow, Frost, was a complete shambles with papers and files everywhere but in their proper place, dirty cups perched on the window ledge and the floor littered with cigarette stubs and screwed-up pieces of paper that had missed the target of the waste bin. 'And this is your desk,' added Burton.

The spare desk, the smaller of the two, was awash with papers and ancient files. Gilmore's jaw tightened. His first job would be to put this pigsty into some semblance of order. The internal phone rang. At first he couldn't locate the instrument which was buried under a toppled stack of files on Frost's desk.

'Control here,' said the phone. 'Got a dead body for you – probable suicide. 132 Saxon Road. Panda car at premises.'

Gilmore scribbled down the details. He could fit it in on his way home. He told Burton to come with him.

On their way out to the car-park, they passed Mullett

who was talking to a scowling Sergeant Wells. 'You should be off duty, Gilmore.'

'Possible suicide, sir. Thought I'd better handle it personally.'

Mullett beamed. 'Keenness. That's what I like to see. A rare commodity, these days. All some people think of is getting off home.' His pointed stare left Sergeant Wells in no doubt as to who he was referring to.

Wells kept his face impassive. 'Crawling bastard!' he silently told Gilmore's retreating back.

Rain hammered down on Frost's blue Cortina as it slowly nosed its way down Saxon Road, a street of two-storey terraced houses in the newer part of Denton. He spotted a police patrol car at the far end and parked behind it. One last drag at his cigarette, then out, head down against the rain, as he butted his way up the path to number 132.

A worried-looking woman opened the door. Behind her, the bitter sound of sobbing. She looked enquiringly at the scruffy figure on the doorstep who was fumbling in the depths of his inside pocket. 'Detective Inspector Frost,' he said, showing her a dog-eared warrant card.

She peered doubtingly at the card. 'I'm just a neighbour. Do you want to see the parents?' She inclined her head towards the back room from which the sobbing continued unabated.

'Later,' he said. And he wasn't looking forward to it.

Up the stairs to the girl's bedroom where a white-faced uniformed constable stood outside. This was PC John Collier, twenty years old. Collier, still very green and usually working inside the station with Wells, had been pitched out on patrol because of the manpower shortage. He hadn't yet got used to dead bodies.

The bedroom door opened, releasing a murmur of

angry voices. DC Burton came out. He seemed relieved to see the inspector and carefully closed the door behind him.

'What have we got?' asked Frost, shaking rain from his mac.

'Suicide, but our new super-sergeant is treating it as a mass murder.'

'He's new and he's keen,' said Frost. 'It'll soon wear off.'

The bedroom was small, neat and unfussy, with white melamine furniture and pink emulsioned walls. A glowering Gilmore was watching Dr Maltby, red-faced and smelling strongly of alcohol, who was pulling the sheet back over the body on the single bed. Gilmore scowled at Frost's entrance. He'd asked for a senior officer. He didn't expect this oaf. 'I thought you were off duty,' he muttered.

'They dragged me out of bed. So what's the problem?'

Gilmore opened his mouth to speak but the doctor got in first. 'There's no problem, Inspector. It's a clear case of suicide.' He jerked his head towards a small brown glass container on the bedside cabinet. 'Overdose of barbiturates. She swallowed the lot.' He glared at Gilmore as if daring him to contradict.

'You don't look very happy, Sergeant,' observed Frost, wondering why the man had requested a senior officer to attend a routine suicide.

'There was no suicide note,' Gilmore said.

'It's not obligatory,' snapped the doctor. 'You can commit suicide without leaving a note.' He was tired and wanted another drink. What he didn't want was complications. 'It's suicide, plain and simple.' He moved out of the way so the inspector could get to the body.

'I'm glad it's simple,' said Frost, pulling back the sheet,

'I'm not very good when things are complicated.' Then his expression changed. 'Oh no!' he said softly, his face crumpling. 'I never realized it was a kid.'

'Fifteen years old,' said Gilmore. 'Everything to live for.'

She lay on top of the bed. A young girl wearing a white cotton nightdress decorated with the beaming face of Mickey Mouse. Over the nightdress was a black and gold Japanese-style kimono. Her feet were bare, the soles slightly dirty as if she had been padding about the house without socks or shoes. A Snoopy watch on her left wrist ticked softly away. It seemed wrong. Almost obscene. Mickey Mouse and Snoopy had no place with death.

Frost gazed down at her face, trying to read some answers. A pretty kid with light brown hair gleaming as if newly brushed, spread loosely over the pillow. Gently, as if afraid to wake her, Frost touched her cheek, flinching at the hard, icy cold feel of death. 'You silly bloody cow,' he said. 'Why did you do this?'

He switched his attention to the bedside cabinet. Standing on top of it was a bright red, twin-belled alarm clock, its alarm set at 6.45, a pair of ear-rings, a Bic pen, an empty, brown pill bottle and, over to one side away from the bed and almost on the edge of the cabinet, a tumbler with an inch of water remaining. Frost crouched to read the label on the pill container. *Sleeping Tablets prescribed for Mrs Janet Bicknell.*

'They were prescribed for the mother,' Gilmore explained. 'There were about fifteen or so left. The kid got them from the bathroom cabinet.'

Frost sank down on the corner of the bed and lit up a cigarette. 'Any doubts it's a suicide, doc?'

'If the post-mortem shows a lethal dose of barbiturates

in her stomach, no doubts whatsoever. If you could speed things up, Jack, I'd like to get off home. I've had one hell of a day.'

'Right,' said Frost. 'How long has she been dead?'

'Rigor mortis hasn't reached the lower part of the body yet. That and the temperature readings suggest she's been dead some nine to ten hours.'

Frost checked his watch. It was now a few minutes past five. 'So she died between seven and eight o'clock this morning?'

'She was still alive at half-past seven, this morning,' interjected Gilmore.

'Then she was dead pretty soon after,' snapped the doctor. His head was throbbing and Gilmore was getting on his damn nerves.

'Slow down,' pleaded Frost. 'Let's take it step by step, starting with her name.'

Gilmore opened up his notebook and read out the details. 'Susan Bicknell, fifteen years old. In the fifth form at Denton Comprehensive.'

'And who found the body?'

'Her stepfather, Kenneth Duffy.'

'Stepfather?'

'Yes. Her father died two years ago. Her mother married again in March.' Gilmore paused, then added significantly, 'He's a lot younger than the mother.'

'Ah,' said Frost. 'I'm getting the scenario . . . teenage girl, randy young stepfather. But let's get the doc out of the way first. I don't want to shock him with our rude talk.'

'I've got nothing more to tell you,' said Maltby, dropping a thermometer in his bag and snapping it shut. 'You'll have my written report today. Any joy with our poison pen writer?'

'No,' Frost told him. 'I'll go and see Wardley in hospital when I get a chance.' The doctor lurched towards the open door. A curse as he appeared to miss his footing on the stairs.

'He's drunk!' hissed Gilmore.

'He's tired,' said Frost. 'The poor bastard is overworked. He never refuses a call day or night and people take advantage of him.' He whispered something to Burton who chased after Maltby and called, 'Give us your keys, doc. I'll drive you home.' Maltby handed them over without a murmur.

'Follow on in the Panda and take Burton back to the station,' Collier was told. Frost lit up another cigarette. 'So what's on your mind, son?'

'The suicide note's missing,' said Gilmore.

'What makes you think there was one?'

Gilmore steered the inspector across to the bedside cabinet. 'One ballpoint pen.' He pointed. On the floor, by the bed, was a pad of Basildon Bond writing paper. 'One notepad.'

'So she had the means to write a suicide note,' said Frost. 'But it doesn't follow she wrote one. I don't have to do a pee just because I pass a gents' urinal.'

'Look at the glass with the water in,' continued Gilmore. 'Right on the edge of the cabinet. If she was lying in bed when she took the pills, she'd have replaced the glass on the side nearest to her. If she took them before she lay on the bed, she'd have put the glass somewhere in the middle.'

'I'm sure this is all significant stuff,' Frost said, 'but I'm such a dim sod I can't see it.' He wandered over to the window and opened it to let out the smell of tobacco smoke. In the darkened street below, the street lights were just coming on.

Gilmore sighed inwardly. He knew the man was thick, but surely he didn't have to explain every detail. 'I'm saying the glass was moved by someone else. I'm saying she left a suicide note and weighed it down with the glass. The stepfather found the body, saw the note and because it implicated him, he destroyed it. There's two sets of prints on the glass. I'm laying odds they're the girl's and the stepfather's.'

Frost squinted at the glass. 'Anything else?'

'Yes,' said Gilmore. 'I've got a feeling about the stepfather. He's hiding something. I just know he is.'

Frost nodded. Feelings and hunches were things he knew all about. His eyes slowly traversed the room. Yes, there was something wrong. He could sense it too. 'All right, son, let's go and have a chat with the stepfather.' He pitched his cigarette out of the window and closed it, then took one last look at the still figure on the bed before covering her with the sheet.

They were in the lounge, a large, comfortable room with heavy brown velvet curtains drawn across a bay window. From the other room the heart-breaking sound of sobbing went on and on. Frost stared gloomily at the blank screen of a 26-inch television set and wished they could get this next part over. He looked up as the stepfather, Kenneth Duffy, a dark-haired, boyish-looking man in his late thirties, came in.

Duffy's eyes were red-rimmed and his cheeks glistening wet. He had been crying. Drying his face with his hands, he dropped heavily into an armchair opposite the two detectives. 'My wife's too upset to talk to you.'

'I quite understand, sir,' murmured Frost, sympathetically. 'I know you've already explained everything to my colleague, but I wonder if you'd mind telling me. I understand you're a van driver with Mallard Deliveries?'

'Yes.'

'And it was you who found Susan?'

'Yes.' His voice was so low they had to lean forward to catch what he was saying. 'I found her.'

'What time would this be?'

'Time? This afternoon . . . just after four. She was on the bed. I touched her. She was cold.' He broke down and couldn't continue.

Frost lit a cigarette and waited until Duffy was ready to go on. 'Tell me what happened this morning. Right from the beginning.'

'Susan always got herself up . . . made her own breakfast. She had a half-term holiday job in the new Sainsbury's supermarket . . . shelf-filling and sometimes helping out on the check-out. She had to clock in at eight and left the house at half-past seven. I'd wait until I heard the front door slam, then I'd get up.'

'You wouldn't come down until after she had gone?'

'I don't start work until 8.30. We'd only get in each other's way.'

'I see,' said Frost, wondering if there was more to it than that, if Susan was deliberately avoiding being alone with her stepfather.

'I heard her going up and down the stairs this morning, but now I think of it, I never heard the slam of the front door. She always slammed it when she went out. Today she must have gone back upstairs to her bedroom. I came down a little after 7.30, washed, dressed and went to work.'

'And you didn't notice anything out of the ordinary?'

'No. There was nothing to suggest she hadn't gone to work.'

'You didn't look in her bedroom before you left?' asked Frost, looking for somewhere to flick his ash.

‘I had no reason . . . but in any case, she hated people going into her room when she was out. So I went to work and my wife went to work and Susan was upstairs dying.’ Again he broke down.

‘So what made you go into her bedroom at four o’clock this afternoon?’ asked Frost.

‘I’d finished early and was home just before four. I phoned Susan at Sainsbury’s to remind her about the groceries we needed and they told me she hadn’t been in to work all that day. I suddenly remembered I hadn’t heard that front door slam. I went upstairs and looked in her bedroom.’ He knuckled the tears from his eyes. ‘I’m sorry,’ he said. ‘I’m so sorry.’ He was apologizing for crying. Frost gave a sympathetic nod and made a mental note to check with Duffy’s firm about him finishing early.

‘Have you any idea why Susan should want to take her own life?’

‘There was no reason – no reason at all.’

‘Was she worried about anything?’

‘She seemed a bit edgy over the last couple of days. We thought something had gone wrong at school . . . a row with a friend or something . . . nothing serious.’

‘Did she have a boyfriend?’

‘Stacks of them – no-one steady.’

‘She must have had some reason for killing herself,’ Frost insisted. ‘Family trouble, perhaps? Girls don’t always get on with their stepfathers.’

‘We got on fine,’ insisted Duffy. ‘She was happy at home . . . doing well at school . . . everything was right for her.’

‘If everything was right,’ said Frost, ‘she’d still be alive.’ He stared at Duffy until the man had to turn his head away. ‘We couldn’t find her suicide note.’

The knuckles of Duffy’s hands whitened as he gripped

hard the arms of the chair to try to stop his body from shaking. 'There wasn't one.'

'My colleague here is pretty certain there was.'

'If there had been a note, I'd have found it.'

'Of course,' said Frost, treating Duffy to an enigmatic smile. 'Of course you would.' He studied the glowing end of his cigarette, then casually asked, 'Was she pregnant?'

'Pregnant? Girls don't kill themselves these days just because they're pregnant.'

'It depends who the father is,' snapped Gilmore.

Duffy's head came up slowly, angry patches burning his cheeks. He sprang to his feet, fists balled. 'What are you suggesting? What filth are you bloody suggesting?'

Frost stepped between them and pushed Duffy back into the chair. 'We're suggesting nothing, Mr Duffy. The post-mortem will tell us if she was pregnant, in which case we might want to talk to you again.'

'I'd like to talk to Susan's mother,' said Gilmore.

'No!' Duffy leapt from the chair and stood by the door to bar their way.

'It's all right, sir,' said Frost. 'It won't be necessary.' He jerked a thumb at Gilmore. 'Let's go, Sergeant.'

Gilmore glared at Frost. Right, you sod. Mullett wants the dirt on you, I'll find it for him. With a curt nod at Duffy, he followed the inspector out. The sobbing from the kitchen was much softer, weaker. The mother had cried herself to exhaustion.

Outside in the car they watched as a hearse pulled up to collect the body for the post-mortem. Two undertakers in shiny black raincoats slid out the coffin.

'Well?' asked Gilmore, impatiently. 'What do we do about it?'

'We do nothing,' said Frost. Before Gilmore could protest, he explained. 'Look, son, just on a hunch and without any evidence, you expect me to believe that Duffy's been having it away with his unwilling, fifteen-year-old, schoolgirl stepdaughter.'

'Yes,' replied Gilmore, biting off each word, 'that's exactly what I expect you to believe.'

Frost took a long drag at his cigarette. 'If it's any consolation, son, I agree with you all the way. I reckon he put Suzy up the spout and that's why she killed herself and that's why stepdaddy destroyed the suicide note. But we could never prove it. She never made a complaint and now she's dead.' He wound down the car window and jettisoned his cigarette end into the gutter. 'There's sod all we can do about it.'

'You want proof?' said Gilmore, his hand on the car door handle. 'I'll get you proof. Let me go and talk to the mother. She must have noticed something.'

'No!' Frost grabbed Gilmore's hand and pulled it away from the handle. 'You do not breathe a word of this to the mother. Don't you think the poor cow's suffered enough? Let it drop, son. That's the end of it.'

Gilmore stared at the rain. 'So the bastard gets away with it?'

'Yes,' agreed Frost. 'The bastard gets away with it.' He started the engine.

The undertakers were sliding the coffin into the back of the hearse.

The light in the upstairs bedroom window went out.

The rain bucketed down.

Monday evening shift

The internal phone grunted and gave its peevish ring. Automatically Wells picked it up and said, 'No, sir, Inspector Frost hasn't come in yet . . . Yes, sir, the minute I see him.' He banged the phone down and stamped his feet to try and restore his circulation. It was freezing cold in the lobby. The central heating had broken down and wouldn't be repaired until the following day at the earliest. How he envied all those lucky devils who were down with the flu and were tucked up in their nice warm beds and didn't have to put up with Mullett bleating every five minutes. He consulted the wall clock. Twenty to ten. Only ten lousy minutes of the shift gone. Still, it was only half a shift. Sergeant Johnnie Johnson was to relieve him at two. So only another four freezing hours of this.

A roar of poncey aftershave as the new chap, Detective-newly-promoted-to-bloody-Sergeant Gilmore marched up to the desk. 'Where's Inspector Frost?'

'No idea,' beamed Wells, delighted to be so unhelpful.

Gilmore scowled at the clock. Frost was ten minutes late already. 'How do I get a cup of tea?'

'You make it yourself. The canteen's closed. The night staff are all down with flu.'

Gilmore scowled again. Detective sergeants didn't make the tea. He would find DC Burton and get him to do it. As he turned to go he bumped into a woman wearing a red raincoat with the hood up over her head. 'Sorry,' he muttered, stepping out of her way.

'Yes, madam?' asked Wells. Then he recognized her

and his voice softened. 'What can we do for you, Mrs Bartlett?'

'I've got to see Inspector Allen. It's very urgent. I've news about Paula . . .'

Gilmore stopped dead. Paula? Paula Bartlett? Of course, the girl on the poster, the missing school kid. 'Perhaps I can help, madam. I'm Detective Sergeant Gilmore. I'm handling the case in Mr Allen's absence.'

She looked up at him, eyes blinking behind heavy glasses, a dumpy woman in her early forties. Her usually pale face was flushed with excitement. 'Wonderful news. Paula's alive. I know where she is.'

'Mrs Bartlett . . .' began Wells guardedly, but Gilmore took her by the arm and drew her away to one of the benches. 'Where is she, Mrs Bartlett?'

'In a big house, overlooking the woods.'

His hand shaking with excitement, Gilmore scribbled this down.

'Where did you get this information from?' called Wells from the desk.

Gilmore scowled. He was handling this. He didn't want any interference from the sergeant.

She turned towards Wells. 'From Mr Rowley. He's a clairvoyant.'

Gilmore's heart sank. 'A clairvoyant?'

She nodded earnestly. 'He phoned us. He told us things about Paula that no-one would know. He said he suddenly had this mental picture of Paula in a tiny room . . . a tiny attic room. She was being held prisoner. He described the room, the house, everything.'

'I see,' said Gilmore. He stood up. 'If you'll excuse me for a moment.' He crossed over to Wells and lowered his voice. 'Do we know a clairvoyant named Rowley?'

'No,' grunted Wells. 'But we know a nut-case called

Rowley who thinks he's a clairvoyant. He spots the girl in about fifty different places every bloody week.'

'Shit!' said Gilmore. He returned to the woman, who was waiting expectantly. 'I don't think you should raise your hopes too high,' he began, but she was in no mood for pessimism.

'Paula's alive,' she said simply. 'You're going to find her and bring her back to me. I've got the full details here.' She pressed a sheet of folded notepaper into his hand.

The lobby doors crashed open and Frost barged in. 'It's peeing cats and dogs out there,' he announced, tugging off his scarf and flapping rain-water all over the papers on Wells' desk. 'Oh heck!' He had spotted Mrs Bartlett walking across the lobby with Gilmore. He turned quickly and pretended to be studying a 'Foot and Mouth Restriction Order' poster on the wall. It was cowardly, but he couldn't face her. He felt like a cancer specialist trying to avoid a terminally ill patient anxious for reassuring news. There was no reassuring news. The girl was dead. He knew it.

'Everything all right, Mrs Bartlett?' called Wells.

'Yes, thank you,' she smiled, pulling the red hood over her hair. 'This gentleman here is going to bring Paula home for me. I've got her room all ready.' She gave Gilmore a look of such implicit trust, he didn't have the heart to contradict her. He opened the lobby door and watched as she crossed the road in the rain to hurry home and wait for her daughter.

'Poor bitch,' murmured Frost. 'She comes in two or three nights a week.'

'You might have warned me,' Gilmore snapped angrily to Wells.

'You never gave me the chance,' said Wells happily. To Frost he said, 'Mr Mullett wants to see you.'

'Sod Mr Mullett,' said Frost.

'That's what I say,' said Wells, 'but he still wants to see you.'

In direct contrast to the arctic conditions in the rest of the station, Mullett's office was a hothouse with the thermostat on the 3-kilowatt convector heater set to maximum. But the heat did nothing to soften the expression on his face which was pure ice as he waited for Frost, who was already nearly a quarter of an hour late.

A half-hearted rap at the door. Unmistakably Detective Inspector Frost. Even his knock was slovenly. Mullett adjusted his chair to dead centre, straightened his back and curtly said, 'Enter!'

The door opened and Frost shuffled in. What a mess the man looked. The shiny suit with the loose buttons, creased and crumpled where it had received a soaking from last night's rain and had then been dried over a radiator. His tie was secured with a greasy knot that looked impossible to undo and Mullett was sure that the shirt was the same one the inspector had been wearing for the past six days. Why was this flu virus perversely selecting all the best men for its victims and leaving the rubbish unscathed?

Frost flopped into a chair. 'Take a seat,' said Mullett a split second too late. His lips tightened as he unlocked the middle drawer of his desk and removed the envelope from County HQ.

Frost watched warily, wondering which of his many transgressions had come to light. He adjusted his face into a pre-emptive expression of contrition and waited.

'I've never been so humiliated and ashamed in all my life,' began Mullett.

No clue here. Mullett had used these opening remarks many times before.

'That an officer in Denton Division – *my* division – should be detected in forgery.'

Forgery? Frost's mind raced. He had often forged Mullett's signature on those occasions when his Divisional Commander's authorization had been required and Frost knew it would not be forthcoming. But the last occasion was months ago.

Mullett pulled out a wad of papers from the envelope and detached the *Strictly Confidential* County memo. The rest he pushed across to the inspector.

Frost's heart dropped with a squelch into the pit of his stomach. He recognized them immediately. His car expenses. His bloody car expenses, back like an exhumed corpse to accuse him

'Ah – I can explain, Super,' he began, frantically trying to dream up an excuse that would satisfy Mullett.

But Mullett was in no mood for explanations. He snatched up the receipts for the petrol Frost was claiming to have purchased during the month. 'Forgeries!' he snapped. 'Twelve different petrol stations, but identical handwriting. *Your* handwriting, Inspector.' He waggled the receipts under Frost's nose and Frost could see that someone in County had done the Sherlock Holmes with his expense claim and had ringed in red ink all the similarities in the handwriting of the various receipts.

'Flaming hell!' gasped Frost. 'Here we are, down to less than half-strength, working double shifts, and some lazy sod in County has got the time to go through a few lousy petrol receipts.' He tossed the expense claim back on the desk. 'If I was you, sir, I'd damn well complain.'

'Complain?' shrieked Mullett. 'I'm in no position to complain. One of my officers, an inspector, fiddling his car expenses . . .'

'I wasn't fiddling,' said Frost. 'I lost the proper receipts and had to make copies.'

'Copies! They weren't copies. They were forgeries . . . and not even good forgeries at that!'

Frost switched off his ears as Mullett ranted on, his face getting redder and redder, his fist pounding the desk at intervals. He wasn't interested in what Mullett was saying, he was only concerned at what Mullett intended doing about it. This could be the chop, the heaven-sent opportunity his superintendent had been dreaming about for years. Then something Mullett was saying penetrated his filtering mechanism.

'This could have been the end of your career in the force, but much against the grain, I have interceded on your behalf with County . . .'

Interceded. Bloody hell, thought Frost. What's the catch?

Mullett stuffed all the receipts back into the envelope and gave it to Frost. 'Resubmit your expense claim, but this time with proper, genuine petrol receipts and nothing further will be said.'

Frost sat stunned. This was too good to be true. He slipped the envelope in his inside pocket. 'Right, Super, leave it to me.' He rose, ready to take his leave before Mullett came to his senses.

'This is your last chance, Inspector. One more slip-up – just one – and . . .' But he was talking to an empty room. Frost had gone.

Mullett sighed deeply. He unfolded the *Confidential* memo from County and read it again. It pointed out that he, as Divisional Commander, had signed Frost's expense claim, certifying that he had checked it and found it correct. How on earth was he expected to check everything he had to sign? It was most unfair. And what was more unfair was that in getting himself off the hook, he had to get Frost off as well. Damn. He returned the memo to his middle drawer and locked it, then phoned Sergeant Wells saying he wanted a briefing meeting with the night shift in ten minutes.

The murmur of conversation stopped abruptly and everyone sprang to their feet as Mullett marched into the Briefing Room. He frowned. There seemed very few people in attendance. A quick count . . . eight in all, six men and two WPCs. No sign of Frost. He raised his eyebrows at Wells, querying the small turnout.

'This is all there is, sir,' he was told. 'Two more down with flu, plus Bryant and Wilkes still in hospital after the pub punch-up last week. Collier's on the desk in the lobby standing in for me.'

'And Mr Frost?'

'I did tell him, sir.'

Mullett's lips narrowed. Typical. Well, he certainly wasn't going to wait for him. He looked around the room. The new man, Gilmore, smartly turned out, was in the front row. Next to him, a sullen DC Burton, all brawn and no brains. Burton was a good man to have at your side in an emergency, but he would never progress beyond the rank of DC.

Mullett shivered and rubbed his hands together briskly. It was damn cold in here. 'Sit down, everyone, please. Well, what we lack in quantity, I'm sure we more than make up for in quality.' He let the half-hearted ripple of laughter die. 'Firstly, I'm sorry to tell you that Mr Allen has suffered a set-back and will not be returning to duty for some time . . .' His brow furrowed in annoyance as the door crashed open and Frost burst in.

'The bloody canteen's shut,' announced Frost, looking round in puzzlement. 'What's everyone doing in here?' Then he spotted Mullett. 'The briefing meeting! Sorry, Super . . . I forgot . . .'

Mullett waited until Frost had found himself a seat right at the back. 'I was just telling everyone the sad news about Inspector Allen.'

'Sad news?' echoed Frost, genuinely misunderstanding. 'Bloody hell, he's not coming back, is he?'

When the laughter subsided Mullett gave a tolerant smile. 'He won't be back for some time. I was about to explain that, in the meantime, you would be taking over his cases. Our resources are going to be spread very thinly, so I don't want any wasted effort. We've got two people tied up in the Murder Incident Room on this Paula Bartlett case. What's the current position?'

'It's more or less fizzled out,' said Frost, striking a match down a filing cabinet. 'I can't see any progress there until the body turns up.'

'Good,' smiled Mullett, ticking off the first item on his pad. 'Then on the basis of your assessment, Inspector, I'm closing down the Incident Room pro tem. This will release much-needed personnel to more urgent duties.' He beamed as if that solved everyone's problems, then frowned as he reached the next item on his list. 'Another senior citizen burglary, over the weekend, Inspector?'

Frost looked up. 'That's right, Super. Old lady living alone. He got away with about £80 in used fivers.'

'Correct me if I'm wrong, Inspector,' said Mullett, 'but this would be the sixteenth such break-in in three weeks, the victims all senior citizens?'

Frost gave a vague shrug. 'I haven't been counting, but you're probably not far out.'

'I am exactly right,' snapped Mullett. 'Sixteen – all

senior citizens, most of them robbed of their life savings. What are we doing about it?'

'What the hell can we do about it?' replied Frost. 'He leaves no clues and nobody sees him. It doesn't give us much to go on.'

'What does he take?' asked Gilmore. 'If it's jewellery, have we got all the local fences covered?'

'Good point!' agreed Mullett.

'Of course I've got the fences covered,' replied Frost. 'Even a dim old twat like me thought of that. If anyone tries to sell any of the loot, I'll be contacted. But he takes very little jewellery. He concentrates on cash – used notes. Many of these old people mistrust banks. They keep wads of banknotes in the house. They stick it in the wardrobe or in the middle drawer of the dressing table under the condoms and the leather knickers. They think no-one will find it there – but it's the first place he looks.'

'You say there's been no clues,' said Mullett. 'I understand people have spotted a blue van in the vicinity. That should give you something to go on. There can't be that many blue vans in Denton.'

'Sixteen burglaries,' said Frost. 'In two instances, we found neighbours who claim they saw a van parked in the vicinity late at night. One thought it was a small blue van, another a biggish van, dark-coloured, could have been blue.'

'But it's a lead,' insisted Mullett. 'Do a check on all blue vans.'

'Do you know precisely how many blue vans there are in the Denton area alone?' asked Frost, producing and waving a small notebook.

Mullett flapped a hand. He didn't want to know, which was a relief to Frost as he had no idea himself, although he was fully prepared to pluck an astronomical figure out of thin air if Mullett called his bluff. 'It doesn't matter how many there are, Inspector. We've got a computer. It can churn out the information in seconds.'

'But the computer can't check through it and knock on bloody doors and question people,' said Frost. 'That's what us poor sods would have to do and it could take weeks – months – and still lead nowhere.'

Mullett gave Frost a vinegary smile. 'It's easy to be negative, Inspector. I offer suggestions, you offer objections. I'm getting a lot of flak from the press on this one. I want him caught now. That's your number one priority. We haven't got many men, but take as many as you like.' He frowned with annoyance as Sergeant Wells' hand kept flapping, trying to attract his attention. Not more of the man's moans, he hoped. 'Yes, Sergeant?'

'With respect, sir. It's all very well saying Mr Frost can have as many men as he likes, but I've still got a night shift to run and I've hardly any men to do it. This flaming flu epidemic doesn't seem to have hit the criminal fraternity yet.'

'I'm well aware of that, thank you, Sergeant, which brings me to my next point. We're under strength so some things will have to go by the board. We are going to have to turn a blind eye to many of the minor crimes, even . . .' and he flashed a paternal beam in Gilmore's direction, '. . . suicides which look slightly doubtful. We will not go out of our way to look for trouble. I don't want any arrests for drunkenness, rowdiness, soliciting, illegal parking, loitering – anything minor like that. We just haven't got the time or the manpower.' He smiled at Wells. 'So that should lighten your load quite a bit, Sergeant.'

'Yes, sir,' mumbled Wells, doubtfully.

'Fine,' said Mullett, closing his notepad and turning to go. Then he remembered one other item. 'Oh –

Inspector Frost. I had a visit from the vicar of All Saints and Councillor Vernon this morning. They are very worried at this current wave of mindless vandalism in the cemetery. There was another incident over the weekend. How are the patrols going?'

'What patrols?' asked Frost.

'The anti-vandalism patrols I asked you to organize. I sent you a memo.'

'I never got it,' said Frost hastily. It was probably buried somewhere in his in-tray together with all the other stupid rubbish Mullett kept sending him.

'And I spoke to you personally about it.'

'Ah – so you did,' agreed Frost, vaguely remembering Mullett chuntering something about graveyards, 'but as you so rightly said, Super, we can't waste time on these piddling trivialities.'

Mullett gave Frost a pitying shake of the head. Hadn't the man any common sense? 'There's no such thing as a piddling triviality when a member of the town council is involved, Inspector. See to it right away – the vulnerable time seems to be between ten and midnight.'

'I've got no-one to send,' said Frost.

'Then attend to it yourself, Inspector. These are difficult times, so we act as a team. We've all got to pitch in.' Mullett looked at his watch and yawned. It had been a long day and it was freezing cold in the Briefing Room. Time for him to get home to bed.

Monday night shift (1)

Rain dripped down the upturned collar of Frost's mac. 'How long have we been here?' he asked peevishly.

Gilmore wriggled his watch free of his sleeve. 'Five minutes.'

Frost hunched his shoulders against the cold, penetrating drizzle and wound his scarf tighter around his face to blunt the teeth of the wind chewing on his scarred cheek. As he stamped his feet to try and bring some feeling to his frozen toes, his wet socks squelched in his shoes. 'This is all a bleeding waste of time,' he muttered, rasping a match on a weather-eroded headstone. The match spluttered, then flared to show the moss-blurred inscription:

George Arthur Jenkins
Born and Died
Feb 6th 1865
Suffer the little children to come unto me

'There's one poor little sod who never drew his old age pension,' he muttered moodily, letting the wind extinguish the match.

The sky was black and heavy with rain and the graveyard looked as lonely and as miserable as a graveyard should look at half-past ten on a cold, wet night. They were in the old Victorian section among weather-eroded angels who wept granite tears over the graves of long-dead children, and where overgrown grass straggled over the crumbling headstones and collapsed graves of their long-dead grief-stricken parents. Through the rain, way over on the far side, Frost could see the serried ranks of stark white marble marking the modern section, where the recently deceased slept an uneasy, decaying sleep. One of the cold marble headstones marked the grave of Frost's wife. He hadn't visited it since the funeral.

Detective Sergeant Gilmore, shutting his ears to Frost's constant moanings, was squinting his eyes, trying to focus through the lashing rain to something over to the left, near an old Victorian crypt. Was it the wind shaking the ivy, or could he see someone moving about?

Frost peered half-heartedly in the direction of Gilmore's pointing finger and grunted dismissively. 'There's sod all there. It's the wind.' He perched himself on the infant Jenkins' headstone and sucked hard at his cigarette. 'How long have we been here now?'

'Eight minutes,' replied Gilmore.

Frost ground his cigarette to death against the headstone and stood up. 'That's long enough. We're going.'

'But Mr Mullett said . . .'

'Sod Mr Mullett,' called Frost, scurrying back to the car. 'If anyone wants to vandalize graves in this pissing weather, then good luck to them.'

Gilmore stared hard across the ranks of marble. The wind rattled the ivy again. There was someone there, he was sure of it. But a cloud crawled across the moon and it was too dark to see. When it passed, there was nothing.

The pub was packed, thick-fogged with eye-stinging smoke, and very noisy. Disco music belted out and voices were raised to overcome it. A group of teenaged girls, clutching vodka and limes, were shrieking with high-pitched laughter at the punchline of some dirty joke. No-one took any notice of the disc jockey framed by flashing disco lights up on the small stage, who was chewing a microphone to announce the next number. In counterpoint to the throbbing beat of the disco, a drunken Irishman in the far corner was singing 'Danny Boy' in a high tenor voice to a fat lady in black who had tears in her eyes.

Gilmore was edgy. His very first night on duty in Denton and they had disobeyed Mullett's express orders. He decided he would choke his drink down and tell Frost he was going back to the cemetery, as ordered by his Divisional Commander, and would continue the surveillance on his own if necessary.

By waving a £5 note Frost managed to grab the attention of the barman who lip-read his order. As he waited, he let his professional eye wander over the throng. The girls with the vodkas were silent, poised ready to shriek anew as the next joke reached its climax. The drunken Irishman had fallen in mid-song and was face down on the table while the fat lady, no longer tearful, thumbed through his wallet.

The main doors were still swinging behind someone who had left hurriedly and Frost recalled a face, a blur in the crowd that had seemed alarmed at the entrance of the two detectives. It was a face he should know, but couldn't place. He shrugged. What the hell. They were here for a drink, not to feel the collar of some petty crook.

The barman pushed the two lagers across and was back from the till with Frost's change when the bar phone rang. He answered it, then, holding the receiver aloft, yelled, 'Is there a Mr Frost here?'

Frost swapped worried glances with Gilmore. Who knew they were here? Flaming hell, had Hornrim Harry sent his narks after them to report on their every movement? Gingerly, he took the phone and pressed it tight against his face, his finger jammed in the other ear to deaden the background noise. The caller was mumbling and he couldn't hear what the man was saying. 'You'll have to speak up,' he shouted and then, as clear as a bell, he heard the words 'dead body'. 'Say that again?'

'Seventy-six Jubilee Terrace. Upstairs bedroom. The old girl's dead. I think the husband's killed her.'

'How did you know I was here? Who's this speaking?'

A click as the caller hung up. Frost swore to himself and slid the phone back across the counter. If it was someone's idea of a joke, it wasn't a very funny one. And that voice. He knew it. It went with the face he glimpsed leaving the pub as they came in. The harder he tried to remember, the further it slipped out of his grasp.

'Trouble?' Gilmore asked anxiously. It was always trouble with Frost. If it was Mullett who had phoned, he'd make it quite clear that he had obeyed Frost's orders under protest.

Frost scooped up his change. 'Knock back your drink, son. I might have another corpse for you to look at.'

The man on the bike tucked his head down against the rain as he took the short cut through the cemetery after his meeting with the vicar. This damn rain seeping through his mac wasn't going to do his cold any good and he hoped he wasn't in for a dose of this flu thing that everyone seemed to be catching. Row after row of headstones slipped silently past as he pressed down on the pedals. Graves and tombs didn't frighten him, not even at this hour of night, but he would still be happier once he was out through the cemetery gates and on to the main road.

And then he nearly lost control of the bike as a sudden sound reverberated around the churchyard. A funeral bell. His head swivelled as he tried to locate the source. There! It was coming from the old Dobson vault! Someone had broken in and was tugging at the rope inside, tolling the bell installed some 150 years ago by old William Dobson who was terrified of being buried alive and wanted to be able to summon help should he awake in his coffin.

Through the rain he could see a light bobbing. He yelled and someone burst from the crypt, and hared off into the darkness.

He turned his bike and pedalled for all he was worth back to the vicarage where he called the police.

Jubilee Terrace was a cul-de-sac of Edwardian terraced houses and would soon be torn down when the next phase of the new town development was reached. Number 76, the fanlight still showing a light, was the end house standing next to a high brick wall which guarded an electricity sub-station. The rain had eased off slightly and the reflection of a lamp standard shimmered in a large puddle where the drain was blocked.

Gilmore knocked at the door and waited, his fingers drumming impatiently on the porch wall. No-one came. He knocked again louder this time.

The door to number 74 opened and a shirt-sleeved man looked out. 'No use knocking there, mate. The old git's as deaf as a post.'

'Actually, it's the lady of the house we want,' said Frost. 'Do you know if she's in?'

'She's got no choice . . . she's bed-ridden. Never goes out.'

'I heard she was dead,' said Frost.

'Dead? You must have the wrong house, mate. He may be deaf but he makes a lot of noise. These walls are paper thin. I can hear them talking and rowing – if my luck's out, I can even hear him gobbing down the sink.'

'I'm not sure I've got their names right.'

'Maskell – Charlie and Mary – he's Charlie, she's Mary.'

'Oh, *he's* Charlie!' Frost pretended to make an alteration in his notebook, then, as soon as the man went in he dropped to his knees and squinted through the letter-box. A dimly lit hall papered in dreary, dark chocolate brown.

'How can she be dead if he's heard them talking?' protested Gilmore. 'This has got to be a wind-up.'

'You're probably right, son,' grunted Frost, still at the letter-box. Then his nose twitched and he knew it wasn't a wind-up. The bad breath of decay. He could smell death.

The detective sergeant took his turn to sniff then shook his head. 'It's damp and stuffy, that's all.'

'It's more than that, son.' He gave one more knock which shook the front door. Noises inside, but no-one came. 'Let's try the back way.'

A lowish wall muddied their trousers as they clambered over to land with a splash in a small back yard, a few square feet of puddled concrete containing a dustbin and an outside toilet, its gaping door hanging from one hinge. Ever the optimist, Frost tried the back door, but it was locked and bolted. A downstairs sash window, curtains drawn and no light showing, defied the efforts of Frost's penknife.

'Let's leave it,' said Gilmore, edging back to the wall. They were trying to break into someone's house just on the say-so of an anonymous phone call.

But Frost wasn't listening. He had now transferred his attention to the upstairs window. Difficult to tell from that angle, but it appeared to be open at the bottom. 'Keep watch, son. Give a yell if anyone comes.' He climbed up on top of the dustbin which seemed ideally sited for the purpose and heaved himself up on the outside toilet roof and then to the sill.

Yes, a gap at the bottom he could get his hand under. For a moment he hesitated. It all seemed too good to be true; the dustbin conveniently placed and the window invitingly open. But there was no turning back now. He lifted the window and dropped inside.

A pitch dark room. The torch he pulled from his pocket was on the blink, but its faltering light enabled him to steer a tiptoeing course through a maze of booby-trapped junk ready to topple at any moment – an old treadle Singer sewing machine, cardboard boxes gorged with useless items too good to throw away, the frame of a push bike and an old-fashioned pram from the late 1930s in pristine condition which, for some reason, made him think of the baby's grave in the churchyard.

Cautiously, he turned the door handle. The door whined open.

A landing from which stairs descended to the hall. To his right a door with a crack of light showing from inside. He moved towards it. From downstairs came the sound of someone lumbering about and talking in the overloud voice of the deaf. Crockery clattered. The old boy was making tea or something.

The smell hit him as soon as he opened the door. And then he saw her. On the bed. An old woman, her head propped up with pillows. She didn't move. She couldn't move. She was a shrivelled, mummified husk and had been dead for many months.

Shit! Just what he bloody wanted! He rammed a cigarette in his mouth, but didn't light it, then steeled himself to walk across and lift the discoloured bed sheet which made a tearing noise as it parted from the body. The stains on the bedding weren't blood. No signs of injury anywhere. There was something round the mouth. Mouldering food and a brown dribble of something still sticky. On a rickety card table alongside the bed was a cup of cold scummy tea and a plate of congealed food. Shit and double shit. He now knew what it was all about and wanted to get out of the room and back in the car and as far away as possible. The bloody cemetery was preferable to this.

Before he could get to the door he heard someone coming up the stairs. The old boy, talking away to himself.

He spun round, frantically looking for another way out. There was a window behind thick, drawn curtains which belched death-scented dust. He parted them to scrabble at the window catch. But it was rusted in and wouldn't budge.

A clatter of crockery then a tap at the door. 'Your supper, love.'

Frost pressed himself tight against the wall, hoping the opened door would conceal him. The old man, tall and stooped, came in. A tray holding a bowl of soup and a plate of bread and butter rattled in unsteady hands. He frowned at the food on the card table then turned angrily to the husk in the bed. 'You didn't eat it!' he shouted. 'I cooked it for you and you didn't eat it.' Then his voice softened. 'You know what the doctor said. You've got to eat to keep your strength up.' He exchanged the old tray for the new and picked up a spoon. 'You must try and eat some of this, love. It's full of goodness,' and he spooned soup over the gaping mouth, dabbing with a handkerchief as it dribbled down the shrivelled chin. He was deaf. He didn't hear the thud of Frost's footsteps down the stairs and into the street.

In the car, Gilmore listened incredulously, his face creased in disgust. 'And he's still bringing her food? Flaming hell!'

'The poor old sod won't accept her death,' said Frost, sucking thankfully at a cigarette.

Before Gilmore could reach for the radio to inform the station, Frost's hand shot out to stop him. 'Forget it, son. We don't want to get involved.'

A shocked Gilmore said, 'You can't just drive away and do nothing about it.'

'We're not supposed to be here,' said Frost. 'We're supposed to be tomb-watching.'

'But she's dead. He's probably still drawing her pension.'

'Big bloody deal,' grunted Frost. 'I'll try and live with it.' And then the car radio which had been pleading urgently for attention to an empty car, tried again.

'Control to Mr Frost. For Pete's sake come in, please . . . over.'

Frost snatched up the handset. 'Frost.'

'At flaming last, Jack!' It was Bill Wells, the station sergeant. 'Where are you?'

Frost looked out of the window on to Jubilee Street. 'On watch at the cemetery, as ordered,' he replied, trying to sound puzzled at such an obvious question.

'No, you're not, Inspector. If you were, you'd see the place was crawling with bloody police cars.'

'Ah yes . . . there does seem to be some commotion at the far end,' said Frost, signalling for Gilmore to put his foot down and get the damn car back to the cemetery at top speed. 'What exactly has happened?'

'Vandals breaking into a crypt.'

Right. 'I'll check it out and call you back.' He switched off hurriedly and urged Gilmore not to heed the approaching red traffic light.

There was only one police car at the graveyard, its blue flashing beacon reflecting eerily off the rain-soaked marble markers. Gilmore parked tight behind it.

'There!' pointed Frost.

Ahead of them, right off the main path, was the Victorian crypt they had spotted earlier, an ugly little building, looking like a small, ivy-covered boiler house and guarded by tall, sharply spiked, cast-iron railings. Two marble angels with naked swords stood sentry on each side of the entrance gate where a uniformed officer, PC Ken Jordan, was talking to an old man in a flat cap who was supporting a push bike. Jordan left the man to meet the two detectives.

'Who's the old git with the running nose?' asked Frost.

'He's George Turner, the churchwarden. He phoned us.' Jordan filled them in on what had happened. 'I've had a quick look around. No sign of anyone.'

'Ah well,' said Frost, anxious to get back in the car and the dry, 'I'll leave you to handle it.' He jerked his head to Gilmore. 'Come on, son.'

But Gilmore was rattling the heavy iron gates. They were held firm by the lock. 'So how did he get in?'

'There's a couple of broken railings round the back,' said Jordan.

'Show me,' demanded Gilmore. They followed Jordan to the rear of the crypt. Next to a stand-pipe supporting a dripping tap, two of the cast-iron railings had been broken away leaving a gap wide enough to squeeze through. They squeezed through, Frost reluctantly bringing up the rear, and marched round to the entrance to the crypt.

The door, solid oak some 3 inches thick, bore a crudely sprayed skull and crossbones in still-wet purple paint. It should have been secured by a heavy duty padlock and hasp, but the screws fixing it had been prised out of the door jamb and the door yawned open.

'Vandals!' bawled Turner. 'I'd horsewhip them till they screamed for mercy.'

'Ah well,' said Frost, fumbling for a cigarette, 'not much harm done.'

'What I want to know,' continued Turner, 'is where were the police who were supposed to be on watch? Something should be done about them. They should be taught a lesson.'

Frost nodded his agreement. 'They should be flogged until they screamed for mercy, then castrated without an anaesthetic.'

'Aren't you going to look inside?' asked Turner. 'They might have done some damage.'

'Right,' grunted Frost, without enthusiasm.

The old man leading, and guided by Jordan's torch, they went in, down two steps to the stone-floored chamber.

Jordan's torch prodded the darkness. It was a very small chamber with some six ornate, black-painted Victorian coffins stacked on stone ledges along the walls on each side. From the roof the bell rope was still quivering.

'I've never been inside a crypt,' observed Gilmore. 'I thought it would be bigger.'

'What for?' asked Frost. 'They aren't going to get up and bleedin' walk around, are they?' His nose twitched. 'What's that smell?'

'I can't smell anything,' said Turner, 'but then I've got a cold.' To prove it he foghorned into a large handkerchief.

'It smells like a corrugated iron urinal in a heat-wave,' Frost said. 'When did you bung the last corpse in?'

'The crypt hasn't been used since 1899,' he was told.

'It's coming from over here,' said Jordan, his torch sweeping the floor.

'There!' called Frost, grabbing the torch and directing it towards the far corner. The light bounced off a large, bulging bundle wrapped in black polythene sheeting, criss-crossed with 2-inch wide brown plastic adhesive tape and tied with cord.

'That didn't ought to be here!' said Turner.

As they dragged it to the centre of the floor it trailed foul-smelling liquid. Frost bent down and prodded it gently with his finger. The bundle felt cold and squelchy and the stench of putrefaction belched out. Frost's penknife slashed open the plastic sheeting. So strong and sickening was the smell that they all had to retreat back to the door to inhale the clean, rain-washed night air.

They steeled themselves to go back in. Holding his breath, Frost cut the slit bigger and peeled back some of the plastic. A gas-bloated putrefying face looked up at him.

PC Jordan gagged, his hand shaking so much that he nearly dropped the torch. Frost snatched it from him and handed it to Gilmore. 'If you're going to throw up, Jordan, do it outside. It stinks enough in here as it is.' Gladly, the constable charged up the steps. 'Are you all right, Sergeant?'

Fighting hard to control his stomach, Gilmore nodded. If the inspector could stand it, so could he.

Jordan returned, white and sweating, wiping his mouth. 'I hope you haven't desecrated someone's grave?' said Frost sternly. Jordan didn't answer. He hadn't looked and he just didn't care.

'Nip upstairs,' Frost told Gilmore, 'and radio through to the station. Tell Sergeant Wells we've found a body in the churchyard. When he stops peeing himself laughing and saying, "But the churchyard is full of bodies," tell him "ha-bloody-ha" from me and I want a doctor, Forensic, Scene of Crime Officer and a gross of air fresheners.'

The mobile generator grunted and coughed before chugging away contentedly, and the Victorian vault was bathed in electric light for the first time in its life. Duck boarding had been placed down the centre of the steps and over the floor and footsteps clacked as they crossed it. Frost stood outside, keeping well out of the experts' way as they measured and photographed, took samples and dusted for prints. The body remained tied up in the sheeting awaiting the arrival of the police surgeon.

A cursing as someone stumbled unsteadily down the path. Frost grinned to himself, happy to see that Dr Maltby was still on duty and not that jumped-up, toffee-nosed sod, Slomon.

'Welcome to the boneyard, doc.'

Maltby waved his bag and lurched over. 'What have you got for me this time?'

'Body in a sack. It's past its best.'

'Aren't we all,' said Maltby, following the inspector down the stone steps. 'Any progress with my poison pen writer?'

'Give us a chance, doc,' pleaded Frost. 'I've been tripping over corpses all day.'

Maltby dropped to his knees and bent over the body. 'Well, he's dead,' he announced.

'I should hope he is,' grunted Frost. 'If I smelt like that, I wouldn't want to live.'

Gilmore snorted his disgust. Frost seemed to thrive on bad taste remarks.

'By the way, Jack,' said the doctor casually as he gently prodded the puffy flesh through the torn opening in the plastic, 'you know that dead girl – the suicide . . .'

'What about her?' asked Gilmore.

Pointedly addressing Frost, the doctor continued. 'Tear up the report I did on her. I'm writing a new one.'

'What was up with the old one?' asked Frost.

'I missed something. The morgue attendant tipped me the wink. He spotted it when he undressed her.' He stood up and wiped his hands on a towel from his bag. 'This one's been dead at least eight weeks – possibly longer.'

'What did the morgue attendant find?' asked Gilmore. He knew there was something dodgy about that suicide.

Maltby's head twisted to the detective sergeant. 'There were marks on her buttocks – weals – about a week old, fading but still visible. She'd been quite severely beaten with a whip or a cane. And there were needle marks on her left arm.'

Gilmore's eyebrows shot up. 'And you missed it?' He pulled the inspector to one side. 'Surely you're not going to let him get away with this?'

'When you've made as many balls-ups as I have, son, you don't hesitate to help fellow sufferers,' Frost told him.

Maltby snapped his bag shut. 'I can't tell you any more about this one unless you unwrap it.'

'Might be best to wait for the pathologist,' suggested the man from Forensic who had been hovering, ears flapping. 'You know how fussy he is about bodies being left untouched.'

'Sod the pathologist,' snapped Frost. 'It'll be hours before he gets here. Cut it open.'

'I'll do it,' said Forensic, cutting through the cord to preserve the knots.

'Must preserve the knots, doc,' Frost explained. 'The murderer might be a Boy Scout.'

'We don't yet know it's murder,' commented Forensic pedantically, as he delicately sliced through the plastic sheeting.

'Bleeding hard to commit suicide and then tie yourself up in a parcel,' sniffed Frost.

Forensic moved away. 'All yours, doctor.'

As Maltby laboriously peeled aside the black plastic which tried to cling to the moist, rotting flesh, both Forensic and Gilmore found it necessary to move nearer the door and the sweet night air.

'Bloody hell!' exclaimed Frost. 'It's a woman.'

Gilmore forced himself to look. He saw the the bloated body of a female, stark naked, hunched in a foetal position, knees bent to breasts and trussed with string which bit deep into wet, oedematous flesh. The hair, stained and discoloured, looked dark, almost black.

'She's wearing shoes!' cried Frost. He bent over. No tights or stockings, just flat-heeled brown shoes, tightly laced over swollen naked flesh. 'I want photographs.'

The doctor moved to one side to let Ted Roberts, the burly Scene of Crime Officer, take photographs, then began a close, careful examination, gently forcing open the mouth, then scrutinizing the neck. 'She's in too bad a condition, but I'd guess at manual strangulation.' His examination continued downwards. He asked for the string to be cut so he could see the lower part of the body. He parted the legs slightly. 'Dear God!' he exclaimed, visibly startled at what he saw.

The lower stomach and genital area was a mass of blackened and charred weeping flesh.

Frost dropped on his knees beside the doctor and gasped. 'Look at this, Gilmore. Some bastard's burnt her.'

A fleeting glance was enough for Gilmore who stood well back, willing his stomach to keep calm while camera motors whirred and flash tubes crackled.

Maltby's nose scraped the blackened area. 'To do this sort of damage you'd need a blow-lamp.'

'Bloody hell!' said Frost. 'Was it done before or after death?'

The doctor shook his head. 'I don't know. I hope it was after.'

No longer hunched up, she looked smaller than Frost had first thought. 'How old is she, doc?'

'Young,' Maltby told him, again exploring the mouth. 'Fifteen . . . sixteen.'

'Fifteen!' echoed Frost. 'And dead eight weeks?' His head sank. 'There ought to be a mole on the right shoulder, doc. Have a look, would you.'

Maltby moved some strands of hair and nodded.

'Shit,' cried Frost. 'Shit and double shit!'

This putrid mess of tortured flesh was the missing newspaper girl.

They had found Paula Bartlett.

'I didn't see what he looked like,' the church warden told Frost. 'He just dashed off into the dark.'

'Was he tall, short, fat, thin . . .? You must remember something. It's bloody important. He'd just dumped a girl's body in there.'

'Just a dark shape, that's all I saw.' Then he hesitated. 'I think there might have been more than one of them.'

'More than one?' yelled Frost. 'Blimey, you kept that up your bloody sleeve.'

'As I was pedalling up, I thought I heard voices – men's voices.'

'So why didn't you tell us this before?' demanded Gilmore.

'Because I didn't think it was important. I thought we were dealing with vandals, not a flaming murder. I didn't hear what they were saying and I didn't see anyone else.'

'You're a fine bloody help,' moaned Frost. 'A body dumped right under your nose and you see damn all! We're looking for one or more men with no description.'

'Don't you blame me for the shortcomings of your lot,' snapped Turner, picking up his bike. 'If the police were doing their job, they'd have caught them. They were supposed to have two men on watch for vandals . . . so where the hell were they? Boozing in some pub, I imagine.'

Frost went cold. He hadn't considered this aspect. 'Bleedin' hell, son,' he muttered to Gilmore. 'I've just given Mullett my head on a platter.'

By the time the pathologist and his secretary arrived, some forty minutes later, Forensic and Maltby had left and the mortuary squad were waiting outside, shuffling their feet impatiently, anxious to pick up the remains and get out of the rain. The pathologist was in a foul temper, furious that Frost had disturbed the body before he had a chance to see it and angry to learn that Maltby, who had been most rude to him after a clash of medical evidence in a recent court case, had done a detailed examination. 'If I'm called in no-one, but no-one – let alone jumped-up general practitioners – touches one hair of the corpse, do you hear? All this clumsy handling has probably destroyed vital clues.'

'Anything you say, doc,' said Frost in his 'couldn't care less' voice.

'And don't call me doc,' snapped the pathologist, pulling on a pair of long, almost transparent rubber gloves.

Frost left him to it, wandering up the steps for a smoke. PC Jordan's personal radio spluttered. Control wanting a word with Mr Frost. 'How's it going?' asked Sergeant Wells.

'The pathologist's just turned up with his blonde secretary. They both went down the crypt and he started putting some rubberware on, so I discreetly left them to it.'

Wells gave a guarded laugh. 'Mr Mullett's at my side, Inspector. He wishes to speak to you.'

Frost waited apprehensively. He certainly didn't want to speak to Mr Mullett.

The superintendent was bubbling over with fury and was almost shouting incoherently. 'You disobeyed my orders, my express orders. Your incompetence has made us a laughing stock, an absolute laughing stock . . .'

Frost turned the volume down and let the superintendent rant away unheard. He couldn't think of any way he could get out of this foul-up. His head turned as Gilmore emerged from the crypt.

'Preliminary report from the pathologist. The body wasn't dumped there tonight. It's been in the crypt for at least six or seven weeks.'

Six or seven weeks? Frost frowned as he worried this through. So the kid must have been hidden there almost immediately after she was killed. So it *was* vandals Turner saw running away. They had nothing to do with the girl. The grin returned to his face as he turned up the volume of the radio where Mullett was still in full flow.

'. . . If you had been doing your damn job you'd have caught the murderer in the act of dumping the damn body . . .'

'Hold on, Super,' Frost interrupted. 'How could I have caught him in the act of dumping the damn body tonight when it's been stinking the flaming vault out for eight weeks?'

So knocked off balance was Mullett by Frost's explanation that he completely forgot that his orders had been disobeyed and ended up by apologizing. 'Forgive me if I was too hasty, Inspector . . . the strain of work, you know.'

'You're forgiven, Super,' said Frost grandly.

'The family will have to be informed, of course.'

'It's half-past midnight,' said Frost. 'I was thinking of leaving it until the morning.'

But Mullett was adamant. 'The press have already got hold of the story. The family mustn't learn of it through the media.'

Frost groaned. Mullett was right, of course. 'Right, sir. We're on our way.'

The Bartlett house was in darkness, but a low-wattage light burnt hopefully in the porch.

Even as they walked up the drive to the front door, Frost kept hoping the girl's parents would be out, preferably staying with friends in some other division so that someone else would have the pleasure of breaking the news. But an upstairs light clicked on to dash his hopes. Sleeping fitfully, the Bartletts must have been awakened by the slam of the car door.

It was the mother who opened the door, a dressing gown over her nightdress. Ignoring Frost, she looked over his shoulder to Gilmore, the young man she had seen earlier. 'It's about Paula, isn't it?'

His face grim, Gilmore nodded.

'You've found her? I knew you would. I told you you'd find her. Thank God!' She was weeping with happiness.

Flaming hell! thought Frost. This is an unmitigated balls-up. That bleeding clairvoyant, I could tear his dick out by the roots.

Behind the woman, her husband, a sad-looking man, read the message in Frost's expression, a message his wife was refusing to see. He moved forward and put his arm around her. She looked at him puzzled, not understanding why he wasn't rejoicing with her . . . and then she looked at Frost again. And then she knew.

'Do you think we might come in?' asked Frost.

They were in Paula's bedroom where everything had been left exactly as it was on the day she went missing. The bed was made, blue pyjamas folded neatly on the pillow and the alarm clock, wound each day ready for her return, set to ring at 6.45 so she wouldn't be late for her paper round. From downstairs the heart-tearing wail of Mrs Bartlett, her grief for her daughter sounding uncannily like that of the mother of the fifteen-year-old who had killed herself. It reminded Frost that they had to visit the mortuary to see the marks on Susan Bicknell's body. He felt in his inside pocket for something to jot a reminder down on and felt an unfamiliar wad of papers. His car expenses. Something else he had forgotten about. How the hell was he going to find the time to get the proper copies made that bloody County were demanding? He stuffed them back in his pocket and forgot about them again.

'What are we doing here?' asked Gilmore.

'I don't know,' said Frost wearily. 'I just wanted to have a think away from all the bloody crying.' He looked around the room. Everything plain and simple, just like the dead girl. No posters, no pop records. On the bedside cabinet was a framed photograph of her mother and father. A small bookcase held some children's books, her school textbooks, a Collins Concise Encyclopedia and a Pocket Oxford Dictionary. Inside the bedside cabinet, standing on its end, was a black and green Adidas nylon holdall. He unzipped it and looked inside. Some gym clothes, a track suit and a couple of exercise books. He stuffed it back again. On the floor by the cabinet was a wastepaper bin. The bin contained a crumpled Milky Way wrapper and a small cardboard carton that had once held a lipstick.

'You're right, son,' he said. 'We're wasting our bloody time here.'

He opened the door and they went downstairs.

The crying went on and on.

They let themselves out.

Monday night shift (2)

Sergeant Wells stared glumly at the cold scummy tea left in the cup, palmed two aspirins into his mouth and flushed them down in a shuddering swallow. It was just a headache. He envied those lucky devils who had gone down with the flu virus and were tucked up in their nice warm beds, leaving mugs like him to do the extra duties they were being paid for. He had been on duty since half-past nine, no-one to help him, the heating on the blink, no canteen and Mullett demanding cups of tea or coffee every five minutes.

'Two teas and a fairy cake, please, Sergeant.'

Wells jerked two fingers up at Jack Frost who came bouncing in with that aftershaved ponce, Gilmore.

Frost ambled over and pulled out his cigarettes. 'Bleeding cold in here, Bill. It was warmer down the crypt.'

'Only the people who matter get heat. It's like St Tropez in Mullett's office. And he wants to see you.'

'He can't get enough of me,' said Frost, trotting off to the inner sanctum.

'Gilmore!' Wells called as the detective sergeant headed for the office. 'Your wife phoned about two hours ago. Wanted to know when you were coming home.'

'Thanks,' said Gilmore. 'If she phones again . . .'

'If she phones again,' cut in Wells, '*you* talk to her. I'm off in fifteen minutes.' In any case, he wasn't acting as messenger boy for a lousy jumped-up ex-detective constable.

It wasn't cold in Mullett's office. The 3-kilowatt heater purred happily, and Frost had to fight to keep awake in the hot room as he gave the Divisional Commander a brief update, sparing none of the details.

'Burnt with a blow-lamp?' gasped the shocked Mullett. 'That's depraved . . . You kept it from the parents?'

'Yes,' said Frost. 'And I want it kept from the press – that and the fact she was wearing shoes.' There'd be the usual spate of nutters coming up with false confessions based on details they'd read in the papers.

'And the pathologist is quite certain the body wasn't placed in that crypt tonight?' asked Mullett, reluctant to let the inspector off the hook.

'The poor little cow was dumped weeks ago . . . that's why she's stinking to high heaven now.'

Mullet winced and moved his chair back slightly. Frost's description of the advanced state of decomposition had been so graphic, he was sure he could smell it. Or perhaps the stench was clinging to that dirty old mac Frost insisted on wearing. Frost took a cigarette end from behind his ear and pushed it into his mouth. He struck a match on his fingernail. Mullett sighed deeply. This case would get extensive press and TV coverage. He daren't risk exposing this slovenly, foul-mouthed lout to the media as typical of the Denton constabulary.

He cleared his throat. 'I have decided to take full executive control of this case, Inspector.'

The lighted match paused an inch from the end of the cigarette. 'Executive control?'

'Yes. You will be responsible for the day-to-day routine, but under my direct control. Do you understand?'

I do all the work and get the bollockings when things go wrong, and you take all the credit when they go right, thought Frost grimly. 'Yes, I understand,' he said aloud.

'I've promised the Chief Constable an early result. This must be our number one priority. What do you need to achieve an early result?'

'A lot of bloody luck and some more men.'

'We can't have any more. Normal schedules will have to go by the board. Everyone will have to follow my lead – work that little bit harder, push themselves to the limit.' He yawned and glanced at his watch. Time he was back home and in bed. 'Everyone must pitch in. We're all one big team.' He gleamed white teeth at Frost in a crocodile smile as he stood up and slipped on his overcoat.

The phone rang. Mullett answered it and passed it over to Frost. The pathologist. He had a heavy schedule for the morning, so he was doing the post-mortem on the newspaper girl in an hour's time.

'I'll be there,' Frost said, yawning.

'Good,' nodded Mullett, moving to the door. 'Well, I must try and snatch a few hours' sleep so I can be fresh for the morning. Report to me tomorrow at nine and we'll go over our plan of campaign.' He clicked off the heater and, when Frost had left, turned out the light and locked the door.

As he passed through the lobby he saw Wells moodily staring at the clock. The wretched man was always clock-watching. He would have a word with him about it in the morning. He responded with a curt nod as the sergeant called good night to him.

Miserable sod, thought Wells. It was 2.59 a.m. Sergeant Johnnie Johnson, who had the morning shift, was coming in three hours early to relieve him. Usually Johnnie was early, arriving a good five minutes before the start of the shift, but Wells wasn't worrying yet. He began stuffing away his pens and notepads in the drawer to leave a clean desk for his relief. The phone gave a timorous, half-hearted ring. 'Denton Police, Sergeant Wells speaking.'

'Hello, Bill. It's Doreen.'

The cold tea curdled in his stomach. Doreen. Johnnie Johnson's wife. What the hell did she want at this time of the morning?

'It's John, I'm afraid, Bill. We've had to have the doctor in.'

That bloody hypochondriac! A headache and he thinks he's got a brain tumour. 'Oh dear, Doreen. Nothing serious, I hope?'

'The doctor thinks it's this flu virus that's going around.'

One sniffle and the bastard's down with flu . . . typical. 'Terribly sorry to hear that, Doreen.'

'. . . so he won't be able to come in to work tonight, I'm afraid.'

'Of course not. We wouldn't expect him to. You tell him to stay away until he is really fit.' He slammed the phone down. 'Skiving bastard!' Leaving the lobby unattended, he dashed off to Jack Frost's office to have a moan.

Gilmore was on the phone as the sergeant came in. He had rung Liz, hoping there wouldn't be an answer, but she was still awake, staring at the clock and complaining about being left on her own for most of the day and half the bloody night. It was three o'clock, and he was overdue for a meal break. He told her he was on his way and she said she'd rustle up a quick meal for him. Not that he felt like eating at this time of the morning, but he didn't want another row. He was shrugging on his overcoat when Frost bowled in and immediately Wells started his moaning.

'It's not on, Jack. I was supposed to be relieved. I've already done a double-bloody-shift. I'm not fit myself, but I stagger in. And what thanks do I get?'

'Bugger all,' said Frost cheerfully, not really listening. 'You can't slope off yet, Gilmore,' he called. 'Post-mortem on the girl in a hour.'

'In an hour?' croaked Gilmore, dropping into his chair with a crash. He reached for the phone to dial Liz before she started cooking.

'And Mullett doesn't give a damn,' continued Wells.

Frost moved some files from his chair to the floor and sat down. 'His door, like his bowels, is always open, Sergeant.'

'Sod Mullett!' snorted Wells.

'The lobby phone's ringing,' said Gilmore, trying to concentrate on what Liz was saying.

'And sod the phone,' snarled Wells, stamping back to the lobby.

Frost had a half-hearted forage through his in-tray which was filled to overflowing, but was thankfully interrupted by a phone call from Forensic. A preliminary report on the black plastic sheeting used to wrap Paula Bartlett's body. It was made up of black plastic dustbin sacks, the standard Denton Council issue for refuse collection, of which more than two million had been issued to households over the past twelve months. Further tests were under way.

'Thanks a lot,' said Frost, gloomily. 'That's narrowed it down to the whole of bleeding Denton.'

'Actually it doesn't,' said Forensic. 'Nearly all the councils in this part of England use an identical sack.'

'Just when I thought it was going to be easy,' Frost said, hanging up. 'I'll be in the Murder Incident Room,' he yelled to Gilmore who was doing a lot of listening on the phone and didn't appear to be saying much.

Two people only in the Murder Incident Room. DC Burton, a phone pressed tightly to his ear, his pen scribbling furiously, and WPC Jean Knight, a redhead in her mid-twenties who was waiting for the computer to finish a print-out.

'Couple of odds and ends from Forensic,' called Burton, waving his sheet of paper.

Frost ambled over and poked a cigarette into Burton's mouth, then offered the pack to the redhead who declined with a smile. 'I know all about the dustbin sacks, son. I'm applying for two million search warrants.'

Burton grinned. 'We can do a bit better than that, sir. Firstly, the padlock. Forensic reckon those screws were prised out at least twice before within the past couple of months and then hammered back.'

Frost's cigarette drooped as his mouth fell open. 'Twice before?'

'Yes, sir. Someone could have got in on two or more different occasions, or it could even have been twice on the same day.'

'Forensic always seem to think they're being bloody helpful,' said Frost. 'Now I'm more mystified than ever.' He looked up as Gilmore came in. 'Did you hear that, son? The padlock to the crypt had been forced at least twice.'

'Oh?' said Gilmore, not really taking it in. His ear was still sore from the phone and his mind was full of Liz's moans and complaints.

'There's more,' announced Burton. 'Forensic found a footprint.'

'Ah,' said Frost. 'So we're looking for a one-legged man.'

'It wasn't exactly a footprint,' continued Burton patiently. 'It was more a clump of mud that had fallen from the sole of a shoe.'

'Where did they find it?' asked Gilmore, stifling a yawn.

'Top step, just inside the crypt door. Forensic reckon it was some eight weeks old which makes it round about the time the body was dumped.'

'How the hell can they tell it's eight weeks old?' asked Gilmore.

'Don't ask!' pleaded Frost. 'Just accept it. You'll be none the wiser if they explain. OK, Burton. We've got a bit of mud. How does that help?'

Burton pulled his notes towards him. 'There were traces of copper filings and lead solder in the mud.'

Frost worried away at his scar with a nicotine-stained finger. 'Copper filings and solder?' If it had any significance, he couldn't see it.

'A plumber!' called WPC Jean Knight from the computer. 'They put central heating in my flat last week. They were forever sawing up lengths of copper tubing.'

'A homicidal plumber!' said Frost doubtfully. He ambled across to the shelf of telephone directories and pulled out the Yellow Pages for Denton and district. There were some fifteen pages of plumbers – nearly three hundred firms. 'At least it's less than two million,' he observed.

'There'll be more names under "Central Heating",' Burton reminded him.

There were nearly two hundred entries under 'Central Heating', although some of these were also entered under 'Plumbers'.

'The gas company does central heating,' added Jean Knight. 'They'd employ plumbers as well.'

'I'm losing interest already,' said Frost.

'It might not be a plumber at all,' added Gilmore. 'It could be someone, like Jean, who's had central heating installed and that's how the filings and solder got on their shoes.'

'It might be a man with a length of copper tubing soldered on the end of his dick who'd popped into the crypt for a Jimmy Riddle,' said Frost unhelpfully. Then he stopped dead and a smile crept over his face. 'Or it might be a lot easier than we think.' Excitedly he expounded his theory, the cigarette in his mouth waggling as he spoke. 'We're not looking for any old plumber. Our killer didn't stagger into the cemetery with a gift-wrapped body just on the off-chance he'd find somewhere to hide it. He knew the crypt was there and he knew he could get into it. Now I've lived in Denton most of my life and I never knew we had a Victorian crypt in the churchyard . . . did any of you?'

Burton and the WPC shook their heads. 'I visit cemeteries as infrequently as possible,' said Burton.

'Me too,' said Frost. 'I only go in one if I can't find anywhere else to have a pee. But our plumber knew where to find it and knew he could get in it.' He jabbed a finger at Gilmore. 'How?'

Gilmore shook his head. He had no idea.

'Right, son, let me mark your card. What was alongside the crypt, by the broken railings?'

'A stand-pipe and a tap,' said Gilmore, beginning to see what the old fool was getting at.

'Exactly, sergeant. And they looked fairly new. So who would have installed them?'

'A plumber,' said Gilmore, 'and he'd know how to get in through the broken railings.'

'And he'd know how to use a blow-lamp,' added Burton.

Frost chucked an empty cigarette packet into the air and headed it against the wall. 'Another case solved. Get in touch with the vicar, find out who did the work, then bring him in for routine questioning and beating up.' He yawned and looked at his watch. Nearly an hour to kill before the post-mortem. He was about to suggest sending out for some Chinese takeaway when the phone rang. Control for the inspector. Another burglary at a senior citizen's home – old lady of eighty-one.

'Damn!' muttered Frost. He could have done without this tonight.

'There's worse to come,' said Control. 'The intruder beat her up. She's not expected to live.'

Clarendon Street. Lights blinked out from quite a few of the houses where the occupants had been wakened by the police activity. Outside number 11 was an empty area car, its radio droning and no-one to listen, and behind that, an ambulance, engine running, rear doors open. As Gilmore parked the Cortina on the opposite side of the street, two ambulance men carrying a stretcher emerged from the house, closely followed by a uniformed constable. By the time they crossed the road the ambulance was speeding on its way to the hospital.

'Anyone at home?' yelled Frost down the passage.

A door at the head of the stairs opened. 'Up here, Inspector.' Tubby Detective Sergeant Arthur Hanlon beckoned them in.

A bedroom, its bed askew in the middle of the floor, the sash window open and Roberts, the Scene of Crime Officer, bending, engrossed in dusting the bottom edge of the frame for fingerprints. There were fragments of a smashed blue and white vase on the floor and the top centre dressing table drawer gaped open, its riffled contents spewing out.

By the dressing table a hooked-nosed woman in her mid-forties wearing a quilted dressing gown was talking earnestly to PC Jordan.

The scene was familiar. This burglar seldom varied his technique. A quick in and out job. Straight for the dressing table to grab indiscriminately whatever jewellery was instantly available, then, starting with the top centre drawer, he looked for the 'cleverly hidden' cache of notes which couldn't be trusted to the bank and which were nearly always at the back of the top centre drawer. Then out again, the whole operation lasting a maximum of five minutes. A familiar scene, but this time with a difference. There was blood everywhere, on the floor, on the bedding and on the curtains.

'How's the old girl?' asked Frost.

'Not good,' said Hanlon, honking loudly into a handkerchief and dabbing a sore-looking nose. 'Stab wounds and a possible fractured skull. The ambulance men don't think she'll regain consciousness.'

'Damn,' muttered Frost, but his eyes were looking over Hanlon's shoulder at the SOC man, who was offering an irresistible target. 'Excuse me a moment.' Frost tiptoed over and accurately jabbed a nicotined finger at the seam of the tight trousers. 'How's that for centre?' he roared.

Roberts shot up, hitting his head on the window sill. He spun round angrily, only to grin when he saw Frost. 'It's you, Inspector. I might have guessed.'

Gilmore raised his eyes to the ceiling in exasperation. A potential murder investigation and the fool was indulging in schoolboy games. Well, someone had to act responsibly. 'What happened?' he asked Hanlon.

'The victim is Alice Ryder, a widow aged eighty-one. She occupies the top half of the house, a Mr and Mrs Francis live downstairs. Mr Francis is on night work – that's the wife over there.' Hanlon nodded towards the woman with Jordan. 'She found the old lady.' Sensing their eyes on her, the woman came over, anxious to relate her part in the drama.

'I woke up about quarter-past three to go to the toilet and I noticed her light was still on. I was worried, so I went up to check. Her telly was going full blast and her bedroom door was open. I looked in . . .' She paused, shuddering at the recollection. 'There she was, on the floor and blood everywhere. I couldn't get to the phone quick enough. She was terrified of anyone breaking in . . . she must have had a premonition.' She wrapped her dressing gown tighter around her. It was cold in the room with the window open. 'That's all I can tell you.'

'You didn't see who it was who did it?' asked Gilmore.

She gave him a thin smile. 'I'd have mentioned it if I had – just in case it was important.'

'Sarcastic cow!' seethed Gilmore when she had gone.

'I thought she was quite nice,' observed Hanlon, who was irritated at the way the new bloke kept trying to take charge.

'I didn't like her nose,' said Frost, 'or her dressing gown.' He nodded to the SOC officer. 'Surprise me. Tell me that this time he left fingerprints.'

Roberts shook his head. 'He wore gloves, as always.'

'Consistent bastard!' snorted Frost. 'All right, Ted, paint me a word picture. Let's have a reconstruction.'

'Right,' said Roberts. 'The old lady was in the front room watching the telly. Our intruder gets in through the bedroom window, but this time he was unlucky. She'd stuck that blue and white vase on the window ledge and as he clambered in, he knocked it over and it fell to the floor. The old lady heard it, came charging in to see what it was, so he went for her with this . . .' Roberts clicked open his 'evidence case' and pulled out a sealed, transparent polythene bag. Inside the bag was a black-handled kitchen knife, its blood-smeared blade honed to razor sharpness. 'It was on the floor, by the bed.'

'You're saying he had this knife in his hand when the old girl came charging in?' When Roberts nodded, Frost shook his head. 'I can't buy that, Ted. If I was climbing through windows I wouldn't want a lethal thing like that in my hand . . . I could cut my dick off.'

'He wouldn't carry it in his hand when he was climbing. He'd have it in a tool bag.'

'All right,' said Frost. 'I'll pretend to accept that for the moment. Then what happened?'

'He stabs her, but she puts up a fight. He drops the knife in the struggle, punches her repeatedly in the face then finishes her off by smashing her skull in with a cosh or something.'

Frost's finger prodded away at the scar on his cheek as he worried this over. 'I can't believe it's the same bloke who did all the others. He's never resorted to violence before.'

'He hasn't been disturbed before,' offered Hanlon. 'His other victims were damn lucky they never heard anything.' He sniffed and dabbed his nose. 'I think I've got the flu.'

'No, you haven't,' said Frost firmly. 'We're too busy. Do we know what's been taken?'

Jordan stepped forward. 'Same as all the others. Bits and pieces of of jewellery – Mrs Francis has given me a description – and money. Mrs Francis doesn't know how much, but says the old lady always kept a fair amount of cash by her – a couple of hundred at least.'

'I want this bastard,' said Frost. 'People who kill for a couple of hundred lousy quid are dangerous.' He looked at the bed, knocked askew with splodges of blood all over the pillows and sheets. Someone must have heard or seen something. 'Get as many men as you want from Bill Wells and start knocking on doors.'

'I've already asked. He says he can't spare anyone until the next shift.'

'He's bloody well going to have to. We're not going to wait for her to die, Arthur, she might sod us about and linger. We're going to anticipate. This is a murder enquiry as of now. I want a team knocking on doors, I want Forensic, I want someone by the old girl's bedside night and day in case she can give us a description. If I've forgotten anything, I want that as well.'

While Hanlon radioed the station, he ambled over to the open window and looked out on to a small, rain-puddled yard. Below him was the dustbin used by the man to gain entrance. It reminded him of the yard in Jubilee Terrace and the mummified corpse. What a bloody night this had turned out to be. First the mummy, then Paula Bartlett . . . Paula . . . Flaming heck! The autopsy! He daren't be late for that. He was in enough trouble with the pathologist as it was.

He checked his watch. Ten to four. They could just do it if they ignored fiddling details like adverse traffic lights. 'I've got to leave you to it, Arthur. Just solve the case and tie it all up before the end of the shift.' He dashed across to the door. 'Come on, Gilmore. We've got an autopsy to watch and ten minutes to get there.'

At four o'clock on a cold, dark, rainy morning, the mortuary lights gleamed across the driveway to the hospital and bounced off the black, supercilious shape of the pathologist's Rolls Royce. Frost's mud-coated Cortina shuffled in and parked alongside. 'Don't forget . . . ours is the one on the left,' he reminded Gilmore.

The night porter, a gangling twenty-year-old with an embryonic moustache, snatched a cigarette from his mouth and dropped it to the floor as the two detectives walked in. He thought it was that toffee-nosed pathologist who had already rebuked him for smoking on duty.

'Midnight matinée,' said Frost, flashing his warrant card. 'Paula Bartlett.'

'We should get paid double for handling bodies in that condition,' complained the porter, leading them through to the autopsy room which was in darkness apart from the end table where the overhead lights poured down on a mass of decomposing and charred flesh that was once a fifteen-year-old schoolgirl. 'Dockers get dirty money, so should we.' He opened a side door and called, 'Police are here, doctor.'

'Overture and beginners, doc,' yelled Frost, perching

himself on a stool for a good view. Gilmore, not so eager, moved back out of the splash of light.

The pathologist, his faithful secretary in tow, entered, scowling. He found nothing about his job amusing. The smile would be wiped off Frost's face when he read a copy of the report he was sending to his Divisional Commander complaining that the inspector had allowed every Tom, Dick and Harry to maul the body before he had had a chance to see it.

'Do you reckon he sleeps with her?' whispered Frost to Gilmore as the secretary adjusted the lights over the end autopsy table to her master's satisfaction. 'It must be off-putting, banging away at someone, knowing you're shaking up her stomach contents and her internal organs.'

Gilmore pressed further back into the blackness, not wanting to get involved in Frost's coarse asides.

While the porter turned on the extractor fan above the autopsy table, the pathologist allowed his secretary to help him on with his green gown and heavy plastic apron. He fiddled with a control under the perforated table top and as water gurgled and trickled, he pulled on a pair of rubber gloves and flexed his fingers. He was ready.

First, he carefully examined the body from top to bottom, without touching any part of it. 'Body of a female in advanced state of decomposition,' he intoned. Miss Grey's pencil zipped across the page of her notebook. He eased open the mouth with a spatula and shone a small torch inside. 'Age about . . .'

'We know how old she is, doc,' Frost told him. 'I even know her birthday. What I don't know for sure is how she died.'

The pathologist's eyes flashed. 'Don't interrupt!'

'Sorry, doc,' said Frost, quite unabashed, 'but we're

operating at half-strength and I've got lots to do. Could you just give me the headlines? I'll read all the boring bits in your report.'

'I don't cut corners. Aged around fifteen.' He snapped his fingers and demanded: 'Dental records!' Miss Grey passed him across a small typed card with marked diagrams. He studied it then handed it back. His spatula clicked on the teeth checking extractions and fillings. 'From the dental record I can identify the body as that of Paula Bartlett, aged fifteen years and two months. Some traces of blood in her mouth.' He wiped the mouth with a swab and dropped it into a container held out by his secretary.

'She anticipates his every move,' Frost whispered to Gilmore. 'I bet he doesn't have to tell her when to thrust or withdraw.'

Gilmore couldn't even pretend to smile.

Frost fidgeted with impatience as the pathologist plodded on, the swollen neck now receiving his painstaking scrutiny, fingers carefully prodding and probing.

'Dr Maltby said death was due to manual strangulation,' prompted Frost. Why was this man so bloody slow?

'If I was one of Dr Maltby's patients,' murmured the pathologist, his nose almost touching the neck, 'I'd insist on a second opinion on everything he told me.' To his secretary he said, 'Signs of manual pressure applied to neck.'

'Ha!' exclaimed Frost. 'So that's what killed her.'

'I'll tell you what killed her when I have completed the autopsy,' said Drysdale, crushingly. 'For all I know, there are eight bullet wounds in the stomach. Just keep quiet.'

Frost gave his watch a pointed stare, sighed deeply then went outside for a smoke. Gilmore was happy to join him. Even with the extractor fan working full blast, the atmosphere in the post-mortem room was foul and would worsen when Drysdale used the scalpel to open the body up.

The porter brought them two mugs of tea and gratefully accepted a cigarette from the inspector. Through the swing doors they could see the autopsy proceeding. A bone saw screamed and Gilmore turned his eyes away, his teeth gritted against the noise.

'Perhaps we could browse while we wait,' requested Frost. 'Have you got a Susan Bicknell in stock?'

The porter flipped open his ledger and ran a nicotine-stained finger down the entries. 'Suicide? Came in this afternoon? This way.'

They followed him to the refrigerated section. On a small side table near the door was a polythene bag containing a folded Mickey Mouse nightdress, a black and gold kimono and, separately wrapped, a Snoopy watch. Snoopy's paws pointed to 4.29. 'Her things,' announced the porter laconically, jerking his thumb.

He stopped in front of one of the bank of metal drawers, checked the name tag and pulled it open. Sliding on rollers, a sheeted body silently emerged. When the sheet was removed the girl was seen to be naked. A red label tied to her big toe seemed an obscene addition as if some joker had put it there for a laugh. Needle marks were clearly visible on her left arm.

The porter folded the sheet and stared down in disapproval. 'I hate seeing them so bloody young.'

'Give my colleague a hand to turn her over,' requested Frost.

Gilmore hesitated, then steeled himself and complied. He wasn't prepared for the hard coldness of the flesh and nearly let her fall back. The porter gave him a scornful look. 'She can't hurt you. She's dead. Bloody hell . . . look at that!'

Now she was turned, they could see it. All across her buttocks, fading but still visible, deep, criss-cross lines of red weals and smudges of pale yellow bruises. They were the marks left by a thrashing, a vicious thrashing, from a whip or a cane. At least twelve weals could be counted. Frost winced. 'It hurts just to look at it. Who the hell could have done this?'

'That bloody stepfather,' snapped Gilmore. 'I'd like to meet him on a dark night.'

A firm shake of the head. Frost couldn't buy that. 'She was fifteen years old, for Pete's sake. She'd never submit to that.'

A sniff from the porter who offered his worldly-wise opinion. 'I reckon she was kinky. Perhaps she enjoyed being beaten.'

'Maybe, but not as hard as this. She'd have been yelling blue murder after the first cut . . . and yet she took more than twelve of them.'

'She could have been into bondage as well,' offered Gilmore. 'Strapped down while it was done to her. Some women like that.'

Frost's eyebrows shot up. 'Blimey, Gilmore, what sort of women do you go out with? I never have such luck. I only have to blow in their ear-hole and they think I'm a pervert.'

'When you've quite finished your voyeurism . . .' The pathologist glowered disapproval, his gown stained and carrying the taint of the grave into the clean coldness of the refrigerated section.

Back to the autopsy table where the body had been crudely stitched and the secretary was writing out neat labels for jars of removed organs. 'She was trussed up and put inside the plastic sack within three or four hours of being killed,' said Drysdale watching Gilmore note this information down. 'Cause of death manual strangulation.'

'That's what Dr Maltby said,' beamed Frost.

Ignoring him, Drysdale plunged on. 'The killer's two hands went round her throat like this.' Obligingly, his secretary allowed herself to be used for a demonstration and stood still as he grabbed her throat, sinking his thumbs deep into her larynx. 'The girl would have struggled desperately, fighting for her life. I imagine she grabbed his wrists, trying to break his grip but her killer, his hands still tight round her throat, swung her from side to side and smashed her head against a wall, probably hard enough to make her lose consciousness.' He swung Miss Grey from side to side as illustration, but spared her the banging of the head. She looked disappointed as he released his grip, but carried on labelling jars of human offal.

Indicating blood-matted hair and a discoloured area on the scalp Drysdale invited them to inspect the damage.

'If she struggled, doc,' asked Frost, 'wouldn't she have marked him . . . scratched him . . . gouged out chunks of flesh?'

A tight smile. 'If you're hoping for pieces of telltale flesh under her fingernails, I must disappoint you, Inspector.' He lifted the girl's misshapen right hand and displayed the fingernails. They were bitten down to the quick.

'Damn,' said Frost.

Carefully Drysdale lowered the hand to its original position. 'Clear evidence of sexual intercourse just before she died.'

Frost nodded glumly. He had expected this. 'Rape?'

'I think so,' replied the pathologist blandly.

'You *think* so?' echoed Gilmore, incredulously. 'You only *think* so .

'There is evidence of bruising that could suggest intercourse took place against her will . . .'

'Then she was raped,' cried Gilmore.

'If I might be allowed to continue,' grated Drysdale. 'The girl was a virgin. She could have submitted willingly, but have been tensed instead of relaxed. This might account for the bruising. Equally, she could have been raped. There is no magic way of knowing at this stage.'

'If she submitted willingly, doc,' said Frost, 'there would have been no real need to have wrung her neck afterwards.'

'That', snapped Drysdale, 'is in your province, Inspector Frost, not mine. I give the medical facts. It's up to you to speculate.'

Frost nodded ruefully. 'Then give me some facts on the way the bastard burnt her so I can speculate how to catch the sod.'

'I was coming to that,' said Drysdale testily. 'As you can see, the genital area is badly charred. In my opinion this occurred very soon after death, within an hour, say.'

'Dr Maltby thought it could have been done with a blow-lamp.'

Drysdale frowned. 'For once, Dr Maltby might have been right. To do that sort of damage you'd need something like a blowtorch.'

'But why would anyone do it, doc? Is it a new kind of sexual perversion?'

'I've come across something like this once before. A murdered rape victim, a thirty-eight-year-old prostitute. She was found in some bushes near a railway embankment. The lower part of the body was badly burnt where her killer had doused paraffin over her and set it alight.

It seems he had heard about genetic fingerprinting. You've probably read about it.'

'No,' said Frost. 'I only read comics and dirty books.'

'There's a newly developed technique,' lectured Drysdale, 'that allows us to determine an individual's genetic fingerprint from traces of body fluid – semen, say.'

Frost's mouth dropped open. 'You mean a dick print instead of a fingerprint?'

The pathologist winced. 'I wouldn't put it as crudely as that, Inspector, but yes, by DNA testing we can positively identify the donor of a semen sample.'

'So if I produced a suspect . . .' began Frost, hoping Burton had traced the plumber.

'If you produced a suspect, we could either positively incriminate him, or positively eliminate him, but he would have to supply us with a blood sample for comparison.'

'I'll get a blood sample for you,' said Frost. 'And if he won't give us one voluntarily, I'm sure we can arrange for him to fall down the station stairs.'

The pathologist's smile wavered. Like many people, he never knew when Frost was being serious or when he was joking. 'Unfortunately, Inspector, it wouldn't work with this poor girl. Even without the burning, the advanced stage of decomposition of the body precludes any possibility of carrying out the test.'

'This bastard's having all the luck,' moaned Frost. 'Anything else, doc?'

Drysdale made a mental note to include in his complaint to the Divisional Commander his displeasure at the way Frost chose to address him. 'Yes.' He held out his hand and clicked his fingers. Miss Grey gave him a large sealed jar full of squishy, lumpy brown unpleasantness dotted with green. 'The stomach contents. She hadn't had time to digest her last meal before she died.'

Frost screwed his face and turned his head. 'Tell me what it is, doc, so I can make a point of not ordering it.'

'Something with chips and peas. You'll get a detailed analysis some time tomorrow. My report will be on your desk by noon.'

'Do you feel like eating, son?' asked Frost as they climbed back into the car. 'Something with chips and peas?'

'No,' said Gilmore. All he felt like doing was going to bed and sleeping the clock round.

Five o'clock. Cold, raining steadily and still dark.

Tuesday morning shift (1)

They got back to the station at 5.15. A less than happy Sergeant Bill Wells was still on duty wearing his greatcoat against the cold of the unheated lobby.

'Still here?' asked Frost.

'Yes, still bloody here. But I'm going home at six on the dot whether anyone relieves me or not. I've had it up to here.' His hand indicated a point well above his head. He spun round to Gilmore. 'And I've got enough to do without keeping on answering calls from your bloody wife demanding to know when you're coming home.'

'When did she phone?' Gilmore asked.

'Do you mean the first time, the second or the third? The last one was ten minutes ago.'

Gilmore hurried off to the office to use the phone and Wells accepted a cigarette from Frost. 'She sounded well sozzled, Jack,' he confided. 'You could smell the gin over the phone.'

'They've not been married long,' said Frost. 'She's suffering from night starvation.'

'Tough!' grunted Wells, pulling his phone log over. 'Couple of messages for you. Jill Knight phoned from the hospital. The old lady is still in intensive care. Doubtful if she'll regain consciousness. And Arthur Hanlon says one of the neighbours spotted a blue van parked at the back of Clarendon Street just before midnight.'

'Clues are pouring in thick and fast,' said Frost, trotting off down the corridor.

In the office Gilmore was making apologetic noises down the phone. 'I know, love . . . I'm sorry. What time will I be back?' He clapped his hand over the mouthpiece and looked enquiringly at Frost.

'Let's pack it in now,' said Frost. 'Grab a few hours' sleep and be back about twelve.'

Gilmore nodded his thanks and assured Liz, cross his heart, he'd be with her in fifteen minutes.

On the way out Frost pushed open the door to the Murder Incident Room. Burton was slumped by the phone, half asleep. Frost gave him a shake. 'Come on, son. I'll take you home.'

Burton smothered a yawn. 'I've located the firm that did the work at the cemetery, but I won't be able to get the plumber's name and address until their offices open at nine.'

'That's what I want,' mused Frost. 'A nine to five job, an expense account with no limit and a sexy secretary with no knickers.' He sighed at the impossibility of his dream. 'Leave a note for your relief to follow it through. Let's go home.'

* * *

The Cortina was juddering down Catherine Street, Gilmore fighting sleep at the wheel, Frost slumped with his eyes half closed at his side and Burton yawning in the back seat. They passed a row of shops; one, a newsagent's, had its lights gleaming. Burton in the back seat stirred and peered through the car window. 'That's where Paula Bartlett worked.'

'Pull up,' yelled Frost. Gilmore steered the car into the kerb. The name over the shop read *G. F. Rickman, Newsagent.* 'Let's chat him up,' said Frost. With a searing scowl at Burton for not keeping his big mouth shut, Gilmore clambered out after him.

George Rickman, plump and balding, was deeply engrossed in a study of the Page Three nude in *The Sun.* On the floor in front of the counter, stacked in neat piles, were the newspapers he had sorted and marked ready for the kids to take out on their rounds. The shop bell tinkled to announce a customer, old Harry Edwards from round the corner for his *Daily Mirror* and some fifty pence pieces for the gas. While he was serving Harry, the bell sounded again and two men he hadn't seen before came in: one, in his early twenties, looking tired and irritable; the other, older, wearing a crumpled mac. They hovered furtively by the door, obviously waiting for the shop to empty before they approached. Rickman smirked to himself. Dirty sods. He knew what they were after.

Harry shuffled out and the two men sidled across. Warning them to wait with a movement of his hand, Rickman darted over to the shop door and squinted through the glass to make sure no-one else was coming, then lowered his voice. 'Who sent you – Les?'

'Yes,' replied Frost, equally conspiratorial, wondering what the hell this was all about.

'You can't be too careful,' said Rickman, unlocking a door behind the counter. He ushered them through. 'Some of this stuff's dynamite.' He clicked on the light. The room was full of shelved books and magazines with lurid covers of naked, sweating, entwined men and women. In boxes on a table were stacks of soft porn videos.

'Les said you had something special,' suggested Frost, signalling to Gilmore, who was fumbling for his warrant card, to hold his horses.

Rickman leered and tapped the side of his nose knowingly. He unlocked a cupboard. More videos, this time in plain white boxes with typed labels.

'There's everything here,' he said proudly. 'All tastes catered for – men with men, women with women, with kids, animals . . . any permutation you want. Fifty quid a time – return it undamaged and I'll allow you twenty-five quid off your next purchase.'

'I don't know that I've got that much money on me,' said Frost, reaching for his inside pocket.

'I take Access . . . American Express . . . any card you like.'

'What about this one?' asked Frost.

Rickman stared at a warrant card. His jaw dropped. 'Shit!' he said.

A ting from the shop bell and a boy's voice called, 'Papers ready, Mr Rickman?'

'By the counter. Take them and go.' He waited until the bell signalled the boy's departure. 'Look, officer. I'm sure we can come to some understanding.' He brought out his wallet and pulled out two £50 notes.

'Give the gentleman a receipt for a £100 bribe,' said Frost, holding out his hand for the money. 'I'll read you the numbers.'

Hastily, Rickman stuffed the banknotes in his pocket. 'You misunderstand me, Inspector.'

'I hope I do,' replied Frost. 'You're in enough bloody trouble as it is.' He read some of the labels on the videos and shuddered. They were very explicit.

Rickman fumbled for a handkerchief and dabbed sweat from his face. 'I don't usually indulge in this sort of stuff. Harmless soft porn, yes, but not the hard stuff. I met this bloke in a pub . . .'

Frost cut him short. 'Save your fairy tales for the officer down the station.' He sent Gilmore to the car to radio for someone to collect Rickman and the books and videos.

'You try and do people a good turn and this happens,' moaned Rickman. 'What bastard shopped me?'

'We've been watching this shop for months,' lied Frost. He had taken an instant dislike to the podgy newsagent. Some of the videos involved schoolgirls. He wondered if Paula Bartlett was tied in with this in some way. He stared at the fidgeting Rickman and slowly lit a cigarette. 'We've found her, you know.'

'Found who?'

'Paula.'

'Paula Bartlett . . . my news girl?'

Frost nodded.

'Is she . . .' He steeled himself to say it. 'Is she dead?'

Another nod.

'Oh, that's terrible.' His face was screwed tight in anguish.

'Yes,' said Frost. 'And you should see what the bastard did to her. It would make a good video for you to sell.'

The shop bell tinkled again as Gilmore returned. He'd also asked Bill Wells to phone his wife and say he would be late, but had got short shrift from the sergeant.

Frost sat on the corner of the ice-cream cabinet. 'Tell me about Paula.'

'A really nice, sweet kid,' said Rickman.

'They're always nice when they're dead,' said Frost. 'Tell me what she was like while she was still alive.'

Rickman shrugged. 'She was a nothing. A dull kid. A bit of a pudding. Never laughed. Hardly ever spoke. Did her work. That was all.'

Again the shop bell quivered and rung and an old woman shuffled in. 'We're closed,' said Frost, taking her by the arm and steering her out into the street. He reversed the *Open/Closed* sign and rammed home the bolts.

'Tell me about the day she went missing.'

'I've already told all this to the other detective . . . the ferret-faced bloke. An absolutely normal day. She left as usual to go on her round and that was the last I saw of her.'

'Had she complained about men molesting her . . . or following her?' asked Gilmore.

'Not to me, she didn't. She hardly spoke a bloody word to me.'

Frost ambled over to the counter and glanced at the paper Rickman had been reading. He studied the naked Page Three girl, his cigarette drooping dispassionately. 'How was young Paula set up? Well stacked, was she?'

'No different to most of the other girls. They mature so bloody quickly these days . . . see them at fifteen you think they're twenty. Mind you, Paula didn't flaunt it. She used to wear loose woolly cardigans and things like that.'

'Did she go out with any of the newspaper boys?'

'No. Between you and me, I don't reckon she'd ever been with a boy or knew anything about sex.'

Frost raised his eyebrows. 'Why do you say that?'

'Something that happened three months ago. I'm in the

shop sorting out the papers for the rounds. Only two of the kids were in, Diana Massey and Jimmy Richards.'

'Who are they?' asked Frost.

'They were both in Paula's class at school – both just turned fifteen. Anyway, I'm sorting out the papers when I realize they've both gone missing. Well, not that I mistrust anyone, but I keep the day's takings in that other back room there until I can get to the bank, so I sticks my head round the door and what do you think I saw?'

'Tell me,' said Frost.

'Diana's on the floor, jeans round her ankles, he's on top of her, jeans ditto and they're having it away on a stack of *Radio Times.* Fifteen flaming years old. Didn't even stop when I yelled at them.'

'I don't think I would, either,' observed Frost.

'Anyway, I hears a gasp behind me. I turned around and there was Paula Bartlett. She was staring at them horrified. She dropped her papers and just ran out of the shop. It was obvious to me she didn't know what the hell they were up to. Innocent, that's what she was.'

'If our plumber lets us down, we'd better check out this Jimmy Richards,' said Frost. 'He might have acquired a taste for innocent newspaper girls.'

While Gilmore was noting down the address, an area car drew up outside and two uniformed officers rattled the door handle. Frost let them in. 'Stack of pornographic gear in the back,' he told them. 'Take it and our friend here down to the station and charge him under the Obscene Publications Act.'

Back to the car. Gilmore slammed the door, hoping this would wake up Burton who didn't deserve to sleep after causing all this trouble, but to no avail. He was fastening his seat belt when the damn radio called for the inspector.

Frost reached for the handset as Gilmore slumped back wearily, waiting for the worst.

'Can you do a quick job for me, Inspector?' asked Sergeant Wells.

'No,' replied Frost. 'Gilmore's got to get home. He's left his wife on the boil.'

'It's on your way, Jack. Probably a false alarm. Number 46 Mannington Crescent. A pensioner, Mrs Mary Haynes. She lives there on her own, but yesterday's milk is still on the doorstep and her cat's miaowing like mad inside. The milkman's phoned us. He thinks something might have happened to her. Take a look, would you?'

'This is uniform branch stuff,' snapped Gilmore.

'The only spare car is loaded down with your filthy books,' Wells snapped back.

Frost sighed. 'OK, Bill. We're on our way.'

The houses in Mannington Crescent were just waking up. A milk float was outside number 46. They parked behind it and Frost shuffled over to the milkman and flapped his warrant card.

Relieved at their arrival, the milkman blurted out the details. 'Might be nothing in it, but she's usually so regular. She'd never go away and leave her cat and it's miaowing like hell in there and yesterday's milk is on the step.'

'Couldn't she have run off with the lodger?' yawned Frost, following the man to the doorstep.

'She's seventy-eight years old!' said the milkman.

'Well – hobbled off with the lodger, then?'

'She hasn't got a lodger,' said the milkman.

Frost yawned again. 'Another brilliant theory shot up the arse.' He moved to one side to let Gilmore tackle the door.

Gilmore jammed his finger in the bell push.

'The bell don't work,' said the milkman.

Gilmore hammered at the knocker.

'I've already tried that,' said the milkman.

Ignoring him, Gilmore hammered again. Silence. A look of smug triumph on the milkman's face. 'What did I tell you?'

Across the road a fat woman in a shortie nightie called, 'Milkie! You haven't left me any milk.' The milkman signalled he was coming over and she waddled back into her house, acres of fat bottom wobbling below the hem of her nightdress.

Frost winced. 'It must be my day for horrible sights. You'd better carry on with your round, Milkie. Thanks for phoning.'

'What do you think?' asked Gilmore, who was staring at the Cortina, where Burton, oblivious to all this, was still asleep on the back seat.

Frost looked up and down the street, hoping to see the reassuring sight of a uniformed constable who would take the responsibility from him, but no such luck.

The downstairs window was heavily curtained and held firmly closed by a security catch of some kind. Frost did his letter-box squinting routine, seeing only an empty passage with a pot plant drooping dejectedly on a side table. There was an open purse on the side table, a small bunch of keys alongside it. He straightened up wearily. It looked bad. The old dear certainly wouldn't leave the house without her purse and her keys. 'We'll have to break in.'

Gilmore picked up the bottle of milk from the step and used it to smash one of the coloured glass door panels. He put his hand through and turned the lock. They stepped inside.

The first door they tried led to the kitchen. From

a dark corner two green eyes flashed, then a plaintive mew. Frost took some milk from the fridge, slopped it into a saucer and watched the cat's frantic lappings. He tried the back door, but it was firmly bolted on the inside. Gilmore looked in the other downstairs room, a musty-smelling, rarely used lounge.

The cat finished the milk and waited expectantly, its tail swishing. Frost topped up the saucer. 'Hundred to one she's upstairs, son. Dead in bed. Nip up and take a look.' As Gilmore's footsteps thudded overhead, Frost found a tin opener on the draining board and opened a tin of Felix which he emptied on a plate for the cat.

A sudden yell from Gilmore sent him running. 'Inspector! Up here. Quick!'

She was on the bed. She had been knifed repeatedly in the stomach and her throat was a gaping, open wound. The body was cold. Ice cold.

'I know you've got no-one to send,' Frost told a complaining Sergeant Wells, 'but I want four of them.' He pressed the handset against his chest so he couldn't hear the sergeant insisting this was impossible. 'I can't manage with less than four. I need people knocking on doors before everyone leaves for work. Over and out.' He clicked the switch, cutting off Wells in mid-moan and returned to the house.

Gilmore was waiting for him in the bedroom, anxious to show him a mess of blood on the carpet, hidden behind the open door. A lot of blood. On the floor, a crumpled heap that was her best black coat. 'He was hiding behind the door. He slashed her as she came in to hang up her coat, then dumped her on the bed.'

Frost nodded glumly. Gilmore was probably right, but knowing where he killed her wasn't going to help them catch the bastard. 'Sod that bloody milkman,' he said. 'We could have been in bed and asleep by now.'

Burton thudded up the stairs. He had been sent out to knock on doors. 'Two things, Inspector. A woman across the road says the old lady visited Denton Cemetery every Sunday afternoon to put flowers on her husband's grave. She saw her leave about three. The bloke next door – a Dean Reynold Hoskins – says the old lady knocked him up on Sunday afternoon just after five, all agitated. She reckoned someone had nicked her spare front door key which she kept hidden under the mat in the porch, but when Hoskins looked, there it was.'

'Have you checked to see if it's still there?'

Burton nodded and held up a bagged key. 'Hoskins called her a silly cow and went back to his own house. She kept ranting on about it not being in the same place she'd left it.'

'The poor bitch was right,' said Frost. 'There's no sign of forcible entry, all doors and windows are internally secured. The killer must have let himself in through the front door. He was already in the house.'

Gilmore grunted begrudgingly. He couldn't fault the inspector's logic.

'Right,' continued Frost. 'He got in after she went off to the graveyard at three. He wouldn't have hung about after slicing her up, so we can assume he left fairly soon after five. Knock on more doors. People usually go deaf and blind when there's been a crime but someone must have seen or heard something. And ask if it was general knowledge that she secretly kept a spare key under the mat.'

'Right,' said Burton, swaying slightly.

The poor sod's dead on his feet, thought Frost. 'I've got some more men coming soon, Burton. You can go home when they arrive.'

The detective constable shook his head. 'I can hold on for a while, sir.'

Stifling a yawn, Frost wished there was someone to tell him to go home. He wouldn't refuse. He turned his attention to Gilmore who was waiting to speak.

'I've checked her purse,' Gilmore told him. 'Empty except for a membership card for All Saints Church Senior Citizens' Club and a hospital appointment card. Nothing else in the house appears to be disturbed or taken.'

'A few quid,' said Frost. 'I can't believe the bastard ripped her up for the few quid in her purse.' He let his gaze wander around the bedroom, which smelt stalely of blood and lavender furniture polish. He lit a cigarette and added the smell of tobacco smoke. On the wall above the veneered walnut dressing table hung a framed black and white wedding photograph, the bride in white and the groom in morning dress amidst a snow shower of confetti. That same bride was now in funeral black, eyes wide open and staring up at the yellowing ceiling. Her dress and the bed-cover were rusted with gummy gouts of dried blood.

'That must be her grave-visiting dress,' muttered Frost. Something brushed against his legs. The cat. He leant down and scratched its neck, then put it outside. Crossing to the window he twitched aside the curtain and looked down on the empty street where black clouds kept the morning dark. His head was buzzing. So much to do and he didn't really feel he was capable of handling it.

An area car nosed into the street and stopped outside the house. PC Jordan and two disgruntled-looking detective constables who had thought their shift was over climbed out. A second car brought Roberts, the SOC officer, with his cameras and flash-guns, and hardly had this pulled up when a green Honda Accord brought the two men from Forensic. Gilmore led them all up to take turns to view the body before sending the constables to join Burton, knocking at doors.

'Find out if anyone saw a blue van,' bellowed Frost as they left.

'You haven't touched anything?' asked one of the Forensic men.

'I haven't even touched my dick,' said Frost, giving his well-worn, stock reply.

The door knocker thudded. 'The doctor's here,' called Gilmore, pushing Maltby up the stairs.

'Bit of fresher meat for you this time, doc,' said Frost as a bleary-eyed Maltby, his face flushed, squeezed between the Forensic men into the tiny bedroom.

'I might have guessed it would be you again,' growled Maltby, who seemed to be in a sour mood.

'Three bodies in one shift,' agreed Frost. 'I'm beginning to suspect I'm on *Candid Camera.*'

The doctor grunted and bent over the body. His examination was brief.

'She's dead.'

'I worked that out myself,' said Frost. 'I offered her a fag and she wouldn't reply. When did she die?'

Maltby took a pad from his bag and scribbled something down. 'You've sent for the pathologist, I understand?'

'That's right, doc.'

'Then let him answer your questions. He gets paid a lot more than I do. Found out who's been sending those poison pen letters yet?'

'Blimey, doc,' moaned Frost. 'It was only six hours ago when you last asked me. I haven't even had a pee since then.'

Maltby blinked at the inspector. His eyes didn't seem to be focusing properly. 'Hours ago? Is that all?' He felt for a chair and sat down heavily.

'Are you all right, doc?' asked Frost with concern.

'Yes, yes, of course I'm all right.' He grabbed the inspector's arm and pulled him down, dropping his voice and engulfing Frost in Johnnie Walker fumes. 'Did you know Drysdale's put in a complaint about me, just because I examined that body in the crypt before he did? He phoned me especially to tell me.'

'The man's a bastard, doc,' soothed Frost. He nodded towards the bed. 'How long has she been dead?'

Maltby lurched over to the corpse and prodded the flesh. 'Rigor mortis has come and just about gone. Some time Sunday evening, say. Anything else you want to know, ask Drysdale.' With a sharp snap he closed his bag and bustled off. 'God's here,' he bellowed from half-way down the stairs. A burble of exchanged frigid conversation and the pathologist swept into the bedroom accompanied by his secretary. He stared pointedly at the Forensic men who took the hint and retired downstairs.

'Was that Dr Maltby who just brushed past me?' he sniffed.

Frost nodded.

'And he's been mauling the body about, I suppose?'

'He never touched it,' said Frost. 'He didn't want to spoil your pleasure. If you could speed it up, doc.'

Drysdale gritted his teeth at the 'doc', but his eyes gleamed when he saw the body. He took off his long, black, expensive overcoat and handed it to his secretary. She, in turn, passed the coat over to Frost who screwed it into a ball, dumped it on a chair and sat on it. He shook a cigarette from his packet.

'Please don't smoke,' snapped Drysdale, glad to have the chance of putting this oaf in his place. Methodically he examined every inch of the body, murmuring the results of his findings to the secretary whose pen translated the great man's words into the loops and whirls of Pitman's shorthand.

After fifteen long minutes, ignoring Frost's repeated and over-loud signs of impatience, he straightened up to deliver his verdict. 'She's been dead approximately thirty-six hours.'

'That's what Dr Maltby said,' grunted Frost.

The pathologist smiled thinly. 'Delighted to have my opinion confirmed by such an expert. The pattern of the bloodstains indicates she was standing upright when she was attacked. The killer would have come at her from behind . . .'

Frost wriggled in the chair. The overcoat buttons were biting into him. 'He was waiting for her behind that door, doc. There's a couple of lovely blood puddles there if you want to have a paddle.'

Drysdale allowed himself a brief look, then carried on. 'The killer would have clamped his hand over her mouth – you can see the thumb pressure mark on the left cheek?' He moved away to allow Frost to inspect this if he wished, but Frost declined with a flick of his hand. He didn't need a pathologist to point out something he had noticed as soon as he entered the bedroom.

The pathologist shrugged. 'The killer then stabbed her three times in the abdomen with a knife. The blade would be single-edged, non-flexible, about 6 inches long – and – and razor sharp.'

'Something like a kitchen knife, doctor?' asked Gilmore who had returned after giving instructions to the door-knocking team.

'Could very well be,' accepted Drysdale.

'There was a similar attack last night . . . an old lady in Clarendon Street. He left a knife behind.'

'Clarendon Street?' barked Drysdale. 'Why wasn't I called?'

'You can have first crack at her as soon as she dies,' replied Frost, 'but at the moment she's still alive.' He related the details.

'If you let me examine the knife,' said Drysdale, 'I'll do some tests to confirm whether it could be the same weapon used to inflict these wounds.'

Frost scribbled a reminder about the knife on his discredited car expenses. 'I'll get it sent over. Carry on, doc. I'm sure you and your secretary want to get back to your bed . . . er, beds.'

Not noticing Frost's lewd wink to Gilmore, Drysdale continued. 'The killer jerked back her head, pushed the tip of the blade into her throat just there.' His thumb pointed to the left-hand side of the gaping wound. 'He twisted the knife so the blade was horizontal – that's why the wound is much wider at that point, then slashed open her throat from left to right.'

Frost yawned openly. The pathologist was making a damn meal of this. She was stabbed from behind and dumped on the bed. He'd deduced that himself within seconds. 'Would he have got blood on his clothes?'

'Yes. Possibly on his upper left arm, but almost certainly a considerable amount of blood from the throat would have gushed on to his right hand – the knife hand – and the sleeve of his coat or whatever he was wearing. He also stepped into the pool of blood when he carried the body across to the bed. You can see the imprints on the carpet.'

'You mean the ones Forensic have ringed round in chalk? Yes, we did spot them, doc.'

'How did blood get there?' asked Gilmore, pointing to a patch of discoloration on the left-hand sleeve of the black dress. 'That doesn't fit in with any of the wounds.'

Annoyed that he had missed it, the pathologist studied the mark. 'That's where he wiped the blade clean of blood.' He straightened up. 'That's all I can tell you for now, Inspector. You'll have a full report when I have completed the post-mortem.' He looked around the room. 'Has anyone seen my overcoat?'

The body had been carefully placed in a cheap coffin and man-handled down the narrow staircase for transport to the mortuary. The Forensic team had departed with their spoils and Frost, alone in the empty bedroom, sat moodily dragging at a cigarette and staring down at bare floorboards. All the bedding had been stripped from the bed and the carpet and underfelt removed for examination.

He stubbed out his cigarette in one of the little glass dishes on the dressing table. The young bride in the photograph, her face wreathed in smiles, beamed down happily through the shower of confetti to the stripped, bleak room where she died, alone and terrified.

He wandered downstairs, his feet clattering on the bare wood where the stair carpet had been taken away for examination. Gilmore and Burton and two of the uniformed men were in the kitchen drinking tea. 'Any joy with the neighbours?'

'No reply from most of the houses,' said Burton, handing him a mug. 'Probably gone to work. We'll have to try again tonight. Three people saw someone suspicious hanging around yesterday afternoon.'

Frost's head came up hopefully. 'Did you get a description?'

'I got three descriptions,' Burton ruefully admitted. 'All different. One medium build, darkish hair who may or may not have a beard aged between thirty and fifty. He was walking up and down the street just after two, staring at windows. The next was a skinhead on a motor bike who kept going round and round the block and the third was a West Indian in a dark suit.'

'And what did the West Indian do to arouse suspicion?' asked Gilmore.

'He just walked by, Sarge, minding his own business. I don't think the lady I spoke to liked West Indians.'

Frost sipped his tea. It was lukewarm. 'It'll be a waste of time, but check them out anyway. Have we traced any relatives, or anyone who might be able to tell us if anything's been pinched apart from her purse money?'

'Not yet,' answered Gilmore. 'I'll check with that senior citizens' club she belonged to. They might be able to help.'

'Good. What sort of woman was she? Did she get on well with the neighbours?'

Burton shook his head. 'A cantankerous old biddy by all accounts, always finding something to complain about. No-one liked her much.'

'We'll have to find out what she's been complaining about recently. Perhaps someone resented it enough to kill her.' He looked around. 'Where's the moggie?'

'The RSPCA bloke has taken it away,' Gilmore told him.

'I expect the little bleeder will have to be put down,' gloomed Frost, swilling down the dregs of tea and pulling a face as if it were bitter medicine. 'Tell me something to cheer me up.'

'Forensic found a few alien prints dotted about,' offered Gilmore. 'One looked very hopeful.'

'It'll be from the sanitary inspector or her family planning adviser, anyone but the killer.' He stood up and stretched. 'I'm too tired to think straight.' He glanced across to Gilmore who was grey with fatigue. 'Let's call it a day. We'll have a couple of hours' kip, then back to the station at noon.'

Noon! The detective sergeant sneaked a look at his watch. That would give him about three hours' sleep if he was lucky. He hoped Liz wouldn't be awake, waiting up for him, spoiling for a row.

He sat tense in the car as Frost drove him back after dropping off Burton, expecting every radio message to be the one sending them out on yet another case. But none of its messages were for them, although one call rang a familiar bell. 'Neighbours complaining of strange smells coming from 76 Jubilee Terrace.'

'Must have been your aftershave,' muttered Frost as the tyres scraped the kerb outside 42 Merchant Street. He had to shake Gilmore awake.

The house was quiet when Gilmore got in. A plate of cold, congealed food stood accusingly on the dining room table. His supper. He scraped the food into the waste bin and dropped the plate in the sink.

Upstairs, Liz was sleeping. Even in repose her face was angry. He undressed and crawled into bed beside her, moving carefully for fear he would wake her and the row would start. Almost immediately he plunged into an uneasy sleep, full of dreams of bodies bleeding from knife wounds and all looking like Liz.

Frost slammed the car into gear and headed for home and bed. He nearly made it.

'Control to Mr Frost. Come in, please!'

The plumber. The suspect in the Paula Bartlett case. Able Baker had picked him up. They were holding him at the station.

'On my way,' said Frost, spinning the wheel for an

illegal U-turn, deaf to the shouts from a minicab driver who had to brake violently to avoid a collision.

Tuesday morning shift (2)

Superintendent Mullett strode briskly into the station, pausing only to remove and shake the rain from his tailored raincoat. At 9.30 in the morning the lobby had a tired, slept-in look, which reminded him that he wanted to have a few words with Frost to ascertain his progress with the Paula Bartlett case.

'Mr Frost in yet, Sergeant?'

'No, sir,' replied Wells, barely managing to camouflage a yawn. 'He's out on another fatal stabbing – an old lady in Mannington Crescent.'

Mullett's forehead creased in anguish. 'Oh no!'

'Nasty one by all accounts,' continued Wells. 'Stomach ripped and throat cut.'

'Send the inspector to me the minute he comes in, Sergeant. Do you know if he left a report for me on the Paula Bartlett case? I've got a press conference at two.'

'I haven't seen one, sir.'

Mullett sighed his annoyance. 'How can I answer press questions if I'm not kept informed? It just isn't good enough.'

'We're all overworked, sir,' said Wells.

'Excuses, excuses . . . all I hear are excuses.' His eyes flicked from side to side, doing a brisk inspection of the lobby. 'This floor could do with a sweep, Sergeant.'

'Yes, sir,' agreed Wells, swaying slightly from side to

side, trying to give his impression of a loyal, dedicated policeman almost dead on his feet from overwork. 'The thing is, with this flu epidemic . . .'

'We mustn't use that as an excuse to lower standards, Sergeant. This lobby is our shop window. The first thing the public see when they come in. A clean lobby is an efficient lobby . . . it inspires confidence.' He paused and stared hard at the Sergeant. 'You haven't shaved this morning. A fine example to set the men.'

In vain Wells tried to explain about the double shift and that his relief sergeant was down with the virus, but Mullett wasn't prepared to become involved in the trivial details of station house-keeping. 'Excuses are easy to make, Sergeant. Those of us fortunate enough to escape the flu virus must work all the harder. Standards must be maintained.'

Waiting until the door closed behind his Divisional Commander, Wells permitted himself the luxury of an impotent, two-fingered gesture.

'I saw that, Sergeant!' rasped the unmistakable voice of the Chief Constable.

Wells spun round, horrified, then flopped into his chair, almost sweating with relief. Grinning at him from the lobby doorway was Jack Frost who had been hovering in the background, waiting for Mullett to leave.

'You frightened the flaming life out of me, Jack.'

'The man of a thousand voices but only one dick. So what's been happening?'

'Well, I've been working all bleeding night . . .'

'Excuses, excuses, Sergeant . . . give me the facts, man.' He pushed a cigarette across and lit it for Wells.

'Rickman's given us a statement.'

'Who's he?'

'The porno video merchant. Says he bought them from

a man in a pub . . . didn't know his name. We've released him on police bail.'

'What about my plumber?'

'Interview Room number two.'

'Thanks,' said Frost, making for the swing doors. He paused. 'This floor could do with a sweep, Sergeant.'

'I'll get you a broom,' grinned Wells. The internal phone rang. Bloody Mullett again. Wells' expression changed. 'The canteen's closed, sir. I haven't got anyone who can make your tea.' He jiggled the receiver, then slammed the phone down. Not interested in excuses, Mullett had hung up.

Outside the interview room an excited Detective Sergeant Arthur Hanlon ran forward to meet Frost. 'We could be on to something here, Jack.' He opened the door a crack so the inspector could see inside. A fat, balding man with shifty eyes in his mid-forties was slouched in a chair. He wore dark blue overalls over a beer belly.

'He's guilty,' said Frost. 'Never mind a trial, just hang him.'

Carefully closing the door, Hanlon continued. 'Bernard Hickman, forty-four years old, married, no children. The day Paula went missing, Hickman was supposed to be working in the cemetery, installing that new stand-pipe by the side of the crypt. His time sheet says he started work at eight, but the vicar is positive he didn't arrive until gone nine.' He opened a folder to show Frost the time sheet.

'Where does he live?'

'63 Vicarage Terrace, Denton.'

Frost chewed this over. The area where Paula went missing was north of Denton Woods. Vicarage Terrace was some four or five miles to the south. 'Has he got a motor?'

'Yes. It's in the car-park.'

Then Hickman could have driven and forced the girl into his car, raped and killed her and got to the cemetery by nine. But what was he doing north of the woods in the first place? The cemetery was in the opposite direction.

'It wasn't a chance encounter,' suggested Hanlon. 'It was planned. He'd seen the girl before and lusted after her. He knew where she'd be and waited for her.'

'Lusted after her?' said Frost, doubtfully. 'Why her? The poor cow was a pudding.'

'There's no accounting for taste, Jack. Some men lust after the ugliest of women.'

Frost looked reproachful. 'That's no way to talk of the Divisional Commander's wife.' Hanlon froze in mid-laugh, alerting the inspector to danger.

'Inspector!'

And there was Mullett charging down the corridor. Please don't let him have heard, pleaded Frost as he slid into his guileless smile. 'Sir?'

'Where's your report for me on the Paula Bartlett case? I've got a press conference at two.'

'Just about to interview a suspect now,' said Frost, jerking his head at the interview room.

Mullett's eyes gleamed. 'A suspect? Already? Marvellous. That's just marvellous. If we can tie this up in time for the press conference . . .' He beamed at the two men, then his expression hardened as Hanlon took out a handkerchief and blew his nose loudly. 'I hope you're not going down with this flu thing, Hanlon?' he snapped accusingly. 'We're enough men short as it is.' He turned on his heel and stamped off down the corridor.

'You can't even blow your blinking nose, now,' moaned Hanlon.

'Don't breath your filthy germs over me,' said Frost. 'Let's question our suspect.'

Hickman shifted his position in the hard, uncomfortable chair and stared unblinkingly at the nervous young uniformed constable, forcing him to look away. He smirked to himself, proud of his small triumph. 'I could smash you with one hand,' he leered.

'Not if we handcuffed you first and gave him a truncheon,' said a voice.

The tubby bloke had returned with a grotty-looking man in a shiny suit.

'Detective Inspector Frost,' announced the man, dropping into the chair opposite Hickman. 'Like to ask you a few questions.'

'I'd like to ask you one,' said Hickman. 'Why am I here? Or is it a state secret?'

'You're here,' Frost told him, 'because we're investigating a very serious matter. I hope we can eliminate you from our enquiries, but if we can't, you're in dead trouble. So just answer my questions.'

'Then ask,' said Hickman. 'Let's get this bloody farce over.'

'September 14th. I want to know everything you did. From when you got up, to when you went to bed.'

'That's over two months ago. How the hell can I remember that?'

'Perhaps this will jog your memory,' said Frost, pushing over a sheet of paper.

Hickman took the time sheet and stared at it in disbelief. 'So this is what it's all about? I fiddle an hour on my time sheet and the bastards call in the flaming Flying Squad! They can stuff their job . . .'

'Your firm didn't call us in,' Frost told him, 'and it's a darn sight more serious than fiddling your time sheet. Tell me what you did on that day.'

'I was working at All Saints Cemetery, fitting a new stand-pipe. They were extending the burial section so the old piping had to be rerouted. On that day – it was a Thursday, I think – I'm ready to drive to work when the flaming car dies on me. I fiddle about with it – no joy. So I have to call in a mobile mechanic and walk to work. I got there an hour late, but it wasn't my fault so why should I let the firm have the benefit?'

'We'll want the name and address of the mechanic.' said Hanlon.

'I've got it at home. Anyway, I worked until half-past twelve, nipped across to the pub for lunch, came back for more work and finished at six.'

'So you were at the cemetery from nine until six,' checked Frost. 'Then what?'

'In the pub for a few more drinks, home for dinner, then back to the pub until closing time. Supper at eleven, then bed, a bit of the other, and sleep.'

'How can you be so sure about the bit of the other?' asked Frost with genuine interest.

'I'm a creature of habit. Every night without fail whether she wants it or not.'

Frost lit a cigarette and dribbled smoke from his nose. 'How old is your wife?'

'Forty-two.'

'Ever fancied a younger bit of stuff?'

'Like bleeding hell, I have,' giggled the man. 'Trouble is, they never fancy me.'

'Big chap like you,' said Frost, 'that shouldn't be a

problem. You could force them to do what you wanted – whether they wanted to or not.'

Hickman's eyes narrowed. 'I don't think I'm getting your drift.'

From a green folder Frost removed a colour photograph and slid it across the table. 'Do you know her?'

Hickman stared down at the serious, unsmiling face of Paula Bartlett. 'Never seen her before . . .' Then he recognized her. 'Bloody hell! It's that kid!' Then he realized the implication and sprang up, sending the chair flying. 'Just what the flaming hell are you accusing me of?'

A nervous PC Collier moved forward to restrain the man and was relieved when Frost waved him back. Frost snatched up the photograph and thrust it under Hickman's nose. He spoke slowly and calmly. 'I've just come from her post-mortem. I haven't yet plucked up the courage to tell her parents what's been done to her. So, no matter how loudly you scream and shout and bluster, you're going to answer my bloody questions. Now sit down!'

His face sullen, Hickman pushed the photograph away and lowered himself into the chair.

'That's better,' said Frost, beaming disarmingly. 'Now tell us why we found fingerprints all over the inside of the crypt which match the fingerprints on your time sheet.' No fingerprints had been found inside the crypt, but Hickman wasn't to know.

'The crypt? Is that where you found her?' He leant back in his chair and smirked. 'If I wanted to rape someone, I'd pick somewhere more romantic than a flaming coffin store.'

Frost's eyes narrowed. 'Who said she'd been raped?'

'I'm not stupid. What have you been asking me questions about sex for if she hadn't been bloody raped?'

'And what were you doing in the crypt in the first place?'

'About eleven o'clock we had this dirty great bleeding thunderstorm. Didn't last long but it was bucketing down. There was no cover and I was getting drenched. I thought the crypt was a tool shed or something, so I forced out the screws with a claw hammer and stood inside the door. When the rain stopped, I hammered the screws back in and went on with my work.'

'What do you think, Jack?' asked Hanlon while Hickman's statement was being typed, ready for his signature.

'I've got an awful feeling the sod's innocent. We'll have to let him go for now, but check every bit of his story out. I want confirmation that his car was up the spout that day, witnesses who saw him working in the bone yard that day, and I want you to find out if it was peeing down with rain like he said.'

'He knew about the rape,' said Hanlon.

'He thought she was raped in the crypt,' said Frost, 'but she was already dead and bagged when she was dumped there. He's our only suspect, but I don't think he did it – so let's go and wipe the smile off our Divisional Commander's face.'

Mullett pulled his overflowing in-tray towards him and flicked through the contents. No sign of the promised amended car expenses from Frost but a complicated-looking batch of multi-coloured forms from County requesting a detailed inventory of the station. He shook his head in dismay. County did pick the worst possible time for their returns. A tap at the door. He straightened his back, smoothed his hair and called, 'Enter.'

A disgruntled-looking Sergeant Wells came in with

Mullett's cup of tea which he banged down rather heavily on the desk. 'Could I have a word with you, sir?'

Mullett's face fell. No more moans from the sergeant, he hoped. Everyone was overworked, but the solution was to buckle down and do that little bit extra, not keep whining about it all the time. He forced a creaky smile and pointed to the chair for Wells to sit.

The phone rang. Mullett glared at it, then frowned at Wells. He had specifically asked that all his calls be held. Wasn't there anyone capable of obeying a simple order? 'Mullett,' he snapped, but immediately his expression changed, his back went straighter than straight and his free hand was adjusting his tie. The caller was the Chief Constable. 'How are we coping, sir? Well – you've seen our manning figures . . . Yes, I appreciate Shelwood Division are in the same position as us . . . I see, sir . . . Well, if Shelwood can cope, then so can we . . .'

Wells gave a silent groan. The Chief Constable was playing Denton off against neighbouring Shelwood, knowing both Divisional Commanders were at daggers drawn in rivalry, each striving to be next in line for promotion.

Mullett swarmed on. 'Yes, sir, this epidemic has hit us pretty badly too, but thanks to . . .' and he gave a modest cough, 'good leadership, marvellous team work and . . .' He raised his voice and shot a significant glance across to Sergeant Wells. '. . . uncomplaining co-operation from the full team, we're coping extremely well.' He swivelled his chair around and lowered his voice. 'Sorry if I sound a mite ragged, sir, but I've been up half the night. You've heard we've found Paula Bartlett's body?'

'Stinking to high heaven and raped.'

Mullett cringed. He hadn't heard Frost come in. He spun his chair round and signalled frantically to the inspector to be silent. 'Apparently the poor child was sexually assaulted, sir, although I don't have the full details at the moment.' He glared to let Frost know whose fault this was. 'However, we do have a suspect . . .'

'No, we don't,' called Frost. 'I've let him go.'

Mullett clamped his hand over the mouthpiece and his eyes spat fire. 'Keep quiet,' he hissed. Back to the phone. 'Events seem to be moving faster than I thought, sir. I'll come back to you.' He smiled sycophantically until the receiver was safely back on its rest, then the smile snapped off. 'You will not make comments when I am on the phone,' he snarled at Frost.

'Sorry, Super. I didn't want you to make a prat of yourself with the Chief Constable.'

The inspector didn't sound sorry and Mullett was irked to note the lighted cigarette wiggling in the man's mouth. He expected people to ask permission before smoking in his office. In Frost's case that permission would have been refused, but that wasn't the point. However, he would see what Wells wanted first.

'Sergeant Johnson is still away. I'm doing double shifts and I'm on again tonight, sir. It's getting a bit much.'

Mullett tried to look sympathetic. 'Don't talk to me about double shifts, Sergeant. It goes without saying that no-one works harder than I do . . .' He paused. He thought he heard a snort of derision from Frost. But the innocent look on the man's face suggested he was wrong. 'If Shelwood Division can cope without extra help, then so can we.' He raised a hand to silence the sergeant's protest. 'A little extra uncomplaining effort and we'll come out with flying colours. If you've got any problems, any worries, come straight to me. My door is always open.' He beamed at the sergeant. 'Perhaps you'd close it as you leave.'

Wells opened his mouth to reply, but thought better of it and accepted his dismissal. He resisted the temptation to slam the door behind him.

Without waiting to be asked, Frost slid into the vacated chair and yawned loudly, not bothering to cover his mouth. What a pig the man is, thought Mullett. 'How are you coping?' he asked.

'We're not coping,' said Frost. 'We're struggling and sinking bloody fast.'

'Shelwood . . .' began Mullett.

'Sod Shelwood Division,' chopped in Frost. 'Shelwood haven't got three major murder enquiries on the go.'

Mullett breathed on the lenses of his glasses and polished them carefully. With his glasses off, the blurred image of Frost didn't look quite so scruffy. But when he replaced them, there was the man, creased, crumpled and slovenly in sharp focus. 'The reason we are not coping, Inspector, is because of sloppiness and inefficiency.'

'You're doing your best, sir,' said Frost generously.

Mullett glared. 'No-one can accuse me of inefficiency, Frost. I prepare the rotas, but no-one sticks to them. I never know who is on duty and who isn't. We've got to organize ourselves . . . allocate the tasks, use our resources to the best advantage. I've prepared new duty rosters.' He pushed a neatly typed list across the desk. 'And they will be strictly adhered to. I will not tolerate any deviation . . . any excuses.'

Frost picked up the roster and studied it. Like most of Mullett's edicts, it was beautifully laid out, but would be impossible to adhere to.

'We'll all have to work that little bit harder,' cajoled the superintendent, 'but it won't be for long. Mr Allen will be off the sick list next week and you'll hand the Paula Bartlett case back to him. Other men are coming off the sick list all the time.' He flashed his 'be reasonable' smile. 'It will only be for a few days.'

Right, you sod, thought Frost. We'll play it your way. He yawned and heaved himself up. 'I see from the roster I'm off duty, so I'll slope off home and get some kip.'

'Wait!' Mullett waved him back to his chair. 'I need an update on the cases you are working on.' He listened distastefully as Frost spared him none of the gory details of the stabbing and the post-mortem. 'One victim's still alive – so it's only two murders.'

'She's eighty-one,' said Frost, 'and her skull's fractured. The hospital don't reckon she'll pull through. I'm anticipating on this one.'

Mullett clenched his fist angrily. 'Catching this swine must be our number one priority, even to the exclusion of other cases.' He pulled his notepad towards him. 'I'm holding a press conference at two on the Paula Bartlett case. No joy with your plumber?'

'Not unless we can pick holes in his story, and I don't think we will.'

'A pity,' said Mullett pointedly, as if it was Frost's fault. 'Have you told the parents yet that she was raped? I don't want them to find out from the media.'

Damn! thought Frost. He'd completely forgotten this aspect. 'No, sir. I don't want to sod up your nice new roster, so as I'm off duty I'll leave that for you.'

The Parker pen doodled in the air and dotted an imaginary 'i'. 'I'd do it willingly, Inspector. But you've got their confidence. They don't want a stranger breaking such bad news. I'll leave that in your capable hands.'

Frost smiled his 'you bastard!' smile. 'Of course, sir.'

Mullett studied his list. 'Only one case demands urgent attention. This maniac with the knife. He's got to be caught before he kills again. That's the case we deploy our manpower on. The rest can go on the back burner until we're back to full strength.'

'But what about Paula Bartlett?' protested Frost. 'She's been murdered and raped – do we stick her on the back burner?'

Mullett nodded emphatically. 'She's been dead for over two months. The trail's gone cold. Waiting a week until Mr Allen returns is sensible and won't make the slightest bit of difference.' At Frost's continued hesitation, he added, 'It's a question of priorities, Inspector. Face facts! We haven't the manpower to handle more than one major investigation. By concentrating our resources, I'm looking forward to an early arrest.'

Frost pulled a cigarette stub from behind his ear and poked it in his mouth. 'I'll give it a whirl,' he muttered doubtfully. He wasn't happy at back-pedalling on the school kid. His every instinct screamed for him to go all out to find the bastard responsible. But Hornrim Harry was right for once. They didn't have the resources for more than one big case and they weren't going to get any help from County.

'Good man!' Mullett smoothed his moustache with his two forefingers. 'But we must keep a high profile with the public. We mustn't let them know we are marking time on the Bartlett case.' His eyes gleamed and he snapped his fingers triumphantly. 'I've got it! There's a video somewhere that Mr Allen had made when the girl first went missing. I'm sure we could get the TV companies to run it again.' The video showed a Paula Bartlett look-alike, wearing similar clothes and riding the identical bike along the route of Paula's newspaper round. It was hoped it would jog someone's memory, but it hadn't been successful. As Paula did her round every day, same route, same time, there was much confusion in the minds of people who had come forward as to the actual day they had seen her. The usual reports of strange men in slow-moving dark cars, but none of the leads had led anywhere.

'If it didn't work when memories were fresh, I can't see it working two months later,' said Frost, 'but I'll arrange it if you like. I could do an appeal to the public.'

'Leave it all to me,' cut in Mullett hastily. 'You've got far too much to do.' There was no way he was going to let Frost appear on TV, slouching in front of the cameras in that terrible suit, retrieving half-smoked cigarettes from behind his ear. He beamed at Frost. 'See the parents, then go and get some sleep. And remember, we concentrate only on vital things. Nothing else matters.'

Frost had almost reached the door when Mullett called him back, waving the complicated inventory return from his in-tray. 'You might fit this in when you have an odd moment, Inspector.'

Frost's gave the return a dubious stare. 'It doesn't look vital to me.'

Mullett's smile didn't waver. 'Shouldn't take you long, now that I've lightened your work load. County want it back this week.'

County can bleeding want, thought Frost morosely as he walked back to his office. He buried the inventory return in his in-tray, screwed up the new duty roster and hurled it at the waste bin, then kicked shut the door and sank wearily into his chair. In two minutes he was fast asleep.

Tuesday afternoon shift

Frost, cold and stiff from an uncomfortable sleep, staggered into the Murder Incident Room where Gilmore and Burton, seated at adjacent desks behind mounds of green folders, barely gave him a glance. They were transferring details from the folders on to roneoed forms which were then collected by WPC Jill Knight who fed them into the computer for collation.

A large-scale map of Denton, well-studded with coloured pins, had been fixed to the wall alongside the computer and Frost wandered over to take a look at it. The pins marked the scenes of all the recent senior citizen burglaries. On the far wall hung the map compiled by Inspector Allen showing the route of Paula Bartlett's last paper round. A newly added black thumb tack pin-pointed the crypt where the body was found. A beefy little blonde WPC brought in another armful of green folders and dumped them on the desk.

'You seem to have things well organized,' said Frost.

'Someone had to do it,' grunted Gilmore who was in a sour mood. A little over three hours' sleep and then treated to a dose of Liz whining and moaning at being left on her own so much and then, when he reported for duty, he had found Frost sprawled asleep in his office without having done a damn thing about getting the Murder Incident Room set up.

'Thanks,' acknowledged Frost. Organization was not his strongest point. 'Well, the good news is that according to Mr Mullett's new roster, we're all off duty until tonight.

The bad news is, we're far too busy to sod about with his rubbish.' He wandered across to Burton and Gilmore, both occupied with their green folders. 'What's all this in aid of?' He dropped a cigarette on each desk, then poured himself a mug of tea from Burton's thermos.

Gilmore looked up from his folders. 'I'm initiating a computer program. What it does . . .'

Frost's hand shot up. If it was to do with computers, then he didn't want to know. 'Please don't explain how it works, son, then I won't have to pretend I understand what you're talking about.'

But Gilmore explained anyway. 'We're feeding the computer with details from all the recent break-ins and burglaries and attacks involving senior citizens to see if we can build up some sort of pattern . . . why did the burglar pick on them, and so on.'

Frost peered over Jill Knight's shoulder, watching the cursor fly across the monitor screen, leaving a complicated trail of facts and figures. 'Any pattern emerging so far?'

'A lot of the victims seem to belong to senior citizens' clubs,' she told him.

'Perhaps that's the sort of club that senior citizens join,' said Frost, unimpressed. He flicked through a file half-heartedly, then pushed it away and jabbed a finger at Burton. 'You were going to check with the vicar about Mary Haynes.'

'I left a report on your desk,' protested Burton.

'You know I don't read reports. Tell me what it said.'

'She'd been a member of the church senior citizens' club for nearly six years. No relatives as far as the vicar knows. She kept herself to herself, never invited anyone back to her place and didn't have any close friends.'

'That wouldn't have been worth reading a report for,' commented Frost moodily.

'There's more,' continued Burton. 'She visited her husband's grave at the cemetery on Sunday . . .'

Frost's head shot up. The cemetery. That reminded him. 'Get the car out – we've got to give her parents the good news that their daughter was raped.'

'If I could finish,' said Burton. 'Her husband's grave had been vandalized . . . swear words sprayed on with an aerosol. She had a row with the vicar about it. She was always having rows. I've started a list of people she quarrelled with, but it's all trivial stuff.'

'Follow it through anyway,' said Frost. 'Did anyone spot our famous blue van?'

'No-one so far.'

A sudden thought. Something else he had forgotten. 'Damn! We should have asked dry-cleaners to look out for bloodstained clothing.'

'Already in hand,' said Gilmore, smugly.

A messenger entered with a large envelope and a package for Frost. He ripped it open. The post-mortem reports from the pathologist, beautifully typed by his loyal secretary on expensive paper. Frost flipped open the first and skipped through it. It was for the suicide, the kid in the Mickey Mouse night-shirt, Susan Bicknell. Drysdale's usual thorough job. He hadn't missed the marks of the beating, but reported them without comment. His sole concern was the cause of death which was confirmed as barbiturate poisoning, probably self-inflicted. Signs of recent intercourse, but she was not pregnant.

He gave the file to Gilmore who studied it grimly. 'She didn't kill herself because she was up the spout, son.'

'Then why did she?'

'We'll probably never know.' Frost opened up the other folder. 'I hope everyone's had their lunch – because it's stomach contents time.' He quickly read the typed sheet. 'Isn't science wonderful? She's been dead two months, yet they can tell us she died within half an hour of knocking back chicken and mushroom pie, chips and peas and – wait for it – a dollop of brown sauce.'

The plump blonde WPC pulled a face. 'I had that for dinner yesterday.'

'If you get raped and strangled, we'll know there's a connection.' He studied the report again. 'Paula must have had another meal. She'd never have eaten all that for breakfast.'

'She was a growing girl,' suggested Burton. 'You'd be surprised what kids eat these days.'

'She died within half an hour of eating,' Frost reminded him. 'The meal wasn't fully digested. I saw it. I can show it to you if you don't believe me.' At Burton's shuddering refusal, he continued. 'If she had eaten it at home, she would have to be dead by half-past seven.'

'We've got a witness who saw her at 8.15,' said Burton.

'Either the witness is lying, or mistaken, or Paula had another meal. A hot, cooked meal.' He opened up the package. 'I hope this isn't the bloody stomach contents.' They backed away as he plunged his hand inside but it was a polythene bag he pulled out. Inside were the shoes found on the body. He gave them to the blonde WPC and asked her to send them to Forensic. And that reminded him. 'Bloody hell – I forgot to ask Forensic to send Drysdale the knife from last night's stabbing.'

'Already done,' said Gilmore. What an inefficient lout the man was.

Frost nodded his thanks. Naked, but wearing shoes. Ate a hot meal. You couldn't force a kid to eat. She must have gone willingly with her killer and that tended to rule the bald plumber out. But Mullett said they shouldn't spend time on this case. Leave it for whizz-kid Allen. Sod Mullett. He'd do things his way. 'Come on, the pair of you,' he told Gilmore and Burton. 'Let's drive over the route she took for her paper round.'

There were a number of strange cars in the car-park. Of course. Mullett's press conference must be in full swing. Mullett would be telling them all about the suspected rape and he hadn't broken the news to Paula's parents yet. 'We'll call on them first,' he said. 'Let's get it bloody over.'

Burton waited in the car and watched Gilmore and the inspector make the short dash through the rain to the Bartletts' house. The girl's father, who answered their knock, was stooped and grey-faced and seemed to have aged some ten years since the previous night. He showed them into the living-room where his wife sat staring into empty space. She forced a ghost-smile of greeting. Frost stood uneasily by the door, not knowing how to begin.

'Would you like a cup of tea?' Mr Bartlett asked them.

'We'd love one,' Frost replied, hoping the mother would leave the room to make it. He wanted her out of the way while he broke the news of the sexual assault to her husband. But she sat, staring, unseeing, and didn't move.

Her husband touched her shoulder. 'Tea for you, love?' She shook her head.

Frost left Gilmore to keep the woman silent company and followed the man into the kitchen. Bartlett filled an electric kettle from the tap. 'She's been like this ever since we heard.'

'There's something I must tell you,' said Frost. He

steeled himself to deliver the blow. The father steeled himself to receive it. 'Your daughter was sexually assaulted before she died.'

The hand holding the kettle shook violently, splashing water all over the tiled floor. Gently, Frost took it from him and guided him towards a chair. Sobs racked the father's body.

His face sharing the man's pain, Frost could only watch and wonder what the hell to say next. The sobbing brought Mrs Bartlett into the kitchen. She cradled her husband's head in her arms and held him tight. 'What is it, love?' But head bowed, tears streaming, he couldn't answer. She looked enquiringly at Frost who had to force the words out again.

'I had to tell him that . . . that Paula was raped.'

Husband and wife clung together, clutching each other like young lovers, saying nothing, their closeness consoling each other. Ignored by them both, Frost fidgeted and wished he was miles away. 'If it's any consolation,' he told them, 'your daughter was a virgin.' Why the bloody hell did he say that? What possible consolation could it be that your daughter was a virgin before some bastard raped and choked the life out of her? He became aware that the father, his tears now of anger, was shouting at him.

'Of course she was a virgin. She was only fifteen. A kid. She'd had no bloody life . . .' And then he was sobbing again.

Hastily, Frost excused himself. 'I'll be in the other room.' In the living-room Gilmore, uncomfortable in a too-low chair, raised an eyebrow in query. 'I sodded it up,' Frost told him. 'It's the wailing bleeding wall out there.' He flopped into a chair. No sign of an ashtray, but he had to have a smoke. He lit one up, offering the pack to Gilmore who declined.

Barely two puffs later the woman was back, her eyes red. She seemed surprised that they were still there. He pinched out the cigarette and stood up. 'Two more things, Mrs Bartlett.' She looked apprehensive. What further horrors could he inflict? 'It's just that we're repeating the video made when Paula first went missing. It'll be shown on the television news tonight.'

She nodded, relieved that it was nothing worse.

'And – just for the record. Can you tell me what Paula ate on that last morning?'

'Cornflakes and toast.'

'You're sure? She wouldn't have cooked herself anything?'

'Oh no. I was down here with her . . . cornflakes and toast. That's all she ever had for breakfast.' As they moved to the front door, she clutched the inspector's arm. 'When can we put her to rest?'

At first he didn't understand what she meant, then realized she was asking about the funeral. 'Not for a while, love,' he said.

'I'd like to see her,' said Mrs Bartlett, her eyes blinking earnestly behind her glasses.

'No, love,' said Frost firmly.

'Please . . .' She gripped so tightly, it hurt.

He gently disentangled her fingers from his sleeve. 'She wouldn't want you to see her as she is now, Mrs Bartlett.'

'I don't care how she looks. She's my daughter. She's my daughter . . .!'

Her shouts followed them to the car. With the car door closed she stood in the doorway, still shouting, but they could only hear the rain thudding on the car roof. Then her husband appeared and led her back into the house.

'That wasn't an unqualified success, was it?' sighed Frost, sticking the cigarette end back in his mouth. 'She had cornflakes for breakfast, Burton. What do you deduce from that?'

'That you were right, sir. She must have had another meal after she was abducted,' replied the detective constable.

'Precisely.' He scratched the match down the car window. 'You're a fifteen-year-old virgin, Burton. You've been abducted and taken somewhere. Would you have an appetite for chicken pie, peas and chips?'

'It depends how long I'd been without food. She might have been held for hours without having anything to eat.'

Frost thought this over and nodded. 'Cooked food, so it's got to be indoors. And if he's keeping the girl hidden there for any length of time, he's got to be alone in the house. Lastly, to get her from his car to the house, he must be pretty certain he won't be seen. Which means the house has got to be remote.' He blew the end of his cigarette and watched it glow. 'The schoolmaster who usually gave her a lift. Is his house remote?'

Burton nodded. 'It's all on its own – miles from anywhere.'

'Then we've got the bastard.'

'What are you suggesting?' asked Gilmore who was feeling left out of the discussion. This was typical Frost, plucking a suspect from thin air, then forcing the facts to fit.

'I'm suggesting that bloody schoolmaster met her in his car and took her back to his house.'

'The schoolmaster was at his wife's funeral that day,' Burton reminded him.

'This was around eight in the morning. The funeral wouldn't have been until ten at the earliest.'

'But he didn't have to go in the car and fetch her,' said

Burton. 'She was due to call at his house with the paper anyway.'

'He was impatient,' said Frost, stubbornly. 'Burning for a bit of the other and couldn't wait.'

'So impatient,' scoffed Gilmore, 'that he gives her chicken pie, peas and chips at eight o'clock in the morning before he has it away with her and then trots off to his wife's funeral.'

Frost sank down in the car seat and expelled smoke. 'All right, so that's shot that theory up the arse. But I'd still like to have a word with this schoolmaster. Do you know where he lives, Burton?'

Burton nodded.

'Then take us there. Follow the route the girl went. Point out the houses where she delivered. Show me where her bike was found.'

Burton backed out of Medway Road and cut through some side streets. Gilmore tried to orientate himself, but soon got lost. And then, after a few minutes, the area looked familiar and the car was splashing through Merchant Street. He looked up as the house flashed by, noting that the bedroom curtains were still drawn. Liz would be sleeping, making sure she would be fully refreshed, ready to renew her moaning when he finished his shift. God, what a cynic he was becoming. How he hated this lousy little town.

The car juddered over cobbles as it negotiated a steep hill, then cut through the market place, empty of shoppers in the heavy rain. The houses they passed became fewer and further between and soon they were skirting the woods.

'She made her first deliveries here,' said Burton as they crawled past a small, walled estate of some forty houses and maisonettes built by the New Town Development

Corporation. 'You don't want to see the individual houses, do you?'

'No,' replied Frost, 'just a general outline of the route.'

They left the estate and drove on to the Forest View area where old Victorian properties had been converted into flats, then they headed away from the wood, along bumpy lanes flanked by hedges, past little clusters of old cottages. Burton slowed down and stopped outside a green-roofed bungalow. 'She made her last delivery there – the *Daily Telegraph* and a photographic magazine. The lady of the house saw Paula pedalling away down the lane about a quarter past eight. That was the last time she was seen alive.'

Frost stared at the bungalow, then signalled for Burton to drive on. The car sloshed in and out of puddles and turned into an even narrower lane where overgrown branches on each side slashed spitefully at the car as it squeezed through. Burton braked. 'This is where we found her bike and the abandoned newspapers.'

They climbed out and stood looking down at a deep ditch running beneath an overhanging hedge. The ditch was brimful and covered with a thick layer of emerald green scum, through which the wheels of an upturned supermarket trolley protruded.

'The bastard must have been waiting for her just about here,' said Burton.

Frost nodded glumly. He had hoped that visiting the actual locale would give him some magic flash of inspiration. He stood in the pouring rain, looking down into the green slimy water, and decorated it with his discarded cigarette end.

Back in the car he asked Burton where the girl's bike was. 'Locked up in the shed at the station. The two newspapers she didn't deliver are in the exhibits cupboard.'

'Only two more houses,' said Burton, as the car bumped into an extra deep puddle which sent a spray of dirty water all over the windscreen.

'Mind what you're doing,' barked Gilmore, who hadn't had a chance to put Burton in his place for some time.

Burton's knuckles whitened on the steering wheel, but he controlled his temper. He pointed up a small side lane which crawled up to a two-storeyed house standing on its own. 'That's called Brook Cottage. They would have had the *Sun* but she never made it.'

Brook Cottage looked a mite dilapidated. They could hear a dog barking as they passed.

The lane widened and passed through empty scrub land. After some minutes a red-bricked house lurched up in front of them. It was an old, solid-looking property and stood alone in extensive grounds. A shirt-sleeved man was working in the garden seemingly oblivious to the pouring rain. 'She finished her round here,' announced Burton as he switched off the engine. 'The man in the garden is Edward Bell, Paula's schoolteacher.'

Frost crushed his cigarette in the ashtray, then turned up the collar of his mac. 'Let's have a word with the bastard.'

The man, wrenching up weeds from the heavy soil, gave a cry of pain as the sharp thorns of a hidden bramble pierced his palm. He stared angrily at the bright red globules welling from the punctures. The damned briar was everywhere. As fast as you cleared it from one section it appeared somewhere else. Well, if it thought it was going to defeat him, it was making a damn mistake. He tore up a thick clump of grass and wrapped it round the briar as protection then pulled and tugged, swearing out loud as the bramble resisted. It took a great deal of effort but at last he tore it free of the rain-sodden earth and hurled it on to the growing pile of garden refuse. His hand was sticky with blood and rain and sweat. He sucked salt and moved on to the next section, only dimly aware of the sound of slamming car doors and approaching footsteps.

'Mr Bell?'

'Eh?' He straightened up and eased the pain in his back. There were two men, one dark-haired, young and neatly dressed, the other older, hair starting to thin, wearing a crumpled raincoat that had seen better days. The younger one held up a piece of plastic bearing a coloured photograph. 'Police, Mr Bell.'

'Is it about Paula?' he asked. 'Has she been found?'

'Let's talk inside,' said the scruffy man.

The house was cold and unwelcoming. They passed through the kitchen, its sink and draining board stacked with dirty saucepans and crockery. On top of the fridge stood a half-bottle of lumpy milk. The room was a mess. It reminded Frost of home.

Muttering apologies for the untidiness, Bell opened one door, decided against it and took them into a musty-smelling lounge. Rain streamed down the patio window, blurring the view of the garden beyond. A miserable room. Frost would be glad to get out.

'Not too cold for you, is it? I haven't had the heating on. I suppose I should, but it seems pointless . . .' Bell's voice trailed off.

'This is fine, sir,' said Frost without conviction, winding his scarf tighter. He and Gilmore sat side by side on the beige Dralon settee, facing Bell who was squatting on a footstool, dripping rain on to the pink carpet.

Bell, who wore a rain-blackened checked shirt and

baggy corduroy trousers, was in his late thirties. Thin and nervous-looking, his face was framed by unstyled light brown hair and a few tufts of a scraggy beard. A hint of dark rings around his eyes suggested he hadn't been sleeping too well.

Unaware of Frost's scrutiny, Bell unwrapped the bloodstained handkerchief, studied his palm, then wrapped it again. Suddenly he remembered the reason for their calling.

'Paula's been found, you say? That's splendid. How is she?'

Frost's eyes flicked to Gilmore, who sat impassive. This was too naïve. Surely Bell must have heard about the discovery of the girl's body? 'Don't you read the papers, sir?'

'Papers?' He shook his head. 'They don't deliver papers here any more. The parents won't let their children do it.'

'Don't you listen to the radio? Or talk to your colleagues?'

'It's half-term and I've been too busy in the garden these past few days to listen to the radio. So what has happened?'

'Paula is dead, sir,' said Frost bluntly, carefully watching Bell's reaction. The man jerked back as if he had been hit, then his face crumpled.

'Oh no. That poor child. Oh no!' His grief and shock at the news seemed genuine.

Without taking his eyes from the teacher, Frost slowly lit a cigarette. 'She was murdered, sir. Raped and murdered.'

Bell stood up. He took the soiled handkerchief from his hand and stuffed it into his pocket. Nervously, he paced the room. 'She was only fifteen.'

'Kids mature earlier these days,' said Frost. 'They have

sex earlier, they get raped earlier, they get murdered earlier.' He exhaled smoke and watched it disperse. 'What sort of girl was she?'

The man dropped back on the footstool and thought for a moment. 'Quiet. Didn't mix much. An excellent scholar.'

'Why did you start giving her lifts to school?' asked Gilmore.

'It was her parents' request. Her newspaper round took her some five miles in the opposite direction. Sometimes the papers would be late which could make her late for school and they didn't want her to miss any of her lessons. I would meet her at the top of the lane and give her a lift from there.'

'What did you do about her bike?' This from Frost.

'It was one of those folding ones. I put it in the boot. She could then cycle home when school was over. This is all in your files . . . I made a full statement to that other officer.'

'What sort of things did you talk about when you drove her to school?' asked Gilmore. 'Did she mention boy friends, or crushes on any of the masters, or anything?'

Bell shifted his position to face the sergeant. 'We hardly passed more than a few words. She was a quiet girl, and that suited me. When I'm driving, I like to concentrate, not talk.'

'Was she a teaser?' asked Frost.

His pale cheeks showed two red spots. 'How the hell should I know?'

'In the car, sir, you and her, close. The old knees rubbing together . . . flashes of elasticated knicker leg and tender young thigh all juicy and throbbing?'

Bell's lip curled contemptuously. 'I find you offensive, Inspector.'

Through a haze of cigarette smoke Frost beamed at him. 'You're not alone in that, sir. But I found it offensive when I saw what that sod had done to that kid, so just answer my questions.'

Bell stood up and towered angrily over the inspector. 'I hope you're not suggesting I am involved in this poor child's death?'

'Let's just say you're quite high on my list of suspects.' In fact, thought Frost, you're my one and only bloody suspect, so if it isn't you, I'm nowhere. 'Can you tell me your movements for the morning she went missing?' His raised hand halted Bell in mid-protest. 'I know you've told it all to the other bloke, but I'd like to hear it first-hand.'

'It was the morning of my wife's funeral. The hearse arrived from the undertakers at 9.30. The interment was at ten. I got back home a few minutes before noon.'

'So, before the funeral, you were alone in the house until 9.30?'

'No. My wife's parents were here. They'd travelled down from Berwick for the funeral and stayed with me overnight.'

'Oh.' Frost tried not to sound disappointed. 'They'd confirm this, of course?'

'I think you'll find they've already given statements to Inspector Allen.'

Frost groaned inwardly. Why the hell hadn't he done his homework? 'I've only just skimmed through the files, sir.' Skimmed! He hadn't even opened them. 'Your morning paper hadn't arrived by the time you left for the funeral. Didn't that worry you? Didn't you wonder why?'

'I didn't give it a thought, Inspector. The only thing on my mind was the funeral.'

'Of course, sir.' Damn, thought Frost. There goes my best suspect. All he was left with now was the plumber. Which reminded him. 'Did it rain during the funeral?'

'There was a sudden cloudburst,' said Bell. 'We all got drenched.'

And damn again, thought Frost. Now I haven't even got the plumber. He poked another cigarette in his mouth and lit up. The smoke curled and drifted and he followed it with his eyes, watching as it was drawn to the fireplace, some of it wafting up to the mantelpiece. In the centre of the mantelpiece a clock in Chinese black lacquer, long unwound, had stopped at ten past eight. Something poked out from behind it. A light blue envelope, the address typed. It looked very similar to the one sent to old Mr Wardley.

A sharp cough to catch Gilmore's attention and a jerk of the head to direct him to the clock. Silently, Gilmore sidled over and pulled out the envelope. He raised his eyebrows and nodded. The typing was identical.

Bell, staring out at the rain-soaked garden, saw nothing of this extended mime show.

'One final thing,' said Frost casually. 'What did the poison pen letter say?'

Bell stiffened, then slowly turned. He saw the envelope in Gilmore's hand and snatched it from him. 'You've no right . . .'

'We've every bloody right,' snapped Frost, standing and holding out his hand. 'The letter, please, sir.'

Bell stared at him, knuckles white, body stiff with fury. He almost threw the envelope at the inspector. 'You bastard!' he hissed. 'You lousy bastard.'

'Sticks and stones,' reproved Frost, mildly. He unfolded the sheet of cheap typing paper. The typed message said, simply, *Fornicator*.

'Terse,' murmured Frost, passing the message to Gilmore. 'Why should anyone accuse you of that, sir?'

'It's none of your damn business.'

'In a murder enquiry, sir, everything is my damn business.'

Bell walked back to the window and again stared at the puddled garden blurred out of focus by the curtain of rain crawling down the pane. He wouldn't look at Frost. He spoke to the glass. 'If you must know, my wife had been ill for a very long time. We were not able to live together as husband and wife. There was a woman in Denton . . .'

'Do you mean a tart?' asked Frost, bluntly.

His back stiffened. 'Yes, she was a prostitute. Someone must have been spying on us, hence the letters. Filthy letters. I burnt the others. This one came on the day of the funeral.' He covered his face with his hands and his body shook. 'The day of her funeral.'

On the way back to the car they detoured. There was the remains of an old bonfire at the end of the garden. Quite a large bonfire. Frost poked at the rain-sodden ashes with his foot. Bits of twigs, stalks and dried leaves. No burnt remains of buttons or the charred remnants of clothes stripped from a schoolgirl's body. He added his cigarette end to the heap.

'We're wasting our time here,' said Gilmore.

'Maybe,' muttered Frost, looking back to the house where a thin, bearded figure was watching them from the patio window. 'But my philosophy in life is never to trust bastards with thin straggly beards.'

Burton started the engine as Frost slid into the passenger seat beside him. 'Back to the station, Inspector?'

'One more call, son. Let's check with the headmaster of Bell's school. I want to find out if there's been any complaints of Hairy-chin teaching advanced anatomy to the senior girls.'

'We shouldn't be doing this,' protested Gilmore from the back seat. 'You're forgetting – Mr Mullett said we should drop this case and concentrate on the stabbings.'

'Mr Mullett says lots of stupid things, son. The kindest thing to do is ignore him.'

As Gilmore had predicted, calling on the headmaster was a waste of time. The man, stout and pompous, was outraged that such an accusation could be levelled at any member of his staff. Mr Bell had an excellent record, was highly regarded, and didn't the inspector realize that the poor devil had recently lost his wife?

Frost felt like retorting, didn't the headmaster know that while his wife was dying, his excellent schoolmaster was having it away with a tart in Denton? But he held his tongue and took his leave.

'Yes, son,' he said, before Burton could ask. 'Back to the station.' And they nearly made it. Another couple of minutes and they would have been in the car-park when Control called.

'Calling all units,' said the radio. 'Anyone in the vicinity of Selwood Road? Over.'

Before Frost could restrain him, Burton had snatched up the handset. They were a minute away from Selwood Road.

'Eleven Selwood Road. Old-age pensioner living on her own. Neighbour reports she hasn't been seen all day, her newspaper's still in the letter-box and her milk is still on the step.'

The neighbour who made the phone call, a sharp-faced little busybody of a man wearing a too-big plastic mac, was hovering in the street and scurried over to the car as they pulled up. 'Are you the police?'

'More or less,' grunted Frost.

'I live next door,' said the man, darting in front of them like an over-enthusiastic terrier as they made their way across to the house. 'She always goes out during the day. I watch her through the window. She didn't today. And none of her lights are on, her milk is on the doorstep. She's an old-age pensioner, you know.'

'Thanks,' muttered Frost, wishing the man would go away.

'I'm an old-age pensioner too, but you'd never think it, would you?'

'No,' said Frost unconvincingly. 'Never in a million years.' The old sod looked at least eighty. They were now at the door, which was painted a vivid green.

'Are you going to break in?' asked the neighbour, pushing between them. 'Only the council have just repainted these doors.'

Frost leant on the bell push.

'No use ringing if she's dead!'

'Nothing good on telly?' asked Frost pointedly, hammering at the door with the flat of his hand.

'You could get over my garden fence if you liked,' offered the man, 'but she always keeps her back door locked.'

Frost moved the man out of the way so he could have a look through the letter-box.

'You won't see anything. Her morning paper's stuck in there.'

Frost tugged at the paper, but it was wedged fast.

'You won't shift it, I've tried.'

Frost gave a savage yank and the newspaper came free.

'You've torn it,' reproved the man pointing to a thin corrugated tongue of paper that had caught on the side of the letter-box.

'If she's dead, she won't mind,' said Frost, peering through the flap. All he could see was solid dark. He sent Burton for the torch.

'I've got a torch,' said the neighbour, 'but it doesn't work.'

Burton returned from the car with the flashlight. Frost shone it through the letter-box. He caught his breath. The beam had picked out a crumpled heap at the foot of the stairs. A woman. And there seemed to be blood. Lots of blood.

'Kick the door in, son . . . quick!'

At the second kick there was a pistol shot of splintering wood and the door crashed inwards. Frost found the light switch as they charged in. She was lying face down, her head in a pool of blood. He touched her neck. There was a pulse. She was still alive. Burton dashed back to the car to radio for an ambulance. Gilmore helped Frost turn her on her back, while the neighbour brought a blanket from the upstairs bedroom to cover her.

Her eyes fluttered, then opened. She seemed unable to focus. Frost knelt beside her. 'What happened, love? Who did it?' He turned his head away as the stale gin fumes hit him.

'I fell down the bleeding stairs,' she said.

Tuesday night shift (1)

Liz was in bed asleep when Gilmore arrived home late in the afternoon and was still asleep at eight o'clock when he staggered out of bed, tired and irritable, ready for the evening shift of Mullett's revised rota. He was clattering about in the kitchen, frying himself an egg and Liz came eagerly downstairs. She thought he had just come home and was furious to learn he'd been working when he should have been off duty and was now starting on another night shift.

'You said it would all be different when they made you a sergeant. You said you'd be able to spend more time with me. It's Cressford all over again.'

'It won't always be like this,' said Gilmore, wearily, cursing as the yolk broke and spread itself all over the frying pan.

'How many times have I heard that before? It's never been any damn different.' She moved out of the way so he could reach a plate, not helping him by passing one over.

Gilmore buttered a slice of bread. 'Could you give it a rest? I've had a lousy day.'

'And what sort of a day do you think I've had? Stuck in this stinking little room.'

'You can always go out.'

She gave a mocking laugh. 'Where to? What is there to do in this one-eyed morgue of a town?'

'You could mix . . . make friends.'

'Who with?'

'Well – some of the other police wives . . .'

'Like his wife . . . that old tramp – the one who's supposed to be an inspector?'

'His wife is dead.'

'What did she die of – boredom?'

Gilmore rubbed a weary hand over his face. 'That old tramp, as you call him, has got the George Cross.'

'So he should. You deserve strings of bloody medals for living in this dump!'

He opened his mouth to reply, but the door slammed and she was back in the bedroom. He pushed the egg to one side, he couldn't eat it. He was pouring his tea when a horn sounded outside. Frost had arrived to pick him up.

Outside the rain had stopped and a diamond-hard moon shone down from a clear sky. Frost shivered as Gilmore opened the car door to enter. 'It's going to be a cold night tonight, son.' He turned the heater up full blast and checked that all the windows were tightly closed.

'Yes,' agreed Gilmore. 'A bloody cold night.'

Bill Wells tugged another tissue from the Kleenex box and blew his sore, streaming nose. His throat was raw and he kept having shivering and sweating fits. And the damn doctor had the gall to say it was just a cold and he hadn't got the flu virus. A couple of aspirins and a hot drink and he'd be as right as rain in a day or so. His pen crawled over the page as he logged the last trivial phone call which was from a woman who had nothing better to do than to report two strange cats in her garden.

The log book page fluttered as the main door opened. Without raising his eyes, Wells finished the entry, blotted it, then forced a polite expression to greet the caller. Then his jaw dropped. 'Bleeding hell!' he croaked.

A small, bespectacled man wearing a plastic raincoat stood in the centre of the lobby. When he had Wells' attention, he parted the raincoat. He was wearing nothing underneath it.

'Oh, push off,' groaned Wells, slamming his pen down. 'We're too bloody busy.'

Defiantly, the man stood his ground, holding the mac open even wider. Another groan from Wells. 'Collier,' he yelled. 'Come and arrest this gentleman.'

The lobby door swung open again as Frost bounded in, a disgruntled-looking Gilmore at his heels. He glanced casually at the man, did a double take and stared hard. 'No thanks, I've got one,' he said.

'When you want a flasher,' moaned Wells, 'you can't find one. When you don't want one, they come and stick it under your nose.'

There were extra staff in the Murder Incident Room where the phones were constantly ringing.

Frost looked around in surprise. 'What's going on?'

Burton, a phone to his ear, noted down a few details, murmured his thanks and hung up. 'It's the response to the Paula Bartlett video. It went out on television again tonight. We're flooded out with calls from people who reckon they saw her.'

'After two months they reckon they saw her,' grunted Frost. 'When the video went out the day she went missing, no-one could remember a damn thing.' He picked up one of the phone messages from a filing basket. A woman reporting seeing Paula in the town two days ago. Frost flicked it back in the basket. 'A waste of bloody time.'

'Excellent response to the video,' boomed Mullett, sailing in and beaming at all the activity.

'Just what I was saying, Super,' lied Frost. 'How did the press conference go?'

'Very well,' smirked Mullett. 'I recorded an interview for BBC radio. They hope to repeat it in *Pick of the Week.*'

'Are you sure they said "pick"?' Frost enquired innocently.

There was the sound of stifled laughter and people in the room seemed desperate to avoid Mullett's eye. One of the WPCs had a fit of the giggles and was stuffing a handkerchief in her mouth. Mullett frowned, uneasily aware he was missing out on something, and not sure what. He didn't see the joke, but he smiled anyway. He remembered the messages he had to deliver. 'Who's been telexing the Metropolitan Police about someone called Bradbury?'

'Simon Bradbury?' asked Gilmore eagerly. 'That was me.'

'Who's Simon Bradbury?' Frost asked.

'The computer salesman. The bloke who picked the fight with Mark Compton. I thought he might be the one who's been sending the death threats.'

'You could be on to something, Sergeant,' said Mullett, handing Gilmore the telex. 'The Metropolitan Police know Bradbury. He's a nasty piece of work and he's got form.'

Bradbury had been involved in drunken brawls, had served two prison sentences for assault and had been fined and disqualified for drunken driving. There was an arrest warrant out on him for beating up a barman who refused to serve him. He had defaulted on police bail and was no longer at his last known address. Full details and a photograph were following.

Gilmore rubbed his hands. 'Sounds like our man, Super. I could have a result on this case very soon.'

'Excellent,' beamed Mullett. 'Results are something we are very short of at the moment.' He glared significantly at Frost then looked around the room where the phones were still ringing non-stop. 'Anything interesting on the Paula Bartlett video?'

'Yes,' sniffed Frost. 'Proof there's life after death. She was still being seen delivering papers up to last week.'

Mullett forced a smile. 'Ah well. Carry on with the good work.' He turned to leave and was nearly hit by the door as Sergeant Wells burst in.

'Urgent message for Mr Frost from Fingerprints,' panted Wells. 'The senior citizen killing . . . Mary Haynes. One of the prints in the bedroom. It's someone with previous.'

'Who?' asked Frost, pushing Mullett to one side.

'Dean Ronald Hoskins. Collier's pulling out his file.'

On cue, a panting Collier rushed in waving a buff folder. Wells snatched it and skimmed through the details. 'Dean Ronald Hoskins, aged twenty-four. Three previous – burglary, breaking and entering and assault with a knife.'

'A knife,' hissed Mullett, snatching the file from Wells. 'By God, we've got him.' He was so excited he could hardly hold the file still. He couldn't wait to phone the Chief Constable . . . 'Sorry to disturb you at your home, sir,' he would begin modestly, 'but a bit of good news I thought you'd like to know . . . Denton Division triumph yet again . . . another murder solved within twenty-four hours . . . watertight case . . . prints . . . full confession . . .'

His soaring flights of fancy were abruptly grounded by Frost who had rudely snatched the file and was now staring at it, a cigarette sagging from his mouth. 'Bloody hell! He didn't have to travel far to kill her. He lives next door.'

'I interviewed him,' said Burton. 'It was Hoskins who told us about the key under the mat.'

Mullett was now bubbling with excitement. 'Bring him in. Take all the men you need.' He pulled open the door. 'I want a result on this one, Inspector. Let's see if we can't give the Chief Constable some good news for a change.'

The patrol car followed Frost's Cortina as far as the road adjoining Mannington Crescent. Two uniformed men got out and sprinted to the rear of number 44 where they climbed the back fence into the garden, blocking Hoskins' retreat that way.

Gilmore coasted the Cortina around the corner, parking it at the end of the street where he switched off the lights and waited for the uniformed men to radio that they were in position. Next to Gilmore sat Burton. In the rear seat were Frost and WPC Helen Ridley, the beefy little blonde, who had changed into plain clothes and was spoiling for a fight.

Most houses in the street showed lights, the exception being number 46, the murder house with its drawn curtains and a heavy padlock securing the front door. From next door, number 44, an overloud hi-fi belted out heavy metal.

'Jordan to Inspector Frost,' whispered the radio. 'We are in position – over.'

'Right,' grunted Frost. 'We're moving in.'

They climbed out of the car and casually sauntered up to the front door of number 44 which seemed to be pulsating as the wham of an electronic bass boomed from inside. Frost lifted the knocker and beat out a rhythmic rat-tat-tat. The others pressed tight against the shadow of the porch. The music blared out louder as an inside door was opened. Footsteps along the passage and a man's shadow against the frosted glass of the front door.

'Yeah? Who is it?'

Frost muttered something unintelligible.

'What?' yelled the voice from inside.

Frost muttered again.

'Just a minute . . . can't hear a bloody word you're saying.' The latch clicked. As the front door opened, Frost moved quickly out of the way and Gilmore pounced, pinning to the wall a man in patched jeans and a washed-out red vest. A potted plant on a stand toppled and crashed to the floor, spilling earth all over the lino. Gilmore tried to yell 'Police!', but the man suddenly sprang forward, his palm clamped under the detective's chin, fingers clawing for his eyes. Gilmore swung him round and crashed him against the opposite wall.

'Let him go, you bastard.' A girl wearing a black T-shirt and very little else raced down the passage slashing at the air with a kitchen knife.

'Police,' spluttered Gilmore, trying to hold Hoskins with one hand and ward the girl off with the other. He had done it all wrong. The knife blade was whistling perilously close to his ear, but the hallway was so narrow, it prevented Burton and the WPC getting past to the girl.

Snorting like a stallion on heat, the little WPC charged into the fray, sending the men crashing to the floor and leaping over them to grab the girl, spin her round and jerk her wrist up high into the small of her back. The WPC's foot hooked round the girl's ankle and sent her toppling.

Frost stepped back and lit a cigarette. As usual, he was superfluous.

'Get this bloody dyke off of me,' screamed the girl, face down in earth and potted plant with the WPC kneeling on her back and twisting her knife arm to near breaking point.

'Drop the knife,' hissed the WPC.

'I've dropped, it, I've dropped it,' screeched the girl.

'I've got it,' said Frost, picking it up.

Reluctantly, the WPC relaxed her grip and dragged the girl to her feet. Gilmore, panting away, now had Hoskins facing the wall in an arm lock. With his free hand he fumbled in his pocket for his warrant card. He stuck it under the man's nose. 'Police. Are you Dean Ronald Hoskins?'

'Yes. How many of you are there?'

'There's two more of the sods in the garden,' the girl told him. 'Who are we supposed to be – Bonnie and bleeding Clyde?'

'Well, you're certainly not Di and bleeding Charles,' said Frost. 'Can we go somewhere comfortable?'

'There's nowhere comfortable in this bloody shithouse,' said the girl.

'You don't have to live here,' Hoskins snarled at her. 'You can pack your carrier bag and go whenever you like.' He nodded towards the far door. 'In there.'

The room housed a settee that doubled as a bed, a hi-fi unit with two shaking, throbbing speakers spewing out heavy metal, a black and white television set and a motor bike which was leaking oil on to bare floorboards.

Frost kicked at the hi-fi flex, yanking the plug from the power point. The music died abruptly and the resulting silence took some adjusting to. He opened the window to the garden and yelled for Jordan and the other uniformed man to come in. 'Search this place from top to bottom. Bag all clothing for forensic examination.'

'Have you got a warrant?' demanded the girl.

Frost smiled sweetly. 'I don't understand these technical terms, love.' He found himself a chair, shook off the dubious pair of underpants it contained and sat down. He pointed to the settee, indicating they too should sit. With an energetic shove the WPC helped them comply.

Frost drew on his cigarette. Their heads moved simultaneously, watching his every move like a rabbit watching a snake. Smoke dribbled from his nostrils. He fanned it away. 'My colleague thinks you might be able to help him with his enquiries.' He nodded for Gilmore to take over.

Gilmore stared at each of them in turn, holding their gaze and forcing them to break away. 'You know why we're here.'

'I've got no bleeding idea,' snapped the man. 'You come bursting in here with that bloody lesbian . . .'

'A woman's been murdered next door and you don't know why we're here.' Gilmore thrust his face to within an inch of Hoskins 'Why did you knife her? A poor old lady who never did anyone any harm.'

'Knife her?' exclaimed Hoskins incredulously. 'Me?'

'Don't give me that innocent crap. You've used a knife before.'

'Only in self-defence.'

'This was in self-defence,' snapped Gilmore. 'She caught you robbing her house. She would have gone to the police. So, in self-defence, she had to be silenced.'

'Oh, marvellous,' sneered the girl. 'The police are bleeding baffled so they arrest the poor sod next door just because he's got a police record.'

'Not just because he's got a police record, love,' said Frost. 'It's because the poor sod next door left his fingerprints all over the murdered woman's bedroom.'

The girl's head snapped round to Hoskins. 'You stupid bastard! You never told me you touched anything.'

'That's right, you mouthy cow!' snarled Hoskins. 'Sign my bleeding death warrant!'

Gilmore gave a yell of triumph. 'Caution them,' said Frost, 'and take them down to the station.' He went out to see how the search for the knife and for bloodstained clothing was getting on. The bedroom was a pigsty. Jordan and WPC Ridley were stuffing unwashed clothing into a black plastic dustbin sack, the same type of sack Paula Bartlett's body was found in.

'Nothing yet,' Jordan told him. Frost nodded glumly. Outside through the window, he could see two police officers sifting through the contents of the dustbin. Something told him that this wasn't going to be as easy as Gilmore seemed to think.

* * *

The interview room was cold. The heating engineers had managed to restore heat to the basement cells, but wouldn't get round to this floor until the morning. So it was cold. But Hoskins was sweating. The girl, now wearing a thick sweater, sat by his side. Gilmore had wanted the pair questioned separately, but Frost favoured having them together.

Gilmore switched on the tape recorder, announced the details of the time and who was present, then dragged a chair across and sat facing them.

'I want to make a statement,' said Hoskins.

'You're on the air, so go ahead.'

'I never touched her. Like I told the other cop, the old girl knocked at our door moaning that someone had got into her house with the spare key, but when I looked, the key was there all the time, so I left her to it. After a while, I got worried about her, so I went back and knocked, but got no answer. I thought I'd better check, just in case, so I used her spare key from under the mat to get in. I called, "Are you all right, Mrs Haynes?" Dead silence. Funny, I thought. I called again. Nothing. So I nipped upstairs just to make sure she's all right and, Christ! There she was on the bed and blood everywhere. I couldn't get down them bleeding stairs fast enough.' He turned to the girl to verify his story.

'Dean was as white as a sheet when he came in,' she confirmed, 'and he was sick as a bloody parrot down the sink.'

'What time was this?' Gilmore asked.

'About eleven o'clock Sunday night.'

'And you didn't think of calling an ambulance, or the police?'

'Ambulance? She was dead – I could see that.'

'Police then?'

'What – a bloke with a record inside a dead woman's house? That's as good as a signed confession to you lot. I'd have been in Death bleeding Row within the hour.'

Gilmore flicked through his notes. 'You told the other officer it was five o'clock Sunday when Mrs Haynes rang your bell.'

'That's right.'

'And you were so worried about her, you waited six hours before knocking to see if she's all right?'

'Well, at least I did go and knock. Other people wouldn't have bothered.'

'I don't believe you,' said Gilmore.

'I don't expect you to,' said Hoskins, loud and clear to the microphone. 'But it's the gospel truth.'

Gilmore frowned as the door opened and the little blonde WPC hovered, waving something – a large brown envelope. He'd give her a mouthful for interrupting at a crucial moment. It was Frost who spoke to her, keeping his voice low, then he called Gilmore over. Murmurs of excited conversation while Hoskins looked on worried, straining his ears in vain, wondering what it was about.

The two detectives returned, Gilmore carrying the envelope which he shook over the table. Five banknotes fluttered out, a £20 note, a £10 note and three £5 notes, all crisp and brand new. Hoskins tried to look puzzled. 'Guess what we found hidden behind one of your chair cushions,' said Gilmore. He picked up one of the notes and sniffed delicately, then smiled. 'Smell it. Lavender!' He looked across to the girl. 'Hardly your style, is it, love?' He waggled the note under Hoskins' nose. 'The old girl's purse reeked of it!'

Hoskins pushed Gilmore's hand away. 'It's my giro money,' he muttered.

'Of course it is,' said Gilmore, 'but just in case you're telling me a porky, I'll check the numbers with the post office where Mrs Haynes drew her pension. If they tally, Sonny Jim, you're for the high jump.' He pushed the money back into the envelope. He felt much happier now. Hoskins was beginning to squirm and the girl looked worried. Frost seemed fidgety, no doubt annoyed that the new boy was scoring all the goals.

Hoskins took a deep breath. 'All right, I'll tell you the truth. It is her money, but she lent it to me. I needed some spares for my motorbike.'

'Lent it?' scoffed Gilmore. 'She wouldn't have lent you forty-five pence, let alone forty-five quid.'

'She bloody lent it to me,' insisted Hoskins. 'And I was very grateful, that's why I went in later to check she was all right.'

Frost leant forward. 'She gave you everything she had in her purse. How was the poor cow going to manage?'

'I intended paying her back in a couple of days. She said she could wait.'

'When did you borrow it?' asked Frost.

'When she thought she'd lost her spare key. I saw her purse in her hand so I asked her.'

'Do you mind if I continue, sir?' asked Gilmore with an edge to his voice that would slice through tempered steel. He didn't want Frost taking over just when victory was within grasp.

Frost's hand waved him to silence. 'Indulge me, Sergeant.' He puffed cigarette smoke down over the seated man. 'All right, Hoskins, let's pretend she lent you the money. And let's pretend you were so full of gratitude that you were worried about her and decided to see if she was all right at eleven o'clock at night. When you knocked, were the lights on in her house?'

Hoskins paused for a moment. 'No.'

'So when you got no reply, from a house with all the lights out, you thought it was your duty to investigate it – to use her spare key and nose around inside?'

'That's right.'

'It never occurred to you that at eleven o'clock at night the most obvious answer was that this seventy-eight-year-old woman might be in bed, asleep?'

Hoskins' mouth opened and shut, then he shook his head. 'No. It didn't occur to me at the time.'

Frost gave a weary sigh. 'Don't waste my time, son. Of course it occurred to you. You were banking on it. You wanted her to be in bed and asleep.'

'I don't know what you're talking about,' Hoskins muttered to the floor.

'You stupid little git. You're going to talk yourself into a life sentence.' He stood up and started to button his mac. 'I don't think you killed her, but if you're sticking to that story I'm charging you with murder and your girlfriend as an accessory.'

Hoskins, his face set, stared stubbornly down at the ground.

'If you don't tell them the bleeding truth, then I will,' said the girl. 'They're not nicking me for something I didn't do.'

Hoskins took a deep breath. 'All right . . . scrub everything I said. This is now the gospel . . .'

Frost sat down again and waited. Gilmore was scowling, arms folded, itching to take over the reins of the questioning.

'Yes, I was going to do the place over – nip in, grab what I could and get out quick. I knew where the spare key was, so I waited until eleven o'clock when I thought the old girl would be asleep. I let myself in. Her bag was on the hall table, so I nicked the money from her purse. Then I crept upstairs. The first door I tried was her bedroom. Christ, when I saw her smothered in blood, it frightened the shit out of me. My feet never touched the flaming stairs as I came down. I took the money, but I never bleeding killed her.'

'I believe him,' said Frost when they were back in the office.

'Well, I don't,' said Gilmore. He was furious. He'd have got a bloody confession to murder if the old fool hadn't butted in.

'Mind you,' added Frost, 'if Forensic find her blood all over his clothes, I'm prepared to change my mind.'

Tuesday night shift (2)

'Woman on the phone for you,' yelled Wells as they crossed the lobby. 'A Mrs Compton.'

'Old Mother Rigid Nipples!' exclaimed Frost, as Gilmore took the phone.

'Mr Mullett wasn't too pleased you're only charging Hoskins with petty theft,' Wells told him.

'Mr Mullett's happiness is rather low on my list of priorities,' grunted Frost, pushing through the swing doors and nearly bumping into an irritable-looking Mullett on his way out.

'Car expenses,' barked Mullett.

'Be on your desk first thing tomorrow, Super,' called Frost, instantly regretting his folly. The expenses, much scribbled on, were still in his pocket and there wasn't a hope in hell of getting the amended receipts by the morning. Ah well, he philosophized, a lot could happen between now and then. Mullett could get injured in a car crash and break both his legs. But he popped the bubble of this optimistic fantasy. The bastard would hobble in on crutches if it meant catching him out.

A quick look in at his office. Exactly as he had left it, cold and untidy. Protruding from under an empty, unwashed mug was a memo headed *From The Office Of The Divisional Commander*. It bore the single word *Inventory???* ringed in red and underlined several times in Royal Blue by Mullett's Parker pen. He ferreted through his in-tray and dug out the inventory return, hoping it wouldn't look so complicated as at first sight. It looked even worse, so he reburied it even deeper.

The door slammed to punctuate an angry Gilmore's return. 'That damn Sergeant Wells!' He flung himself into his chair.

Frost stifled a groan. He had enough troubles of his own. 'What's the matter now, son?'

'That phone call from Mrs Compton. Her husband's away and she's alone in the house.'

'It sounds a bloody good offer,' said Frost. 'We'll flip a coin to see who has the first nibble.'

Gilmore's scowl cut even deeper. 'It's not funny. She's had another threatening phone call. The bastard told her tonight will be her last night on earth. She's frightened out of her wits. I've told Sergeant Wells I want a watch kept on the house tonight and he says he can't spare anyone.'

Frost picked up the internal phone. 'I'll have a word with him.'

At first Wells dug his heels in. He wasn't going to let any jumped-up, know-nothing, aftershave-smelling detective sergeant tell him how to organize his own men. And did the inspector know how many men he had available to cover the whole of Denton – the *whole* of bloody Denton? Four! Two in cars, two on foot. The others had to be kept in to answer the flaming phones which were ringing non-stop after that stupid Paula Bartlett video on television. Frost put the phone down on the desk and let Wells rant on, while he lit up another cigarette. When the whining from the ear-piece stopped, he picked up the receiver and made a few sympathetic sounds with the result that Wells now grudgingly admitted that perhaps he could spare one man and one car to keep a spasmodic watch on The Old Mill, but he couldn't guarantee one hundred per cent coverage.

'You're a prince, Bill,' said Frost. 'Your generosity is exceeded only by the size of your dick.' He hung up quickly before Wells could change his mind then twisted his chair round to tell his sergeant the good news, but if he expected thanks, he was disappointed.

'What a bloody way to run a station,' snarled Gilmore, stamping out of the room.

The office was too cold to stay in for long so Frost sauntered along to the Murder Incident Room where the temperature wasn't much better. Two WPCs and one uniformed man, all well wrapped up against the cold, were beavering through the senior citizen burglary files and answering the spasmodic phone calls that were still coming in following the TV broadcast. Another WPC was slowly working through the vast computer print-out of light vans and estate cars, either blue or of a colour which could be mistaken for blue under street lamps. 'Mr Mullett's orders,' she explained.

'You don't need to tell me,' sniffed Frost. 'Anything stupid and useless, it's always Mr Mullett's orders.'

Even if a blue van was involved, it could well have been repainted but still be registered under its original colour.

He dipped into the filing tray and read a couple of the messages. Paula was still being sighted. A woman had spotted her in France, and a man was positive that Paula was the same girl who had delivered his paper that very morning.

At a corner desk, DC Burton, a sandwich in his hand, was reading the *Sun*. He stuffed it away hastily as Frost approached and busied himself with the senior citizen files. 'On my refreshment break, sir,' he explained. He accepted a cigarette. 'Hoskins and the girl have been charged. We're holding them in the cells overnight pending the result of the forensic examination.'

Frost nodded and plonked himself down on a chair. 'I want to get filled in on the Paula Bartlett case, but I'm too bleeding lazy to read through the file. Start right from the beginning.'

'September 14th,' said Burton. 'She was on her paper round. Left the shop at 7.05.'

'Hold it,' interrupted Frost. 'Five past seven? Her parents said she usually started her round at half-past seven.'

'That was when her teacher gave her the lift. She would have had to cycle to school that day, so she gave herself more time.'

Frost blew an enormous smoke ring and watched it wriggle lazily around the room. 'I'm still listening.'

'At five o'clock her parents are expecting her home from school. By half-past five they're phoning around and are told she hadn't been to school at all that day. At ten past six they phone us.'

'And two months later, we found her,' commented Frost, wryly.

Burton grinned patiently. 'Anyway, we sent an area car. They got details of her delivery route from the paper shop and followed it through with the customers. As you know, she never made the last two houses.' He heaved himself from his chair and crossed to the large-scale wall map. 'Her last delivery was here at around 8.15.' His finger jabbed the map. 'Her next delivery should have been Brook Cottage . . . here. She never made it.'

Frost joined him at the map which was studded with yellow thumb tacks marking Paula's progress. 'She was doing her round half an hour earlier than usual?'

Burton nodded.

'Then unless the bloke who abducted her knew that, it must have happened by chance – he saw her, acted on impulse and grabbed her.'

Burton destroyed that theory. 'She'd been doing it half an hour earlier for the previous four days, sir. Mr Bell stayed away from school when his wife died, so Paula didn't get her lift in.'

'Whoever it was, he must have had a car. He either bundled her in and dumped the bike, or it was someone she knew and trusted. Someone, perhaps, with a wispy beard who offered her a lift. The bike went in the boot and he dumped it later.'

A tolerant smile from Burton. Inspector Allen had reasoned all this out months ago. 'If she was picked up in a car, sir, it couldn't have been by Mr Bell. He never left the house before the funeral. His wife's parents confirm it.'

'He's still got a wispy beard,' said Frost, 'and I don't trust the sod.' He returned to his desk. 'Right. She's reported missing. What happened from there?'

'Mr Allen took over the case at 20.15. The area between Grove Road and Brook Cottage was searched. At 23.32 we found her bike and her newspaper bag with the two undelivered papers, dumped in the ditch. The ditch was dragged in case the girl was there as well. It was then too dark to continue so it was resumed at first light with the search area extended to include part of the woods. Mr Allen had all known sex offenders, child molesters, flashers and the like brought in for questioning.' He pulled open a filing cabinet drawer jam-packed with bulging file folders – the results of the questionings.

Frost regarded them gloomily. Far too many for him to read through.

'There's more,' said Burton, tugging open a second drawer.

Frost winced and kneed them both shut. 'Say what you like about Mr Allen, but he's an industrious bastard. I take it he cleared them all?'

'Yes.'

'Then that's good enough for me.' He struck a match down the side of the filing cabinet and lit up another cigarette. 'Where's the bike?'

Burton led him to the freezing cold evidence shed in the car-park and unlocked the door.

The bike, swathed in dimpled polythene, was leaning against the wall. Burton pulled off the covering and stood back. A neat little foldable bike in light grey stove-enamel with dark grey handle-grips and pedals. Frost stared at it, but it told him nothing. He waited while Burton replaced the dimpled polythene, then followed him back to the Incident Room.

'Let's see the physical evidence.'

Unlocking a metal cupboard Burton took out a large cardboard box that had once held a gross of toilet rolls and dumped it on the desk. Then he pulled a bulging box-file down from the shelf and handed it to the inspector. 'The main file.'

Frost opened it. From the top of a heap of papers a serious-looking Paula Bartlett regarded him solemnly through dark-rimmed glasses. The school photograph provided by the parents when she first went missing, which was used for the 'Have You Seen This Girl?' poster. There were many more photographs, including those taken at the crypt and at the post-mortem. Frost shuddered and dug deeper, pausing to examine the flashlight enlargements showing the handlebar of the bike poking through the green scum of the ditch. 'Any prints on the bike?'

'You've already asked me, sir. Just the girl's and the schoolmaster's.'

Frost paused. Why did little buzzes of intuition whisper in his ear every time the schoolmaster was mentioned?

The rest of the file consisted of negative forensic reports on the bike and the canvas newspaper bag, plus statements from Paula's school friends – no, she had never talked of running away; no, she wasn't worried or unhappy about anything; no, she had no boyfriends. In the early days of the investigations, as no body was found, it was hoped that she had dumped her bike and, like so many kids of her age, run away from home. There were reports from various police forces who had followed up sightings of Paula look-alikes, teenage girls on the game or sleeping rough. A few missing teenage girls were restored to their families, but the Bartletts just waited, and hoped, and kept her room ready exactly as she left it.

He closed the file and handed it back to Burton, then pulled the cardboard box towards him. Inside it, loosely folded in a large transparent resealable bag, was the black, mould-speckled plastic rubbish sack, Paula's shroud, ripped where the knife had cut through to reveal her face.

'A rubbish sack,' commented Burton. 'Millions of them made. No clue there.'

'Tell me something I don't know,' gloomed Frost, taking the next item from the box. A canvas bag which had held the newspapers. The stagnant smell of the scummy ditch in which it had been immersed wafted up as he examined it. He slipped his arm through the shoulder strap. The bag was too high and uncomfortable. Paula was much smaller than he was. What the hell does that prove? he thought. He shrugged off the strap and put the bag on top of the rubbish sack. Next were the brown, flat-heeled shoes, the stained laces still tied in a neat double bow.

'Naked, raped and murdered, but still wearing shoes,' muttered Frost. 'It doesn't make sense.'

'What's going on?' Gilmore was staring pointedly at Burton. 'I thought I told you to go through the senior citizen files.'

'He's helping me,' said Frost. He held up the shoes. 'Why was she wearing shoes and sod all else?'

'She tried to get away,' offered Gilmore, not very interested. Mullet had told them to forget the Paula Bartlett case. 'She put on her shoes so she could make a run for it, but he came back and caught her.'

'She'd been raped,' said Frost. 'She was terrified. If she wanted to run, she'd bloody well run barefoot. She wouldn't waste time putting on shoes and tying them both with a double bow.'

'Then I don't know,' grunted Gilmore, moving away and busying himself with the senior citizen files, making it clear that he knew where his priorities were, even if others didn't.

The brown shoes refused to yield up their secrets, so Frost put them to one side and took out the last item in the box, a large plastic envelope which held the two undelivered newspapers, the *Sun* and the *Daily Telegraph,* each folded in two so they would fit the canvas bag.

Frost slipped them from the envelope. The same stagnant smell as the bag, both papers yellowed and tinged with green from their immersion. With great care he unfolded the *Sun* which the soaking in the ditch had made slightly brittle. Scrawled above the mast-head in the newsagent's writing was the customer's address, *Brook Ctg.* He turned to page three and studied the nude dispassionately. She too was stained green. 'There's a green-tinged pair of nipples to the north of Kathmandu,' he intoned, closing the paper, careful to ensure it settled along its original folds.

He nearly missed it. It caught the light as he was returning it to the envelope. A quarter of the way down the back page, running across the width of the paper. A roughened, corrugated tongue-shaped tear an eighth of an inch wide and barely a quarter of an inch long. He pulled out the schoolmaster's *Telegraph* and scrutinized the back and front pages. Nothing on that, so back to the Sun. It was telling him something, but he didn't know what. 'What do you make of this, Burton?'

Burton made nothing of it.

'Come and look at this, Gilmore,' called Frost.

Making clear his resentment at being dragged away from more important work, Gilmore took the newspaper, gave it a cursory glance and handed it back. 'A bit of damage in the handling,' he said.

No, thought Frost. Not damage in the handling. It was more than that. A faint bell began to tinkle right at the back of his brain. The drunken fat woman earlier that day. Her paper was jammed tight in the letter-box. He'd had to pull it out and he'd torn it. A very similar tear to that on the back page of the undelivered *Sun*. Or was it undelivered? Hands trembling, he took up the newspaper and gave it a second, loose fold. The rough corrugated tongue ran exactly down the line of the new fold.

Frost felt his excitement rising. 'Did Mr Allen notice this?'

'I don't know, sir. Why, is it important?'

'It could be bloody important, son. The papers are folded once so the girl can fit them in the canvas bag. But they have to be folded again so they can be poked through the letter-box.' Frost pointed to the tear. 'I'd stake my virginity that this paper has been pushed through a letter-box and then pulled out again.'

The DC took the paper and twisted it in the light to examine the abrasion. It was possible. Just about possible. 'But we know it *wasn't* delivered,' he said.

'Who lives at Brook Cottage?'

Burton pulled the details from the folder and read them aloud. 'Harold Edward Greenway, aged 47. Self-employed van driver. Lives on his own. His wife walked out on him a couple of years ago.'

This was getting better and better. Frost rubbed his hands with delight. 'Has he got an alibi for the day the girl went missing?'

Burton turned a page. 'According to his statement he had no jobs lined up, so he stayed in bed until gone eleven, then pottered about the cottage for the rest of the day. He never saw the girl and he didn't get a paper.'

'And we believed him?'

'We had no reason to doubt him, especially when we found her bike and the papers in the ditch.'

Frost sat on the corner of the desk and shook out three cigarettes. 'OK. Try this out for a scenario. Harry boy lives all on his own. Wife's been gone for two years and his dick's getting rusty through lack of use. One morning, what should come cycling up his path but a nice, fresh, unopened packet of 15-year-old nooky with his copy of the *Sun*. She rolls it up and pokes it through the door. The sexual symbolism of this act hits him smack in the groin. He invites her in, or drags her in, or whatever. She can scream if she wants to, there's no-one for miles to hear. Afterwards, when all passion's spent and she's screaming rape, he panics, and strangles her.'

Burton, caught up with Frost's enthusiasm, could see where the plot was leading. 'Greenway puts the newspaper back in the bag, dumps it with the bike in a ditch and we all think she never made the delivery.'

Even Gilmore looked impressed. 'It's possible,' he decided reluctantly, 'but it still doesn't explain the shoes.'

'Sod the shoes,' said Frost, hopping down from the desk. 'Let's get our killer first, then get explanations.' He stuffed the papers back into the plastic envelope and handed it to Burton. 'Tell you what you do, son. Send both newspapers over to Forensic. Tell them our brilliant theory and get them to drop everything and make tests.'

'And then come back and get down to these bloody files,' called Gilmore. 'We're never going to get through them at this rate.'

The stack of folders didn't seem to be getting any lower. Gilmore ticked off the squares on the roneoed form and dropped it into the filing basket ready for the girl on the computer. Something sailed past his nose. It was a paper aeroplane which attempted to soar upwards before losing heart and nose-diving with a thud to the ground at his feet. He bent down and picked it up. The paper looked familiar. He unfolded it. One of the roneoed forms. He turned suspiciously to Frost who grinned back sheepishly.

'Sorry, son.'

Frost was bored. He'd been staring at the same robbery folder for the past forty minutes. He was dying for an excuse to get out of the station, but the phone stubbornly remained quiet. 'About time Forensic came back to us on those newspapers.'

'They've only had them five minutes,' said Gilmore.

'How long does it bloody take?' asked Frost peevishly, pulling the phone towards him and dialling the lab.

'Give us a chance, Inspector,' replied Forensic testily. 'We've got half our staff down with this flu virus thing. We're still working on the clothing and other items collected from 44 Mannington Crescent. Negative so far.'

'That old rubbish can wait,' said Frost. 'It's not important. Get cracking on those newspapers.'

A scowling Gilmore looked up. 'We're supposed to be concentrating on the senior citizen murders and you're telling Forensic it can wait?'

Frost was saved from answering by the phone. WPC Ridley from Intensive Care, Denton Hospital. Alice Ryder, the old lady with the fractured skull, had regained consciousness.

The moon, floating in a clear sky, kept pace with the car as they raced to the hospital. Frost, puffing away nervously in the passenger seat, was willing the old dear to stay alive until they could question her. A detailed description of her attacker would be worth a thousand of those lousy forms they had been filling in for the computer. A detailed description! He was kidding himself. She was eighty-one, concussed and dying. The bastard had attacked her in the dark. The poor cow would tell them sod all.

The dark sprawl of the hospital loomed up ahead. 'Park there, son.' He pointed to a 'Hospital – No Waiting' sign by the main entrance and was out of the car and charging up the corridor before Gilmore had a chance to switch off the ignition.

Gilmore pushed through the swing doors in time to see the maroon blur of Frost's scarf as he darted down a side corridor. With a burst of speed, he caught up with him. 'Straight ahead,' panted Frost, indicating a small flickering green neon sign reading 'Intensive Care'.

The night sister looked up angrily and glared them to silence. She nodded grimly at Frost's warrant card. 'Mrs Ryder is over there.' A jerk of her head indicated a curtained-off corner.

'How is she?' asked Frost.

'She's dying, otherwise I wouldn't let you near her.' As they moved across, she added, 'Not too many of you. Send the WPC out.'

They slipped through the curtains. A concerned WPC Ridley was bending over the bed talking quietly. She looked up with relief at Frost's appearance. 'Her eyes are open, sir, but I don't think she's really with us.'

'Take a break, love,' said Frost flopping down in the chair alongside the bed. Gilmore stood behind him. The old lady, a small frail figure, seemed unaware of their presence. She lay still, her head barely creasing the plumped hospital pillow, an irregular bubbling sob marking her shallow breathing. Her face was a dull grey against the starkness of the turban of bandages around her head. Taped to her cheek, a thin, transparent tube ran into her left nostril. Another tube descended from a half-filled plastic bag on an iron stand and dripped fluids through a hollow needle to a vein on her wrist. Her hand, a yellow claw, was trembling and making tiny scratching noises on the bed-cover.

Everything was clean and white and sterile and Frost felt gritty and dirty and out of place. He leant forward. 'Mrs Ryder?'

Her red-rimmed eyes stared blankly up at the ceiling. She gave no sign that she had heard him. Her head was twitching slightly as if trying to shake off the tube fastened to her nose which was clearly uncomfortable and worrying her.

Why can't they let the poor cow die in comfort, thought Frost. He brought his face close to hers. 'Mrs Ryder, I'm a police officer. If I'm to get the bastard who did this to you, I need your help.'

No response.

'A description, Mrs Ryder – anything. If you can't talk, blink. A blink means yes. Do you understand?'

If she understood, she didn't respond.

Undeterred, Frost plunged on. 'The man who attacked you. Was he tall?' He waited. No response. 'Short? Fat? Thin?'

Her breath bubbled. Her fingers drummed. Her eyes, unblinking, were fixed on the ceiling.

Frost slumped back in his chair. Why was he hassling her? She wasn't going to tell him anything, so why not let the poor cow die in peace. He dug his hands in his pocket and felt his cigarettes. No chance of a smoke in here. The night sister would have him out on his ear.

'Let me try,' said Gilmore, but before Frost could answer the old lady made a choking sound. 'I'll get the sister,' said Gilmore, trying to open the curtains.

'No!' hissed Frost, grabbing his arm. 'Wait!'

The old lady was attempting to raise her head, but the effort was too much. Her eyes fluttered wildly and her lips quivered. She was trying to speak, but the words wouldn't come. Frost brought his ear right down to her mouth and felt the hot rasp of her faint breath on his façe.

'Try again, love. I'm listening.'

One word. Very faint. It sounded like 'stab' but he wasn't sure if he heard it correctly. 'I know what he did, love. Can you describe him? Did you get a good look at him?' He kept his voice down. He didn't want the sister running in to order him out.

She nodded.

'Was he taller than me?'

Her lips moved, then her eyes widened and there was a choking noise at the back of her throat. And then she was still . . . dead still, the fingers no longer drumming.

The old girl was dead. Damn and sodding blast. She'd told him nothing. He dragged back the curtains. 'Nurse!'

He signalled for WPC Ridley to take over and hustled Gilmore out of the ward.

In the corridor outside he fumbled in his inside pocket to make a note of what the old lady had said and found he had pulled out those damn car expenses, the ones he had promised Mullett he would hand in tomorrow morning. Well, he'd have to think of yet another excuse for the Divisional Commander to disbelieve. Something was scribbled on one of the phoney petrol receipts. The name 'Wardley'. He racked his brains, but it meant nothing. 'Who's Wardley?'

Doesn't the old fool remember anything, thought Gilmore. 'He's the old boy who attempted suicide after he got the poison pen letter.'

Frost grinned. Something else to delay their return to the cold, dreary station. 'I promised the doc I'd have a word with him. Come on, son.'

Gilmore almost lost Frost in the labyrinth of corridors. Denton General Hospital was originally an old Victorian workhouse, but had been added to and rebuilt over the years. Frost darted up dark little passages, across storage areas and up clanking iron staircases to get to the ward where Wardley was lying. The staff nurse in her little cubicle with the shaded lamp greeted Frost as an old friend. She wasn't too keen on the idea of waking Wardley up, but Frost assured her it was essential.

Wardley, a little man of around seventy-five, his thinning hair snow white, was sleeping uneasily, turning and twitching and muttering. Frost shook his shoulder gently. Wardley woke with a start, mouth agape. He looked concerned as Frost introduced himself.

'Have you come to arrest me?' he croaked in a quavering voice.

'Attempted suicide isn't a crime any more,' said Frost, dragging a chair over to the bed. 'Besides, for all we know, it was an accident.'

Wardley frowned. 'You know it was suicide. I left a note.'

'Did you? We couldn't find it.'

The old man pulled himself up. 'It was on the bedside cabinet. My note . . . and that letter. How could you miss them?'

Frost scratched his head. 'They might have fallen under the bed. We'll look again later. Suppose you tell me what the letter said?'

The old man shook his head and his hands gripped and released the bedclothes. 'Terrible things. I'm too ashamed.'

'Blimey,' said Frost, 'I hope I can do things I'm ashamed of at your age.'

'It happened a long time ago, Inspector.'

'Then it doesn't bloody matter,' said Frost. 'Tell me what it said.'

A long pause. Someone further down the ward moaned in his sleep. A trolley rumbled by outside.

'All right,' said Wardley at last. 'It goes back thirty years – before I came to Denton. I lived in a little village. It was miles away from here, but I'm not telling you its name. I ran one of the classes in the Sunday school.' He paused.

'Not much sex and violence, so far,' murmured Frost. 'I hope it warms up.'

Wardley pushed out a polite, insincere smile and immediately switched it off. 'There were these two boys in my class. One was twelve, the other thirteen. After the class they would come back with me to my house. We would chat, watch television. All innocent stuff.' His voice rose. 'As God is my witness, Inspector, that's all it was.'

'What else would it be?' soothed Frost, thinking to himself, You dirty old bastard!

'One of the boys told lies about me. Filthy lies. I was called up before the Sunday school superintendent. I swore my innocence on the Bible, but he didn't believe me. I was forced to resign.' He stopped and studied the inspector's face, trying to read signs that he was being believed now.

'Go on,' murmured Frost.

'I couldn't stay in the village. People whispered and pointed. I had to move. So I came to Denton. After thirty years I thought it was all over and done with. And then I received that awful letter.'

'What did it say, Mr Wardley?'

'Something like "What will the church say when I tell

them what you did to those boys?" I'm a churchwarden, Inspector. It's my life. I couldn't face it happening all over again. If it gets out, I won't fail next time.'

Gilmore asked, 'Is there anyone in Denton, or locally, who could have known about your past?' Wardley shook his head.

'These two boys you messed about with,' Frost began, stopping abruptly as Wardley, quivering with rage, thrust his face forward and almost shouted.

'I never touched them. It was all lies. I swore on the Bible.' So loud did he protest that the staff nurse hurried anxiously towards the bed, only turning back when Frost gave her a reassuring wave.

He rephrased his question. 'The boys who lied, Mr Wardley. I want their names. And the name of the Sunday school superintendent, and all the people from your old village who would have known about this. We've got to check and see if any of them have moved to Denton.'

He left Gilmore to take down the details and went down to the car where he could smoke and think. Why on earth was he wasting time on this poison pen thing when he was way out of his depth with more important cases?

The car lurched to one side as Gilmore climbed in. 'Where to?' he asked, trying to get comfortable in the sagging driving seat.

His reply should have been 'Back to the station,' but he couldn't face going back to that cold Incident Room and wading through those endless, monotonous robbery files. 'Wardley's cottage. Let's have another look for that letter.'

'We shouldn't be wasting time on this,' moaned Gilmore. 'And how are we going to get in?'

'Dr Maltby will have a key,' said Frost, hoping this was true.

Frost was in luck. Maltby did have the key. He sat them in his surgery while he went upstairs to fetch it. 'Watch the door,' hissed Frost, darting for the doctor's desk.

'What are you doing?' asked Gilmore, horrified, watching the inspector methodically opening and closing drawers.

'Looking for something,' grunted Frost, busily opening a locked drawer with one of his own keys.

A creak of a floorboard above, then footsteps on the stairs.

'He's coming,' croaked Gilmore, wishing he could run and leave Frost to face the music.

'Got it,' crowed Frost, waving a blue envelope. He glanced at it and stuffed it back, quickly locked the drawer, then slid back into his seat just as the door opened and Maltby came in with the key to Wardley's cottage.

'What the hell was that about?' asked Gilmore when they were outside.

'The poison pen letter the doc gave us yesterday. He wouldn't tell us who it was sent to, so I sneaked a look at the envelope. Sorry to involve you, son, but you've got to grab your chances when they come.'

'So who was it addressed to . . . anyone we know?'

Frost grinned. 'Mark Compton. Mr Rigid Nipples.'

Gilmore's eyebrows shot up. 'What?'

'Doesn't it make you hate the swine even more . . . married to that cracking wife and having it off every Wednesday with a female contortionist in Denton?' He halted outside the door of a small, dark cottage, pushed the key in the lock and they went in.

They started in the bedroom, with its iron-framed single bed, and worked downwards. Everything inside the bedside cabinet was taken out. Frost showed mild interest in some loose tablets he found in the drawer, then seemed to lose interest. The cabinet was pulled away from the wall in case the note and the letter had fallen behind it. The bed likewise was moved, exposing a rectangular patch of fluffy dust. Even the bedclothes were stripped and shaken.

Gilmore, watched by Frost from the doorway, crawled all over the room on his hands and knees, looking in corners, behind curtains. He even stood on a chair and looked on top of the wardrobe. 'Nothing here,' he said, brushing dust from his jacket.

A quick poke around in the bathroom and then downstairs. Again Frost didn't seem inclined to join in the search, but let Gilmore do it while he sat on the arm of a chair, smoking and flipping through some bird-watching magazines he'd found in the magazine rack then looking all the way across the room at some nail holes in the wallpaper through a pair of high-powered binoculars he'd taken from a shelf.

'It would be quicker with two,' said Gilmore.

'When you get fed up, we'll go,' said Frost. 'The letters aren't here. I'm only staying because you seem so keen.'

Gilmore glowered. 'All right,' he admitted. 'I'm fed up.'

'We'll have a word with Ada next door,' said Frost.

You're messing me about, thought Gilmore as he followed the inspector to the adjoining cottage with its black-painted door and shining, well-polished brasswork. A quick rat-tat-tat at the brass knocker and the door was opened by Ada Perkins, her sharp pointed chin thrust forward belligerently. 'Oh, it's you, Jack Frost. I thought I could hear heavy feet plonking about next door.'

'And we thought we could hear the sound of an ear-hole pressed against the wall,' replied Frost. 'We'd like a couple of words . . . preferably not "piss off".'

With a loud sniff of disapproval she showed them into a spotlessly clean, cosy little room where a coal fire glowed cherry red in a black-leaded grate and where chintz curtains hid the damp and depressing weather outside. In the centre of the room stood a solid oak refectory table draped in a green baize cloth on which was a quantity of different coloured wine bottles bearing white, hand-written labels.

'Not interrupting an orgy, are we?' asked Frost.

She ignored the question and pointed to the high-backed wooden chairs by the table. 'Sit down!'

While Gilmore fidgeted, and kept consulting his watch, anxious to get back to his files, Frost settled down comfortably and warmed his hands at the fire. He picked up one of the bottles and pretended to read the label. 'What's this? "Cow's Dung and Dandelion. A thick brown wine, sticky to the palate." That sounds good, Ada.'

She snatched the bottle. 'It's *Cowslip* and Dandelion, as well you know. I'm sorting out my home-made wine.' She turned to Gilmore, who was drumming his fingers impatiently. 'Would you like to try some?'

Gilmore shook his head curtly. 'We're not allowed to drink while we're on duty.'

'This isn't alcoholic,' Frost assured him. 'This is home-made.' He beamed at Ada. 'Perhaps just a little sip – to keep out the cold.'

From the top of the matching solid oak sideboard, she produced two of the largest wine glasses Gilmore had ever seen and, after giving them a quick blow inside to shift the dust, banged them down on the green baize. She filled them to the brim, and slid them across. 'Try that.'

Gilmore lifted his glass and eyed the cloudy contents with apprehension. 'That's more than a sip.'

Frost told him, 'You've got to have a lot to get the full

benefit,' and raised his glass in salute to Ada who waited, arms folded, for their verdict. 'Cheers!' The wine tiptoed down his throat as smooth as silk, tasting of nothing in particular, then, suddenly, the pin slipped from the hand grenade and something exploded inside him, punching him in the stomach, making him gasp for breath and firing little star shells in front of his eyes. 'Gawd help us!' he spluttered as soon as the fit of coughing stopped.

'What's it like?' whispered Gilmore who hadn't plucked up the courage to try his yet.

'Delicious,' croaked Frost, his throat raw and stinging as if he had swallowed a glass of hot creosote. Quickly he covered his glass as Ada offered a second helping. 'If you're trying to get us drunk so you can have your way with us, Ada, forget it. I lust after your body, but all I want at the moment is the letters.'

Her expression hardly changed as she rammed the cork home in the bottle. 'What letters?'

Pausing only to slap the coughing, red-faced Gilmore on the back, Frost said, 'The poison pen letter and the suicide note.'

She stared blankly, as if mystified.

'You don't have to be a bleeding Sherlock Holmes to deduce you've got them, Ada. Wardley left them on his bedside cabinet. You were the first one in. They were gone by the time the doc arrived a couple of minutes later. Don't sod me about. I want them.'

Her lips tightened stubbornly. 'Did Mr Wardley say you could have them?'

'Yes, Ada. And he also said if you didn't hand them over, I was to give you a clout round the ear-hole.' He held out his hand. She hesitated, then took a folded sheet of notepaper from her apron pocket and thrust it at him.

Frost was slowly becoming aware that he was beginning

to feel a trifle light-headed. Everything in the room was starting to blur slightly round the edge. It took a great deal of effort to bring the typed letter into focus. Thank God he'd refused a second glass of Cowslip and Dandelion.

'Give it to me,' said Gilmore impatiently. He unfolded the note and read it aloud. '"Dear Lecher. What would the church say if I told them about you and the things the boys said you did?"'

'Is that it?' asked Frost, sounding disappointed.

Gilmore nodded. 'Typed on the same machine as the others. The "a" and the "s" are out of alignment.'

'It all looks out of alignment to me,' muttered Frost, wishing he hadn't made such a pig of himself on Ada's lethal brew. He squinted up at the blurred outline of the woman. 'And where's his suicide note, Ada?'

Stubbornly, she folded her arms. 'I burnt it.' At Frost's angry exclamation, she explained, 'Suicide is a mortal sin. Mr Wardley is a churchwarden. I wanted people to think the overdose was an accident.'

Frost pulled himself to his feet and waited to give the room a chance to steady itself. 'I wish you hadn't done that, Ada.'

She walked with them to the front door. 'Think yourself lucky I kept the poison pen letter. I was in two minds whether to burn that as well.'

'Thanks for the wine,' said Frost. 'I only felt sick for a little while.' A cold, swirling mist was waiting for them outside. Its chill dampness embraced them, sobering Frost instantly and making him shiver.

Gilmore edged the car out of the village and headed for Denton. Up on the hill, looking down on them, The Old Mill, a dark blur in the mist. No lights showed. 'Old Mother Rigid Nipples has gone to bed,' Frost murmured. 'Her husband's probably got one of them stuck up his nose right now.'

'Her husband's away,' grunted Gilmore, trying to spot the area car that was supposed to be watching the place, but there was no sign of it.

As they drove back, the radio was pleading for all available patrols to help break up a fight between two gangs of youths outside one of the town's less reputable pubs. 'Steer clear of there,' said Frost, not wanting to get involved.

And then the radio was calling them. 'Can you get over to The Old Mill right away?' asked a harassed-sounding Bill Wells. 'I had to call Charlie Alpha away to help with this pub fight. Mrs Compton's seen someone prowling about the grounds.'

Tuesday night shift (3)

The smell of burning oil from Frost's clapped-out Cortina grew stronger as Gilmore roared the car up the hill. 'I can see the sod!' yelled Frost. A hunched shape was moving across the lawn towards the house. Gilmore braked violently, slewing the car across the gravel driveway, and flung open the door. The sound of breaking glass shivered the silence, followed by the shrill urgency of an alarm bell.

'There he goes!' said Gilmore as something darted back across the lawn and was swallowed by shadow. 'I'll cut across that field, round to the side of the house. You nip that way to the end of the lane and cut him off as I flush him out.' Frost, his running days long past, listened without enthusiasm, and was still fumbling with his seat belt as Gilmore streaked away into the darkness.

The radio called to report that the alarm at The Old Mill was ringing. 'Yes, we know,' said Frost.

Gilmore, out of breath, was clinging to a tree, sucking in air for dear life as Frost eventually ambled over. Frost lit a cigarette and pushed a mouthful of smoke in the sergeant's direction. Gilmore fanned it away and, at last, between gasps, was able to croak, 'Where were you?'

Frost ignored the question. 'Did you see him?'

Gilmore's head shook in tempo with his panting. 'No. I told you to head him off.'

'I must have misheard you,' said Frost. 'Let's go to the house and see what he's done.' He spun round abruptly as a figure crashed towards them out of the black. 'Who the hell's this?'

'Did you get him?' It was Mark Compton, flourishing a heavy walking stick.

'He was too fast,' panted Gilmore. 'We thought your wife would be here on her own.'

'That's probably what that swine thought,' snapped Compton. 'I changed my schedule. I've just got in.' He led them back to the house and through to the lounge where curtains billowed from a jagged hole in the centre of the large patio window. Glass slivers glinted on the carpet. The cause of the damage, a muddied brick, probably from the garden, lay next to what looked like a bunch of flowers. Frost picked it up. It wasn't a bunch of flowers.

'My God!' croaked Compton.

It was a funeral wreath of white lilies, yellow chrysanthemums and evergreen leaves. Attached to it was an ivory-coloured card, edged in black. A handwritten message neatly inscribed in black ink read simply, and chillingly, *Goodbye.*

'The sod doesn't waste words, does he?' muttered Frost, passing the wreath to Gilmore. He stared out at the empty, dead garden, then pulled the curtains together. The night air had crept into the room and that, or the wreath, was making him feel shivery. 'Did you see anything of the bloke who did it?'

'No. Jill said she'd heard someone prowling around, but I couldn't spot anyone. I thought she'd imagined it, then the glass smashed, then the damned alarm. I saw someone running away, but that was all.'

'And you've no idea who it might be?'

'I've already told you, no.'

Frost scuffed a splinter of glass with his shoe. 'He's going to a great deal of trouble to make his point. He must really hate you . . . or your wife.'

'There's no motive behind this, Inspector,' insisted Compton. 'We're dealing with a nut-case.'

'Mark!' His wife calling from upstairs.

'I'm down here with the police.'

Gilmore pushed himself in front of the inspector. 'A quick question before your wife comes in, sir. Simon Bradbury – the man you had the fight with in London . . .'

'Hardly a fight, Sergeant,' protested Compton.

'Well, whatever, sir. It seems he's got a record for drunkenness and violence . . . and now we learn that his wife – the lady you obliged with a light – has given him the elbow. Any reason why he might believe you were the cause of her leaving him?'

Compton's face was a picture of incredulity. 'Me? And Bradbury's wife? I lit her damn cigarette over four weeks ago and that is the sum total of our relationship. You surely don't think Bradbury's responsible for what's been happening here? It's ridiculous!'

'The whole thing's bloody ridiculous,' began Frost

gloomily, quickly cheering up as the door opened and Jill Compton entered in a cloud of erotic perfume and an inch or so of nightdress. Her hair hung loosely over her shoulders and while Frost didn't know how breasts could be called 'pouting', pouting seemed a good word to describe Jill Compton's breasts as they nosed their way through near-transparent wisps of silk.

She smiled to greet Frost then she caught her breath. 'Oh my God!' She had seen the wreath. Her entire body began to tremble. Mark put his arms round her and held her tight. 'I can't take much more of this,' she sobbed.

'You won't have to, love,' he soothed. 'We'll sell up and move.'

'But the business . . .'

'You're more important than the bloody business.' He was squeezing her close to him, his hands cupping and stroking her buttocks, and Frost hated and envied him more and more by the second.

From somewhere in the house a phone rang. It was 00.39 in the morning. Everyone tensed. The woman trembled violently. 'It's him!' she whispered. Her husband held her tighter.

'I'll take it,' Frost barked. 'Where's the phone?'

Mark pointed up the stairs. 'In the bedroom. We switched it through.'

Frost and Gilmore galloped up the stairs, two at a time. The bedroom door was ajar. Inside, the room held the sensual smell of Mrs Compton. Frost snatched up the onyx phone from the bedside table and listened. A faint rapid tapping in the background. It was the sound of typing. At this hour of the morning? And indistinct murmurs of distant voices. Frost strained to listen, trying to make out what was being said. There was something familiar . . . Then a man's voice said, 'Hello

. . . is there anyone there?' and he flopped down on the bed in disappointment. The caller was Sergeant Wells.

'Yes, I'm here,' replied Frost. 'Sorry if I'm out of breath. I'm in a lady's bed at the moment.'

'Got a treat for you, Jack. Another body.'

'Shit!' said Frost. The only body he was interested in just now was Mrs Compton's. 'What's the address?' He snapped his fingers for Gilmore to take it down.

'The body's out in the open. It was dumped in a lane at the rear of the corporation rubbish tip.'

'Ah,' said Frost. 'Sounds like a job for Mr Mullett. I'll give you his home phone number.'

'Don't mess about, Jack. Jordan and Collier are waiting there for you. Could be foul play, but I've got my doubts.'

'Collier? You're pushing that poor little sod in at the deep end?'

'I had no-one else to send. Both area cars are ferrying the wounded down to Denton Casualty after the pub punch-up. There's blood and teeth all over the floor down here.'

'Excuses, excuses,' said Frost, hanging up quickly. 'Why do I always get the shitty locations? Rubbish tips, public urinals . . . I never get knocking shops and harems.' Well, he was in no hurry for this one. He stretched himself out on the bed and inhaled Jill Compton's perfume. 'Nip down and tell the lady of the house I'm ready for her now,' he murmured to Gilmore. 'And ask her to wash her behind. I don't fancy it with her husband's sticky finger-marks all over it.'

'Don't you think we should hurry?' asked Gilmore.

'I can't work up much enthusiasm about a body in a rubbish dump.' Reluctantly, he hauled himself up from the soft, still warm bed and had a quick nose around.

Other people's bedrooms fascinated him. His own was cold, cheerless and strictly functional, a place for crawling into bed, dead tired, in the small hours, and out again in the morning to face a new day's horrors. But here was a bedroom for padding about, half-undressed, on the soft wool carpeting, and for making love on the wide divan bed with its beige velvet headboard. By the side of the bed, a twin-mirrored, low-level dressing table where pouting-breasted Jill Compton would splash perfume over her red-hot, naked body, before sprawling on the bed, her hair tumbled across the pillow, awaiting the entrance of her rampant, adulterous sod of a husband.

He shook his head to erase the fantasy and walked across to the wide window to look out, across the moonlit garden. The wind had dropped and everything was quiet and still. 'Any chance the bloke we saw could have been the husband?'

'The husband?' Gilmore's eyebrows shot up. What was the idiot on about now? 'Smashing his own window? Scaring the hell out of his own wife?'

'I just get the feeling there's something phoney about this.'

'I don't share your opinion,' sniffed Gilmore. 'And in any case, there was no way it could have been the husband. He was with his wife when the window was smashed.'

'Then I'm wrong again,' shrugged Frost.

Downstairs, husband and wife were in close embrace, the shortie nightdress had ridden up to pouting breast level and hands were crawling everywhere.

Frost scooped up the wreath and passed it over to Gilmore. 'We'll see ourselves out,' he called.

They didn't hear him.

* * *

Police Constable Ken Jordan, his greatcoat collar turned up against the damp chill, was waiting for them at the lane at the rear of the sprawling rubbish dump. The lane was little more than a footpath with rain-heavy, waist-high grass flourishing on each side. In the background the night sky glowed a misty orange.

'Blimey, Jordan, what's that pong?' sniffed Frost, inhaling the sour breath of the town's decaying rubbish. 'It's not you, I hope?'

Jordan grinned. He liked working with Frost. 'Pretty nasty one this time, sir. The body's a bit of a mess.'

'I only get the nasty ones,' said Frost. 'Let's take a look at him.'

They followed Jordan, stumbling in the dark, as he led them down the narrow path, the wet grass on each side slapping at their legs. 'The old lady died, sir – at the hospital. I suppose you know.'

'Yes,' said Frost. 'I know.'

The lane curved. Ahead of them sodium lamps gleamed and flickering flames of something burning bloodied the haze. The tip was perimetered by 9-foot high chain link fencing, giving it the appearance of a wartime German prisoner of war camp.

Behind the wire fence, towering proud through streamers of mist, rose mountains of black plastic rubbish sacks and chugging between them, pushing, scooping and rearranging the landscape, a yellow-painted corporation bulldozer splashed through slime-coated pools of filthy water. As it demolished heaps of rubbish, rats scampered and scurried, their paws making loud scratching sounds on the plastic sacking. The smell was stale and sickly sweet like unwashed, rotting bodies.

Frost wound his scarf around his mouth and nose as

he nodded towards the bulldozer. 'I didn't know they worked nights.'

'It's this flu virus,' explained Jordan. 'Half of the work-force are off sick and the rest have to do overtime to keep ahead. It was the bulldozer driver who spotted the body.'

'Then sod him for a start,' said Frost.

'This way, sir.' Jordan led them off the path, trampling a trail through the lush, sodden grass to where a pasty-faced PC Collier stood uneasily on guard over rusting tin cans and a tarpaulin-covered huddle.

Frost lit up a cigarette and passed around the packet. Everyone took one, even Collier who didn't usually smoke. Frost looked down at the tarpaulin and prodded it with his foot. 'I can't delay the treat any more.' He nodded to Collier. 'Let's have a look at him.'

Collier hesitated and didn't seem to want to comply.

'You heard the inspector,' snapped Gilmore. 'What are you waiting for?'

Keeping his head turned well away, Collier fumbled for the tarpaulin and pulled it back.

Even Frost had to gasp when he saw the face. The cigarette dropped from his lips on to the chest of the corpse. He bent hurriedly to retrieve it, trying not to look too closely at the face as he did so.

Jordan, who had seen it before, stared straight ahead. Gilmore's stomach was churning and churning. He bit his lip until it hurt and tried to think of anything but that face. He wasn't going to show himself up in front of the others.

The body was of an old man in his late seventies. There were no eyes and parts of the face were eaten away with bloodied chunks torn from the cheeks and the lips.

'The rats have had a go at him,' said Jordan.

'I didn't think they were love bites,' said Frost. He straightened up. 'Still, we're lucky the weather's cold. Did I ever tell you about that decomposing tramp in the heat-wave?'

'Yes,' said Jordan hurriedly. Frost was fond of trotting out that ghastly anecdote.

'Did I tell you, son?' said Frost, turning to Gilmore. 'The hottest bloody summer on record. I can still taste the smell of him.'

'Yes, you told me,' lied Gilmore.

The dead man, the exposed flesh yellow in the over-spill of the sodium lamps, lay on his back, lipless mouth agape, staring eyeless into the night sky. He wore an unbuttoned black overcoat, heavy with rain, which flapped open to reveal a blue-striped, flannelette pyjama jacket which bore the bloodied paw marks of the feeding rats. The pyjama jacket was tucked inside dark grey trousers which were fastened by a leather belt.

'Do we know who he is?'

'Yes, Inspector.' Collier came forward. 'It's that old boy whose daughter-in-law reported him missing from home last week. He was always walking out and sleeping rough.'

'I bet the poor sod has never slept as rough as this,' observed Frost. 'Sergeant Wells said you think it's foul play?'

'His face looked battered, sir,' said Collier, pointing, but not looking where he was pointing.

Frost haunched down, slipped a hand beneath the head of the corpse and lifted it slightly. He dribbled smoke as he stared long and hard at the mutilated face, then stood up, wiping his palm down the front of his mac. 'That's just where the rats have been tucking in, son. There's no other marks . . . see for yourself.'

'I'll take your word for it, sir, if you don't mind,' said Collier.

Jordan's personal radio squawked. He pulled it from his pocket. Sergeant Wells wanted to speak to Inspector Frost urgently.

Frost took the radio. 'Everything's bloody urgent,' he moaned.

'Fifteen Roman Road, Denton,' said Wells tersely. 'Mrs Betty Winters, an old lady living on her own. A neighbour's phoned. He reckons he saw a man breaking in through the front door. The intruder is still in the house. Sorry about this, but I've got no-one else to send.'

'On our way,' said Frost, stuffing the radio back in Jordan's pocket. 'Jordan, come with us. Collier, stay here and wait for the police surgeon.' At the young PC's look of dismay at being left alone with the body, he added, 'You can handle it, son. If death isn't due to natural causes, let me know right away.'

With Jordan driving they made it to Roman Road in three minutes, coasting past number 15 and stopping outside the public telephone box where a middle-aged man emerged and hurried over to them. 'It was me who phoned,' he announced. 'I knew he was up to no good the minute I saw him. I thought he was going to pee in the porch. They do that, you know – dirty sods. You put your empty milk bottles out . . .'

'What did he look like?' cut in Frost as the man drew a breath.

'A big, ugly-looking sod. I couldn't get to that phone quick enough. Stinks of urine in that phone box. When they're not peeing in your porch or your milk bottles they're peeing in the phone box . . .'

'Are you sure he's still inside?' asked Gilmore.

'Positive.'

'Is there a back way out?'

'Through the gardens and over the rear wall. But I don't think he's got out that way. You'd hear next-door's bloody dog barking . . . bark, bark, bark, all bleeding night.'

'Go with the gentleman, Jordan,' said Frost, anxious to get rid of the verbose neighbour. 'Get into the garden over his fence and block the escape route.'

As soon as Jordan radioed through that he was in position, Frost did his letter-box squinting act. Utter blackness. A quick examination of the front door. No sign of a forced entry, so if there was an intruder, how did he get in? Hopefully he looked under the porch mat for a spare key. Nothing.

'Shall I smash the glass panel?' offered Gilmore.

'No,' grunted Frost, poking his hand through the letter-box and scrabbling about until his fingers touched something. A length of string looped at the end. He gave the string a tug. There was a click as the door knob was pulled back. Cautiously he pushed open the door, grabbing it as a sudden gust of wind threatened to send it crashing against the wall of the hall.

They tiptoed inside and Frost flicked the beam of his torch to show Gilmore how the string ran through staples and was tied round the door catch. 'The burglar's friend, son.' If the tenant forgot his key, he just had to pull the string. But so could anyone else who wanted to gain entry.

They held their breaths and listened. The house stretched and creaked and breathed and sighed. Then an alien sound from upstairs made Frost grab at Gilmore's sleeve, willing him to silence. A small click like a door closing. Signalling for the sergeant to stay by the front door, blocking that escape route, Frost padded along the passage and began creeping up the stairs.

Every stair seemed to creak no matter how carefully he placed his feet. At the top his torch picked out a small landing and two doors side by side. He clicked off the torch and slowly turned the handle of the nearest door.

Pitch black and a feeling of cold and damp. A hollow plop. Water slowly dripping from a tap. And a smell of sweat. Of fear. His thumb was on the button of the torch when he caught the metallic glint of a knife just as something hit him, sending his head smashing against the wall.

The torch dropped from his grasp as arms locked round him and dragged him down to the ground. Someone was on top of him, punching. There was hardly any room to move. His arm was trapped between his body and the wall, but he strained and wriggled frantically until he managed to free it. He reached up. Cloth. Flesh. Then a clawing hand clutched his face. He grabbed it, trying to tear it away while his other hand scrabbled in the blackness over cold, wet lino. Where was the damned torch?

He started to yell 'Gilmore!' when a fist crashed down on his face. He jerked up a knee, blindly. A scream of pain as his assailant fell back. His groping hand touched something metallic. The torch. Thankfully he grabbed it and swung it upwards like a club. A sharp crack and a groan as his attacker collapsed on top of him. Frost pushed and wriggled and managed to get on top.

Thudding footsteps up the stairs. 'Are you all right, Inspector?'

'No, I am bloody not!' panted Frost. 'I'm fighting for my bleeding life in here.'

Gilmore pushed in and fumbled for the light switch. They were in a small white-tiled bathroom. Frost, astride the intruder, was wedged between the wall and the bath.

His tongue took a trip round his mouth, prodding at teeth, tasting salt.

He stood up to get a better look at the unconscious man on the floor. His attacker was around twenty, fresh complexion, his hair black and cut short, dressed in grey slacks, a grey polo-neck sweater and a windcheater. Gilmore searched his pockets. No wallet, no identification. No sign of a weapon but over the sweater a heavy silver crucifix on a chain glinted like the blade of a knife.

The man on the floor groaned and stirred slightly.

'Hadn't we better get him to a doctor?' asked Gilmore.

Frost shook his head. 'He's only stunned.' Then he remembered the old lady who should have heard all the noise and be screaming blue murder. 'Let's find the old girl.'

She was in the bedroom. In the bed, eyes staring upwards, mouth wide open and dribbling red. The bedclothes had been dragged back, exposing a nightdress drenched in blood from the multiple stab wounds in her stomach. On the pillow, by her head, was a browning smear where her killer had wiped the blade clean before leaving.

While the little house swarmed with more people than it had held in its lifetime, Frost and Gilmore closeted themselves in the bathroom with their prisoner, now securely handcuffed. He lay still, apparently unconscious. A dig from Frost's foot resulted only in a slight moan. On the bath rack was an enormous sponge which Frost held under the cold tap until it was sodden and dripping, then he held it high over the man's face and squeezed.

The head jerked, and twisted, the eyes fluttered, then opened wide. He blinked and tried to focus on the piece of white plastic bearing a coloured photograph.

'Police,' announced Frost.

A sigh of relief as the man struggled up to a sitting position. 'In the bedroom – she's dead . . .' He winced and tried to touch his head and then saw the handcuffs. 'What's this? What's going on?'

'Suppose you tell us,' snapped Frost. 'What's your name?'

'Purley. Frederick Purley.'

'Address?'

'The Rectory, All Saints Church.'

'Are you trying to be funny?' snarled Gilmore.

Purley raised his dripping face to the sergeant. 'I'm the curate at All Saints Church. Please remove these handcuffs.' He tried to rise to his feet, but Gilmore pushed him down.

'Since when do curates break into people's houses in the middle of the night?' asked Frost.

'I only wanted to see if Mrs Winters was all right. I never dreamed . . .' His head drooped.

'Why did you think she wasn't all right?' asked Frost, dropping his cigarette end into the toilet pan and flushing it away.

'I'd been sitting with one of my parishioners – an old man, terminally ill – giving his daughter a break from looking after him. As I walked back I saw Mrs Winters' milk was still on the step. After that dreadful business with poor Mrs Haynes, I had to make sure she was all right.'

Gilmore's head jerked up. 'You knew Mrs Haynes?'

'Yes, Sergeant. I was with her on Sunday. Her husband's grave was vandalized. She was so upset.'

'It wasn't the poor cow's day,' said Frost. Then his eyes narrowed. 'There was no milk on the step when we arrived.'

'I brought it in with me. I put it in her fridge.'

Frost yelled down the stairs for the SOC man to check there was an unopened bottle of milk in the fridge and if so, to go over it for prints. Back to Purley. 'How did you get in?'

'There's a string connected to the front door catch. I've used it before . . . Mrs Winters is a cripple – she's under the hospital, chronic arthritis. She can't always get to the door.'

'Right,' nodded Frost. 'So what did you do next?'

'The hall was in darkness. I couldn't find the light switch, but I made my way upstairs. I tapped on her bedroom door. No answer. I went in and switched on the light and . . .' He shuddered and covered his face with his hands, 'and I saw her. And then I heard the door click downstairs. I thought it was the killer coming back. I switched off the light and hid in the bathroom. You know the rest.'

A brisk tap at the door. The SOC man came in holding a full pint bottle of red-top milk, shrouded in a polythene bag. 'This was in the fridge, Inspector. Two different dabs on the neck – neither of them the dead woman's.'

Frost squinted at the bottle. 'One should be the milkman, the other ought to be the padre here. Take his dabs and see if they match.' He ordered Gilmore to remove the cuffs.

Another tap at the door. 'The pathologist has finished,' yelled Forensic.

'Coming,' called Frost.

It was cold in the tiny ice-box of a bedroom with its unfriendly brown lino and the windows rattling where the wind found all the gaps. Drysdale buttoned his overcoat and rubbed his hands briskly. 'I estimate the time of death as approximately eleven o'clock last night, give or take half an hour or so either way.' He pointed to bruising on each side of the dead woman's mouth. 'He clamped his hand over her face so she couldn't utter a sound, then he jerked back the bedclothes and stabbed her repeatedly – three times in the stomach and lastly in the heart. The wounds are quite deep. To inflict them he would have raised the knife above his head and brought it down with considerable force.' Drysdale gave a demonstration with his clenched fist. 'As he raised his hand, some of the blood on the knife splashed on to the wall.' He indicated red splatters staining the pale cream wallpaper.

'Would he have got any of that on himself?'

'Without a doubt,' said Drysdale, pulling on his gloves. 'Considerable quantities of blood spurting from the wounds would have hit his right arm and blood from the blade would have spattered him as he raised his arm to deliver the next blow.'

'No traces of blood in the bathroom waste-trap,' offered the man from Forensic, who was measuring and marking blood splashes on the wall, 'so he didn't wash it off before he left.'

'Dirty bastard!' said Frost. 'What can you tell us about the knife, doc?'

'Extremely sharp, single-edged, rigid blade approximately six inches long and about an inch and a quarter wide, honed to a sharp point.'

'The same knife that killed the other old girl – Mary Haynes?'

'It's possible,' admitted Drysdale, grudgingly. 'I'll be more positive after the post-mortem – which will be at 10.30 tomorrow morning. You'll be there?'

'Wouldn't miss it for the world,' replied Frost.

Gilmore was waiting for him at the head of the stairs. The vicar of All Saints had been contacted and had confirmed that his curate, Frederick Purley, had gone out to visit a terminally ill parishioner, and the SOC officer had confirmed that one of the thumb prints on the milk bottle belonged to the man in the bathroom.

Frost groaned his disappointment. 'The old lady died yesterday. So unless Purley killed her last night, then came back today just to put the milk in the fridge, we've lost our best hope for a suspect.'

He waited in the kitchen while Gilmore brought down the verified curate, who was vigorously rubbing his freed wrists, and who declined the offer of a doctor to look at his head on which a lump had formed nicely.

They sat round the kitchen table where the plates were already laid for the breakfast the old lady hadn't lived to enjoy. Frost utilized the egg cup as an ashtray. A rap at the door as PC Jordan entered.

'We've been all over the house, Inspector. No sign of forced entry anywhere. The back door's locked and bolted and all windows are secure. He came in through the front door.'

Frost nodded, then turned to Purley. 'Who else knew about instant entry with the old dear's piece of string?'

'Very few people, I should imagine. She wasn't a very friendly or communicative woman.'

'So how did you know her?'

'She used to be a member of our church senior citizens' club until her legs got too bad. I like to keep in touch.'

'Anything about her that would make her attractive to a burglar, padre? Was she supposed to have money, or valuables in the house?'

Purley shook his head. 'Not as far as I know.'

Frost scratched his chin. 'Was Mrs Haynes a member of your church club?'

'Yes, but an infrequent attender. She hasn't been for months.'

'What about a Mrs Alice Ryder?'

'Ryder?' His brow furrowed, then he shook his head. 'No. I don't recall the name.'

'We believe the same bastard killed them all,' said Frost. 'There's got to be a link.'

Purley gave a sad, apologetic smile. 'Then I'm afraid I don't know it.'

On the way back to the station they detoured to drop off the curate at the vicarage. As the car passed the churchyard Frost was reminded of the wreath dumped in the Comptons' lounge. He couldn't remember picking it up and was relieved when Gilmore jerked a thumb to the back seat where the wreath lay between a pair of mud-caked wellington boots.

'You might as well take the Compton case over, son. I'm not going to have much time for it.'

'Right,' said Gilmore, trying to keep the delight from his voice. A case of his own. He'd show these yokels how to get a result.

'You don't buy wreaths off the peg – they have to be ordered specially,' continued Frost. 'If I were you I'd get Burton to check with every florist in Denton.'

'That's what I intend to do,' said Gilmore.

As they crossed the lobby with the wreath, Sergeant Wells looked up from his log book. 'Who's dead?' he asked.

'Glenn Miller,' grunted Frost. 'It just came over on the radio.' He was in no mood for Wells' jokes.

'I'll tell you who is dead,' said Wells, anxious to impart his news.

Frost groaned, and walked reluctantly across to the desk. More cheer from Wells. The man was a walking bloody obituary column. 'If it isn't Mullett, I don't want to know.'

Wells paused for dramatic effect, then solemnly intoned, 'George Harrison! Heart attack as he was going downstairs. Dead before he hit the bottom.' He leant forward to observe the effect this had on the inspector.

Frost's jaw dropped. Police Inspector George Harrison had only retired a few weeks ago after twenty-four years service. 'Bloody hell!'

'First you come round with the list for their retirement present,' said Wells, dolefully, 'next thing you know you're going round with the list for their wreath. You might as well collect both at once and be done with it.'

'Bloody hell!' said Frost again. The force was his life and retirement was the one thing he dreaded. The thought made him depressed. He jerked his head to Gilmore and headed for the stairs. 'Come on, son, let's get something to eat.'

'If you're going to the canteen, don't bother,' said Wells, happy to be the bearer of more bad news. 'It's shut.'

'Shut?' echoed Frost in dismay.

'The night staff are still down with flu. If you want anything, you've got to bring it in from outside.'

'And eat it in this ice-box?' moaned Frost, giving the dead radiator a kick. 'Sod that for a lark!' Then a slow grin crawled across his face. Somewhere in the building there was a room with comfortable chairs, a carpet and a 3-kilowatt heater. He pulled the car expense sheet from his jacket pocket and licked the tip of a stubby pencil. 'I'm taking orders for the all-night Chinky. Who wants curried chicken and chips?'

'I don't like this, Jack,' said Wells. 'If Mullett finds out . . .'

'He's not going to find out.' retorted Frost, peeping inside a foil container. 'Who ordered the sweet and sour?'

They were in the old log cabin, Mullett's wood veneer-lined office, Gilmore, Burton, Wells, and the four members of the murder enquiry team, the heater going full pelt, the room hot and steamy and reeking of Chinese food. The top of the satin mahogany desk was littered with foil containers and soft drink cans. Frost, in Mullett's chair, smoking one of Mullett's special cigarettes, was sorting out the food orders. 'Who wanted pancake rolls?'

Gilmore stood near the door, hovering nervously, his eye on the corridor, expecting any moment to see an irate Divisional Commander bursting through the swing doors.

'Come on, Gilmore,' called Frost. 'The chop suey's yours.'

Gilmore smiled uneasily and sat himself where he could still see down the corridor. He shuddered to think what discovery would do for his promotion chances.

'All we want is a disco and a few birds,' said Frost, spilling sweet and sour sauce on the carpet, 'and this job would be just about tolerable.' He swung round to Burton who was demolishing a double portion of sweet and sour lobster balls. 'Mrs Ryder died in hospital. Any news from Forensic on that knife the killer dropped?'

Burton swallowed hard. 'Nothing that helps much, Inspector. Their report's on your desk.'

'You know I don't read reports,' said Frost, dipping a chip in his curry sauce. 'What did it say?'

'An ordinary cheap kitchen knife of a standard pattern. No fingerprints, but traces of blood type O.'

Frost sniffed disdainfully. 'That's a coincidence – the victim was type O.' He peered suspiciously into his foil dish. 'This looks like stomach contents.' He sniffed. 'Smells like it, too.'

'Oh God, Jack,' shuddered Wells, pushing his food away from him.

Frost addressed the murder enquiry team. 'Any joy from the neighbours?'

'Most of them are in bed,' Burton told him 'We're going to have to go back first thing in the morning to catch the rest before they set off for work. Those we've spoken to hardly knew the old girl. She stayed in most of the time. No-one seemed aware of the string.'

'And no-one saw anyone suspicious hanging about,' added Jordan.

'Suspicious?' said Frost, pulling a piece of gristle from his mouth and flinging it in the vague vicinity of Mullett's wastepaper bin. 'This bastard isn't going to mooch about looking suspicious. He won't have a stocking mask on and a bleeding great knife poking out of his pocket. He's going to be inconspicuous. I want to know about everyone who's been seen going up and down the street – and that applies to the other two victims as well. I don't care if it's the road sweeper, the postman, doorstep piddlers or even a bleedin' dog – I want to know. People, vans, cars, the lot. We can then start comparing – see if anyone's been seen in all three streets.'

'The computer . . .' began Gilmore.

'The computer's a waste of time,' cut in Frost. 'I'm only going along with it to keep Hornrim Harry quiet. The only way to solve these cases is by good, solid detective work. By beating the hell out of some poor sod until he signs a fake confession.'

Gilmore faked a smile. 'It will be quicker with the computer, I promise you.'

'All right,' said Frost. 'I'll leave it to you.'

'What about a search team for the murder weapon?' asked Burton, wiping his mouth. 'He could well have chucked it.'

'Put a couple of men on it, but don't waste too much time. My gut feeling is that the bastard has kept it – ready for next time.'

The room went quiet. 'Next time?' said Wells.

'Yes, Bill.' He pushed the empty container away and fished out his cigarettes. 'I've got a nasty feeling in my water that he's going to kill again.'

Mullett's phone rang. A collective gasp and all eating stopped in mid-chew.

'It's all right,' assured Wells, 'I had the main phone switched through here.'

Frost picked it up. 'Mullett's Dining Rooms,' he said.

Wells' eyes bulged with alarm until he realized the inspector had his hand over the mouthpiece.

The caller was a technician from Forensic reporting that he had extensively examined all the items removed from 46 Mannington Crescent, Denton and found nothing that would link them with the murder of Mrs Mary Haynes. As Frost listened he raised his eyes to the ceiling in despair. 'Sod clearing the innocent – what about nailing the guilty for a change? I asked you to drop that and check on those two newspapers as a matter of priority. No, I don't know who I spoke to. All right, all right.' He banged the phone back on its rest. 'He never got the message. Flaming Forensic. They're about as bloody efficient as we are. They can't start on the newspaper until tomorrow.'

'Well, it is two o'clock in the morning,' Wells reminded him.

'Then I'm bloody going home,' said Frost, not bothering to cover up a yawn. 'I've had enough for today. The rest of you, go home too. Grab some sleep and be back here by six. You can pinch some men from the next shift and start knocking on doors before people go off to work.'

'But Mr Mullett's rota . . .' began Wells.

'Sod Mr Mullett's rota. See you in the morning.'

He looked in his office on the way out. His in-tray was overflowing. He tugged the top paper from his tray. It was PC Collier's report on the dead body outside the refuse tip. He had almost forgotten about it. Natural causes – heart attack. Well, that was a relief. Clipped to the report was the SOC's photograph of the dead man *in situ,* sharp, clear and full of graphic detail. He showed it to Gilmore.

'I shall dream about that damn face tonight,' moaned Gilmore as they walked out to the car.

'I hope I don't,' said Frost. 'I want to dream of Mrs Compton.'

He did dream of Jill Compton. But she was eyeless and screaming and crawling with bloody-snouted rats. He woke up just before five in a cold sweat and couldn't get back to sleep again.

Wednesday morning shift

Police Superintendent Mullett stamped up the corridor to his office. He was angry. His sleep had been continually disturbed by calls from the media, and then from County, the Chief Press Officer, demanding his comments on a possible serial murderer in Denton, the brutal killer of three old ladies. When he had phoned the station to try to get some information from Frost, he was informed that, despite the rota, the inspector and his team had left for the night and calls to Frost's home indicated that the phone had deliberately been left off the hook. He finally managed to get the information required from Detective Sergeant Gilmore, but only after Gilmore's wife had been extremely rude over the phone, asking why her husband was expected to be at everyone's beck and call twenty-four hours a day.

Scooping up a fearsome stack of mail from his absent secretary's desk, he unlocked his office door, then paused, nose twitching, testing the air. What was that smell? A stale, rancid oniony aroma which reminded him of curry. He dumped the post in his in-tray and flung open the window. The curtains flapped wildly as the wind roared and drove in the rain. Below, in Eagle Lane, the noise of traffic was deafening. He hastily closed the window and returned to his desk where he reached for the internal phone to ask the station sergeant to come in with his morning report.

While he waited he flicked through the post, shuddering at a photograph of a mutilated body found outside Denton rubbish tip, then frowning at the totally inadequate, scrawled report from Frost – *Mrs Alice Ryder, victim of burglary assault, died in Denton Hospital – full report to follow. Mrs Betty Winters, aged 76, 15 Roman Rd, Denton. Murder by stabbing – full report to follow.* Mullett's frown deepened. As he knew from bitter experience, Frost's 'further reports' never materialized. The man's paperwork was hopeless. Which reminded him, where were those car expenses? He rummaged through his tray but, as expected, they were not there.

He looked up as Sergeant Johnson came in with the morning report and the mail from County. He greeted him with a smile. 'Good to see you back, Sergeant. Are you fit?'

'Well, actually, sir . . .' began Johnson, who was starting to feel a trifle light-headed and was wondering if he hadn't reported back to work too soon.

'Excellent,' cut in Mullett hastily. He didn't want a catalogue of the man's ailments. He'd had enough of moans from Sergeant Wells. 'Manning level?'

'Three men back from sick leave,' Johnson reported, 'but two more off – injured in that pub punch-up last night.'

'First class,' snapped Mullett, concerned only with the plus side of the arithmetic. 'We're winning, Sergeant.' He smiled as he signed the report and blotted it neatly. 'We'll soon be back to normal.'

'We're going to be very thin on the ground today as far as normal duties are concerned,' warned the sergeant. 'Mr Frost has commandeered most of my men for house-to-house enquiries – another old lady stabbed to death last night.'

'I know,' said Mullett bitterly. 'The press phoned me at three o'clock in the morning to tell me – and Mr Frost kindly scribbled a note for my in-tray.' He held aloft the piece of paper. 'County want us to tread very carefully with this one, Sergeant. A serial killer at large in Denton – could cause panic. It's vital I see the inspector the minute he comes in.'

'Sir,' said Johnson, taking the signed report.

The office door opened. Mullett hoped it was Frost, but it was his gum-chewing temporary secretary in a disturbing polo-necked sweater who wiggled in with the correspondence he had dictated yesterday. 'Sorry I'm late,' she said, dumping the poorly typed, heavily corrected letters on his desk, 'but we've run out of Snowpake. I had to buy some more. Oh – and this has just come.' She dropped the Denton *Echo* in front of him.

He snatched up the paper from her and stared goggle-eyed, mouth dropping with dismay at the screaming banner headlines. *Town of Terror – Granny Ripper Claims Third Victim!!! Terror spread like wild-fire amongst the senior citizens of Denton today as news of yet another brutal murder* . . . The phone rang. Still staring at the paper he groped for it. 'Yes?' he croaked. He jerked to attention. 'Good morning, sir . . . Yes, I've just seen the paper.' He clapped a hand over the mouthpiece and bellowed at Johnson, 'Find Frost. I want him here, now!'

To Johnson's surprise, Frost was already in his office, a wad of blank petrol receipts in front of him which he was filling in with different coloured pens. Sitting in the other desk was the new detective sergeant, looking disgruntled and also scribbling out petrol receipts.

'Hello, Johnny,' greeted Frost. 'Welcome back. We thought you were dying. We'll have to send the bloody wreath back now.' He indicated the withering floral tribute in his in-tray. 'Talking of wreaths reminds me of a joke.'

'Never mind jokes,' said Johnson, 'Mr Mullett wants to see you.'

'Sod Mullett,' said Frost. 'There was this woman . . .' He paused as DC Burton came in.

'Got a minute, sir?'

'Sure, son, but I've got a joke first. There was this woman . . .' He paused again as Detective Sergeant Arthur Hanlon, nose red and sore, poked his head round the door.

'Oh, if you're busy, Jack . . .'

'No – come in, Arthur. I've got a joke for you.'

Hanlon pulled a face. 'If it's the one about the man drinking the spittoon for a bet, you've told it to me.'

'A different one,' said Frost, beckoning him in. 'It's about the funeral of a woman who's had fifteen kids.' He frowned as the phone rang. Burton answered it.

'Forensic for you, Inspector. They say it's urgent.'

'Everything's bloody urgent!' He took the phone and in a strangulated voice said, 'Mr Frost will be with you in a moment.' He pressed the mouthpiece to his jacket. 'Where was I?'

'Fifteen kids,' reminded Johnson, anxious to get the story over so Frost could report to Mullett.

'Right. Funeral. Woman who'd had fifteen kids being buried. As the coffin's being lowered down into the grave, the vicar turns to the husband and says, "Together at last!" The husband says, "What do you mean, together at last? I'm still alive." "I wasn't referring to you," says the vicar. "I meant her legs."'

Gilmore sat stone-faced as Frost's raucous roar of mirth almost drowned the others. Old women butchered and the fool was cracking jokes! Frost raised the phone, poking his finger in his ear to shut out the laughter. 'Hello. Frost here. Sorry, I can't hear you. I think the Divisional Commander's throwing a party.' He flapped a hand for silence. 'That's better, I've shut the door. You were saying?' He listened. 'That's bloody marvellous. Check it out and let me know.' He hung up and beamed happily at Gilmore and Burton. 'Those newspapers we sent to Forensic. Nothing on the *Daily Telegraph,* but when they shoved the *Sun* under the microscope, not only were the Page Three girl's tits enormous, but they spotted tiny flakes of black paint and rust on the outside page.'

'Black paint and rust?' frowned Burton.

'If our luck's in, it's from Greenway's letter-box,' explained Frost. 'It could have rubbed off as the paper went in and out. Forensic are sneaking someone round to his house to check. If the paint matches, we've got the bastard.' He rubbed his hands with delight and passed his cigarettes round.

Johnson was getting fidgety. 'Mr Mullett wants to see you, Jack.'

'I'm not ready for him yet.' He peeled off some blank petrol receipts. 'Fill these in for me, Johnny. Disguise your writing. Six gallons, eight gallons and four gallons.'

The sergeant's pen flew over the receipts. 'What crime am I committing?'

'Forgery,' said Frost, giving three blanks to Burton. 'Disguise your handwriting, son. Two lots of eight gallons and one of six.' He pushed two more blanks across to Arthur Hanlon. 'Five gallons and seven gallons, Arthur – and blow your nose, it's starting to drip.'

'Just tell me what I've done,' said Johnson, handing the completed receipts back.

Frost collected the balance from Gilmore and Burton and riffled through them. 'I lost all my receipts last month so I had to forge my car expenses. Some silly sod in County with nothing better to do spotted it. Mullett said I could get off the hook if I came up with the genuine ones.' He waved the receipts. 'These are them.'

'But they're still fakes,' insisted Johnson.

'But better fakes than the first lot. Besides, I didn't have time to go round all the flaming petrol stations asking for copies.' He turned to Hanlon. 'What's the latest on the house-to-house, Arthur?'

Hanlon handed over his two receipts. 'We've almost finished. The first of the results are going through the computer now.'

'Anything significant?' asked Gilmore.

Hanlon shrugged. 'One person thought they saw a blue van cruising down Roman Road late on the night of the murder, another saw a strange red car. I'll check them out.'

After Hanlon squeezed out of the office, Frost remembered that Burton was still patiently waiting. 'Sorry, son, I forgot about you. What was it?'

'I've been checking all the florists about that wreath, sir. I traced the shop and found out who ordered it.'

Frost had to readjust his thoughts back to the Compton business. 'Who?' But before Burton could answer, Gilmore had leapt from his chair and was glowering angrily at the detective constable.

'This is my case, Burton,' he hissed. 'You report to me, not to the inspector.' He was in a lousy mood. Liz had been insufferably rude to the Divisional Commander when he'd phoned last night. Mullett was furious and it was pretty clear that his promotional chances were fast gurgling down the drain. How the hell could he report Frost's misdemeanours when the inspector involved him in them all . . . eating in Mullett's office, forging petrol vouchers. And now this cretin of a detective constable was going over his head.

Burton, taken aback by Gilmore's outburst, looked from the sergeant to the inspector.

'My fault,' said Frost. 'The sergeant is quite right. It is his case.'

'So who ordered the damn thing?' asked Gilmore, returning to his chair.

Burton flipped open his notebook. 'Mr Wilfred Blagden, 116 Merchants Barton, Denton.'

Gilmore smiled sarcastically. 'I suppose if I wait long enough you'll tell me who he is?'

The constable hesitated before deciding that the pleasure of smashing Gilmore's face in was marginally outweighed by the need to retain his job.

'He's an old man, eighty-one years old. His wife, Audrey, died last week.'

Gilmore still appeared mystified, but the penny dropped for Frost. 'The wreath was stolen from her grave?'

'Yes, Inspector. The old boy's very upset – wants to know what the police are doing about it.'

The police are sitting on their arses cracking dirty jokes, thought Gilmore. He waved Burton away with an irritated flap of the hand then skimmed through a report from Forensic reporting that the death threats to the Comptons had been cut from copies of *Reader's Digest.*

The office door crashed open and a flustered-looking Johnny Johnson burst in. 'Mr Mullett is screaming for you, Jack.'

Frost quickly checked through the newly forged car expenses, then stood up, moving the knot of his tie to somewhere near the centre of his collar. 'I'm ready for him now. Do I look innocent and contrite?'

'You never look innocent and contrite,' Johnson replied.

As he breezed through the lobby on his way to the old log cabin, he passed an old man sitting hunched on the hard wooden bench by the front desk. The man looked familiar, but Frost couldn't place him. He sidled over to Collier who was standing in for Johnny Johnson and jerked a thumb in query.

Collier leant forward, 'His name's Maskell.'

Frost clicked his fingers. 'Jubilee Terrace – Tutankhamun's tomb – mummified body?'

Collier nodded. 'He refuses to accept that his wife is dead. He keeps coming in to report her missing.'

Sensing their attention, the old man looked up. 'Her name's Mary. I left her in bed, but she's not there any more.' He cupped a hand to his ear so he wouldn't miss a word of their reply.

'She's dead, Mr Maskell,' said Collier.

But the old man refused to hear what he didn't want to hear. 'Her name's Mary Maskell – 76 Jubilee Terrace, Denton.'

Frost moved on hurriedly, leaving Collier to deal with him. He was half-way up the passage to Mullett's office when . . . 76 *Jubilee Terrace . . . Upstairs bedroom. The old girl's dead* . . . The tiny tape recorder at the back of his mind had been triggered into replaying, over and over, that mysterious phone call in the pub. How had the caller known about the old girl? Maskell wouldn't have let him in. She was upstairs and the bedroom windows were heavily curtained. The only way in would have been through the same window Frost had used. *Upstairs bedroom. The old girl's dead.* The voice. He knew that damned voice. He screwed up his face trying to squeeze his memory into action. Then it clicked. Wally Manson . . . Wally bloody Manson! He spun round and raced back to his office.

Johnny Johnson, gazing out of the window, saw Frost with the new bloke tagging behind, dashing across the car-park. The interview with Mr Mullett must have been a brief one, he thought. His internal phone rang. 'Yes, Mr Mullett?' His face froze. 'You're still waiting for him?' Through the window the Cortina belched smoke as it roared towards the exit. 'I think he's just gone out, sir.'

The grey Vauxhall Cavalier bumped up a side lane, stopping well short of the cottage. Tony Harding, a junior technician with the Forensic Laboratory, climbed out of the car and walked purposefully up the garden path of the isolated building, a clipboard in his hand. He hammered loudly at the door and took a pen from his pocket as if ready to conduct a market survey. The knocking rumbled through an empty house and awakened a dog in the back garden and started it yapping. Harding waited, then, to play safe, knocked again and called, 'Anyone in?'

With one last look around to make certain he was unobserved he knelt by the letter-box. The paint was black. Parts of it were flaking. With a pocket knife he gently scraped off a tiny portion into an envelope.

In half an hour he was back in the lab where the spectroscope was already set up.

'Who's Wally Manson?' asked Gilmore, swerving to avoid a road-crossing dog.

'Small-time villain who's been in and out of the nick most of his life. Stealing cars, shop breaking, receiving stolen goods, assault with a dangerous weapon. Wally's never turned his hand to burglary before, that's why I never reckoned him for those senior citizen larks. But it was definitely him who phoned me at the pub.'

Gilmore slowed down at the traffic lights. 'So what does that prove?'

'How did Wally know there was a date-expired corpse on the bed? Even the bloody neighbours didn't know. The only way he could have found out would be by doing what I did – climbing through the back window and sneaking into the bedroom.'

At last Gilmore twigged. 'He was going to rob the place?'

'That's what I reckon, son . . . and I bet he ruined a perfectly good pair of underpants when he saw the sleeping bloody beauty. Round the corner, here.'

This was part of the newer section of Denton, modern two-storey houses with front lawns in a street lined with sapling trees. 'Last but one on the right,' said Frost. Then he leant back and almost purred with satisfaction.

Parked outside the house was a battered van. It was a dark blue colour.

Belle Manson, Wally's wife, was a plump, bleached-haired woman of around forty with heavy ear-rings hanging, like tarnished brass curtain rings, from ear-lobes which looked as if they had been pierced with a 6-inch nail. She was on her knees, scrubbing the front doorstep, her over-sized breasts swinging in sympathy with the gyrations of her scrubbing brush. Without pausing in her labours, she scrutinized the two pairs of shoes plonked in front of her, one pair scruffy, unpolished, cracked and down at heel, the other so highly burnished she could see her fat face in them.

She didn't need to look up to see who it was. She'd seen those broken-down shoes many times before. The scrubbing brush worked vigorously at a stubborn spot in the corner. 'He's out. I don't know where he is. I don't know when he'll be back. I haven't seen him for days.'

'Thanks very much, Belle,' said Frost, stepping over the wet patch into the hallway. 'We'd love to come in.' She snorted annoyance and straightened up, flinging the scrubbing brush into the bucket and splashing Gilmore's trousers with dirty water in the process.

'You got a warrant?' she screamed.

'Would I come in without one?' asked Frost in a hurt voice, patting the forged car expenses in his inside pocket as he marched up the passage and into the kitchen.

'Yes, you bloody would,' she yelled, charging after him.

Frost drew a chair up to the formica-topped table and plonked himself down. He jerked his head for Gilmore to have a quick look round for a lurking Wally.

'Where the hell do you think you're going?' she yelled as Gilmore clattered up the stairs.

'He wants to use your toilet,' Frost explained. 'He had curry for breakfast and it's given him the runs.'

Ear-rings and breasts quivering, Belle glowered. She flopped down in the chair opposite him. Frost gave her a friendly smile. 'You're looking well, Belle.'

'You're not,' she snapped. 'You're looking old and scruffy.' She waved away the offered cigarette. 'I don't smoke.' Then her face softened. 'Sorry to hear about your wife.'

'Thanks,' muttered Frost. An awkward silence. She'd thrown him off balance. He lit up and waited for Gilmore's return.

A kettle on the gas-ring rattled its lid and whistled. Belle heaved herself up and turned off the gas.

'Two sugars in mine,' said Frost.

'You've got the cheek of the bloody devil,' she snapped, banging three mugs on the table and hurling a tea-bag in each. Gilmore came in, shaking his head. Wally wasn't in the house. 'What did I tell you? I haven't seen him for days.' smirked Belle, filling the mugs from the kettle and slopping in milk. 'Help yourselves to sugar.' She slid the mugs over.

'So where is he, Belle?' said Frost, spooning out the dripping tea-bag and depositing it on the table.

'I've told you, I don't know.' She leant back to reach an opened box of Marks and Spencer's Continental chocolates from the dresser and wrenched off the lid. A chocolate truffle disappeared into her mouth and was washed down by a swig of tea.

'When did you last see him?' persisted Frost.

Her face contorted as she gave her impression of

thinking deeply. 'Last Friday. He goes away a lot on business. I hardly ever see him. He only comes back for you know what and that only lasts five minutes on a good day.'

Frost nodded sympathetically. 'We've got him down in our files as a quick in and out merchant, Belle.' His finger worried away at his scar. 'He doesn't take his van when he goes away, then?'

'His van?'

'The blue one outside.'

'Oh that,' sniffed Belle. 'No. It's broken down.' As she spoke, the front door slammed. Her head jerked round. She looked worried. Quick footsteps along the passage. At a sign from Frost, Gilmore was up out of his chair, standing by the door, ready to grab the newcomer.

'Mum, have you . . . Oh, sorry, I didn't know you were with clients.' It was a young girl.

Belle forced a smile. 'It's the police, Deidree . . . I was just telling them we hadn't seen your dad since Friday.'

Deidree Manson, fifteen years old, in a leather jacket and a short skirt, was a scaled-down replica of her plump mother, even down to small, curtain-ring ear pendants, but with sandy-coloured hair which had not yet made the acquaintance of the bleach bottle. She stared blankly at her mother. 'Dad? Oh yes . . . of course. We haven't seen him for days.'

Frost flicked ash into his tea mug. 'Clients? Are you back on the game, Belle?'

'Thank you very much!' mouthed Belle to her daughter. To Frost she said airily, 'I oblige the odd gentleman. Just for pin money.'

'Yes. Some of your clients are bleeding odd,' said

Frost, pushing his mug away. 'I hope you disinfect your crockery.' He swung round to Deidree. 'No school today?'

'Half-term,' she replied laconically, helping herself to a strawberry cream.

'What school do you go to?'

'Denton Modern.'

The same school as Paula Bartlett. Frost asked Deidree if she knew her.

Her tongue snaked out to catch a straying dribble of chocolate juice. 'She was in my class. Bit of a drip. Nose always stuck in a book. Had no interest in boys or sex or pop music or anything.'

'What about the teacher, Mr Bell?' asked Frost casually. 'What sort of a bloke is he?'

Deidree chomped and shrugged. 'Boring. I think Paula had a crush on him. Two drips together.'

A brisk rat-tat-tat at the door made Belle frown and consult her wrist-watch. She beckoned Deidree over for an enigmatic message. 'If it's "you-know-who" for "you-know-what", tell him it's inconvenient at the moment. Can he call back later?'

Frost watched Deidree's plump little bottom wriggle through the door and wondered how long it would be before she was invited to join the family business. 'We're going to have to search the place, Belle. Wally's been naughty.' He stood and signalled for Gilmore to follow.

Belle leapt up to block their path. 'I want to see your warrant, first.'

He pulled his car expenses from his inside pocket and flashed them under her nose. 'Satisfied?' Before she had a chance to examine them, they were back in his pocket.

'All right,' she nodded reluctantly. 'But don't make a mess – and don't pinch anything.'

A door in the hall led to the lounge. 'We'll start in here, son.' They were about to enter when there was a sudden angry burst of protestations from the disappointed client at the front door. 'If he won't go away,' called Frost, 'tell him I'll cut off his "you know what" and stuff it up his "he knows where".' Silence. The front door slammed.

It was a smallish room jam-packed with Belle's pin-money purchases of new furniture and dominated by an enormous 28-inch twin-speakered colour TV and a stereo video both housed in a mahogany-veneered, Queen Anne style cabinet. Frost nudged Gilmore and pointed. On top of the cabinet lay a familiar-looking box holding a video cassette. The box was white with a typed label which read: *Till The Blood Runs – Canings & Whippings.* The same title as one of the pornographic videos removed from the newsagent's. 'Belle!' he yelled.

'I know nothing about it,' said Belle as she waddled in. 'Something Wally brought home.' She looked at the label. 'Canings and Whippings? A bit too strong meat for my clients – it would give the poor old sods a heart attack. If you want to know about dirty videos, ask our Deidree. Some bloke wanted her to make one.'

The young girl was called in. 'Pornographic videos,' said Frost. 'Your mother says you were approached. Tell me about it.'

Deidree leant against the door frame and eased some toffee away from her back teeth with her finger. 'Nothing much to tell. We were coming out of a disco one night when this bloke came across from a posh car and asked me if I wanted to earn myself fifty quid posing in the nude with him for a video. I told him to stuff his video camera right up his arse.'

'I've always brought her up to be a decent girl,' said Belle proudly.

'What did he look like?' asked Frost. 'Would you know him again?'

'Old – about forty. Dressed to the nines – shirt and tie and all that stuff. Darkish hair. I might recognize him again, but I'm not sure.'

Frost dismissed them both with a flick of his hand. He couldn't waste time on this – porno videos were very low on his list of priorities. A quick search of the lounge revealed nothing. 'Right, son. Up the wooden stairs to Bedfordshire.'

He sat on Belle's soft-mattressed double bed with its plump purple eiderdown and watched Gilmore opening and shutting drawers. A packet of Hamlet cigars lay on the dressing table. Frost shook it hopefully. It rattled. There was one left. He lit it, stretched out on the bed and contentedly puffed smoke across to the detective sergeant.

'Excuse me,' said Gilmore huffily, annoyed that Frost wasn't helping. He leant over to tug open the drawer of the bedside cabinet. Packets of contraceptives . . . small aerosol cans. He seized one of the cans and showed it to the inspector. 'Look at this!'

Frost sat up and blinked at the label. 'Nipple Hardening Spray! I don't believe it.' He examined the can from all angles. 'This could make a man's thumb obsolete.'

'And this!' Gilmore flourished another can.

'Bloody hell, son, don't point it at me. It's the last thing I need at the moment. What else has she got?' Happy now to join in, he was soon rummaging through the various sex aids and stimulants.

The bedroom yielded nothing else of interest. The bedroom next door was Deidree's with its pop posters and record player. 'Leave it, son,' said Frost. 'Wally wouldn't have stuck any bent gear in here.'

'It still wouldn't hurt to look,' said Gilmore stubbornly, dragging out the wardrobe so he could see behind it.

'Whatever turns you on, son,' said Frost. He ambled over to the window and opened it so he could jettison the cigar. Below was the back yard, a miserable patch of concrete landscaped with oily rain-puddles, a couple of rusty, bottomless buckets, and two treadless car tyres. Car tyres! The blue van! He'd forgotten all about the bloody blue van. That was the next thing to search. He watched the cigar butt nose-dive to its death.

An excited shout from Gilmore had him spinning round.

Gilmore had found a crumpled bundle of blue cloth. He opened it out. A pair of men's jeans, grubby and thickly spattered with dried blood.

'Belle!' roared Frost, his bellow echoing down the stairs.

'Won't be a minute.' She was talking to someone, her voice low and urgent.

'I want you now!' he yelled.

'Coming.'

The front door clicked shut and as it did a bell shrilled a warning deep in his subconscious. From outside, an engine coughed, then roared into life. A van engine.

'Shit!' cried Frost, galloping down the stairs two at a time, Gilmore hard on his heels. At the bottom of the stairs was Belle, lumbering up very slowly, deliberately blocking their way. Frost almost pushed her over as they charged for the front door. Outside an empty street. A patch of oil where the van had been standing.

'Double shit!' howled Frost.

'There!' pointed Gilmore. Something blue disappearing round the corner trailed by a billow of exhaust.

The Cortina shuddered as they hurled themselves in and roared off in pursuit. Round the corner, but no sign of the van. Up to the main road. 'Which way?' asked Gilmore.

'Left,' said Frost. He had seen something blue jumping the lights. Drumming his fingers impatiently on the steering wheel, Gilmore waited for the lights to change. The blue van ahead was getting smaller and smaller in the distance.

What a foul-up, thought Gilmore. The van was there when they arrived, but they'd ignored it. 'That bloody fat cow,' he muttered. 'We ought to run her in for obstruction.'

'He's her husband, son,' said Frost, mildly. 'Your wife would have done the same to help you.'

Would she? thought Gilmore bitterly. She certainly didn't help me last night when bloody Mullett phoned. Before he could follow the thought further, the traffic lights flickered. He jammed his foot down, passing car after car after car. The blue van was getting bigger.

'Control to Mr Frost. Come in, please.'

Gilmore braked abruptly as an estate car shot out of a side turning right in their path.

'Control to Mr Frost. Come in, please.' repeated the radio.

'Shut your bleeding row,' said Frost to the radio as Gilmore swerved round the estate car. Frost twisted in his seat and jerked two fingers at the driver.

More traffic lights ahead. The blue van had stopped.

'Control to Mr . . .'

Frost snatched up the handset. 'Hold on, Control. We are . . . Shit!'

'Say again?' said Control.

'I said, "Tut tut",' muttered Frost bitterly and feeling like banging his head against the windscreen. The blue van they had been chasing had the name of a dress shop written on the side and was being driven by a woman. Gilmore glared poison darts at the inspector as if it was all his fault. Frost was philosophical. 'He'll turn up. He's got nowhere to go.' He was much more used to cock-ups than the sergeant. He raised the handset to his ear. 'Put out a call to all units. I want Wally Manson brought in. Last seen driving a blue Ford transit van about ten years old . . . I don't know the registration number, but you should be able to get it from the computer.'

'Will do,' said Control. 'Hold on, please. Sergeant Johnson wants to speak to you urgently.'

A rustling sound, then Johnson took over. 'Jack. Forensic have matched up the paint on the newspaper. It definitely came from Greenway's letter-box. Mr Mullett wants you back here right away.'

'My one aim in life is to gratify Mr Mullett's every whim,' replied Frost. 'We're on our way.'

Mullett was almost dancing with excitement. He waved the Forensic report at Frost. 'We've got him, Inspector. We've got him . . . and we can all take credit. A chance observation on your part, scientific skill and expertise from Forensic plus solid devoted team work under my supervision.' He lowered himself down into his chair and swung from side to side in smug satisfaction. Frost thought this was a good time to hand over the forged car expenses.

'Excellent,' said Mullett, giving them barely a glance as he signed them with a flourish of his Parker and tossed them into his out-tray. 'Things are really moving our way at last. How's the inventory going?'

'Almost finished it, Super,' said Frost, trying to remember where he had hidden the damn thing.

'Good,' beamed Mullett. 'I want this man Greenway picked up and brought in right now. How many men will you need?'

'The fewer the better, Super. He lives out in the wilds. If he spots half the Denton police force converging on his cottage, he might do a runner.'

'Very well, but don't let there be any foul-ups.' He was itching for Frost to go so he could pick up the phone and casually let drop to the Chief Constable that, despite the appalling manpower shortage, Denton Division had once again come up trumps. Then his euphoria crash-dived as he remembered what he had originally wanted to see Frost about. He snatched up the Denton *Echo* and jabbed at the headlines. 'Have you seen this? "Granny Ripper! Town of Terror!" What are we doing about it? The press are screaming for our blood and County are breathing down our necks.'

'I might be able to give you a quick result,' Frost said, filling him in on Wally Manson. 'We've sent the jeans over to Forensic.'

Mullett could hardly contain himself. Wait until the Chief Constable heard about this. 'I want Manson picked up and brought in,' said Mullett, scooping up the telephone and dialling.

'I'll make a note of it,' said Frost solemnly.

'Chief Constable, please,' said Mullett. He put his hand over the mouthpiece. 'That will be all, Inspector.' As the door closed behind Frost, he straightened his tie and smoothed back his hair. 'Oh, hello, sir.' He put on his weary voice. 'Sorry if I don't sound all that brilliant . . . lack of sleep, you know . . .' He gave a modest laugh. 'Someone's got to keep an eye on things, sir . . . Some double good news on the Paula Bartlett case and the senior citizen killings that I thought you should have right away . . .'

Wednesday afternoon shift

Harry Greenway dropped a tea-bag into a mug and drowned it with boiling water from the kettle. He felt uneasy. He didn't know why. On top of the fridge the portable radio was tuned into the local station where The Beatles were singing 'Eleanor Rigby'. Greenway pulled a face and switched it off. A miserable, lonely song about death. He wasn't in the mood for it. He was raising the mug to his mouth when his ears picked up the soft gentle click of a car door being carefully closed. Instantly, his hand shot out to the light switch. From the darkened kitchen he twitched back the curtains.

Two men were walking up the path, one middle-aged and scruffy, the other in his late twenties with the look of a thug. Greenway cupped his hand to the window pane to see better. The older man, a maroon scarf hanging unevenly round his neck had a scar of some kind on his cheek. He didn't recognize either of them, but they spelled trouble.

A half-hearted knock at the front door which sounded almost too deliberately reassuring. The dog at his feet, a nine-month-old Dobermann, sprang up and started to growl, then to bark. He grabbed its collar and shut it in the lounge where it barked even louder. Another knock, a little stronger this time. Greenway reached for the heavy walking stick he kept on the hall table as he cautiously opened up. The scruffy man was smiling apologetically.

'Mr Greenway? Sorry to bother you so late, sir. We called earlier, but you were out.' He held something up. Greenway's heart faltered and skipped a beat. It was a police warrant card.

'Police?' he stammered. *God, how had they found out?*

'Routine enquiry,' purred the man who he noted from the warrant card was Detective Inspector Frost. 'All right if we come in?' And without waiting to be asked, they were in the hall.

Routine enquiry? They don't send detective inspectors on routine enquiries, not even rag-bags like this one. He felt his hands trembling. He forced a smile of unconcern. 'I was just going to cook my dinner.'

'This won't take long, sir,' said Frost.

Hearing strange voices, the dog was barking and frantically scratching at the lounge door.

Greenway smiled. 'I'd better put Spike outside. He can get quite nasty with strangers.' They stood well back as he opened the lounge door and grabbed the Dobermann's collar as it leapt out. 'Find yourselves seats,' he called, dragging the snarling dog past them and into the kitchen.

'Thank you, sir,' said Frost, giving the dog a wide berth and following Gilmore into the lounge, a grotty room with a well-worn and sagging three-piece suite and old newspapers heaped on every chair. The settee had been dragged in front of the television set, at the side of which a waste bin overflowed with empty lager cans. Frost strode around, prodding, poking.

'Look at this!' Gilmore was holding up a girlie magazine with a picture of a busty blonde dressed in school uniform on the front cover.

But Frost was beginning to feel uneasy. 'He's taking a bloody long time putting that dog out . . . Shit!' He spat out the expletive at the growl of an engine starting up outside. Twice in the same flaming day! 'The bastard's done a runner!'

They dashed to the back door where a snarling Dobermann barred their way. Back along the passage and out the front door, just in time to see the rear lights of a delivery van disappearing into the dark.

Back in the car, bumping and jolting in hot pursuit, Frost fumed and castigated himself for letting the sod walk out so easily. Why hadn't he taken more men and posted someone at the back? If Greenway got away, he'd never hear the last of it from Mullett. 'Faster, son,' he urged Gilmore as the red rear-lights ahead shrunk to pinpricks.

'This car's not in the best of condition,' Gilmore retorted as the Cortina shook and shuddered in protest at the unaccustomed increased speed. A warning light on the oil gauge kept flashing and there was a hot metal burning smell. 'Hadn't you better radio Control for some back-up?'

Frost hesitated. Of course they needed back-up, but he was hoping they could get by without the station knowing what a twat he had made of himself. A teeth-setting grinding noise from the engine made up his mind. He radioed for help.

'Do you mean to say,' howled Mullett, snatching the microphone from Sergeant Wells, 'that you just let him drive off?' He had been hovering in Control, awaiting confirmation of a successful arrest.

'Just get me back-up – over and out,' muttered Frost, banging down the handset, aware that he had only delayed a Grade A bollocking from his superintendent.

'Where's the bugger gone?' The red lights had vanished. 'Look out,' he screamed as a dark shape loomed up in front of the windscreen.

Gilmore jammed on the brakes. The tyres screeched and the car slewed to a halt, throwing Frost heavily against Gilmore who almost lost control of the wheel. They had pulled up within inches of Greenway's delivery van.

'What's the silly bugger playing at?' asked Frost, all fingers and thumbs as he tried to release his seat belt. He was answered by Greenway blurring into vision at the side of the Cortina, swinging what they later realized was a long-handled sledge-hammer. A clanging thud which shook the car and nearly deafened them, then a splintering and shattering as the windscreen crazed into an opaque honeycombed sheet. When Frost finally managed to release the seat belt and leap from the car he was just in time to see the rear lights of the van dwindling into the distance.

'Shit!' yelled Frost yet again, after they had knocked out enough of the shivered windscreen to see where they were going. They limped off after Greenway, eyes streaming, faces stinging from the ice-hard punch of cold gritty air. Control had advised them that area car Hotel Tango was on its way to afford them assistance.

But they had lost too much time. The road was dead straight ahead and the van was nowhere to be seen. Turning his head to one side for protection against the slip-stream, Frost groped for the handset. 'We've lost him, I think. Last seen heading towards the motorway.'

'Hotel Tango receiving,' replied Simms. 'We are in position by motorway exit. Will block.'

'Bully for you, Hotel Tango,' said Frost, turning up his coat collar and sinking low in his seat to try and escape the worst of the slip-stream. He attempted to light a cigarette but the match died in its battle against the wind.

A gargle of squelch from the radio, then Hotel Tango, very excited. 'He's spotted us. He's skidded round. He's heading back in your direction. Am in pursuit.'

'There he is!' yelled Gilmore. Fast-approaching headlights flared and blinded and a horn screamed for them to get out of the way.

'Block him,' shouted Frost.

Not too happy about this, Gilmore spun the wheel, turning the car side on to the oncoming vehicle.

The headlights got nearer and nearer, the van's horn screaming and pleading. From behind came more headlights and the piercing wail of Hotel Tango's siren in pursuit.

'He's not going to stop!' screamed Gilmore, blinded by the dazzle of the headlights as he hit his seat belt release.

'Jump,' yelled Frost, thankful he hadn't refastened his seat belt after the last incident. He pushed open the door and dived out on to the road, rolling over and just regaining his feet as the van impacted, smashing into the car and sending it spinning. Tyres squealed and smoked. The van's engine raced impotently, then it started to back away. But the approaching police car was too close and Hotel Tango skidded to a halt, siren still blaring, blocking the road right behind the van.

Car doors opened and slammed. Two uniformed men emerged from the area car and approached cautiously from the rear. Gilmore, rubbing grazed elbows, advanced from the front. The cab door jerked open and Greenway leapt out, tightly gripping the sledgehammer which he brandished threateningly.

Crouching slightly, ready to leap, Gilmore edged nearer.

Greenway spun round, whirling the sledge-hammer above his head, his eyes wild and threatening.

'Drop that, you silly sod!' roared Frost. Momentarily distracted, Greenway jerked his head towards the inspector giving the two uniformed men the opportunity to risk a dash forward, but they were not quick enough. Greenway twisted round, swinging the hammer in a two-handed grip. As they backed away, Gilmore made his move, leaping on Greenway from behind, locking his arm tightly round the man's neck in a strangulating grip making him drop the hammer as he tried to prise Gilmore's arm away. A back elbow jab from Greenway almost paralysed Gilmore who cried in pain and slackened his hold which was enough for Greenway to dive to regain the hammer. He almost had it when he shrieked in agony as the heel of Frost's shoe stamped down on his hand with the inspector's full weight bearing down. 'You bastard!!'

'Naughty, naughty!' admonished Frost, only easing off his foot so Gilmore could pull Greenway's wrists behind him and snap on the handcuffs.

Gilmore stood up and brushed dirt from his grey suit then yanked his prisoner to his feet. 'You've broken my bloody hand,' whimpered Greenway. 'I want a doctor.'

'You'll want an undertaker if you don't shut up,' said Frost. 'It's police brutality week. Now get in that bloody car.' They all squeezed into the area car and drove back to the station. It was a silent drive. Greenway said nothing, just stared straight ahead. He didn't even ask what the charge was.

'Number 2 Interview Room,' called Wells as they marched their prisoner through the lobby.

'I want a doctor. The bastards have broken my hand,'

called Greenway, giving a good impersonation of a man in agony.

'Get him a doctor,' ordered Mullett, who was hovering excitedly in the background, grinning like a man with two dicks. 'We're going to play this one by the book.' He called the inspector over. 'The Chief Constable's thrilled to bits about this, Frost.'

'Then let's hope we don't disappoint the old git,' replied Frost. 'Our suspect's playing the injured innocent at the moment.'

'I've got a full Forensic team going over Greenway's cottage, inch by inch,' said Mullett. 'As soon as they come up with something, I'll let you know.' He squeezed Frost's shoulder. 'I have every confidence in you, Inspector.'

Then you must be bloody mad, muttered Frost under his breath as Mullett returned to the old log cabin. Whenever people expressed confidence, the doubts welled up.

'Shall I get a doctor?' asked Wells.

'Later,' said Frost. 'When I've finished with him. The odd jolt of pain might improve his concentration.'

Wednesday night shift (1)

Greenway twisted his head round to look at the clock high on the wall behind him in Interview Room number 2. Half-past nine. He resumed his sprawl in the chair and rubbed his injured hand. Opposite him, leaning against the mushroom-emulsioned wall, the young thug of a detective sergeant scowled down at him. Unblinking, Greenway scowled back.

'How much longer?' asked Greenway.

Gilmore said nothing.

'As long as that?' said Greenway in mock surprise. He turned to the little blonde WPC standing guard by the door. 'How long have I got to waste my time here, darling?'

WPC Ridley stared through him and didn't answer.

'Natter, natter, natter,' said Greenway. The door swung open and Frost breezed in, a bulging green case file under his arm. He chucked the file on the table, together with his matches and his cigarettes.

'Where's the doctor?' asked Greenway.

'He's putting someone's cat down at the moment,' said Frost, dropping into the vacant chair. 'He'll be along as soon as he can.' He poked a cigarette in his mouth and dragged a match along the table top. He lit up, then pushed the packet towards the prisoner.

'What's this?' asked Greenway with a sneer. 'The good guy and the bad guy routine?'

'No,' said Frost, grinning sweetly. 'We're both the bad guys. We both hate your guts.' He lit Greenway's cigarette. 'Make us hate you some more. Tell us all about it, blow by blow, thrust by thrust.'

Greenway spread his palms in mock bewilderment. 'Tell you about what? I haven't the faintest idea what this is all about.'

Frost puffed out a smoke ring and watched it drift up and curl around the green-shaded light bulb. 'If you don't know what it's about, why did you do a runner?'

'I panicked. I'm not used to the police barging into my house at night.' He stood up. 'If you're going to charge me, charge me. If not, I'm walking out of here.'

Gilmore pushed him back in the chair. 'The charge, as you bloody well know, is murder.'

A scornful laugh from Greenway. 'Murder?' His eyes flicked from Gilmore to Frost. 'Who am I supposed to have murdered?'

A damn good act, thought Frost, grudgingly. If I didn't have the forensic evidence I might start having doubts. He flipped open the folder and took out the photograph of Paula Bartlett, then steered it with his finger across to Greenway. 'Only fifteen. Must have been easy meat for a great hulking bastard like you.'

Greenway stared at the colour photograph with an expression of utter disbelief. 'The school kid? This is getting bloody farcical. I gave a statement to that other bloke . . . the miserable-faced git, Inspector Allen. She never even reached my place. I never got a paper that day.'

Gilmore moved his face forward close to Greenway's. 'Yes, you bloody did. She delivered the paper. On your own admission you were home that morning. You dragged her in . . . a fifteen-year-old kid, a virgin . . .'

'A fifteen-year-old virgin? There's no such thing!' smirked Greenway.

The detective sergeant's control snapped. He grabbed the man by the lapels, lifted him and slammed him against the wall. 'Don't come the funnies with me, you sod. I saw her body. I saw what you did to her.'

WPC Ridley coughed pointedly, reminding Gilmore that she was there to make notes of everything that happened between the detectives and the prisoner. Gilmore pushed Greenway away and wiped his hands down his jacket as if they were contaminated.

Greenway smouldered. 'I'm not answering any more questions.'

'Yes, you are,' said Frost, 'otherwise I might accidentally tread on your bad hand again.' He leant back, balancing the chair on its rear legs, and shot a column of smoke at the yellow ceiling. 'Let's talk about mitigating circumstances. Perhaps you didn't mean to kill her. What did she do – lead you on? Waggle it under your nose, then snatch it away?'

'I don't know what you're talking about,' yawned Greenway, feigning boredom. 'Whoever poked and killed that kid, it wasn't me. I like them older with big knockers – like that little policewoman there – not flat-chested schoolgirls.'

Frost's chair crashed down, the sudden noise almost making Greenway leap from his seat. 'Flat-chested, was she? When you stripped her off you saw she was flat-chested.' He jabbed a finger at Gilmore who was busy with his notebook. 'Underline that, Sergeant.'

'You don't have to strip anyone off to see if they're flat-chested or not,' sneered Greenway. 'That kid used to deliver here in the summer wearing only a T-shirt. You could see she had nothing.'

'You're quite right,' Frost agreed. 'She didn't have much to show when I saw her stretched out on the slab in the morgue. It didn't stop you raping her, though, did it?'

'Rape?' He snorted a hollow laugh. 'You must be bloody hard up for suspects.'

Frost pulled a sheet of typescript from the folder. 'This is the statement you gave to my colleague, Inspector Allen, the miserable-faced git. You say you're a self-employed van driver?'

'That's right.'

'You were asked to account for your movements for September 14th, the day Paula went missing.' He let his eyes run over the typed page. 'You said you didn't go out at all that day. Is that correct?'

'Bang on! There was no work for me.' Greenway flicked his ash on the floor and looked as if he was enjoying the questioning. His expression said, 'Ask what you like, pigs, you'll get nothing out of me!'

Frost scratched at his scar. 'The girl usually delivered your paper – the *Sun* – around eight o'clock?'

'Yes. But that day, she didn't turn up.'

'And you didn't get a paper?'

'Brilliant,' said Greenway, sarcastically.

Frost produced the copy of the *Sun* in its transparent cover. 'This is the paper you say wasn't delivered. And this . . .' He fluttered the forensic report, 'is scientific evidence which proves you are a lying bastard.'

Greenway snatched the report, his head moving from side to side as he skimmed through it. He gave a scoffing laugh and handed it back. 'A load of balls.'

Gilmore moved forward. 'Solid scientific evidence. The court will love it.'

Greenway smiled disarmingly. 'All right. Let's pretend it's genuine. So the newspaper was pushed through my letter-box and pulled out again. That doesn't prove the girl was in my house and it doesn't prove I bloody touched her.'

'We'll soon have all the proof we want,' said Frost. 'A Forensic team is going over your place inch by inch right now. One hair from her head . . . a thread of cotton from her clothes, and we've got you, you bastard.'

'Tell you what then,' smirked Greenway. 'If you find anything, I'll give you a full, sworn confession. Now I can't say fairer than that.'

Frost switched on his sweetest smile. 'We'll find it,' he said, trying to sound convincing. But he was worried. Greenway was too damned cock-sure. He looked up with irritation as the door opened and Wells beckoned.

The sergeant didn't look the bearer of good news. 'Just heard from the Forensic team, Jack. They've been all over the cottage and found nothing.'

Frost slumped against the wall. 'There's got to be something.'

'It's been over two months since she was there,' said Wells. 'Forensic are bringing in more men to go over the entire place again, but they're not optimistic. Are you getting anything from Greenway?'

'Only the bleeding run-around.'

Mullett's office door opened. He saw Frost and hurried towards him. 'What joy?' he asked eagerly.

'No joy, all bloody misery,' replied Frost. 'Unless Forensic can come up with something quick, the best I can charge Greenway with is dangerous driving.'

Mullet's smile flickered and spluttered out. 'I hope this is not going to be another of your foul-ups, Frost. I've really stuck my neck out with the Chief Constable on this one.' He spun on his heel and marched back to his office.

'Let's hope the bastard chops it off for you,' muttered Frost to the empty passage.

Back to the Interview Room where Greenway was making great play of nursing his injured hand. 'I'm in agony. I want medical treatment and I want to go home. You've got nothing to hold me on.'

'Lock the bastard up and get him a doctor,' said Frost. He felt tired and miserable and even more incompetent than usual.

His office was a hostile dung-heap of bulging files, snarling memos, and complicated-looking returns. Rain splattered against the window and drummed on the roof. He stared out to the rain-swept car-park, and was puzzled because he couldn't see his Cortina, then remembered it had been towed away for repairs after Greenway smashed into it. Gilmore poked his head round the door. He had his hat and coat on in the hope he could nip back home for an hour or so. He'd been on duty solidly since six and a busy night was still looming ahead. 'Greenway wants to know what's happening about his dog.'

'A dog-handler's on his way to pick it up and take it to kennels,' Frost told him. 'You off home then?'

'Yes . . . only for an hour . . . if it's all right with you.' Gilmore's tone implied that it had better be all right.

'Drop me off on the way, would you, son. I haven't got wheels.'

Gilmore readily agreed. It was only when he turned the car into the Market Square to take the short cut to the inspector's house that Frost broke the news that he wanted to be dropped off at Greenway's cottage. It was miles off Gilmore's route, but all right, he'd dump Frost off and then get the hell out of there. Frost could find his own way back.

Lights were spilling from every room of the cottage. From the back yard the dog kept up its monotonous yapping. The Forensic team were busy. Hardly any surface was free of fingerprint powder, small vacuum cleaners whirled gulping up dust, hairs and fibres for analysis, men crawled over the carpet with tweezers. Tony Harding, in charge of the team, looked up wearily as Frost entered. Gilmore hovered impatiently behind, scowling at the inspector who had said he would be a couple of minutes at the most and wanted a lift back.

'Still no joy,' said Harding, 'but we haven't finished yet.'

Frost received the news gloomily. 'Keep looking. Any clue – no matter how small. A pair of schoolgirl's knickers, a confession, a half-eaten chicken and mushroom pie.' He scuffed the carpet with his foot. 'At the moment, all we've got is the paint samples on the newspaper.'

'Ah,' said Harding, sounding shamefaced. 'I've been meaning to talk to you about that.' He took the inspector by the arm and led him to one side. 'The paint sample evidence might not be as conclusive as we first thought. It might not have come from this letter-box.'

A cold shiver of apprehension trickled down Frost's back. 'What do you mean? You did a spectrograph analysis. You told me it was conclusive.'

'Yes . . . well . . . it was . . . up to a point . . .'

Frost's shoulders slumped. 'Get to the bad bloody news. I don't want the death of a thousand cuts.'

'We did a spectrograph analysis of the paint sample from the newspaper. There were traces of three layers of paint, the bottom layer brown, the middle a grey undercoat, the top layer black. The spectrograph analysis of the sample taken from Greenway's letter-box showed three identical paint layers, same colours, same chemical composition.'

'Yes,' nodded Frost. 'That's the point in the story where I started believing Forensic weren't the big, useless twats I'd always thought them to be.'

Harding's faint smile accepted the rebuke. 'The test was fine as far as it went, but we should have tested other letter-boxes on the girl's delivery route. This I've now done.'

'And?' asked Frost, ready to wince, knowing he wasn't going to like the answer.

'Quite a few letter-boxes came up with identical spectrograph readings.'

'But how the hell . . . ?'

'Most of the properties on the girl's route are owned by the Denton Development Corporation. Every four years their maintenance department repaint exteriors . . . standard colours, standard specification. What I hadn't appreciated was that Greenway's cottage is also owned by the Development Corporation. They bought the land some twenty-five years ago for a new housing estate, but haven't yet found the money.'

'So it's received the same coats of identical paint every four years as all the other houses?'

Harding nodded. 'I'm afraid so. And that means that the girl could have pushed the newspaper through any of those letter-boxes by mistake, then tugged it out again. It doesn't have to be this cottage.'

'Thank you very much,' muttered Frost bitterly, knowing that Mullett would blame him for this. 'So unless you can find evidence that the girl has actually been inside here, we've got sod all to hold Greenway on?'

'Unfortunately, yes,' agreed Harding.

Frost wandered across to the window and looked out on to the puddled, muddy back yard where a black shape prowled up and down like a caged wolf. At the end of the garden a sorry-looking shed crouched under pouring rain. 'You done the shed yet?'

'Not with the Hound of the Baskervilles out there,' replied Harding. 'We're waiting for the dog-handler.'

As if answering his cue, the dog-handler's van drew up outside and a short stocky man wearing a padded jacket and thick leather gloves came in, swinging a muzzle and a leash. 'What sort of dog is it?'

'A bloody man-eater,' said Frost, leading him to the back door.

The dog-handler opened the door a fraction, squinted through the crack, then closed it firmly as the door bulged inwards when the dog hurled himself at it. He didn't look very happy. 'I hate Dobermanns. They're vicious sods.' He zipped up the padded jacket and pulled the gloves up over his wrists, then nodded. 'Right. Here goes.'

'Geronimo!' said Frost, opening the door just wide enough for the handler to squeeze through. He then shut it quickly and listened to the noises off – several minutes of ill-tempered barking and a lot of swearing.

'OK. I've got it!'

The bedraggled dog, muzzled and shaking with rage, snarled as it was pulled through by the leash. It charged at Gilmore then shook rain all over him as it was dragged off.

Frost beckoned to Gilmore who, frozen-faced, waited with ill-concealed impatience. 'Let's take a quick look in the shed, son.'

Shoulders hunched, they splashed to the end of the yard. The rusty padlock which secured the shed door yielded to the first key from Frost's bunch.

The torch beam danced over rubbish. The shed was stacked roof-high with junk. The dirt-encrusted frame of a deck-chair rested against a rusting lawn-mower. Twisting, crumbling remains of old chicken wire strangled sodden strips of mouldering carpeting, rotting fence posts and jagged-edged sheets of warped plywood. The torch beam bounced from item to item. Junk. Stacks of half-empty paint tins, torn bags spewing damp fertilizer. Useless, hoarded rubbish. Frost tugged at the deck-chair, but this caused paint tins to topple and he had to jump back quickly.

'Satisfied?' asked Gilmore, smugly.

Frost's shoulders drooped. 'Yes, I'm satisfied, son. A quick poke around the house, then we'll go.'

He really thought he had found something in the kitchen. On the work top, thawing from the freezer and ready to be popped into the microwave, was Greenway's planned evening meal. A box of microwave crinkle-cut chips and a chicken and mushroom pie. 'Stomach contents,' exclaimed Frost delightedly. He yelled for Harding, who listened and shook his head.

'They don't help us, Mr Frost.' He picked up one of the packets. 'Both common brands . . . the market leaders. Even if we could prove the girl's last meal was an identical product, the supermarkets sell tens of thousands of these every week.'

'Damn!' growled Frost.

'You ready to go yet?' asked Gilmore pointing yet again to his watch.

'A quick sniff around the bedroom and then you can get off to your conjugals,' Frost promised.

The bedroom reflected the state of the rest of the house with the bed and the floor strewn with dirty clothing and unwashed, food-congealed crockery. Was this where Greenway dragged her and raped her? Was this pigsty of a room the last thing that fifteen-year-old kid saw before he choked the life out of her?

One of the Forensic team pushed past him and began stripping the clothing from the bed. 'We're taking the bedclothes for further examination, Inspector, but I get the feeling they've been washed during the past four weeks or so.'

'I only wash mine once a year,' said Frost gloomily, 'whether they need it or not.'

Another long, deep, irritating sigh from Gilmore.

'All right, son,' said Frost. 'We're going now.'

In the hall, Harding looked even gloomier than Frost. 'We haven't come up with a thing, Inspector. There's no evidence at all that the girl was ever in the house.' He plucked a Dobermann hair from his jacket. 'There's dog's hairs all over the place. Would have been helpful if we'd found some on the girl, but we didn't.'

'Find me something, for Pete's sake,' pleaded Frost, 'otherwise I'm in the brown and squishy up to my ear-holes.'

Gilmore put his foot down hard on the drive back in case the inspector thought of some other outlandish spot to visit. Frost slumped miserably down in the passenger seat, stared at the rain-blurred windscreen, smoked and said nothing. Gilmore could almost feel sorry for him.

Then Frost sat up straight, pulled the cigarette from his mouth and rammed it into the ashtray. 'I'm a number one, Grade A twat!!' he announced.

Tell me something I don't know, thought Gilmore, slowing down at the traffic lights in the Market Square.

'Turn the car around,' ordered Frost. 'We're going back to the cottage.'

'You're kidding!' gasped Gilmore, looking at Frost whose face was bathed red by the traffic signal.

'Under my bloody nose and I missed it . . . All that junk in the shed. You'd expect it to be dry, but it was wet, dirty, muddy and rusty. It must have been out rotting in the open for months . . . so why gather it up and bung it in the shed?'

'Perhaps he just wanted to tidy up his garden,' said Gilmore.

'Do me a favour. His place is a rubbish tip, just like mine. I'd never tidy up my garden and neither would he. That junk was dumped in his shed to hide something . . . so let's go and find out what.' Frost's face was now bathed in green. Wearily, Gilmore spun the wheel round and headed back to the cottage.

The Forensic team had almost completed their work and Harding shook his head at them as they passed through. 'Nothing. We're now going to try the shed.'

'Then you can give us a hand,' Frost told him. 'Bring a torch.' Harding slipped on a plastic mac and followed them down to the bottom of the yard.

'This would be easier in the morning,' moaned Gilmore as rain trickled down his collar.

'Shouldn't take us long,' said Frost dragging out the deck-chair frame and flinging it into the dark of the garden.

It took nearly half an hour. As one item of useless junk was removed more and more was revealed.

'I can't think why he bothered to keep this,' grunted Harding, struggling with a muddy iron-framed bed-spring, heavily corroded with rust.

It was not until the shed was nearly empty that they found what Greenway had been hiding. Stacked high against the far end of the shed, white cardboard boxes, piled almost to the roof. Frost moved back to let Gilmore reach up and drag one down. He tore open the stapled lid. Inside, tightly packed, were cartons of Benson and Hedges Silk Cut cigarettes. Gilmore took out a carton and tossed it over to Frost who ripped off the wrapping. No 'Government Health Warning' on the side of the packets. These cigarettes were made for export.

Frost stared at the packets, feeling even more depressed. He wasn't sure what he was expecting to find, but certainly not this. This would effectively shoot his case against Greenway right up the anal passage. He went to the shed door and swore bitterly into the rain and the wind and the dark.

The Interview Room now reeked strongly of stale shag tobacco smoke and cheese and onion crisps. There was a spit-soaked, thin hand-rolled cigarette end in the ashtray. Someone else had been interviewed since Frost's questioning of Greenway.

'All right, all right. Stop shoving.' Greenway, rubbing the sleep from his eyes with a neatly bandaged hand, stumbled into the room, urged roughly from behind by a foul-tempered Gilmore. Frost waited until the man was sitting down, then he pulled a packet of Benson and Hedges from his pocket and pushed it across. Greenway stared at it for a while, turned the packet gingerly with a finger so he could confirm the absence of the health warning. 'You took your bloody time finding them,' he grunted.

Frost retrieved the packet and shook out a cigarette. He lit up and sucked in smoke. 'Feel like talking?'

Greenway helped himself to a cigarette and accepted a light from the inspector. 'I take it I'm no longer being charged with killing the school kid?'

'No. The bloke you coshed has identified your photograph.'

Greenway thought for a moment. 'All right. I'll give you a statement.'

But as Gilmore turned the pages of his notebook, Frost waved a hand for him to stop. 'This isn't our case. Detective Inspector Skinner from Shelwood Division is on his way over. You can give a statement to him.'

Gilmore snorted in exasperation. 'Would someone mind telling me what this is about?'

'Sorry, son,' apologized Frost. 'On the day Paula Bartlett went missing a van-load of Benson and Hedges king-size cigarettes for export was hijacked on its way to the docks. The driver was flagged down, coshed, and his load nicked. This happened on the motorway at Shelwood, miles outside Denton Division.'

'But Greenway told Inspector Allen he never went out that day,' protested Gilmore.

'I think he was lying,' said Frost. 'People don't always tell us the truth.'

'Of course I was lying,' said Greenway. 'The bloody van, full of nicked fags, was standing outside my house when the other inspector called that evening. I thought he was on to me, so when he asked me, I said I hadn't been out all day. But it was about the missing kid . . .'

'Can you help us at all about the girl?' asked Frost.

Greenway shook his head. 'I left home at six in the morning . . . didn't get back until nine o'clock at night. The paper hadn't arrived when I left and it wasn't there when I got back.'

A tap at the door. 'Detective Inspector Skinner is here,' announced Sergeant Wells.

Skinner, a burly man in a trench coat, looked exactly how a detective inspector should look, a contrast to the rag-bag Gilmore had to work with. His sergeant, lean and mean, looked like a detective sergeant who would always be in his boss's shadow, not how Gilmore intended to end up. 'Understand you've got a little present for us, Jack?' said Skinner, his eyes on the prisoner.

'He's all yours,' said Frost 'I can't solve any of my own cases, but I solve other people's.' He offered his cigarettes around and Skinner nearly choked when he was told he was smoking some of the stolen property.

Wells returned with papers to be signed for the transfer of the prisoner and whispered to Frost that Mr Mullett would like to see him in his office.

'Shit,' muttered Frost. 'It's been a rotten enough day already.'

In fact Mullett was hovering outside in the corridor and was full of charm and smiles for the two detectives from Shelwood. 'Delighted to have been able to help,' he smarmed. But as soon as they had gone, his smile froze to death. 'My office!' he hissed and spun on his heel away.

Frost was dead tired, but he kept his eyes open to pretend he was listening as Mullett droned angrily on. 'You've made me look a complete and utter fool in the eyes of the Chief Constable . . .'

He let his gaze drift around the old log cabin and noticed to his horror that there was a foil take-away food container, yellowed with cold curry sauce, poking from under Mullett's desk. He moved forward, looking very contrite, and nudged it out of sight with his toe.

'. . . and it wasn't even our case. We've improved Shelwood's crime figures, which made ours look sick anyway, and done nothing for our own. What on earth am I going to tell the Chief Constable?'

The drone of Mullett's voice roared and faded and Frost had to jerk his head up to keep awake. He fought back a yawn. This was all his life seemed to be lately, making balls-ups, getting bollockings from Mullett, and then sent out to make a fresh balls-up.

'. . . and, in any case, I had told you to concentrate on the senior citizen killings. So leave the Paula Bartlett case for Mr Allen and try and find that other suspect you let slip through your fingers. I want no more mess-ups.' He leant across his desk, his chin thrust out. 'Are you receiving me, Inspector?'

'Loud and clear,' said Frost. 'Loud and bloody clear.'

1.15 a.m. The lobby had a sour smell. A mixture of stale beer and spilt whisky. Wells was shouting at PC Jordan who, helped by young PC Collier, was struggling with a man in evening dress. The man's legs kept giving way and he seemed ready to collapse in the pool of vomit at his feet. At last they managed to sit him down safely on the bench.

'Anything in from the Met on Simon Bradbury?' asked Gilmore.

'How the hell do I know?' snapped Wells, irritably. 'I don't keep track of every bit of paper that comes in and out of this building. And another . . .' He stopped short and yelled, 'Take him outside! Quick!' The drunk was being sick again. Jordan and Collier grabbed him, but too late. More vomit pumped out and they jumped back just in time as it splattered on the lobby floor. Eyes squinting, the drunk tried to make out what the mess was at his feet.

'Bloody marvellous!' cried Wells, and he looked around for someone to vent his anger on. PC Collier decided this was a good time to take a refreshment break and sidled out towards the rest room, but didn't quite make it.

'And where do you think you're going, Collier?'

'Refreshment break, Sergeant.'

Wells consulted his watch and found, to his disappointment, that Collier was entitled to his break. 'Right. When you come back you can clean up this mess.'

'That's not my job, Sergeant,' Collier protested, firmly.

'Your job is to do what I bloody well tell you to do,' yelled Wells as Collier stamped out, slamming the door behind him. Red-faced Wells charged, fists clenched, after him. 'I'll have you, Collier.'

Frost cut across to bar his way. 'Hold it, Bill. Hold it,' he said, soothingly. 'We're all tired and overworked.' He poked a cigarette in the sergeant's mouth and led him back to the desk. 'Any chance of a cup of tea?'

'There's a kettle in the rest room,' said Wells. 'You might bring me one.'

The only occupant of the rest room was Collier who was huddled in a chair in front of a 14-inch colour TV set, warming his hands round a mug of instant coffee and brooding over the injustices of working under Sergeant Wells. On the screen, a young girl in pigtails who didn't look much older than twelve was sprawled naked on some grass, sunbathing. The camera moved to show a man with a riding crop watching from the cover of some bushes. Behind the man a board read *Trespassers Will Be Punished.*

'Where did you get that video?' demanded Gilmore, sharply.

Snatched too abruptly from his morose meditation, Collier started, spilling instant coffee down the front of his uniform. He reached out to switch off the set, but Frost grabbed his wrist. 'Leave it, son. Where did you get it?'

'We only borrowed it, Inspector. We were going to put it back.' He held up a video case which had the typed label *A Thrashing For Fiona.* It was one of the haul of pornographic videos removed from the newsagent's.

On the screen the naked girl was on her knees, pleading with the man who was slapping the riding crop against his leg.

'Go and fetch Sergeant Wells,' ordered Frost, dragging another chair in front of the set.

Collier registered dismay. It was unlike the inspector to report people. 'I only borrowed it, sir.'

Dragging his eyes from the TV set where the girl was across the man's knees, being thrashed with the riding crop, Frost gave a reassuring grin. 'Don't worry, son. I'll tell him I took it. Just send him in.'

Gilmore spooned instant coffee into three mugs and filled them with boiling water. He passed one to Frost and sat beside him in the chair vacated by Collier.

A clatter of footsteps up the passage and Wells came in. 'Look, Jack, I haven't got time . . .' He stopped dead as he caught sight of the screen. 'Bloody hell . . .!' He grabbed the other chair and sat down.

Engrossed, Frost gulped down his coffee, unaware that he hadn't added his usual three heaped teaspoons of sugar. The man was now using the riding crop to do something unspeakable. 'He caught her trespassing,' Frost told Wells, explaining the plot.

'Serves her bloody right,' said Wells. 'She'll think twice before she does it again.'

The video finished abruptly. Frost fed another one in. The title read *Animal Passions*. An interior scene this time. The same pigtailed girl, naked and with a dog, a large white and brown Great Dane with a torn left ear, its tail wagging furiously. The girl lay on her back. The dog, slowly and deliberately, was licking her.

'I bet he prefers that to Pedigree Chum,' croaked Wells.

'Who wouldn't,' said Frost.

Gilmore looked at his watch. Nearly two o'clock. He'd told Liz he'd try and pop in during the shift, even if it was only for half an hour. He tried to catch Frost's attention as the fool sat there, eyes bulging, like a schoolboy with a dirty book. 'Do you mind if I take a break, Inspector? About half an hour or so? I'd like to pop home.'

'Sure,' muttered Frost, his eyes glued to the screen where the dog, tongue lolling, whites of eyes showing, was coupling with the girl.

This was too much for Gilmore who turned away in disgust. As he reached for the door handle it was abruptly snatched away from him as the door opened and there, framed in the doorway like an avenging angel, stood a furious and angry Mullett.

The internal phone rang.

Gilmore stared at Mullett, open-mouthed. Bloody Frost had dropped him in it again. He was sure the Divisional Commander had gone home.

Frost and Wells, eyes fixed rigidly on the screen, were blissfully ignorant of this visitation and Gilmore could do nothing to alert them.

Mullett pushed Gilmore to one side and strode into the rest room. He stood between the two men and the TV set and glowered down at them, his face thunder black.

Wells nearly had a heart attack.

'Hello, Super. This is a pleasant surprise,' said Frost, managing an unconvincing grin.

The phone kept on ringing. Glad of something to do, Gilmore answered it. It was Collier warning them that the Divisional Commander was on his way in.

'Thank you,' hissed Gilmore through clenched teeth, 'but we know.'

'What the devil is going on here?' spluttered Mullett. 'I look in on my way back from a function and what do I find? The lobby floor plastered with vomit, a junior officer left on his own to cope and the station sergeant and other officers in the rest room, watching . . .' His eyes bulged as he looked over his shoulder to see just what they were watching, '. . . obscene, bestial videos.'

Wells was on his feet, his mouth opening and closing in the hope that his brain would provide him with something mitigating to say. Gilmore wished the ground would open and swallow him. At the first opportunity he would request an interview with Mullett to explain that he was not there from choice.

Frost didn't appear to be paying his Divisional Commander much attention, but leant forward to study the antics on the screen more closely.

Mullett's lips compressed as he bottled up his rage. This was the last straw. 'Would you please wait outside,' he asked the other two men. A mad scramble for the door as they raced to comply, leaving the inspector as hostage for the superintendent's fury.

Frost dragged his chair closer to the TV set. Angrily, Mullett pushed in front of him, blocking his view. 'If I might have your attention,' he began icily then nearly burst a blood vessel as Frost had the temerity, the brazen-faced insubordinate impudence, to reach out and push his Divisional Commander to one side.

'How dare you,' he spluttered when the words finally came.

Flapping a hand for Mullett to be quiet, Frost roared out, 'Gilmore . . . in here! Quick.'

The detective sergeant came back in the room, looking first at the purple-faced, rage-quivering Mullett, then at Frost who was on his knees operating the rewind button on the video recorder. Like a silent film in reverse, the naked girl and the dog moved jerkily backwards at high speed.

'Watch,' ordered Frost, releasing the rewind. The dog, panting with excitement, again approached and straddled the girl.

'For the last time, Inspector . . .' roared Mullett.

Curtly jerking his hand for silence, Frost jabbed the pause button. On the screen, in full close-up, the vacant face of the girl froze, quivering slightly as the video head passed over and over the same section of tape.

'The pigtails and blonde hair are a wig, son,' said Frost, his hands moving to block them out.

Gilmore stared hard at the girl's face, her lips slack, eyes glazed and unseeing, tiny flecks of sweat on the forehead.

'Recognize her, son?'

Gilmore nodded. Yes, he recognized her. The suicide. The Snoopy watch. The Mickey Mouse night-shirt. Fifteen-year-old Susan Bicknell. The marks of the beating were now explained.

Frost straightened up. 'Come on, son. I think we should ask her stepfather a few questions.'

'I demand to know what this is all about!' shrieked Mullett. But they were gone, the door slamming firmly shut behind them, leaving him alone in the room. Behind him the dog had worked itself up into a frenzy. He tried to switch it off, but none of the buttons seemed to work. He pushed the door open and thundered down the corridor. Tomorrow. He would see Frost tomorrow. And then it would be his turn. The lobby wall suddenly zipped upwards and the ceiling stared down at him as his back hit the floor. His feet had found a slippery patch of vomit.

'Whatever you do,' hissed Frost to Wells, just before he darted out to the car-park, 'don't laugh.'

A cold black night, made blacker by purple rain clouds that covered the face of the moon. They didn't have to drag anyone out of bed. A downstairs light was still on at the house and a shirt-sleeved Kenneth Duffy, tired and drawn, opened the door to them.

'Remember me, Mr Duffy?' asked Gilmore, showing his warrant card.

Duffy stared through the card and nodded.

'We'd like to come in, please,' said Gilmore. 'Just a couple of questions.'

Duffy twisted his head. 'It's for me, love,' he called, ushering the two detectives into an unheated lounge. 'I don't want my wife troubled,' he explained. 'She's broken up about this. We both are.' He dropped into a chair and stared at the drawn red curtains. He shivered. 'Sorry there's no heat.'

Frost sat down on the settee, facing Duffy. 'You're up late?'

'My wife can't sleep. I stay up with her. I don't like leaving her alone.'

Frost gave a sympathetic nod and looked up for his sergeant to start the questions.

'We're worried at the absence of a suicide note,' Gilmore said.

'Oh?' He tried to rub some warmth into a shirt-sleeved arm.

'You're quite sure there was no note?'

'Positive.'

Silence, broken only by the measured ticking of the clock on the mantelpiece. Then another sound. Frost had taken something from his mac pocket and was tapping it on his knee. It snatched Duffy's attention away from his study of the curtains.

The object was black, made of plastic, and Frost, a half-smile on his face, was tapping it slowly and regularly, again and again, on his knee.

At first Duffy couldn't make out what it was. Then his eyes widened and he sucked in air. It was a video cassette.

'Woof woof,' said Frost, and grinned.

'You bastard!' With a howl of rage Duffy hurled himself across the room at the inspector, his fists swinging wildly. Gilmore leapt forward to grab his wrists and fling him back into the chair.

'Was it something I said?' asked Frost in pretended puzzlement.

'You bastard,' repeated Duffy, this time near to tears. He shrank down into the chair and covered his face with his hands and his body convulsed with the sobbing he was no longer able to hold back. 'Don't tell my wife. It would kill her.' His voice was muffled by his hands.

Gilmore turned away. Raw emotion embarrassed him. Frost dribbled smoke and tried to look as if he knew more than he did.

Kenneth Duffy knuckled his eyes dry. 'What do you want to know?'

Frost waved the video. 'Tell me about it.'

Duffy bowed his head. 'I watched a few seconds – that was enough.'

'Where's the suicide note?'

The man shivered again and folded his arms around himself. 'I destroyed it.'

'Why?' snapped Gilmore who was standing behind him. 'Because it incriminated you?'

He twisted his head round and looked up at the sergeant. 'No. Because Susan asked me to. The note was addressed to me.'

Frost lit up a fresh cigarette from the stub of the old. 'What did it say?'

'It said, "The letter will explain. I can't face mum after what I've done. Please help me. Destroy this. She must never know." '

'Letter? What letter?'

'It was with Susan's note. An anonymous letter.'

Anonymous letter! Frost started, as did Gilmore. 'Tell us about it.'

Duffy paused to control his agitated breathing. 'It was addressed to my wife. Susan must have known it was coming so she waited for the postman. She opened it, read it and . . .' He shrugged as if referring to something trivial. '. . . and killed herself.'

'I want that letter,' said Frost grimly.

'I'm sorry. I haven't got it. I burnt it with the suicide note.'

'Shit!' said Frost vehemently. 'Describe it. The notepaper, the handwriting.'

'Is it important?' asked Duffy wearily.

'Yes, it bloody is.'

'Blue notepaper. Typed. Posted in Denton.'

Frost nodded grimly to Gilmore. 'What did it say?'

'What do you bloody think it said?' replied Duffy, again near to tears. 'It said, "Dear Mrs Duffy. Did you know that your dear darling, pure daughter Susan has taken part in depraved, bestial practices with men, with other women . . . even with animals, and is so proud of what she did that she allowed herself to be filmed. If you doubt me, I'm sending you a video."' He paused and listened to the clock tick.

'And did he send a video?' prompted Frost.

'Yes. It came the next morning . . . the day after Susan died. Imagine the effect on my wife if she'd received it. I waited for the postman, just like Susan must have done.' He shuddered. 'It was the one with the dog.'

All heads turned to the door as it clicked open. Mrs Duffy came in, a shrunken, stooped figure, face tired and lined, eyes red. Duffy rose from his chair. 'It's the police, love. Just asking a few questions.'

'Routine,' muttered Frost, avoiding her eyes. She'd have to know, but he wasn't going to be the one to tell her.

She forced a smile. 'I'll make some tea.'

'We can't stop, I'm afraid,' said Frost. 'Lots of things to do.'

'I won't be long, love,' said Duffy, helping his wife out of the room. 'You go in the warm.' When he came back he said, 'How old does she look? Sixty?' Not far short, thought Frost. 'She was forty last month and she never looked her age. Losing her only daughter was bad enough, but when this other business comes out, it'll kill her. You'll have another death on your hands.'

'You'll have to tell her,' said Frost.

'You bloody tell her,' said Duffy. He went to the sideboard and opened a drawer where he took out a small box. 'You see these?' He rattled it. 'The bloody doctor's put her back on the same tablets Susan took.'

Frost looked away. There was nothing to say.

Outside, in the car, Gilmore said, 'That video. Did you notice Susan's feet?'

'Her feet were the last thing I thought of looking at,' said Frost. 'Why?'

'The ground was rough so she was wearing shoes,' said Gilmore. 'Stark naked, but wearing shoes . . . just like Paula.'

Frost worried away at his scar, then shook his head. 'Coincidence, son. No-one would want to make a porn video with Paula. The poor little bitch didn't have the looks, or the figure.' He salvaged a decent-sized butt from the ashtray and lit up. 'The doc was right. He said that poison pen bastard would kill someone some day.' He huddled down in his seat, suddenly feeling cold. 'And I haven't the faintest idea how to go about catching the sod.'

Gilmore started up the engine. 'Where to?'

'Drop me off at the station, then go home, son. You'll be fit for sod all in the morning if you don't get some kip.'

Wednesday night shift (2)

Gilmore drew up outside the house and checked the windows. Despite the hour he half expected to see all the lights blazing and a still-smouldering Liz waiting for him. But the house seemed to be in darkness and he sighed with relief. He wasn't ready for another slanging match. But as he quietly clicked the front door shut behind him he heard mumbled voices and a slit of light showed from under the lounge door.

He tiptoed down the hall and turned the handle. An old black and white film was playing on the television and Liz was curled up in the armchair, a couple of empty tonic water bottles on the table and a bottle of vodka on the floor by her side. She turned and held up a brim-full glass in a mock toast. 'Home is the hunter!' In one gulp she swigged it down, waving the empty glass triumphantly aloft.

'It's gone four o'clock,' he said. 'What are you doing up?'

She pouted. 'You said you'd be in early. You promised me you'd be in bloody early.'

He shrugged off his jacket, loosened his tie and took a clean glass from the display cabinet. 'I said I'd try. It just wasn't possible.' He flopped wearily into the other armchair and reached for the vodka bottle. It was empty. He held it up accusingly. 'This was a full bottle on Saturday!'

'So I bloody drank it. What else is there to do in this stinking town, sitting in this lousy room, waiting for you and you never bloody come.'

He rubbed his hands over his face, trying to wipe away the fatigue. 'It won't be for long.' None too hopefully he pushed himself from the chair and foraged through the display cabinet, looking for something alcoholic amongst the half-empty bitter lemon and Coke bottles. Defeated, he poured himself a glass of Coke. It was warm and flat. On the television screen Humphrey Bogart was slapping Peter Lorre around. He relaxed, rested his head against the back of the armchair and tried to fight off sleep.

'You know what I thought,' slurred Liz in a husky whisper, putting her empty glass on the table. 'I thought I'd wait up for my randy, rampant, lover-boy husband and I thought we'd have some randy, rampant sex. How does that grab you, superstud?'

He was too tired. He wasn't in the mood and he didn't even think he was capable of making love. But he forced a grin. He didn't want a row, a hurtful, scratching row, all in hoarse angry whispers to avoid disturbing the neighbours. 'You're on,' he said, and held out his arms.

She slunk over and nestled in his lap. He kissed her. She tasted of vodka. Her body was hot and burning and her perfume was heady and erotic. Her hand crawled over him, tugging the shirt free from his trousers, her fingers exploring, caressing and lightly scratching his lower stomach. Then he wasn't faking any more. Then he was unbuttoning and easing off her dress. Then he was biting and licking and groaning.

And then, jarring like a dentist's drill, the door bell. A long, persistent ring. And someone banging on the door. And Frost's voice yelling for him to open up. This is a nightmare, he thought. A bloody nightmare.

'Sorry, son,' said Frost, barging in as he opened the front door. 'An emergency . . .' He stopped dead as he saw Liz smouldering in the armchair, her dress unbuttoned down to the waist, making no attempt to cover her naked breasts. Frost made no attempt to hide his gaping admiration.

Gilmore made the unnecessary introduction. 'My wife Liz.'

'Sorry about this, love,' apologized Frost. 'You must hate my guts.'

'Yes,' she said simply.

'I'm known as Coitus Interruptus in the trade,' added Frost, hoping to warm up the atmosphere, but neither of them responded.

'What do you want?' asked Gilmore curtly.

'Another arson attack at the Comptons'. I know it's your case, but I'll attend to it if you like.'

Gilmore hesitated.

'Bloody go,' snapped Liz. 'Bugger off and go!' The door slammed as she stormed out of the room.

'I'll wait outside,' said Frost. 'Be quick.'

'I'm coming now,' said Gilmore, grabbing his coat.

The rain had stopped, but a cold wind chased them to the car. 'Sorry if I sodded things up for you, son,' said Frost, settling into the passenger seat. Gilmore gave a noncommittal grunt and slammed the car into gear. He looked back at the house, half hoping Liz would be at the window so he could give her a wave. A forlorn hope.

The road was clear so Gilmore was able to ignore traffic signals and speed limits and drove with his foot jammed down hard while Frost briefly outlined what he knew. 'Compton phoned the station about half an hour ago. Someone was prowling about outside. A couple of minutes later the station alarm went off, so the prowler must have broken a window or forced a lock or something. Control sent an area car. It found the place in flames. The fire brigade's on its way. That's all I know so far.' As they left the town and climbed the hill to skirt the woods an orange glow throbbed in the sky ahead. 'Bloody hell, son,' said Frost. 'That's one hell of a fire.'

Soon they could see the flashing electric-blue beacons of the fire trucks and hear the deep-throated roar of the burning wooden structure fanned to a frenzy by the wind. The scorching heat hit them as they climbed out of the car and stumbled over a spaghetti confusion of hoses.

'Look out!' someone yelled.

A long-drawn-out creaking screech of agony as the supporting timbers of the mill gave way, then a slow rumbling as the roof collapsed and whooshed up a tongue of flame which licked the night sky with thousands of red, dancing sequins. Firemen in yellow oilskins turned their backs as the dragon's breath of scorched air and smoke blasted out at them.

With the roof down and the building open to the sky, the firemen were able to direct their hoses into the seething heart of the fire gradually damping down the flames and sending up clouds of steam and oily smoke.

'Inspector! Over here.' PC Jordan was waving to them from the side of a fire truck. There was something on the grass by his feet. Something covered by a crumpled sheet of grey plastic, dripping wet from the back-spray of the hoses.

'Shit,' said Frost. The plastic was draped over a dead body.

'The firemen found him in the lounge,' Jordan told them. 'He's burnt to buggery.'

Frost bent and carefully lifted the sheet, then turned his head away, but not before he had breathed in the sickening smell of burnt flesh. Gilmore, watching, felt his stomach start to churn. The dead face gawping up at him was blistered red raw and distorted by intense heat. Where the hair should have been was grey powdery ash.

'The firemen reckon he must have fallen into a pool of blazing petrol,' explained Jordan, staring straight ahead, determined not to look down. 'They dragged him out of the lounge.'

'Poor bastard,' muttered Frost. He pulled the plastic sheeting down further to see better. Welded into the bubbling black flesh, pieces of charred material. 'Looks like pyjamas.'

'Yes, sir. We presume he's the householder.'

Frost forced himself to bend again and study the face closer. If it was Mark Compton it would require medical and dental records for a positive identification. Slowly, he straightened up. 'So what happened?'

'The place was well alight when we got here. Simms radioed for the fire brigade. No way of getting in at the front, so I tried the rear and found Mrs Compton, in her night clothes, unconscious on the lawn just outside the back door.'

'Where is she now?'

'She's with someone in the village, I think.'

Frost nodded for him to continue.

'When the fire brigade got here they sent a couple of men with breathing apparatus into the house. The body was in the lounge. They dragged him out but he was already dead.'

'I thought the sprinklers were supposed to stop this sort of fire,' said Frost.

'They'd been put out of action, Inspector. The water supply was turned off at the mains.'

Gilmore thought it was about time he reminded everyone that this was his case. 'Radio through to Control,' he snapped. 'Tell all patrols that anyone out and about at this time of the morning, on foot or in a car, is a suspect and is to be detained for questioning.'

'And advise all hospitals, chemists and doctors that we want to know immediately about anyone requesting treatment for burns,' added Frost.

A car horn sounded and Dr Maltby's Vauxhall crept into the side road. Maltby, wrapped up against the cold in a thick overcoat, climbed out and surveyed the smouldering wreckage of the once beautiful house. He spotted Frost and made his way across, stepping with exaggerated care over the hose-pipes.

'He's drunk again,' hissed Gilmore.

'Then arrest him,' snapped Frost. 'We need the extra work. Over here, doc!'

The doctor lurched over. 'Terrible business, Jack.' He nodded at the sheeted shape. 'The husband?'

'All that's left of him, doc. He fell face first in some four star. What I want to know is, did he fall or was he pushed?'

Maltby pulled the sheet completely away from the body and arranged it over the wet grass so he could kneel down. He shook his head testily. 'He's too badly burnt. You'll need a proper post-mortem.' He lifted the head slightly, his fingers exploring the skull. 'Hello . . .' Carefully he moved the head so he could examine it more easily. 'The back of the skull's caved in.'

'Where?' asked Frost, squatting down beside the doctor. His nicotine-stained fingers probed. Yes, he could feel the pulpy fracture where the skull gave way under pressure. He wiped his hand on his mac and straightened up. 'Damn, damn and double damn!'

'Could it have happened when he fell?' asked Gilmore.

Frost shook his head. 'He fell face down, son . . . straight into the burning petrol.'

Maltby nodded his agreement. 'I'd say he was struck from behind . . . a heavy blow from a blunt instrument. If the blow didn't kill him outright, then the fire finished him off.'

Frost's shoulders sagged wearily. 'It's murder whichever way you look at it, doc.' He shook water from the plastic sheeting and jerked it back over the body. 'Where's the poor sod's wife?'

'Ada's looking after her,' said Maltby. He turned to watch the firemen. The Old Mill was now a skeleton of blackened, smoking timbers which had to be continually dampened down as a malevolent wind kept fanning sparks into flames. 'Get the bastard, Jack,' he said, as he stumbled back to his car.

'I'll try,' called Frost. He turned to Gilmore. 'Come on, son. Let's go and have a word with Old Mother Rigid Nipples.'

Gilmore exploded. He had had just about enough of Frost's callous crudeness for one day. 'Haven't you got any bloody feeling? A man's dead. His wife is a widow. Must everything be a cheap joke?'

Frost accepted the rebuke with a half-hearted shrug. 'I see so many rotten things, son. If I dwelt on them, I'd probably go and chuck myself under a bus, which might make Mullett happy, but wouldn't do the victim any good . . . so I joke. It makes the job a bit more tolerable . . . sorry if it upsets you, though.'

A concerned-looking Ada, a thick mouse-grey dressing gown over flannelette pyjamas, a man's cap covering her curlers, led them through to the bedroom where Jill

Compton, all respectable in one of Ada's passion-killing high-necked winceyette nightdresses, lay with eyes closed, on Ada's iron-framed single bed. Frost thought it was the most erotic sight he had ever seen and wished he wouldn't keep thinking dirty thoughts at inopportune moments. Jill's eyes fluttered, then opened wide in startled anxiety as Frost gently called her name. She sat up. 'Where's Mark? Is he all right?'

Frost groaned inwardly. He hadn't realized she hadn't been told. 'It's bad news, I'm afraid, Mrs Compton.'

She stared at him, then at Gilmore, her eyes pleading to be told that what she feared, what she dreaded, wasn't so. 'No . . . no . . . please . . .' And her head shook, rejecting what she knew they would tell her.

Frost knew of no way to deaden the hurt other than killing hope quickly. 'Your husband is dead, Mrs Compton. The firemen got him out, but it was too late.'

At first she looked angry, as if her refusal to accept what they were telling her would make it untrue. Then her body shook as she buried her face in her hands, tears streaming between her fingers. 'No . . .'

Ada pushed forward to comfort her. 'You'd better go now,' she ordered the two detectives.

'No,' said Frost, firmly. 'She's the only witness. The only person who can help us.'

Ada stood her ground, chin jutting defiantly, one arm protectively around her charge. 'I've told you to go. This is neither the time nor the place.'

But, sniffing back her tears and biting hard on her lower lip, Jill spoke quietly. 'It's all right. I want to help. What do you want to know?'

Signalling Gilmore to get out his notebook, Frost dragged a wicker-seated chair to the side of the bed. 'Tell us what happened.'

The detective sergeant gave a sharp cough and glared angrily. 'This is my case,' he reminded the inspector.

'Sorry, son,' said Frost mildly, moving his chair back a little.

Gilmore gave the woman a sympathetic smile. 'Tell us what happened, Mrs Compton.'

She fumbled under the pillow for a handkerchief, dabbed at her eyes, then, twisting the tiny scrap of cloth in her hands, related the course of events. 'We went to bed just before midnight. I woke up suddenly. Mark was using the phone by the bed. He was calling the police. He had heard someone prowling about outside.'

'Did you see who it was?' asked Gilmore.

'Not clearly. We looked out of the window and could see a shadow of someone moving about. Mark was angry. He grabbed a heavy torch and said he was going to teach whoever it was a lesson.'

'He was going to use the torch as a weapon?'

She nodded. 'I imagine so.'

'You didn't go downstairs with him?'

'No. He insisted I stayed in the bedroom with the door locked. I waited. Suddenly I heard shouting and crashing, as if there was a fight. Then it went quiet. I waited, hoping Mark would come back. I called him. No answer. Then I smelt burning so I unlocked the bedroom door. Thick black smoke. I could hardly see. I had to feel my way down the stairs. When I opened the lounge door, flames and smoke roared out. I could see Mark, face down on the floor. But the heat was intense. I couldn't get to him.'

She paused, her face drawn and pained as she relived the moment. Frost started to say something, but Gilmore brusquely signalled him to be quiet.

'I saw the lounge window was open, so I tried to get out into the garden through the back door. But the smoke was so thick. I was choking. When I found the bolts, they wouldn't undo. I struggled and finally got them undone . . .' She looked at her broken nails, then hid her hands under the bedclothes. '. . . but I must have passed out. That's all I remember. There was a fireman . . . and then there was Ada.' The effort of talking had exhausted her. Her eyes closed and her head dropped back on the pillow. 'That's all I remember,' she repeated in a whisper.

'The firemen found you collapsed just outside the back door,' Gilmore told her. 'Did you see anything more of the person who broke in?'

Eyes still closed, she shook her head. 'No.' Her body trembled with the reaction and she tried to sit up. 'If only I could have got to Mark. He was so close. But the flames . . .'

Gilmore patted her arm. 'There was nothing you could have done, Mrs Compton. He was already dead when you first saw him.'

She raised her face to the sergeant. 'I pleaded with him to wait for the police. If only he had stayed with me . . .' And then she threw back her head and howled in anguish, her sobs racking her body . . .

With a belligerent stride Ada pushed in front of Gilmore. 'No more. She's had enough.'

Gilmore replaced the chair up against the forget-me-not patterned wallpaper. 'Thanks for your help, Mrs Compton. And I really am most sorry.'

Ada wrapped her dressing gown around her spare frame. 'I'll stay with her for a while. There's tea and biscuits in the kitchen if you want some.'

The kitchen, with the coal fire roaring away, was almost overpoweringly warm and Gilmore had to fight hard to keep his eyes open as he sipped Ada's hot, sweet tea. Frost had twitched back the curtains to reveal the early morning sky, part-streaked with smudges of smoke from the fire. He was sprawled in the chair by the kitchen table, using a saucer as an ashtray. He too was tired. He'd have given anything to be able to climb into bed, preferably with the naked Jill Compton whose tear-stained, unmade-up face seemed to hold an erotic attraction.

His foot twitched and made contact with something under the table, something that swayed, then toppled heavily with a glassy clunk. Yawning, he lifted the tablecloth. Nudging his foot lay a wine bottle on its side. One of Ada's home-made brews. There were about twenty or so more bottles of wine bunched together under the table. 'The stingy cow's hiding it from us,' he said, pulling the cork out with his teeth and taking a swig. The room shimmered, then jerked still. He replaced the cork and pushed the bottle back with the others under the table.

'You know what I've been thinking?' said Gilmore.

Frost shook his head to stop the fuzziness. 'If it's something rude, I'm all ears, son.'

'If that poison pen letter was sent to Mark Compton, then who is the woman he's been knocking off?'

'I wish I knew,' replied Frost. 'I'd love to get some of what he's been getting.'

'He's been going with another woman,' said Gilmore. 'There could be a jealous husband, or boyfriend.'

'A good point, son,' began Frost, then he stopped dead and looked under the table again as a nagging thought struck him. 'Why has she dumped the bottles there? She's usually so neat and tidy . . . everything in its place.'

'I don't know,' muttered Gilmore, his tone implying he didn't care either.

A wall cupboard in the corner caught Frost's eye. 'That's where she usually keeps her wine. Quick, son.

Take a look inside.' Gilmore showed his astonishment. 'It could be important, son.'

Anything to humour the old fool, thought Gilmore as he tugged at the handle. 'It's locked!'

'Catch!' Frost tossed him a bunch of keys. 'Try one of these.'

The first key didn't fit, so he tried another. 'We shouldn't be doing this without a search warrant.'

Frost raised his eyebrows in mock astonishment. 'You learn something new in this job every day. Someone was telling me you can't plant false evidence any more, but I'm not that gullible.' He lit up another cigarette. 'Hurry it up, son.'

Another key. Still no joy. But the next glided in smooth as silk and the lock clicked. Gilmore pulled open the door then whistled softly. Inside the cupboard was a battered old Olympia typewriter. He was carrying it over to the table when a door slammed and an angry voice shrilled, 'And just what do you think you're doing?'

'I tried to stop him, Ada,' said Frost, 'but he wouldn't take any notice.'

'I let you into my house. I give you tea. I give you biscuits . . .'

'But you don't give us your body, Ada. The one thing I've been lusting after.'

She wasn't listening to Frost. Angry eyes stabbed at Gilmore who was ripping a blank page from the back of his notebook and feeding it into the roller. Her voice, shaking with rage, rose an octave. 'Don't you dare touch that!' She plunged forward but Frost's arm shot out to restrain her.

'We've got to check it to make sure he hasn't broken it, Ada. I want you to get every penny of compensation.'

The page in to his satisfaction, Gilmore pecked out a test sentence. *The quick brown fox jumps over the lazy dog.* He snatched the paper from the machine and studied it carefully, a grin of triumph creeping across his face. 'The "s" and the "a" are out of alignment, Inspector. We've found the poison pen typewriter.'

Frost took the page from him and nodded. 'He's right, Ada. But I bet you've got a perfectly plausible explanation?' He waited expectantly.

She folded her arms stubbornly and compressed her lips.

'Can't quite hear you, Ada,' said Frost, cupping his hand to his ear.

Her eyes narrowed, but she remained silent.

Gilmore pushed himself between her and Frost. He was barely in control of himself. He kept seeing Susan Bicknell in her Mickey Mouse nightdress, stretched lifeless on the bed. 'You don't need to say anything, you evil-minded bitch. Because of you an old man tried to kill himself. Because of you a fifteen-year-old kid took her own life.'

She stared back at him, her eyes unflinching. 'Then you'd better arrest me, hadn't you?'

'Stop fighting, you two,' said Frost, flopping back in his chair. 'You never wrote those bloody letters, Ada. The longest note you ever wrote said "No milk today, please, the cat's got diarrhoea."' He shook an export Benson and Hedges from the packet. 'That's old Mr Wardley's typewriter, isn't it? He's the sod who's been sending the letters.'

Her expression didn't change.

'Wardley?' exclaimed Gilmore. 'That's impossible. He got one of the letters. He tried to kill himself.'

'He didn't try very hard, did he, son? He didn't try as hard as that poor cow Susan Bicknell.' He folded the piece of paper into a spill and lit his cigarette from the fire. 'I reckon Wardley didn't swallow more than a couple of those tablets.'

'The bottle was nearly empty,' said Gilmore.

'Only because he'd tipped most of the tablets out into the drawer of his bedside cabinet. He sent the poison pen letter to himself, then faked the suicide.' He puffed smoke towards the woman. 'I'm right, aren't I, Ada? You can caress any part of my body if I'm wrong.'

Her lips twisted into a tight, bitter smile then she moved across to the table and started stacking the dirty cups and saucers on a tray. 'How did you find out?'

'Guesswork mainly, Ada. But I was bloody suspicious of that unfranked poison pen letter Wardley was supposed to have received. Everyone else's letter went into juicy detail . . . every thrust, every withdrawal, each nibble of naked ear-hole all lovingly described. But there weren't any juicy bits at all in his own letter. It was almost polite. "What would the church say if I told them what you did to those boys!" Not a mention of dick anywhere.' He dragged hard at the cigarette. 'And then there was the missing suicide note. It didn't make sense you should destroy it. There was no point.'

Ada crossed the room to the sideboard. 'I didn't destroy it. I just didn't want you to see it.' From the drawer she took a sheet of blue notepaper. Frost glanced at it, then passed it over to Gilmore. '"A"s and "s"s out of line, son. The silly sod used the same machine for the suicide note and the poison pen letters.'

'He thinks himself so clever, but he's not all there,' said Ada. 'I found out about him last year. I went in to do his cleaning and there he was, bashing away at the typewriter, so engrossed in one of his nasty letters he never heard me.'

'Then why didn't you inform the police?' asked Gilmore.

She dragged a chair to the fire and sat down. 'He's lived next door to me for years. I didn't want to get him into trouble.'

'So you just let him carry on writing his dirty letters?'

'I made him promise he'd stop. I thought he had stopped.' She stared into the fire then picked up the poker and shattered a lump of coal sending sparks shooting up the chimney.

'What brought things to a head?' asked Gilmore. 'Why the letter to himself and the faked suicide attempt?'

She rubbed her hands as if she was cold and held them to the fire to warm them. 'I was working up at The Mill when the post came. There was a letter addressed to Mr Compton. I recognized the blue envelope and the wonky typing right away, so I hid it in my pocket. I wasn't going to let him cause trouble with the Comptons.'

'Did you confront Wardley?' Frost asked.

'As soon as I finished work. I charged over to his cottage and told him I was going straight to the police. He said the police would never believe me. It would be his word against mine and he was a churchwarden and I was a charlady. Just then, in comes Dr Maltby with the sleeping tablets. I took the letter from my pocket and said, "Can I talk to you in private, doctor. I've got something to show you." Mr Wardley went as white as a sheet. Of course, when we got outside, I gave the doctor the letter and explained how I'd got hold of it, but I didn't tell him anything about Mr Wardley writing it. I only meant to frighten him. I can't tell you how I felt when I went back later and it looked as if he'd killed himself.'

'Like I said, he faked it to make you out a liar, Ada,' said Frost, pushing himself out of his chair.

Gilmore gathered up the typewriter and followed Frost out into the cold, damp morning air where the smell of smoke and burning clung to the wind.

The Old Mill was a depressing blackened shell, dripping water which plopped mournfully into soot-filmed, debris-choked pools. The ground squelched under foot as firemen in yellow oilskins and blackened faces rolled up hoses and stowed away equipment while others, helped by members of the Forensic team, were picking through the sodden wreckage. DC Burton in an anorak over a polo-necked sweater spotted their car as they pulled up and hurried to meet them. 'The pathologist has examined the body, Inspector. He thinks the blow on the head knocked Compton unconscious and death was due to smoke suffocation. He'll be doing the autopsy at eleven this morning.'

'I'll be there,' said Gilmore to remind everyone once again that this was his case.

'Any joy with petrol- and smoke-smelling suspects?' asked Frost.

'No, sir. Charlie Alpha picked up a tramp on the Bath Road, but what he smelt of isn't nice to say.'

'Forensic turned anything up?'

'Yes – those.' Burton pointed to three heat-distorted metal petrol cans, bagged up for laboratory examination. 'And this . . .' He picked up a plastic bag containing a blackened cylinder of metal, caved in at one end. 'They think this is the murder weapon.'

'Compton's torch!' said Frost. He told Gilmore to get Mrs Compton to identify it as soon as Forensic had finished their tests.

'That's what I intended doing,' hissed Gilmore through clenched teeth.

'What's the name of our one bloody suspect?' asked Frost. 'The one who picked the fight?'

'Bradbury,' Gilmore reminded him. The fool had a memory like a sieve.

'That's him! There's an all-forces bulletin out on him. Find out if he's been located yet.'

While Gilmore radioed through to the station, Frost peered through a smashed window at the remains of the lounge, which was now a miniature indoor lake of greasy water dotted with islands of ash and charred wood. He lit a cigarette, took one deep drag, then hurled it away. The smoke had the greasy taint of burnt flesh.

Gilmore returned, shaking his head. No joy yet on Bradbury. Frost took one last look round. Everyone seemed to be coping quite well without him. 'We're doing no good here, son,' he muttered. 'Let's go to the hospital.'

'The hospital?' echoed Gilmore. 'Why?' Now that he had committed himself to attending the autopsy in six hours' time, all he wanted to do was go home and get some sleep.

'To question Wardley,' explained Frost. 'You said Mark Compton's bit of spare might provide the motive for his death and Wardley knows who she is. I'll do it on my own if you like.'

No way! thought Gilmore, slamming the car into gear. No bloody way.

At that hour of the morning Denton Hospital was a place of uneasy, muffled noises, whispers, coughs and groans. The very young probationer nurse in sole charge of the wheezing, snuffling ward wasn't at all happy about

Frost waking up one of the patients, but Frost breezily assured her that he had permission.

Wardley, deep in a trouble-free sleep, was rudely awakened by a rough shaking of his shoulder. His eyes flickered open as he tried to focus on the two strangers looking grimly down at him. One of them he recognized immediately and his heart-beat faltered before thudding away. It was that detective inspector, back again, in the middle of the night. And the look on his face. God, they knew. They had found out. He closed his eyes tightly and feigned sleep, but the renewed shaking of his shoulder nearly jerked him out of bed. 'Yes?' he asked in a quavery, weak, old man's voice.

'Get dressed,' said Frost. 'I'm arresting you.'

'Arresting me?' He pulled himself up. 'It's that woman next door telling lies about me, isn't it? Don't you believe her . . . she's evil. She hates me.'

'Not as much as I bloody hate you,' said Frost. 'And the only lies Ada told us was when she was covering up for you, you sod. She even hid your typewriter – the one you used for your suicide note – and for your poison pen letters.'

'Poison pen?' He tried to sound indignant. 'The intention was to make people stop their filthy practices.'

'You made Susan Bicknell stop hers,' said Frost. 'The poor cow killed herself.'

The skin on the old man's knuckles stretched almost to blue transparency as he clutched at the sheet. 'I didn't mean that to happen. She over-reacted. I'm sorry.'

'Oh, you're sorry?' hissed Frost. 'That makes it all right. We'll dig the poor bitch up so you can apologize.' He dragged a chair across the floor with such a loud, teeth-setting squeak that half the ward stirred uneasily. 'Right,' he said wearily. 'I'm tired, my sergeant is tired, and we haven't got time to sod about. I'm going to ask you questions, and I want answers.'

'I'm saying nothing,' whimpered Wardley. 'I'm a sick man.'

The chair squeaked again as Frost stood up. 'Arrest the bastard, Sergeant.'

'Wait,' said Wardley. 'What do you want to know?'

Another squeak from the chair. Frost made himself comfortable, then shook the last export cigarette from the packet and lit up. 'Let's start with the pornographic video. Who's been making them?'

'A purveyor of filth. If I knew his name I'd tell you. I bought the video, Inspector. It wasn't for enjoyment. I have to do these things to ferret out evil. When I screened it, I recognized the girl. Her mother goes to our church. I've no idea who makes and distributes them.'

'Where did you buy it?' Gilmore asked.

'A newsagent's in Catherine Street. I don't know the name.'

'We do,' said Frost. 'We've already arrested him.' That part of Wardley's story checked out anyway. 'We'll leave that for the moment. You sent one of your well-meaning letters to Mark Compton?'

The old man pulled himself upright, his eyes wild, his expression intense. 'That lecher. All smug and high and mighty, but sneaking off behind his wife's back for disgusting perversions with a prostitute.'

'A prostitute?' said Gilmore, glumly. This ruined his theory. If Compton's bit of spare was a prostitute, a vengeful boyfriend or husband would have his work cut out.

'Never mind, son,' said Frost. 'We'll check her out anyway.' He asked Wardley where she lived.

'Where all these high-priced harlots live. In Queen's Court – those new flats at the back of the big supermarket . . . end flat, third floor.'

'If they were up on the third floor, how could you see through the bedroom window?'

Wardley smiled. 'The multi-storey car-park overlooks her flat. All you need is a strong pair of field-glasses.'

'And a dirty vicious bastard to use them,' said Frost.

PC Dave Simms tucked the area car into the lay-by off the Bath Road and reached for the thermos flask. His observer, PC Jordan, yawned and stretched his arms. 'I'll be damn glad when this shift is over,' he sniffed. 'I'm sure I've got this flu bug coming on.'

'Don't breathe over me then,' replied Simms, slopping steaming hot coffee into a plastic cup and passing it over.

Jordan sipped at the cup, then his eyes narrowed. 'Hello. What's this?'

Headlights approaching. Coming from the opposite direction to the fire, but they had been given instructions to stop everyone. Anyone out and about at this time of the morning was a potential suspect.

It was a small black van which slowed down and stopped as they sounded the siren and cut in front of it. The driver, a short, sharp-featured man with long greasy hair, in his late forties, eyed them warily. 'What's the trouble, officer?'

Simms asked to see the man's driving licence, his nose twitching, trying to detect the smell of smoke, or petrol, but smelling only fresh paint.

'I haven't got my licence with me. What's this all about?'

'Just routine, sir. Do you mind telling us what you are doing out at this time of night?'

Jordan was checking the van. The smell of new paint was strong. The vehicle had been freshly painted. A pretty ropey job, done with a paint brush, not a spray gun. He tried the rear doors. They opened.

'Leave them alone!' yelled the man, reaching forward to switch on the engine, but Simms' hand clamped round his wrist.

The beam of Jordan's torch found a stack of cardboard boxes. He pulled one forward and looked inside. Jewellery. Lots of jewellery. Mainly old-fashioned, but good quality – brooches, lockets, bangles, rings.

'Well, well, well,' smirked Jordan. 'And what is your perfectly reasonable explanation for these, sir?'

The hospital was slowly waking up as they clattered down the stone stairs past the first shift of cleaners with mops and buckets. They could hear the car radio as they crossed the pavement.

'Frost,' he yawned into the handset.

'We've got him, Jack,' reported Sergeant Wells triumphantly.

'You've got Bradbury?' asked Frost, unable to believe his luck. 'Is he dripping with petrol, smothered in blood and carrying a blunt instrument?'

'Not Bradbury,' replied Wells, testily. Frost was always joking at the wrong moment. 'No joy with him yet. But we've got Wally Manson. Jordan and Simms picked him up. His van's a bloody treasure trove – full of stolen gear from the senior citizen break-ins. Mr Mullett is cock-a-hoop.'

'What's that about Mr Mullett's cock?' asked Frost innocently. 'This is a very bad line.' He replaced the handset. 'The station, son.'

But Gilmore was already on the way.

Frost sank down in his seat again. He dug down in his pocket, but the Benson and Hedges packet was empty.

Thursday morning shift

A quarter to six in the morning and Mullett, freshly shaven, highly polished, and immaculately dressed in his best tailored uniform, emerged from his office, mentally rehearsing the speech he would make to the press and the television cameras after they had charged Manson with the 'Granny Ripper' killings. He waylaid the dishevelled Frost and Gilmore, both looking tired and edgy, on their way to the Interview Room. 'No doubts about the right man this time, Inspector. Hanlon has definitely identified an item of jewellery from Manson's van as belonging to one of the murder victims and there's a positive forensic report on those jeans.'

'Great!' muttered Frost, trying to share his commander's enthusiasm. He always got worried when things appeared to be going too well.

They looked in on the exhibits store where Arthur Hanlon, his nose red and sore from repeated blowing, was hovering over a collection of cardboard boxes, the spoils from Wally Manson's van. 'Mr Mullett tells me it's all cut and dried,' said Frost. 'Wally's confessed and hanged himself to spare the state the cost of a trial.'

'Not quite, Jack,' giggled Hanlon, blowing his nose with a sodden handkerchief. 'He's denying everything at the moment – you know what a slimy little sod he is.'

'Yes,' nodded Frost. 'I sometimes think he's Mr Mullett's illegitimate son. Anyway, what have we got?'

Hanlon pushed one of the boxes over and raised the flaps. 'This was a surprise, Jack.' The box was packed tight with pornographic videos. 'Forty-nine in all,' reported Hanlon. 'The same titles as we got from the newsagent's.' Frost grunted and pulled the next box towards him. This one held assorted house-breaking tools – screwdrivers, jemmies, hammers, glass cutters. The last box, the smallest of the lot, contained various small plastic supermarket bags. Selecting one at random, Frost looked inside, then handed it over to Gilmore. Jewellery. Gold rings, chains, lockets, crucifixes. Another bag held necklaces and ear-rings. Yet another, old-fashioned cameo brooches, and heavy dress jewellery.

'We've only positively identified this, so far,' Hanlon told them, fishing out a pearl-studded crucifix on a silver chain. 'But it's the one that matters. This belonged to Mrs Alice Ryder.'

Frost held the crucifix in his open hand. It looked like silver, but it wasn't and the pearls were false. It was worth a few pounds at the most and the old lady who fought to stop it being stolen had had her skull smashed in and had died in Denton Hospital. 'Mullett was yapping about positive forensic evidence?'

'The stains are definitely blood, the same group as the old lady, and there were small fragments of china which matched up to that vase he smashed getting through the window.'

'What have you told Manson?'

'I haven't told him anything. I've only questioned him about being in possession of stolen property.'

'You haven't mentioned the killings?'

'No.'

'Good. Let's keep the sod guessing. Bring him to Interview Room Number 1.' Frost patted his pockets and realized he was out of cigarettes. He sent Gilmore back to the office to fetch a packet from his desk drawer.

Gritty, tired and irritated at being treated as a messenger boy, Gilmore yanked the drawer open. Underneath the camouflage of two ancient files were a couple of packs, each containing 200 Benson and Hedges export only cigarettes. He paused. A way to get back into his Divisional Commander's good books. This was exactly the sort of thing Mullett had asked him to look out for. Evidence of Frost's dubious practices. A quiet word in Mullett's ear. 'I don't know if I ought to be saying this, sir, against a fellow officer, but . . .' He could already see the Cheshire cat grin spreading over the Divisional Commander's face. He stuffed a spare packet in his pocket as evidence. Then he noticed something protruding beneath one of the packs in the drawer. A battered, blue material-covered case. Something else Frost had helped himself to? He clicked it open. Snug on red plush a silver cross on a dark blue ribbon, the inscription in the centre reading *For Gallantry.* Frost's famous medal. The George Gross. The civilian equivalent to the VC. Gilmore stared at it, then quickly clicked the case shut and replaced it at the bottom of the drawer together with the spare pack from his pocket. Frost would never know it, but yet again his medal had got him out of possible trouble.

'Gentleman to see you, Inspector,' announced Hanlon, pushing Wally Manson into the Interview Room.

Manson blinked as his eyes adjusted to the bright light after the shaded bulb of his cell. Through a haze of blue smoke he could see the unwelcome sight of Detective Inspector Jack Frost sprawled untidily in a chair, a cigarette dangling from his lips. On the table in front of him were a couple of the boxes taken from his van.

'Nice of you to drop in, Wally,' said Frost, waving a hand at the other chair by the table. 'Sit down.' Behind the inspector, leaning against the wall under the tiny window, was a younger man he didn't recognize, in a smart suit. The younger man looked tired and frazzled and nasty.

Gilmore contemplated Manson with disgust. The man was a slob with his weasel-like face, lank greasy hair and eyes that kept shifting from side to side; a cornered rat looking for an escape route.

'I don't know what this is all about, Mr Frost,' Manson said, shrinking down into the offered chair. 'Like I told the other gentleman, I found those boxes dumped in a lay-by. I was on the way to the police station to hand them in when those two coppers picked me up.'

'I'm sorry to hear that, Wally,' said Frost, shaking ash all over the floor, 'I was hoping you were guilty, because we're going to frame you anyway.'

Wally grinned at the inspector's joke, but Frost didn't seem to be joking. He dipped into one of the cardboard boxes and pulled out a pearl crucifix which he swung by the chain under Wally's nose.

'She identified you, Wally.'

Manson jerked his head away. 'Like I told the other officer, Mr Frost, I found these boxes in a lay-by . . .'

'They'll find you in a bleedin' lay-by if you don't stop sodding me about, Wally. You've been identified, we know you did it and we're going to get a confession and a conviction by fair means or foul. So tell us about it.'

'If only I knew what you're talking about, Mr Frost,' said Manson, giving his unconvincing impression of puzzled innocence, then nearly jumping out of his chair as the young thug behind him suddenly bellowed in his ear, 'We're talking about the woman whose skull you fractured, you scum-bag.'

'There's no need to raise your voice, Sergeant,' reproved Frost mildly. 'He's going to give us everything we want without bullying, aren't you, Wally?'

'I'll help you if I can,' said Manson, rubbing his ear.

Frost beamed a friendly smile that made the prisoner's blood run cold. 'Good. Then help me with Mrs Alice Ryder, the old lady from Clarendon Street who you put in hospital.' At this stage he wasn't going to let Manson know that she was dead.

Manson looked hurt. 'Not me, Mr Frost. That's not my style.'

Frost snorted a cloud of Benson and Hedges smoke. 'Style! You haven't got any bleeding style. If you're going to sod me about, I can sod you about. Notebook, Sergeant.'

Gilmore took out his notebook and flipped it open.

'Stand up,' snapped Frost to Manson.

Manson hesitated so Gilmore yanked him to his feet.

'Walter Richard Manson,' droned Frost, 'alias the Granny Ripper . . .'

'Granny Ripper?' croaked Manson, his astonishment sounding genuine this time.

'Shut up!' barked Gilmore.

'Alias the Granny Ripper,' continued Frost, 'I am arresting you on three counts of murder . . .' To Gilmore he said, 'Fill in the details – I forget the names and dates.' Gilmore nodded, his pencil scribbling furiously. 'You are not obliged to say anything – etc. etc., but anything you do say, blah, blah, blah. Take it as read, Wally – you know the words better than I do.'

'I am totally innocent of these preposterous charges,' said Manson smugly, twisting his head to make sure Gilmore was writing it all down.

Frost put his hand on Gilmore's notebook to stop him writing. 'Hold on, Sergeant. I'm sure we can do better than that.' He scratched his scar thoughtfully. 'Put . . . "The prisoner replied I didn't mean to kill them. I'm terribly sorry for what I did. I deserve to be punished."'

The man's jaw dropped. 'I never said that.'

Frost lit up another export only. 'What you actually said doesn't matter, Wally. It's what he puts down in his book that gets read out in court.'

Manson shrunk back in his chair. 'I shall deny saying it. I shall say it's all lies.'

'Of course you will, Wally. And it will be the word of a cheap slimy little crook with a record against a detective inspector with a medal. Courts seem to think that people with George Crosses are incapable of telling lies.'

'That's not fair,' said Manson, almost in tears.

'Life's not fair when some bastard breaks into your house and smashes your skull in,' snapped Frost.

Wally's tongue flicked snake-like across dried lips. 'You wouldn't perjure yourself, Mr Frost?' he pleaded, but the expression on the inspector's face said, 'Yes, I bloody well would.'

Frost leant his head back and treated the ceiling to a squirt of smoke. 'Not perjury, Wally – it's called oiling the wheels of justice. Take him away, Sergeant, and charge him. We'll have him in court first thing tomorrow.'

Hanlon stepped forward and took the man's arm, but Wally shook him off. 'What do I get if I co-operate?'

'My undying gratitude, Wally – and perhaps a whisper to the judge about how helpful you were.'

Manson hesitated. 'This old lady in Clarendon Street. You say she identified me?'

'She described you perfectly, Wally. She said her attacker was an ugly little bastard with bad breath and dandruff. We showed her some photographs and she picked you out right away.'

Manson gnawed at his lower lip. 'I didn't mean to hurt her, Mr Frost. She came at me like a bloody tiger.'

'An eighty-one-year-old tiger,' said Frost. 'What did she attack you with – her pension book?'

'A knife, Mr Frost . . . a flaming great knife.' He tugged the shirt from his trousers and lifted it to expose his stomach. 'Look what she did to me!' A thick pad of dirty red-mottled cotton wool, blood still weeping from the edges, was strapped to his stomach by strips of sticking plaster. 'She'd have killed me. I had to hit her to defend myself.' He fumbled at the dressing. 'Do you want to see what it's like underneath?'

Frost waved the offer away. 'No, thanks, Wally. It's a bit too near your dick and I haven't had my breakfast yet. I'll get the doctor to have a look at it.' He slid from his chair and went to the door, making a small jerk of his head to signal Hanlon to follow.

Outside in the passage, Frost closed the door firmly and lowered his voice. 'Here's a turn-up for the bleedin' book, Arthur. Did you check that knife to see if it matched up with any of the old girl's cutlery?'

'No, Jack. There were no prints on it and the damn thing had been honed razor sharp. I just assumed it came from her attacker.'

'She was terrified of burglars. She probably kept a sharpened knife to protect herself. Check it out now – and find out what blood group Wally is. It should be on his prison file.' He followed the worried-looking Hanlon down the corridor and asked Sergeant Wells to call the duty police surgeon.

* * *

The police surgeon dropped unused bandages into his bag and clicked it shut. 'I don't think there's any danger, but just to be on the safe side, the hospital should check him over.' He gave Frost his 'Payment Request' form to sign and checked it carefully before nodding his goodbye.

An agitated Arthur Hanlon was waiting outside the Interview Room. His shamefaced expression told Frost all.

'The knife came from her cutlery drawer,' Hanlon admitted. 'She's got a carving fork and a sharpening steel all in the same pattern to match. I'm sorry, Jack, I should have checked.'

'Never mind, Arthur,' said Frost. 'It makes me feel better to know I'm not the only twat in the force.'

'And Wally's blood group is O, the same as the dead woman's, so the blood on the knife could well have come from him.'

'Damn. The knife was the only thing that tied him to the other two killings and we haven't got that now. Never mind, let's do our best with what little we've got – as the bishop said to the actress.'

In the Interview Room, which now reeked of antiseptic, their prisoner was noisily drinking a cup of tea, watched by a sour-faced Gilmore. Frost dropped wearily into his chair. 'Right, Wally. The doctor says you're not going to die, but I've got over my disappointment. Tell me about the old dear at Clarendon Street – right from the beginning.' He pushed a cigarette across the table and lit it for the man. 'And cover up your stomach – it's wobbling like a bloody blancmange.'

Manson sucked gratefully at the cigarette. 'Thanks, Mr Frost.' He tucked his shirt back in and readjusted his belt. 'This was last Monday night – one of those nights when everything went wrong.'

Frost nodded in sympathy. He had many nights like that.

'The first house I tried I thought was going to be easy. Up on the dustbin and through the back window. I could hear the old boy talking to his wife downstairs, so I thought the coast was clear. Straight in the bedroom and there's this weird niff . . . I flashes my torch around and, bloody hell – there's a decomposing corpse grinning at me. I couldn't get out of there fast enough. I had to nip in the pub for some Dutch courage and who comes walking through the door but you and that bloke there with the fancy aftershave. This just ain't my bloody night, I thought. But I phoned you. I told you about the body.'

'I know, Wally,' nodded Frost. 'I recognized your voice.'

'I should have packed it in, but I needed some readies – I owed the bookie a couple of hundred and he was screaming for it. I'd already marked out this house in Clarendon Street. It looked easy and they said this old lady had cash all over the place. It must have been well bloody hidden – I never found it. The bedroom was empty. She was in the other room watching the telly, then, just my flaming luck, I knocks this vase over and the next thing I know she's charging in with the knife, slashing away. I lashed out in self-defence and she went out like a light.' He took another drag at his cigarette. 'It was all her fault, Mr Frost. I could have sued her for what she did to me. You know the law – you're only supposed to use reasonable force in ejecting a burglar, and gouging chunks out of his gut with a carving knife ain't reasonable force.'

'Neither is smashing someone's skull in,' barked Gilmore from behind him.

'A tap, Mr Frost, that's all I gave her. A tap with me jemmy, just to discourage her. The bloody knife was stuck in my stomach and I had to pull it out. I'd tore my rubber gloves in the struggle, so I wiped the handle clean in case my prints were on it, then grabbed up a few bits of jewellery and got the hell out of there. When I read in the paper next day she was in Intensive Care, it frightened the shit out of me – if you'll pardon the expression. I never did another job from that night to this. That's the honest, gospel truth.'

Frost shook another cigarette out of the packet and tapped it on the table. 'Tell me the honest gospel truth about the other poor cows, Wally. Did they all come at you with knives and then commit hara-kiri?' He watched the prisoner closely, but unless Manson was a brilliant actor, he didn't seem to know what Frost was talking about.

'Others? What are you trying to pin on me?'

Frost opened the file and spread out colour photographs of the two dead women showing their wounds in vivid close-up, his eyes still locked on Manson's face.

Wally shuddered and turned his head. 'Bloody hell, Mr Frost. That's horrible.' He fumbled for a grubby handkerchief to mop his brow. 'You ain't suggesting they're down to me? I've never killed anyone in my life.'

'Yes, you have, Wally,' said Frost, grimly. 'The old girl you discouraged by caving in her skull died in hospital.'

'Come off it, Inspector,' said Wally, grinning to show that he had seen through Frost's bluff. 'There's no way a little tap would . . .' And then he saw Frost's expression and knew he was serious. 'Oh my God!' The grin froze solid and his face drained of colour. 'Dead?'

Frost nodded.

'Bloody hell, Mr Frost. She came at me – with a knife. I had no choice – it was self-defence.'

'Were these self-defence?' asked Frost, smacking his hand on the photographs.

'You're not pinning them on me, Mr Frost. I'll cough to the old girl, but that's all.'

Frost gave him a disarming smile. 'Fair enough, Wally. Tell you what – as we're mates – cough to the others and I'll give you self-defence on the first one.'

'I never bleedin' did the others. How can I make you believe me?'

'I'd consider an alibi, Wally. Where were you Tuesday night?'

Manson looked appalled. 'I can't give you an alibi without incriminating myself. I was doing another job.'

'Don't be a twat, Wally. We're talking murder and you're talking petty burglary.'

Manson gave a hopeless shrug. 'I can't bloody win, can I? All right, on Tuesday night I did some cars over at Forest View – I got a CD player from one and a couple of cassette players from the others.'

'What about Sunday?'

'I did a house in Appleford Court. Got away with around £80. Then I tried a car round the back but the flaming alarm went off.'

Frost nodded. He knew about the Appleford Court burglary and he'd check on the cars. But this was Sunday night. Mary Haynes was killed in the afternoon. 'What about Sunday afternoon?'

'I stayed in. I had it away with Belle.'

'Let's say that took a minute – half a minute if you kept your boots on. What did you do with the rest of the time?'

'I stayed in until six – Belle will vouch for me.'

Frost gave a snort. 'She's as big a liar as you are. You've got no alibi for the time of the killing, and we've found a pair of your jeans soaked in blood.'

'That was my blood, Mr Frost . . .' Wally was almost in tears. 'You've got to believe me.'

'The court has got to believe you, Wally, not me.' Frost scratched his chin thoughtfully. 'Feel like doing a deal?'

Manson regarded Frost warily. 'What sort of a deal?'

'A bloody good one, Wally. We've got a whole stack of outstanding burglaries and car thefts on file. I want you to cough to every single one that's down to you . . .'

'Now hold on, Mr Frost,' Manson protested.

'Do yourself a favour and listen, Wally. Whatever sentences you get will run concurrently: one burglary or a hundred, you won't even feel it. In return, I'm prepared to tell the court how helpful you've been and to recommend to the DPP that we accept your plea of manslaughter in the case of Alice Ryder. To help you make up your mind, if you say no, we're going for murder.'

Manson chewed at his finger while he thought this over. 'What about them two?' He pointed to the photographs on the table.

'Call me a sentimental old sod, Wally, but providing nothing happens to make me change my mind, I'm prepared to give you the benefit of the doubt over them two.'

Wally sighed. 'All right, Mr Frost. You win.'

'Good boy,' smiled Frost, scooping the photographs back into the file and standing.

Behind the prisoner, Gilmore's eyes gleamed with satisfaction. The inspector had given almost nothing away – the DPP would probably have settled for manslaughter anyway – and in return a whole stack of outstandings would be cleared in one go and Denton's 'Crime Return' would start looking healthy again. Anxious to share the undoubted credit this would accrue, he dropped into Frost's vacated chair, ready to start taking

Manson's statements. His scowl deepened when Frost informed him that the little fat slob, Hanlon, would be taking over from now and it was with the greatest reluctance he vacated the chair.

At the door, Frost stopped and smote his forehead with his palm. He had almost forgotten the videos. 'Where did you get them?'

Wally hung his head. 'I nicked them from a car. Wouldn't have touched them had I known what they were like. Blimey, I like a bit of the old sex and violence as much as the next man, but I draw the line at dogs . . . they may be man's best friend, but that one was being too bloody friendly.'

'Details, Wally.'

'I'm driving in the van the Saturday night before last, about ten o'clock, and I spots this big flash motor parked round the back of the Market Square.'

'What sort of car?' Gilmore asked. 'What make?'

'I don't know. An expensive motor, all gleaming. Black, I think . . . the seats looked like real leather. Anyway, I wasn't there to admire it. I jemmied open the boot, grabbed this box and I'm back in my van before anyone spots me.'

Frost prodded Manson for more details, but there was nothing else he could tell them, only that it was an expensive set of wheels.

Outside in the corridor, Gilmore's anger boiled over. 'You're letting Hanlon take his statement? We get a confession on the Ryder murder and Manson is going to cough on all his other jobs. We do all the work and you're going to let Hanlon take all the credit!'

'I can't be sodded about with all that paperwork,' said Frost. 'We've got enough on our plates without having to take yards and yards of statement down.' He yawned. 'I don't know about you, son, but I'm going home for some kip.'

Gilmore, still angry, watched the old cretin shuffle off down the corridor. Just his lousy luck to be stuck with that apology for a policeman. He was being associated with Frost's many failures, but wasn't getting the chance to be involved with his all too few successes. Just because the fool had killed all his own promotion prospects, there was no need to deny them to everyone else. Damn and blast the stupid burk. He stormed off to the car-park.

As he was settling down in bed, Frost remembered he hadn't reported back to Mullett about Wally Manson. Ah well, he'd worry about that in the morning.

The jangling of a bell woke Gilmore up. He fumbled for the alarm, but the bell rang on. The bedside clock tried to tell him it was ten o'clock but he felt as if he had only been asleep a couple of minutes. The ringing went on and someone was banging at the front door. He pulled on his dressing gown and staggered downstairs.

A motor-cycle policeman holding a crash helmet asked him if he was Detective Sergeant Gilmore and told him to pick up Inspector Frost immediately.

There had been another Ripper killing.

'Why knock me up?' growled Gilmore. 'Haven't you heard of the telephone?'

'Haven't you heard of putting it back on the hook?' called the policeman, kick-starting his bike and roaring off.

Yes, the damn handset was off. Mentally cursing Liz, Gilmore replaced it and dashed into the bathroom for a quick cold shower which he hoped would jar him into consciousness. He had finished dressing when the front door slammed and Liz returned from shopping, the bottles clinking in her carrier bag.

'You're going out again?' she shrilled. 'Out all night and now you're going out again?'

He patted on aftershave, then knotted his tie and adjusted it in the bathroom mirror. 'I've got to. There's been another murder.' His head was aching from not enough sleep and he could have done without any more aggro.

She pushed past him, her face ugly, not saying a word.

He slipped on his camel-hair overcoat and made sure he had his car keys. 'I'll get back as soon as I can – I promise.'

'Don't bloody bother,' she snapped, slamming down the shopping. 'Don't bloody bother.'

Frost, looking as gritty and crumpled as he had done the night before, was waiting outside his house and he grunted thankfully as he slumped into the front passenger seat. 'Another old girl slashed,' he told Gilmore. 'Haven't got the full details yet.'

The address was Kitchener Mansions, a block of old people's flats. The lift, its wet floor smelling of pine disinfectant, juddered them up to the third floor. DC Burton, waiting for them outside flat number 311, looked shattered. 'It's a messy one, Inspector.'

'Tell me something new,' muttered Frost gloomily, following Burton into the flat.

They walked into a tiny passage, squeezing past a small table holding a telephone and a plastic piano-key index, then on to a small living-room which seemed to be full of people, all keeping well back from the object in the centre of the floor. 'Let the dog see the rabbit,' said Frost, barging through.

The old lady, fully dressed, sat in an armchair, her head back, empty eyes staring at the ceiling. Her neck grinned with the blood-gummed lips of a cut throat. Her stomach had been slashed open so that her intestines bulged out on to her lap. At her feet the grey-carpeted floor was sodden with the blood pumped out by her panic-stricken heart as the knife ripped and tore. The tiny room had the smell of an abattoir.

'Flaming hell!' muttered Frost. He backed away. He had seen enough.

Even Ted Roberts, the SOC officer, no stranger to violent death, was shaken and had difficulty in keeping his hands steady as he adjusted his camera lens for close-ups of the neck wound.

Gilmore pulled his eyes away from the corpse, and looked around the room. He recognized the uniformed constable, PC Simms, who had arrested Manson the night before. He also recognized the two men from Forensic who had been at Greenway's house. The duty police surgeon, a thin solemn-looking man busily engaged in filling in his Police Expense Claim form, he hadn't seen before.

A light oak sideboard stood against the far wall. On it a cut-glass fruit bowl held some apples and a black leather purse. Gilmore nudged Frost and pointed it out to him.

Carefully stepping wide to avoid the puddles of blood, Frost picked up the purse with his handkerchief. It bulged with the pension money the old lady had drawn from the main Denton post office the previous morning. He counted it quickly. Nearly one hundred pounds. Gloomily he pushed it back into the purse. 'How come the killer didn't take this?'

'Perhaps he was disturbed?' suggested Gilmore. 'He heard someone coming and legged it away.'

'Perhaps,' muttered Frost, who wasn't convinced. He nosed through the other compartments of the purse. An uncollected prescription for some sleeping tablets, a hospital appointment card, a membership card for the Reef Bingo Club, and some ancient raffle tickets. In the last compartment he found two Yale keys; one was for the front door, but the other was a maverick. He clicked the purse shut and returned it to the fruit bowl. 'What has been nicked?'

'Nothing, as far as we can tell,' answered Burton. 'Nothing seems to be disturbed.' He moved away so Frost could look into the bedroom where everything was as neat and tidy as the murdered woman had left it. Frost opened a couple of drawers. The contents clearly had not been touched.

'Like I said,' offered Gilmore, 'he heard someone coming and legged it before he could nick anything.'

'Perhaps,' muttered Frost, still doubtful. Back to Burton. 'All right, son. Let's have some details.'

Burton flipped open his notebook. 'Her name is Doris Watson, seventy-six. She's a widow and has a son living in Denton.'

'Anyone contacted him?' interrupted Frost.

Burton shook his head. 'We've been waiting for you, sir.'

Frost sent Gilmore to look the son up in the telephone index in the hall. 'Ring him. Ask if he can come over. Don't tell him what it's about.' He nodded for Burton to continue.

'Her neighbour, Mrs Proctor, in the next flat saw her at eight o'clock last night when she called here to borrow a *Daily Mirror* to read. A little before ten she knocked again to return it, but got no answer.'

'By ten, she was dead,' called the police surgeon, picking up his bag ready to leave.

'You're bloody precise all of a sudden,' commented Frost. 'You usually won't even pin yourself down to the day of the week. Are you certain she was dead by ten?'

The doctor shrugged. Nothing was certain in determining the time of death. 'Give or take an hour each way,' he hedged.

'Thanks for sod all,' sniffed Frost as the doctor took his leave. He raised his eyebrows at Gilmore who had finished phoning.

'All I get is his answering machine,' Gilmore told him. 'I left a message for him to phone the station.'

Frost's eyes travelled round the room. No sign of forcible entry. The killer must have come in through the front door.

They moved through the hall to take a look at the door which had additional bolts fitted and also a security chain, but not a very strong one. There was a peephole lens so any caller could be verified before the door was opened. She was nervous of callers, but when someone knocked some time after eight o'clock at night she had drawn the bolts, unhooked the security chain and let them in. It had to be someone she knew. Someone she trusted.

'Her son?' offered Gilmore.

'He'll do for starters,' grunted Frost. 'Who found her?'

'The old dear in the next flat – Mrs Proctor,' Burton told him.

'OK. Burton and Jordan – knock on doors. Find out if anyone saw or heard anything. Gilmore, come with me. We'll chat up Old Mother Proctor.'

Mrs Proctor, her untidy grey hair in need of combing, squinted and blinked watery eyes at the warrant card held out for her inspection. 'I'll have to take you on trust,' she finally decided. 'My eyes aren't too good this time of the morning.' And to prove it, she bumped into the hall table as she unsteadily led them through to her untidy lounge. 'The old dear's pissed!' hissed Frost to Gilmore.

'Sit down,' she mumbled, breathing gin fumes all over them. Frost sat on something hard. An empty gin bottle. He carefully stood it on the floor. She flopped down in the chair opposite and tried unsuccessfully to stop her body swaying from side to side.

A messy room with dirty underwear draped over chairs and unwashed glasses in abundance. The gas-fire was going full blast and the room was hot and close.

She hiccuped gin fumes and fanned them away. 'Can I get you something to drink?' Thinking she meant tea, Frost nodded, but she slopped gin into two dirty cups and handed one each to the detectives. 'Get that down you!' Frost eyed the tea-coloured gin swilling about in the cup with tea-leaves floating on its surface. It was a bit early in the morning, but what the hell. He downed it in one gulp.

Mrs Proctor nodded her approval and topped up her own cup from the bottle. 'I don't usually indulge this time of the morning, but after seeing her, in that chair and all that blood . . .' The recollection required a quick swallow and a second helping.

Frost nodded sympathetically. He noticed a line of birthday cards on the mantelpiece. 'Someone's birthday?'

She suddenly burst into tears. 'Mine – and not a very happy one. A bloody fine present, finding your next-door neighbour butchered.' She dabbed her eyes. 'I'm sorry.' Tottering over to the mantelpiece she took down one of the cards with a picture of a basketful of kittens. 'This is her card. The very last card she ever sent me.'

'Very nice,' said Frost, unenthusiastically.

She sniffed derisively. 'I hate cats – they stink the bloody place out. Still, I expect she only bought it because it was cheap.' She leant forward confidentially.

'I know I shouldn't speak ill of the dead, but she really was a tight-fisted old cow.'

'You don't say!' said Frost.

'I do say. Her purse always looked as if it was pregnant . . . it was packed with notes, but you never saw her put her hand in her pocket to buy you a drink.'

Frost gave a disapproving shake of the head. Mrs Proctor started to say something else then burst into tears. 'Here am I running the poor woman down and she's lying dead in her chair.' She raised a tear-streaked face. 'It was awful . . . when I went in there and saw all that blood . . .'

'I know it's upsetting,' soothed Frost, 'so I'll get this over as soon as I can. You borrowed the *Daily Mirror* from her?'

'I borrowed it at eight o'clock. I went to return it at ten, but she wouldn't answer the door.'

'Was that unusual?' asked Gilmore, distastefully eyeing the gin slurping about in his sugar-encrusted cup.

'Bloody unusual. She was such a mean old bitch, she wouldn't have been able to sleep if I hadn't returned her paper . . . afraid I might run off with it. I banged at the door. No reply. So I went to bed.'

'Then what?'

'This morning I expected her to send Interpol round to arrest me for hanging on to her lousy paper, so I tried her door again. Still no reply. I thought she might be ill with that flu virus thing, so I let myself in.'

'How did you get into her flat?'

She fumbled in her apron pocket and produced a key. 'I've got the spare key to her flat and she's got the one to mine.'

Frost nodded. The maverick key explained.

'I didn't think I'd be able to get in with the key as she always put on the bolts and the chain. But it opened, and

I went in and . . .' Her body shook at the recollection.

He leant across and patted her hand. 'I know it's difficult, love. Just take your time.' At last, after several false starts, she managed to stem the flow and bravely nodded her willingness to continue. 'When you saw her last night to borrow the newspaper, did she say she was expecting anyone?'

'No. She just gave me the paper like she always did . . . bloody begrudgingly.'

'After that, did you hear anything?'

She blinked at him. 'Like what?'

Like a bloody woman being disembowelled, you stupid cow, thought Frost. 'Anything at all that might help us?' he asked sweetly.

'No – I had the telly on. I like to read the paper with the telly on – it gives me something to occupy my mind.' She shivered. 'Poor Doris was terrified of something like this happening ever since she heard about this Granny Ripper maniac. She was going to get a stronger chain put on her door, but she left it too late.'

'The chain wouldn't have helped her,' said Frost. 'She let this bloke in like an old friend. Did she have many friends?'

'Hardly any. She was such a tight-fisted cow, no-one liked her and she hardly ever went out – except to bingo and the club. The senior citizens' club – it's run by the church.'

'Did you go to her club?'

'No, but she used to get me to go to bingo with her – she was nervous of being out on her own – but I gave it up a year ago. I don't approve of gambling. Besides, I never bloody won anything.'

Frost shook his head both in sympathy and to keep himself awake. The gas-fire, aided by the gin, was strongly soporific. 'She only went to the daytime bingo sessions, I suppose?'

'Yes. She didn't even like coming back in the dark late afternoon, but that nice driver used to bring her right to her door – leave his coach and escort her right up to the flat.'

Frost's drooping head suddenly snapped up. 'What driver?'

'Of the coach. They lay on this free coach for the bingo . . . picks you up in the town and brings you back.'

'Only back to the town centre, surely?' asked Frost.

'That's all they're supposed to do, but if you've got a nice driver and he passes your door, he'll drop you off. It's almost as good as getting a taxi.'

'And this nice driver . . . would he go with you to your door, wait until you got safely inside, help you get the key out from under the mat, or pull the string through the letter-box, or something?'

'Some of them do. Some just drop you off at the corner.'

'Hmm.' Frost spat out a tea-leaf. 'Mrs Watson was nervous, even of coming home late afternoons, and yet she let someone into her flat at night. Any ideas on who that might be?'

'The only person I can think of is her poncey son. He lives in Denton somewhere. He often came to see her.'

'What is he like?'

'A nasty piece of work. Do you know what he had the nerve to say to me? He said, "Why don't you buy your own *Daily Mirror* instead of scrounging one from my poor mother?"'

'Sounds a real right bastard,' Frost confided, rising from his chair. 'Thanks for your help. An officer will be along soon to take a written statement. If you think of anything else – anything – that might help, let the officer know.'

Gilmore pushed his untasted cup of gin to one side and followed him out.

In the murder flat they had to flatten themselves against the wall as the body was manhandled out on a stretcher by two ambulance men who had difficulty getting it round the tight bend to the front door, the corner of the stretcher ripping a section of the floral wallpaper in the process. Immediately following the stretcher came the pathologist, looking like an undertaker in his long black overcoat. 'I've given preliminary details to your detective constable. I'll phone your office with a time for the autopsy.'

In the lounge the Forensic team were packing up. The chair and the bloodstained carpet had been removed and the blood which had soaked through to the exposed floorboards had been ringed in yellow chalk. The warm, sticky slaughterhouse smell still tainted the air. Moodily, Frost tore off the dangling strip of wallpaper. The poor cow. She'd have a fit if she saw the state of her little flat now.

From the bathroom door came grunting and a metallic clanging. He looked inside. Harding from Forensic was on his knees, swearing softly to himself as he tried to manoeuvre a long-handled spanner underneath the tiny wash-basin in an effort to remove the waste trap. 'Blimey,' Frost exclaimed, 'isn't there anything you won't pinch?'

Harding grinned. 'There's traces of blood in the sink waste, Inspector.'

Frost showed surprise. 'You mean he had a good wash afterwards?'

'The way he sliced her he'd have been splattered with blood. He couldn't go out like that.'

'What about his clothes?'

Sucking barked knuckles, Harding gave the spanner one final push and sighed his relief as he felt something give. He looked up at the inspector.

'I reckon his clothes are smothered in blood – unless he took them off before he butchered her.'

'Oh,' sniffed Frost. 'And what is she doing while he strips off? Staring hypnotized at his John Thomas?'

Harding grinned. 'Just a theory, Inspector.' He dropped the spanner and found he could now turn the large nut by hand.

Frost stuck his head out of the bathroom. 'Don't forget to check all dry-cleaners.'

'Already done!' replied Burton. A waste of time. This killer was too smart.

Back to the bathroom where Harding was easing off the waste trap. 'So, if he washed himself, the blood you're going to find in the waste trap will be the old girl's blood – right?'

'Yes, sir.'

'Do we need any more? We're nearly swimming in the bleeding stuff out there as it is.'

Harding shrugged. 'We've got to be thorough, sir.'

'Smile when you say that,' said Frost wandering out to the empty-looking lounge. 'I might think you're getting at me.' Gilmore watched him meander about aimlessly, picking up pieces of bric-a-brac and putting them down again. The old fool had no idea what to do next.

PC Jordan and another uniformed officer returned from their door-to-door enquiries to report no joy. As usual, everyone was shocked at what had happened, but no-one had heard or seen anything.

'This bloke's too bloody lucky.' Frost dropped his cigarette end on the floor and ground it underfoot. He felt tired, useless and inadequate. Mrs Proctor's gin was sloshing about in his stomach, he was beginning to feel sick and his head was starting to throb. He flopped into an armchair.

'What do you want us to do now?' asked Gilmore.

Just leave me alone, he wanted to answer, then sat up frowning at a burst of voices from outside. He groaned out loud as Mullett, bright and morning fresh, bounced into the room. He could have done without Hornrim Harry at this particular moment.

Mullett's lips tightened. Typical. A serious murder enquiry. Forensic busy and conscientious as always in the next room and here was Frost, sprawled in an armchair, and – Mullett's nose quivered to confirm his suspicion – reeking of drink. 'Another body, Inspector?' he said testily, his tone implying it was all Frost's fault.

'Where?' said Frost, jumping up and pretending to look around the room. 'I can't see it, Super.'

Teeth gritted, Mullett raised his eyes to the artex ceiling and sighed loudly. Frost never knew when it was the wrong time to act the fool. 'What progress have you made?'

'So far, sod all. This bloke's bloody lucky. No-one sees him, no-one hears him and he leaves no prints. Unless Forensic can come up with something spectacular we might have to wait for him to make a mistake. His bleeding luck's bound to run out sometime.'

A derisive snort. 'Wait? You mean until he kills again? No way! I want these killings stopped!'

'Oh?' muttered Frost. 'And how do we achieve that, Super?'

'By finding the killer and arresting him.'

'Oh! Make a note of that, Gilmore,' said Frost, the gin making him reckless. 'Any other bright ideas, sir – I'm always ready to learn.'

Mullett glared angrily, his jaw twitching. The man's insouciance always infuriated him. He jerked his head at Burton and Jordan. 'Wait outside, would you, please.' He waited until they had gone. 'You made a damn fool of me last night, Inspector.'

'Did I?' asked Frost, sounding very interested. 'How did I do that?' His tone implied he would mark it down for future reference.

'That Ripper suspect. You led me to believe you had a water-tight case against him, and I now understand that your big clue, the knife, belonged to the victim all the time.'

'I'm afraid so, Super,' agreed Frost, ruefully.

'And you left me dangling. You didn't even come in and tell me what had happened. I was waiting for your report and the Chief Constable was waiting for my report.'

'Sorry about that,' mumbled Frost. 'I forgot all about you.'

Mullett's mouth opened and closed. He was almost speechless. 'Forgot?' he spluttered. 'Forgot to inform your Divisional Commander about a suspect in a major murder investigation?'

'I have got a lot on my plate,' snapped Frost. 'We're going flat out, we're working double shifts and we get lots of stupid interruptions.' He hoped Mullett might take this subtle hint and go, but the superintendent hadn't finished yet.

'Detective Sergeant Hanlon works under the same conditions as you, Frost, but he managed to get results. He's obtained a murder confession from Manson and confessions on at least thirty burglaries. Excellent work that will put us right at the top of the league for crime rate figures this month. It's results that count,

Inspector, not excuses. It seems to me,' and here his glare of displeasure clearly included Gilmore, 'that you may not be up to the task, in which case I will have no hesitation in replacing you.' With that he spun on his heel and marched out, oblivious to the near-audible raspberry that followed him out.

Now it was Gilmore's turn to be angry. If he were to share in Frost's failures, he wanted to share in his few triumphs. 'Why didn't you tell him about Hanlon? He was the one who sodded up the knife and Manson was our collar, not his.'

'We're supposed to be a team, son,' said Frost, 'not all fighting for Brownie points.'

Gilmore's reply was stifled by the return of DC Burton and PC Jordan. But all right, he muttered to himself, if it takes Brownie points to get on, I'll give the bastard Brownie points.

Desmond Watson scooped up the post from the mat and closed the front door behind him. He dumped his brief-case by the hall stand and checked through the letters on his way through to the living-room. Two bills, a bank statement and a commission cheque from his firm. Watson was the Northern Area Sales Representative for a double-glazing company. In the living-room the little green light on his telephone answering machine told him there were messages waiting. He fast-forwarded on cue and review, his ear able to recognize from the high-pitched gabble the girl from his firm passing on sales leads which he would note down later, and then the familiar sound of his mother's voice. He released the button and listened as he opened up the envelope to check that his firm hadn't yet again made a mistake with his commission payment.

Hello, son. It's mother. You needn't worry any more about . . . Just a moment, there's someone at the door . . . A pause. A long pause. And then the automatic cut-off operated.

He raised his head from his checking of the commission payment and waited for the next message which should have been his mother phoning back. But it was a strange voice. A man's voice. It asked him to ring the Denton Police Station. The commission cheque fluttered from his fingers. His stomach churning with foreboding, he reached for the phone.

Thursday afternoon shift (1)

Gilmore spooned sugar into a cup of hot, strong tea and placed it in front of Watson who was still in a state of shock after formally identifying his mother's body. The cup clattered on the saucer as his shaking hand raised it to his mouth. He tried to concentrate on what the scruffy inspector was saying.

'I know it's been an awful shock, sir, but if you could answer one or two questions.'

The cup was rattling against his teeth. He lowered it back to the saucer, the tea untasted, and pushed it away. 'Yes . . . anything.'

'We've been listening to a tape from your answering machine, your mother's last message. You said she made the call at 9.35 p.m. If you weren't at home, how do you know that?'

'My answering machine logs the time and date of all calls.'

'I see, sir. And where were you at 9.35 last night?'

'Me?' His head jerked up 'You suspect me?'

'I'd be happy if I had anyone to suspect, sir,' said Frost, wearily. 'I just want to eliminate. Your mother was a nervous woman. She kept her front door chained and bolted and yet someone calls at 9.35 at night and she cheerfully lets them in. It had to be someone she knew and trusted . . . someone like you, sir. So where were you?'

'I was in Birmingham. The Queensway Hotel.' He pulled a receipt from his inside pocket and handed it across. 'You'll want to check, of course.'

Frost glanced at it and passed it to Gilmore who went out to phone.

'I'd like it back,' said Watson. 'I need it for my expenses claim.'

Frost nodded. He knew all about expenses claims. 'On the tape, sir, your mother starts by saying, "You needn't worry any more about . . ." Any idea what she meant by that?'

'I think she was referring to a new security chain. The one on her front door was inadequate. After hearing about those burglaries and then those two women killed, I'd been on to her to get a stronger one.'

'Can you think of anyone your mother would be happy to admit into her flat at 9.35 at night?'

'No-one. She was a very nervous woman.' He looked up as Gilmore returned with the receipt and murmured something in the inspector's ear.

'The hotel confirm your visit, sir.' Frost handed the receipt back and stood up. 'Thank you for your help. We'll let you know how our enquiries progress . . . and, of course, you have our deepest sympathy.' As the door closed behind Watson, Frost's solemn expression changed to a grin. 'So he had a double room and a woman and he asked the hotel for a single room receipt?'

'Yes,' confirmed Gilmore.

'The crafty bastard,' said Frost, shaking his head in admiration. 'He gets his firm to pay for his nookie. I wish I could wangle something like that. Anyway, Sonny Boy's in the clear.' He picked up the cassette from the answering machine. 'Let's find out if this can tell us what we want to know.'

The Murder Incident Room was swirled with a fog of duty-free cigarette smoke. Frost sat on the corner of the front desk watching Gilmore slot the tape into the Yamaha cassette deck. He clapped his hands for silence.

'Right. As you know, we've had another Ripper murder.' He held aloft some enlarged colour prints where red was the predominant colour. 'We've got photos of the victim, but unless you get a kick out of steaming entrails, I suggest you take them as read. The bastard almost disembowelled her.' He stood up, the cigarette waggling in his mouth as he spoke. 'The victim is a Mrs Doris Watson, aged seventy-six, a widow with one son. She rarely went out, except to the twice-weekly senior citizens' afternoon sessions at the Reef Bingo Club. The poor cow was terrified of being attacked so she had extra bolts, a spy-hole and a security chain fitted to her front door. Last night, at 9.35, she made a telephone call to her son. The son was out, but his answering machine picked up the call. This is it.' He nodded for Gilmore to start the tape.

A bleep. Then, *Hello, son. It's mother. You needn't worry any more about . . . Just a moment, there's someone at the door . . .* Vague sounds as the tape continued, then another bleep. Gilmore jammed down the Stop control.

The room was dead quiet.

'She put down the phone,' continued Frost, 'and went to the front door. She squints through the spy-hole, likes what she sees, so this nervous woman undoes the chain, draws the bolts and welcomes in the bastard who's going to rip out her intestines.' He took the cigarette from his mouth and spat out a shred of tobacco. 'You're all a lot smarter than I am, so let's have some brilliant suggestions. Come on – you're a nervous woman of seventy-six. Who would you let into your flat at night – apart from a toy-boy with his own teeth and a big dick?'

Burton raised his hand. 'Something we've never considered, sir. She'd never let in a man – but what if the Ripper was a woman?'

Frost chewed on his lip as he thought this over. 'It's possible, son. It would explain a lot, but my gut reaction is against it. We'll keep it in mind, though.'

WPC Jill Knight raised a hand. 'If she'd phoned for a doctor, she'd let him in.'

A buzz of excitement.

'You're right,' said Frost. 'She'd let a doctor in.'

'Or a priest,' added Gilmore. Purley was still his number one suspect.

'Or a priest,' agreed Frost. 'OK, son. You can check on the curate. We want to know where he was last night. And you, Jill. Find out who her doctor was. See if she asked him to call last night and even if she didn't, find out where he was at 9.35. Anything else?'

He waited. Nothing. He took out a fresh cigarette then threw the pack to Burton to offer around. 'I'll tell you something that worries me.' He struck a match on the table leg. 'This time he took no money. He didn't ransack the bedroom. Over a hundred quid in her purse in full view on the sideboard and it wasn't touched. Now Sergeant Gilmore suggests something disturbed the Ripper and he had to hoof it off before he could nick anything.' He blew out the match and let it drop to the floor. 'But stupid sod that I am, I can't buy that. This bloke is icy cold. Nothing panics him. I reckon money's never been his motive.'

'So what is his motive?' asked Gilmore.

'Killing,' said Frost. 'I reckon he gets his kicks out of cold, bloody killing.'

The room went quiet. Chillingly quiet. This had the ring of unpalatable truth.

'Right.' Frost slipped down from the desk. 'Let's play the tape again.'

It was played again, and again and again. Frost, smoking, chewing his knuckles, hunched in front of the loudspeaker. *Just a moment, there's someone at the door* . . . Vague sounds. A bleep. Gilmore's voice . . . *Mr Watson, this is Denton Police* . . .

'Again,' snapped Frost. There was something there. Something his subconscious had caught but which kept slipping away. 'This is no damn good,' he moaned. 'I want it louder.'

'It won't go any louder,' said Gilmore.

'We could use the hi-fi equipment in the rest room,' suggested Burton.

They crowded into the rest room. Gilmore slotted in the cassette and turned the amplifier up almost to its maximum. He pressed Play and the hiss of raw tape crackled from the twin speakers.

The bleep screamed out like an alarm signal. Tape hiss. *Hello, son. It's mother,* shouted the old lady, the sound almost hurting their ears.

'Leave it,' ordered Frost as Gilmore's hand moved to turn down the volume. *You needn't worry any more about* . . . Through the mush, a buzzing vibrating sound. Then another.

'The door bell,' muttered Frost. At ordinary volume level it was inaudible.

Just a moment, there's someone at the door . . . A rustling, then an echoing bang as if someone had hit a microphone. She had put the phone down. Fading footsteps as she padded up the hall to the front door, eager to let in her murderer. Now the tape background roar was paramount. Frost pressed his ear to the speaker. 'Nothing. I imagine she's giving him the eyeball through the peep-hole. Ah . . .' He moved back. Just about audible, the sound of bolts being drawn and the chink of the chain being removed. The lock clicked. The door opened. The woman said something, but it was so faint and the background so loud, they couldn't distinguish a word. Then a screaming bleep as the automatic cut-off operated.

'Let me have a go,' said Burton, elbowing Gilmore away and adjusting various controls on the hi-fi's graphic equalizer which could cut and boost individual frequencies. 'Now try it.'

By now, they almost knew every squeak, rustle and click off by heart. When the woman spoke after opening the door it was clearer, but tantalizingly not clear enough for them to make out a single word. 'Again,' ordered Frost. But Mrs Watson might have been talking in a foreign language for all the sense it made. God, thought Frost. She could be naming her killer – 'Come in, Mr Ripper of 19 High Street, Denton' – yet they couldn't understand what she was saying.

'Try the earphones,' said Burton.

The earphones were better, but still not good enough.

'Let me have a go,' said Jill Knight, adjusting the earphones over her tightly curled hair. She listened and frowned. 'Again,' she said. The frown was deeper, but this time her lips were moving as if she was repeating what she heard. She took off the earphones. 'She's saying, "Oh, it's you. I didn't expect you so soon."'

They played it again through the speaker. The WPC was right. *Oh, it's you. I didn't expect you so soon.* Frost's head bowed. He had been hoping for so much and this was nothing.

'She knew him,' said Burton.

'And he came sooner than expected,' muttered Frost. 'I think that's called premature ejaculation.' The resulting laughter lifted his depression. 'Let's hear it again.' He waved aside the moans that they knew it off by heart. 'Indulge an old man's whim. We might have missed something.'

Again they listened, but only half-heartedly. The tape had told them everything it could. There was nothing they had missed. *Oh, it's you. I didn't expect you so soon.* The thud of the door closing behind him, then the hiss and clanking as raw tape scraped past the replay heads when the automatic cut-out operated. A bleep . . .

Frost was sitting bolt upright in his chair, an unlit cigarette drooping in his mouth. 'Again – just the end bit – and the volume as high as you bloody well like.' Gilmore spun the volume control to its maximum. At first they didn't spot it. 'You must be stone bleeding deaf,' roared Frost. 'Again . . . and listen this time . . . There!' And this time they heard it. A fraction of a second before the message switched off. The closing of the front door. The hiss, roar and crackle as the tape bumped past the heads then . . . a boxy, metallic chink.

Burton scratched his head. 'Could be anything, Inspector. He could have bumped against the table as he came in.'

'Even if he did,' said Frost, 'there was nothing on the hall table that would chink. That is definitely a metallic sound.'

'There could have been something on the table – something valuable – but he took it away with him,' suggested Gilmore, who was feeling left out of things.

'I thought I heard something chinking as he came through the door,' said the WPC.

'Did you?' exclaimed Frost excitedly and he was up on his feet, jamming his finger on the Rewind button and playing the tape through again. 'Yes . . . there!' And through the mush, as the man stepped through the door, a faint metallic chinking sound . . . then another.

They didn't hear the door open. 'What's going on in here?'

'Piss off!' said Frost. 'Oh, sorry, Super . . . didn't know it was you.' He played the tape through yet again for Mullett who tried to look as if he knew what Frost was driving at, but obviously didn't.

'That noise, sir. At first we thought he'd bumped into the hall table and jolted something on it, but we now reckon that whatever it was, he brought it in with him and dumped it on the hall table.'

Mullett considered this. 'It might help if we knew what it was. But we don't.'

'I think I do,' said Frost. He looked around the room to make sure he had everyone's attention. 'What about a new security chain?'

Mullett frowned. 'A security chain?'

'Old Mother Watson had arranged to have a stronger one fitted,' Frost told him. 'And that's who she let in last night with open arms . . . the man who was going to fit the new security chain . . . so she would be safe from attack.'

'It could be a chain,' said Mullett doubtfully, 'but we don't know for sure.'

'I know for bloody certain,' announced Frost. 'I've got a hunch.'

A thin smile from Mullett. 'Hunches are all very well,' he began, but Frost wasn't listening, he was giving instructions to his team.

'Knock on doors again. Go round to all the neighbours of the victims. Did the victims talk of having chains fitted? Has anyone been canvassing before, or since, offering to fit security chains? Don't cause a panic, but get what gen you can. I want someone to contact all the local security system firms. Do they send salesmen around canvassing? Have their salesmen found that some bloody amateur has been undercutting their prices? Mrs Watson was supposed to be a tight old sod, so this would have to be a cheap job. One last thing – Burton. Mrs Watson talked to the old biddy in the next-door flat about having a new security chain. Chat her up, see if she can come up with names. OK – on your bikes, everyone. Chop chop.'

As the team scurried out he flipped a cigarette from his packet and tried to catch it in his mouth. It missed. Scooping it up from the floor, he lit up and inhaled deeply. He felt happy. Things were now on the move. They were on the track of the killer, he felt sure of it.

The phone rang. Detective Sergeant Hanlon from the mortuary. 'The pathologist has completed the autopsy on Mark Compton, Jack. Definitely murder. A heavy blow to the head from behind. That didn't kill him, but the fire and the fumes finished him off – death from asphyxiation.' Frost pushed Mullett to one side so he could yell for

Gilmore, his voice echoing down the empty corridor.

Mullett cleared his throat pointedly. He wasn't used to being ignored.

'Sorry, Super,' grunted Frost. 'Be with you in a minute.' As Gilmore appeared in the doorway, he told him about the autopsy findings.

Gilmore checked his watch. He'd forgotten all about the damn autopsy. Frost's bad habits were contagious. 'How come Hanlon attended it?'

'I told him to, son. We're far too busy.'

'But it's my case.'

'Sorry, son, but we've too much work and not enough men to be able to specialize. It's everyone's case.'

But if I crack it, it's my bloody case, thought Gilmore. 'I want to see the woman that Compton was knocking off. She might know something.'

'Right, son. We'll do it now. Bring the car round to the front.' Back to Mullett. 'Anything I can do, Super . . . as long as it's quick?'

Huffily, the Divisional Commander produced the curt memo he had received from County. 'Still some discrepancy with your car expenses, Inspector. County are furious. They want an immediate reply.'

'They want stuffing,' corrected Frost, his mind elsewhere. 'Stick it on my desk as you go out, would you, sir? I'll deal with it later.' And he dashed out of the rest room to the car.

Mullett was halfway down the corridor before he realized that Frost had ordered him about like an office boy. But it was too late to go back and protest.

The flats behind the supermarket were owned by a firm of property agents and were usually let out on short leases. The Denton *Echo,* in one of its bouts of outraged crusading, had exposed several of these tenancies as being taken up by high-class call girls and for a while many of the apartments remained empty, but slowly, and more discreetly, many of the old tenants returned.

In the carpeted foyer a lift purred down and the door opened with a barely audible hiss. They stepped inside and Gilmore pressed the button for the third floor. So different from the disinfectant-masking urine smell of the lift in the senior citizens' flats, this lift was heady with the perfume of its previous passenger.

They walked over thick footstep-muffling grey carpet to the end flat. There was something outside the door. Four bulging rubbish sacks. Black plastic sacks, the sort Paula Bartlett's body was in. Frost peeped inside one. Assorted packets, cartons and jars as if someone had been clearing out a cupboard. He fished out a detergent packet. It had been opened, but was almost brim-full. 'The cow's done a bunk,' he said, jamming his thumb in the bell-push. He was surprised to hear footsteps from inside.

The woman who opened the door was around twenty-six years of age, and wore a tightly fitting knitted dress in emerald green. She was slightly plump, with red hennaed hair and breasts that could best be described as ample. Admiring their generosity, Frost had difficulty in locating his warrant card. Gilmore produced his.

'Police. May we come in?'

She stared at Gilmore's warrant card wide-eyed. 'Police? What's it about? That nosy old bitch downstairs hasn't been complaining again, has she?'

'Not to us,' answered Gilmore curtly. 'Can we come in?' Pre-empting her reply he pushed forward into the hall.

Bristling slightly at his tone, she led them through to the lounge, a comfortable room with pale blue carpeting and dark blue upholstered furniture. The light grey walls were hung with aluminium-framed abstract prints. Frost shuffled across to the large picture window and looked down on to the sprawl of the supermarket. 'Very nice,' he murmured. 'I bet you get a good view of the multi-storey car-park from your bedroom.'

Her lips shaped a brief, flat, non-understanding smile. 'This won't take long, will it? I'm in a hurry.'

'Mind if I sit down?' said Frost, sinking into one of the blue armchairs. He dug deep into his pocket for his cigarettes and frowned with disappointment. The packet was empty. He had been too generous in the Murder Incident Room. 'Do you mind telling us your name?'

'East. Jean East.' She studied her watch. 'Look – what is this all about?'

'A few questions,' said Frost, letting his eyes wander around the room. He imagined this was where clients waited while the bedroom was occupied. He straightened up. Two bulging suitcases stood side by side to the left of the lounge door. 'Moving out?'

'The lease is up. I can't afford to renew it. I'm going back to London.'

'Then we caught you just in time,' beamed Frost. 'Do you know a gentleman called Mark Compton?'

A barely perceptible pause. 'No. Why – what is this about?'

'He might not have told you his real name,' said Gilmore, moving in front of Frost to remind him that this was his case. He showed her a photograph.

She studied the colour print briefly, shook her head, and handed it back. 'Sorry. Never seen him before.'

'Perhaps you don't recognize him with his clothes on,' Frost suggested.

Her face tightened and her eyes blazed. 'You can get out right now.' She flung open the door dramatically, her breasts heaving, straining the woollen dress to the limits.

Frost heaved himself from the chair. 'We're going, love, but you're coming with us. Get her coat, Sergeant.'

She hesitated. 'Where are we going?'

'To the station. I want a policewoman to examine you.'

'Examine me? Why?'

'If you haven't got a little strawberry birthmark on your lower stomach, my apologies will bring tears to your eyes.'

She closed the door and turned slowly. 'How do you know about that?'

'You should keep your blinds closed when you're entertaining,' sneered Gilmore.

'You had an audience,' added Frost. 'An old boy with field-glasses watching from the car-park.'

Her hand covered her mouth. She looked horrified. 'Watching us?'

'From start to finish. And then he sent a poison pen letter to your client. It described you in graphic detail.'

Her face crimsoned to match her hair. 'Let's get one bloody thing straight. I'm not a tart. Yes, I knew Mark Compton. We were lovers. He came here and we made love and it was wonderful and if some dirty little snivelling shit in a filthy raincoat was watching, then sod him. I'm ashamed of nothing.'

'Eat your heart out, Mills and Boon,' said Frost. 'But you said you *knew* him. You *were* lovers. Past tense?'

'Yes – past tense, because the bastard threw me up last week. Came here, made love, then calmly told me it was all over. Look – what the hell is this all about?'

Gilmore raised his head from his notebook. He was content to let Frost ask the preliminary questions, but he would step in when the time was ripe. So she was a discarded lover. Not an uncommon motive for murder.

But Frost, digging fruitlessly through his pockets in the hope of finding a pinched-out butt, didn't seem to have realized the significance. 'Why did he chuck you?' He watched enviously as she took a cigarette from a black lacquered box on a side table and lit it with a tiny, initialled, blue and gold enamelled lighter.

'He was afraid his wife might find out.' She flung her head back and laughed bitterly. 'His bloody wife! He always told me he was going to divorce her and marry me . . . and like a fool I bloody believed him. Even when the bastard's cheques bounced, I believed him.'

'Cheques?' queried Frost, tapping his empty Lambert and Butler packet hopefully, but she didn't take the hint.

'He was always borrowing money, and when I asked him to pay me back, his cheques bounced.'

'How much money are we talking about?'

'Getting on for £500, which I could ill afford.'

Frost scratched his chin. 'He sounds a right charmer. How long have you known him?'

'A couple of months. We met in London.' She dropped down into the other chair and her breasts bounced like Mark Compton's cheques. Do that again, Frost pleaded silently.

'Does your husband know of this association?' asked Gilmore who, unlike Frost whose gaze was directed higher, had noticed the wedding ring on her finger.

She gave a tight smile and shook her head. 'No.'

'How can you be so sure?'

'My husband is a very violent and jealous man. That's why I left him.' Her hands travelled over her body and she winced in remembrance. 'I could show you bruises . . .' Yes please, pleaded Frost, again silently. 'I changed my name so he couldn't trace me. If he ever found out that Mark had been my lover, he would have killed us both.'

Frost's head jerked up. 'Changed your name?'

'East is my maiden name. My married name is Bradbury. Mrs Jean Bradbury.'

Behind her, Gilmore choked back a gasp and slowly expelled air. He felt a warm glow inside. The equation was almost too good to be true . . . an unfaithful wife plus a violent husband equals one dead lover. Now was the time for him to take over. 'Are you aware that your lover, Mark Compton, and his wife have been subjected to verbal and written threats over the past few weeks and that their property has been maliciously damaged?'

She seemed genuinely surprised. 'No, Sergeant. I was not aware of that.'

'Are you aware there was a fire at The Old Mill last night? The place was gutted.'

She couldn't disguise a malicious smile. 'I didn't know that either, but serve the bastard right.'

'The bastard's dead, Mrs Bradbury,' said Frost, bluntly. 'He died in the fire. We think it was murder.'

The cigarette dropped from her fingers and she stared unbelieving at the inspector. 'No! Oh no!' Then her eyes widened in horror. 'And you think my husband killed him . . .? Oh my God!' Her hands covered her face.

'We've got to find him,' said Gilmore.

'If he's killed Mark, he'll kill me,' she said, scrabbling for the cigarette which had burnt a black mark into the landlord's carpet.

'We won't let that happen,' Frost assured her. 'Any idea where he is?'

'I don't know and I don't care.' She studied the end of her cigarette, her full, pursed lips blowing it back to life.

God, thought Frost, squirming in his chair, you can blow me back to life any time you like, love. A muffled voice calling his name slowly caught his attention. His personal radio. He tugged it from his pocket. Johnny Johnson with some news. He moved away so the woman couldn't hear.

'We've located Simon Bradbury, Inspector.'

'Then grab him where it hurts and hold him,' said Frost, signalling for Gilmore to come over.

'No need, Jack. He's not going anywhere. He's at Risley Remand Centre . . . drunken driving, malicious damage and assaulting a police officer. He's been in custody for the past two weeks.'

'Damn!' Gilmore's foot lashed out at the waste bin in anger, spilling the contents over the floor. His one and only suspect now had a cast-iron alibi. They were back to square one.

There was no further point in staying. Frost rewound his scarf and began to button up his coat while Gilmore, on his knees, stuffed the spilt papers back into the bin.

'One last question,' said Gilmore. 'Do you own a car, Mrs Bradbury?' She nodded. 'And where were you last night?'

'Here. I did my packing and went to bed early.'

'No, you didn't,' smirked Gilmore. 'You drove over to Lexing to get your own back on your ex-boyfriend.'

She stared at him as if he were mad. 'I don't know what the hell you are talking about.'

'Don't you? Then I'll spell it out for you. Mark Compton chucked you up. You weren't going to let the bastard get away with it, so you made abusive phone calls and sent death threats.'

Her head moved slowly from side to side in disbelief. 'Death threats? I'd scratch his bleeding eyes out, but I wouldn't make threats.'

'You did more than scratch his eyes out,' continued Gilmore. 'You burnt his house down. But he caught you in the act, so you smashed his skull in and left him to burn to death.'

She looked in appeal to Frost who stared stoically back, hoping his own mystification didn't show.

'The death threat letters were made up of words cut from this month's *Reader's Digest,*' Gilmore continued. 'And what have we here?' With a triumphant flourish he waved under her nose a magazine he had retrieved from the waste bin. The current copy of *Reader's Digest.*

Frost slumped on to the arm of his chair. He thought Gilmore might have been on to something, but this was grabbing at straws.

'I've got news for you,' said the woman. 'They don't only print one copy. Lots of people buy it.'

'Oh, I agree, madam,' purred Gilmore. 'Lots of people read it. But how many people cut words out?' He thrust a scissor-slashed page under her nose, then flipped through and found another, and another. . .

Frost took the magazine. Gilmore was right. The death threat letters had been from this copy of the magazine. He looked up at the woman. 'Have you got anything to say?'

She stared at him, then at Gilmore, her face white. 'You're framing me, you bastards! I want a solicitor.'

'You can phone from the station,' said Gilmore. At the door holding her tightly by the arm, he called to Frost, 'You'd better bring her suitcases down. Forensic will want to examine her clothes.' He waited while she put on her coat before leading her out to the lift.

With a distinct feeling of being upstaged, Frost gathered up the cases. At the side table he paused and hopefully looked inside the black lacquered cigarette box. It was disappointingly empty. Not his lucky day. Shoulders drooped in resignation, he picked up the cases, kicked the door shut behind him, and left the flat.

The lift taking him down now smelt fleetingly of plump, jolly, hennaed-haired murderess, Jean Bradbury. Frost was vaguely worried. He had his own theories on the Compton killing and the woman didn't figure in them. But downstairs, with the woman locked safely in the car and glaring poisoned darts at them a smirking Gilmore called to him from one of the residents' garages.

'This is her garage,' said Gilmore as he squeezed past a beige-coloured Mini Cooper and pointed to patches of damp on the concrete floor. The pervading smell was petrol. 'This must be where she stored the petrol cans.'

Frost nodded gloomily. 'Well done, son.' He was forced to admit it. Gilmore was right and he was wrong.

'I'd better get my prisoner back to the station,' said Gilmore, leaving his inspector to close the garage doors.

The significance of 'my prisoner' instead of 'our prisoner' was not lost on Frost.

Police Superintendent Mullett sat to attention in his chair. He was on the phone to the Chief Constable. Opposite the satin mahogany desk stood a self-satisfied Detective Sergeant Gilmore, and a pale-looking Police Sergeant Wells who clutched a sodden handkerchief and kept interrupting the phone call by coughing and spluttering and noisily blowing his nose. If Wells thought he could wheedle his way on to the sick list, when they needed every man they could lay their hands on, he could think again.

'We're very much below strength,' he told the Chief Constable, staring at Wells as he said it, 'but I think you can rely on the Denton team to turn up trumps on Friday night.'

The door clicked open and Mullett looked up in annoyance as Frost shuffled in. Late again. 'Ah, Frost,' he said, putting his hand over the mouthpiece. 'The Chief Constable wishes to know what progress you have made with the Paula Bartlett case.'

'Bugger all,' said Frost, dragging a chair over to the desk and sitting down wearily. 'You told me to leave it for Wonder Boy's return.'

Mullett's smile flickered on and off like a dying neon tube. He held it unsteadily in place as he spoke into the phone. 'Detective Inspector Frost reports no further progress at present, sir. However things should improve when Mr Allen returns from the sick list.' He glared at Frost who, unabashed, seemed more intent on trying to read, upside down, a private and confidential memo in the superintendent's out-tray. Mullett pulled the tray towards him and turned the memo face down, then he flashed his gleaming white teeth into the receiver's mouthpiece. 'Yes, sir. Thank you, sir. You can depend on me, sir.' He grovelled his goodbyes, then replaced the phone.

He smoothed down his moustache. 'Trouble, gentlemen. County have been hearing rumours that those gypsies – or travellers as they prefer to be called – who were involved in the fighting in the town centre last Friday are out to seek their revenge on our Denton lager louts.

The Chief Constable wishes us to ensure that we have a sufficiently large police presence here on Friday night to nip any such trouble in the bud.'

'How many men is he sending us, then?' asked Wells, between coughs.

Mullett treated the sergeant to one of his thin, superior smiles. 'County are stretched to the limit, Wells.'

'And we're not, I suppose?' said Frost, flicking ash all over the carpet.

'Everyone's in the same boat,' snapped Mullett. 'I am not giving County the impression that we will go whining to them each time we have a minor problem. I want them to see that Denton can cope. So tomorrow, all leave will be cancelled. All off-duty men will be called in. And the sick list is closed.' He stared hard at Wells, letting him know that the last comment included him. 'I have assured the Chief Constable that the maintenance of public order will be our number one priority.'

'Priority even over our murder investigations?' asked Frost in his deceptively innocent voice.

'Of course a murder case takes precedence,' barked Mullett, 'but you will manage with the barest minimum.' He jerked his head away from Frost and gave Gilmore the full benefit of his white flashing smile. 'The Chief Constable was delighted when I told him of your success in the Compton case, Sergeant.' He beamed. 'There was some mention of him writing you a personal letter of commendation.' He noticed that Frost looked unhappy at this. Jealousy, of course. His assistant had succeeded where he had failed. 'That will be all, gentlemen.'

In the corridor outside, Frost grabbed Gilmore's arm. 'Has the Bradbury bird confessed yet, son?'

'No,' Gilmore told him. 'But we don't need a confession. The forensic evidence is overwhelming. The death threat letters definitely came from that magazine . . . they even confirm they were cut out by her own scissors. We've found identical notepaper and envelopes in her flat and the marks on the garage floor are definitely consistent with cans of petrol being stored there. We've got motive, opportunity and strong evidence. What more do we want?'

'I'm not happy about this one,' said Frost.

Gilmore bit back the urge to say 'tough'. 'If you'll excuse me, Inspector, I'm on my way to see Mrs Compton. I want to tell her the good news.'

'I'll come with you,' said Frost.

'Why?' asked Gilmore, icily. It was his case. He didn't want Frost along.

'Just for the ride, son. I haven't seen a decent pair of nipples all day.'

Ada Perkins wasn't very welcoming. Her vinegar expression and sharp sniff of disapproval showed them exactly what she thought of them barging in on her patient. She marched them into the living-room where a washed-out-looking Jill Compton in a thick towelling dressing gown sat staring into a roaring fire.

'Good to see you up and about,' said Frost, sinking into the other comfortable chair.

Gilmore dragged a hard kitchen chair over and sat opposite her. 'How are you feeling, Mrs Compton?'

'It hasn't really sunk in yet. Everyone's being so kind.'

Gilmore moved his chair closer. 'I've some news for you. We've arrested Mrs Jean Bradbury for the murder of your husband.'

She stared at him in total disbelief. 'Bradbury? You mean the wife of that man who tried to pick that fight with Mark?'

'Yes. She moved into Denton some weeks ago.'

'But why should she want to harm Mark?'

Gilmore looked at Frost, hoping the inspector would want to tell her of her late husband's infidelity, but, for a change, Frost seemed content to lean back and listen. He took a deep breath. 'Your husband was having an affair with her.'

She shrank back as if he had struck her, and stared wide-eyed, uncomprehending. 'No,' she whispered at last. 'Oh no!'

'I'm afraid it's a fact,' continued Gilmore doggedly. 'He even promised her he would divorce you and marry her. When he broke off the relationship, she began this hate campaign. Jean Bradbury started the fire last night. She killed your husband.'

Jill Compton shivered even though the room was sweltering. 'No,' she said firmly, as if trying to convince herself. 'I don't believe you. My husband would never look at another woman.' Then she covered her face with her hands and her body shook. 'This is more than I can stand. I've lost everything . . . my home . . . my husband . . . and now you tell me he was unfaithful.'

Gilmore turned his head away in embarrassment. He didn't know how to handle crying women. Frost leant forward to pat her arm sympathetically. 'There were lots of things your husband didn't tell you, Mrs Compton. This may come as a bit of a shock to you, but did he tell you that your business was bankrupt?'

Her expression was one of utter bewilderment. 'Bankrupt? That's nonsense. We had a thriving business.'

'It was thriving so much,' Frost told her, 'that your husband had to borrow small sums of money from his mistress . . . and then paid her back with cheques that bounced.'

She shook her head defiantly. 'You're wrong. We had no secrets. Mark would have told me.'

'I'm afraid I'm right.' Frost patted her arm again. 'I was in Bennington's Bank today. One of the cashiers there owes me a favour and he accidentally left your business file on his desk and then went out for a few minutes. He must have completely forgotten what a nosy bastard I am.' He dug deep in his pocket and fished out a crumpled scrap of paper. 'I've scribbled down the details. The Old Mill is in hock to the bank as security for unpaid loans, your current account is £17,000 in the red and creditors galore are breathing down your neck.' He stuffed the paper back in his pocket. 'My friend in the bank is a bit of a cynic. He said the only thing that could have saved your bacon was an insurance policy and a bloody good fire. Well, we've had the fire. Do you know the details of your insurance, Mrs Compton?' He offered her his cigarette packet.

'I know nothing of the financial side of the business. Mark handled all that.' Distractedly, she accepted a cigarette, looked at it in puzzlement and pushed it back in the packet.

'Then I can enlighten you,' said Frost, striking a match against the fire surround. 'A mate of mine works for your insurance company. He tells me that the building and the contents are insured against fire, theft, explosion, earthquakes and stampeding cattle for the sum of £350,000.'

Her eyes widened. 'I can't believe it.'

'Neither could I,' said Frost. 'I doubt if there was more than a couple of thousand pounds' worth of stock in the entire house . . . and even that wasn't paid for.' Again he patted her hand. 'You're a very lucky woman, Mrs Compton.'

'Do you think I give a damn about the money?' she asked incredulously. 'I want my husband. I want my home. That spiteful bitch of a woman . . .'

'I've got more bad news for you,' said Frost. 'That spiteful bitch had nothing to do with the fire.'

Jill Compton shifted her gaze from Frost to Gilmore who was seething in his chair. Why the hell was the swine undermining him like this?

'Your husband started the fire,' continued Frost. 'It was an insurance fiddle. One last throw to clear all the debts and make a dirty great profit. It was your husband who was sending all the death threats and the wreath and doing all the damage.'

'This is ridiculous. Why would he do that?'

'A providential fire, your business on the rocks and the sprinkler system turned off at the mains. No insurance company is going to pay out on that. So your husband had to invent this imaginary nutter who makes weird phone calls and death threats. He even involved the police to give it authenticity.' Frost shook his head in grudging admiration. 'Bloody clever. He almost deserved to get away with it.'

An ingenious theory, thought Gilmore, but where's your proof?

'I'm sorry,' said Jill, her chin thrust forward defiantly, 'but I won't believe a word against my husband. It was that damn woman . . .'

'We've got proof coming out of our ear-holes,' said Frost. 'He had the key to the girl's flat. The magazines he cut the messages from . . . his fingerprints are all over them . . .'

Gilmore stared down at the floor and tried to keep his expression impassive. He wanted no part of this. Forensic had found no prints other than the Bradbury woman's.

'Secondly,' Frost continued, 'we've a witness who saw your husband stacking petrol cans in Jean Bradbury's garage. But the clincher, the absolute clincher . . .' He scrabbled around in his mac pocket. 'I found these in the boot of your husband's car.' He opened his hand to show some bright green leaves nestling in his palm. 'Three different sorts of leaf. And not any old leaf. According to our Forensic Department they are identical to the leaves on that wreath which we found in your lounge. We've even traced the grave where your husband pinched it, haven't we, Sergeant?'

'Yes,' acknowledged Gilmore, curtly. That was the only part of Frost's tissue of lies that he was prepared to endorse.

She stared at the leaves and shook her head. 'This is too much. I just can't believe it.'

Carefully, Frost replaced the leaves in his pocket then gave her one of his disarming smiles. 'It shouldn't be too hard to believe, Mrs Compton. It wouldn't have worked if you weren't in it with him.'

She jerked back, her face white. 'How dare you!'

Ignoring her, Frost continued. 'You were his alibi, he was yours. When he was away, you vandalized the garden. You each claimed to have received the phone calls in the other's presence . . . and when the wreath was chucked through the window, you both claimed to have seen someone running away. Which was impossible, because your husband planted the wreath. Even a dim sod like me can see that you were in the fiddle with him.'

Her mouth opened and shut, then she thought for a while and finally took a deep breath. 'I was hoping this would never have to come out, Inspector. Everything you say is true. It was Mark's idea. I didn't want to go along with him, but he said things were desperate and this was the only way out. He was my husband and I loved him. I did what he asked. Any wife would have done the same.'

Frost nodded. 'But that still makes you an accessory, Mrs Compton.'

She gave the secret smile of a poker player holding a royal flush. 'An accessory to what, Inspector? I have no intention of making a claim on the insurance policy, and if I don't claim, then there is no conspiracy to defraud.'

Frost looked deflated. 'Law isn't my strong point, Mrs Compton. I suppose there's no law that says you can't destroy your own property. So who burnt it down – you or your husband?'

'Mark. I tried to stop him, but he did it.'

A match flared. Frost sucked at his cigarette. 'That only leaves one problem.' He flicked the match in the fire and slowly expelled a lungful of smoke. 'Who killed him?'

She frowned.

'I may be a bit slow on the uptake, Mrs Compton, but there was no mysterious nutter with a grudge . . . you and your husband invented him, so you couldn't have heard him breaking in last night. You must have gone downstairs with your husband . . . you wouldn't lie in bed while he was splashing petrol about. Only two people in the house and one of them is murdered. So who did it, Mrs Compton?'

Gilmore was watching the woman. God knows how Frost had stumbled on to the truth, but her expression was as good as a signed and sealed confession.

'Why did you do it, love?' asked Frost, his voice softening. 'Did you find out about him and the Bradbury woman?' Her reaction was barely perceptible, but he saw it.

She stared at him unblinking. 'I had no motive to kill my husband. I never knew about Mark and her.'

Frost pushed himself out of his chair. 'I think you did, love. You probably got a poison pen letter telling you all about it, but we can check on that.' He jerked his sleeve back to consult his wrist-watch. 'But here am I rambling away and it isn't even my case.' He gave an apologetic grin to Gilmore as he shuffled out. 'Sorry, son. I'll leave you to get on with it.'

Gilmore stood up and opened the bedroom door. 'Would you please get dressed, Mrs Compton. I'd like you to come to the station with me.' While he waited he was irritated to hear Ada's startled shriek from the kitchen, followed by the raucous roar of Frost's laughter and his cry of 'How's that for centre, Ada?' Stupid childish bloody fool, he thought.

Outside, Frost pulled the handful of leaves from his pocket and hurled them into the wind. There were plenty more on Ada's privet hedge where he had plucked them on his way in.

Thursday afternoon shift (2)

The Incident Room was buzzing with activity when Frost entered carrying a mug of tea and a corned beef sandwich from the canteen. Burton, eyes gleaming with excitement, hurried over to him.

'You look happy,' said Frost. 'Has Mr Mullett died?'

Burton grinned. 'It's better than that, sir.'

Frost sat on the edge of a desk and sank his teeth into his sandwich. 'Nothing could be better than that.'

'First of all,' Burton told him, 'we've checked all the local security firms. A couple of them send salesmen around cold calling to sell complete burglar alarm systems, but they leave chains and padlocks to the hardware stores.'

Frost washed down a mouthful of sandwich with a swig of tea. 'That doesn't send my pulse racing, son. What else?'

'We've knocked on as many doors as we can asking if any one-man-band outfits have been touting for custom in fitting security chains and locks. A complete blank.'

Frost chewed gloomily. 'Wake me up when you get to the good bit.'

'I called on Mrs Proctor as you asked . . .'

Burton paused for maximum effect. 'A couple of days ago Mrs Watson told her that one of the bingo coach drivers had offered to fit a stronger security chain on the cheap.'

Frost punched the air and whooped. 'Geronimo! Did she say which driver?'

'No, sir.'

'No matter, we can probably pin-point him. Now I want you to check all the coach companies . . .'

'Already done,' cut in Burton. 'The main bingo run contract is with Superswift Coaches, but they sub-contract the work out to other firms on a day-to-day basis. I've got details of the other firms.' He offered the typed list to Frost who warded it away with his sandwich. 'Each firm has a rota of drivers for its various runs, so you wouldn't necessarily get the same driver each time . . . additionally, most drivers are self-employed so the same driver could do work for different firms.'

Frost gave a weary shake of the head. 'All these details give me a headache. Skip the foreplay – go straight to the big bang!'

'Right, sir. Sally fed all the names and duty rotas through the computer so we could eliminate those who definitely weren't anywhere near Denton when the killings took place. We've come down to four possibles.' From a folder he pulled four typed A4 sheets with photographs clipped on them. 'We pulled the photographs from the firms' personnel files.'

Frost wiped his buttery fingers on his jacket and took the first page. The photograph showed a man in his late thirties, a podgy face, receding dark hair.

'David Allen Hardwicke,' recited Burton. 'Works for the Denton Creamline Coach Company. He's done a lot of bingo runs, but he's mainly used for coach parties from the clubs for West End shows and pantomimes. During the summer he does the outings to the seaside resorts.'

Frost stared down at Hardwicke's details. The man was thirty-eight, married with two children aged nine and ten. Frost poked at the typescript with the crust of his corned beef sandwich. 'He was away from Denton for two of the killings.'

Burton retrieved the sheet and shook off the breadcrumbs. 'Yes, but sometimes drivers swap turns with each other and don't let their firms know. That's one of the complications you didn't want to hear about. We're checking it out.'

Frost took one last bite, then hurled the remains of his sandwich in the general direction of the waste bin. It missed by a foot. He ambled over and tried to boot it in, but missed again. He picked it up and dropped it in. 'Who's next?'

The next was Thomas Riley, the photograph showing a thin, sharp-featured man, light hair plastered well back and well-spaced teeth. 'Riley runs a one-man business – Riley's Coaches,' said Burton. 'Forty-one years old, married, no children. Does the odd bingo and theatre run, but nowhere as many as Hardwicke.'

Frost drained his tea. He couldn't work up any enthusiasm about Riley.

'And he's got form,' announced Burton, waiting for the reaction.

'Form?' Frost snatched Riley's details and studied them again.

Burton's finger pointed out the information. 'Receiving stolen goods. Video recorders, TV sets, electronic gear.'

'Hmm.' Frost dumped his mug on a stack of computer print-outs and fished out his cigarettes.

Burton took one. 'And he beat up a night-watchman once.'

'Hardly beat him up,' corrected Frost, scraping a match down the side of the computer casing. 'Knocked the old boy over when he tried to stop him.' He turned to the continuation page. 'Anyway, Riley was out on a job last night. Didn't get back in until after the time of the murder.'

'He dropped his last passenger off at 9.15,' said Burton, leaning forward to share Frost's match, 'but didn't garage the coach until 9.45. Mrs Watson was killed around 9.35. He could just have done it.'

Frost snorted smoke. 'He'd have had to rush, and I can't see our Ripper rushing things. He likes to take his time.' He handed back the details. 'Next.'

Burton passed across another page and waited expectantly. If he had to put money on it, this was his nap selection. Robert Jefferson, thirty-three, married, one teenaged daughter. A thickset man with close-cropped black hair, he stared morosely from his photograph like a criminal having his mug-shot taken. Jefferson drove for Superswift Coaches, mainly long-distance and Continental work, but had done a couple of bingo runs from time to time. His off-duty schedule put him in Denton for every one of the Ripper killings. A man of violent temper, he had broken his wife's jaw and she was instigating divorce proceedings because of his cruelty.

Frost seemed unimpressed. 'I don't think so, son. I can't see Old Mother Watson inviting that thug into her flat. Bung him at the bottom of the pile.'

'You'd better like this one,' said Burton. 'He's the last. Ronald William Gauld, twenty-five, single, lives with his widowed mother. Does casual work as a relief driver for Clarke's Coaches – mainly bingo and old people's outings. He's supposed to be a ball of fun on the coach trips. All the old dears love him.'

'I'm beginning to hate him already,' said Frost, extending his hand for the details.

'He's only employed as a casual by Clarke's, so he could well work for other firms we haven't checked on yet . . . but Clarke's time-sheets have him off-duty on all the times and days of the Ripper killings.'

Frost glanced at the colour photo clipped to the sheet. Gauld, grinning with well-spaced teeth into the camera, looked more a boy than a man. His expression was frank and open, his brown eyes twinkled and his thick, light brown hair hung boyishly over his forehead. Excitement like static electricity crackled through Frost. Instinct. Gut reaction. He knew. He just knew. 'Bingo!' he yelled.

Everyone in the room looked up.

Frost waggled the photograph, then held it aloft. 'This is him. This is the Granny Ripper!'

Burton could only look puzzled. 'Why, sir?'

'Gut reaction, son. I'm very rarely right, but I am this time. Forget the rest . . . We go nap on Laughing Boy Gauld.' He slid down from the desk, rubbing his hands together and pacing backwards and forwards to discharge his nervous excitement. 'Put every available man on him. I want him watched twenty-four hours a day.'

Burton urged caution. 'Don't you think we should hedge our bets, sir?'

'No,' said Frost firmly. 'We go for broke.'

'He's only a possible suspect. We've got nothing on him.'

'So we find something on him. Show copies of his photograph to the victims' neighbours. Do they remember seeing this roguish little bastard hanging around? Find out if he's been offering to fit new security chains for any of the old dears who find him such a scream. Go back to Old Mother Proctor and ask her if Gauld was the name of the man who offered to fit Mrs Watson's chain. Check with Gauld's neighbours. Has he come home at night dripping with blood with a knife sticking out of his back pocket? Get everyone on it . . . even the girl on the computer.'

'Hold it, Inspector!' Detective Sergeant Arthur Hanlon, eyes watering, nose streaming, looking like death warmed up, had been standing by the door. 'You'd better hear what I've found out first.'

'If it's bad news, I don't want to know,' said Frost.

'You might have to look for another suspect, Jack. You asked me to check on the three murder victims. I did. The only one who went to bingo was Mrs Watson.'

'Rubbish, Arthur. The second old girl – Betty Winters. We found a Reef Bingo membership card in her purse.'

'She hadn't used it for five years. She was crippled with arthritis – never left the house except to go to hospital for treatment.'

'And the first one – Mrs Thingummy?'

'Mrs Haynes. Very prim and proper. Didn't believe in gambling. Wouldn't even play bingo down at the church club for packets of tea.'

Frost's shoulders slumped. 'Sod you, Arthur. Why must you be so flaming thorough?' He glanced down at the photograph of Gauld which seemed to be smirking smugly back at him. 'It's got to be Gauld. There's got to be some common factor that links him to all three.' He became aware that everyone in the Murder Incident Room was waiting for him to give them orders, to tell them what to do. And he didn't know. His one and only lead had gone down the pan. He stared through the window out at the miserable, depressing, rain-swept car-park, drawing deeply on his cigarette, punishing his lungs for his own inadequacy. As he pulled the cigarette from his mouth, a thought buzzed and screamed. 'You said Mrs Winters never left the house except to go to hospital for treatment. How did she get there – the poor cow couldn't walk?'

'She certainly didn't go by bingo coach,' said Hanlon.

'Very funny, Arthur – remind me to pee myself when I've got more time.' Frost's finger stabbed at Burton. 'Phone the hospital transport officer and find out.'

Burton reached for the phone, but he thought it was a waste of time. 'She'd have gone by ambulance, Inspector.'

'Not necessarily, son. Just phone and ask.' He paced the room impatiently as Burton held on, waiting for someone to fetch the transport officer from the canteen. And then he remembered something else. Mrs

Mary Haynes. The first victim. Her purse. There was a hospital appointment card in her purse. 'And ask about Mrs Mary Haynes,' he shouted.

Burton nodded, then held up a hand for silence. The transport officer was on the line. Burton put his questions and waited . . . and waited . . . There seemed to be a long delay with Frost hovering anxiously before the answers came through. 'Ambulances? I see. Do you have the drivers' names? I see. Thank you very much, you've been a great help.' He replaced the receiver and tried to look noncommittal as Frost hurried over. But he couldn't keep up the pretence.

'You bastard!' yelled Frost. 'We've hit the jackpot, haven't we?'

Burton grinned broadly. 'They have a pool of volunteer drivers who help out with their own cars when the ambulances are too busy to collect patients for treatment.'

'I know,' said Frost. 'A volunteer driver used to pick up my wife.'

Burton smiled sympathetically before adding, 'One of those volunteers is a Mr R.W. Gauld.'

Frost crashed down on a chair. 'Then we've got the bastard!'

'Not quite, Inspector. The hospital doesn't keep records of individual pick-ups – they handle hundreds of patients every day. All they can say is that Gauld was among the volunteer drivers on duty on the last two occasions when Mrs Winters and Mrs Haynes attended for treatment. He didn't collect them, but it's possible he took them back home afterwards.'

'And that's when he found out about the spare key under the mat and the string inside the letter-box,' said Frost, excitedly. 'Let's bring the bastard in.'

Hanlon was more cautious. 'We could blow it by acting too soon. Jack. We need some solid evidence.'

'All right. Go to the hospital, see if you can find anyone who saw Gauld take the old dears back home. Check with the neighbours in the hope someone saw Gauld deliver them back. Get details of his car – did anyone see it in the vicinity on the nights of the murders? You know the form – whatever I've forgotten, do it. Lastly, I want Gauld tailed. I want to know everything he does every minute of the day and night, and when he goes out on his next killing job, we grab him, and if he's got his bloody knife on him, that's all the proof I need.'

In the corridor, he collided with Detective Sergeant Gilmore who looked as happy as his inspector.

'We've got a full statement from Mrs Compton, Inspector.'

'Thank God for that, son. I was afraid I might have to perjure myself at her trial.'

'She admits everything, but says the husband's death was an accident.'

'How? Did she accidentally welt him round the head with one of her rigid nipples?'

A broad grin from Gilmore. Anything Frost said was funny today. 'Thanks for your help,' he added sincerely.

'All I did was tell a few lies,' demurred the inspector. 'Any self-respecting policeman would do the same.'

'And after your stunt with the leaves,' added Gilmore, 'I got Forensic to go over the boot of Mark Compton's car. We actually found a couple of leaves from the wreath.'

'That's what's known as nature imitating art,' said Frost. 'When you get a minute, see me in the office.

I'll update you on the Ripper case. We're nearly ready to nail the bastard.'

In the office, weighed down in the centre of his desk by a stapling machine, was the memo from County beefing about the balls-up with his car expenses. He screwed it into a tight ball, tossed it in the air and headed it towards the open goal of the waste bin. It dropped dead centre with a satisfying plonk. He beamed happily. Things were starting to go right.

Later, when everything blew up in his face, he would remember this brief moment of euphoria.

Thursday night shift (1)

The downstairs light went out. A pause, then the upstairs light came on and the silhouette of a man passed the window. Gilmore ducked down behind the steering wheel until the curtains were closed and the bedroom light went out. He shook Frost awake. 'He's gone to bed.'

Yawning heavily, Frost consulted his watch. A few minutes to midnight. They had been parked down the side turning for nearly two hours, since taking over from Burton. Gauld had collected a party of senior citizens from the Silver Star Bingo Club at nine o'clock, and had delivered them all safely back to their homes by 9.56. He had then driven his grey Vauxhall Astra back to his terraced house in Nelson Street and was indoors by 10.15.

Frost fidgeted and tried to get comfortable. He was tired and hungry and there was no chance of a relief until six a.m. His fault. He had forgotten to ask Mullett to authorize more overtime and Wells was playing it by the book. He smeared a gap in the misted windscreen with his cuff and peered out at the still, dark street. 'It's too late for him to murder anyone now,' he decided. 'Let's get ourselves something to eat. I know a place that's open all night.'

The 'place' Frost knew was a converted van selling hot dogs and hamburgers on a windswept stretch of waste ground near the cemetery. The stale greasy smell of frying onions slapped them round the face as they got out of the car. On the side of the van a drop-down flap provided a serving counter and a canvas awning sheltered the clientele from the worst of the weather. Behind the counter a tall, thin man with a melancholy face and a red, running nose sucked at a cigarette as he pushed some onion slices around the fat with a fork.

'Lord Lucan and party,' announced Frost. 'We did book.'

'Very funny,' said the man, pulling the cigarette from his mouth so he could cough all over the food. He banged two cups on the counter, dropped a tea-bag in each and filled them with hot water from a steam-belching urn.

They sipped the scalding tea while the man fried them two hamburgers in tired, spitting fat. It was a cold night with the wind flapping the canvas awning.

'You caught that girl's killer yet?' asked the owner, putting the burgers on a plate and sliding them over.

Frost lifted the top of his bun and peered suspiciously at the onion-topped meat sinking in a puddle of fat. 'We're on a different case, Harry. Suspect meat sold as hamburger filling.' He took a tentative bite and chewed cautiously. 'I hope yours comes from a legitimate source?'

Harry sucked nervously at his cigarette. 'Of course it does Mr Frost. That's top-class stuff, that is – minced steak.'

'Good,' said Frost. 'Only this dodgy outfit is importing so-called meat from the Continent . . . all sorts of rubbish – dead horses, cats, dogs, some of it even worse.'

'Worse?' asked Harry.

Frost leant forward confidentially and lowered his voice. 'Don't spread this around, Harry, it would cause a public outcry, but we've got evidence they're even buying unclaimed bodies from undertakers and putting them in the mincing machine.'

Harry pulled the cigarette from his mouth and flicked off the spit from the end. 'You're having me on, Mr Frost!'

'I wish I was,' answered Frost gravely. He took a bite at his hamburger, then pulled it from his mouth. 'Bloody hell!' He snatched the top from his bun and gaped in disbelief. Lying across the onion, drenched in a bloody pool of tomato ketchup, was a severed human finger.

Gilmore shuddered and dropped his on the counter. Harry's face went a greasy white and his head jerked back in horror, rattling the tins on the shelf behind him. 'Christ, Mr Frost! They told me it was good meat. They said it was prime beef steak . . .' His voice suddenly changed to outrage. 'You bastard!'

The severed finger was wiggling at him and Frost was convulsed with laughter as he pulled it free and wiped off the ketchup.

'It's not funny,' bellowed Harry. 'You nearly gave me a bloody heart attack.'

Frost wiped the tears from his eyes. 'I was going to put my dick in, Harry, but the buns were too small.'

'Bleeding funny!' snarled the man as they walked back to the car, Frost still convulsed at his joke. 'Pity you don't put your bloody energy into finding that poor kid's killer.'

Frost stopped laughing.

The cemetery was crawling past the car window. Frost asked Gilmore to stop. He lit a cigarette and stared moodily across white marble and granite. 'Harry was right, son. That bloody girl. I haven't the faintest idea what to do next.'

Gilmore said nothing. At the far end of the empty road he had spotted a man, dressed in black, crouching by the cemetery railings. Gilmore clicked off the headlights, then nudged Frost, who nodded. 'I see him, son.'

The man seemed to be doing something to the railings.

'What's he up to?' asked Gilmore.

'Whatever it is, let him get on with it,' muttered Frost, huddling down into his seat. 'I can't solve the cases I've got. I don't want any more.'

But Gilmore wanted more. Another arrest on top of the successful outcome of the Compton case would do his promotion chances a world of good. He wound down the window and stuck his head out, trying to make out what the man was doing. Frost shivered as the cold air rushed in. 'He's either got his dick stuck between the railings, or he's having a pee, son. Let's get back to the station.'

Suddenly the man seemed to push against the railings and was through to the cemetery where his black shape flitted briefly across the white of the headstones before being gulped up by darkness.

Gilmore was out of the car while Frost was still fumbling for his seat belt.

One of the cast iron railings had rusted away and could be lifted from its concrete base. Gilmore pulled it up and wriggled though, then held it so Frost could follow.

The cemetery was vast. Their man could have gone anywhere. 'We've lost the bugger, son.'

'Shh!' hissed Gilmore, squinting to focus his eyes. 'There!'

Frost's eyes followed Gilmore's finger. The moon pushed its way through a cloud and illuminated the cemetery in a cold blue light. Uncut grass twitched and shivered in the wind. Trees creaked and groaned. And then Frost saw him. About sixty yards away, zigzagging between the graves.

'Follow me!' ordered Gilmore, haring off in pursuit. Reluctantly, Frost stumbled after him. He couldn't see what Gilmore was getting all excited about. The man could simply be taking a short cut.

They jogged on, past angels and cherubs. The path veered to the right and there ahead of them was the Victorian crypt. 'Stop, son,' pleaded Frost, 'I've got to rest.' They paused alongside some new, raw graves, panting, sucking in air, looking left and right where the path split. Nothing but white headstones as far as the eye could see.

'We've lost him,' said Frost happily. 'Let's get back to the car.'

An irritated flap of Gilmore's hand hushed him to silence and pointed to the crypt. The man, his back to them, was bent over doing something to the padlock. A loud click, then a groaning of hinges as the door was pushed open. A torch flashed and the man disappeared inside the burial vault.

'Still taking a short cut?' scoffed Gilmore, smugly. He moved quietly round to the side of the building and squeezed through the railing by the tap, where Paula Bartlett's killer squeezed through with her body. Frost, slower, followed.

Round to the door where the newly fitted brass padlock still held the hasp firmly, but as before, the screws had been prised from the rotting door frame. Intermittent splashes of light spilled from inside. Echoing in the confined space, sounds of something heavy being dragged across the stone floor.

Gilmore and Frost looked at each other. What the hell was he doing?

Cautiously, Gilmore edged his head until he could see inside. Pitch black, then the man's torch clicked on again and lit up a scatter of something on the floor. Bones. Human bones. And on top of them, a grinning, yellow-toothed, human skull.

Gilmore's involuntary gasp was enough to make the man spin round, the glare of his torch hitting Gilmore straight in the eyes, momentarily blinding him. Then, with a yell, the man charged and Gilmore found himself flying through the air, his back, then his head hitting the stone floor with a teeth-jolting crack making pin-points of light dance in the blackness at the pain.

Crouching, ready to give him a second dose, the man moved forward.

'Stay where you are. Police!' yelled Frost, dragging his torch from his mac pocket and kicking bones out of the way as he advanced into the vault. The man blinked into the beam and Frost stopped in his tracks. Gilmore's assailant was wearing a clerical collar.

The curate gawped surprise at the sudden appearance. 'Mr Frost!'

Gilmore creaked open his eyes and saw a skull and a thigh bone within inches of his face. He sat up, gingerly touching the back of his head then studying the blood on his fingertips.

'I'm terribly sorry, Sergeant,' apologized the curate. 'I thought you were one of the vandals.' He helped Gilmore to his feet and examined the cut on his head. 'Only a graze, I think.'

With an angry jerk, Gilmore shook him off. 'Perhaps you'd care to explain what you're doing here at this time of night?' He picked up the torch and swept the stone floor with its beam. The lids of two coffins had been unscrewed open and the skeletal bodies inside tipped out with bones and pieces of shroud strewn all over the floor. 'And how do you propose to explain this?'

'I use the graveyard as a short cut to get back to the vicarage. I've been sitting with another sick parishioner. She died, I'm afraid – this terrible influenza epidemic.' He shook his head sadly. 'So many deaths.'

'Let's have the address of this sick old lady,' said Gilmore, pen poised over his notebook. He wrote down the details. 'Right. Now explain this.' He nodded at the mess.

'Does it need explaining?' said the curate bitterly. 'You're supposed to be protecting us against vandals. I passed the crypt and saw the door was open. I came in to investigate and found this.' He shook his head. 'Such pointless desecration. One tries to be forgiving, Sergeant, but this is sick.'

Gilmore snapped shut his notebook. 'All right, Mr Purley. That's all, for now.' He emphasized the 'for now'.

They followed him out and watched as he tried to make the door secure. 'You'll need a new door frame,' said Frost.

'Yes, Inspector. More expense.' Another sigh. 'I'll

come back tomorrow and try and fix it. I'll tidy up inside as well.' Round to the side of the building where they squeezed through the gap in the railing.

They watched him picking his way between the graves before veering off towards the vicarage.

'I don't trust him,' growled Gilmore. 'He's always out too late at night for my liking. If there's been another Ripper murder . . .' Frost was pinning his hopes on the coach driver, but Gilmore had serious doubts. 'Let's go. This place is giving me the creeps.'

'It must have given Paula Bartlett's killer the creeps, coming here at dead of night with a body in his arms.' Frost poked away at his scar and stared at the ranks of white headstones crowding in on the crypt. 'He knew how to find the crypt, son, and he knew he could get in.' He pushed his hands deep into his mac pockets and wandered along the railings, booting at pebbles in his path. 'So how did he know?'

'Perhaps he was someone who often used the graveyard as a short cut,' offered Gilmore, pointedly rubbing the back of his head.

Frost chewed his knuckles in thought, then took out his cigarette packet and shook it. One left. He poked it in his mouth and flung the empty packet into the long grass. A blast of cold wind cut across the cemetery, shaking the trees and making him shiver. 'Let's go.'

They walked on to the path where the first of the new graves encroached. Frost struck his match on a convenient headstone. The match flared. He saw the wording, but at first didn't take it in. Then he stared, open-mouthed, until the match burnt his fingers. 'Where the bloody hell did this come from?'

He struck another match so Gilmore could read the inscription.

In Loving Memory
Of
Rosemary Fleur Bell
April 3 1962 – September 10 1990
Adored Wife Of Edward Bell M.A.
R. I. P.

'The schoolmaster's wife! Her grave right on the bloody doorstep of the crypt and we haven't spotted it. We must be bleeding blind as well as stupid!'

'It's probably only just been put up,' said Gilmore, wondering what all the fuss was about. 'You have to wait ages for the grave to settle before you can erect a headstone.'

'That wispy-bearded bastard. I knew it was him all the time.' He turned and stared at the crypt.

'I don't follow you,' said Gilmore.

'You could spit on the flaming crypt from here,' said Frost. 'At the funeral Bell would have had a grandstand view of that fat-gutted plumber forcing open the door to get inside out of the rain. Later he needed somewhere to hide the kid's body. A crypt. Who'd look for a body in a Victorian crypt?'

'You're saying he killed her the very day of his wife's funeral?'

'Yes,' said Frost.

'But he was in the house all the time she was doing her paper round.'

'I don't know how he did it, I just know he did it.'

Gilmore swivelled his head towards the vault door with its solid brass lock hanging impotently. 'Even if you are right, how are you going to prove it?'

'Proof!' barked Frost. He took a long drag at his last

cigarette and dashed it to the ground half-smoked. 'Everyone's obsessed with bloody proof.' Then his shoulders slumped. Gilmore was right. Without proof, the bastard was going to get away with it.

Thursday night shift (2)

The minute hand on the lobby clock was quivering as it gathered its strength to claw up to two o'clock. The damn phones had been ringing non-stop and Wells was finding it hard to keep his voice sounding polite. 'I'm sorry, madam,' he told a caller who had phoned previously to complain that her neighbours were having a noisy row and were keeping her awake. 'We're short-staffed and we had to divert the car to a more important incident. We'll get someone there just as soon as we can.' Hardly had he replaced the phone and logged the call when there was an angry commotion outside, then a scowling, red-faced bull-frog of a man in an expensive black overcoat and a white silk scarf exploded into the lobby, closely followed by an anxious-looking PC Collier.

'Who's in charge?' the man bellowed, dumping a bulky briefcase on the floor. He reeked of whisky.

Wells put his pen down and sighed. He could do without this. 'I am, sir.'

The man looked disdainfully at Wells' sergeant's stripes and screwed his face into a sneer. 'I want someone in authority, not you. Not a bloody sergeant.'

'What's this all about?' Wells asked Collier.

The man barged between the two officers. 'Don't you damn well ignore me. *I'm* talking to you, Sergeant. You ask me, not him. Now get me someone in authority.' He fumbled in his pocket for a cigar.

'Would an inspector satisfy you, sir?' asked Wells, struggling to hold his temper in check.

'If that's all you've got, then he'll have to do,' snapped the man, clicking a gold Dunhill lighter and drawing on the cigar. Wells felt like pointing to the 'No Smoking' sign but wasn't in the mood for any more aggravation and the odds were that Frost would come slommocking out with a cigarette in his mouth. He used the internal phone and whilst the man glowered and puffed cigar smoke and whisky fumes all over him, asked Inspector Frost to come into the lobby.

'I'm Detective Inspector Frost. What's up?'

Frost, in his crumpled suit, greasy knotted tie and unpolished shoes, didn't look at all impressive and he certainly didn't impress the complainant who pulled the cigar from his mouth and stared contemptuously. 'Isn't there anyone else in charge?'

'No,' said Frost. 'So if you've anything to say, spit it out, I'm busy.'

'Not too busy to attend to me,' snarled the man. 'I'm making a complaint against that police officer.' His finger jabbed at Collier. 'He drove his car into me while I was stationary, then accused me of drunken driving.'

Frost wrinkled his nose and turned his head away from the whisky fumes. To Collier he said, 'Has he been breathalyzed?'

'No, Inspector. He refused.'

'Right,' said Frost to Wells. 'Get a police surgeon . . . one with warm hands. We'll have a urine sample.' Back to Collier. 'So what happened, Constable?'

'I've just told you what happened,' shouted the man, his face getting redder.

Frost pushed him away. 'Shut up. You're giving me a bleedin' headache.' Back to Collier.

'I was on patrol in the Bath Road when I saw this Bentley crawling along, swinging from one side of the road to the other. I signalled for the driver to stop. He pulled into the kerb. I drew up behind him. As I was getting out, he started up the engine. I think he was trying to get away, but he put it into reverse by mistake and rammed into me. He was obviously drunk – speech slurred, eyes glazed. He flatly refused to use the breathalyzer, and knocked it out of my hand, so I brought him in.'

'Well done,' nodded Frost. 'Book him.' As he turned to go, the man grabbed him by the shoulder and jerked him round.

'Do you know who I am?' he demanded, pushing his sweating face close to the inspector's.

'I know what you are,' replied Frost, shaking himself free. 'You're a drunken, boring prick. Take your sweaty paw off my suit.'

No-one heard the lobby door swing open. 'What's going on here?'

Frost groaned. Bloody Mullett had to choose this particular moment to do his rallying call act on the troops. A little touch of Mullett in the night. 'I'm handling it, sir,' he said firmly.

Mullett hesitated. He preferred not to get involved in anything unless he knew what it was about. Then his face lit up with recognition. 'Good lord! It's Councillor Knowles. What are you doing here?'

'I'm making an official complaint against this police officer,' said Knowles, 'and I'm being treated abominably. That man . . .' and his lip curled at Frost, 'has been incredibly rude. He has threatened me, sworn at me and made me the subject of a false charge.'

Mullett looked suitably shocked. His lips tightened. 'You'd better come to my office, councillor. I'm sure we can sort this out.' He glowered at Frost as he spun on his heel. 'Two coffees to my office at once, please, Sergeant.'

Frost jerked forked fingers to the door as it closed behind his Divisional Commander. 'Pompous git!' he bellowed impotently to the ceiling.

'Did you hear that? Two coffees!' croaked Wells. 'What does he think this is – an all-night flaming café?'

Young PC Collier was white-faced. 'What will happen, Sarge? It was a proper arrest. The man was drunk and he ran into me.'

'Go and make their coffee,' said Wells, 'and do one for me.'

The internal phone buzzed. Inspector Frost to report to the Divisional Commander . . . at once! 'When I'm ready,' said Frost, after he had hung up. Slowly he finished his cigarette, then ambled off to obey the summons. Mullett was waiting for him in the passage outside. He took Frost by the arm and drew him away, beaming a smile of smug satisfaction. Hello, thought Frost. What's the slimy sod been up to?

'I've managed to get the councillor to drop his complaint against Collier, Inspector.'

'What bloody complaint?' demanded Frost, his voice rising with anger. 'The drunken slob rammed into him then refused to take a breath test.'

Waving a hand for Frost to keep his voice down, Mullett led him away from the office door, then leaned forward to talk to Frost in his 'man to man' voice. 'Young Collier is inexperienced. Mr Knowles is a councillor. He is also on the Police Committee. It will be his word against Collier's. Who do you think will be believed?'

'Collier will be believed – especially when the urine test shows Fat-guts is as pissed as a newt.'

Mullett winced. He deplored Frost's too-frequent crudities. He carefully composed his face into a brittle smile and looked at the far wall across Frost's shoulder. 'Ah . . . there won't be a urine sample. We won't be proceeding with the charge . . .' His hand jerked up to silence Frost's explosion of outrage. 'Politics, Inspector. It pays to have a man of his influence on our side, instead of against us.'

Frost jerked his arm free from Mullett's grasp. 'You can have him on your bloody side. I don't want him on mine. And if I ever arrest the bastard for anything, I'll make the charge stick, politics or no bloody politics.'

The brittle smile slipped and shattered. 'There will be no vendettas,' hissed Mullett. 'And before you go, Inspector, there's one more thing. In order to persuade the councillor to drop his complaint against Collier, I agreed that you would personally apologize to him for your rudeness.'

'Up your shirt!' shouted Frost, ready to march back up the corridor.

Mullett's whole body was quivering with anger. 'That was not a request, Inspector. That was an order.'

'Very good, Super,' replied Frost, with an expression of such sweet reasonableness that Mullett was instantly uneasy.

Knowles was sprawled in one of Mullett's special visitor's chairs, his piggy eyes agleam at the prospect of Frost's impending humiliation. He looked up from his cup of Sergeant Wells' instant coffee in mock surprise as Frost entered, looking very contrite. 'Yes, Inspector?'

'I'd like to apologize', said Frost, 'for calling you a big, fat, ugly bastard.'

Knowles frowned and looked puzzled. 'I didn't hear you say that.'

'Oh, sorry,' said Frost innocently, sounding genuinely apologetic. 'It must have been what I was thinking.'

Knowles rose from his chair, eyes bulging, ready to erupt. Then he gave an evil smile. 'I shall remember this, Inspector.' As he spoke the threat, he swayed from side to side like a snake ready to strike.

'You're too kind,' cooed Frost.

With a furious, laser beam glare, Mullett ordered the inspector to wait for his return, then ushered his visitor out. Left alone in the old log cabin, Frost riffled through Mullett's in-tray, but found nothing of interest. He was delighted to discover that Mullett's cigarette box had been newly replenished for the recent visitor, so helped himself to a few, just managing to stuff them in his pocket and put on his contrite expression as the Divisional Commander stamped back, slamming the door behind him.

'That', said Mullett, 'was unforgivable. Mr Knowles is a councillor, a member of the Police Committee and a personal friend of mine.'

And a big, fat drunken bastard to boot, thought Frost. But he hung his head and tried to look ashamed of himself.

'Don't worry,' said Frost, trying to console a gloomy PC Collier with one of Mullett's cigarettes. 'You just misinterpreted the law. The law is that if you're a friend of Mr Mullett's, then you can get away with bloody murder.'

Collier squeezed out a smile, but was still upset. Frost inhaled deeply, then dribbled out smoke. Something propped against the desk caught his eye. He bent to examine it more closely. It was a brief-case. 'What's this?'

Sergeant Wells stretched over the desk to take a look and immediately panicked. 'Flaming heck, it could be a bomb.' His hand shot out for the phone.

'Hold on,' muttered Frost, crouching on his haunches to examine the object. 'Collier, did that fat sod have a brief-case with him when you brought him in?'

'Yes,' answered Collier, relieved to provide the explanation. 'He clung to it like grim death.'

With a grunt, Frost heaved it up on to the desk. 'I wonder if there's anything worth pinching inside.' He tried the catch. It was locked, so he produced his bunch of skeleton keys.

'You're not going to open it, are you?' asked Wells, his head anxiously flicking from side to side in case the Divisional Commander caught them in the act.

'Why not?' grunted Frost, trying to force a clearly unsuitable key to turn.

Wells backed away. 'I want nothing to do with it, Jack. Mullett's still in the building.'

'A suspected bomb,' said Frost, his concentration all on the lock. 'At great personal risk to life, limb and dick I am trying to defuse it . . . ah!' The lock yielded with a click. He lifted the flap and looked inside. His jaw dropped and he emitted a long, low whistle. 'Look what we've got here!' He produced a handful of banknotes. Dirty, creased, well-used banknotes of mixed denominations, fives, tens, twenties, fifties . . . The sort of money that rarely saw the inside of a bank, or was declared on an income tax return. He dived in and produced a second handful, then riffled his thumb through them. At a rough guess there was something in excess of £5,000. 'I wonder how much of this he gave to Mullett for letting him go? Right, let's share it out.' He proceeded to deal out the notes in three piles as if they were playing cards.

'Put them back, Jack,' pleaded Wells, now very agitated, his ears straining to catch the first sounds of Mullett's approaching footsteps.

'Why?' asked Frost. 'The sod's obviously been up to no good. This is crooked money. It sticks out a mile.'

'You've got no proof.'

'The man's a bastard, that's all the proof I need.' Reluctantly he stuffed the money back and let Wells lock the brief-case away for safe-keeping. A quick peep up the corridor. The light was still on in Mullett's office. 'Ah well. No-one will dare commit a crime while Hornrim Harry's still here, so I'm going off home.'

He poked his head round the door of his office where Gilmore was pecking away at a typewriter. 'Come on, son. You can surprise your wife in bed with the lodger. We're having an early night.'

Gilmore didn't really consider nearly three o'clock in the morning to be an early night, but he didn't argue. He scooped up his coat and hurried out after the inspector.

There were a few cars dotted about the station car-park. In its specially reserved parking space, sneering at Gilmore's Ford, stood Mullett's blue Jaguar. But making the Jaguar look like a poor relation was a gleaming black Bentley. Frost ambled over to it and peered through the tinted windows to the cream leather upholstery and polished figured walnut fascia. A jingle of keys and there was young Collier. 'Why didn't you tell me my new motor had arrived?' asked Frost.

Collier grinned. 'It's Councillor Knowles' car, sir. He went home by taxi. Mr Mullett wants me to drive it back for him.'

'How can that bastard afford to run a bloody car like this?' said Frost, walking around the vehicle and giving it his grudging admiration. He stopped in midstride.

'Gilmore!' Gilmore, waiting patiently by his own car, came reluctantly over. 'Remember how Wally Manson told us he nicked those porno videos from an expensive motor?'

Gilmore nodded wearily. There were lots of expensive motors about. He hoped Frost wasn't going to plunge head first in another of his wild, tenuous, proofless hunches.

'And you remember how Wally said he jemmied open the boot?' Frost pointed to the rear of the car. Gilmore moved forward to look. He had to agree. The boot had been forced open – and not too long ago.

'And the bastard's got a brief-case full of dirty money,' Frost continued. 'What's the betting he's been doing the rounds, flogging his dirty videos?' Frost held out his hand to Collier. 'Keys, son.' He took them and unlocked the driver's door. The aroma of rich leather and cigar smoke. He slid into the driver's seat and rummaged about in the dash compartment. He found a button to press and a concealed drawer glided open. Inside were a dozen or more of the familiar pornographic videos. Triumphantly he showed them to Gilmore. 'Proof enough for you?'

'It's a start,' agreed Gilmore, reluctantly. He didn't want to get involved. People like Councillor Knowles would always come out on top.

Frost told Collier to fetch the brief-case from Sergeant Wells. 'Tell him I'm going to kindly deliver it in person.'

'Are you sure you know what you're doing?' asked Gilmore.

'Yes,' said Frost. 'I'm risking my bloody job.'

Knowles lived in a large rambling house just north of the Bath Road on the outskirts of the town, standing in its own extensive grounds, completely hidden from the road by trees. Although it was well past three in the morning, lights still showed from the downstairs windows. They pulled up in front of a massive black oak door which was flanked by replica flaming torches lit by electric bulbs.

Up two stone steps, guarded on each side by stone watchdogs, to the door where the bell-pull, a heavy black iron ring on a chain, descended from the top of the porch. Frost tugged it and somewhere far in the bowels of the house a bell echoed. The ringing started a dog barking. A door slammed. Someone inside shouted angrily and the dog stopped in mid-bark.

Gilmore's agitation was showing. Not only were they barging into someone's house in the dead of night for the flimsiest of reasons, but it was the house of an important friend of the Divisional Commander who would have apoplexy if he knew they were there. Why the hell had Frost dragged him into this? Frost, striking a match on the rump of one of the stone dogs seemed blissfully unaware of the possible consequences of what he was doing.

They waited. Shuffling footsteps, then a light glowed through the coloured glass on either side of the door and a voice called, 'Who is it?'

'Police, Mr Knowles,' said Frost. 'You left your brief-case at the station.'

Bolts and chains clinked and the door opened wide enough for a hand to pass through. It closed round the handle of the brief-case. 'Tell Mr Mullett, thank you.' The brief-case vanished inside and the door jerked back. But it would not close. A scuffed, unpolished shoe prevented it.

'What the hell!' Knowles felt the door being pushed open. That damn, scruffy inspector, a cigarette drooping insolently from his mouth, was barging his way into the house.

'If we could come in for a moment, sir,' said Frost, kicking the front door shut behind him and snatching the brief-case back from Knowles who was clasping it tightly against a black and red silk dressing gown.

Knowles, the alcohol smell stronger than ever, quivered with rage and pointed dramatically to the front door. 'If you aren't out in thirty seconds I am getting on the phone to your Chief Constable.'

'I'm sorry, sir,' said Frost, not sounding it, 'but this is a very serious matter.' He opened the brief-case.

Knowles sobered up instantly. 'What right have you to open a locked brief-case?'

'No right at all,' replied Frost. 'It came open in the car and the contents fell out.'

Gilmore squeezed even further into the background, hoping Frost wouldn't seek his corroboration.

'In the brief-case was a large amount of money in used notes. Can you account for it, sir?'

Knowles took a red-banded cigar from his dressing gown pocket and lit it with a snap of his gold Dunhill. 'I can, but I have no intention of doing so. You have far exceeded your authority and you will very soon suffer the consequences.'

Ignoring the threat, and the mute pleading for caution from Gilmore, Frost ploughed on. 'We found a quantity of these in your car.' He held up two tapes. 'They are locally made, pornographic videos involving bestial and disgusting acts against children.'

'Just what are you insinuating?' asked Knowles, his voice soft and menacing.

'I'm insinuating sod all. I'm stating that you are involved with a pornographic vice ring. So get your clothes on. I'm taking you back to the station.'

With a chilling smile Knowles drew deeply on the

cigar, then flicked a cylinder of ash on to the carpet. 'I'll happily come to the station with you, Frost, and then you can kiss your career goodbye. Those videos were given to me by an outraged member of the public. If you check, you will find that I have already given notice that I intend raising this matter at the next meeting of the Denton Police Committee. I will also be raising the matter of your outrageous behaviour.'

Oh my God! thought Gilmore. This is it. The stupid fool's done it now. Well, he's not dragging me down with him. But he couldn't help feeling a pang of pity for the inspector who was shaken rigid and looked older, even more shabby and useless than usual.

With the cigar clenched in a gloating grin, Knowles retrieved the brief-case and quickly checked through the contents. 'I hope, for your sake, all the money is intact, Inspector. I suggest you leave now. I'll be speaking to your Chief Constable first thing in the morning.' He opened the front door. Outside it was raining again.

Defeated, Frost couldn't think of a thing to say. Mullett would demand his resignation and he would have to give it.

But luck, which all too often deserted him in his hour of need, suddenly remembered it owed him a favour. Somewhere at the end of the darkened passage, a door opened and a rectangle of light fell out. 'Is everything all right?' a woman called. Then a scamper of feet and she yelled sharply, 'No . . . come back!'

But the dog bounded up the passage towards its master, wagging its tail happily and whimpering. An enormous dog. A Great Dane. A brown and white Great Dane. Its left ear was torn.

Frost stared, then grinned happily in warm, sweat-trickling relief. He marched back into the house, closing the front door firmly behind him. 'What a beautiful dog, Mr Knowles. He looks just like he did in the video.'

Dawn was scratching at the small window of the main interview room as Knowles and his wife were hustled in. They sat sullenly, refusing to say a word until their solicitor was roused from his bed. Outside, from a police van in the car-park, boxes and boxes of videos, raw tape, and video cameras were carted into the station.

The door opened and Frost slouched in and mumbled a few words to PC Collier who was guarding the prisoners. Collier nodded and left to stand watch outside, ready to warn the inspector of the solicitor's arrival.

Frost dragged a chair over and sat facing Knowles and his wife. 'Alone at last, Councillor.'

'I've nothing to say,' said Knowles in a flat voice. His wife, a superior-looking blonde some ten years his junior, stared aloofly ahead and wrapped her fur coat tighter around her. The early morning cold still clung to the room.

Slowly, Frost lit up a cigarette. A clatter of footsteps in the corridor outside made him look up in concern, but he relaxed as they passed on. He lowered his voice. 'I might be able to do a deal.'

Knowles' tiny eyes glinted. He was a pretty shrewd judge of character and he had this foul-mouthed tramp summed up as someone who could be bought right from the start. He leant forward. 'I'm listening.'

'The girl you filmed performing with your dog. Did you know she killed herself?'

Knowles lowered his gaze and found something on the floor that held his full attention. 'I heard something to that effect,' he said vaguely.

'It would do you a lot of good if we could stop it coming out in court,' said Frost.

'You could arrange that?' whispered Knowles.

'I can arrange for the videos of the girl and the dog to go missing. That part of the charge could not proceed and would not be mentioned in court – unless your side raised it, of course.'

'We're not likely to do that,' said Knowles, mentally working out how much this piece of good fortune was likely to cost him. 'Naturally, I would be extremely grateful if the tapes did go missing . . . extremely grateful. The death of the girl was unfortunate – nothing to do with me – but the court might not see it in that light.' He gave Frost a patronizing smile. 'Tell me how you would like me to express my gratitude?'

'You admit to all the other charges. Both of you. You don't dispute any of the facts. You plead guilty. You don't make us call any of the kids involved to give evidence. In return, the tapes go missing, which should knock at least three years off your sentence . . . and the girl's mother will never know what perverted things you pair of bastards made her daughter do.' He stood up and moved to the door. 'I want a "yes" or "no" right now, or the deal's off.'

Mullett strode up and down his office, pounding his fist, shaking his head in disbelief. 'You've lost a box of video tapes? Vital evidence in a serious case? I can't believe it. Even by your sloppy standards, this is disgraceful. I take it you've looked everywhere?'

'Everywhere,' mumbled the inspector, head bowed, looking very ashamed of himself.

'This entire operation was mismanaged from the start. You dashed into it, head first without any thought of the consequence should proof not be forthcoming.' He returned to his desk and looked again at the typed, signed statement on his desk. 'You can count yourself lucky that Knowles has decided to do the right thing and make a full confession of the other offences. It does show a certain amount of character. I'm sure it will count in his favour at court.'

'I'm sorry it turned out to be your personal friend, sir,' mumbled Frost, trying hard to suppress a grin of delight.

Mullett glared at him grim-faced. Two could lie if they wanted to. 'He's no friend of mine, Frost. I never trusted him from the start.'

Friday morning shift

Liz slammed the eggs and bacon on the table and stamped off back to the kitchen without a word. 'Thanks,' grunted Gilmore, eyeing with wary disfavour the flabby bacon floating in grease and the under-cooked eggs. He liked the bacon crisp and the eggs well done, but he held his tongue. She was spoiling for a fight and was just waiting for him to complain.

His knife sawed away at a tough chunk of meat which squeaked across the plate and defied all efforts to cut it. Liz returned with his tea. 'Anything wrong with the food?' she snapped.

'No, no – it's fine,' he lied. 'I'm not very hungry.' He risked a sip of the tea. Near-cold and milky when he liked it hot and strong. He replaced the cup on the saucer and made one more effort to restore peaceful relations. 'Look, Liz, I'm sorry.'

This was her chance. 'Sorry! I'm left on my own all night. You come in hours late, too tired to talk or do any bloody thing, then you tell me you've got to be out again. I never bloody see you.'

'It won't be for long, love, then things will be different.' He reached for her, but she shook him off.

'It's always *going* to be different, but it never bloody well is. I'm sick of your job, I'm sick of this dead and alive town, I'm sick of everything.' The door slammed in an angry explosion behind her.

Gilmore sighed and took his plate to the kitchen where he emptied it into the pedal bin. He hated to admit it to himself, but he was getting sick of Liz.

Frost wasn't feeling very happy either. That damn inventory form had reappeared. Mullett must have quarried deep into the filing tray in Allen's office where Frost had buried it and had transferred it to the top of his in-tray with a large, block-capitalled inscription in red felt-tip yelling WHY HASN'T THIS GONE OFF? Because I haven't bleeding sent it off, thought Frost, reading on. MUST GO OFF TODAY WITHOUT FAIL. SCM – the OR ELSE was implied.

Gilmore came in carrying a thick bacon sandwich and a mug of tea from the canteen. Frost brightened up until he realized Gilmore intended it for himself. 'Doesn't that wife of yours feed you?' he growled and was quite unprepared for Gilmore's slashing expression of vehemence.

Burton broke the tension by coming in to report.

'What's the position with Gauld?'

'He left home at 8.56,' Burton told him, 'and drove straight to Denton Hospital. He's been ferrying outpatients backwards and forwards. We're keeping him under surveillance.'

'Good,' nodded Frost. 'What have you found out about him?'

'Not much. He lives with his widowed mother. They moved to Denton some ten years ago from Birmingham. He's never had a permanent job – just temporary work, mainly driving. The neighbours like him. Apart from his hospital work, he helps out at the local Oxfam shop in his spare time.'

Frost gave a derisory snort. 'What else does he do? Cure the sick and raise the dead?' He thought for a while. 'Do the neighbours see him coming and going late at night?'

'Sometimes, sir. But you'd expect that with all the late-night coaches he drives.' Burton paused. 'I know you want to go for broke on him, Inspector, but it wouldn't hurt to keep a watch on some of the other coach drivers.'

'Then do it, son. As long as you don't let up on Gauld.'

'We could do with more men.'

'I could do with a new dick,' said Frost, 'but I've got to manage with what I've got.' He stared miserably at the inventory. 'You busy, son?' he asked Gilmore.

Gilmore backed towards the door. 'I'm due in court with Mrs Compton in twenty minutes.'

Frost flicked through the wad of information-demanding pages and shuddered. He chucked it back in his in-tray and reburied it. His internal phone buzzed. He scooped his mac from the hat-stand. 'Tell him I'm out,' he yelled from the corridor.

Burton picked up the phone. 'I'm afraid Mr Frost isn't here, sir,' he told the Divisional Commander.

The sound of the Westminster chimes reverberated inside the flat. A fat, motherly little woman in a green overall waddled into the hallway and opened the door. A shabbily dressed man twitched a shy smile. Not one of the regulars. She hadn't seen him before. 'I phoned,' he said.

She gave a welcoming smile to put him at ease. He looked so nervous. 'French lesson, isn't it? Miss Désirée's expecting you.' She led him through the hall into a dimly lit room with the curtains drawn. 'The gentleman who phoned,' she announced, then retired discreetly, closing the door with a gentle click behind her.

The woman sitting on the bed was in her late thirties and looked like a young Mae West. The loose-fitting red dressing gown she wore was carefully flapped open to display black bra, black knickers and black stockings which were held up by rosette, red garters. An over-brilliant smile clicked on automatically as she greeted her visitor. 'Don't be shy,' she purred in a thick French accent, 'I am Mademoiselle Désirée.'

'Hello, Doris,' said Frost, giving her a quick flash of his warrant card. 'How's your bunions?'

The smile withered and died with the French accent. 'Jack effing Frost! Well, you can piss off as soon as you like.'

'You can't get round me with sweet talk,' said Frost, helping himself to one of her cigarettes from a packet on the bed. He flopped into a chair and pulled a photograph from his pocket. 'Recognize him?'

She took the photograph and gave it a cursory glance. 'Can't place him,' she said, disdainfully handing it back.

'It's dark in here,' said Frost. 'Perhaps the light might be better down at the station.'

'All right. Haven't seen him for a while, but he used to be a regular. Every Wednesday just after five. His name's John Smith.'

'It's his John Thomas I'm interested in. What did he

pay for, Doris – straight sex, or did you have to tart it up, if you'll pardon the expression?'

'More or less straight sex – but I had to dress up.'

'As what?'

She crossed the room to a large fitted wardrobe and slid open the doors. Like the stock for a fancy dress ball, all sorts of bizarre costumes rustled and swung on hangers. On the floor of the wardrobe were whips, canes, a canvas strait-jacket, some handcuffs and various ropes, straps and chains. She selected a hanger and unhooked it from the rail. It held a black gym-slip, a white blouse, black knickers and thick dark stockings. 'He was kinky about schoolgirls,' she said. 'I had to wear this school uniform and act all bleeding coy. It didn't half get him excited.'

'It's getting me excited,' said Frost, standing up and stuffing the photograph of Bell back in his inside pocket. 'I only wish I had the time . . .'

Gilmore found Frost in the Murder Incident Room rummaging through the exhibits cupboard. 'You wanted me, Inspector?'

'Yes, son. Get the car. We're going to call on the schoolmaster.' He pulled out the plastic bag which held the shoes Paula Bartlett was wearing when they found her. He told Gilmore about his visit to the prostitute. 'That's clinched it for me, son. I'm going to nail the bastard.'

Gilmore hesitated. Frost's case was strong on suspicion, but pathetically weak on proof. 'How are you going to do that?'

'I might have to cheat a little,' said Frost, pushing the bag back into the exhibits cupboard, 'and if that doesn't work, I might have to cheat a lot.'

Bell led them through into his cold, cheerless lounge,

apologizing for the state of the place. 'I still haven't got over it.' He cleared some old newspapers from a chair, but they declined his invitation to sit.

'An official call, I'm afraid, sir,' said Frost, looking grim.

'Oh?' He straightened a few cushions and seemed more concerned at the state of the room than the unexpected visit of the two detectives.

'Probably nothing in it,' continued Frost. 'We get these crank calls all the time and we have to follow them up?

'Crank calls?' blinked Bell.

'Paula Bartlett, sir. We have a witness who claims he saw the girl in your house on the afternoon she went missing.'

'Here?' Bell frowned, finding the idea incredible. 'Oh no, Inspector, that's ridiculous.'

'I'm sure it's ridiculous,' continued Frost, 'but as I said, sir, we have to follow these things through. Just a formality, but do you mind if we have a look around the house?'

'Mind? Of course not. Look anywhere you like. It's all such a mess though, I'm afraid.'

'We're used to mess, sir,' Frost assured him. 'No need to come with us. We'll do it quicker on our own.' And he trotted up the stairs, Gilmore following close behind. The first door they tried led to the master bedroom, the unmade bed a shambles, discarded clothes everywhere. Frost grinned. 'This will do fine. Start searching.' He sat on the bed, smoking, as Gilmore poked around, dragging out the dressing table, peering behind the wardrobe.

'It would help,' grunted Gilmore, shouldering the wardrobe back into position, then climbing on a chair so he could look on the top, 'if I knew what I was supposed to be looking for.'

Frost puffed out three smoke rings then speared one with his finger. 'We're looking for proof the girl was in the house.'

Gilmore climbed down from the chair and rubbed the dust from his hands. 'We're never going to find it after two months.'

'I don't know,' said Frost, pushing himself up from the bed and wandering over to the dressing table. 'There's something poking out down there.'

He bent down and came up holding a shoe. A flat-heeled, lace-up brown shoe. Neatly written inside, in biro, the name 'Paula Bartlett'.

Gilmore stared in confusion. 'I looked there,' he said. 'I couldn't have missed it.' He snatched the shoe from Frost, his nose wrinkling in distaste as a clinging smell of decay floated up. 'This is one of the shoes we found on the body. You took it from the exhibits cupboard.'

'Keep your voice down,' hissed Frost.

'You're going to plant evidence?' croaked Gilmore. 'You fool! You'll never get away with it.' He thrust the shoe back into Frost's hand. 'You can forget it as far as I'm concerned. I want no part of it.'

'Play along with me,' pleaded Frost.

'No bloody way.' Gilmore's mind was racing. He couldn't wait to get back to the station. This was something Mullett had to be told about.

'Please!' said Frost.

The old twit looked so pathetic, Gilmore relented. 'Just don't involve me,' he said.

Bell, slumped in a chair, straightened up as the two officers came back in. He forced out a smile which wasn't returned. The older detective's face was grim and doom-laden. 'Is there anything the matter?'

Frost didn't answer. He just held out the shoe in mute accusation.

Bell backed away, shaking his head in disbelief. 'I don't understand.'

'Paula was only wearing one shoe when we found her, sir. We kept this information from the press. In searching your bedroom we found this. It matches perfectly the other shoe we found on the body.'

The schoolmaster's face was a picture of incredulity. 'It's impossible. I don't understand . . .'

Frost felt the familiar, icy quiver of doubt. He was so sure he had the killer that he hadn't fully considered the serious consequences of what would happen if his bluff failed. 'In your bedroom,' he repeated. 'There's no way it could have got there by accident.' He was aware of the irony even as he said it.

Still the man shook his head.

'I've had a chat with your prostitute friend, sir. Very interesting. Did your wife dress up in kinky schoolgirl clothes for you as well?'

Bell's head jerked back as if he had been struck. He bit his lip tightly and shuddered, his face screwed up as if on the verge of bursting into tears. He went through the pantomime of searching hopefully in the empty cigarette box, then gratefully accepted one from Frost. 'We all do things we're ashamed of, Inspector. I was hurting no one. As I told you, my wife was incapable of making love during the last months of her illness. I had to find an outlet somewhere.'

'And you found it in poor little Paula Bartlett? You raped her.'

'No!' screamed Bell

'You strangled her, and rammed her in a sack like so much rubbish.'

'No! No, no, no.'

'So how did the shoe get in your bedroom?' asked Frost, hooking it on his finger and slowly swinging it from side to side.

Bell stared at Frost, his gaze unwavering. Because you put it there, you bastard, his expression seemed to say. Unflinching, Frost stared back. Gilmore's pen hovered over a page where nothing was written down.

Slowly, Bell pulled his eyes away from Frost, away from the shoe. He drew deeply on the cigarette, holding the smoke in his lungs, then gradually releasing it and watching the air currents catch it and tear it to shreds. Then he reached out a hand towards Frost. He wanted the shoe. He took it, turned it over slowly, then gave it back. 'You have a witness who saw her in the house?'

'Yes,' lied Frost.

He crushed out the cigarette in an ashtray and buried his face in his hands. 'I'd better tell you about it. Yes, Paula was here that day. I should never have kept quiet. It was stupid. But I was terrified you'd think I'd killed her. She was alive when she left here, I promise you.' Again he looked in the cigarette box, again seeming surprised to find it empty. Gratefully he accepted another from Frost.

'When I got back from the cemetery, I was soaked to the skin. There'd been a cloudburst during the funeral.'

Frost nodded. This part, at least, was true.

'To my surprise, Paula Bartlett was in the kitchen. All she was wearing was one of my dressing gowns and her shoes. She was putting her wet clothes in the tumble drier. She told me she'd been caught in the storm on her bike and had got absolutely drenched. She thought I wouldn't mind if she dried off in my house. I could have done without it that day of all days, but of course, I agreed.'

'How had she got in?' Frost asked.

'The back door wasn't locked.'

'Why was she out in the storm – she should have been at school?'

'She said she intended skipping the first lesson – she didn't like the relief teacher who was taking my place.'

'I see.' Frost signalled for him to continue.

'We had a meal from the deep freeze in the kitchen, then she went upstairs to put on her dry clothes. She left here shortly after one. I thought she was going straight to school. I last saw her pushing her bike up that path.' He pointed through the window. 'And that's the gospel truth, Inspector.'

'I don't think so, sir,' said Frost, shaking his head sadly and sounding genuinely sorry. 'You say she pedalled away into the sunset on her bike?'

'Yes!' insisted Bell.

'Wearing only one bloody shoe?' asked Frost, holding it accusingly under the man's nose.

Gilmore, his pen hovering, held his breath. Frost was pushing his luck. If the schoolmaster remembered both shoes were on the body, he'd realize that there was no way the other shoe could have been found in the bedroom and that Frost's case was built solely on a bluff.

But Frost's luck held. Bell was confused. His expression kept changing as various alternatives to his story flitted across his mind and were hastily discarded. His best bet would have been to keep quiet. To say nothing. To let the police do the proving. But he'd kept quiet for too long. He had to tell someone.

'The girl had sex before she died, sir,' Frost gently prompted. 'And we found her shoe in your bedroom.'

Bell shrank visibly, and stared down at the carpet. 'I'd like to make a statement.'

Concealing his relief, Frost gave the statutory caution and signalled for Gilmore to start a fresh page. 'When you're ready, sir.'

'We had lunch. I should have suspected something. Paula kept *"accidentally"* letting the dressing gown slip open. Then she went upstairs to get dressed. She called me. She was in our bedroom. Sitting on the bed. She was naked. She was wearing lipstick – thick lipstick. She looked like a child tart. The girl was offering herself to me.' He paused, then glared defiantly. 'What the hell! What the bloody hell! I suppose you think I'm some sort of animal?'

Frost said nothing.

The man's shoulders shook as he covered his face. 'When it comes down to it we're all bloody animals.' He stood up and stared out of the window. 'We made love. Half-way through she began to struggle. She yelled for me to stop. Then she started screaming rape. I panicked. I grabbed her by the throat to stop her screaming. We struggled. She wouldn't stop screaming. Suddenly she went still. I must have squeezed too hard. I didn't mean it . . . as God is my witness, I didn't mean it. I tried the kiss of life, I tried everything . . . but she was dead.'

'Did you think of sending for a doctor?' asked Frost.

'A doctor?' Bell frowned and his hand flicked away the question as futile. 'It would have been no use. She was dead.' He paused. The only sound in the room was the slight rustle as Gilmore turned the page of his notebook. Bell's head twisted to the sergeant, as if suddenly realizing that everything he was saying was being taken down. 'I didn't know what to do. I was so frightened . . . so appalled. I tried to think. I had to find somewhere to hide the body and I suddenly thought of that crypt. I thought it would at least be a Christian place of burial for the poor child.' At this Frost gave an involuntary snort of derision, but Bell didn't care what Frost thought. This was the statement that would be read out in court, the statement the jury would hear. 'That night, I took the poor child's remains out to the car and drove to the cemetery. As reverently as possible I put her in the crypt. I said a prayer for her. I never meant to hurt her.'

'Before you did that, you reverently burnt the poor child with a blow-lamp,' said Frost. 'What sort of kindly, Christian act was that?'

He bowed his head. 'Genetic fingerprints. I'd read somewhere you could positively identify a sperm sample. I was trying to destroy the evidence.'

'The newspapers?' prompted Frost.

'I wanted it to look as if she hadn't finished her round, so I took the newspaper she had brought and put it in her bag, meaning to dump it somewhere with the bike. As I was passing Greenway's cottage, I noticed his paper sticking out of the letter-box, so I took that as well.' He waited until Gilmore's pen had finished writing this all down before adding, 'I bitterly regret the pain and anguish I caused Paula's family. It was an accident. I shall live with the scars for the rest of my life.'

Frost stood up and took him by the arm. 'So will the poor cow's parents, sir.' They helped him on with his coat and led him out to the car.

Mullett was angry. He paced up and down Frost's tiny office, shaking with rage. 'I've told you time and time again, Frost, catching the criminal isn't enough. We've got to be able to prove our case in court. What on earth did you think you were doing?'

'I thought I was solving a murder case,' answered

Frost. He didn't expect praise, but he was unprepared for Mullett's fury.

'By slipshod, unorthodox methods? By sneaking official evidence from the evidence cupboard? Planting it in a suspect's house? For heaven's sake, man, don't you realize the risk?'

'Risk?' asked Frost.

'What other solid evidence do you have against him apart from his own admission?'

'Nothing yet,' said Frost.

'Has he signed the statement he's given you?'

'Not yet. It's being typed now.' He nodded towards Gilmore who was typing at speed and pretending not to listen to Frost's bollocking. He ripped the last page from the machine and hurried from the room.

'What if he refuses to sign?' demanded Mullett. 'What if he decides to plead not guilty in court and claims that the statement was obtained by means of a trick . . . by the planting of false evidence? If this all blows up in our faces, Inspector, I'm distancing myself from the whole affair. It was done behind my back, against official instructions and contrary to my specific orders. Don't expect me to carry the can for your shortcomings. Don't expect me to stand by you.'

'I'd never expect that, sir,' said Frost, and he had never sounded more sincere. He looked up anxiously as Gilmore came back, the statement in his hand. 'Well?'

'He signed it,' said Gilmore, slipping the typescript in a folder.

'He can still retract it,' snapped Mullett, cutting short Frost's audible sigh of relief. 'And then we haven't got a shred of legitimate evidence against him.'

'We've got quite a bit, sir, actually,' said Gilmore.

'Forensic have just phoned an interim report. They've turned his house over and found strands of the girl's hair on the plush velvet headboard of the bed. Bell had changed and washed all the bedding, but there's definite traces of blood on the mattress corresponding to the girl's blood group.'

'Oh!' said Mullett, sounding almost disappointed. 'That's . . . good news. Perhaps more than you deserve, Inspector, but good news.' He took the statement from Gilmore and ran his eye over it.

'I almost feel sorry for the poor sod,' said Frost.

Mullett's eyebrows arched. 'You feel sorry?'

'A choice young naked piece of nooky offering herself. I wouldn't like to bet I'd have turned my nose up at it,' said Frost. 'Just his rotten luck she turned out to be a teaser.'

'That's just Bell's version. You surely don't believe it?'

'Yes, I do.' He turned to Gilmore. 'He said she'd put on lipstick. Do you remember when we searched Paula's room – in her wastepaper bin?'

Gilmore thought, then nodded. He remembered. 'An empty lipstick packet!'

'Plain little Paula never used make-up! The poor cow had a crush on him. She had it all planned in advance what she was going to do. And now she's dead, his life is ruined and when it all comes out in court it will break her parents' hearts. I thought I was going to enjoy bringing the bastard in on this one, but now . . .' He shrugged and pulled open his drawer for a packet of export only.

Mullett gave an uneasy smile. He didn't quite see what Frost was driving at. 'Another crime solved, and that's all that matters, Inspector.'

The phone rang. Gilmore answered it, then offered it to Mullett. 'For you, sir. The Chief Constable.'

Mullett tugged his uniform straight and stiffened as he

took the phone. 'Yes, sir . . . we've got him . . . and he's given us a full confession. And I modestly claim credit for our team work, sir. The good old Denton team have turned up trumps again.' He listened and smirked, oblivious to the faces Frost was pulling behind his back.

The other phone rang. Frost answered it. He listened and his face went grim. He snatched his mac from the hat-stand and jerked a thumb for Gilmore to follow. 'Another Ripper victim. An old lady. The bastard's nearly decapitated her.'

It was like seeing the same tired B-movie over and over again. The tiny over-furnished room. The smell, a mixture of blood and of too many people packed in too restricted a space. The atmosphere was frowsty with sweat, aftershave and tobacco smoke. 'Open a window,' yelled Frost. 'It stinks in here.'

Everyone was busy. The SOC officer, draped with an array of Japanese cameras and leather cylinders of lenses, blazing away with a Canon, the Forensic team, crawling over the carpet, the fingerprint man, whistling tunelessly to himself as he dusted away with his little brush, splashing white powder everywhere. Frost had almost to fight his way through to the corpse. 'Everyone outside,' he yelled. 'You can come back in when I've finished.' He waited while they shuffled out, then he approached the body.

She sat in the rust and grey armchair, her dull eyes fixed on an old 19-inch black and white television set which, encircled by a stockade of knick-knacks and framed photographs, stood on a rickety coffee table. Frost touched the set. It was still warm.

'It was still on when I got here,' said Detective Constable Burton. 'I switched it off.'

Frost nodded and haunched down to study the Ripper's

handiwork. A jagged gash on her neck had gouted blood which glinted stickily down the front of her brown floral dress. Blood from stab wounds in her stomach had leaked to form a puddle on her lap. Her left hand dangled down the side of the chair, the fist tightly clenched. His eyes travelled slowly up to her face, the wrinkled flesh bluish white against her sparse grey hair. He leaned closer to examine the hair, which was in untidy disarray. 'What do you make of that, son?' Gilmore crouched down beside him.

'He came on her from behind,' said a familiar voice and they looked up at the slightly swaying figure of Dr Maltby who had been waiting in the bedroom. He nodded a greeting, then prodded a finger at her hair. 'The killer came at her from behind, grabbed her hair and yanked up her head. Then he cut her throat. The head's only hanging by a thread of flesh at the back of the neck, so I wouldn't shake her if I were you.'

They backed gingerly away from the body, Frost carefully lowering himself into the matching armchair.

'When he cut her throat,' continued the doctor, 'he sliced through her vocal cords in the process, so she wouldn't have been able to scream, even if she wanted to.'

'I'm sure she bloody wanted to,' said Frost, poking a cigarette in his mouth and passing the packet around. 'I reckon the poor cow would have given her right arm to have been able to scream.'

Grunting his thanks, Maltby accepted a light and moved round to face the body. 'The killer then came round to here and stabbed her four times in the stomach.' He mimed four stabbing thrusts. 'That done, being a neat and tidy person, while she was still bleeding to death and drowning in her own blood, he wiped the knife blade clean, just there.' He indicated a wide smear on the skirt of the dress.

Frost took this all in with a sniff. 'I won't ask how you deduced all that, doc, because I don't suppose I'd understand a flaming word. Time of death?'

Gently, the doctor felt the woman's legs. 'Rigor's fully developed and she feels cold. It would need rectal temperature readings to be precise, but I shall leave that treat to our pathologist friend . . . he can be the one to have her head fall off in his lap. At a rough guess she's been dead fourteen to eighteen hours.' He jerked back his sleeve to read his watch. 'Say between nine o'clock last night and one o'clock this morning.'

Frost dropped to his knees and, very carefully, lifted the woman's left arm. 'Look at the way her fist is clenched.'

'Show me,' said Maltby, lowering himself, none too steadily and kneeling on the floor. He took the hand and focused his eyes with difficulty. 'Looks like a cadaveric spasm . . . you sometimes get it with violent death. Hello . . .' He looked closer. Something white. The corner of a piece of paper was protruding slightly. Frost snatched the hand and tried to force the cold fingers open.

Maltby stood up and distanced himself from the operation. 'Careful,' he said. 'You'll have her damn head off.'

Frost snapped his fingers at Gilmore. 'Hold her head, son.'

'Eh?' said Gilmore.

'She won't bloody bite you.'

Steeling himself, Gilmore took the head in his hands while Frost tugged at the tightly closed fingers. The head felt cold and as fragile as a blown egg. He gritted his teeth and willed the inspector to hurry.

'The pathologist won't like you interfering with his corpse,' warned Maltby gleefully.

'Sod the pathologist,' muttered Frost, grunting as the fingers opened and the hand suddenly went limp. Gilmore almost cried out as the body seemed to quiver and he swore he could feel the head parting from the trunk. Carefully and very slowly, like a man building a tottering house of cards, he took his hands away.

The piece of paper fluttered to the ground. It was a carefully folded £5 note. There was something else pressed tightly into the palm, leaving an impression in the flesh. Three pound coins.

Frost placed the coins in his open palm and stared at them. They told him nothing. He retrieved the banknote from the floor, pushed all the money back into the dead hand and tried to close the fist around it so the pathologist wouldn't know what he had done. But the dead hand remained limp and let the money drop.

'You've done it now,' called Maltby, moving quickly to the door. 'If you'd asked me I'd have told you that you couldn't put it back again.'

'I'll throw the bloody head at you if you don't hop it,' bellowed Frost as the door clicked shut.

Gathering up the money, he deposited it on the coffee table alongside the knick-knacks, then sank back in the chair. 'All right, Burton, let's have some details. I don't even know the poor cow's name.'

Burton flipped open his notebook. 'Mrs Julia Fussell, aged seventy-five, a widow, one son, married, two kids.'

Frost groaned. 'Don't tell me I've got to break the news to him.'

'He emigrated to Australia last year.'

Frost brightened up. 'Good for him. Carry on, son. Who found her?'

'Her next-door neighbour, Mrs Beatrice Stacey. She knocked to see if the old dear wanted any shopping, didn't get a reply, so let herself in with a spare key. I haven't got much sense out of her. She's having hysterics next door.'

'I'll see her in a minute,' said Frost.

'The pattern's the same as Mrs Watson, yesterday,' Burton went on. 'No sign of forcible entry, apparently nothing taken – the bedroom's undisturbed – and money left in her purse.'

A glum nod from Frost. He wandered over to the front door which was fitted with bolts top and bottom, and a security chain. 'As you say, son, exactly the same as that poor old cow yesterday. He comes late at night, but she lets him in and then she calmly sits down to watch the telly so he can creep up behind her and cut her bloody throat.' He examined the security chain. Quite a flimsy affair. 'You said her purse was untouched. Where is it?'

Burton walked over to a small walnut-veneered sideboard and tugged open a drawer. Using his handkerchief, he took out a worn red leather purse and handed it to the inspector. 'There's eighty-five quid in there.'

Holding it by the handkerchief, Frost flicked through the banknotes. All new £5 notes, crisp and consecutively numbered. The numbers tallied with the note taken from her hand. He chewed at a loose scrap of skin on his finger as he thought this over. 'Right. Try this out for size. It's the same pattern as yesterday. The Ripper's coming to fit a new security chain for her. She's waiting for him, the money all ready from her purse. She lets him in, sits down, holding the money tight in her hot little hand, and watches the telly while the nice man fits the chain for her. But the nice man just creeps up behind the poor cow and cuts her throat, then he stabs her in the stomach, wipes his knife on her dress and off he goes, all happy.'

'Then this puts Gauld in the clear,' said Gilmore. 'He was driving his coach until ten and we watched his house until past midnight.'

'He could have gone out again after we left,' said Frost, furious with himself for giving up the surveillance so early. 'If Doc Maltby is right the time of death could have been as late as one o'clock.'

'You don't call at one in the morning to fit a chain,' pointed out Gilmore. 'And old girls of seventy-five don't sit up all night watching television.'

Frost gave a rueful sniff. The sergeant was right. This was his star suspect flushed down the sewer. He pushed the money back into the purse, then noticed something else in the centre compartment. Membership cards for the Reef Bingo Club and for the All Saints Senior Citizens' Club.

'All Saints?' exclaimed Gilmore excitedly. Frost's suspect might be a non-runner, but his own one was fast coming up on the rails. 'That bloody curate comes from All Saints.'

The pathologist studied the rectal thermometer, gave it a shake, then wiped it clean before replacing it in his bag. His lips moved silently as he did a mental calculation. 'In my opinion death occurred between midnight and one o'clock this morning.'

Gilmore registered dismay. 'Not earlier?' They had seen the curate outside the cemetery just after midnight last night and it was over half an hour later that they left him to go on to the vicarage.

'If it was earlier,' sniffed the pathologist, snapping shut his bag, 'then I would have said so.' He shouted down the stairs for the mortuary attendants to come up and collect the body then shafted a glare of disapproval at Frost who had come bounding back into the flat, grinning all over his face. 'I've relayed my preliminary findings to your sergeant.'

'Thanks, doc,' said Frost, not sounding very interested. He grabbed Gilmore by the arm and pulled him to one side.

'Autopsy at four,' called the pathologist, buttoning up his coat.

'Right,' said Frost. He wasn't interested in the autopsy. By four o'clock the killer should be behind bars.

But Gilmore got in with his own bad news first. 'Death occurred after midnight, so that clears the curate.' He waved away Frost's offered cigarette. 'So now we haven't got a single flaming suspect.'

'Yes, we have, son,' beamed Frost, sending his cigarette packet on a round tour of the room. 'Our luck had to change some time and now it's happened. I've been chatting up the old dear next door. First, the dead woman had a job getting off to sleep. She was always up watching television until three or four in the morning. Second, she'd told her neighbour she was going to have a stronger chain fitted and guess who was going to do it?'

'Gauld?'

'She didn't know his name but it was that nice young man who drove the mini-coach that took her to bingo.'

'Did she say when he was coming to do the job?'

'No, son. But he came last night. Late. After Joe Soap pulled off the bloody surveillance.'

'How do you know?'

'She didn't tell her neighbour *when* he was coming. But she told her how much he was going to charge her. Eight quid.'

Gilmore whistled. The £5 note and three pound coins in the dead hand. 'It sounds too good to be true.'

'You know my motto,' smirked Frost. 'Never kick a gift horse up the fundamental orifice.' He noticed Burton hovering. 'What is it, son?'

'Forensic have turned up a rogue fingerprint, sir. On the sideboard. Looks recent.'

Frost beamed. 'Luck could be running our way for once. I think the time has come to bring Gauld in.'

Friday afternoon shift

The coach drew up at the old lady's house. The driver sprang from his seat and opened the door, steadying her as she descended the steep step from the coach to the pavement. 'Can you manage all right from here, my love?' he asked. She nodded and waved her thanks and hobbled up to her front gate as the coach went on its way.

There was only one other passenger. A dishevelled individual hunched up in the rear seat, puffing away solidly on the journey back from the bingo hall. Gauld hadn't seen him before. He slowed down at the traffic lights. Damn. The scruffy man was making his way down the aisle. Not one of those chatty sods, he hoped. The seat behind him creaked as the man lowered himself down.

'Drop you off at the Market Square?' Gauld asked.

'Eagle Lane,' mumbled the man. 'Opposite the police station.'

As he turned into Eagle Lane he noticed in his rear-view mirror a police car close behind him. When he pulled up outside the police station, the car stopped even though it had plenty of room to pass. His passenger shuffled out, squeezing past two uniformed policemen who suddenly appeared at the coach door. 'Mr Ronald Gauld?' asked one of them. 'I wonder if you'd mind popping into the station for a couple of minutes.' The other policeman leant across and switched off the ignition.

They took him through to a small, functional room, sparsely furnished with a plain light oak table and three chairs. In the corner of the room a young thickset chap in a grey suit was sitting, a notebook open on his knee. Another man, whose scowl seemed permanent, was standing, leaning up against the wall. He pointed to a chair for Gauld to sit. The door opened as a third man came in. Gauld blinked in surprise. It was the scruffy passenger from his coach. 'Frost,' announced the man, 'Detective Inspector Jack Frost.'

The lino squealed as Frost dragged a chair over to sit opposite Gauld. He then laid out on the table a green folder, a pack of cigarettes, a box of matches and the large manila envelope containing the possessions the station sergeant had asked Gauld to empty from his pockets. This done, Frost smiled benevolently and helped himself to a cigarette.

Gauld wriggled in his chair. He cleared his throat and tried to keep his voice steady. 'What's this all about?'

Frost frowned. 'Haven't you been told?' He swung round to the man with the notebook. 'Didn't you tell him?' A headshake. Frost tutted with mock exasperation, then slowly took a match from the box and struck it on the table. 'It's about Mrs Fussell.'

Gauld frowned as if trying to remember. 'Never heard of her.'

'Oh dear,' exclaimed Frost, looking worried. He turned to the scowler. 'We might have the wrong man, Sergeant.' Looking puzzled, he scrabbled through the green folder and plucked out some typed pages. 'All these witnesses must be lying.' Back to Gauld. 'You'd swear on oath you don't know her, sir?' Before Gauld had a chance to answer, he added, 'What about Mrs Elizabeth Winters, Roman Road, Denton? Surely you're not going to tell us you don't know her?'

'I know lots of people. I'm a coach driver. I drive people about all the time. I don't necessarily know their names.'

'Then here's an easy one – Mary Haynes.'

'I've just told . . .' He blinked and stopped dead, his expression freezing as if he had just realized what the inspector was on about. 'Wait a minute! I've just twigged. Haynes . . . Winters! They were both murdered! Are you trying to pin them on me?'

'Yes,' replied Frost, simply. 'That's exactly what we're trying to do.' He shook out the contents of the manila envelope and raked through Gauld's possessions. There was a colour photograph of a grey-haired lady smiling doubtfully at the camera. He picked it up and studied it carefully. 'I don't recognize this one. When did you murder her?'

Gauld snatched up the photograph. 'That's my mother, you bastard!'

'Ah!' said Frost with an enlightened nod. He studied his notes. 'Father died when you were three, mother alive and well.'

'She's not well!' retorted Gauld. 'She's got a bad heart.'

'Sorry to hear that,' said Frost. 'Still, better a bad heart than having your throat cut. Any objection to our taking your fingerprints?'

'What happens if I object?'

'We'll take them anyway, so why cause bad feeling?'

A young uniformed officer was summoned to take the prints. Frost waited patiently until the task was completed, then whispered something to the officer who nodded and left.

'I ought to have a solicitor,' said Gauld.

Frost seemed astonished. 'You're innocent! What do you want a solicitor for?'

'Because I think you bastards are trying to frame me for something I haven't done, that's why.'

'Oh no.' Frost sounded hurt. 'I might frame you for something you had done, but not otherwise.'

The scowler moved forward. 'All the murder victims travelled on your coach.'

Gauld twisted in his chair to face the questioner. 'So what? Hundreds of people travel on my coach.'

'Where were you last Sunday afternoon?' barked the detective sergeant.

'I don't know,' smirked Gauld. 'Where were you?'

The door opened and the fingerprint man returned to murmur in the inspector's ear. Frost's eyes gleamed with satisfaction. 'All right, Gauld. You can stop the pretence. We've got you.'

'Have you really? he said cockily. 'I'm shaking with fright.'

'You'll be shitting yourself in a minute,' said Frost. 'You told me earlier you didn't know a Mrs Julia Fussell.'

'I said I didn't know the name.'

'You were going to fit a stronger security chain on her front door.'

Gauld leant back in his chair. 'Ah – now I'm with you. Little old dear – about seventy-five. Lives in Victoria Court.'

'So you do know her!' said Gilmore.

'I didn't know her name. I always call her Ma.' He

looked disturbed. 'What about her? Nothing's happened to her, has it?'

'You called on her late last night to fit the security chain.'

'No, I didn't. I was going to, but I felt tired, so I had an early night.'

Gilmore, standing directly behind him, bent down. 'You lying bastard. You went there and killed her.'

Gauld's knuckles whitened as he gripped the edge of his chair. 'Killed? You mean . . . she's dead? That poor old lady is dead?'

'Don't act the bloody innocent. You know damn well she's dead,' hissed Gilmore.

Gauld just stared straight ahead, slack-jawed, head moving from side to side in disbelief. Then his eyes narrowed. 'And you're accusing me of killing her?'

'That's right,' beamed Frost. 'You got careless this time. You left a fingerprint behind.'

'A fingerprint!' echoed Gauld, eyes wide open as if understanding for the first time. 'So that's why you think I'm the killer? Would you like me to give you a statement?'

'If you want to give us one, we'll take it down, sir,' said Frost, signalling to Burton who turned to a fresh page in his notebook. Frost was vaguely worried. The man was looking far too smug and self-assured. Could he possibly have made a mistake? No. His every instinct told him that this smirking little bastard had cut, slashed and mutilated.

When he saw Burton was ready, Gauld began. 'I am making this statement freely, without any inducements being offered, solely to help the police find the perpetrator of this terrible crime.' He paused to let Burton catch up with him. 'On 14th November, around ten o'clock in the evening, I was returning from the Reef Bingo Club with a party of senior citizens. Amongst my passengers was a lady I now know to be Mrs Julia Fussell, who expressed herself as being very nervous because of the killings of old people that were taking place and which the police seemed powerless to prevent. When we pulled up outside her destination, Victoria Court, I offered to escort her up to her flat. She accepted. At her door, she gave me her key. I opened the door, had a quick look around inside, and was able to assure her that all was well. I told her that her door chain was inadequate and suggested I fitted a stronger one when I got the chance. She accepted my offer. I then returned to my coach and continued dropping off my passengers. This may serve to explain why my fingerprints were found inside the flat and assist the police to eliminate me from their enquiries so they can concentrate on finding the real killer.'

A pause. The detectives shuffled their feet and cleared their throats. Gilmore shot a glance across to Frost who was looking very worried. 'You're saying that this happened on the 14th . . . the day before the killing?'

'That's right. I've got a coach-load of witnesses if you don't believe me.'

'We'll check them out,' said Frost, but he knew they would corroborate Gauld's story. This slimy sod was too clever by half and Frost wasn't anywhere near clever enough. He tugged the list of murder dates and times from the folder and began rattling them off one by one. 'Where were you on these dates?'

Gauld shrugged. 'I don't know. Probably at work, driving.'

'You weren't,' barked Gilmore. 'We've checked.'

Mockingly, Gauld knuckled his brow, then beamed. 'If

I wasn't at work, then I probably stayed in and kept my mother company. I'll ask her when I get home.'

'We can save you the trouble,' Frost told him. 'We've got a team searching your house now. One of my men is having a word with your dear old mum this very minute.' He jerked back as Gauld lunged forward, all composure gone.

'My mother's got a heart condition. If any harm comes to her, I'll kill you . . .'

'You know all about killing, don't you,' said Frost, getting in quickly while the man was rattled.

The only sound was Gauld's heavy breathing as he fought to control his temper. Then he smiled. 'I'm not taking any more of your insults, Inspector. You either charge me, or I'm walking straight out of that door.'

'You'll go when I say you can go,' snapped Frost, frowning as someone knocked. He didn't want to be disturbed. He wanted to get Gauld rattled again. The door opened. Detective Sergeant Hanlon, not looking like a man with good news to impart, beckoned him out. Hanlon had been leading the team searching Gauld's house.

'We tore the house apart,' reported Hanlon. 'We found nothing. No bank books, no money we can tie in with the killing, no sign of blood on his clothes or shoes . . . nothing!'

'There must be some bloodstains,' insisted Frost. 'The pathologist said he would have been swimming in the bleeding stuff.'

'Forensic have double-checked. Not a trace. And to make matters worse, his mother swears blind he was with her on each of the murder nights.'

'Then she's lying,' said Frost. 'He's as guilty as arse-holes.' He scuffed the brown lino moodily. 'What about his car? Did you check that for blood?'

Hanlon nodded. 'Forensic have given it the works – nothing.'

Frost treated the lino to an extra hard kick. Things were not working out. His heart sank as the brisk clatter of polished shoes announced the approach of the Divisional Commander, all eager for news of yet another triumph for the Denton team.

'We've hit a couple of minor snags,' Frost told him. 'We've found sod all clues and his mother's given him a watertight alibi.'

Mullett's jaw dropped. 'But you told me you had conclusive evidence. A fingerprint!'

'It wasn't so conclusive as we thought, Super. He explained it away.'

'The house search?'

'We found nothing,' said Hanlon.

Mullett switched his gaze from Hanlon to Frost. 'So what hard evidence have you got?'

Frost shuffled his feet. All he now had was a gut reaction. He knew Gauld was the Ripper. He couldn't prove it, but he knew.

'Your silence gives me the answer I expected,' snapped Mullett. 'You've blown this, Frost. You jumped in feet first without checking your facts. If he is the Ripper, which is by no means certain, all you've done is put him on his guard. Without evidence, there's no way we can hold him.' His lips tightened. 'Thank goodness Inspector Allen is coming back on Monday and we can start getting things done properly.' He spun on his heel and marched back up the corridor, pausing only to punch out one last below-the-belt blow. 'The inventory?'

'Almost done,' called Frost.

'I can tell County it will go off tonight?'

'Without fail,' Frost assured him. Tell the buggers what they want to hear, then make your excuses later was his philosophy. Absently, he pulled out his cigarettes, only to realize he was already smoking.

'What are you going to do?' asked Hanlon.

'I'm nipping round to see Gauld's mother and try and get her to change her story.'

'Be careful – she's got a weak heart,' Hanlon reminded him.

'And I've got a weak bladder, so that makes us quits.' Halfway down the corridor he turned and yelled, 'Probably a waste of time, but send someone down to check out the Oxfam shop where Gauld works.'

Gauld's house was just round the corner from Jubilee Terrace where they had found the mummified body all those weeks . . . no days . . . ago. A small cul-de-sac of older-type properties, jammed on both sides of the road with parked cars so Frost had to leave the station runabout round the corner.

The hinges of the black iron gate grated as he walked through. The woman who answered the door stepped back in alarm. She had been expecting the return of her son and here was this man in a dirty mac, a knitted maroon scarf trailing untidily from his neck. She was about to shut the door on him when he held up a piece of plastic with a coloured photograph on it. 'Detective Inspector Frost,' he announced.

She peered at the photograph, then at the man. There was a slight resemblance. 'I've had enough of police. Where's my son?'

He gave his reassuring smile. 'Ronnie's fine. He's having a cup of tea down at the station.'

'I've got his supper waiting,' she said.

Frost sniffed the savoury warm smell floating from inside the house. 'Lucky devil. I'd like a couple of words, if I may.'

She took another look at his warrant card. 'Are you *sure* you're a policeman?'

'Fairly sure,' said Frost, following her down the passage, 'although my boss has his doubts at times.'

The radio was mumbling away, just around the limit of audibility. The tiny kitchen was warm from the gas oven which breathed out sausage and onion. On the small table a red and white checked cloth was laid with knife and fork and HP sauce. One place only. Frost unwound his scarf, pulled the green file from his pocket and sat down. He sniffed again. 'Smells good.'

She opened the oven door and peeked inside. 'It'll spoil soon. When is he coming home?'

'Difficult to say,' Frost hedged. She moved a chair to the table and sat opposite him. Grey-haired, she was probably in her early sixties, but looked older. A nervous smile twitched on and off and her hands were constantly moving, plucking at her apron, smoothing out the table-cloth, straightening the knife and fork. A bag of nerves, he thought. He tried his smile out again. 'I'm not stopping you from making us both a cup of tea, am I?'

'You've got a cheek!' she said. But she filled the kettle from the sink. 'This isn't a restaurant, you know.' A plop as she lit the gas. 'Why are you still holding him?'

'Murder is a very serious charge, Mrs Gauld.' Her back stiffened as she reached for the tea caddy, but her face was composed and apparently unconcerned when she turned. From the hooks on the dresser she took two cups, her hands shaking a little as she set them down.

'He's a good boy,' she said flatly, 'a very good boy.'

A larger version of the photograph taken from Gauld's

wallet looked down from the top of the dresser. 'Does he miss his father?' asked Frost.

She frowned. 'His father died when Ronnie was three. He hardly remembers him.'

Frost 'tutted' sympathetically. 'He couldn't have been very old. How did he die?'

She looked away. 'He killed himself.' At Frost's start of surprise, she added, 'He used to get very depressed. He threw himself under a train at New Street station.'

'And you had to bring Ronnie up on your own?'

The tea in the pot was given a vigorous stir. 'I had to go to work. His gran brought him up.' She put the lid back on the teapot and filled the two cups. 'It wasn't a very happy time for him. She was very strict. She used to beat him. Poor little mite.' She pushed the tea across.

'I'm sorry to hear that.' He tried to conceal his excitement, but his hand wasn't steady as he spooned in the sugar. Whatever vague doubts he might have had about Gauld being the Ripper were now dispelled. He endeavoured to keep his voice casual. 'I suppose, being beaten by his granny made him hate old people?'

Her expression changed. 'What are you trying to make me say?'

'We both know what this is about, Mrs Gauld. He's your son and you want to protect him. I understand that. But he's killed four people. He could kill more.'

She thrust out her chin defiantly. 'Drink your tea and go!'

Frost took out the list of dates of the killings and waved it at her. 'You didn't tell my colleague the truth, Mrs Gauld. Ronnie wasn't with you on any of these nights. He was out killing old people. He gets a kick out of it.'

'I don't tell lies,' she said. He stared at her. She wouldn't meet his gaze and turned her head away.

He opened the green folder and dealt out the colour photographs of the victims. 'Look at these,' he ordered, jabbing the worst of them with his thumb. 'This is what your precious boy is doing to get his own back on granny.'

He heard her gasp with horror and then the gasp changed to an ominous choking sound. He looked up in alarm. Her face was contorted and blue and she was clutching at her chest. A heart attack! The old dear was suffering a heart attack. 'Where's your bloody tablets?' he shouted.

A gargling sound from her throat. Her finger shook weakly in the direction of the dresser.

By the time he had found them, she was slumped unconscious in her chair. He slipped the wafer thin tablet under her tongue, his other hand digging in his pocket for his radio. 'Frost to Control.' He paused. He couldn't remember the damned address. 'I'm at Gauld's place. Send a bloody ambulance quick.'

Mullett was feeling feverish. This wretched business with Gauld's mother couldn't have come at a worse time. The smoke from Frost's cigarette wafted across and made him cough, and when he coughed, his head ached. He fanned the smoke away pointedly. Frost took the cigarette from his mouth, flicked ash all over the carpet, then replaced it. The phone rang. Mullett snatched it up, his expression hardly changing as he listened. 'Thank you.' He hung up, then stared grimly across to Frost. 'That was the hospital. A very mild attack. They're keeping her in overnight for observation, but will probably send her home in the morning.'

Frost dropped down in the chair, almost sweating with relief. 'Thank God for that. I'll try her again tomorrow. I think I can bust the alibi story.'

Mullett took off his glasses and wearily rubbed his eyes. 'You're going nowhere near her. You've caused enough trouble. You knew she had a heart condition, yet you showed her those horrific photographs.'

'Of people butchered by her son. Don't worry, Super. I'll be gentle with her next time.'

'There's not going to be a next time,' said Mullett emphatically, thumping the desk and wincing as it made his head ache.

'I need to break his alibi,' insisted Frost.

'Even if you broke his alibi. Even if his mother confirmed he was out on each and every one of the murder nights, that simply means he *could* have killed the victims . . . you still don't have a shred of proof which says that he *did* kill them. I want proof, Frost, not suspicion, not gut reaction – good, old-fashioned solid proof.'

'Let me talk to her and I'll get your proof.'

'No!' Mullett's head was now throbbing constantly and he wished the inspector would accept the position and leave him alone.

'Without proof, I'll have to let Gauld go,' said Frost despairingly.

'That', said Mullett curtly, 'is your problem.' He winced as the door slammed behind Frost and set his headache roaring off again. He could feel the sweat beading his brow as he tugged open the drawer for the aspirins. It was this wretched virus, he knew it, but if he went down, then that would leave Frost as the senior officer. And there was no way he was letting Frost run the division.

Gilmore was waiting for him outside the interview room. 'Gauld's shut up like a clam. He's going to sue us for what we did to his mother and he's not saying another word unless we get him a solicitor.'

'We're letting him go,' said Frost. He filled the sergeant in on his interview with Mullett. 'But I still want him tailed twenty-four hours a day. At best we might get the bloody proof we want. At worst we can probably stop him killing another poor sod until Mr Allen returns on Monday and takes over the case.'

'Will I be transferring to him?' asked Gilmore, hopefully.

'I'm afraid so,' said Frost.

Gilmore tried to look disappointed.

'We haven't got the men to carry out a twenty-four hour surveillance,' said Johnny Johnson.

'You'll have to find them,' said Frost. 'Plain-clothes, uniformed, dog-handlers, walking wounded . . . I don't care. The important thing is we don't let the bastard out of our sight even for a second.'

'Are you sure he's the Ripper?' asked Johnson. 'A fine lot of fools we'd look with the entire force following the wrong man while the Ripper kills someone else.'

'Trust me,' said Frost.

'I've trusted you before, Jack, and you've dropped me right in the muck.' He sighed. 'But I'll see what I can do.'

The phone rang. Burton from the Oxfam shop. 'Can you come over, Inspector? There's a locked cupboard here full of stuff belonging to Gauld, and I can't get it open.'

'We're off to the Oxfam shop,' Frost called to Johnson.

'Buying another suit?' called Johnson after them.

* * *

The Oxfam shop used to be a carpeting and furniture retailers until the firm went broke. Pushing past racks of used clothing and stacks of kitchen utensils, Frost and Gilmore, hastily pursued by the manageress, a thin, angular woman in a green overall, followed Burton to the rear of the shop where he led them down a short flight of stone steps to the basement. There, Burton clicked a switch and an unshaded bulb lit up a small, stone-flagged room in which an old-fashioned solid fuel boiler, belching sulphurous fumes, clanked away, a heap of anthracite glittering at its side. To the left of the boiler was another door which took them into a narrow passage where six metal lockers, painted light grey, backed against one wall.

'That one is Gauld's.' Burton indicated the last locker in the row.

Frost examined the solid-looking padlock and fumbled in his pocket for his bunch of keys.

The manageress looked uneasy. 'I presume you've got a warrant?'

'Yes,' said Frost, curtly, staring back at her, defying her to ask to see it. The second key did the trick. He turned the handle. The manageress pushed forward, eyes goggling. 'You'd better keep back, madam. It might be a body.' Alarmed, she hopped back, stepping on Gilmore's toe as she did so.

'Abracadabra,' said Frost and pulled open the door.

The locker was crammed tight with men's clothing; jackets, trousers, shirts, assorted styles and colours. Some of the clothing was old and threadbare, some in reasonable condition, all second-hand.

The manageress gasped and stared open-mouthed.

'Looks as if he's been nicking your stock, madam,' suggested Frost.

'I can't understand it. Ronnie seemed such a nice boy. I'd have trusted him with my life.'

'Lots of people thought the same,' smiled Frost. 'What exactly did he do here?'

'He drove our little van – collected items that people wanted to give to Oxfam. And he would deliver some of the larger items that people bought. Oh, and he helped with the boiler . . . keeping it well stoked.'

'Sounds a little treasure,' said Frost. 'I wouldn't worry too much about the clothes. I'm sure he's got a good explanation.' He cocked his head to one side. 'I think I can hear a customer in the shop.' As soon as she had left he began examining the clothing. 'It's all about Gauld's size – he was taking it for himself.'

'So he's been pinching the stock,' sniffed Gilmore. 'Big deal.'

'You're missing the point, son.' Frost was getting excited. He held up a pair of torn and paint-splattered jeans. 'Much of this is rubbish. So why did he nick it?'

'I give up,' shrugged Gilmore, not sounding very interested.

'None of his own clothes were bloodstained. Supposing he kept a supply of old clothes that he could change into just for his Ripper jobs?'

Gilmore's eyes widened. 'And after each job he disposed of them in the boiler! It's so simple, it's almost brilliant.'

They went back to the boiler room. 'Any point shutting this thing down?' Gilmore asked. 'We could rake through the ashes. There'll be bits that don't burn . . . buckles . . . clips . . . zips.'

'It wouldn't prove anything,' said Burton. 'I was talking to the manageress before you arrived. They get lots of clothes offered to them that are verminous, or too dirty to sell . . . so they shove them in the boiler.'

'Damn.' Frost gave the boiler a kick. 'This bastard is either too clever or too lucky. If we want proof, we're going to have to catch him in the act.' He stretched his arms and yawned loudly. 'Come on, Gilmore, let's get some kip. I get the feeling we're going to have a busy night.'

The house was strangely still and quiet when Gilmore closed the front door behind him. Liz was either out, or had gone back to bed. He tiptoed up the passage so he wouldn't disturb the dormant fury. In the living-room the ticking of the clock seemed unnaturally loud. Or was it because the rest of the house was so quiet?

Her farewell note was tucked into the frame of the mirror above the mantelpiece. She'd used the expensive blue monogrammed notepaper he'd bought for her birthday, his name scrawled across the envelope in green ink. He read it, then dashed up to the bedroom to make sure. The unmade bed was empty, her clothes gone from the wardrobe. He crossed the passage. Her toilet things had been removed from the bathroom.

Back downstairs he read her note again, his free hand pouring out a drink. He tried to feel sad, but couldn't. He swilled down the remains of the drink, stuffed the note on top of the unpaid bills in the bureau and went upstairs to the empty bedroom.

Even as his head touched the pillow he was in a deep, dreamless, trouble-free sleep.

Friday night shift (1)

Police Sergeant Bill Wells shivered and turned the lobby thermostat up to full in the hope that it would encourage the radiator to belt out some more heat. A waste of time, because as soon as Mullett came in, he'd complain about the lobby being like a tropical greenhouse and would turn the thermostat right down again. It was all right for him, with his 3-kilowatt heater, but let him try working in this draughty lobby with the door opening every five minutes and that gale-force wind roaring through.

The lobby door slammed open, the wind roared through, and there was Jack Frost, his scarf wound round his face to cover his nose. He was unwrapping himself when Burton pushed through the swing doors carrying the sergeant's tea.

'What news on Ronnie boy?' asked Frost, warming his hands on the radiator.

'He drove to the hospital at 7.22 and brought his mother back home,' said Burton.

'His mother? I thought they were keeping her in overnight?'

'She couldn't have been as bad as they thought.'

'I knew the old cow was faking. So where's Gauld now?'

'Indoors. Collier's watching the house.'

The phone rang. Wells answered it, then pulled a face at the mouthpiece. The caller was Mullett. 'Mr Frost, sir?' Frost shook his head vigorously 'I'm afraid he's not here at the moment.'

'I won't be in until later,' said Mullett. 'I'm feeling a bit under the weather. What have we got on the menu?'

'There's this threatened gang violence when the pubs shut, sir. Can I call on other divisions for assistance if necessary?'

'It shouldn't be necessary,' replied Mullett. 'Put every available man on to it.'

'Mr Frost is going to need much of the available manpower to keep tracks on Gauld, sir,' persisted Wells.

'You must give Mr Frost every assistance possible, Sergeant. Both operations are top priority. I'm relying on you to ensure that each operation does not hamper the effects of the other.'

A click as he hung up, leaving Wells spluttering helplessly at the dead phone 'Both top priority and neither must hamper the success of the other! He knows it's flaming impossible, that's why the bastard's staying away. Why is it always me?' He swung indignantly round to Frost. 'You're the senior officer. You should have taken the call.'

'I wasn't here,' said Frost. 'I heard you tell him.' He hurried off to collect Gilmore, leaving Wells staring at an empty mug and slowly realizing that the inspector had drunk his tea.

PC Collier champed at the cheeseburger. He was parked at the end of the little cul-de-sac, tucked tightly behind a cream-coloured Ford Consul whose owner had decided it would look better in green, but had abandoned the idea after painting just the front wing. The car radio, on which he reported every fifteen minutes that there was nothing to report, was turned down low so that its stream of messages were not audible to passers-by. His eyes were fixed on the house in mid-terrace. Gauld's house. Parked opposite the house, but out of sight from Collier's position, was Gauld's Vauxhall Astra.

He twisted his wrist so he could see his watch. A quarter to ten. He'd been stuck down this side turning for some two hours. In mid-bite something made him pause. Movement reflected in the rear-view mirror. Two men, keeping tight to the wall, stealthily approaching, obviously up to no good. Collier sank down in his seat so his head was below the window and waited. Suddenly the car echoed like a drum as someone pounded a fist on the roof and jerked the door open.

'Are you playing peek-a-boo, Collier?'

He grinned sheepishly and kicked the yellow polystyrene food container out of sight under the dash. It was Detective Inspector Jack Frost with the new chap, Gilmore. 'I spotted you coming, sir. Thought you were villains trying door handles.'

The car lurched as Frost and Gilmore climbed inside and settled themselves down on the back seat. 'What's happening?'

'Nothing, sir. He's still inside. Went in with his mother just after eight. Hasn't come out.'

Frost's nose began to twitch suspiciously. 'Can I smell cheeseburger?'

Collier blushed. 'Yes, I did have one, sir.'

'Did you cook it in the car,' asked Frost, innocently, 'or was it delivered?'

'Delivered?' frowned Collier, not sure what the inspector was getting at.

'You didn't bloody go off watch to get it, did you?' barked Gilmore.

'I've had nothing to eat for hours. I wasn't gone more than five minutes.'

'Five minutes!' repeated Frost, sadly. 'A lot can happen

in five minutes. I could have five women in five minutes – on an off day. Is his car still there?'

Collier craned his neck, but the Ford Consul blocked his view. 'I think so,' he stammered.

'You *think* so?' exploded Gilmore. 'If you've blown this, Collier . . .'

'Nip out and see,' said Frost, trying not to let his anxiety show. Collier was soon back and Frost's heart nose-dived as he read the answer in the young constable's white face.

'His car's gone, sir. A couple of kids said he drove off about five minutes ago.'

'You stupid fool!' yelled Gilmore.

'It's my fault,' said Frost, 'I should have had two men in the car, not one.' He leant forward to grab the handset. 'Frost to Control, receiving?' He barked out his orders for all cars, all patrols, to be on the lookout for Gauld's Vauxhall and to report the sighting immediately.

Half-way back to the station, Frost smote his forehead with his palm. 'The Oxfam shop! He might try to burn the evidence there.' He radioed through to the station requesting a man on permanent watch at the Oxfam shop.

'I haven't got anyone to spare,' protested Wells.

'Just do it,' said Frost, switching off the set before Wells could reply.

As they roared past a public house they noticed a gang of youths pouring out of an old van and making for the public bar. They seemed to be spoiling for a fight.

He sat in Control, listening to the stream of radio messages, a mound of mangled corpses of half-smoked cigarettes in the ashtray at his side. He hardly looked up when Wells banged a cup of tea in front of him.

'Bloody Collier,' snarled Wells. 'He must choose the busiest flaming night of the week to sod things up.'

'I sodded it up,' said Frost, lighting another cigarette and offering the packet to Wells. 'Collier didn't have the experience and I shouldn't have left him on his own.'

PC Lambert, the officer on Control duty, twisted his head. 'Inspector! Punch up at the Denton Arms. A gang of yobbos smashing the place up. Can I send a couple of cars?'

'Send one,' said Frost. 'I need all the rest.'

'One won't be enough,' protested Lambert.

'It's better than sod all,' Frost told him. 'Tell it to drive with its sirens screaming full blast. With a bit of luck the pub will empty before they burst in.' He tossed his cigarette packet across to Lambert. 'And I want them back searching for Gauld's car as soon as they've mopped up the last drop of blood and guts from the sawdust.' He sipped his tea and shuddered at the taste while Control directed Charlie Able to the pub.

No sooner was that task completed than Control was in trouble again. 'Serious domestic at Vicarage Terrace. Neighbours report couple seem to be smashing the happy home up. They can hear kiddies crying. I'd like to send a car.'

'You're car-mad,' admonished Frost. 'Haven't you got a foot patrol who could handle it?'

'It will take a quarter of an hour for the foot patrol to get there. There's kiddies involved!' protested Control.

'The kids won't get their throats cut. Some senior citizen will if we don't find Gauld quickly. The bastard's going to try it on again tonight, I just know it.'

Anxious squawks from Control's headphones. Lambert turned a permanently worried face to Frost. 'The fight at the pub is getting out of hand, sir. It's sprawled into the street. Windows have been smashed and they're damaging cars now.'

Frost sighed. 'All right, son. You handle it. Send what you want.' His mouth felt stale and bitter. The last thing he wanted was another cigarette, but he lit one up. Nothing was going right.

It was Burton who saved the day. Control switched the call to the external loudspeaker.

'Have located Vauxhall Astra registration K, Kansas, X, X-Ray . . .'

'Sod the phonetic spelling, Burton,' yelled Frost, snatching the handset from Control. 'Where is the bastard?'

'He's parked half-way down Wedgewood Street. I only spotted him by chance.'

At Frost's raised eyebrows, Control indicated Wedgewood Street on the large-scale map. A derelict side street in an area scheduled for demolition. 'I can't think what he's doing down there, Inspector. All the houses are boarded up and empty.'

Frost nodded and went back to Burton. 'You got him in full view?'

'Yes, I'm parked right at the end with my lights off. I don't want him to see me.' A pause, then, 'Damn!'

'Now what?'

'He's turned his lights off. There's no street lamps down there. It's pitch black.'

Frost peered up at the wall map. 'He's got to pass you to come out.'

'Only if he stays in the car. If he goes on foot he can cut through any of the empty houses.'

'Right. We can't be sodded about any more. If he's still in the car, arrest him and bring him back here . . . parking without lights . . . any excuse you can think of. And hurry.' Frost drummed his fingers impatiently as he waited. Then a crackle from the loudspeaker.

'Have subject car in view.'

'But is the sodding subject in the sodding subject car?' demanded Frost.

A pause. Then, 'Subject car is empty . . . repeat empty.'

'Shit,' moaned Frost, 'repeat shit! I suppose he hasn't got out just to have a pee or something innocent like that?'

'No sign of him anywhere,' said Burton.

With a weary grunt, Frost flopped back in his chair. 'Right, son. This is what you do. You immobilize his car . . . wee in his petrol tank, let his tyres down, anything, just so he can't use it. We don't want him driving off the minute your back is turned.'

He waited nervously sucking at his cigarette until a blast of static from the loudspeaker announced Burton to report that he'd immobilized the car.

'Good boy. Still no sign of him?'

'No, sir. No sign of anything. It's a ghost street – just empty houses. Hold on . . .'

'What is it?' asked Frost excitedly.

'I thought I saw a light in one of the houses. It flickered like someone striking a match. I'll go and take a look.'

'Be careful,' ordered Frost. 'And keep in touch.' He lit a fresh cigarette and fidgeted in his chair as he waited. Gilmore came in with two more mugs of tea. 'Thanks, son.' He stirred it with a pencil, feeling vaguely worried. Why the hell was Burton taking so long? He hesitated about asking Control to call the detective constable. Burton might be stalking his prey and a police radio sounding could give the game away. He stared up at the big wall clock, just above Lambert's head. He'd give Burton another two minutes before asking Control to radio. But before fifty seconds were up he had one of his feelings . . . one of his icy cold fingers scraping the back of the spine feelings. 'Call him,' he barked. 'Now!'

'Control to Burton, come in, please . . .' Lambert flipped the switch to receive. A crackle of empty static from the loudspeaker. He tried again. 'Control to Burton . . . are you receiving . . . over?' More empty static. 'He doesn't seem to be responding, Inspector,' said Lambert, redundantly.

'Keep bloody trying,' yelled Frost from the door. 'Come on, Gilmore. Let's get over there.'

The traffic light changed to red and Gilmore slowed to a halt with Frost grunting his impatience as they waited. As soon as the cross-road was clear he ordered Gilmore to jump the lights. They passed a huge building site with skeleton tower blocks and giant cranes. Frost peered through the side window. 'Wedgewood Street should be along here somewhere . . .' They nearly missed it. 'There!'

Slamming on the brakes, Gilmore backed the car and turned into a dark side road. A dead street of empty windowless houses. Burton's car stood by the corner. Further down the road another car. A grey Vauxhall Astra.

At the top of his voice Frost repeatedly shouted, 'Burton!' The empty houses flung his words back.

'On the pavement – there!' Gilmore pointed to something black and rectangular.

They ran over. It was a police radio, its casing smashed and caved in as if it had been stamped on. When Frost picked it up his hand touched stickiness. He stared at his fingers. Blood, fresh and ruby red that glittered in the ray of Gilmore's torch. Frost yanked his own radio from his pocket and fumbled for the transmit button. He blurted out instructions to Control. 'I want every available officer to come immediately to Wedgewood Street.'

'There isn't anyone to send,' answered Control. 'They're all out. There's a near-riot at the Denton Arms.'

'Call them away and send them here . . . now! We've got an officer in trouble!' He switched off before Control could come up with any more stupid objections.

All of the houses had been boarded up with corrugated galvanized sheeting blanking out the windows and heavy planking nailed across the front doors. But on quite a few of the properties vandals had torn away the planking and kicked in the doors. Frost poked his torch beam tentatively into one of the houses and ventured inside. The passage was thick with debris and breathed a sour, mildewy smell. As he shuffled in, the debris moved as rats squealed and scuttled to safety. He lashed out his foot to hasten them on their way. Before he could proceed further the sound of a car, then the slamming of doors. Back to the street where PC Jordan and four other uniformed men were waiting with Gilmore. Five men! Was this all Control was sending?

'We're stretched to the limit,' Jordan told him. 'The pub fight is getting right out of hand.'

Frost stripped cellophane from a fresh packet of cigarettes and passed it around as he quickly briefed them. 'My guess is that Burton went in one of these empty houses after Gauld. The flooring's rotten, the stair treads and banisters are broken, so he could have fallen and hurt himself. But that doesn't explain his radio.' He held it up and showed it to them. 'We found it on the pavement, there, and it frightens the shit out of me. Anyway, sod the speculation until we find him. Take a house each and be careful . . . they're bloody death traps.'

He took the middle property himself, the one nearest to where they had found the smashed radio. It reeked of damp and decay. His torch beam blinked feebly into the blackness, picking out rotting floorboards and slimy rubbish. A door to his right was closed. Warily he turned the handle and pushed. A groaning creak as it swung back on to an empty, dead, urine-smelling room. He moved on, things rustling and scurrying in front of him. To his left, stairs with broken jagged banisters lurching outwards. Another door in front of him. He kicked it open. The kitchen, piled high with rubbish and smelling of bad drains and cats and rotting food.

Back to the hall and up the stairs, testing each tread carefully before putting his weight on it. Half-way up he stopped and held his breath as he listened. A creaking. There was someone up there. There it was again. The soft creak of a floorboard. 'Burton?' He waited. Silence. No! A rustling, then another floorboard creaked. His torch kept flickering. The beam shuddered and died. He gave the casing a welt with the flat of his hand which frightened it into brief life again before it died finally a second time.

He waited to let his eyes adjust to the darkness and took another step. Then he froze. Something. He stopped dead, ears sharply focused for the slightest sound. Silence. Silence that screamed in the blackness. But there was something . . . someone up there. 'Burton?' If it was Burton, why the hell didn't he answer?

He rammed the useless torch in his pocket and fished out his matches. Up the stairs to the landing. The match burnt his fingers. Swearing softly, he shook it out and struck another. A door, slightly ajar, to his right. He nudged it open with his foot, then poked the hand with the match inside. He nearly dropped the match. On the floor, in the flicker of the flame, a face. Another match. God, it was Burton, his face a sweat-soaked dirty white, his lips mumbling incoherently.

Frost dropped to his knees on to a puddle of something wet which soaked his trousers. Another match. He was kneeling in a pool of blood. Burton's hands were clasped round his stomach. A red trickle oozed from between slippery, red fingers. He was trying to say something. Frost brought his head down to Burton's lips. 'Gauld. The bastard stabbed me.' His eyelids flickered and closed.

'Up here!' yelled Frost at the top of his voice. He tugged out his radio. 'Control. Burton's been stabbed. Get an ambulance over to Wedgewood Street . . . now!'

The ambulance men adjusted the strap around the red-blanketed Burton, then wheeled the trolley up into the ambulance. One of the uniformed men hopped in the back with it.

'Got a stack of your chaps in Casualty,' the ambulance driver told Frost cheerfully as he climbed into his seat. 'Blood and broken noses everywhere. A bunch of yobbos breaking up a pub or something.'

Oh, sod! thought Frost. I'd forgotten all about that. He radioed through to the station.

'We're being massacred,' Wells told him. 'Things are getting out of control and bloody Mullett's not answering his phone in case he should have to make a decision.'

Gilmore tugged at Frost's sleeve. 'Gauld's been spotted. He's got into that building site.' He pointed in the direction of the giant crane.

'Damn,' said Frost. There were a hundred places Gauld could hide in in the sprawl of the building site. Back to the radio. 'We know where Gauld is. Without more men we'll lose him. Pull more people out from the pub.'

'I can't,' insisted Wells.

'Just bloody do it. Then phone County and get reinforcements from other divisions,' said Frost.

'Mullett won't like that. He'll do his nut.'

'Sod Mullett. Just do it.'

Wells hesitated. 'If it blows up in our face, will you take the can back, Jack?'

'Don't I always?' said Frost.

The building site covered almost twenty acres and would eventually house a hypermarket, shops, and two tower office blocks which, at the moment, were skeletons of scaffolding and girders. The car picked its way along a muddy, temporary road to the main gates.

Chain link fencing encircled the area. A notice in red warned *Keep Out. Guard Dogs Loose On This Site.* The main gates were locked and chained, but there was a smaller gate to one side which sagged where it had been kicked in. Beyond the gate a brown and white shape twitched and whimpered in the mud. The knife-ripped guard dog.

Gilmore's radio reported the arrival of reinforcements. Three pub-battle-scarred warriors were in position at the back entrance of the site, ready to move in from there. 'It's not enough,' said Gilmore.

'As the bishop said to the actress, son, it may not be much, but it's all I've got.' He took the radio and warned the newcomers to be careful. Gauld had a knife and was prepared to use it. 'Right. Let's go in.'

Near the entrance stood a green-coloured Portakabin. Frost tried the handle. Locked. He flashed a torch through a window. Desks, phones and drawing boards.

Other torches bobbed in the distance as the rest of his thinly stretched team carried out the search. The site was littered with hills and mountains of building materials; earthenware drainage pipes, concrete blocks, bricks on pallets covered with polythene sheeting, bag after bag of cement. And then there was machinery. Bulldozers, earth-moving equipment, cranes, and overshadowing everything, a giant skyscraper of a crane on its tower of scaffolding. The muddy ground had been churned into a Somme battlefield by the wheels of countless lorries.

It was a slow, laboured search. Heavy items had to be man-handled out of the way, planking covering drainage trenches removed, builders' huts forced open and searched, canvas and polythene sheeting stripped away. They squeezed between stacks of splintery timber shuttering, crawled under wooden sheds and, finally, mud-caked, dishevelled and disheartened, there was nowhere else to look and Gilmore was wearing his 'I told you so' smirk.

They gathered round Frost who was dishing out cigarettes, forming a tight circle as he struck a match to stop the rising wind from blowing it out. 'Now what?' asked Gilmore.

'We go back and search again, son.'

'He could be miles away.'

Frost's chin poked out stubbornly. 'No. He's here. Laughing at us. I know it.' He held up a hand. 'I thought I heard something.' Someone's radio was burbling away about casualties and ambulances and shortage of manpower. 'Turn that thing off.' The offending radio was silenced. 'Now listen.'

They listened. The wind, working itself up into a paddy, rattled chain link fencing, flapped polythene sheeting, and made the temporary overhead telephone wires sing and hum. Almost 200 feet above them, the jib arm of the giant crane, with its warning light on the far end, creaked and groaned and shrieked as if in pain.

A sudden clatter. All heads turned. Jordan grinned sheepishly. He had knocked over a stack of empty lubricating oil drums.

Frost shook his head. Whatever he thought he'd heard wasn't going to repeat itself. Then he clicked his fingers. 'The crane. We haven't looked up there!' Heads turned up and up and up. The distant warning light, a pin-prick of bright against the night sky, seemed almost another star.

'It's bloody high,' croaked Jordan.

'Yes,' agreed Frost, now wishing he hadn't suggested it. The damn thing seemed to go up and up and up for ever.

A yell from Gilmore. 'Someone's up there!' And as the moon elbowed through black clouds, there was Gauld, on the ladder, nearly 100 feet up, clinging for dear life and looking down at them.

Making a megaphone with his hands, Frost yelled up into the night sky. 'You can't get away now, Gauld. We've got you. Come on down.'

The wind fielded Gauld's defiant reply and hurled it away.

'He's coming down,' exclaimed Jordan.

'He's not,' said Frost. 'He's going higher.'

Necks craned, they watched until he was swallowed by blackness. 'Let's have some lights,' Frost ordered.

With much difficulty an area car zigzagged, bumped and slid its way towards the crane, and then a powerful spotlight sliced upwards, cutting a steamy white swathe in the night sky and picking out the doll-man as he climbed up and up.

Gauld was nearly at the top of the ladder and could see the platform of the driver's cab just above his head. He gripped the rungs tightly with hands that the wind was trying to tear loose. Above him the jib groaned and whined and shuddered. He heaved himself up on to the small platform outside the cab. The protective metal handrail seemed flimsy and inadequate and he kept well back as he looked down, eyes squinting against the blinding spotlight beam. The police were still staring up at him, the one in the dirty mac yelling something which any fool should realize couldn't be heard at this height. One of the uniformed men was running from a car with something in his hand. A loud-hailer.

'Be sensible, Gauld. You can't go anywhere. Come on down.'

Pointless shouting. They wouldn't hear him. But the cop was right. He couldn't go anywhere. They had him trapped. God, how had it all gone wrong?

'Come on down, Gauld.'

The fool was yelling again. Come on down? He ventured another look over the edge. Just looking made him dizzy and he pressed back against the cab, his hands scrabbling for something to hold on to. If they wanted him, they'd have to bring him down.

Above him the jib gave another tortured scream of pain, then another sound pierced the night. A two-tone siren.

The fire engine halted outside the gate and a bearded fireman made his way across to the inspector. He looked angry. 'You called a vet for that dog? It's still alive, you know.'

'He's on his way,' snapped Frost, annoyed with himself for not attending to it. He signalled to Jordan who moved out of earshot and radioed through to Control. Frost pointed to the crane platform. 'We want to get up there. Would your turntable ladder reach?'

The fireman squinted up, then shook his head. 'You'd need a bleeding helicopter to get up there.' He moved to the ladder lashed to the scaffolding and gave it a shake. It didn't seem very firm. 'That's the only way up.'

'Sod that for a lark,' said Frost. 'Take me up on your turntable ladder as far as it goes. I'll see if I can't sweet-talk the bastard down.'

The turntable platform gave a jerk, then the ground suddenly hurtled down and Frost had to grab the rail to steady himself as the ladder zoomed upwards. Briefly he chanced a look down, then quickly pulled his eyes away and concentrated on staring straight ahead at the bolts and nuts and rusted metal of the scaffolding as they zipped past.

After what seemed ages, the ladder slowed and juddered to a halt and the fire officer tugged Frost's sleeve. 'As far as we go.'

Frost looked down. Toy cars, tiny people, miles and miles away. He looked up. Lots more scaffolding roaring up to the sky and the white blob of Gauld's face staring down at him. 'There's nowhere to run,' shouted Frost. 'Chuck your knife and we'll bring you down.'

Gauld yelled something, but the wind snatched and tore the words to shreds. Then the blob of his face withdrew and they couldn't see him any more.

'Now what?' asked the fire officer.

Frost's neck was aching from craning upwards. He lowered his head. In front of him was the flimsy metal ladder which Gauld had climbed. It didn't look very safe and was rattling in the wind. He shivered. 'If we both went up, we could overpower him.'

'Not our job to overpower nutters with knives,' said the fire officer, firmly. 'Disarm him and you can have as many of my men as you like. Until then, you're on your own.'

Sod it, thought Frost. Let's pack it in and starve the bastard into submission. But he'd come this far. He wanted to get it over and done with. Fumbling at the buckle, he released the safety belt. 'Help me across to the other ladder.'

The fireman looked doubtful. 'Are you sure you know what you're doing?'

'I never know what I'm bleeding doing,' said Frost.

The gap between the platform and the scaffold ladder grew markedly wider as he looked at it. Before common sense made his nerve fail he ducked quickly under the rail, holding it tight with one hand, and plunged forward in the blind hope his other hand would find something to hang on to. He managed to find one of the ladder rungs and squeezed it to death as he released his grip on the guard rail and grabbed at the same rung. He was now hanging over the gap, feet on the platform, hands on the ladder rungs and definitely at the point of no return.

'You're doing fine,' called the fireman unconvincingly. 'Now hold tight and swing your feet forward.'

He didn't need to be told to hold tight. The skin over his knuckles was paper thin and the bones threatened to burst through. He swung forward, his feet kicking about as they tried to find the rungs. They found only space . . . pulling, plunging space. He was hanging by sweat-slippery hands, kicking wildly and he was terrified. Then he felt hands grabbing his ankles and placing his feet on a narrow rung. He managed to croak a word of thanks to the fireman and froze to the ladder, heart hammering, his face pressed against the cold metal, not wanting to look up or down or left or right, just wanting to be back on the ground, looking up at some silly sod doing what he was doing and telling everyone what a prat the man was.

'Anything wrong?' The fireman sounded anxious.

'No,' lied Frost. 'Just catching my breath.' He forced one hand to release its grip and move further up the rail. Then the other. One leg lifted and found the next rung. This was easy. As long as he didn't look down, this was easy. It was just like climbing a ladder a couple of feet off the ground. But confidence cloaked near-disaster and he almost screamed when his foot slipped from the rung and he had to hug the ladder, shaking, feeling the ladder rattle like chattering teeth against the scaffolding. He forced himself to press on, rung by rung, his body stiff and rigid, leg muscles aching with the effort. 'I'll be fit for sod all when I get up there,' he kept telling himself, trying to erase the mental picture of himself sprawled on the gantry, gasping for breath, while Gauld slowly hacked away at his windpipe. But even that prospect was currently preferable to going down, which meant moving backwards, descending the ladder in reverse. God, he was never going to get down again.

'You're doing fine!'

The voice seemed to come from a long way down. He risked a glance and saw the top of the man's helmet floating in space below his feet. With an effort he forced himself on.

There was one frightening section which required him to swap from one ladder to another, holding with one hand to the first and reaching out for the next and swinging across. But not far now, thank God. He must be near the top. The teeth-setting grinding and squealing of the jib, like a giant fingernail scratching down a blackboard, screamed in his ears.

The ladder stopped and his sweat-blurred eyes were

level with a wooden platform. His hands seemed fused to the ladder, but he tore them free and flung himself forward on to the gantry where he rolled across to huddle up tight to the side of the cab, keeping as far from the edge as possible.

'Are you all right?' A faint voice calling from a hundred miles down.

'I'm fine,' he yelled, not feeling it. A quick fumble through his pocket for a cigarette, turning his back to the hurricane force wind which, at this height, was making everything shake violently. Far away to his left were the winking dots of light from the Lego town of Denton. His radio squawked.

'Inspector!' It was Gilmore from the smug safety of the firm ground. 'Gauld's round the other side of the gantry to you. Just seems to be standing there.'

'Not much else the poor sod can do,' he answered. He'd almost forgotten about Gauld, the whole purpose of this nightmare climb. Another squawk from the radio. Gilmore back again. 'Mr Mullett is here, Inspector. He'd like a word.' Mullett! Trust Hornrim Harry to be in at the kill. All ready to take the credit should the operation prove a success, and to dissociate himself from it in the more likely event of failure. The thought of realizing a long-held ambition to defecate on Mullett from a great height flashed across his mind as he waited.

'What's the position, Inspector?'

'I'm just about to go round and talk him down.'

'Good. Let's tie this up neat and tidy. Bring him down safely, and do it by the book.'

Stupid sod. How the hell do you get a knife-wielding mass-murderer down from a 200-foot crane by the book? He stuck the radio back in his mac and dragged himself to his feet. The wooden platform creaked and gave slightly under his weight, then the whole structure lurched and the stars danced in the sky as the wind pounded the jib. Through the cracks between the planks he could see straight down to the swaying, yawning black of the bottomless drop. One last drag of his cigarette before he flipped it away. The wind caught it and hurled it over the side where it nose-dived down to oblivion, spitting red sparks.

He inched round to the other side, keeping tightly to the solid reassurance of the driver's cab. And there was Gauld, his back to the rail, hair streaming, legs braced against the force of the pummelling wind. 'Keep away from me!' In his upraised hand something bright reflected the twinkling blood gobs of the warning light at the end of the jib.

Frost leant against the cab and wearily shook his head. 'It's all over, son. You've got nowhere to go.' He waited for a response, eyeing the man warily. If Gauld decided to put up a fight, there wasn't much he could do. There was hardly room for a punch-up on this barely 2-foot-wide platform. They'd probably both end up over the edge, splashing blood, brains and guts all over Mullett's patent leather shoes.

Gauld moved forward, the arm with the knife still raised, a manic grin clicking on and off. Then his face crumpled and tears streamed. 'Why didn't you leave me alone?'

Shit, thought Frost. Don't make me start feeling sorry for you, you murdering bastard. He kept his eye firmly on the blade and edged forward a fraction. Gauld, the guard rail pressing into his back, couldn't retreat. He could only move forward.

'The knife!' said Frost firmly, optimistically holding out his hand.

Again the flickering, manic grin. Gauld scrubbed at his face with the back of his hand to wipe off the tears. His eyes glinted slyly and the knife-hand shook. 'You want the knife? You want the bloody knife?' He held it out. 'Here it is. Take it.'

'Don't try anything,' warned Frost, 'or I'll push you over the bloody edge.'

Gauld raised the knife higher, then, as Frost steeled himself, flung it far out into the night where it spun and glinted before vanishing into the void. 'It was only a penknife. You couldn't cut bloody butter with it.'

A cold trickle of relief, but Frost moved warily towards Gauld who looked as if he still had a few aces hidden up his sleeve. Tugging out his radio he let the firemen know it was safe for them to come up and give him a hand.

'You've got him?' cried Mullett's excited voice. 'What's the position?'

'Later,' snapped Frost. 'I'll tell you bloody later.' He clicked off the set and felt for the handcuffs, still watching Gauld like a hawk.

'I panicked,' said Gauld, suddenly. 'I had the knife in my hand and I panicked.' He glared at Frost. 'It was your fault. Why didn't you leave me alone?'

Frost frowned. What the hell was the man talking about? 'My fault?' He now had the handcuffs and reached for Gauld's arm.

'Of course it was your flaming fault,' yelled Gauld, snatching his arm away. 'You hounded me. You frightened the shit out of my mother. That's why it happened.'

Frost's mind raced, trying to make sense of all this, but then the wind suddenly wailed and hit the crane jib with a tremendous punch, wrenching the gantry round until the anchor chains braked it with a shuddering jerk. Frost was flung to the floor of the gantry, the stars zip-panning across the sky. And through the creakings and squeals and resounding clangs, the sound of a man screaming.

In an instant he was up on his feet, trying to regain his balance on the shaking platform. Gauld. Where was Gauld? The guard rail where he had been standing was broken and a section dangled down. Still that screaming. And yells from below as firemen clambered up the ladder.

'Help me!'

Frost leaned over the edge. A spotlight from the fire appliance on the ground blinded him. He shielded his eyes with his arm. Someone on the ground saw what was happening and yelled for the beam to be directed downwards. It slid down and locked on to a screaming, pleading Gauld who was clinging by his fingertips to the protruding edge of a girder just below the platform, feet kicking wildly in a futile effort to find a foothold before his fingers gave way.

'Hold on!' roared Frost. A stupid thing to say. What else could the poor bastard do? He flung himself down on the gantry, kicking into a gap in the planking to wedge in the toes of his shoes. With the platform cutting into his stomach he leant out over the edge and reached down.

Below him, the white, upturned face of the dangling man who was whimpering with terror. It didn't seem possible that Frost could reach him. The thudding of firemen's feet on the ladder over on the far side was getting louder. He prayed that they would hurry. Way, way below, tiny dolls held out a circular white canvas, only part of which protruded from an overhanging section of the scaffolding. A tiny, inadequate, very missable target.

He groped and stretched. The bitter, cutting wind stung his cheeks, roared pain into his scar, and gradually sucked the feeling from his bare hands. He gritted his teeth and stretched further. Something. Cold flesh. Icy cold knuckles gripping raw-edged metal scaffolding.

'Take my hand!'

Gauld moaned and gave a feeble shake of the head. 'I can't.'

'Don't sod me about,' shouted Frost. 'Take the bloody thing!'

Gauld's hand fluttered, then snatched. Frost grabbed at wet, blood-slippery fingers, cut by the saw-edge of the metal. It was not a secure grip, but the first fireman was now up on the platform and could take over. As long as Gauld didn't release his other hand, Frost could sustain him. 'Wait,' he yelled down.

But Gauld wasn't going to wait. He wanted to be pulled to safety. He let go of the girder and snatched up at Frost, but he couldn't reach and his body started to swing and his fingertips just brushed the hand Frost was straining out to him and his life depended on Frost holding on to his cut and bleeding fingers.

Frost could feel him going. He gripped tighter, but this squeezed more blood from Gauld's torn hand. Slippery blood. The fireman flung himself alongside Frost, but even as he did so, Gauld was screaming. Frost, free arm flailing, desperately tried to find something to hold. Gauld's hair raced through his fingers and the white terrified face grew smaller, smaller, smaller, still screaming. He screamed as he fell. He screamed as he hit and bounced off the protruding girder which broke his back. He screamed as he smashed into the ground. After he was dead, after his heart stopped pumping blood out of his broken body, his screams still rang and rang round and round the building site.

Friday night shift (2)

The ambulance took away the pulp in a body bag and the firemen hosed away the mess. Frost, white and shaken, greedily sucked at a cigarette and was hardly listening to what Mullett was saying.

'You're absolutely certain Gauld was the Ripper?'

Frost took one last gloomy drag then chucked the cigarette away. Up until half an hour ago he was positive, but now the shrill, insistent nagging voice of doubt kept raising the terrible possibility that he might have hounded an innocent man to his death. 'Yes, I'm certain,' he said without conviction.

'Did he admit it?' persisted Mullett. 'We're a little short of solid proof and it would make things neat and tidy if I could tell the Chief Constable that we got a verbal confession.'

Admit it? It was those last words of Gauld that triggered the doubts. 'It was your fault,' Gauld had said. 'You hounded me . . . that's why it happened.' That sounded more like an apology for stabbing Burton, not an admission that he was the Ripper. 'No, he didn't admit anything.' He searched for his cigarette packet.

Mullett gave a deep sigh. Couldn't Frost take the smallest hint? Gauld was dead. No-one would know whether he had actually admitted guilt or not, and if Frost was certain Gauld was the Ripper, then where was the harm in a little white lie? 'Are you *sure* he admitted nothing?' he asked, slowly and deliberately, giving the inspector the chance to amend his answer.

'Of course I'm bloody sure,' snapped Frost, turning his back on his Divisional Commander.

Mullett's lips tightened. But he wouldn't create a scene here. Just wait until he got Frost back to the office. 'By the way,' he hurled at Frost's back, 'the hospital called. Burton is quite comfortable . . . all he required was a few stitches. His wounds were quite superficial.'

'Good,' grunted Frost, his mind whirling, his doubts multiplying. Superficial! None of the Ripper's other victims had superficial wounds. That poor cow with her head hanging off – that wasn't superficial. The canker of doubt gnawed and chewed and got bigger and bigger. But it had to be Gauld. It just had to be. Only vaguely was he aware of Gilmore answering a radio call in the car, then hastening across to Mullett and murmuring something in his ear.

'What?' Mullett couldn't believe what he had been told. He listened, open-mouthed, as Gilmore repeated it, then spun round to Frost, his whole body shaking with uncontrollable anger. 'You were so damn sure!! While you were chasing Gauld with his Boy Scout's penknife, the real Ripper has struck again.'

Frost went cold. Icy, shivery cold. He could only gape at Mullett. He looked pleadingly at Gilmore, willing him to say it was all a mistake.

'Elderly lady,' said Gilmore. 'Slashed to ribbons. They've rushed her to Denton Hospital.'

Hospital! Then she was still alive. He almost knocked Mullett over as he dashed for the car.

'Come here, Frost,' choked Mullett. 'I haven't finished with you yet . . .' Doors slammed and the car roared off. 'My office!' screamed Mullett to the dwindling red lights. 'I want you in my office . . . now!!' Panting with fury, he gasped for breath, then was aware of someone at his side. A stocky figure in a dark blue anorak poking a miniature cassette recorder at him.

'Mr Mullett, I'm from the Denton *Echo*. Is it true you've caught the Ripper?'

Hunched over the steering wheel, dragging savagely at a cigarette he didn't want, he went over the night's events again and again. Could he have saved Gauld if he had tried that much harder to reach out and grab him? Was it his stubborn certainty that Gauld was the Ripper that stopped him from trying harder? And now, it seemed, Gauld was innocent.

He lurched to one side as the car spun into the main hospital access road. Out of the corner of his eye he was vaguely aware of an ambulance parked outside the mortuary and the stretchered body-bag being carried in.

The car had barely stopped when Frost was running up the steps and barging through the swing doors. A uniformed constable seated on a wooden bench by the night porter's cubicle snatched the cigarette from his mouth. 'She's in Intensive Care, Inspector.'

His running footsteps clattered and echoed along the empty corridors. The night sister in Intensive Care looked up angrily as they barged into her domain and was completely unimpressed with the warrant card Frost flashed at her.

'One minute, that's all I'm giving you.' She led him across to a bed where liquid-filled plastic bags dripped through tubes into the veins of a barely breathing woman who was swathed in white bandages through which blood seeped. The nurse adjusted the flow of one of the drips and gave the plastic bag a squeeze.

'Will she live?' asked Frost.

The nurse shrugged. 'Cut throat . . . slashed abdomen.

She's barely alive now. She regained consciousness for a couple of minutes, then drifted off in a coma again.'

'Did she say anything?'

'She tried to. It was all garbled. Something about her son. She said he did it.'

Her son? Frost pushed the nurse to one side and bent close to look at the face. Shrivelled and sunken with her dentures removed, she looked a hundred years older than when he last saw her.

It was the mother. It was Mrs Gauld.

Her eyelids quivered, then fluttered open to reveal watery colourless eyes. She didn't seem surprised to see the blurred face of Frost hovering over her. Her lips moved and her voice was so weak he had to press his ear close to her mouth and feel the hot rasp of her breath on his cheek. 'I told him it had to stop or I'd tell the police. That made him angry. He always had a temper.' With a strain of effort that made the nurse look worried, she lifted her head from the pillow and stared pleadingly at Frost. 'He didn't mean it. Not his own mother.'

'Of course not,' whispered Frost.

'You won't hurt him?'

'No,' said Frost. 'Of course we won't hurt him.'

She managed the ghost of a smile as her head dropped back.

He sat with her until she died.

'So it was Gauld?' Mullett's mind was racing. Frost had dropped him in the mire yet again. The phone on his desk was still warm from his call to the Chief Constable, explaining that Frost had screwed up and Gauld wasn't the Ripper. Having dumped the blame for the debacle on Frost, it was going to be difficult to claw back any credit for himself.

'Yes, Super,' said Frost, dragging the visitor's chair across the carpet and flopping wearily into it. 'Those photographs of the victims I showed his mother apparently did the trick. She told him she was going to shop him, so he knifed her. Then he panicked and went on the run.'

'I see.' Mullett pointedly fanned away the smoke which drifted across from the cigarette Frost was puffing at without permission. 'Well, somehow or other you seem to have muddled through to a correct result on this one.'

'Thank you, Super.' He pushed himself out of the chair and brushed away the cigarette ash that was all over the front of his coat. It snowed down all over the blue Wilton carpet. Making no attempt to cover his mouth, he gave a loud yawn and moved towards the door. 'If there's nothing else, I'm going home.'

Mullett looked down at the long list of casualties from the pub fight. The men returning from sick leave would not make up the deficiency and the manning level would be worse than before. Damn Frost. Why did he have to be saddled with such an incompetent? His eyes glinted malevolently. He'd almost forgotten. He'd poked through Frost's in-tray earlier that evening and, to his fury, had found the inventory return, completely untouched. 'Oh.' He tried to keep his voice casual. 'Before you go, Frost, I'd like you to drop in the completed inventory return. I've promised County they'll get it tonight.'

'Sure, Super,' muttered Frost. He pulled the door shut behind him and felt his shoulders slump. How the hell was he going to get out of this one?

Back in his office, watched by Bill Wells, he retrieved the bulky wad of blank forms from the depths of his in-tray and thumbed through them despairingly. 'The bastard,' he moaned. 'He knows damn well I haven't done it.'

'But you told him you'd finished them,' said Wells.

'He knew I was lying,' said Frost. His eyes skimmed round the room. 'Two desks, two chairs and a filing cabinet.' He flipped through the pages and scribbled in the figures.

'You've missed out the hat-stand, the typewriter, the filing trays, the telephones, the stationery stocks. You'll never do it, Jack.'

The cigarette packet was generously proffered. 'But if you helped me, Bill.'

'If I did, it would cost more than a lousy cigarette. There's no way you're going to get it done tonight, Jack, even if we all pitched in. It used to take Mr Allen the best part of a week with three people to help him.'

Frost admitted defeat. He dragged his scarf from the hat-stand and wound it round his neck. 'I'll give the bastard the blank form and tell him to stick it up his arse. He can only sack me. Then I'm going home. I think I've got a dose of flu coming on. With luck, it'll kill me.'

He shuffled along the corridor to the Murder Incident Room to collect Gilmore. The detective sergeant, anxious to take advantage of his new-found freedom, was chatting up Jill Knight, the red-headed WPC who operated the computer. She didn't appear very interested.

'I'm off home,' announced Frost.

'Message just in from Birmingham Police,' Gilmore told him. 'They traced a copper who remembers something about Gauld. Apparently, when he was twelve he attacked his grandmother with a knife but she wouldn't press charges, so the case never went to court.'

'Wouldn't have hurt to have had that earlier,' sniffed

Frost. He pulled the inventory from his pocket. Now to face Mullett.

A cry of recognition from Jill Knight. 'So that's where it's been. I've been looking for it everywhere.'

Frost could only watch and wonder as she took the blank inventory return from him and began pounding the computer keyboard. At her side, the dot-matrix printer clunked, then the print-head screeched as it shuttled back and forth, hammering out columns of figures on continuous stationery.

'Inspector Allen put the inventory details on computer before he went off sick,' she explained. 'I've been hunting high and low for that return.'

Frost pulled out his cigarettes and poked one in her mouth. 'Will it take long?'

She leant forward to receive a light. 'You can have it now.' She tore the sheets from the printer, clipped them together and handed them over.

Frost wound the scarf round his neck and buttoned up his mac. 'I don't know whether to kiss you or the bloody computer.'

With a happy, off-key whistle hampered by the cigarette in his mouth, Detective Inspector Jack Frost sashayed up the corridor. Gilmore, a thin look of contempt on his face, watched him go. Thank heaven Inspector Allen would be back on Monday and he'd be working with a real copper for a change.

THE END